Beneath Dark Waters

KAREN ROSE

HEADLINE

The right of Karen Rose Books Inc to be identified as the Author of
the Work has been asserted by her in accordance with the
Copyright, Designs and Patents Act 1988.

First published in 2023 by
HEADLINE PUBLISHING GROUP

First published in paperback in 2024 by
HEADLINE PUBLISHING GROUP

2

Cataloguing in Publication Data is available from the British Library

ISBN 978 1 4722 8298 9 (B format)

Offset in 10.08/15.22pt Carre Noir Pro Medium by Jouve (UK), Milton Keynes

Printed and bound in Great Britain by Clays Ltd, Elcograf S.p.A.

Headline's policy is to use papers that are natural, renewable and recyclable
products and made from wood grown in well-managed forests and other
controlled sources. The logging and manufacturing processes are expected to
conform to the environmental regulations of the country of origin.

HEADLINE PUBLISHING GROUP
An Hachette UK Company
Carmelite House
50 Victoria Embankment
London
EC4Y 0DZ

www.headline.co.uk
www.hachette.co.uk

Beneath
Dark
Waters

Karen Rose was introduced to suspense and horror at the tender age of eight when she accidentally read Poe's *The Pit and the Pendulum* and was afraid to go to sleep for years. She now enjoys writing books that make other people afraid to go to sleep.

Karen lives in Florida with her family, their cat, Bella, and two dogs, Loki and Freya. When she's not writing, she enjoys reading, and her new hobby — knitting.

To find out more about Karen Rose, check out her website www. karenrosebooks.com, follow her on Facebook @KarenRoseBooks, and on Twitter @KarenRoseBooks

PRAISE FOR KAREN ROSE

'Intense, complex and unforgettable' **James Patterson**

'Karen Rose delivers the kind of high-wire suspense that keeps you riveted' **Lisa Gardner**

'Rose . . . effortlessly balances romance and crime . . . An excellent example of how far-reaching and varied romance can be' *New York Times*

'Fast and furious' *Sun*

'Takes off like a house afire. There's action and chills galore in this nonstop thriller' **Tess Gerritsen**

'A pulse pounding tale that has it all' *Cosmopolitan*

'A blend of hard-edged police procedural and romance — engaging' *Irish Independent*

'Rose juggles a large cast, a huge body count and a complex plot with terrifying ease' *Publishers Weekly*

'A high-octane thrill ride that kept me on the edge of my seat and far too late at night!' **Lisa Jackson**

By Karen Rose

The Raleigh Series
Have You Seen Her?

The Chicago Series
Don't Tell
I'm Watching You
Nothing to Fear
You Can't Hide
Count to Ten

The Philadelphia/Atlanta Series
Die For Me
Scream For Me
Kill For Me

The Minneapolis Series
I Can See You
Silent Scream

The Baltimore Series
You Belong to Me
No One Left to Tell
Did You Miss Me?
Watch Your Back
Monster in the Closet
Death is Not Enough

The Cincinnati Series
Closer Than You Think
Alone in the Dark
Every Dark Corner
Edge of Darkness
Into the Dark

The Sacramento Series
Say You're Sorry
Say No More
Say Goodbye

The New Orleans Series
Quarter to Midnight
Beneath Dark Waters

The San Diego Case Files
Cold Blooded Liar

Novellas available in ebook only
Broken Silence
Dirty Secrets

To Dan.
My life is so much richer because I know you.
Thank you for all the things you do, but especially for your friendship.

As always, to Martin. I love you.

PROLOGUE

Mid-City, New Orleans, Louisiana
MONDAY, OCTOBER 24, 6:45 P.M.

'WHY ARE WE here again?' Jace asked Rick, nervously checking traffic as he drove down a quiet street in a suburb he'd never been to before. Most of the buildings were small businesses that had already closed for the day. A few people walked the streets, most seeming to have been shopping at the corner store, which, other than a laundromat, was the only place still open. It didn't feel dangerous, though. The streets were well lit and no one looked nervous walking around. 'Rick?' he prodded when Rick didn't answer.

Rick should have been behind the wheel, but he'd shoved the keys to their brother Corey's van into Jace's hand, telling him to shut up and drive. Jace knew how to drive, but he didn't have a license because he was only fifteen. All he needed was to get stopped by a cop. He would have his license in six months, but he didn't think a cop would accept that excuse.

Plus, the cops weren't too happy with the Gates family right now. Jace couldn't say that he blamed them. What his oldest brother Aaron had done . . .

Jace might have believed it of his brother Corey, because Corey beat the shit out of Jace and his other brother Rick on the regular. But he wouldn't have thought Aaron capable of beating a man to death.

Except Jace had watched the video with his own eyes. Several times, because he hadn't been able to believe what he'd seen at first. Aaron had beaten that doctor to death with his fists.

Jace understood Aaron's grief. They'd all loved Aaron's little boy, Liam. The doctor hadn't cured Liam of his leukemia and the little boy had finally died.

But Jace didn't understand Aaron's rage. A week later, he was still in shock.

'Rick?' Jace asked again, because Rick still hadn't answered. 'Why are we here?'

Of his three brothers, Jace was closest to Rick. They were less than a year apart, and Rick took care of him. Had always taken care of him, ever since their mother had died.

Sure, Aaron and Corey had been made their legal guardians because they were a lot older—both in their early thirties—but it was Rick who'd looked out for Jace. They lived with Corey, but it was Rick who'd fixed his breakfast, made his lunch. Bandaged his skinned knees and tucked him into bed at night when he'd still been young enough. Rick had even done his homework because Jace couldn't do it on his own.

Aaron's arrest had hit Rick the hardest, Jace thought. Corey was furious with their oldest brother, but Rick had been devastated.

'We're picking something up for Aaron,' Rick said.

'What?' Jace insisted.

'Slow down,' Rick ordered, pointing to the sidewalk. 'See that woman there?'

Tapping the brake, Jace squinted at the woman who was about fifty feet ahead of them. 'The pregnant one?' Because, wow, the woman was *really* pregnant.

'Yeah, her. Didn't you read Corey's email? Oh right,' Rick said sarcastically. He'd been sarcastic a lot lately. Mean, even. And more jittery than usual. But they were all stressed out. 'You can't, because you're so stupid you can't even read.'

Jace winced. It wasn't like the words were lies. He was stupid and he couldn't read. Corey told him that every day. But the words hurt a lot more coming from Rick.

'Sorry,' he mumbled.

Rick huffed. 'Whatever. Just . . . do what I say, okay?'

Jace hunched in on himself, feeling small even though he was bigger than Rick. At six-one, he was only a few inches shorter than Corey, but it didn't matter. He couldn't read and could barely write his own name. It sucked to be the stupid one in the family. 'Okay. Can you tell me what we're picking up for Aaron?'

Rick pointed at the pregnant lady. 'Him.'

Jace frowned. There was a little boy walking next to the pregnant lady. He looked like he was only eight or nine years old. 'Why?'

'Because he can get Aaron out of jail,' Rick spat. 'He's *currency*.'

Jace blinked, confused. 'What?'

'*Currency*,' Rick repeated. 'That fucking no-name public defender Aaron got can't help him, so we need to do something. We need Aaron back. *We need him.*' Jace was struck by the desperation in his brother's tone. 'We can't—' Rick cut himself off, shaking his head hard. 'Somebody needs to do something. You're either with me or you're against me.'

Jace was still back on 'currency.' 'What are you talking—'

'Shut up and listen. If you don't want to do this, then back the fuck out right now,' Rick snapped. 'I need to be able to depend on you.'

'You can,' Jace said, hating his own desperation. 'But—'

'Shut up,' Rick hissed. He shoved something black and soft into Jace's hand.

Jace stared at it. A ski mask, just like the one Rick was pulling over his own head.

'Put it on,' Rick ordered. '*Now.*'

And then Rick pulled a gun from the waistband of his jeans.

Jace gaped. 'What the fuck?'

'Stop the van.' Wild-eyed, Rick grabbed at Jace's arm, making him jerk the steering wheel to one side, and the van veered into the curb. 'Put it on if you don't want to live in prison with Aaron. I mean it, Jace. *Now.*'

Stunned into obedience, Jace pulled the ski mask over his head as Rick yanked the passenger-side door open and jumped out of the van. The kid on the sidewalk stopped abruptly, turning to look up at the pregnant woman. She looked around with a frown.

Don't hurt her. She's pregnant. Please don't hurt her.

Dazed, Jace watched as Rick, still holding the gun in one hand, ran up to the pair and grabbed the boy, shoving him under his arm like a football. He'd made it two steps when everything went to shit.

Rick screamed and dropped to the ground a second before a siren began to wail.

Jace looked around, trying to figure out what had happened. *Fuck. Fuck. Fuck. I have to get out of here. Drive. Leave him.*

But Jace couldn't do that. Rick was his brother.

He'd leave you in a heartbeat.

True. But if Jace left Rick and the cops picked him up, two of his brothers would be behind bars. And Corey would be even madder.

Jace couldn't make Corey even madder. He just couldn't.

Making his decision, he burst from the driver's seat and rounded the van. By the time he got to the curb, the kid had rolled out from under Rick's arm and was kneeling on the sidewalk, visibly trembling— and holding Rick's ski mask in his small hand.

Shit. Rick's face was out there, for all the world to see. *Corey's going to kill us.*

'Run, Elijah, run!' the woman shouted. She grabbed at the boy's shoulder, yanking him to his feet, and Jace glimpsed the weapon in her hand.

A stun gun. She'd tased Rick.

The woman took off running faster than Jace thought a pregnant woman could run. 'Elijah, come on!' she screamed. But the boy was frozen in place, staring down at Rick.

Jace rushed to where Rick lay and the little boy slowly looked up at him, eyes wide. Looking every bit as shocked as Jace felt.

'Elijah!' the pregnant lady shouted from the doorway of the laundromat. The look of horror on her face made Jace think that she'd thought the little boy was behind her. She started to run back toward them but slipped and fell back into the laundromat with another scream.

Jace could grab the kid. He could do it.

But . . . he couldn't do it. *It's wrong.* Meeting the boy's terrified eyes, he made another decision. 'Run,' he snapped. 'I said *run!*'

It was when the kid finally started to run that Jace realized people were beginning to gather, to stare.

To take video. Things had just gone from bad to worse. *Goddammit.*

Rick was still on the ground, twitching and moaning. The smell of urine was thick. He was going to be so mad.

Don't think about that. Just move.

Jace hauled his brother onto his shoulder in a fireman's carry, grateful that Rick was the smaller of the two of them. Jace threw him in the van, closed the side door, and ran to the driver's side, revving the engine as he made their escape. *What have I done?*

Rick was gonna be pissed off. Jace had let the kid go.

No, he'd *made* the kid go.

Corey was . . . Jace shuddered at what Corey was going to do to them. *Don't think about that. Just drive.*

1

'MORNING, JOY,' VAL Sorensen singsonged.

Their office manager was at her desk in the lobby of Broussard Investigations, frowning at her computer monitor. 'Welcome back, Val,' she said without looking up. 'How was your assignment?'

'Boring. Some CEO said that someone was threatening his wife, but he was just worried that she was getting some from the pool boy on the side and wanted a chaperone.'

Joy glanced up. '*Was* she getting some from the pool boy?'

'Not my job to know,' Val said, then laughed. 'But yeah, she totally was.' Waving the box she held, she was rewarded when Joy's normally stoic expression became rapturous. Val gestured to the box like it was a game show prize. 'See something you like?'

Joy's lips twitched. 'Depends. Does that box in your hands contain Marica's cupcakes?'

Val smirked. Her pals MaryBeth and Jessica owned one of the best bakeries in the Quarter. 'They *were* Marica's, but then I paid for them, so now they're mine.' She put the box on Joy's desk, centering it carefully on the blotter, because a crookedly placed anything was annoying as hell. 'And now they're yours. Happy birthday, Joy.'

Joy grinned. 'You stood in that ridiculous line for me?'

'I did indeed.' She propped her hip on the corner of Joy's desk. 'I didn't have to, because MaryBeth already had these set aside for me and told me to just come to the front of the line to pick them up. But the crowd looked unruly, so I decided it would be safer to wait.'

Besides, it was a beautiful fall morning and she'd wanted to breathe it in before getting stuck behind her desk all day. She loved her job at Broussard Investigations—except for the paperwork, and she had a ton of it waiting for her.

'Well, thank you,' Joy said. 'Although you could have hip-checked anyone who gave you any shit, Miss Roller Derby Queen.'

Val rolled her eyes. 'I don't hip-check random strangers. Plus, there were a few old ladies in front of me who must have come from morning mass. They were clutching rosaries and didn't look scared to use them.'

'Such foolishness.' Joy lifted the box's lid, sniffed deeply, then sighed. 'Chocolate.'

'Of course. I'm not stupid.'

'No, you're not.' Joy tilted her head in a speculative way that had Val sliding off the desk and taking a wary step back.

'What?'

Joy smiled up at her. 'Nothing.' She took two of the cupcakes from the box and handed them to Val. 'One for you and one for the child.'

Val frowned. 'What child?'

The door to their boss's office opened and Burke Broussard appeared. A big and brawny retired Marine, Burke was somewhere in his midforties. A very handsome man, he turned heads everywhere.

Just not mine.

Burke was perfect as a friend, but she'd never even considered anything more. He was . . . too big. Way too big. Val had to swallow back the memories of the others who'd been too big, all while keeping a smile plastered on her face.

Burke knew her history, and he'd never been anything but kind and respectful of her boundaries. She trusted him implicitly, and that was a big deal for her. She'd been lucky the day he'd asked her to join his team. Broussard Investigations was a tightly knit group, and everyone was protective of the others. They were as close to a family as one could get without blood ties, and Val found the love and comfort here that her own broken family could no longer provide.

'Morning, Val,' Burke rumbled in that deep Cajun drawl of his. 'You have a new client. Bring a cupcake for him.'

Okaaaay. Holding the two cupcakes, Val walked to Burke's office door, hearing the whir of Joy's motorized wheelchair as the older woman followed her, unabashedly curious. A shiver of trepidation raced down Val's spine.

A moment later, she knew why. Assistant District Attorney Jean-Pierre Cardozo was coming to his feet, having been seated in one of the chairs in front of Burke's desk. She'd first met him at a party back in the summer. Burke and his staff had been celebrating with some clients after closing an all-hands-on-deck case when Cardozo had arrived, dressed in an expensive black suit that made him look like a Fortune 500 CEO.

He'd been charming as hell and impossible to ignore, despite her best efforts—that day and later. Unable to resist, she'd found herself googling him later that evening, learning surprisingly little personal information. Other than a few of the cases he'd tried up in the New York City courts, the man had no real internet presence, which took a lot of talent. Burke's IT guy, Antoine, would surely have been able to dig up a lot more, but she'd been unwilling to ask. Unwilling to voice aloud that the man had fascinated her.

She knew only that he'd recently moved from New York and that his first name was spelled K-a-j but pronounced 'Kai', rhyming with 'pie'. And she only knew those tidbits because she'd overheard Burke telling someone else in the firm.

After that day, she'd seen Cardozo twice. Once a couple weeks ago at another party at a friend's restaurant, Le Petit Choux. He hadn't stayed long, and she'd managed to avoid him. Their most recent crossing of paths had been in a courtroom the week before, a plea hearing for one of the criminals whose crimes Burke's group had exposed. No words had been exchanged between them either time, but Val had noticed the man's every movement.

He moved so very nicely. And he was a good guy, prosecuting bad guys, but that smile he'd worn . . . He could get her to trust that smile. Which meant he was dangerous.

He didn't look anything like that now. He was as handsome as before, his dark brown hair neatly combed, his face freshly shaven. His khakis were unwrinkled, the sleeves of his casual button-up shirt rolled up, exposing tanned forearms. He even wore a tie printed with whimsical dinosaurs. But his expression appeared haggard, as if he hadn't slept at all.

And his dark eyes were full of fear.

Val glanced to the corner of the room, revealing the source of his fear. A boy of about nine or ten sat at Burke's little meeting table. His hair was white-blond, unlike Cardozo's. But their faces were too much alike for them not to be related. *Father and son*, she thought.

She hadn't realized that Cardozo had a child, and she didn't want to think about why that disappointed her. It didn't matter that the child had a mother, that Cardozo had a significant other. It didn't matter because she was not interested in ADA Cardozo, first name 'Kaj' that rhymed with 'pie.'

The child, however, had captured her attention. He clutched a tablet in his hands, staring down at it with a vacant look that Val recognized all too well.

She'd seen it in the mirror plenty of times.

He'd been traumatized. He didn't look up, so Val turned back to his father.

'Hey,' Val said quietly, because the mood in the room was brittle. 'It's good to see you again, ADA Cardozo.'

The man's throat worked as he swallowed. 'Likewise. This is my son, Elijah. Elijah, this is Miss Sorensen.'

My new client? Val wondered. She looked at Burke, who inclined his head toward the boy, gesturing her to engage.

'Hi, Elijah,' she said, approaching the table. 'I'm Val.'

The boy didn't look up until Val put the cupcake in front of him. 'Hi,' he whispered.

It was one tiny word, but said with a determination that won her respect. She pointed at the cupcake. 'That's yours.'

'And that one, too?' Elijah asked, pointing at the cupcake still in her hand.

'Pfft. No,' she said, using her best *duh* tone. 'This one is mine. You're a greedy one, aren't you?' She smiled so that he would know she was teasing.

The boy's lips quirked up before returning to a grim line. 'Was worth a try.'

'It's always worth a try when cupcakes are on the line. Are you my new client?'

Elijah pushed Harry Potter-style glasses up on his nose. 'I guess so.'

'May I sit down?' She waited until Elijah nodded before taking the seat beside him. From this vantage point she could see the boy's face as well as that of his father.

Cardozo lowered himself back into his chair in front of Burke's desk, his face still frozen in a rictus of fear.

Whatever had happened, it had been bad.

She peeled the wrapper from the cupcake she'd kept, watching as Elijah did the same.

He hummed his pleasure when he took the first bite.

'Good, huh?' Val said. 'My bestie makes them fresh every morning.'

'Really good,' Elijah said, setting the rest of his treat aside. He gave his father a quick, sharp look across the room. 'I'm saving the rest for later.' His tone was dry but not unkind. 'You can get your own cupcake.'

Cardozo's chuckle sounded forced. 'I'll get right on that.'

Elijah shrugged sassily, but then his shoulders sagged as he sighed, his playfulness clearly feigned. 'Ask your questions, Miss Sorensen. I figure you have some.'

'Okay. Why are you here?'

'My dad said I had to come. He didn't have anyone to leave me with, and it wasn't safe for me in school.' There was a reluctance in his voice, and Val wasn't sure if it was because he was here or because he wasn't in school.

She wanted to ask where his mother was but held back. 'Do you like school?'

Elijah's expression became abruptly defiant. 'I do. Is that a problem?'

'Nope. I'm a teacher. I like kids who like school.'

'I thought you were a bodyguard.'

'Now, yeah. And an investigator sometimes, too, but I still do some teaching.'

Elijah's defiance melted away. 'What do you teach?'

'Music. I teach kids at the community center. Piano, violin, flute, some guitar, and a little tambourine for those who don't have success with the other instruments.'

'That's really nice,' Elijah said with a small smile, then dropped his gaze to the cupcake. Silence followed, and Val waited patiently, keeping her attention on Elijah.

She had experience with traumatized kids and knew that he'd speak when he was ready.

Finally, he looked up, swallowing audibly. 'Someone tried to kidnap me yesterday.'

Val drew a sharp breath, managing not to gasp. 'That sucks.'

Elijah snorted, then looked surprised that he had. 'It really did.'

'Can you tell me what happened?'

'It happened really fast. I was with my aunt, walking home after the math club competition at my school.' He dropped his gaze again. 'There were two men in a white minivan. Both had on ski masks. One got out and grabbed me, then started carrying me to the van.'

He stopped and looked up, his eyes now as fearful as his father's.

'That had to have been terrifying,' Val murmured. 'How did you get away?'

His lips curved again, this time with pride. 'My aunt Genie carries a Taser.'

'Excellent,' Val said with a nod. 'She hit the guy with the ski mask?'

'Yep. And I have a noisemaker, one of those things that's as loud as a siren. I pressed it right after she tased him.'

'Good job.' Val held out her fist, and Elijah bumped it.

'The guy dropped to the ground after Aunt Genie tased him, and she yelled for me to run. But . . .' He dropped his gaze to his hands once again. 'I froze.'

The boy's shame was palpable. That would not do.

'It happens,' she said quietly. 'When you're dropped into a situation you aren't expecting or you haven't been trained for, sometimes the brain can't process.' Elijah only huffed his disgust, presumably at himself. She decided to come back to the shame later. 'You're sitting here enjoying a cupcake, so I'm guessing that you got away.'

'Yeah.'

'And because you're here with your dad, I'm guessing the masked guys got away and you're still in danger. What happened after your aunt tased the bad guy?'

'The driver got out of the van and started to come after me, but lots of people had started to gather around.'

Then the boy went quiet, his expression becoming puzzled.

'Did the driver try to get you?' Val asked.

'No.' And this seemed to be the source of his puzzlement. 'He told me to run.'

Val blinked. 'That's . . . unexpected.'

'I know, right?'

'Then what did he do?'

'He picked up the guy who got tased and threw him over his shoulder, put him in the van, and drove away.'

Val had so many questions, but she figured she'd be following up with Cardozo and Burke once this interview was completed. And she had no doubt that this was an interview. Cardozo wanted to see how she interacted with his child, and she didn't blame him at all.

But first things first. She settled in her chair, giving Elijah an up-and-down visual exam. 'Were you hurt?'

'No, but Aunt Genie . . .' He shuddered. 'She's really pregnant and her doctor put her on bed rest. She was crying and kept asking him if she'd lose the baby.' His throat worked as he swallowed hard again. His eyes had gone glassy with unshed tears. 'I couldn't stand it if she lost the baby because of me,' he finished in a whisper.

Val wouldn't tell him that his aunt would be fine because she didn't know that for sure, and she wouldn't lie to him. 'Feeling guilty sucks, too. Even when it's not your fault. You know it's not your fault, right?'

Elijah nodded miserably. 'I get that. I do. But . . .' He blinked and sent fat tears sliding down his cheeks. 'She thought I was behind her and she ran. But I froze and she started to come back for me. Then she tripped and fell and . . .'

Oh, honey. She wanted to hug him, but she kept her hands folded on the table. 'What did her doctor say?' she asked, keeping her tone soft but firm.

He wiped his cheeks angrily. 'That the baby was okay. That bed rest was just a precaution. That it wasn't my fault.'

'Then those are the facts. You're entitled to however you feel, but the facts are that the baby is okay, and your aunt is resting. So . . . what do you want from me, Elijah?'

He glanced at his father, their eyes holding for another long moment. 'My dad wants me to have a bodyguard. Mr. Broussard says he thinks you'd be the best for the job.'

Val smiled at the boy. 'And what do you think?'

Elijah sized her up, his eyes sober behind his glasses. 'How tall are you?'

'Five-eleven in bare feet. Six-one with my boots on.' She'd hated being tall when she was Elijah's age, but now she liked the view from six feet up.

'You look like you have muscles. And Mr. Broussard said you were in the Marines.'

'I do have muscles, and I did serve.' Although muscles weren't always enough to keep one safe, she thought, then briskly swept the unwanted truth aside with a practiced mental swipe. 'I'm also told that I'm decent with kids.'

'I guess you'd have to be, to be a teacher. Do you have a gun?'

'I do. But I'd prefer not to have to use it, because I've kept you safe and out of the grabby hands of people who want to hurt you.'

He snorted again. 'Grabby hands?'

'I call 'em like I see 'em, kid.'

He sobered. 'Have you ever killed anyone?'

She looked him square in the eye. 'I have. I don't recommend it, but I don't regret it, either. The few times I've had to, the people I was protecting remained safe and well because I did. Like I said, my preference is to avoid that kind of conflict, because it means I've kept you safe. What will my duties entail?'

Again, Elijah looked at his father before returning his gaze to Val. 'Keeping me safe?'

'Well, yeah. But will I be going to school with you? Will I need to cook for you, do your laundry, that kind of thing?'

'I do my own laundry. But I can't cook. Not really.'

She noted that Elijah hadn't answered her question about school— and that his father had opened his mouth before abruptly closing it. There was disagreement there that she'd tackle later. 'Luckily for you, I can cook. I've been taking lessons lately from another one of my friends who co-owns a restaurant here in the Quarter. My food's not as good as hers, but we'll be just fine.' She tilted her head. 'Do I pass muster?'

'I might need help with my homework. Can you do math?'

This was another interview question, she was certain. A kid in the math club was unlikely to need help with his homework. 'Yes. Before I was a bodyguard-slash-investigator-slash-part-time-music-teacher, I was a full-time middle school math teacher.'

He blinked. 'Seriously?'

'Seriously. I can take a test later, if you need proof. In fact, we can take the same test and see who wins. Loser buys cupcakes. And I won't let you win, I promise.'

He regarded her steadily, then stuck out his hand. 'You're hired.'

She shook his hand, pleased that she'd won him over. Elijah Cardozo fired up all her protective instincts. But, of course, the boy's father had the final say. 'Thank you. Let me work out the details with your dad and then we'll see where we go from there.'

His tense shoulders relaxed a fraction. 'Thank you, Miss Sorensen.'

'You're welcome. And my friends call me Val.'

He nodded once. 'Thank you, Val.'

The Quarter, New Orleans, Louisiana
TUESDAY, OCTOBER 25, 9:15 A.M.

Thank you, Val.

Kaj Cardozo closed his eyes at his son's sober gratitude, trying to control the fear that clawed at him from the inside out. *Someone touched my son. Someone tried to take my son.*

Val Sorensen came recommended by Burke Broussard, and Broussard Investigations had a stellar record for closing cases. They got justice for those who'd been long denied. They also specialized in personal protection, which was why he was here.

Kaj had seen Burke in action, had witnessed his dedication and integrity.

Burke Broussard hires capable people. Which includes Val Sorensen.

Kaj had been chanting those words in his mind ever since he'd made the call to Broussard the night before, asking for this appointment. Right after he'd left his pregnant sister's home, trying not to hold his son too tightly.

Genie had been amazing, protecting Elijah, incapacitating his would-be attacker. His son was still here because Genie had saved him with her quick thinking. And her Taser.

If Genie hadn't been so vigilant . . . Kaj drew a deep breath, determined not to have a panic attack where Elijah could see him. He couldn't think that way. It wasn't good for Elijah.

Nor for me.

'Hey,' Val said softly right next to his ear, and the scent of vanilla filled his head. 'Breathe, Mr. Cardozo.'

Kaj's eyes flew open, and he shuddered out a breath when he saw the woman take the seat beside him, sweeping her hair over one shoulder in a practiced way. He'd noticed her hair the first time he'd seen her at a party back in the summer. It was long and white-blond, nearly the same color as his had been as a child, the same as

Elijah's was now. She was smiling at him, sympathy in her blue eyes.

'Elijah's here,' she murmured. 'He's here and he's okay. Scared, but okay.'

'And we're going to keep it that way,' Burke added.

Kaj scrubbed his palms over his face. 'Okay. What's next?'

'That depends on you.' Val glanced at Elijah, who sat watching them warily.

Kaj tried to smile, but his mouth wouldn't curve. 'You okay over there, kiddo?'

Elijah rolled his eyes, and that very genuine preteen gesture finally prodded a smile onto Kaj's face. 'I'm fine, Dad,' he said, his tone dripping with condescension. 'Are you?'

Yes, Kaj started to say, then shook his head. 'Not really. But I will be.'

Elijah sobered. 'I know.'

Kaj returned his gaze to Val Sorensen, who sat patiently waiting, carefully watching. 'You've protected children in the past?'

Val nodded once. 'Four times in the past three years.' She pursed her lips, as if remembering. 'All are safe today.'

But they hadn't been. He could see it in her eyes. Something had happened to one of her charges.

'What happened?' Elijah called over. 'Which time did you have to use your gun to keep a child safe from grabby hands?'

Val's smile was rueful. 'Why are you so smart, kid?' she called back.

'It's my cross to bear,' Elijah said dryly, and Kaj's chest tightened. *Heather used to say that.* In that same dry tone. Damn, but he missed her.

Val coughed, hiding a laugh. 'How old are you, Elijah? Twenty-five?'

'Only ten,' he said with a put-upon sigh.

She huffed. 'I'm gonna need to see a birth certificate.' She eyed Kaj. 'You might as well have your son sitting here with us, Mr. Cardozo. We're not hiding anything from him.'

Kaj sighed. 'I know. He really is too smart for *my* own good. C'mon over, Elijah. This is all about you, so you might as well be involved.'

'Which is what I *told* you when we *got* here,' Elijah muttered, dragging his chair from the small conference table over to Burke's desk. He dropped into the chair, crossing his arms. 'Well? Grabby hands?'

Val glanced at Burke, who shrugged. 'Okay,' she said, her accent also New Orleans, Kaj noted, but not Cajun—and not very strong. It made him wonder how long she'd been in the city. 'I was protecting a teenage girl and her brother, who was nine. I'm only telling you because it's public record. It was covered by the media. Otherwise, I wouldn't be able to share this.'

Elijah nodded very seriously. 'I understand.'

'Good. The girl's father had been threatened because of an upcoming corporate merger. Lots of people were losing their jobs and tempers were high. His children had been specifically targeted in the threats, so he hired me. The nine-year-old did everything I asked, but the teenager . . . not so much. She didn't think all the fuss was necessary and had a boyfriend.' She looked at Elijah sadly. 'She's a smart young woman. She figured out how to disengage the alarm system and climbed out her window and shimmied down a tree to see her beau.'

'But she's still alive?' Elijah asked, eyes wide.

'Yes. But her boyfriend is not. I was able to shield her, but the boyfriend got caught in the line of fire. He . . .' She sighed. 'He'd been approached by one of the disgruntled employees to lure the young woman away from the house. He'd taken money to deliver her into the hands of those who would have harmed her to get back at her father. He was only seventeen.'

'And you feel guilty,' Elijah murmured.

My perceptive son. It was exactly what Kaj had been thinking because the emotion was clear on Val's face.

'I do. I would have saved him, too, but he ran back to the kidnappers, thinking they'd protect him, that they'd take him with them when they ran away. But he was a loose end and they killed him.'

'I'm sorry,' Elijah said quietly. 'That it happened, and that I made you talk about it.'

'You're fine,' she said firmly. 'If I'd been nearly kidnapped yesterday, I'd want to know that my bodyguard had the experience to keep me safe, too. You have every right to ask questions. If I can't answer them, I'll tell you so. If I don't know the answer, I'll find out. If I can't answer because I'm protecting someone else's confidentiality, I'll tell you that, too. Just like I'll keep your circumstances confidential when we're finished and you're safe again.'

Elijah bowed his head. 'Thank you.'

Val ran a hand over his son's hair, her touch sweet, her expression fond. Which wasn't a surprise. Elijah elicited that response in nearly everyone who met him. Except for the bastards who'd tried to kidnap him.

'It's my job, but you're welcome,' she said. 'I need you to promise that you'll follow any rules that I set. If you want to know why, then ask. If I have time to explain, I will. But don't just disregard what I tell you to do. It could mean your life, Elijah.' Her eyes softened. 'I know that this isn't fair, but it's the way it is—for now anyway.'

Elijah looked up, determined. 'I promise.'

'Thank you.' She turned to Kaj. 'Do you know who was responsible?'

'He does,' Burke said, and there was something in his tone that had Val studying her boss. It was almost as if Burke were warning her.

Kaj would come back to that later. 'Aaron Gates,' he stated baldly.

Her brow furrowed in confusion. 'He's in jail. I've been out of town on a job, so I'm behind on the news, but I caught a clip. He murdered a doctor last week, right?'

'Beat him to death with his bare hands,' Elijah said grimly.

Val shot Elijah a surprised look, then shot Kaj one of censure that he probably deserved. His son was too young to know the details of violent crimes, but Elijah found ways to enrich his knowledge despite Kaj's best efforts to limit his online exposure.

'You're a kid,' she said. 'You shouldn't know about stuff like this.'

Elijah shrugged. 'I read the newspaper online. Every day. Knowledge is power.'

Another one of Heather's favorite isms. She'd be so delighted with how their son was turning out. Of course, she'd also be kicking Kaj's ass for putting their boy in danger in the first place. *I'm sorry, Heather.*

Burke cleared his throat, bringing them back on topic. 'It was Aaron's younger brother Rick who tried to grab Elijah last night.'

Val sucked in a breath, realization stark in her blue eyes. 'He . . . Holy sh—crap.' She stumbled over the barely missed swear word as she stared at Kaj. 'They thought that kidnapping your son would get you to release Aaron Gates?'

'That's the theory.' And Kaj liked to believe that he wouldn't have even considered bowing to the kidnappers' demands but knew that he would have. His son was everything.

'How was Rick identified?' she asked, running a comforting hand over Elijah's back.

'Rick's sixteen,' Burke said, 'so he has a driver's license. Elijah ID'd his DMV photo.'

'Sixteen,' she murmured then turned to Elijah with a frown. 'Wait. You saw his face?'

'I did.' Elijah preened. 'I ripped his mask off right before I got away.'

'Whoa,' Val said, clearly impressed. 'On purpose?'

'Yep. All the people recording on their phones got his face, too.'

'Way to go, Elijah.' She held out her fist for him to bump, giving him a wink when he did so. 'What about the other guy, the one driving the van? The one who told you to run?'

Elijah's face fell. 'I didn't see his face. I should have ripped off his mask, but . . . I ran.'

'Hey.' She tipped Elijah's face up with a finger under his chin. 'You did good. You gave the cops a place to start their investigation. Otherwise, they'd be spinnin' their wheels, because I'm betting the van had stolen plates.'

'True enough,' Burke confirmed in a lazy drawl.

Val was still holding Elijah's gaze. 'And running away was the very smartest thing to do. If you have the choice, *always* run. There is *nothing* shameful in getting away from danger. Got it?' There was a ferocity in her words that suggested personal experience. Kaj would come back to that later, as well.

Elijah nodded, and Kaj felt a burst of gratitude for Val. Elijah had been obsessing that he hadn't done enough. 'Got it.'

'We don't know who was driving the van—yet,' Kaj said, giving his son a proud nod. 'There are four Gates brothers. Aaron's the oldest, and in jail. Corey's thirty-one, two years younger than Aaron. He runs a construction business here in town. He was very cooperative with the NOPD when they wanted to search Aaron's home and office after the murder. Seemed shocked that Aaron would melt down like he did. Corey probably wasn't the driver because he's a few inches too tall. Rick is sixteen, and Jace is just fifteen. We don't know much about Jace, but he was too young to be driving the van.'

'Legally, anyway,' Burke said quietly.

'True,' Kaj conceded. 'But there is another possibility.'

Burke stiffened and, seeing him, Val did the same. 'Which is?' she asked warily.

Kaj wanted to know what the hell the two of them knew, but he'd confront them in private. He wasn't sure he wanted Elijah to know any more than he already did—which was way too much. 'Have you heard of Sixth Day?'

If he hadn't been watching Val's face so closely, he'd have missed the infinitesimal flinch. That flinch might be bad or good, depending on why the name of the gang had affected her. This was what Burke had been warning her about. *And I'll definitely be following up.*

'Yes,' she said evenly. 'I have. They sold a lot of drugs, but they're now defunct. Been so for about four years. Rico Nova, the old leader, was jailed for murder, and then the gang disintegrated. How is Aaron Gates connected to Sixth Day? I thought he was some kind of financial advisor.'

'He was,' Kaj said. 'We found the connection when we were searching the home of the woman arrested with him.'

'Sandra Springfield,' Elijah broke in helpfully. 'She was his personal assistant. She held Aaron's coat while he killed the doctor. People watching said she was cheering him on.'

'So she's a nice person,' Val said sarcastically.

'She's also Aaron's *girlfriend*,' Elijah added. 'Even though Aaron already has a wife.'

Dear Lord. Kaj hadn't realized Elijah knew that, too. He was going to have to totally block his son's internet access.

'Drama in a drug gang. Who'd have thunk it?' she deadpanned. 'What did you find when you were searching Sandra's home?'

'A thumb drive,' Kaj said, 'containing photos of Aaron with one of the known Sixth Day members—Dewey Talley.'

Again she flinched, and it was, once again, infinitesimal. 'Rico Nova's second-in-command.'

Kaj nodded, still watching her. 'I understand that most people dealt with Talley for day-to-day operations. Nova was a fairly silent partner.'

Her jaw tightened. 'Most people didn't know Rico Nova's name until he was arrested for murder.'

Kaj noted her tension. It was very well covered, but it was there. 'Everyone said that Talley went under after Sixth Day fell apart. Nobody's seen him for almost four years.'

'Maybe he's dead,' she said, her tone flat and grim.

Kaj sighed. 'If he is, it's a real recent thing.' He handed his phone to Val, one of Sandra Springfield's photos they'd found on his screen.

She went perfectly still, her gaze locked on the off-center photo of Aaron Gates and Dewey Talley laughing. Her mouth tightened and she exhaled silently. 'He looks different. Older. A lot more than four years older.' She glanced at Kaj. 'The beard, the shaggy hair, and the ratty clothes are new. He used to be clean-shaven and well-dressed. I wouldn't recognize him if I passed him on the street, which I suppose has helped him hide for the past four years. How do you know this is recent?'

'That's Aaron Gates's living room,' Kaj told her. 'The movie on the TV was only released a few months ago. In all the photos, they appeared to be friends.'

She handed him his phone. 'Is Talley still dealing?'

'I checked with an old friend from my days in Narcotics,' Burke said quietly. Almost warily. 'Talley is rumored to still be the go-to guy for high-quality meth, heroin, and any pill a user could want. He's just become smarter about not getting caught. His client list—again, this is rumor—is high-society types. Businessmen, trophy wives, that kind of thing. Aaron might not be part of Sixth Day, but he is somehow involved with Talley.'

'That makes sense,' she agreed begrudgingly. 'The fact that Aaron's girlfriend hid those photos indicates that they're somehow important. My guess would be blackmail or some kind of insurance. Photos like that generally are. But that doesn't necessarily mean Talley was involved in last night's abduction attempt.'

'Rick dropped a gun at the scene last night,' Kaj said, and his blood ran cold once again. *Rick Gates had a gun in one hand and my son in the other*. 'Ballistics matched it to a gun used to murder a low-level dealer last year.'

Val opened her mouth to say something, but Burke silenced her with a look. 'Talley's body type matches last night's driver—who had a dragon tattoo on his right upper arm.'

'Like Talley's.' Val seemed to deflate before squaring her shoulders. 'Y'all could have just led with that, y'know,' she grumbled. 'But it still doesn't make sense. The driver told Elijah to run. That's the opposite of what Dewey Talley would do.'

'I agree,' Burke said. 'But for now, these are the two leads we have. A definitive identification of Rick Gates working with someone who has a tattoo like Dewey Talley's, who is at least friendly with Aaron Gates. Let's see where that takes us.'

She nodded once. 'All right, then. Where is Rick Gates now?'

'We don't know,' Kaj admitted. 'He and the driver got away. NOPD is searching.'

'What about their camp?' she asked. 'Sixth Day has a place out on the bayou. Or at least they did four years ago.'

Val Sorensen was very knowledgeable about Sixth Day. She'd known about Talley's tattoo and the existence of their bayou camp, neither of which had been released to the press. Kaj knew because he'd pored over the Sixth Day files all night long to learn whatever he could. More than her knowledge, Val's interest seemed personal. He needed to find out why before hiring her to protect his son.

Burke cleared his throat. 'The land was private property and the owners back then claimed to have no knowledge of Sixth Day squatting. NOPD believes that they have another camp, and they're looking for it, but so far, no dice.'

Her mouth turned down. 'So Dewey Talley's out there somewhere, maybe planning another attempt. Do you want me to take Elijah out of the city?'

'No,' Elijah said forcefully. 'I won't leave my dad or Aunt Genie.'

Val started to say something to Elijah, but Kaj lifted his hand. 'Actually, Elijah can't leave. Not easily, anyway. He's undergoing treatment for juvenile diabetes. His doctor is here in New Orleans. If we can keep him safe at home, that would be our preference.'

Elijah's lips trembled, and Kaj's frozen, terrified heart cracked. His son's life wasn't in immediate danger from his disease, but Elijah hated the constant monitoring.

Val darted a glance back at the little table, her gaze focusing in on the cupcake missing just one bite. 'You should have said something,' she said quietly, and Kaj wasn't sure who she meant to gently chastise— him or his son.

Elijah bristled. 'I didn't because I'm not stupid. I know what I can eat and what I can't. I did the carb math in my head before I took a bite. Gave myself a unit of bolus insulin once you'd left to sit over here. I don't need a needle. I can control my insulin pump with my phone.'

Val glanced at Kaj before turning her full attention on Elijah. 'Okay,' she said with a single nod. 'I'll do the research and you can help me plan our meals. What impact did the adrenaline from your scare yesterday have on your blood sugar?'

That she asked the question made Kaj relax a little. Despite being thrown off her game at the mention of Dewey Talley, this woman was a thinker and appeared to be a planner, which was exactly what they needed right now.

Elijah shrugged sullenly. 'It spiked. I have a pump, and it did its thing. After a few hours it went back down. I'm not stupid.'

A simplistic explanation, because the spike had been frighteningly severe, made only worse by Elijah's worry over Genie. The doctor had wanted to keep Elijah overnight to observe him, relenting when that made Elijah even more upset. But Kaj wouldn't bruise his son's ego in front of Val by pointing it out right now.

'I can see that you're not stupid, so you don't need to keep saying that.' She tilted her head, studying Elijah. 'Who prepares your meals?'

'My aunt does.' Elijah flinched. 'Did.'

'She's been your caregiver while your dad's at work?' Val asked carefully.

Kaj thought that she wanted to ask about Elijah's mother but seemed hesitant. The woman could read a room. Another point in her favor.

'Yes,' Elijah said. 'Since I was small.' He lifted his chin defiantly, as if daring her to say that he was still small.

He was, of course. His mother had been petite as well, barely five feet tall in her socks.

I'm sorry, Heather. I'm sorry that I've put him in danger. I'm so sorry.

His wife couldn't hear him, of course. But it helped to talk to her, even if it was only in his mind. It helped him feel not so alone.

He was so damned tired of feeling alone.

Val smiled down at Elijah. 'Then, if Aunt Genie's up to it, we'll Skype with her to get some tips.' She slid her arm around Elijah protectively. 'We *will* keep him safe, Mr. Cardozo.'

Kaj exhaled, relieved when Elijah rested his head on the woman's shoulder. They'd made a connection, and from everything Burke had told him, she'd protect Elijah with her life.

'Burke, I'd like to see your contract for both investigative and bodyguard services.'

Val's brows rose. 'We're investigating, too? The whole team?'

'You are,' Kaj answered. 'I've asked Burke to put as many people as he can on this case. While I trust the NOPD to fully investigate, I'm taking no chances with Elijah's safety.'

Which was a diplomatic way of saying that, after six months in his role, he still wasn't sure who he could trust within the NOPD. He'd taken the job with the Orleans Parish DA's office to help identify internal corruption, and he'd been successful so far. Unfortunately, he'd made a few enemies within the NOPD along the way.

He was not going to apologize for hiring a private firm to find out exactly who was behind the plot to abduct his son. He wasn't worried about being able to afford Burke's services. He didn't earn a lot as a prosecutor, but he had the funds from Heather's life insurance. He hadn't touched a dime, planning to give it to Elijah someday for college. But Heather would approve of him using the money to protect their son. If it wasn't enough to cover Burke's bill, Kaj would sell everything he owned if it meant keeping Elijah safe.

So first, he'd review the contracts. But before he signed anything, he'd find out what the hell Val Sorensen knew about Dewey Talley and Sixth Day and why she knew it.

2

Downtown, New Orleans, Louisiana
TUESDAY, OCTOBER 25, 9:15 A.M.

'ARE YOU READY?' Ed asked, looking worried. 'Do you need to go over it again?'

Corey gave himself a final look in his foyer mirror, smoothing his tie with a hand that did not tremble. He'd survived enemy sniper fire in Iraq. A dozen reporters were no threat.

'I'm ready,' he said. He'd spent most of the night on the phone with Ed and their other business partner, Bobby. Their heads had been far cooler than Corey's after Jace had called him with the story of the failed abduction. Of a prosecutor's son, no less.

Of the one prosecutor whose attention Corey sought most to avoid. This week was critical for him and Bobby and Ed. The success of their business depended on the job they were about to close. They couldn't afford to be sucked into whatever hell Rick's stupidity had brought down on their heads.

Corey had been convinced that Rick's fuckup was a disaster for him as well, but Bobby was a former cop and knew how police investigations worked. Plus, Bobby still had eyes and ears in the department who slipped him information every now and then. Last night, one of his sources had come through for them, giving them the single piece of intelligence that would turn this debacle into the perfect smoke screen.

They were going to spin this story, reimagining it in their own favor. They'd already laid the foundation with the cops, painting Rick as a troubled teenager with a serious drug problem when they'd come to question him the night before. Now they were going to use the media to seal the deal.

He nodded to Ed. 'Let's do this.'

'Corey,' a small voice all but whispered. 'Wait.'

He turned to find Dianne standing in the living room archway, pale and shaking. 'I ironed your pocket square.' His brother Aaron's wife crossed the foyer with remarkable grace, considering she was already drunk as hell at nine fifteen in the morning. Pasting on a too-bright smile, she tucked his pocket square into place, then smoothed his lapels. 'You'll be fine. We'll bring Rick home. We'll find him.'

He kissed her cheek gently, pity and love for her momentarily dulling the rage and hatred he harbored toward his brothers. Dianne hadn't been the same since Liam died. Neither had Corey. He'd loved that boy like he was his own son.

None of them had been the same, but that didn't give Aaron an excuse to kill a goddamn doctor or Rick an excuse to try to kidnap the prosecutor's son.

'We'll find him,' he echoed confidently because she needed to hear it. There had always been a fragility to Dianne, long before Liam had been diagnosed with a rare form of leukemia, but it had always been paired with a sweetness that made everyone feel compelled to take care of her. Everyone except Aaron, of course, who was as shitty a husband as he was a brother. Even before he'd killed the doctor, he'd been a drug-dealing, lying, thieving SOB, but Dianne didn't know any of that.

She'd only just learned that Aaron had been cheating on her for years with his personal assistant.

Liam's death and Aaron's betrayal had pushed her past her limit. She was no longer fragile. She was downright brittle. Rick's idiocy might very well break her.

Corey wished he could tell her that he knew exactly where Rick was to ease her mind, but he couldn't afford to. Especially given his plans for Rick. 'You stay inside with Ed, okay? You don't need to run that gauntlet again.' She'd been staying with him to escape being pestered by reporters ever since Aaron's asshole move last week.

Killing a damn pediatric oncologist, for God's sake. In front of people. If Aaron had to do it, at least he could have been discreet. But Aaron was a dick, and now Corey was having to clean up his mess. Which was now doubled thanks to Rick.

Corey walked through the front door of his house, which he'd allowed the police to search during the night. It would take a week to clean the forensic fingerprinting dust from his walls, doors, and appliances. Because his brother Rick was a fucking idiot.

All his brothers were fucking idiots.

Rage bubbled up from his gut, nearly choking him, but he pushed it back. Now was not the time for rage. Now was the time for calm. Because if he was going to spin the hell out of Rick's little fiasco, Corey needed to bring his A game.

He stopped at the edge of his front porch, counting heads. There were nearly two dozen people on his lawn. Half were reporters and the other half held cameras. They were here because he'd asked them to come. He'd promised them a statement regarding Rick.

He was going to give them one that would make headlines.

The two detectives who'd already questioned him waited behind the crowd of reporters. Corey figured the cops were watching him as much as they were looking for Rick. This performance was for them, too. He needed them firmly in his corner.

His gaze swept down the street, noting how many of his neighbors had come out to witness his humiliation.

Vultures, every last one of them. But they'd serve his purpose today.

He ran his hand over his shaved head awkwardly, projecting nerves that he didn't feel. 'Good morning,' he said gravely. 'My name is Corey Gates. Please let me read my statement without interruption.' He didn't expect the reporters to comply. It was all part of the game. 'As I'm sure you've heard, my younger brother Rick attempted to kidnap the son of an ADA last night. He was, thankfully, unsuccessful. I've fully cooperated with the police, who've searched my home, turning it upside down. Rick is not here.'

'Where is he?' one of the reporters shouted.

Anticipating the interruption, Corey tightened his jaw for effect, delivering the lie with the emotion expected of the guardian of a boy gone wrong. 'I don't know where he is, which is one of the reasons I asked you to come. I'd like your viewing audience to help me locate my brother. I've raised Rick since my mother's death, and, quite honestly, I've been at the end of my rope for a long time. Rick's been troubled and . . .' He cleared his throat, straightening his shoulders. 'He's gotten involved with drugs. I've tried to get him help, but I've failed. I'm not saying that the drugs excuse what he did last night, because nothing can excuse that. He did a terrible thing and needs to face the consequences.'

He swallowed hard, hoping the cameras caught his distress. 'But he's only sixteen. He's out there somewhere, maybe alone and scared. He's been depressed since our mother's death, but I didn't realize it had gotten so bad. Look, I'm not a child psychologist. I'm just a contractor. I run a home improvement business.' He gestured to the truck that sat in his driveway. 'Three Vets Renovation. I install drywall and toilets for a living.'

Which was true on paper, but he, Bobby, and Ed put minimal effort into actually renovating anything. Three Vets Renovation was merely a front, hiding their far more lucrative—and far less legit—business. On paper, they were stand-up citizens, but Three Vets existed solely to launder the monies they earned doing very dirty jobs for very powerful people.

This week their dirty job was to cause the death of Bella Butler, an actress who'd accused her director, Trevor Doyle, of rape. It was shaping up to be a blockbuster trial, one that would hurt Doyle's career, even if the jury acquitted him—and these days, one could never be too sure how a jury would go.

So Doyle had hired them to get rid of Bella before the trial began. He'd wanted it to look like a car accident—low-key and completely untraceable back to him to keep the Feds from investigating him for witness tampering. Corey had come up with a better idea because Bella might survive a car accident. She wouldn't survive what he'd planned.

As for diverting suspicion from their client, Corey, Bobby, and Ed had built a solid strategy for that as well, and Doyle had been very pleased. But none of it would be possible if the cops were following Corey's every move as they had been, first with Aaron and now with Rick. Of all the weeks his brothers could pick to colossally fuck up, this week was the worst.

Doyle's trial started in a few days, but Bella had been in hiding for weeks. They knew where she was, but she was surrounded by too much security to get to her. Their window of opportunity for eliminating her was very slim—the hour she'd be driving from her hideaway to New Orleans. Her security would still be impressive, but they had a plan for that, too. She'd be coming to the city sometime this week, so they had to throw the NOPD off their scent.

Which was why he was now begging strangers to help him find his brother. But, if everything went to plan, he'd also provide the police and the public an alternate villain to pursue, one they wouldn't be able to resist.

Searching the crowd, Corey spread his hands imploringly. 'I didn't know anything about parenting. But then my mother died, and Rick became my responsibility. I was completely unprepared to raise a troubled teenager. I still am.'

It was working. The reporters' expressions hadn't cracked, but a few of the camera folks looked sympathetic.

'If I could find Rick,' Corey continued, 'he could get the help he desperately needs. He'll have to face the consequences of his actions, but hopefully he'll emerge clean and sober. Please, if you see him, call the NOPD. I'm putting up a reward of ten thousand dollars for any tips that lead to his return. He's not safe out there.' He hesitated, bit his lip, then blurted, 'I don't think he's just using drugs. I think he's fallen in with a gang who will not have his best interests at heart. He's only sixteen. He should have his whole life in front of him. If you're afraid to call the cops, please call my personal cell phone at 504-555-1020.'

He figured his voice mail would be full within an hour with crackpots and true crime wannabes trying to cash in on the ten grand reward, but he would not be calling anyone back. Because none of them would know where Rick was.

Corey knew, of course. Rick was with Jace at Corey's camp on the bayou, being guarded by Corey's best friend, Bobby. The camp had been the only place Corey had been able to think to hide them last night after Jace's frantic call for assistance. Corey had been rattled and angry, able to think only about the blow his brothers had struck to his business.

ADA Cardozo, for fuck's sake. It just *had* to be ADA Cardozo. It had been bad enough when Aaron had landed the same prosecutor who was also prosecuting Trevor Doyle. Their client had been very displeased. But then Rick had to go and grab Cardozo's kid? The ADA and the NOPD would be coming after anyone named Gates.

Which included Corey, unfortunately.

'Where's your youngest brother Jace?' another reporter called out.

'He's with some friends.' Luckily, no one knew that Jace had been driving the van. He'd managed to keep his ski mask on, unlike Rick, who was supposed to be the smart one. 'Jace isn't involved in any of this. Please respect his privacy. Now, if you'll excuse—'

'Mr. Gates!' A redhead forced her way to the front of the crowd, her microphone extended. 'Did Rick's abduction attempt have anything to do with the fact that your older brother Aaron is in jail awaiting trial for the murder of Dr. Singh last week? Was Rick trying to use ADA Cardozo's son to get Aaron out of jail?'

Of course he was, he wanted to snap. *You're as big an idiot as Rick is.* But he said no such thing. The redhead was Noni Feldman and her news program was viewed by thousands.

So he shrugged sadly. 'Who knows what was going through his mind? We've all been on edge since Aaron's crime last week, but that doesn't excuse Rick's behavior, either. We've undergone a great deal of stress this year. Six months ago, we lost our nephew Liam to cancer, and he was only eight years old. His death sent Rick spiraling deeper into depression. Rick's not a bad kid, but he's not making good choices right now. Please, help me find him.'

Corey started to back away, knowing that they'd continue to pepper him with questions.

'Mr. Gates!' Noni called again. 'You mentioned Rick was involved with a gang. Which one, and how do you know?'

Finally. This was the question he'd been waiting for, the major element of the spin.

Corey let his shoulders sag and hoped he looked as worried as he'd practiced in the mirror. 'Sixth Day.'

That got everyone talking.

'But Sixth Day isn't operating anymore,' a male reporter protested. 'They collapsed four years ago.'

'I didn't know anything about Sixth Day until last night,' Corey told the camera, with exhaustion that was not feigned. The tip that the

NOPD believed Dewey Talley had been driving the van hadn't been passed on to them until nearly dawn. But it had made all the difference. 'I'd never even heard of them.' More lies.

Corey knew Sixth Day very well. He knew Dewey Talley particularly well, because the man was Aaron's partner. Prior to their partnership, Sixth Day had sold drugs to anyone from schoolkids to rich socialites. Over the last four years, Dewey and Aaron had grown the business into a boutique racket, no longer focusing on the schoolkids. Sixth Day's clientele was now exclusively the rich and famous of New Orleans, the movers and shakers.

Well, it had been. With Aaron in jail and Dewey about to be set up for Rick's crime, local high society would have to get their happy pills somewhere else. Corey had no desire to keep that business going.

'But we found evidence that Rick was communicating with one of Sixth Day's leaders—a guy named Dewey Talley.' Gasps rippled through the gathered crowd. This was going better than he'd hoped. 'After I read about what Sixth Day did in the past . . .' He shuddered. 'I'm terrified for my brother, as I'm sure you understand. I need to find him so that he can get the help he needs. Now, I really have to go. Thank you for your time.'

He turned around, conscious of the reporters' shouts and the camera flashes.

'Mr. Gates!' Noni Feldman again. 'Are you going to bail your brother Aaron out of jail?'

Corey turned slowly to face the cameras, allowing them to see his true reaction—disbelief and contempt. 'No. I have no intention of bailing him out. He killed a man with his bare hands. That he was high at the time was no excuse.' He shook his head. 'And even if I wanted to, I don't have that kind of money. His bail was set at two million dollars. Even ten percent of that for a bail bond is completely out of my reach. This house and Three Vets Renovation are all that I have.'

Which totally wasn't true. His business doing dirty jobs for powerful people had enabled him to amass a fairly hefty bank account. Enough that he could pay Aaron's bail. But Aaron's betrayal was still way too fresh. Corey had always known that Aaron was a dick and a user, but he hadn't expected Aaron to steal from his own family.

From me. From Dianne.

Corey was perfectly content to let Aaron rot in prison.

And when Aaron tried to draw on his own funds to bail himself out? He'd find he'd been cleaned out. *By me.*

He turned for his door once again, grinding his teeth when Noni Feldman's voice rang out once more. 'Your father did time for murder. Twelve years in Angola.'

Corey froze, his back to the crowd. The statement was true, of course, but every time he heard it spoken his gut turned to ice. He'd always despised Aaron, but the hatred he felt for his father eclipsed everything else.

'Do you think having a convicted felon for a father influenced your brothers to commit felonies?' she pushed. 'Aaron killed Dr. Singh with his bare hands, just like your father killed his victim.'

Staring at his front door, Corey opened his mouth. *Fuck you, bitch* was on the tip of his tongue. His pulse pounded in his head, drowning out all other sounds. He wanted to kill Noni Feldman. Strangle her, just like his father had done to that stranger in a bar brawl when Corey had been only five years old. He remembered the reporters back then. Remembered the shame.

Remembered the ceaseless poverty after his father was no longer an earner.

He wanted to turn on the reporter and tell her to go to hell, but he spied Ed peeking from the side window next to the front door. Ed was shaking his head, his expression pinched.

Don't react. Don't fuck this up. Corey drew a breath, then another until the pounding in his head lessened and he could hear himself think again.

He's dead. His father was dead and couldn't cause him any more trouble, but his brothers had taken up the old man's mantle, all right.

Focusing on each step, Corey climbed his porch stairs, ignoring the reporters' incessant questions. Let them shout. He was done.

He closed the door and leaned against it, meeting Ed's eyes. 'Well? How'd I do?'

Ed's nod was relieved, like he'd expected Corey to fall apart. 'It was good. Let's talk more once we're on the road.'

Corey nodded. 'I'm expecting those two detectives to knock any second. I don't think they wanted me to share the info about Sixth Day, but they didn't tell me not to. Go sit with Dianne in the living room and shut the door. Keep her occupied. I don't want her listening.'

'Sure thing.' He disappeared into the living room, pulling the pocket door closed just as two sharp raps rattled his front door.

Corey opened the door to find the two detectives on his front porch, just as he'd expected. They were Detectives Clancy and Drysdale, but they were clearly playing Good Cop and Bad Cop, so that was how Corey thought of them.

Detective Bad Cop lifted his brows. 'We didn't expect you to divulge the gang connection, Mr. Gates.' Because they didn't want the public to know about Sixth Day, but it was what Corey most needed all of New Orleans to know.

Police phone lines would ring with residents demanding the police round up the gang and clean up the city. Public scrutiny—and police attention—would be on the drug dealers.

Not on me.

Corey widened his eyes in pretend dismay. 'I'm sorry.' He shook his head, dropping his gaze subserviently. 'I didn't think to hold it back. I was nervous and . . .' He sighed wearily. 'I was trying to be as transparent as possible. I'm sorry.'

The other detective nodded sympathetically. He was the good cop, Corey had learned during his interrogation on Rick's whereabouts the evening before. 'We understand, but you have to understand that you've likely made yourself a target. Sixth Day won't like that you've put them back in the spotlight. They could retaliate.'

Corey opened his mouth, honestly a little stunned. 'I didn't think about that. But it doesn't change anything. I want Rick back. Even if it's dangerous for me.'

It wouldn't be dangerous, of course, but he hadn't thought about the threat to himself. He hoped this didn't make the police follow him 'for his own good.'

'That's noble, Mr. Gates,' Good Cop said, still sympathetic. 'But please don't say any more to the press. They'll aid with getting Rick's photo out there and hopefully that will help us bring him in peacefully.'

Corey glanced up, drawing a pained breath. 'That's all I want. For him not to be hurt.'

Lie. He wanted Rick to hurt a lot. And he'd make sure the little bastard did before this day was over.

Detective Bad Cop looked like he wanted Rick to be hurt, too. 'I assume you'll be staying here?'

Corey had planned for this. *Keep it cool.* He grimaced. 'I will be, but my sister-in-law is exhausted. She's been staying here with me because the media was at her house, but now they're here. She has a sister down in Houma. I'm planning to take her there later today. But for now, she wants to help us continue looking for Rick. I'll keep my cell phone on and charged. I'll call you the minute I either find him or hear from him. You said last night that the judge might be able to get him into rehab. Is that still possible?'

Detective Good Cop nodded. 'It's possible. It'll be up to the DA on the case, but we'll put in a good word.'

Which was utter bullshit, but Corey smiled gratefully. 'Thank you.'

Good Cop smiled back. 'I'm glad we found the burner phone that Rick left behind. We wouldn't have thought to look at Sixth Day for this. They've been off our radar for four years.'

More bullshit. But Corey simply nodded.

Detective Bad Cop harrumphed grumpily. 'I can't believe your brother hid his burner and drugs in your mother's funeral urn. That's messed up, man.'

Rick hadn't, of course. Corey had planted them there after Ed had walked him through how to configure one of their burners to look like Rick had been corresponding with drug dealers. The drugs had been Rick's, though. Corey had found them in Rick's bedroom. He'd known for a while that Rick was using, but if his brother wanted to poison his body, he wasn't going to tell him no.

'Like I said, he hasn't been right in a long time.'

Bad Cop took a step forward. 'We're going to need to talk to Jace.'

Oh no. No, no, no. 'He's not here. I don't want him drawn into this.'

'It doesn't matter what you want, Mr. Gates. We need to talk to him.'

'He's fifteen.'

Bad Cop scowled. 'That's old enough to—'

'He's special,' Corey blurted out. 'Cognitively challenged. He can't read or write and is emotionally a child. I don't want him dragged into this.'

Again, lies. Jace wasn't cognitively challenged. He was just stupid. He'd been that way when Corey had taken custody and no amount of bribes or punishment had made his youngest brother any smarter, so Corey had given up. Jace was a lost cause.

'We'll bring in a specialist,' Good Cop said soothingly. 'We won't upset him.'

'He's already upset,' Corey said angrily. 'That's why I sent him to stay with a friend. All the reporters chasing us, yelling at us, asking questions? Police all over Aaron's house? All the TV coverage? He was in a right state, Detective. So, no. I will give you access to Rick's room and his things. But Jace is off-limits. I'll have to insist on a warrant.'

Detective Good Cop lost his sunny disposition. 'I thought you wanted to be cooperative, Mr. Gates.'

'I do. I have been. But Jace is off-limits. I fucked up with Rick. I'm not repeating my mistakes with Jace.' Untrue. Corey hadn't fucked up at all. His brothers had been ruined when he'd gotten them, and they were too old to fix.

Liam had been his chance to raise a child the right way. Since Aaron had never been home, child rearing had fallen to Dianne and she'd leaned heavily on Corey. But now Liam was dead. *And I can't think about Liam right now,* he thought as a wave of fresh grief hit him hard. *Have to keep my wits. Have to make these assholes go away.*

He held his breath, hoping the detectives would back down. If they didn't, he'd make them work for a warrant. In that time, he'd school Jace on the proper responses. Jace was easily controlled. A couple of slaps, a few kicks, and a punch or two rendered him completely compliant. Corey could handle Jace.

'We'll get back to you,' Bad Cop promised ominously. 'Until then, do not leave town.'

Yada yada yada. 'If I do, it'll only be to Houma and back,' he promised sincerely, then opened the door to show them out. 'Have a good day, gentlemen.'

They left without another word and Corey closed the door, truly exhausted now. He tugged at his tie as Ed emerged, looking grim.

'They don't give up, do they?' he asked.

'No.' Corey stuffed his tie in his suit coat pocket. 'Let's get out of here before they come back with more questions.'

Ed immediately started for the door, but Corey shook his head. 'We can't leave her here,' he murmured.

Ed looked over his shoulder with a sigh. Dianne sat in Corey's living room, clutching a photo of Liam to her chest. It was one of the pictures taken before the chemo had robbed the child of his hair and his vitality. He was grinning sweetly and it was Corey's favorite photo because Liam looked just like Dianne.

'Why can't we leave her here?' Ed whispered.

'Because she's my alibi for last night,' Corey whispered back. 'I left as soon as Jace called and she was asleep. I handed the boys off to Bobby, then hightailed it back here because I knew the cops would figure out who Rick was pretty damn quick.' And they had. He'd made it back home with only thirty minutes to spare. He was damn lucky they hadn't asked to touch the hood of his car because it would have still been warm to the touch. 'I woke her up and made her believe she'd only nodded off for a moment, then started sobering her up. She told them what I told her to say, that she and I had been home the entire time. If the cops catch her when she's totally drunk, she might tell them I had to wake her up. They'll assume I was with Rick.'

The Gates brothers hadn't had the best track record in the last week. If it came down to it, the cops would believe he'd lied about the alibi. Which he had. 'She'll spill everything.'

Ed sighed again. 'So what do you want to do with her?'

'Bring her to the camp.'

Ed's eyes widened. 'What the fuck?' he hissed.

Corey pulled a bottle of Dianne's sleeping pills from his pocket and tossed them to Ed. 'We'll fix some coffee for the road. Put some in hers and, combined with the vodka she's been drinking all morning, she'll be out like a light.'

'And when she wakes up?'

'We'll keep her confined, keep her sedated.' He shrugged uncomfortably. 'Keep her drunk. Just until we deal with Rick. Like we planned.'

Ed gave him a reluctant nod. 'Fine. But I wish you'd chosen a sober alibi.'

'I did the best I could with what I had.' He had, in fact, panicked, but he wasn't going to admit that. 'You make the coffee. I'll sit with Dianne.'

Bayu des Allemands, Louisiana
TUESDAY, OCTOBER 25, 9:30 A.M.

Lying on the inflatable mattress on the floor of Corey's fishing cabin, Jace closed his eyes, misery clogging his throat. They were in so much trouble. He and Rick had never been in so much trouble. Then again, they'd never done anything like what they'd done last night.

I did a crime. He hadn't meant to. He hadn't even known that was what Rick had planned, but he didn't think the cops would believe him. Aaron had killed a man and Rick had tried to kidnap the prosecutor's son. *I was there. I drove the getaway van.*

That makes me a criminal, too. Didn't it? The cops were looking for Rick. *And me. What am I gonna do?*

Jace had called Corey for help after driving away from Cardozo's house, expecting Corey's fist—or worse. But that hadn't happened. Yet. Instead, Corey had met them behind a deserted strip mall near their house, given them each a bottle of water, then silently handed them over to his best friend Bobby Landry, who'd taken the wheel of the minivan.

The next thing Jace had known, it was nearly dawn and he and Rick had been waking up here. In some kind of fishing cabin in the middle of nowhere. Corey had drugged them.

Jace wasn't sure where to even start with that. His brother had drugged them and had taken their phones.

This felt . . . bad. Really bad.

Jace had no idea where they were. He'd never known this place existed. Neither had Rick. But it seemed like Corey spent a lot of time here with his friends, which would explain all the times Corey disappeared for days at a time, leaving him and Rick to fend for themselves.

The cabin was clean, at least. There was a living room big enough for a sofa, a chair, and the air mattress on which they lay. The kitchenette would have been fine to cook in if Corey had left them any food. There was a small bedroom and another 'mystery' room. A locked room.

The front door to the cabin was locked as well. They were not free to leave. And even if they could get out of the cabin, they couldn't leave the camp. They were somewhere in the bayou, based on the view of the river from the front window.

This was a prison, complete with a scary guard because Bobby was still here. Not only Corey's best friend, Bobby was his business partner. Along with Ed, they owned Three Vets Renovation, where Jace worked sometimes. They never let him do anything important. It wasn't like he could read directions, but he could read a blueprint. Mostly he just did demolition work and simple framing. Rick was usually too busy with school to work, but Jace didn't go to school anymore, so he had lots of free time.

Bobby joked and grinned a lot at work, but there'd always been something about the man that made Jace avoid him. The former cop was intimidating when they weren't in trouble. Today . . .

Bobby had claimed that the enormous gun he carried in a chest holster was for shooting gators, but he'd had this sly look on his face that made Jace sick to his stomach.

Bobby just wasn't right. So when Bobby had told him and Rick to stay put, they'd obeyed.

When Bobby had told them that the cops had already identified Rick, they'd believed him.

When Bobby had said it was inevitable that the cops would ID Jace, too, and that if the cops got their hands on them they'd go to prison for twenty years, Jace had felt tears prick his eyes, but he'd refused to let them fall. He couldn't show any more weakness. Bobby was enjoying how scared he was.

'When's Corey coming back?' Rick asked Bobby, who was lounging on the sofa, scrolling on his phone.

If we could get his phone, we could call for help. But who would they call? The cops would put them right in jail. For twenty years. So Jace kept his mouth shut.

Bobby smirked. 'You that eager to get your ass handed to you, boy?'

Rick's jaw bunched, but his hands trembled. 'What's he gonna do to us?'

'Not sure yet. Don't think he's sure yet, either.' Bobby glanced at his phone. 'We got visitors. Dewey's here.'

Jace felt a trickle of relief. The old man was their mechanic, fixing Corey's construction trucks and just about everything else. *And he's nice to me.* Maybe Dewey could get them out. 'How do you know?'

Bobby went to Corey's front door, ignoring his question. 'You two stay put. Do not make me mad.' He was gone then, closing the door behind him.

His whole body shaking, Rick went to the door and listened.

'Rick,' Jace hissed. 'Do not make Bobby mad.'

'I won't. But I want to know what's going on. Corey could kill us both and feed us to the gators and nobody would miss us.'

Jace was not thinking about those gators. Or that Corey might actually kill them. But he wasn't sure that Rick was wrong. 'Dianne would miss us,' Jace said instead.

Rick snorted. 'When she's sober.'

Jace blew out a breath. That was fair. Dianne was drunk most of the time. 'Can you hear anything?'

'Nah. But Bobby and Dewey are talking about something. They're definitely not having a friendly conversation, which just adds to how much this sucks.' Rick returned to the air mattress and landed with a grunt. He eyed Jace sternly, his gaze wild and desperate. 'Remember the story.'

'I remember,' Jace snapped. 'You've only told me ten million times.'

'Well, you're not too smart. If you forget, he'll kill us.'

Jace flinched. He wasn't smart, and Corey might just kill them. But even he could remember Rick's simple instruction—tell Corey it was all Rick's idea.

Which was true, but Jace hadn't known that yesterday. Rick had talked about Corey's email and made it sound like Corey had sent them to grab that kid last night. Probably because he knew that was the only way to get Jace to cooperate.

But Jace hadn't cooperated. He'd told the kid to run. Rick hadn't said a single thing about that, and Jace had been waiting for him to. Maybe Rick hadn't heard him. He *had* just been tased, after all.

'I'll remember.' Jace stared up at the ceiling, wishing he'd never agreed to drive. Wishing everything was different. 'Do you think Aaron woulda done it if he wasn't in jail? Woulda taken us back, I mean?'

He and Rick had lived with Corey since Liam got sick, and it was hell. Corey used his fists whenever they pissed him off. Which was a lot. Aaron had never hit when they'd lived with him. Their oldest brother had said they could live with him and Dianne again, but then he went and got himself arrested. Now they were stuck with Corey again.

'Yeah. I think he would have. That's why I took the risk yesterday.' Rick rolled over onto his side. His eyes were bloodshot and his whole body was shaking. He was sweating, too, like he had a fever. 'Look, Jace, if Corey doesn't literally kill us, he's going to make us wish we were dead. And one beating ain't gonna be the end of it. I've been beat enough. We need to run.'

The very thought made Jace excited, anxious, and terrified, all at once. 'Where to?'

'I don't know. I have a little money put away back at home, in my room. We can take it and hit the road.'

Jace stared. 'Number one, how do you plan to get away from here? Number two, the cops are looking for us, Rick. We leave here and we'll end up in jail with Aaron.'

Rick scowled. 'I can't take living with Corey anymore. Plus, the cops won't find us anyway, if we're dead. If we stay here, we just might be.'

Jace sighed. 'He's not gonna kill us. He might beat us good, but I guess we're kinda used to that.'

'He might beat you,' Rick said bitterly. 'But he'll kill me. He already thinks the wrong Gates died.'

Jace winced. Corey *had* said that. Several times since Liam died. Corey would say that God took the wrong kid. *Why couldn't it have been you?* Usually 'you' referred to Rick, but every so often he'd say it to Jace. At first, Jace thought it was the grief. Corey had taken Liam's death harder than anyone except for Dianne. Harder even than Aaron.

But the more time passed, the more Jace thought that Corey really meant it, that he wished the two of them weren't alive, that he'd trade them for Liam if he could.

Maybe Rick wasn't wrong. Especially after last night. Still, Jace tried to stay positive.

'He wouldn't beat you so much if you just did what he said. Or even if you just shut your mouth.'

Rick looked hurt, then angry, before he shut down completely. 'Never mind.'

'Hey.' Jace squeezed Rick's shoulder. 'I didn't mean to make you mad. You've only got a few years till you're eighteen. You can go then.'

'I'm not gonna leave you with him. I'm serious, Jace. Corey will kill us sooner or later.'

The door opened and Bobby stood in the doorway, blocking the sun. 'Jace, Dewey's gonna fix up Aaron's boat so he can sell it, and he wants your help. Says you're good with engines.'

It was true. Jace was good with engines. He helped Dewey sometimes, whenever the mechanic came to fix one of Corey's construction trucks or one of the backhoes. It didn't happen every day because

Dewey had other jobs to do, but it was often enough that Jace had learned a lot about fixing stuff from the older man.

He lurched to his feet, eager to get out of the small room. 'Sure!' he said too brightly. 'What about Rick?'

Bobby smiled, an evil sight that made goose bumps ripple over Jace's skin. 'Rick stays here with me. Go on, now.'

Bobby slammed the door behind him and Jace heard the click of the lock, reiterating that they really were prisoners here. But at least he was outside. He couldn't run away, but he didn't have to feel stifled, either.

And if he checked out possible escape routes, that would help, too.

'Hey, kid.' Dewey waved from down on the dock. He was older, maybe fifty or so. He looked . . . well, he looked like the homeless guys Jace had seen in the city. His T-shirt was dirty and a little torn, his jeans even dirtier. He had a bushy beard and his hair was long and scraggly, held back in a ponytail. But the man knew engines.

He was also the only person who actually gave a damn about Jace. Dianne tried, but when Liam got sick, she'd been too busy for him and Rick. And in the six months since Liam had died, she'd been too drunk. Rick was right about that.

But Dewey spent time with Jace. He taught him stuff. Dewey never treated him like he was too stupid to remember to breathe.

Maybe he could go live with Dewey. Jace wasn't excited about running away with Rick. He'd seen the shows about what happened to teenage runaways.

Then it occurred to him that he had no idea where Dewey even lived. He'd always seen him at Corey's construction business or at Aaron's house.

'Whatcha got, Dewey?' Jace asked, stopping at the end of the dock. There were three boats tied up—Bobby's, Aaron's, and Dewey's old jon boat. It had a smaller motor than the other two boats did. It also had oars. It was the kind of boat a fisherman would like.

Dianne had taken them fishing, before Liam got sick. Jace missed that life.

'Aaron's starter. I'll show you how to fix it. I figured you'd be getting stir-crazy right about now.'

'You don't even know,' Jace murmured.

'C'mon, kid. I'll take you to my little workshop and you can tell me about it.' Dewey threw an arm around Jace's shoulders and they started walking. 'Why did you boys do it?'

Jace sighed. 'I was just the driver. I didn't even know that's what Rick was doing until a few seconds before he did it. I guess Rick did it because he wanted Aaron to come home.' Because as angry and unpredictable as Aaron had become after Liam died, he was still so much nicer than Corey. 'Aaron . . . don't beat us.'

Dewey made an understanding noise. 'I know.'

They passed a second cabin, identical to Corey's. 'Whose is that?'

'Aaron's.'

'And that?' He pointed to a little shack that looked a breath away from falling down.

'Where I sleep sometimes when I spend the night.'

'Oh.' They came to a fourth building, a little smaller than the two cabins. 'Is this your workshop?'

'Yeah. I bring things here to fix. It's quiet. Kind of meditative.'

Jace had no idea what that meant, but he nodded anyway, then smiled once he'd followed Dewey through the door. There were two long tables covered with engine parts. It smelled intensely of motor oil. 'I like this. Do you have a workshop where you live?'

Dewey seemed to still, then shook his head. 'Nope. I live in a space not much better than that shack over there. A bit upriver.' He shrugged out of his jacket and hung it on the wall, the movement causing the sleeve of his T-shirt to ride up, exposing his dragon tattoo.

'Oh. I got one, too.' Jace tugged his own sleeve up and angled his body to show off his tat, which looked pretty similar to Dewey's, if he said so himself. Of course, the sketch he'd made from memory was much closer to Dewey's, but the tattoo artist had been kind of drunk. So not exactly the same.

Dewey's eyes widened. 'Is that real? I mean, permanent?'

'It is,' Jace said proudly.

Dewey frowned. 'Boy, you're only fifteen. Who gave you a goddamn tattoo?'

Stung, Jace dropped his hand, letting his sleeve ride back down. 'Some guy in the city. He didn't ask for ID. I pass for eighteen all the time.'

'I guess you do. You're sure big enough. Here, let me see it again.' Dewey whistled. 'It's just like mine. Why?'

Jace shrugged awkwardly. 'I liked yours. You're always nice to me, y'know? I just . . . well, I wanted it.'

Dewey's eyes changed, softening. 'Don't let your brother see it if you don't want an ass-whoopin',' he said gruffly, 'but it's real nice. Now, what d'you say we fix Aaron's starter?'

'Sounds good.'

Maybe if Jace was very helpful, Dewey would take them away. If Rick was right and Corey was planning to do more than just beat them, Dewey's place—no matter how run-down it might be—would be a lot safer.

3

THROAT TIGHT, VAL pressed the single-side earbud harder into her ear—as if the action could keep Elijah from hearing what he'd probably already seen online. He was sitting at the small table in the far corner of her office, wearing headphones over his ears, so there was no way he could hear or see what she was watching.

She and Elijah were waiting on Burke and Mr. Cardozo to deal with the contracts. Val was using the time to review the two viral videos—the doctor's murder last week and last night's abduction attempt.

Dr. Singh had been a slightly built man. Certainly no match for Aaron Gates's bowling-ball-sized fists. Aaron was big and muscular and . . . strong. There was a look in his eyes that she'd seen before—cruel and sadistic. And triumphant as he'd been pulled away from the doctor's lifeless body after he'd gotten what he'd wanted. The man was dead.

Aaron hadn't disclosed why he'd beaten the doctor, but Val could make a guess. Aaron's son Liam had recently died of leukemia and Dr. Singh was a pediatric oncologist. She'd have to find out if Singh had been one of Liam Gates's doctors.

The audio was dominated by observers' screams for Aaron to stop, but a woman could be heard chanting, 'For Liam! For Liam!'

Aaron's punches had fallen into a rhythm, a macabre accompaniment to the woman's chanting. The woman had been identified as Sandra Springfield, who'd been Aaron's personal assistant in his financial consulting business.

She'd also hidden the photos of Aaron with Dewey Talley. Val already knew how bad Dewey was. His Sixth Day gang had owned the drug trade in several parishes four years ago, selling their poison to anyone with the money to pay. Rich people, poor people. Even children Elijah's age.

Val's throat tightened. And they'd gotten rid of anyone who tried to stop them. Permanently.

That Aaron Gates had welcomed Dewey Talley into his home was telling. Even if they were only friends, Dewey was vile and anything he touched was tainted. So was Aaron Gates, based on the video she'd just forced herself to watch. Vile, tainted, and brutal.

That Aaron was a drug user was fairly certain. He'd been high on meth when he killed the doctor. That he was getting his meth from Dewey Talley—a known drug dealer—wasn't a huge leap.

Which meant that Sixth Day—and Dewey Talley—were not truly gone. Not as she'd spent the last four years hoping. If Dewey Talley had been with Rick last night and they'd tried to abduct Elijah? That was significant. Dewey wouldn't go to the trouble for a simple client. Probably not even for a friend. There had to be more to the relationship that they had to figure out.

But he'd told Elijah to run. That did not sound like the Dewey Talley she'd studied so obsessively. Again, more to figure out.

Val wanted to bring Dewey and Sixth Day down more than she wanted to breathe. But, at this moment, her duty was to Elijah, to keeping him safe. Which was why she was subjecting herself to the violence of this video. She knew a lot about Dewey Talley. Now she needed to understand everything about both Aaron Gates and his brother Rick. She needed to know who else might come for Elijah.

The press was speculating that the meth in Aaron's system at the time of his arrest was the cause of his breakdown. But Aaron appeared somewhat coherent in the video, like he'd known what he was doing in that moment.

She knew that look, too.

That final look of triumph in the bastard's eyes was nearly identical to the one that haunted her worst nightmares, the one that too often had her waking up shaking and clammy with sweat. With her dog at her side. Czar was a protection dog, but he always responded when she had the dream, climbing up into her bed and lying by her side until she stopped shaking.

She tabbed from the YouTube page to her desktop. Her wallpaper was a photo of Czar wearing a Santa Claus hat. She wished her dog were at her side right now, but he was at home. Probably barking at the neighbor's cat, Mr. Boots.

Double-checking, she clicked on the link to the security cameras that had already been installed when she inherited her house. Sure enough, Czar was barking at the cat. Again. Mr. Boots made a game of taunting Czar, pawing at Val's patio door when the dog was inside the house and prancing along the top of the eight-foot security fence when he was out back.

That cat had no idea how lucky it was that Czar was so well trained. He could crash through the glass and eat Mr. Boots in one bite but chose not to. Didn't stop Czar from pretending, though.

The sight of Czar was the mental palate cleanser she'd needed. Drawing a breath, she returned to YouTube and clicked play on one of the many videos of Elijah's attempted abduction taken by onlookers. The most complete version began a split second after Aunt Genie had tased Rick Gates.

Even though Val knew that Elijah had escaped, her pulse still raced as she watched the attempted abduction play out. Her lips curved when the boy pulled Rick's ski mask off his face. *Go, Elijah. You rock.*

And then the driver ran around the van and paused in a moment of indecision, which must have been when he told Elijah to run. He then scooped Rick up in a fireman's carry and his shirtsleeve rode up, exposing his dragon tattoo.

The same tattoo that marked Dewey Talley. The tattoo was no secret. Several of the photos she'd obtained of Dewey showed the tattoo. He'd never tried to hide it.

Except he should have tried last night, shouldn't he? He'd worn a ski mask to hide his face. So why not wear a long-sleeved shirt to hide the tattoo that could so easily identify him?

More questions that needed answers.

She paused the video, staring at the masked driver, whose biceps strained against his short-sleeved T-shirt as he lifted the man who'd tried to take Elijah Cardozo. Hatred pulsed in her mind and, for a moment, she left it alone to throb. To consume.

Dewey Talley, second-in-command of Sixth Day. Now likely first-in-command because the old leader was gone. Not dead. Just gone. For life. Without parole.

She needed to remember their brutality.

As if she could ever forget.

That was the thing about trauma and loss. One might push the memories into a box and lock them away somewhere in the recesses of the mind, but they were never truly gone. They lingered, lurking until triggered to reappear.

But this isn't about me. She fixed her gaze on Elijah. *He's what's important right now.*

She hit play and watched as the van sped away. Leaving Elijah and his aunt Genie safe.

She restarted the video, watching the driver. Damn. If he really was Dewey Talley, the man was in good shape for his age. Rick Gates was smaller than the driver, but Rick was still at least five-nine. Maybe one-sixty.

Dewey Talley had been in his early fifties four years ago. The photos she'd seen back then had shown a beefy middle-aged man with a bit of a beer gut. The more recent photo, the one recovered from Sandra Springfield's thumb drive, showed him to be leaner. More muscular. It was difficult to tell from the newer photos if he was as muscular as the driver, though. The clothes he wore in Sandra's photos were loose-fitting, his sleeves long, the angle not the best for seeing details. But there were enough similarities for Val not to completely rule him out.

If he was the driver, he'd clearly been working out during the time he'd gone under.

Good to know. Especially if he came after Elijah and she had to take him down.

The driver was a big man. Big and muscular. Her blood chilled as much older memories swirled to the top of her mind. Like always, she shoved them away.

It was with a swell of relief that she heard the footsteps approach her office door. Val never used earbuds in both ears. She wasn't willing to be unaware of her surroundings at any time, even though here, in Burke's office, she was safe.

Once a person had been sneaked up on . . . Well, Val didn't know how other people handled it, but she'd found solace in control.

She looked up and waved Molly Sutton into her office, smiling as her friend sat on the corner of Val's desk. Molly was Burke's second-in-command. A former cop, she mostly investigated cases, providing security when Burke was low on bodyguards. She was kind but had a spine of steel.

She was also one of Val's dearest friends.

'Hey, you,' Val said quietly.

'Hey, yourself, stranger.' Molly glanced at Elijah, who still sat at

Val's little table, then pointed to her screen and whispered, 'Brave little boy.'

'He is,' Val whispered back. He was immersed in whatever he was watching on his tablet, or at least he pretended to be. He still wore his headphones, but the kid was smart enough—and curious enough—to figure out a way to eavesdrop without an ounce of shame. 'He reminds me of myself when I was that age.'

'You had Harry Potter glasses?' Molly teased.

'I had Velma from *Scooby-Doo* glasses,' Val corrected. 'Velma was the coolest of the Scooby gang.'

'She was,' Molly said. 'Elijah's okay? Last night was . . . too close.'

'He's doing as well as can be expected.' She restarted the video and pointed to the van's driver as he ran around the vehicle. 'Burke and Mr. Cardozo think it might be Dewey Talley.'

'Yeah. I got the skinny from Joy. Are you sure you're going to be okay with this case?' Because Molly knew who Dewey Talley was and what he'd done.

'I'll be fine,' Val said brusquely. 'I wonder if Antoine can get this video any clearer. I want to see the driver's eyes.'

'Because?'

She paused again on the driver as he slung Rick Gates over his shoulder. 'Because I know what Talley's eyes look like.' She'd stared at the man's image for too many hours. 'And because the driver told Elijah to run.'

Molly's eyes widened. 'Oh. That's an un-Dewey-Talley-like thing to do. You doubt that Talley was involved?'

'Keeping an open mind. If Antoine can get me a clear view of his eyes, that would help.'

Their IT guy was a jack-of-all-trades and expert of all when it came to computers. Val had no idea how he accomplished ninety percent of what he did.

Molly hummed her approval. 'If anyone can, it's Antoine.'

Val opened an email to Antoine and listed the video enhancement as her first request. 'I also want to know where Dewey Talley's been for the last four years.' *Because I looked for him.*

'Even Antoine might not be able to get you that.'

'Maybe not, but I'm going to ask. I also want everything about the Gates brothers and all of their minions. Faces, past jobs, criminal records. Everything.' She added full background checks to the list. 'In case they try to grab Elijah again.'

'They'd be crazy to try,' Molly said. 'Then again, it was crazy to try it the first time.' She lifted a brow. 'Not that anything Sixth Day ever did made a lot of sense.'

'True enough.' Val understood why Molly was emphasizing the point. Today wasn't the first time she'd done so. But Val wasn't interested in a therapy session. She leaned back in her chair, studying her friend's face. 'What have you been up to? And how is *Gabe?*' She said Molly's beau's name slyly, chuckling when her friend blushed.

'He's fine. I, however, have gained five pounds from his chocolate cake.'

Gabe was part owner and head chef of Le Petit Choux, a restaurant in the Quarter. His chocolate cake was absolutely decadent. 'It would only be two and a half pounds if you'd shared with me.'

Molly grinned. 'Sorry, not sorry. ADA Cardozo isn't exactly chopped liver.'

Val's gaze darted to Elijah, relieved to see his headphones still in place. She glared at Molly. '*Hush.* I'm his son's bodyguard.'

Molly lifted a shoulder. 'The supporting scenery is pleasing, I'm just saying.'

Val rolled her eyes. It was true, but she wouldn't admit it. 'Shut up and help me think of things to ask Antoine to research. I can't allow these assholes to come near Elijah again. I don't want to think of what they'd have done to him if they'd been successful last night.'

Sobering, Molly nodded once. 'Get the police reports. Antoine knows how to find what isn't public record. Given ADA Cardozo's connection, I'm thinking they'll put a rush on any DNA evidence they got from the ski mask that Rick Gates was wearing. It's not likely, but his partner might have handled the mask. With any luck, he will have left something behind—hair or skin cells.'

Val added it to the list for Antoine. 'I'll ask if they found fingerprints on the gun Rick left behind. Rick wore gloves but the driver didn't. The van's license plate belonged to a car that was reported stolen last night, so that's a dead end.'

Molly slid off the desk. 'That list is a good start and Antoine won't mind if you add stuff later. I gotta run. I'm on parent lunchroom duty at Harper's school today because my sister can't make it.'

Val had a soft spot for Molly's niece. 'Tell Harper I said hi and that I'm saving her a seat at my next game.'

Molly chuckled. 'My sister is still annoyed that Harper has added roller derby queen to her list of careers. Call if you need me.'

'Will do.' With a wave, Val returned her attention to her computer screen, sending the email to Antoine and then running a new search on Sixth Day and Dewey Talley. She'd ceased her stalking of the organization two years ago on the advice of her therapist.

Squaring her shoulders, she prepared to dive back into the world of the insidious drug-running bastards who'd taken so much from her and her family. She'd do this for Elijah and his father.

Maybe even for me.

And then she saw the first search result—a breaking headline from only a half hour before. *Attempted Abduction of ADA's Son Linked to Drug Gang.*

'Well,' she murmured as the last of her hopes that Sixth Day wasn't involved slithered away. She clicked on the link and a video filled her screen. A big, muscular man with a shaved head wearing a severe black suit stood on the front porch of a house as he spoke to reporters.

Corey Gates, brother to Aaron and Rick, looked exhausted and devastated as he pleaded for the public's help in locating his brother, even offering a ten-thousand-dollar reward for information leading to Rick's return.

Because not only had Rick started using drugs. He'd fallen in with a drug gang. And not any old drug gang. Rick Gates had fallen in with Sixth Day.

The boy was only sixteen. But Sylvi hadn't been much older when she'd started buying from Sixth Day. Val's little sister had forever broken their family, just like Aaron and now Rick had broken the Gates family. It was such a waste.

Corey Gates seemed sincere enough. He was clearly out of his element in raising a teenager, which most people would understand. He also appeared to fully accept that his brother would need to face justice for his crime.

And then the reporter asked him about his father, and the man's whole posture changed. His body stiffened, his shoulders going back, his chest puffing out. His hands clenched into fists at his sides. He was *angry*.

She added a background check on his father to her list for Antoine. The father had reportedly served time for murder, so the apples hadn't fallen far from the tree, at least when it came to Rick and Aaron Gates.

She supposed that only time would reveal if Corey Gates was a decent person. But at least she no longer doubted who was behind Elijah's abduction. Even if the driver wasn't Dewey Talley himself, he'd been associated with two of the four Gates brothers, and that was enough. The only silver lining in this mess was that the driver had had a split second of conscience and let Elijah go.

Val wouldn't give him a second chance to try.

Metairie, Louisiana
TUESDAY, OCTOBER 25, 10:25 A.M.

Corey pulled the Chevy SUV's door shut and fastened his seat belt. 'Let's go, Ed.' Settling into the back seat, he studied Dianne, who sat beside him. Her eyes were still vodka-dulled, but some of the color in her cheeks had returned after their flight from the media.

They'd departed in Corey's beat-up old Ford F-150, leaving his Three Vets truck in the driveway and Dianne's Mercedes in his attached garage. The Mercedes was nine years old, bought for her by Aaron as a wedding gift, but the perception of wealth was not an image they wanted to portray.

Once they'd made it past the reporters and the two scowling detectives, they'd taken a very winding route to Ed's house, where they'd changed to a Chevy Suburban that Ed had appropriated from somewhere. Corey didn't ask. He knew that Ed wouldn't allow them to be connected to the vehicle.

They hadn't been followed by either the cops or the media, and that made Corey suspicious. He'd assumed that someone would try to tail them, so they'd come up with the getaway plan in advance.

Still, better safe than sorry. Their camp's location had remained a secret for nearly four years, and Corey wasn't about to see that change now.

Dianne looked around, seeming to only now realize that they'd swapped vehicles. 'Where are we?'

'My house,' Ed said gently.

'Are we leaving Corey's truck here? Why?'

Corey patted her knee. 'I don't trust that we aren't being followed. So we're going to use Ed's SUV for now.' None of their vehicles could be tracked through GPS. They routinely dismantled the location systems every time they either bought or appropriated a new set of wheels. But he wouldn't put it past the cops or the media to have slipped a tracking device under his truck. 'You just rest. It's been a busy morning.'

'I am tired,' she admitted.

Some people were nasty drunks. Some got giggly. Dianne simply went to sleep, her escape of choice ever since they'd lost Liam.

Corey wished he could make her stop, but he was going to have to use her alcoholism to keep her out of the way for the next day or two.

Ed glanced up to the rearview mirror. 'I still don't understand why Rick and Jace did it. Why were they so desperate to get Aaron out of jail?'

This line of questioning had also been planned. If Rick and Jace were going to talk to anyone, it would be Dianne. She was just drunk enough to spill secrets without passing out first.

'Did they say anything to you, Di?' Corey asked.

She hesitated, looking away. 'I overheard Rick talking to Aaron a few weeks ago. Rick kept asking if they could live with us again. Aaron eventually said that they could.'

Having his brothers go live with Aaron again would have been a gift. They'd started out with Aaron and Dianne after their mother had died but had come to live with Corey when Liam had gotten sick. Dianne hadn't been able to cope with Liam's treatment plus two more kids.

Corey had done his time taking care of the little assholes. He'd housed, fed, and clothed them for more than three fucking years. He'd tried to teach them some respect, but they'd fought him at every step. Especially Rick. Corey was done. 'But that still doesn't explain why they were so desperate to get Aaron out of jail.'

She looked apprehensive. 'Aaron didn't say yes at first when Rick asked if they could live with us again. He said he wasn't sure. Used my drinking as an excuse. Now I know he didn't say yes at first because he was already planning to run away to the Bahamas with that whore

Sandra. At least that won't happen now that they're both in jail. At least God gave me that.'

Corey agreed that Aaron's girlfriend was a whore, but he needed Dianne to focus. 'What about Rick?'

She sighed. 'When Aaron first said no, Rick asked him about emancipation.'

'*What?*' Corey had to rein in the quick flash of temper. 'From who?'

She recoiled at his fury. He rarely let her see it. 'Um . . . from you.'

Anger roiled up in his gut. *Ungrateful little bastards.* Corey had given up a lot to take care of his asshole brothers and *this* was the thanks he got?

'What did Aaron say?' he gritted out.

'Aaron told Rick that they could live with us again. Not like there was ever an "us",' she said bitterly. 'Aaron was blowing smoke like he always does. He lies like he breathes. I should have told the boys that Aaron was planning to run to the Bahamas with that whore. He never intended to keep his promises to them or to me. If they'd known that Aaron was a dirty, cheating liar, maybe they wouldn't have been so stupid and done what they did last night.'

'What about Jace? Where was he in all this?'

'Jace is never the leader, Corey. You know that. I don't think he even knows what "emancipation" means.' She bit her lip. 'Will you still help them if you find them?'

'Yes. Of course,' he lied. At least this newest tidbit would make what he had to do to Rick easier to swallow. He'd had a tinge of doubt that he could kill his own brother. Now? Not so much. *Emancipation, my ass.*

She exhaled in relief. 'Thank God. They're just children. Don't be too harsh with them.'

They weren't children. Rick was sixteen and Jace was fifteen. *At that age, I was working to help my mother put food on the table because my bastard father was in prison.* But he understood Dianne's emotion.

Having lost Liam, she wanted to mother Rick and Jace. When she was sober, anyway.

'Thank you for telling me,' he murmured.

Her smile was tired. 'Are we going to look for them now?'

'Of course.' Another lie. They were going back to his camp, but she wasn't drunk enough to sleep through the trip. He needed her passed out and couldn't risk her waking up at any point along the way. 'We know a few more places he could be hiding. We made some coffee for the road. Ed?'

Ed handed a travel mug over the seat. 'Here's yours, Dianne. I made it just like you like it. Three creams, two sugars.'

And a couple of sleeping pills.

'Thank you,' Dianne murmured. 'That was nice of you, Ed.'

'No problem,' Ed said, then handed another travel mug over the seat, this one sedative free. 'Corey, here's yours.'

The three of them sipped in silence, Ed driving in circles until Dianne's blinks grew heavy. 'I'm so tired,' she said, slurring her words.

Corey took the cup from her hand and unbuckled her seat belt. 'Then sleep. We'll be there before you know it.' He waited until Dianne was snoring softly, curled up with her head on his thigh. 'She'll sleep for a few hours. At least until we've got her safely stowed in my quarters.'

'Tell Bobby our ETA so he can move Rick and Jace into the comm room,' Ed suggested. 'We don't want her seeing them in case she wakes up.'

Their communication room was a man cave with leather sofas, an eighty-five-inch flat-screen, a very strong Wi-Fi signal, and doors that locked securely so that no one could break in and snoop. Because it was also where Corey and his team conducted their dirty business—the planning, the surveillance, and the execution.

Meaning, sometimes they executed people there, then dumped the bodies into the water for the gators if the client never wanted the body found.

Others, like their current client Trevor Doyle, wanted to avoid any suspicion of witness tampering. So that was exactly what they would provide. They'd even set someone else up to take the blame, so Doyle would walk away a free man.

Corey fished his burner phone from his pocket and dialed Bobby, putting him on speaker.

'It's about time,' Bobby grumbled. 'I saw the interview. You did good, boy. Especially there at the end. That reporter hit low, asking about your no-good daddy.'

Corey and Bobby had been friends since they were kids, and Bobby knew how much Corey hated his father. How hard he'd worked never to become a loser like his father had been. 'I agree. Feldman's a real bitch. Look, we're an hour and a half from the camp. Can you have the assholes moved to the comm room before we get there?'

'Sure. But why? I thought we were keeping them out of there.'

Corey sighed. 'Because we're bringing Dianne back with us. NOPD's been snooping around and if they catch her when she's drunk—'

'Which is always,' Bobby interrupted.

'Yeah, I know,' Corey snapped. 'But she's my alibi. I can't have her fucking it up. We'll keep her sedated until it's safe to take her home.'

'Okay,' Bobby said dubiously. 'She could just have an accident and fall down the stairs. It happens to drunks every day.'

'*No.*' Corey drew a sharp breath, sickened at the very thought. 'Just no. We'll keep her quiet, then take her home and convince her that she blacked out and lost a few days. It's happened before. Anyway,' he said, changing the subject, 'have you checked Ed's social media accounts? How was the interview perceived?'

'Pretty much like we hoped,' Bobby reported happily. 'That you're a terrible guardian but everyone understands how hard it is to raise a teenager. And that if he's fallen in with Sixth Day, his life is already too fucked up to repair. People are remembering how bad they were and how much of the city's drug trade they controlled. So my pal on the force saved the day with that heads-up about Dewey.'

'I wouldn't have even begun to guess that they'd think Dewey Talley was the driver,' Corey grumbled. 'I didn't know that Jace had a tattoo.'

'I saw the tat on Jace's arm myself,' Bobby said. 'It's real.'

Corey frowned. 'I believe you. But I also can't believe the kid found someone to tattoo him without ID. He can't read or write, but he can convince a tattoo artist to give him ink?'

'Let it go, Corey,' Bobby said with an impatient sigh.

Corey scowled. 'At least we're making it work in our favor.'

'We are. Like I said, it's working better than we expected. I checked the pro-Doyle subreddit and the dudebros have been very active. One suggested finishing what Rick Gates started so Cardozo would be forced to throw the trial Doyle's way.'

The Doyle trial had been covered to death in the mainstream media, but they'd found that Doyle's fans—and Bella's enemies—were most active in communities on Reddit. They fumed about lying women in general and Bella in particular. A few had been very graphic, suggesting 'how awful' it would be if some someone 'did to her' what she'd accused an innocent man of doing, 'to teach her a lesson.' Most of the comments were couched in 'how awful would it be' language to keep the moderators from kicking posters out of the community, but their intent was clear.

It had been a perfect setup, really. Ed had created accounts for the three of them, and they went online nearly every day to fan the flames. Ed had even managed to score an invite to one of the private servers on Discord where Bella-haters could discuss their basest fantasies without worry of reprisal.

Ed had identified one of the most vocal of Bella's detractors, whose car trunk would conveniently be found to contain remnants of the bomb they planned to use to kill her. They'd nicknamed him Comic

Book Guy because he literally lived in his mother's basement and spent his waking hours online. His real name was Jerry Engel and he lived just over the Texas border.

Framing Jerry Engel would make Bella's death appear to have been caused by the online haters, not Doyle. That the haters had glommed onto Rick's idiocy last night was truly an unexpected boon.

'That started last night after Rick's video went viral,' Ed said. 'Is there anything new?'

'Oh yeah,' Bobby said. 'I checked Ed's Discord account. The one guy who said on Reddit that they should finish what Rick started got an invite, too. The private server has been super active.'

Corey had learned more about online forums and their users over the past few months than he'd ever wanted to know. Reddit was a series of open boards where users could read or talk to others about everything from food to bridezillas. Anyone could read posts and no privacy was expected. Discord, on the other hand, had real-time chat rooms, both public and private. The private rooms were where the Bella-haters went to plan their revenge in graphic detail.

Some of that shit turned even Corey's stomach.

Ed was the manager of the accounts, but Bobby took the most pleasure in fanning the flames, especially on Discord. He could go fullthrottle insane with conspiracy theories about Bella Butler and had been responsible for starting some truly horrific fantasies.

'What are they saying on Discord?' Corey asked when Bobby paused dramatically.

'They've listed Cardozo's address and posted a photo of the boy. One clever bastard suggested a reward fund for whoever takes either Cardozo or his kid out of the picture.'

'Let me guess,' Corey said dryly. 'You're the clever bastard?'

'Aw, shucks,' Bobby drawled. 'Thank you, Corey.'

Corey snorted. 'How much did you offer in reward?'

'I didn't. Another poster took up the idea and they've started a pledge drive. So far they're up to five grand. Now, none of it's real money, but there's definite interest. If we can't get to Bella by the end of this week, grabbing Cardozo's kid could be our plan B. We cut Cardozo at the knees and we can still blame it on Comic Book Guy. If the DA's office is out an ADA, they'll delay the trial and buy us a little more time.'

'It sounds good on the surface,' Corey admitted, 'but that won't work any more than Rick's plan would have. They'll just assign another ADA.'

'I know,' Bobby said patiently. 'Which is what some clever bastard—also me—said in the private channel. The trial would likely go to Cardozo's second chair. The users went wild, talking about taking both Cardozo and his second out in simultaneous hits. Like I said, plan B. It would definitely throw the DA's office into a tizzy.'

'Only as a last resort,' Corey said. 'But get the second chair's info in case we have to go that route.'

'I already did,' Bobby boasted. 'My pal came through again and I dropped it into the private channel.'

Corey was impressed, he had to admit. 'Who is this mystery pal of yours, B?'

'He won't let me say. Says if I blow his cover, he'll stop feeding me info, no matter how much I pay him.'

Corey didn't like that, but he respected the need for anonymity. 'You've been busy this morning, B. Did you get Dewey to the camp?'

They needed to keep the older man from seeing the news. He'd either disappear again or he'd make sure the cops knew that Jace was the driver. Either way, they needed him gone. Probably permanently.

'I did. I told him that we needed to fix Aaron's boat so we could sell it. He wasn't happy about the selling part. He seems to think that the boat belonged to their business, so it should now belong to him. I told him to take it up with you when you got back.'

Corey frowned. 'I thought you were just going to take care of him.'

'I was, but then he started talking. He was asking all kinds of questions about Rick and the abduction. Wanted to see Rick, asking if he could talk to him. He never pays attention to Rick, only to Jace.'

Corey frowned. 'Did he see the press conference? Does he know we blamed Sixth Day?'

'No. He got here at about nine thirty and the first clips of the interview didn't upload until nine forty-five. But there's something going on with him. Was Rick getting his drugs from Dewey? If so, maybe Dewey wants Rick to keep quiet about it.'

'I figured he was getting them from either Dewey or Aaron. Or stealing them, since he doesn't have a job.'

'Makes sense. I didn't want Dewey intimidating Rick into silence before you got here to question him. My gut says that we should talk to him together. So I'm stalling for time.'

'I trust your gut.' Bobby had kept them from getting caught more times than Corey could count. 'And I've been wondering how Rick knew where to find Cardozo's kid. Makes sense that Dewey would want to get Aaron out, too, but I honestly thought Dewey was smart enough to know that wouldn't work.'

'I never thought he was all that smart,' Bobby said. 'If he was, he could've taken over their business a long time ago and gotten rid of Aaron. Which is what I would have done.'

'Me too, but Dewey needed Aaron's contacts. It's not like any of those high-society types would give Dewey the time of day, looking like he does.' Dewey made the product and left the networking and sales to Aaron, whose clientele were the wealthy people who'd rather buy his drugs than pay him to invest their money. Aaron made tons more as a drug dealer than he had as a financial consultant. 'Did you take his phone? He'll be able to see the story if he goes online. It's everywhere.'

'I'm using the signal jammer.' They frequently used the device while on a job, disrupting cell reception for whichever mark they'd been hired to kill. No good to have the victim call 911 before the hit. 'I wasn't born yesterday, Corey,' he added, sounding irritated.

'Sorry, B. Cut me some slack, okay? I haven't slept a wink. Look, we'll question Dewey together when I get there, find out what he knows.'

'He'll tell us. I can be persuasive.'

Corey grimaced. Bobby could be downright scary. 'That you can. Talk to you soon.'

He slid the phone into his pocket, then leaned his head back and closed his eyes. 'I'm beat.'

'You'll have time to catch some z's before the meeting tonight,' Ed said. 'We're still having our meeting with Zach and Allyson, right?'

'Yes. We need to review the plan one more time.' Zach and Allyson were key to making their plan work. Both were members of Bella Butler's security staff. Both had secrets they'd do nearly anything to keep hidden. In other words, they were perfect accomplices. 'I'm going to catch some shut-eye. Wake me up if anything happens.'

Corey's eyelids had begun to droop when Ed swore viciously. 'What?' Corey demanded. 'What's wrong?'

Ed passed his cell phone over the car seat to Corey. 'The perimeter alarm at Three Vets just went off. Check the camera. The app is open. Who is it?'

'It's that bitch reporter, Noni Feldman. She's peeking in the windows. And cussing, it looks like.' There was no audio, but the woman was definitely saying 'fuck'. 'She must have thought we'd go to the office and she could snag a one-on-one interview. As if.'

'Has she broken in?'

'No. She's looking in the window of the break room. All she'll see is Bobby's nudie pics on the wall.'

Ed scowled. 'And all the pictures of Bella Butler he taped up. I kept taking them down and he kept putting them back up.'

That was a bit of a concern. Bobby had insisted on hanging the photos to get 'in the zone.' Sometimes it was easier to let him do his own thing than to argue. *I should have argued.* But many of the Bella pics were racy poses, so they didn't look too out of place on the wall.

Corey watched the woman looking into the other windows before finally leaving, disappointment on her face. 'She may need to be dealt with. She's way too interested in us.'

Ed raised his hand, mimicking a kid in school. 'Pick me! Pick me! I'll do it!'

Corey almost chuckled. 'Fine, if it comes down to it. Just don't pull an Aaron, okay? No more videos.'

'Don't worry. I won't. What a dumbass.'

'No argument there.' Corey returned Ed's phone. 'Aaron's always been a dick, but he didn't used to be stupid.'

'Comes from taking your own meth,' Ed said derisively.

That was the truth. 'He was always so careful with his passwords.' But after Liam's death, Aaron's meth use had skyrocketed, and he'd become careless.

So careless that he'd left a guidebook and travel brochures to the Bahamas out where Dianne could find them. She'd initially hoped that Aaron would be taking her, but he'd been cruel in his rejection of that idea. So cruel that Dianne had finally had enough and spied on him when he was typing his password into his laptop, which, in the past, he'd kept locked up tighter than Fort Knox. Dianne had gone searching for dirt and had found the hard evidence of what she'd feared for years, but that everyone else had known—Aaron was a cheating bastard and was planning a grand escape to the Bahamas. Which she'd then shared with Corey in between drunken sobs.

That had been the day *before* Aaron's arrest.

Hours *after* Aaron's arrest, Corey had searched the laptop. He hadn't cared about Aaron's affair. What he did care about was Aaron's money from his and Dewey's drug business. He'd hit the jackpot, finding the usernames and passwords to his brother's offshore bank accounts, where there was lots and lots of money. Millions of dollars.

Aaron's meth business had been far more profitable than he'd ever let on, but the prick had never intended to share any of it. Even though Corey had allowed Aaron and his partner Dewey to deliver their product in Corey's construction trucks to keep from paying so many outsiders to do the distribution. Corey had even made deliveries himself.

He'd never asked for a dime. He'd done it for Liam.

Aaron had done it for Aaron. He'd allowed Corey to think that he needed the drug money to pay for Liam's experimental treatments. That his insurance wasn't covering them.

It hadn't started out as a lie but had quickly become one that Aaron had never corrected. Initially, Aaron's insurance hadn't paid for the treatments. That was back when Aaron had been an independent financial consultant and was not making enough to get the deluxe policy. But once he'd started selling drugs with Dewey Talley, he'd been able to upgrade Liam's coverage. Everything had been paid for.

Aaron had made far more money than Corey could have ever dreamed of, but Aaron hadn't planned to share any of it. He'd taken advantage of Corey and his love for Liam, which really pissed Corey off.

So Corey had taken all of Aaron's money and shared it with Bobby and Ed—which Aaron would learn as soon as he tried to access the cash to pay his bail bond. *Sucks to be Aaron.*

Aaron might have started in the drug business for a good reason, but he had quickly become greedy, which was classic Aaron. He always wanted more than he had and had always found a way to get it. He was a slimeball, but a charming one. Everyone had liked him. Their mother had been so proud of him. *Corey, why can't you be like Aaron? Corey, ask Aaron for help with your homework. He gets straight As and you've got Ds. Why can't you go to college like Aaron and make something of yourself? Ask Aaron to give you a job in his firm.*

Everyone thought that Aaron had it together, that he was this fancy, intelligent guy. But now Aaron was in jail, and this time, Aaron wasn't going to get what he wanted.

This time it was Corey's turn to be successful. Once he'd eliminated Bella Butler, he'd be able to write his ticket for any dirty job he wanted. The operation would be so smooth, no one would suspect that Doyle had even thought of killing his accuser.

He, Bobby, and Ed just had a few loose ends to tie off first.

4

PULLING OFF HIS headphones, Elijah frowned. 'What's taking them so long?' he grumbled.

Val glanced up from her laptop. 'Burke and your dad are talking money.'

Elijah's frown morphed from irritated to worried. 'How much are you going to cost?'

Val sighed. She'd been researching New Orleans' current drug trafficking networks to see if any of the old Sixth Day members' names appeared, and she hadn't considered her words. She needed to remember that—no matter how old a soul this kid was—he was still just a ten-year-old kid. A kid who clearly worried about the family finances along with all the other shit that troubled him.

'I don't know exactly. Sometimes Burke gives a break to people in law enforcement. He figures they can send business his way later. But I do know that he won't ever cheat your father. I'm betting they've figured out the money and are talking about how best to keep you safe.'

Elijah bit his lip, but he nodded. 'Okay. Thank you.'

'No worries, Elijah. If it's okay, I want to research the people who tried to snatch you.'

'So you're investigating *and* being my bodyguard?'

'Well, Burke makes the call on who does the investigating. I'll probably be behind the scenes, feeding Burke any information that I find.' *Or that I already know.* 'The more I know about their organization, the better equipped I am to protect you. I need to know their faces, their motivations, their approaches.'

'Their MO,' Elijah said gravely.

Val had to fight back a smile. The kid really was too freaking cute. 'Exactly.'

'Then I'll be quiet and let you read,' he promised.

'Thank you.' She refocused on her laptop screen, kicking herself for not staying more on top of Dewey Talley's activities, but blocking out anything Sixth Day-related had become necessary to save her sanity. For that, she'd cut herself a little slack.

A movement in her peripheral vision had her glancing to the bookshelves that lined one wall of her office. Elijah was studying her trophies, his hands gripped behind his back.

'You can touch them,' Val offered. 'They won't break.'

Elijah looked over at her. 'What are they for?'

'Roller derby,' she said, then chuckled when his mouth dropped open.

'For real?'

'For real,' she confirmed. 'The photo next to the trophies is my team.'

Elijah picked up the frame carefully. 'The New Orleans Quarter-Masters?'

'Yep.'

He shot her a delighted grin. 'Awesome.'

She grinned back. 'It really is.'

'Your hair is really short in the picture.'

'It's braided and pinned up under my helmet. I wear it up when I'm working or skating. I should put it up now, in fact.' She began braiding it. 'Keeps people from yanking it.'

Because that was a trigger she avoided at all costs.

'Have you ever hip-checked someone into the boards?'

'We don't have boards like in hockey, but yeah, I have hip-checked many a player.'

'What's your roller derby name? I know that you all have special names.'

'I'm Val-Killer-Rie.'

'Like Valkyrie?'

'Exactly.'

'So you were a Marine, you're super tall, you've got a gun, *and* you play roller derby.' He drew a breath, his chest expanding. 'I feel better now.'

She couldn't hold back her smile as she pinned her long braid to her head. 'I'm glad to hear that. I've got bona fides, after all.'

Roller derby had also been key to saving her sanity long before she'd ever heard of Sixth Day. Back then, she'd needed an outlet for her anxiety and aggression, and the ladies had embraced her with open arms. 'Maybe, when it's safe, you can come to a game.'

His eyes grew wide behind his glasses. 'Yes, please!' Then he picked up the one photo she didn't want to have to explain. *Don't ask. Please don't ask.*

She held her breath, waiting, then exhaled when he set the photo down and moved to her collection of books. She was off the hook for now. She wasn't sure if she was relieved or not. After all, the photo involved him, in a way.

A sound on her right had her turning in time to see Burke and Cardozo step into the open doorway. 'Everything settled?' she asked them.

Elijah turned from the books. 'She plays roller derby, Dad!'

Cardozo's smile appeared forced. Poor man was still terrified. She couldn't blame him. Bad people had put their hands on his son. Any good parent would be terrified.

'I heard,' Cardozo said. 'Hey, buddy, will you go with Burke? He's got a snack in his office. You should eat something, especially after that cupcake.'

And that was another thing Val needed to research. How to provide necessary nourishment to a child with diabetes. If Elijah was seeing a doctor regularly enough that he couldn't leave the city, his condition had to be severe.

Elijah's cheeks pinked up, his mouth turning down. He glanced at Val before glaring at his father. 'I *know*, Dad. I already ate something.'

Val wanted to hug the kid. And Cardozo. As hard as dealing with his diabetes must have been for Elijah, it was also a heavy load for his father to carry.

And, while she was in their lives, a load for Val to carry as well.

'I think your father wants to talk to me alone, Elijah,' she said.

'Oh.' Elijah shrugged. 'You should have just said so.'

Cardozo gave her an appreciative look. 'Yes, I should have.'

Elijah shouldered his backpack and headed out with Burke. 'See ya, Val-Killer-Rie.'

'Ask Burke *all* the questions,' she called after the boy. 'He *loves* to answer questions!'

Burke snorted as he followed Elijah, because of course he didn't like questions at all.

Cardozo closed the door behind him, leaving them alone for the first time. He pointed to the chair in front of her desk. 'May I?'

'Please.' She closed her laptop and waited for him to begin.

'Burke has briefed me on your qualifications.' He smiled faintly.

'He didn't mention the roller derby fame, but that seems to have earned you a seal of approval from my son.'

'He's a good kid.'

'He is.' The pain and fear in his eyes was like a punch to the gut. 'He's everything to me. I can't . . .' He swallowed. 'I can't let anyone hurt him.'

'I'll keep him safe. If you think you'd be more confident with someone else, that's okay. Leaving your child in the hands of another person is a risk you have to be comfortable with.'

But she didn't want him to pick someone else. She'd already become invested in Elijah's safety.

'I appreciate that,' Cardozo said. 'Did you see the interview Corey Gates gave this morning?'

It was an abrupt segue, his question asked almost accusingly. She took a moment to consider her reply, because while the question itself was fine, his tone was not. 'I did. I'm still not convinced that Dewey Talley was the driver, because he told Elijah to run, but knowing that Rick has been communicating with Sixth Day is pretty damning. I was hoping that we were wrong, that they weren't involved, but that's where we appear to be.'

'I agree.' Then Cardozo narrowed his eyes. 'Who is Sixth Day to you? Specifically, Dewey Talley. I saw your reaction when Burke mentioned his name. I asked him and he said that I should ask you. So I'm asking you. What is your connection to Sixth Day?'

Ah. Okay. This was the question she'd been expecting. Bracing herself, she met his gaze directly. 'The former leader of Sixth Day killed my brother.'

Metairie, Louisiana
TUESDAY, OCTOBER 25, 11:20 A.M.

'Fuck.' Noni Feldman cursed again as she got into her car in the Three Vets parking lot, waving her cameraman back to his SUV. 'I'll meet you back at the station.'

It had been a long shot, but she'd hoped for another go at Corey Gates. Unfortunately, she wouldn't be talking to him again this morning. The Three Vets Renovation office was empty. Corey Gates wasn't here, and she'd waited as long as she could.

She'd peeked in the windows, but all she'd seen were a bunch of girlie photos on the walls. Most had been centerfolds, but there had been a few where the woman was clothed. It seemed that the three vets were Bella Butler fans.

She thought they might have come by the construction office to search for the still-missing Rick after the press conference, but maybe they'd already done so. If Corey had been right and Rick was entangled with Sixth Day, the kid was in even bigger trouble than a botched abduction attempt.

Corey had pretended to be sincere this morning, but Noni wasn't buying it. Two weeks before, she'd gotten an anonymous tip that Corey Gates was up to no good and if she investigated, she'd get an amazing story. That was before Aaron had killed the doctor and Rick had tried to abduct the prosecutor's son, which made Noni wonder just how much Corey knew.

So Noni had been investigating the hell out of Corey Gates, putting out feelers to several of her usual sources. One of whom—her source in Veterans Affairs—had texted her early that morning, asking her to call. They'd played phone tag for the past few hours, so she wasn't hopeful when she dialed.

To her surprise, he answered. 'Yeah?'

'It's Noni. What do you have?'

'Corey Gates's army discharge papers.'

'You had those already. He got an ODPMC discharge.' She'd become a walking lexicon of military alphabet soup. The ODPMC was a discharge for Other Designated Physical and Mental Conditions. Which included mental illness of most kinds. 'I assumed he had PTSD.' Given the man's eight years of service, that he'd come home with PTSD wouldn't have been a shock. 'Is that not right?'

'Not a bad assumption, but not the whole story. He's listed as having a personality disorder. Some of the PTSD symptoms overlap, but in Corey's case, he lost his temper and beat one of the local Iraqi women so badly that she's permanently disfigured. He'd been counseled about the fights he'd gotten into before, so this was the final straw.'

Noni pulled up the Notes app on her phone and began typing this information. 'Why wasn't he prosecuted?'

'I guess that the army didn't want the bad publicity and just wanted him to go away. ODPMC is sometimes used to get rid of unruly soldiers in general.'

'How do you know this about Corey?' she asked.

'I called the clerk who filed the paperwork. He owed me a favor and I collected it. I appreciated the story you did on the conditions in the VA hospitals. You gave our soldiers a voice, so I used my marker for you.'

Noni was touched. 'Thank you.'

'Just don't use my name.'

'I never would. Can I get a copy of the paperwork?'

'I'll upload it to your private Dropbox account.'

'Thank you so much. This establishes Corey's history of violence. I can do something with this.'

'I saw the interview he gave this morning. You hit him hard with the daddy question. He's got more control now than he did when he was in uniform. But he wanted to punch you.'

'I know,' she said, satisfied. 'I'll keep poking and see what I can get him to give away.'

'Just be careful. I saw a photo of what he did to that Iraqi woman and it was not good.'

'I'll be careful. Thanks!' She ended the call and, her mood improved, headed back to the station. She had to refresh her makeup before she went live at noon.

The Quarter, New Orleans, Louisiana
TUESDAY, OCTOBER 25, 11:20 A.M.

Kaj stared at Val Sorensen. 'Rico Nova killed your brother?'

She nodded grimly. 'Sixth Day was a major player in the drug trade four years ago. They distributed all over the city, but the operation they ran out of a little twenty-four-hour café in Freret was the one that impacted my family. It was close enough to Tulane to attract college kids needing speed to study all night. That's how my sister got addicted. My brother had followed my sister to the café the night he died, to try to keep her from buying. She'd been sober for almost a year by that point. He didn't want to see her fail.'

'But?'

She sighed quietly. 'He got into some kind of altercation with Rico Nova, who owned the café. Some accounts said that Talley was there, too. I don't know if he was, but he seemed to know everything that went on in Sixth Day, so I figured he knew about this, too. My brother probably threatened to report Nova to the cops, but I don't know that for sure. Nova stabbed him.' She met Kaj's gaze, hers unfaltering. 'Gutted him, Mr. Cardozo. Then tossed him out onto the sidewalk and left him there to die.'

Kaj swallowed hard. *Gutted him.* These were the people who'd tried to steal his son. His Elijah.

It had been terrifying when he'd thought the kidnapping was just Aaron Gates's brother wanting him back, but when the NOPD had shown him the tattoo on the driver's arm . . .

He now understood why Burke had been so adamant that Val Sorensen be his son's bodyguard. She understood the danger better than anyone else.

On one hand, that did make her a good choice.

On the other, however . . . If she wanted vigilante justice? That could put Elijah in even more danger. That made her the worst possible choice.

He needed more information before he decided what to do.

He started to say as much, then stopped short. *Wait. Wait just a minute.*

'I read the file on that murder, but the victim wasn't named Sorensen. It was . . .' He faltered, then snapped his fingers when the name came back. 'Kristiansen. Ivan Kristiansen.'

Her expression softened. 'I called him Van. He was my twin.'

'But Kristiansen isn't your last name. Were you married? *Are* you married?'

The notion didn't sit right with him, but he wasn't going to dissect his reasons right now. He remained focused on Val Sorensen's face. On her clear blue eyes. He made a living detecting lies. He needed to be sure she was telling him the truth.

She stiffened. 'No, I've never been married. I changed my name. Legally.'

'Why? And when?'

For a moment he thought she wouldn't answer, her full lips thinning into a mutinous line. But she finally spoke. 'It was after I got back from my tour in Iraq. I had an issue with one of the Marines I'd known back there. I was home for almost a year before he was discharged, and he . . . sought me out. He wouldn't leave me alone. So I took my grandmother's maiden name and moved to New Mexico to make it harder for him to find me. Voilà, Val Sorensen was born.'

I had an issue. That could be code for so many things, none of them good.

He sought me out. Clearly code for stalking of some kind.

New rage filled him. Someone had scared her so badly that she, a Marine, had legally changed her name and uprooted her life. *Who is he? Where is he? What did he do to you?*

But he held the questions inside. The only information he had a right to was whether the man was a threat to Elijah.

'Is he still a problem? I only ask because you are guarding my son and—'

She held up a hand. 'I understand. The man is no longer a problem. He's dead.'

Kaj's brows shot up. She'd uttered those last two words in a tone that made it sound as if she was satisfied at the man's death. There was relief there, too. 'How did he die?'

Her lips curved sardonically. 'I didn't do it, if that's what you're asking.'

'What happened to him?'

She met his gaze directly. 'He must have bothered the wrong person, because he was shot while he slept. I had an airtight alibi. Because I didn't do it.'

He studied her for a long moment, then decided she was telling the truth. 'All right.' He'd investigate her alibi later, because he operated on facts and this was an important one.

'You still want me to guard your son?'

'I think so. Because I think that maybe you wanted to kill the man, too.' There had been too much satisfaction in her declaration of the man's death. 'But you didn't.'

She blinked. Then nodded. 'I did want to, but you're right. I didn't. I changed my name and moved across the country to get away from him instead.'

'I see,' he said calmly, even though his internal radar was screaming that this woman had borne something truly terrible. *Not my business. Elijah is my concern.* 'So, back to your brother and Sixth Day. As I recall, Rico Nova is serving a life sentence in Angola for the murder.'

Her smile was grim. 'Yes. He pleaded guilty to avoid the death penalty. It spared my parents having to go through a trial. It won't bring my brother back, but at least *one* Sixth Day bastard can't hurt anyone else.'

'True. Although the case against him seemed a little weak.' He watched her face as he said the words. Her jaw went tight and her eyes flashed in anger, but her reaction didn't seem aimed at him. 'It came down to an anonymous tip called in to 911,' he went on. 'Then Nova confessed.'

Her nostrils flared as she suddenly exhaled. He wasn't sure which part of his sentence she was reacting to—the anonymous tip or Nova's confession.

'You're wondering if he was taking the fall for someone else,' she stated flatly. 'I wondered that, too. That's why I know about Dewey Talley and Sixth Day. I wanted to know who else was involved. I wanted to know why Nova killed Van himself instead of relegating it to a flunky. I wanted to know what Van said to make him mad enough to gut him. I wanted to know why Nova toppled like a house of cards at the first visit from the cops. I wanted to know what hole Dewey Talley disappeared into and who helped him hide. So I asked questions and I searched for anyone who'd seen Talley. But I kept hitting brick walls. NOPD either didn't know anything or they weren't willing to share. None of his old dealers would talk. A few of them disappeared, too. A few were found dead.'

'A message to the others to keep their mouths shut.'

'Exactly.' She shrugged. 'At the end of the day, Nova confessed. He was explicit in every detail in how he killed my brother, and his statement at his plea hearing matched with the ME's findings. I would have preferred if he'd resisted a plea, or at least if he'd given up who else was involved to get a lighter sentence, but he didn't. He took one hundred percent of the fall, and now he's in prison. Forever. That's good for something.'

Kaj had come to the same conclusion about Rico Nova when he'd read the case file. She appeared to be resigned about Nova's confession, so it had to have been the tip that made her so angry. 'Well, somebody was brave enough to call in that anonymous tip.'

Her eyes flashed again, hotter this time. Angrier. 'Sure,' she said bitterly. '*Somebody* finally found their fucking backbone and did the right thing.'

Ah. This was personal. It was in every nuance of her response. 'You know who it was. Who made the call.'

Her nod was clipped. 'My sister Sylvi was there that night. She was the reason my brother was there in the first place. Like I said, she'd gone to buy. Van went to stop her. He went inside the café to find her. She saw him go in, but she didn't try to stop him. She saw Rico Nova toss Van's body on the sidewalk, but she didn't try to help him. She ran away. Called 911 eventually—and anonymously—but she ran. She never even tried to save him.'

Kaj could understand her anger, although he could also understand the sister's actions. She'd just seen her brother's gutted body and, if she'd been there to buy, had probably been needing a fix. Running away was a human response. Maybe even the wisest response.

But he wasn't going to express such thoughts. *Not my business. Elijah is.*

He considered his next question carefully. 'What do you want to see happen to Sixth Day? And what are you willing to do toward that end?'

Her shoulders relaxed a fraction. 'I'm no vigilante, Mr. Cardozo. But I'd be lying if I said that I didn't want to see them brought down. I wanted to be the one to do it four years ago because I was angry. I got more than a little obsessed with Sixth Day after Van's death. I'd drive past Rico Nova's house and watch his family from my car. I questioned every two-bit drug dealer I could find for information on Dewey Talley, because I didn't believe that Sixth Day was truly defunct—and it seems I was right. Those two-bit dealers did say that he was rumored to have a camp out in the bayou, so I searched for it a time or two. Or fifty.' She lifted a shoulder. 'But my common sense finally kicked in, along with the words of a good therapist. At least one of Van's killers is behind bars. I eventually let Talley and the rest of Sixth Day go. I had to.'

'I understand letting it go,' Kaj said quietly. 'Not every case I've tried has ended the way I want. If I didn't let them go, I couldn't go on to the next, and even more people wouldn't be getting justice. Sometimes letting go is the best thing you can do. That was then, though. What are you willing to do now?'

'As I said, I'm no vigilante. I'm a private investigator and a bodyguard. If someone comes after Elijah, I will kill them if I must. I'll do whatever I have to do to keep your son safe. If I find information that leads to Dewey Talley or Sixth Day, I will not go off on my own, gunning for them. I would work with Burke and the others to coordinate a response. I would call in backup. I would never leave your child unprotected.'

Kaj had a lot of experience talking to liars. He wasn't talking to one now. He believed Val was telling the truth.

He wanted her help. He wanted the benefit of her knowledge and insight into Sixth Day. And if she could help Burke stop the men who'd come for his son, he'd be forever grateful.

'How will you handle Elijah's diabetes?' he asked.

'I'll find recipes and ask someone I trust to buy the ingredients I need to feed him properly so that I don't have to leave his side. I'll research what symptoms to watch for, in case his blood sugar goes too high or low. I'll talk with your sister to find out what their routine has been. And I'll ask Elijah what he thinks needs to be done. He seems very mature for his age.'

Those were good answers. 'He is very mature.' And Kaj hated that Elijah had to be. As if losing his mother and dealing with his illness weren't enough, he now had to deal with the terror of kidnapping. 'Do you have questions for me?'

'A few. What about school? Will Elijah go to class, or will he stay home with me?'

'That's a point of contention between us. He wants to go to school, but I can't risk it right now. I talked to his teacher this morning and she said that he's so far ahead he can work from home for a while without it impacting his grades. Were you really a math teacher?'

She smiled. 'I was. Taught middle school math in New Mexico.'

Kaj exaggerated a shudder. 'You *are* tough. Why did you leave teaching?'

Her smile faltered. 'After Van was killed, my mom . . . Well, she wasn't okay after that. I moved back to New Orleans to take care of her and my dad. They've settled into a new normal, whatever that is. Anyway, I knew Molly Sutton from the Corps.'

Kaj also knew Molly Sutton. She was one of Burke's PIs. 'She brought you into Burke's agency?'

'She did. I make more money working for Burke than I did teaching, but I like to keep my hand in, so I work with kids in the community center's music program and I tutor math.'

'How do you handle your job at the community center when you're working for Burke?'

'It's a volunteer position, so the community center is flexible with me. When I can't make it, one of my friends from the QuarterMasters subs for me.'

'The QuarterMasters?'

Her grin made him feel lighter. 'My roller derby team.'

He grinned back. 'Oh, right. Anything else?'

'Will Elijah also have police protection?' she asked. 'Will there be any officers stationed at your house?'

He winced at the sudden pain in his jaw and realized that he'd clenched his teeth. 'No. Not at this time.'

'May I ask why?'

He hesitated, then sighed. 'I've uncovered a lot of corruption in the six months that I've been here. I haven't made a lot of friends in NOPD.'

'You don't trust them?'

'Some, sure. Probably most. I'd even say that several of the police are friends. André Holmes, for one.' The NOPD captain had proven himself trustworthy as they'd worked closely together on more than one case. 'But André can't camp out at my house and he wasn't able to spare anyone that I know to stand guard. So I declined.'

'I understand that. I only needed to know how to coordinate with other security on the ground. One more question—where is Elijah's mother? Is she in the home? Shared custody?'

Kaj swallowed. The pain of loss wasn't nearly as harsh as it had been, but yesterday's events had him missing his wife anew. 'She died five years ago, when Elijah was only five. She had cancer. My sister Genie put her own career aside and lived with us through the whole thing. She took care of Heather and Elijah, and when Heather died, Genie became like Elijah's second mother. She lived with us in New York until she got married and relocated here.'

'She's special, then.'

Kaj nodded. 'She is. I'm so glad she had that Taser.'

'Me too. Do you believe that she's in danger? Will we need to provide protection for her while she's on bed rest?'

'No. Her husband's family has rallied around them. They know how to use weapons in self-defense and that's . . . well, that's really all I want to know. She's safe for now. I'd have asked them to watch over Elijah, too, but I don't want to bring more trouble to her door.'

'Good. Will she be available to answer any questions I have about Elijah's nutritional needs or his routine?'

'She will.' He huffed a laugh. 'She's already insisted on it.'

'Then she'll be the first person I'll call.' She hesitated a moment, biting at her lip before shrugging apologetically. 'I don't want to break Elijah's confidence, but you should know that he's worried about how you're paying for all this.'

Kaj sighed. 'He would. He worries about everything, which I suppose he gets from me.' He grimaced self-deprecatingly. 'I worry about everything, too. Heather, on the other hand, was a planner. She made sure we both had life insurance policies that were sufficient to take care of Elijah if anything happened to us. Hers was more than enough to cover Burke's fees. I'll make sure that Elijah knows not to worry.' He stuck out his hand. 'Thank you, Miss Sorensen. I'd be happy if you guarded my son.'

She stood to lean over the desk and shook his hand, her grip firm. 'Call me Val.'

He considered her for a moment. 'My friends call me Kaj. It's spelled K-a-j but rhymes with "pie".'

A smile bloomed, brightening her already pretty face. She was a very attractive woman. And he shouldn't notice that. This was business. This was about Elijah.

'Your parents must have wanted names with a European flair, what with a Scandinavian first name and a French middle. And Cardozo?'

He stared at her smile, still gripping her hand. He hadn't let go. But neither had she. It should have been awkward, but it wasn't. And he wasn't going to think about why that might be.

He released her, letting his hand drop to his side. 'Cardozo is Portuguese. My father was from Portugal and my mother was Danish. Kaj was her father's name. My godfather was Jean-Pierre, so I've kind of got a mishmash of names. When I was Elijah's age, no one could pronounce my name properly. Bullies like to push buttons, so when I started middle school, I started going by Jean-Pierre.

The bullies still teased me and called me Jean, like the pants, but the girls swooned, so I called it a win. Jean-Pierre just carried over into college and then my career. But my closest friends and family know me as Kaj.'

She grimaced good-naturedly. 'My birth name isn't Val,' she confided. 'It's Ingrid, but nobody calls me that except for my family. I played a Valkyrie in a high school play, because I was the only one tall enough to fit into the costume. Kids started calling me Val and it stuck.'

'What's your legal name now, after the name change? Ingrid or Val?'

'Val. The Marines in my unit knew me as Ingrid Kristiansen, so using Val felt safer once I got out.'

'Why didn't you change your name back after the stalker was no longer a threat?'

She shrugged. 'By then I'd built an identity as Val Sorensen. I had a teaching career and my roller derby friends. I've considered it a few times since Van died, but it's a lot of bother, so I just haven't.'

'I'm sorry. I didn't mean to dredge up difficult memories about your brother.'

'Thank you, but you don't have to be sorry. I miss him every day, but life does go on. Which you know as well.'

'Yes, I do.' He sometimes still reached for Heather in those hazy moments between sleep and waking up. Brusquely he pulled a business card from his pocket and wrote his cell phone number on the back. 'My office number and work cell are on the front. My personal cell is on the back. Please don't give out the personal number. Not many people have that.'

'I'll keep it safe.'

He knew she would, just as she'd keep his son safe. 'I'm going to take Elijah home. When can we expect you?'

'I can follow you right now. I have a go-bag in my car. That way you can get back to work or wherever you need to go. I'll ask Burke to arrange a backup bodyguard so I can go home and pack more clothes if this stretches on more than a few days.'

He gestured to the door. 'Then . . . after you.'

5

COREY RELAXED AS he steered the boat around the final bend, his camp now in sight. It was back in the bayou, off one of the many little tributaries, nearly impossible to find if you didn't know exactly where it was. No one 'just happened' upon them, which was how Corey liked it.

The camp had been just a plot of cleared land four years ago when Aaron had taken it over from the former head of Sixth Day. The old leader had apparently planned to build his own camp, but never got the chance.

In that first year, Corey, Bobby, and Ed had built two structures. The first had been for Aaron, yet another contribution that Corey had made to his brother's drug business. For Liam.

Aaron had needed a place to make and store his meth, far away from Dianne and Liam. He hadn't wanted his family to know how he was paying the bills, and the fumes generated by meth production would have given him away.

Corey had thought at the time that the health risks to Dianne and

Liam from the fumes and the explosion risks from the meth production process were better reasons for Aaron to do his making far away, but he'd held his tongue. Aaron had been under such financial pressure and Liam had been so sick. Plus, Aaron had no handyman skills. He was a white-collar man all the way. At least he had been four years ago. It was Corey who'd worked for a construction company as a teenager to help his mother pay the bills. It was Corey who'd had the skills.

Please, Aaron had begged. *For Liam.*

I'll build it, he'd replied, *but I want half the land.* Aaron had been desperate enough then to agree.

So Corey had built his brother a small cabin with a working kitchen for his meth production. It had taken a few months to build, partly because it was the first thing Corey had ever built from the ground up by himself, but mainly because he'd had to transport all the materials by boat. But it was a good cabin, strong enough to withstand the hurricane or two that had blown through. Within hours of its completion, Dewey and Aaron had set up production. The two had made meth and Corey had helped them distribute it.

For Liam.

Corey had built the second cabin for himself, with Bobby and Ed's help. They'd decided that they also needed a location far away from prying eyes, a place where they could plan their dirty jobs. Plus, Corey loved the bayou. It was a good fit. After building the two cabins, they figured a construction business would be a decent cover for their real business. Corey had spent the last few years adding on to his cabin and making it more comfortable than his actual house. He would have lived here all along had it not been for Rick and Jace.

Who might not be a concern after today. It was a liberating thought.

Corey had also built Dewey's workshop, but for that he'd demanded another piece of land Aaron had inherited from the old Sixth Day leader. It was farther away, near Lake Cataouatche. Corey had drawn the line at building a house for Dewey, so Dewey had built himself the little shack that looked like it would fall down at any moment. As soon as they'd taken care of Dewey, that eyesore would be history.

'Do you think he knows?' Ed asked, breaking the silence. 'Aaron, I mean. About our business?'

'No,' Corey said flatly. 'If he did, he'd already have given us up to the DA to get a better deal. He's always seen what he wants to see. He sees our cabin as a fishing getaway.'

Aaron was too arrogant to see that other people were successful all around him. He was about to be taken down a few pegs. *Enjoy prison, asshole.*

Ed pointed to the older man ambling toward the dock, watching their approach. 'And Dewey?'

'If he suspects, he's never let on. Doesn't really matter anymore, though.' Corey turned his head, lowering his voice. 'After today, he won't be an issue.'

He cut back on the throttle, guiding the boat against the dock. Aaron's boat floated beside his, the engine exposed, parts carefully set on the boat's bench seat.

Dewey moved to the edge of the dock and stared down into Corey's boat with a frown. 'What the fuck, Corey? Is Dianne okay? What'd you do to her?'

Corey sniffed the air cautiously, relieved when he smelled no noxious odors. At least Dewey hadn't started a new batch of meth. He only smelled motor oil layered over the earthy, slightly fishy scent of the bayou. It seemed that Bobby's ploy of having Dewey work on Aaron's boat to keep him occupied had been the wisest course of action.

'She's blackout drunk again.' Corey jumped onto the dock, then took Dianne from Ed's arms and started walking toward his quarters. 'How's Aaron's boat?'

'Almost done,' Dewey said, keeping pace with him while casting worried looks at Dianne's still form. 'Jace's been helping me. You and I need to talk about sellin' Aaron's boat.'

'Bobby mentioned that you think it should be yours.'

Dewey lifted his chin, his scraggly beard unkempt. 'Because it should be. With Aaron gone to jail, I'm going to need a way to support myself until I can get another partner. I can either sell the boat or hire someone to run my product into the city usin' it. Either way, that boat is my due.'

Corey wondered if Dewey knew how much money Aaron had squirreled away. He wondered if Aaron had shared any of it with his partner, but the man always looked homeless, so Corey didn't think so.

'You could have a point.' Dewey did not have a point, but Corey would let him think so until they'd satisfied Bobby's concern regarding Dewey's interest in talking to Rick. Bobby was rarely wrong, but Corey planned to question Rick first. He'd be a far easier nut to crack than Dewey. 'Let me set Dianne down and we can talk it through.'

'Okay. How long are you keeping her here?'

'Until the cops stop poking around. Don't want her saying the wrong thing when she's drunk. Like now.'

'She never knew about this place, you know,' Dewey said, his tone a little softer. 'She never knew what Aaron was doing. She can't tell what she don't know.'

'She was too drunk to leave alone,' Corey said, not wanting to discuss Dianne being his alibi. 'I'll take her back once I've dealt with Rick and Jace.'

Dewey nodded silently, standing back as Ed unlocked Corey's front door. Ed took his laptop to the comm room to begin finalizing the plans for the Trevor Doyle/Bella Butler job. Corey didn't worry about his younger brothers seeing Ed work. Rick wouldn't be able to say a thing to anyone after today and Jace couldn't read.

Dianne was growing heavy in his arms, so Corey looked at Dewey over his shoulder. 'Stay there. We'll discuss your boat now that Aaron's out of the picture.'

Corey had briefly considered a partnership with Dewey, now that Aaron was gone. For maybe a minute and a half. There was a lot of money at stake, for sure. But drug dealing was a complicated business that required constant monitoring to keep product flowing and dealers from stealing one blind. His own dirty-jobs business was based on a one-and-done model. They signed a client, did the job, got paid, and then went on to the next client, whose job would likely be completely different.

Corey liked his business the way that it was. He'd built it from nothing, and he was on the cusp of something big. It was the only thing he'd ever been successful with. His other endeavors had never gone to plan.

He wasn't a born schmoozer like Aaron was. He'd only known construction before he enlisted. Then he'd been in the army for eight years and would have made it his career had they not given him a fuckin' ODPMC discharge. Pompous assholes.

But he'd learned a lot from the army. He knew how to kill. So that was what he did now, for a helluva lot more money than he'd made as a soldier.

No way would he have the patience to deal with selling drugs to rich people, with their simpering and whining. *I'd probably shoot them all, just to shut them up.* Dewey's business simply wasn't worth it, no matter how much more money he could make.

Corey deposited Dianne on his neatly made bed—a habit drilled into his head from his first days in boot camp. Straightening, he stretched his back and bit back a groan.

Shit. He wasn't old enough to feel this tired from carrying a woman a hundred feet, even if she was dead weight. He turned on the overhead fan, made sure the security camera pointed at the bed so that he'd know when she woke up, and set a bottle of water on the nightstand. Then he rejoined Dewey outside.

The man would make the perfect distraction for NOPD this week.

'I was going to sell Aaron's boat for ten grand,' Corey told him. 'You got that much?'

Dewey shrugged. 'I got it.'

'One other thing.' Corey couldn't have Dewey thinking he was completely soft. Dewey would know something was up. 'I want veto power on whoever you choose as your new partner. My friends and I come up here for relaxation and I don't want to be looking over my shoulder if you bring in some Mexican cartel type.'

Dewey bobbed his head from side to side, considering it. 'I guess that's fair enough.'

'Also, we can't have you using our construction trucks anymore. I only let Aaron do it for Liam's sake. If we're caught hauling your stuff, we could all go to jail with Aaron.'

Corey had never charged Aaron a single penny for his time or the use of his equipment, asking only that Dewey do the maintenance for free. Corey had done everything for Liam. At least that was what he'd thought. He'd thought every penny Aaron made went to the doctors.

Aaron had used him. It still made Corey want to rip Aaron's head off.

Dewey frowned, then nodded. 'I guess that's fair, too.'

Corey let his expression soften, preparing his first question about Rick. 'I'm not trying to bust your chops, Dewey. I'm also worried about Rick. He's been using.'

'He didn't get it from me,' Dewey denied quickly.

Corey didn't know that he believed the man, but it really didn't matter. Dewey wouldn't be a concern after today, either. 'I think he was stealing from Aaron. Y'know, since Aaron started keeping the shit in his and Dianne's house.' Since Liam died. Aaron had at least been careful about having drugs in his home when Liam had still lived. 'Rick didn't have any money of his own. I've got to get him off that junk.'

'It'll fry your brain, for sure,' Dewey agreed heavily. 'I kept trying to tell Aaron not to dip into the product, but . . .' He eyed Corey warily. 'And what's with Rick? What was he trying to do last night?'

Corey immediately saw what Bobby had been talking about. There was a cagey air to the older man, like he already knew the answer to the question he'd asked. *Like he's trying to play me.* 'I don't know,' he lied. 'But I'm about to find out, so if you'll excuse me.' Without waiting for an answer, he turned back to his cabin. His brothers were waiting in the comm room with Bobby, as they'd agreed on the phone.

He hoped Bobby hadn't started questioning them without him. If he had, Rick and Jace might be carved up like jack-o'-lanterns already. Corey wanted to do some of the damage himself. *Emancipation, my ass.*

'Corey,' Dewey called, his voice sounding uncertain. 'Jace couldn't have come up with that idea. So . . . maybe go easy on him.'

Dewey had always had a soft spot for Jace and had shown the kid how to rebuild engines. Jace wasn't good at book learning, but he had a real aptitude for machines. Corey had let Jace hang out with the old man when Dewey was working on their trucks. At least the kid would have a useful skill. He was never going to graduate from high school. Hell, Jace hadn't graduated from elementary school.

'I'll see,' was all Corey would promise. He went back in the house, first locking the front door's interior dead bolt with his key. It would keep Dewey out and Dianne in, should she wake up before he was finished with his brothers.

He'd stepped around the air mattress on his living-room floor on his way to the comm room when his business burner vibrated in his pocket. Dread prickled at his nerves as he dug for the phone, coalescing into a solid wave of panic when he saw the number on the caller ID.

It was Trevor Doyle.

He hadn't heard from his client since yesterday evening, shortly after Rick's video had gone viral. The text had simply said: *Fix this.*

Drawing a breath, Corey hit accept and lifted the phone to his ear. 'Yes?'

Don't cancel the contract. Do not cancel the contract. This was the biggest job he'd ever had and he needed the win. With everything spiraling out of control around him, his job was the one thing he uniquely controlled.

'I saw your interview.'

Corey swallowed, his mouth suddenly dry. 'And?'

'I told you last week to stay out of the spotlight.'

Doyle had, minutes after the video of Aaron killing the doctor had gone viral. 'I was in the spotlight, whether I liked it or not. I did the interview to redirect the spotlight.'

'Was the part about your brother and Sixth Day true?'

'The police believe that it is.'

There was a beat of silence, then a chuckle that didn't sound all that amused. 'You made lemonade out of shit. It's still shitty lemonade, though.'

'The important thing is that the cops are now looking at someone else for last night's fiasco. They're not looking at me.'

'See that they don't. Just because your life is fucked up beyond belief is no excuse to fuck up mine. I don't have time to find someone else to take care of things, so make sure you stay out of the spotlight from here on out.'

Corey ground his teeth because Doyle wasn't wrong. His life was fucked up beyond belief right now, but he *would* make it right again. 'I will.'

'Do not fail me or the NOPD will be the least of your concerns. If you disappear, nobody's going to be looking at me for it. Understand?'

The threatening words should have made him angry, but they only made him scared. And *that* made him angry. He hated being scared. 'Yes,' he bit out. 'Anything else?'

'No. Just get it done.' The call ended, leaving Corey staring at the phone in his hand, fury roiling in his gut.

His rage shouldn't be directed at Doyle. The man had hired him to do a job and thought that job's success was in jeopardy. Rick and Jace were the real assholes here. *Focus all that anger on them.* So he did, and he was instantly back in control and ready to deal with his brothers.

The comm room was quiet except for Rick's heavy breathing. Both Rick and Jace sat in straight-backed chairs that Bobby had dragged to the center of the room. His friend stood behind the chairs, one beefy hand on Rick's shoulder, the other on Jace's.

Bobby was also armed, and Corey nearly laughed. Bobby wore a crossbody chest holster and in it he'd parked his Raging Judge, a revolver that was almost cartoonish in size. It was huge, weighing four and a half pounds, and was fourteen inches long from hilt to barrel. One almost expected a little flag that said 'boom' to exit the barrel rather than the .454 Casull bullet that could take down a grizzly bear. It was overkill in the extreme but appeared to have done the trick. Rick looked like he was about to have a stroke. He was red-faced and clearly stressed the fuck out. Jace, on the other hand, looked quietly terrified.

That was a good place to start.

Corey sat on the arm of one of the two leather sofas and stared at his brothers, his eyes narrowing. 'Whose idea was it?' he demanded.

Rick flicked a glance at Jace, then met Corey's gaze. 'Mine.'

'Jace?' Corey asked, keeping his tone even. 'Is that true?'

Jace swallowed. 'Yes, sir.'

Liar. If he couldn't get the truth from Jace, he'd separate them. Jace had to be handled more delicately than Rick. When Jace felt cornered, he'd shut down, and no amount of beatings could make him speak. It was almost like his whole brain froze.

Rick, on the other hand, spewed words at the least bit of pressure.

'If it wasn't your idea, Jace, why did you go? And don't look at Rick. You look at me, boy.'

Jace's face crumpled. 'Rick said we should. He said that y—' He cut himself off, then drew a deep breath. 'He said we should help Aaron.'

Corey knew what Jace had been about to say. *You.* Rick had claimed that this idiocy had been ordered by Corey. 'Did you want to go?'

Jace looked miserable. 'No, sir.'

'I see. So what was your role, Jace?'

'I drove. That's it.'

'It was my idea,' Rick stated baldly, and Corey had to admit to being a little impressed with his brother's guts. 'Jace just drove. He's telling the truth. He didn't do nothin' but drive.'

Corey came to his feet, staring down at Rick. 'I wasn't talking to you. So keep your mouth closed. Got it? Nod.'

Rick's mouth tightened, but he nodded once.

Kid had found his balls. Too bad it was too little, too late. He might have become a decent addition to Corey's team in time.

Corey took a step toward Jace, making the boy look up at him. 'Do you realize what you've done?' he asked severely.

Jace trembled. 'We broke a law.'

Corey barked out a harsh laugh. 'You broke so many laws, I don't even know where to start. How the hell was this going to help Aaron?' Jace turned his head to look at Rick, his expression beseeching, but Rick kept his gaze fixed on the far wall, staying silent. Corey grabbed Jace's chair and turned him so that he could no longer see Rick. 'You look at me, boy.'

Jace gulped. 'We . . . we thought the father would trade Aaron for his son. That he'd let Aaron out of jail.'

'You're both fucking idiots. Aaron *killed* a man, Jace. He *deserves* to be in jail.' Rick's head jerked sideways, their gazes colliding. Corey didn't think he'd ever seen so much hate in Rick's eyes. Jace, on the other hand, was frowning as if confused. 'What?' Corey snapped.

'I . . .' Jace exhaled unsteadily. 'I don't know if you're mad because we did it or because we didn't do it right.'

Rick's eyes narrowed. It was clear that he thought the first one. And he'd be right.

Corey lost his temper. 'Both! I'm mad because you tried to kidnap a kid to get fucking Aaron out of fucking jail. I'm mad that Rick let his face be exposed. I'm mad that I have cops sniffing around. *Again*. And I'm mad that you thought that you had the right to do *anything* without my permission.'

Jace leaned away, his fear obvious. 'What are you going to do to us?'

'What do you think I should do, Jace?'

Jace cowered. 'I don't know. I got us out of there as soon as I could, because people were taking video and now it's all over the internet. I'm sorry. I didn't know what else to do.'

'Will you ever do such a thing again?'

'Oh no,' Jace breathed, like a prayer. 'I promise on Mama's grave.'

That was a big deal in their family. Even though he'd never quite measured up to Aaron in his mama's eyes, Corey had loved her. She'd done nothing but sacrifice for them her whole life. *And then* I *sacrificed for these assholes, and this is how they repay my generosity.*

'All right, then. Come with me.' He walked Jace to the back door of the comm room and unlocked the dead bolt. 'Dewey says you're helping him with Aaron's boat. Get back to that.'

Jace's gaze flitted between him and Rick. 'What about Rick?'

'Not your business, boy. Go help Dewey. Do as I say.'

Jace squared his wide shoulders. 'What are you going to do to Rick?'

Huh. Kid's tougher than I thought. Time to knock that courage down a few notches. 'Not. Your. Business. Go now or I'll get angry *with you*. You don't want me to get angry *with you*, do you?'

Jace shrank back, just as Corey had hoped. The kid had been on the receiving end of his backhand enough times to know his place. 'No, sir.'

'Good. Now go.'

He watched as Jace went down the back stairs, the boy turning a few times to look over his shoulder, uncertainty clear in his expression. When Jace was halfway to Dewey's workshop, Corey shut and locked the door.

Rick was still sitting, his back ramrod straight, arms folded tightly over his chest. At five-nine, Rick was the smallest of them all. He took after their mother more than the rest of them. Unfortunately, he was also wily and had way too much attitude.

Corey had been trying to beat that attitude out of him for years, ever since he'd returned from the Middle East to find himself a joint guardian of two boys. They'd lived with Aaron then, but Corey had hung around Aaron's place enough to recognize discipline issues. Rick had only been ten, Jace nine. Rick had been stubborn even then. Didn't seem to matter how many beatings he took.

Corey grabbed the chair Jace had been using, straddling it so that he faced Rick head-on. 'Why?'

Rick lifted his chin with his typical defiance. 'I wanted to help Aaron.'

Corey made sure that his smile was nasty. 'Because he can't help you get emancipated from prison.'

The color in Rick's face abruptly drained away. 'What?'

'You want emancipation, I understand.'

'No,' Rick sputtered. 'I don't—' His head flew to one side as the back of Corey's hand connected with his jaw. He only stayed in the chair because Bobby held him there.

'How'd you know about Cardozo's son?'

Rick worked his jaw from side to side, his nostrils flaring in rage. 'Internet.'

Corey hit him again. 'Liar. Ed looked. There's no sign of Elijah Cardozo on the internet. How did you know?'

Rick's lips pressed together mutinously, and he said nothing.

'How did you get to Cardozo's last night?' Corey demanded.

Rick looked away, a cry escaping him when Corey hit him a third time. 'I took your van and stole some license plates so that nobody would know it was yours.' He closed his eyes. 'What are you going to do to me? Keep me hostage?'

'Nope. I'm gonna hand you over to the cops.' Rick's body, anyway, along with a note Corey was going to sign as Sixth Day that would have Cardozo laser-focused on Dewey Talley. *Not on me.*

Rick's eyes flew open. 'You can't!'

'Oh, I can.' Corey leaned in until he was nose-to-nose with Rick. 'But first, you're going to tell me who helped you. Who told you where you could find Cardozo's kid?'

Rick looked away. 'Nobody.'

Corey smiled. 'Fine. Bobby's real good at making people talk. Aren't you, Bobby?'

A slow Cheshire Cat grin spread over Bobby's face. 'I am.'

Rick had grown deathly pale. 'What? What are you talking about?'

Corey patted Rick's cheek hard enough to hurt. 'Don't you worry your emancipated little head about it. You'll find out soon enough.'

With a smirk, Bobby gathered the items he needed from one of the drawers in the entertainment center. He placed the wires and alligator clips on an end table and dragged it over so that Rick could see them. The kid's eyes widened in fear.

Bobby leaned down to murmur in Rick's ear. 'I don't give you more than ten seconds. Current to the balls? It really hurts. You're going to wish you'd told Corey what he wanted to know when he first asked.'

'No, please!' Rick blurted. 'I'll tell you.'

Corey flashed his brother a smile. 'Oh, I know you will.'

Mid-City, New Orleans, Louisiana
TUESDAY, OCTOBER 25, 12:45 P.M.

Val stared up at the ceiling of Elijah's bedroom in awe. 'Wow.'

'You like it?' Elijah asked shyly.

A model airplane collection hung from the ceiling, arranged in battle formation. 'Did you do this, Elijah?'

'He did,' Kaj said from the doorway. 'He made all of the planes and hung them.'

Val turned to Elijah in amazement. 'Is it Midway?'

Elijah sucked in a breath. 'How did you know?'

'My dad's a history professor at Tulane. We watched *all* the war movies growing up and Dad pointed out *all* the ways the filmmakers had gotten it wrong. I recognize the planes.'

'Did you fly any planes in the Marines?' Elijah asked.

'Nope. Only rode as a passenger in one of the troop transports.' She made a face. 'No in-flight movie or free drinks.'

'The very nerve,' Kaj said, and Val chuckled.

'I did jump out of one once, though,' she said brightly. 'But that was a normal skydive.'

Elijah beamed. 'I want to do that, Dad.'

'When you're eighteen,' Kaj said. 'Then I can't stop you.'

'I have to wait for everything,' Elijah grumbled.

'I have video of my jump,' Val offered. 'Later, we can watch it.'

Kaj opened his mouth, most likely to object, then closed it. 'Okay.'

She bit back a smirk. 'Maybe Elijah can write a paper on the aero-dynamics of parachutes,' she said as she took a slow turn around his room. 'Elijah, this is so cool. And all these ribbons.' She walked to his shelves to inspect them.

'For the math club, mostly,' Elijah said, sounding embarrassed. 'No sports.'

She cast him a glance. 'Math geeks end up ruling the world, kid.'

Elijah rolled his eyes. 'That's what my dad says.'

'He's right.' She turned her focus to the windows. 'Hurricane glass?'

Kaj nodded. 'This area was heavily damaged in Katrina. The house that was here before was demolished. A lot of the new construction has hurricane windows.'

'Good.' She met Elijah's eyes. 'That means anyone wanting to break that glass to get to you will have to use something noisy like a Sawzall. Which I doubt they'll risk doing, because it'll wake me up.'

Elijah frowned. 'What do you mean, it'll wake you up? Where are you sleeping?'

'In the guest room next door,' she said quickly, reassuring him. 'But I'm a super light sleeper. I'm going to give you a panic button, like you used last night. It'll screech loud enough to wake the dead, but I'll also be wearing a receiver that will vibrate to wake me up. And I'd like to put a monitor in your room. I'm not spying on you. But I will hear if you yell or if anyone tries to come through that window.'

Elijah hesitated and Val could see the indecision on his face.

'I want you to feel safe enough to be able to sleep, Elijah,' she said quietly. 'The monitor is only one tool that will help with that. If you don't want to, I'll find another way.'

He hesitated a beat longer but finally nodded. 'Okay.'

'Thank you.' She checked her watch. 'I want to check the alarm contacts on the windows, make sure they're all hunky-dory, then I can try my hand at making lunch.'

'I am hungry,' he admitted. 'And tired. I didn't sleep much last night.'

'There's chicken wraps in the fridge,' Kaj said.

Elijah clenched his teeth, and Val saw real anger flash in his dark eyes for the first time. 'I know,' he gritted out. 'I made them. I'll go eat. I'm also going to call Aunt Genie.'

'If she's asleep, don't bother her,' Kaj warned.

'I *know*, Dad,' he snapped. 'I won't bother her if she's asleep. I'll text René first to make sure she's awake.'

'Who's René?' Val asked.

'My uncle,' Elijah said, still sounding irritated. 'He's the reason Aunt Genie moved here and why we had to follow. René was in college in New York, but then he graduated and came back home. Here, to New Orleans. He's an architect.'

Val kept her tone mild. 'When you talk to your aunt, can you ask her for a convenient time for me to call?'

Elijah huffed. 'Fine.'

Kaj watched Elijah head down the stairs, then sagged against the doorframe. 'He never used to snap at me like that. I know that he's probably just hungry and tired and stressed, but . . .' He sighed. 'I hate that he's hungry and tired and stressed.'

'He's more rattled than he wants to show.'

Kaj stared at her blearily. Even haggard and worry-worn, he was still a very handsome man. 'He'd never lived anywhere else until we came here. I . . .' He shrugged helplessly. 'I thought I was doing the right thing, uprooting him to follow Genie. And then all of this happened.' He crossed the room and sank onto Elijah's bed, which was made with military precision.

She wasn't yet sure if Elijah's perfection at age ten was a good thing or not.

She moved to the doorway, taking a moment to make sure Elijah was all right. She'd already secured the downstairs, so he was safe. She could hear him talking to his aunt, so she turned her attention back to Kaj, her heart hurting for him.

Kaj was hunched over, head in his hands. 'I should never have left New York. My son wouldn't be in danger like this.'

She wasn't going to tell him that this wasn't the case, because she didn't know if it was true. She wasn't going to tell him that it wasn't his fault, because she didn't think he'd hear her.

'Right now, he isn't in danger. You're here and I'm here. Right now, he's talking to his aunt, and I just heard him laugh. He's fine, and we're going to keep it that way.'

He looked up, his exhaustion obvious. 'Thank you.'

'You look tired, Kaj. Why don't you lie down and have a rest? I'll watch over Elijah.'

His smile was tight. 'I might.'

'Good. But before you do, I wanted to finish talking about security. Do you own any weapons?'

'A Glock 17. It's in a gun safe in my closet. I haven't fired it in over a year, but I can shoot. I used to go to the range with one of my friends in the NYPD and he taught me the basics.'

'You shouldn't need to use it, but I'm glad to know you have it. There is one other security measure we could take. You've got an alarm system with cameras, you've got nearly impenetrable windows, and you've got me. But you don't have a dog.'

He frowned. 'I can't just go out and get a dog.' He paused, tilting his head. 'Can I?'

'You can, of course, but I have a dog and he's very well trained.'

'Trained for what?' he asked warily.

That was a loaded question. 'Protection,' she answered simply.

He opened his mouth, then closed it. She could tell that he was thinking, reviewing everything she'd said about having to change her name and move across the country. About the man who'd sought her out.

She hoped he didn't bring it up again. She didn't want to think about it again.

Which was bullshit. The memory was always there. Always ready to pounce. Still, having it in her head wasn't the same as having to speak of it out loud. With actual words.

'What kind of dog?' he finally asked, and she breathed a sigh of relief.

'He's a Black Russian Terrier.'

Kaj looked at her oddly. 'A little ankle biter as a protection dog?'

She laughed, pulling her phone from her pocket and finding a photo. 'Not that kind of terrier. This is me with Czar.'

Kaj's eyes bugged. 'What is that?' his asked, his New York accent thickening. 'That isn't a dog. That's a horse. His head comes up to your waist.'

'Black Russians are big. He weighs about one-thirty-five. He's almost eight years old, so he's getting up there, but he can still do the job.'

Kaj stared at the photo before handing her back her phone. 'He won't hurt Elijah?'

'No,' she said kindly. 'Once I introduce Elijah, Czar will protect him, too. He'll alert me to anyone approaching the house, and if I have to take Elijah anywhere, Czar is a deterrent simply by being with us. Nobody bothers me when I'm walking a dog this big.'

'Have you taken him with you on jobs before?'

'A few times. Sometimes there are other dogs in the house, so he's not needed. But when he comes along for the ride, my clients have been pleased. I'm sure Burke can get you references if you like.'

'Not necessary. Let's give it a try. Will you need to go and get him from your place?'

'No. Remember the friend I talked about, the one who subs for me at the community center when I'm on a job? Jessica also takes care of Czar when I'm not home. She can bring him here, if that's okay with you.'

'You trust this woman?'

'I do. I've known MaryBeth since high school. She's a good person.'

'She does roller derby with you, right?' He tilted his head. 'What's her derby name?'

She grinned. 'Mary Popshins.'

He snorted quietly. 'By all means, ask Miss Popshins to bring the small horse.'

'I will. For now, get some rest. I'll check the alarm contacts on the windows, then I'll go downstairs and sit with Elijah.'

She watched him go to his room and shut his door, then checked all the contacts on the windows, just as Burke had taught her to do when she'd first joined the firm. One was a little loose, so she tightened it before heading downstairs, where Elijah was staring at his tablet, which had gone dark.

She sat in the dining room chair next to him. Kaj's house was an open-plan design, so the dining room flowed into the living room, which was classy without being uncomfortable. One wall was covered in photos of a younger Elijah with a petite brunette who Val guessed to be his mother. And against one wall was a very nice piano that made her fingers itch to play.

'Finished talking to your aunt?' she asked Elijah.

'Yeah.'

She studied him. 'I told your dad to take a nap. Do you want to do the same?'

He let out a huge sigh. 'I can't sleep. I close my eyes and it's like it's happening again.'

'I get that.' She really did. 'I wish I could snap my fingers and say that it will be better tonight, but I can't. That was a really scary thing yesterday. If it doesn't get easier to sleep, maybe you could talk to someone.'

Elijah scowled. 'Like a therapist?'

'Yes. I saw one, back in the day. It helped.'

He blinked, looking surprised. 'You did? Really?'

'Really. I, um, saw some things in the military that got stuck in my head.' Big men. Big, powerful men. 'I had to talk to someone. And then after my brother died, I had to talk to someone again.'

His eyes widened. 'Your brother died?'

'He did.'

He watched her so intently she could almost see the wheels turning in his head. 'The man in the picture with you. The one in your office. That was your brother?'

Damn, the kid was smart. 'Yeah, my twin brother. His name was Van. He died almost four years ago.' *Please don't ask me how.*

'How?'

Dammit. But she wouldn't lie to the boy. 'He was murdered. He happened to be standing near a drug dealer when a fight broke out.'

Elijah stiffened. 'Sixth Day. That's why you know so much.'

Fucking smart. 'Yeah.'

His shoulders sagged. 'I'm sorry for your loss,' he said.

His adult phrasing broke her heart a little more. 'Thank you. And I'm sorry for yours.'

'Thanks. I saw a therapist after . . .' He sighed. 'Afterward. My dad made me go.'

'Did it help?'

'No. It didn't bring her back.'

'No, therapy can't bring them back. But it can help you find ways to move forward, and that's what I needed.'

He nodded sagely. 'Your brother died, like, in a surprise. A shock, I mean. I knew my mom was dying. She had cancer.'

'That's what your father said.' Her heart broke for the little family. 'Five is awfully young to lose your mom.'

He shrugged. 'Genie's like my mom now. She says that you can call her anytime. She's bored.'

'I'll do that.'

He tilted his head. 'Do you have any other brothers and sisters?'

Her whole body tensed, just like it did whenever she thought of Sylvi. 'Just a sister.'

'Is she nice?'

Val considered lying, but she'd promised Elijah she wouldn't do that. 'No. She's not very nice.'

He looked down. 'Oh. That's not good.'

'No, it's not, but sometimes people make bad choices. My sister did and . . . we don't talk often anymore.' She needed to change the subject. 'So, do you like dogs?'

He lit up. 'Yeah! My dad says we can't get one yet. Not until Genie has the baby and it's old enough. Why?'

'Because your dad gave me permission to bring my dog over, but I wanted to run it by you before I make the call. Czar is big. Like, really big.'

'Bigger than me?'

She smiled. 'Almost bigger than me.'

His white-blond brows crunched together. 'Is he nice?'

'If I introduce you properly, he is. But if someone tries to hurt you, he is definitely not.'

He seemed to mull that over. 'Can he sleep in my room?'

'If you want him to.'

'I do. Then I think I can sleep.'

Oh, honey. 'Then that's settled. I'll call my friend and have her bring him over.' She passed him her phone. 'Here's his picture.'

Elijah expressed the typical shock at Czar's size, then brushed his thumb over the photo. 'He looks friendly.'

'He is, unless you're being threatened, and then he is not friendly at all to whoever is threatening you. I've been where you are, Elijah. I remember not being able to sleep because I didn't feel safe. Part of my job is making sure you stay healthy, not just alive. Sleep is necessary, and Czar can help with that.'

He looked up, tears in his eyes. 'Thank you, Val.'

She wanted to hug him, but she only squeezed his shoulder. 'You're welcome.'

Bayou des Allemands, Louisiana
TUESDAY, OCTOBER 25, 2:00 P.M.

'Shit.' Jace yanked his hand back from the starter he'd been assembling, grimacing at the sight of blood dripping from his palm.

'Go find Corey.' Dewey fetched a paper towel and wrapped it around Jace's palm. 'He'll fix you up.'

Jace hesitated. 'Corey's . . . talking to Rick.' He was scared for his brother. He couldn't stop thinking about the look on Rick's face as he'd left Corey's office.

Rick had been scared shitless.

Jace was, too, and he hadn't even been the one in trouble.

Dewey wrapped his hand with duct tape to hold the paper towel in place. 'Talking to him? I figured he'd just . . . punish him.'

'No. He's questioning him about who helped him. Corey didn't believe he thought it all up on his own.' Jace hesitated, then figured it couldn't hurt to try to get Dewey to take them with him. 'Corey hits,' he whispered. 'I mean, we survive. But he's never been this mad before, and I don't know what to do. He said that Aaron deserves to be in jail, that we shouldn't have tried to kidnap the kid to get him out.'

Dewey frowned. 'I didn't think he'd be mad about that. I thought he'd want Aaron freed, too.'

'I thought the same thing, but Corey's mad. Really mad.' Jace hesitated. 'Rick wants to run. I don't know where he'd go. Where we'd go. Can we . . . can we stay with you?'

Dewey's mouth opened, then closed. 'I'll see what I can do. Look, you need to go get your hand fixed up. Infection's a real thing, especially out here on the bayou. You go on now.'

'Do you think it needs stitches? Maybe I can just put a Band-Aid on it.'

'It's deep, Jace. Go find Corey. If it needs stitches, he can do it. You get an infection out here, you could lose a hand.'

Jace didn't want to ask Corey to do anything. He wanted to run from Corey. But he also didn't want to lose his hand.

Swallowing his dread, Jace headed toward Corey's quarters, to the door he'd come out of. He had his fist raised, ready to knock, but stopped at the sound of a thin, muted scream coming from inside.

Oh my God. Rick. That scream had to have come from Rick.

Jace stared at the door, his mind spinning. He needed to get Corey to stop. But if he tried, Corey might start hitting him, too. But he had to do something. He glanced down at his bleeding hand and hoped Corey wouldn't hit him for interrupting.

He knocked hard. 'Corey!' he shouted. 'I'm hurt. I need help. Corey?' Ten seconds passed with no response, so he knocked again, his heart beating louder than the sound of his fist on the door. 'Corey?'

'What the fuck, kid?'

Jace wheeled around to see Bobby coming around the house from the front door. 'I need to see Corey. Please.'

Bobby eyed him, both angry and suspicious. 'He's busy, kid.'

Jace stuck out his hand, the towel now a bloody, sodden mess. 'I cut myself. Dewey said to find Corey. That he could fix me up.'

Bobby rolled his eyes. 'I'll tell him, but you're in for a hurt worse than that scratch on your hand.'

Jace followed him to the front and waited as Bobby disappeared inside. A minute passed. Then two. Jace had slumped against the bunker wall when the front door opened again.

'Well?' Corey's voice cut through his fear. His brother stood in front of him, fists on his hips. 'Let me see it.'

Jace held out his hand, bracing himself for Corey's rough hands, and was shocked when his brother's touch was gentle.

'That looks like it hurts,' Corey said quietly.

'It does.'

'Let's go inside. I'll fix you up.' Corey shocked him again when he put an arm around Jace's shoulders. 'You've had an eventful two days, little bro.'

Jace felt tears sting his eyes at Corey's unexpected kindness, but he refused to let them fall. 'I guess so.'

Jace sat at Corey's kitchen table while his brother gathered first-aid supplies. Corey had worked in a New Orleans hospital before he'd started his construction company. He'd been a security guard in the ER but said he'd picked stuff up.

'It's not so bad,' Corey said. 'It's already stopped bleeding. You don't need stitches, but I am going to clean it out. It's gonna sting.'

Jace saw little white lights dancing in front of his eyes by the time Corey had cleaned and bandaged his hand. He hadn't watched his brother work, but he was still light-headed.

'All done,' Corey said softly. 'Jace, did Rick tell you that I said to abduct that child?'

Taken off guard, Jace whipped his gaze up to Corey's. 'How—'

He closed his eyes. *Shit.* Corey had tricked him.

When he opened his eyes, Corey's jaw was tight. 'I thought so. You should have told me when I first asked. I get that you were trying to protect Rick, but you can't lie to me.'

Jace tried to be brave, but he was trembling and couldn't stop. 'I'm sorry.'

'Who else was involved in the idea of taking the prosecutor's son?'

'Nobody,' Jace said desperately. 'I promise. Rick showed me an email that he said was from you. I guess it wasn't.'

'It was not. What was in the email?'

Jace grimaced, not wanting to admit that he hadn't been able to read it. 'It talked about using the kid to get Aaron back.'

'You didn't read a word of it, did you?' Corey asked mildly.

Jace swallowed. 'I tried,' he whispered. 'I'm sorry. I just . . . can't.'

'I figured as much.' Corey stood, casting a shadow over Jace. 'Not everybody is smart, Jace. You're good with your hands. It'll have to be enough.'

Jace squinted up at him, not trusting this gentler side of his older brother. 'You're not . . . you're not gonna beat me, too?'

'No.' Corey smiled, but Jace didn't think it was real. 'I will need you to do something for me, though.'

'What?' Jace asked warily.

'Drive me somewhere.'

'That's all?'

'That's all. We'll leave at four. Meet me at my boat. Don't be late.'

'I won't. I promise.'

'Good. Keep your hand dry and take some Advil. It's going to throb like a bitch.'

It already was. And so was Jace's head. Something was up, but he wasn't sure what it was. 'What about Rick?'

Corey's smile disappeared and Jace shrank back, closing his eyes. Expecting a blow. When none came, he opened his eyes to see Corey staring down at him. 'Get back to Dewey's workshop, Jace. And don't cut yourself again.'

'Yes, Corey.' Legs shaking, he made his way back to the workshop, but it was empty. 'Dewey?'

But nobody answered. Nothing but silence.

Jace checked Dewey's desk, finding his wallet and keys. There was no sign of the mechanic, so Jace went back to working on the boat starter. His stomach growled, but he wasn't about to go back to Corey's little house and get food until he got permission.

He was in enough trouble for one day.

6

COREY LOOKED OVER his shoulder, pausing in front of his quarters until he saw Jace enter Dewey's workshop. Slipping in through his front door, he made his way back to the comm room, where Bobby and Ed waited with the instigators of last night's botched abduction attempt.

Dewey Talley was handcuffed to the high-backed chair Jace had been using. The drug-dealing mechanic was red-faced, the duct tape over his mouth muting what were probably curses. Bobby and Ed had fetched him while Corey had been bandaging Jace's hand.

Corey wasn't sure what he'd do about Jace. He might keep him around to do the grunt work if he was certain he'd broken Jace enough to trust him not to go to the cops. He hadn't liked that Jace had put his loyalty to Rick first. That was a bad sign. He'd give the kid another chance later in the day and if that didn't cow him . . . Corey would have to dispose of him, too.

Then I'll be free.

'Excellent job, guys,' Corey said to Bobby and Ed, then turned to

Rick, who was still in a daze from the pain of their interrogation. They hadn't needed to be so rough, but it worked for their plan. And it had felt damn good, too. 'Thanks, bro. We appreciate the heads-up.'

Dewey silently glared at Rick, his jaw tight.

Corey laughed. 'Oh yeah. Little Ricky gave you up before Bobby even started turning up the current to his balls. But Bobby kept going anyway, just because Rick really deserved it.'

Bobby nodded in sham solemnity. 'He really did.'

Ed gave Dewey a sour look. 'This one thought he could get away. I followed him to that shack of his, next to the workshop. He was piling cash in a backpack like his ass was on fire. And'—Ed dug in his pocket and pulled out a handful of spark plugs—'I found these in the front flap of the backpack. They go to our boats, Corey. I checked the camera and he took them right after we got back with Dianne. He wanted to make sure that we couldn't follow him.'

'Sonofabitch,' Corey muttered. 'Can you guys stow Rick in Aaron's quarters for now? We have things to discuss with Dewey. Make sure that Jace is in the workshop. I don't want him asking questions.'

Bobby's lips curved in the smile that had terrified suspects when he'd been a cop. 'My pleasure. But you can't start on Dewey until I come back.'

Corey rolled his eyes. 'Fine.'

Bobby paused at the door. 'Corey, I'm gonna shoot him up, just like we talked, okay?'

Corey felt a tug of unwelcome guilt. Bobby was going to give Rick an overdose of Aaron's heroin. Bobby was going to kill Rick. Corey nodded once, grateful on some level. He wanted Rick gone, but doing it himself . . .

He could hear his mother telling him to take care of his little brothers. Well, he had. For three fucking years. That the two of them couldn't be taught to behave wasn't Corey's fault. His brothers had been damaged goods from the get-go.

'Thanks,' he murmured.

Bobby gave him a nod. 'You check on the workshop,' he told Ed. 'If the coast is clear, just whistle and I'll dump Rick in Aaron's bedroom.'

Unsettled and not wanting to be, Corey left Dewey cuffed to the chair in the comm room to check on Dianne.

She still slept deeply. The vodka she'd drunk that morning would make the sleeping pills they'd put in her coffee more potent. He hoped they hadn't given her too much, but her pulse was steady and strong. Closing the bedroom door, he headed back to the comm room.

Where Dewey had knocked his own chair over.

'Trying to escape so soon?' Corey asked mildly. With one hand he yanked on the chair, setting it upright none too gently. Dewey's grunt of pain was satisfying.

Corey dragged another chair close to Dewey. 'We're gonna have to hose down the chair Rick was using,' he said companionably. 'Rick pissed himself in the first minute. But don't worry. We installed a drain for easy cleanup. Sometimes we bring guests here, y'see. They have information that we've been paid to learn. Bobby is particularly good at convincing these guests to give up whatever our clients want to know, but he leaves a bloody mess. So we built the room with a drain so we could just hose the floor down when he's finished.'

Dewey's eyes widened, filling with horror.

'Now,' Corey continued, 'Rick told us that you didn't mean to give him the idea of kidnapping Cardozo's son. He went through your things one night. Said he was looking for either meth or heroin—he wasn't picky—but he found your notebook instead.'

Dewey gave Corey a defiant evil eye.

Corey chuckled. 'You're not scaring me. Okay, so I'm going to recap what Rick told us and you'll get a chance to talk when I'm finished. Rick was there when you broke into my construction office on Saturday night. Imagine how surprised I was to hear that you were there— without my permission—using my office as if it were your own.'

Surprise flickered in Dewey's eyes. 'You didn't know Rick was there, huh? I was surprised to hear that Rick used my office, too. Apparently, he goes there when he "needs space".' Corey huffed. 'Which is code for when I've beaten him for whatever stupid-ass thing he's done recently. But I digress. You went to my construction office to use my shower and Rick rifled through your stuff.'

More grunts and general posturing from Dewey. Corey ignored him.

'Rick didn't find any drugs, but, like I said, he did find your notebook—and your gun, by the way. Did you even miss it?' A muscle in Dewey's jaw bulged, his eyes narrowing. 'I guess you didn't. Maybe you have so many that you didn't miss one. Well, the cops now have that gun, which works for us tying Rick to drug dealers. Back to your notebook. Rick said you'd made a list of all the ways to get Aaron out of jail. One you'd crossed off was grabbing Cardozo's kid. That you crossed it off your list shows you do have a brain. But not too big of one, because you came up with the plan to begin with. According to Rick, it was a pretty detailed plan. You knew where Cardozo's kid would be on Monday night and that he'd be with his pregnant aunt. You were going to chloroform the aunt, then grab the kid and take off, calling Cardozo right away to tell him not to call in the cops. You were then going to use the boy to get Cardozo to drop the charges against Aaron.'

Dewey's jaw worked, but he couldn't speak. Duct tape was an amazing invention.

'Rick was very upset to see that you'd crossed it off, because the plan sounded solid to a stupid sixteen-year-old.'

The door opened, Ed and Bobby returning. 'What's he got to say?' Bobby asked.

'Haven't given him a chance to talk yet. I was setting up the conversation that we're going to have.'

Bobby laughed. 'Corey means we're going to have fun making you talk.'

'Bobby loves his work,' Ed said dryly. 'Maybe a little too much.'

'There is no such thing as too much job satisfaction,' Bobby declared. 'Can I take off the tape now?'

'Go for it,' Corey said and had to admit that the sound Dewey made when Bobby ripped the tape off was satisfying.

'We have questions,' Bobby said with unrestrained glee. 'And you'll have answers.'

Dewey was grimacing. His lips were now raw and bleeding. 'Fuck off.'

Corey shrugged. 'So many of our guests have started with those very words,' he said lightly, then dropped the act. 'Why are *you* so desperate to get Aaron out of jail? I don't believe it was just out of friendship. So *why?*'

Dewey clenched his jaw.

'Can I try?' Bobby asked, sounding like a kid on Christmas.

Corey rolled his eyes. 'In a minute.' He turned to Ed. 'Go upriver to Dewey's camp. Search for anything useful, but especially his computer.'

'You think Dewey knows how to use a computer?' Ed asked skeptically.

Corey spared Ed an irritated glance. 'Just because he's over fifty doesn't mean he's tech illiterate.'

'It's not his age,' Ed protested. 'Just . . . well, look at him.'

Dewey was unshaven and his clothes were filthy, but there was an intelligence in his eyes. 'He's stayed out of the hands of the law for years. And even if Aaron only gave him ten percent of the profits, he's made at least a million since I've known him.'

Dewey didn't react, not even a twitch. If Aaron had been cheating him, Corey figured that Dewey would show some surprise.

'Looks like Dewey might have been doing the same thing,' Bobby said idly. 'Socking away money offshore, I mean. I bet we can get his passwords out of him before Ed comes back with his laptop.'

Corey smiled. 'I bet you're right.' Then he had a thought. 'Ed, take

Rick with you, as long as you're headed upriver. Take him to the boat launch. Wrap him up and stick him in the back of the van. I don't want Jace seeing him when we leave for Cardozo's. Hit Dewey's place on your way back.'

When Ed had left, Corey turned to Dewey. 'Let's try again. Why were you so desperate to get Aaron out of jail?'

Dewey clamped his lips shut.

Bobby got to work, starting by laying out his knives. It was his thing.

Dewey sneered. 'If you kill me, you won't ever find out what you want to know.'

Corey dragged his chair out of the splash zone. 'Ah, bravado. We don't plan on killing you. Not yet, anyway.'

Bobby was humming a happy tune, a smile on his face.

'Why are you so happy?' Corey asked.

'One, because I get to carve Dewey up like a Thanksgiving turkey and that always makes me happy. Two, I got a call from my buddy on the force when I was dumping Rick in Aaron's quarters. It'll make you happy, too.'

'What did he say?'

'Cardozo has declined police protection. Seems like he's made some enemies and doesn't know who to trust. He's got no one outside his house.'

'Huh.' Corey considered. 'Might be safer to drop Rick off at Cardozo's than at NOPD.'

Dewey reacted to that. 'What the hell? You're turning Rick in?'

'We are,' Corey said with a smile. 'Because Bobby's buddy also told us that the cops think you were the driver last night. Because of your tattoo.'

Dewey closed his eyes. 'Jace.'

Corey nodded. 'Exactly. So we're going to give the cops someone to chase. Sixth Day is the Big Bad, and you, Dewey, are Sixth Day. The biggest remaining fish, anyway. They've been looking for you for four years now, not realizing that you've been hiding out with Aaron in plain sight. So we're going to give them Rick with *your* compliments.'

Dewey shook his head. 'That doesn't make sense. Why would they think Aaron and I were working together? He would never tell the cops anything. We've never been seen together. So what if the driver had a tat? Lots of people have dragon tats. I don't believe you.'

'But they do have a photo of you and Aaron together,' Bobby said, looking up from his knives. 'Sandra Springfield took a few of the two of you. Hid them on a thumb drive. Cops found it when they searched her house after she was arrested with Aaron. Looks like she snapped the pics when you weren't watching and planned to use them somehow.'

Dewey's nostrils flared. 'That money-hungry bitch.'

Corey could agree with that. 'So the cops *do* have evidence tying you to Aaron. That they tied the tattoo to you was a legit leap. We're going to make sure that they keep looking for you and, importantly, they'll stop looking at me.' He rubbed his hands together. 'I have an hour before I need to take Rick to Cardozo's. Let's see what we can get out of Dewey before then.'

Grinning widely, Bobby chose a particularly wicked-looking blade and ran the tip along Dewey's cheek. 'Let's get started.'

Mid-City, New Orleans, Louisiana
TUESDAY, OCTOBER 25, 4:45 P.M.

'Elijah?' Kaj called, a thread of panic in his voice. 'Where—'

Val rose from the Cardozos' dining room table when Kaj came down the stairs, looking sleep rumpled. She pressed her finger to her lips, then pointed at the sofa, where Elijah was sound asleep. He wore his headphones, but she wasn't sure how much noise they'd block out.

Some of the tension left Kaj's shoulders and he blew out a breath. 'Thank you,' he whispered. 'How long has he been asleep?'

She beckoned him to follow her back to the table, retaking her seat. And trying not to notice how good he smelled when he pulled up a chair next to hers. The lingering spice of his aftershave was faint, and she had to stop herself from sniffing him to get more of the scent. 'An hour,' she said. 'I downloaded one of those background sound apps to his phone.'

'Like the ocean?'

'Well, there was that sound, too, but I thought he might be missing the noise of the city. It's the sound of traffic. He kept saying that he couldn't sleep—up until he conked out.'

'He didn't sleep last night. Neither of us did.'

'I know. I figured he could sleep until MaryBeth and Jessica get here with Czar.'

'The small horse,' Kaj said, his lips turning up just a smidge. 'When will that be?'

'Sometime before six. Are you hungry? I can make you something.'

'That's okay, Val. I appreciate the offer, but I can make my own sandwich later.'

'Don't wait too long. Dinner tonight is a treat, so you shouldn't spoil it with snacks.'

His brows lifted. 'What's for dinner?'

'I don't know, but it'll be good. One of my friends co-owns Le Petit Choux in the Quarter. She's coming by to show me how to cook tasty low-carb meals for Elijah. If that's okay,' she added. 'She's trustworthy and completely safe to be around Elijah.'

'You mean Gabe Hebert's cousin, Patty?'

'You know Patty?'

'I know Gabe better, but Patty was at the party last summer when I first met you.'

Val's cheeks heated. How had she forgotten that Patty had been there that day, too? Probably because she'd been too fascinated with Kaj. 'Well, she's cooking for us tonight.'

'I can't wait. I get their lunch specials whenever I can. You bring all kinds of perks,' he added with a smile. 'Dogs, roller derby, and friends who make good food.'

His smile lit up his face, making him gorgeous. Making awareness sizzle across her skin. She bit back a needy sound that his son's bodyguard definitely shouldn't make.

Kaj Cardozo might have been sexy as hell in the courtroom in his fancy suit, but he was more appealing sitting at his table in wrinkled clothes, his body warm and smelling way too good.

She cleared her throat, dropping her gaze to her laptop screen. 'Well, I get to eat the good food, too, so I'm selfishly bringing the perks.'

'Still,' he said quietly, as if sensing her withdrawal. 'Thank you.' He leaned closer to look at her screen. 'What are you doing?'

'Research. I first talked to your sister and she sent me some educational links on what Elijah should and shouldn't eat. But then I got an email from Antoine—he's our IT guru—and I stopped reading about food to read the background checks on all the major players. Antoine sent information on Aaron and Corey Gates, plus anything he could find on Dewey Talley. Which doesn't appear to be anything more than I've already gathered myself over the years.'

'Anything jumping out at you about Aaron?'

She glanced at Elijah, who still slept deeply, before turning her screen so that Kaj could see it more easily. 'I'm sure you've seen most of what I've got here, since you're prosecuting Aaron.' She scanned the email and froze for a moment, staring at the words on the screen. 'Huh. Aaron used to work at Cunningham and Spector, a financial firm in the Quarter.'

'I know.' He regarded her warily. 'Why is that upsetting to you?'

'Not upsetting, just surprising. My brother Van worked there, too.

At the same time as Aaron. I guess I'm just wondering if they knew each other.' She shook her head, aware of Kaj's watchful gaze. 'Anyway, Aaron resigned six years ago, then opened his own firm.'

She continued reading the information Antoine had sent, pausing at Aaron's mug shot from last week. His cheeks were dark with scruff, his eyes angry and bloodshot. 'I wonder if he started using after his son died or before.'

'I don't know when he started using, but he was high when he was arrested. It took three cops to subdue him once they'd pulled him off Dr. Singh.'

'I was thinking that he killed Dr. Singh because the doctor was treating his son at the time of his death. Grief can have a terrible effect on logical thinking, especially if he was using.'

'That's my take. It was a senseless murder on so many levels. I never met the doctor, but he was apparently well loved. My office is still fielding calls from locals demanding we get justice for him, that we don't let Aaron Gates walk.'

'Aaron's guilt's pretty clear,' Val said.

'Yeah. But I don't want some defense attorney claiming he was lost to grief. I believe Aaron's actions were premeditated. He saw that Singh was being given a humanitarian award, got into his car, and drove to the ceremony—all of which took a while.'

'He didn't just happen to see him, then kill him in the heat of the moment.'

'Exactly. Plus a few bystanders said he was calm while waiting for Singh to park his own car. They said Aaron was even joking with the woman he was with. All of that makes a difference when it comes to the charges I can make stick.'

'And what sentence you can ask for. But now you have to worry about the threat to Elijah. Sixth Day wants Aaron out of jail, so whichever way you proceed in his case may anger them into trying to hurt Elijah again.'

He grimaced. 'I don't expect to be on the case too much longer. My boss and I are having a meeting this afternoon and I expect he'll recuse me.'

'How do you feel about that? And if it's none of my business, just say so.'

'No, it's okay to ask. Truth is, I'm torn. A part of me wants to stay on the case and get justice for Dr. Singh. A part of me hates that Sixth Day was able to bully the system by threatening my son, because what are they going to do to the next prosecutor and the one after that? But if they'd been successful, if they'd gotten their hands on Elijah . . .' He swallowed. 'I don't want to think about what I'd have done. Recusal would be a relief, honestly, because a bigger part of me wants to take a leave of absence and make sure Elijah is okay. It's not only his safety— it's his emotional state, too. He's afraid and traumatized and it's going to impact his health. It already has.' He pointed to his cell phone on the table. 'His sugar levels feed to an app. They're lower than they were last night, thank God, but they're still high. That's why I haven't left town and hidden him in a safe house. His doctor wants him here, just in case.'

'Why can't you take a leave of absence?'

He sighed wearily. 'I can for a few days, but I have a trial that starts next week that I've been preparing for months. I need to be in court, and I need to be focused.'

'Can someone else handle the trial? Or is it not that easy?' she added when he frowned.

'Someone could. I have a second chair. But this is a high-profile rape case. I've spent hours talking with the victim, and she trusts me.'

Val's eyes widened as she realized what he was talking about. 'You're the prosecutor on the Bella Butler case?' It had been in the headlines for weeks, the coverage having intensified in the past few days.

'I am. She deserves justice.'

Val nodded. 'She's brave. It's hard enough to come forward in a regular courtroom, but knowing that the entire country is following every detail of one of the worst experiences of your life, being dissected on TV and online . . .' She could hear the tremble in her own voice and cleared her throat. 'I respect her.'

He studied her for so long that she thought he'd ask her more questions, but he didn't. 'I respect her, too,' he finally said. 'But as much as I want to see Trevor Doyle's trial through, I won't choose my job over my son. If he needs me next week, I'll have second chair step up.'

'I suppose you'll have to address the biggest threat first,' she said warily, wanting to help, but aware that she was stepping through a minefield. She'd never been a parent, but she could certainly empathize with his very valid concerns. 'When will you know if you're recused from Aaron Gates's case?'

He glanced at his watch. 'In about ten minutes. I have a Skype call with my boss.'

She glanced at the sleeping boy on the sofa, then back at his father. 'If you are recused, Sixth Day or Rick Gates or whoever was behind last night's attempt won't have any reason to go after Elijah. What will you want to do about protection? I'm not asking for myself,' she hastened to add. 'Burke can place me in another job by tomorrow, so this isn't about me. But you might want to start thinking about what you'll do, either way, so Elijah knows what to expect.'

Kaj pinched the bridge of his nose. 'I *have* been thinking about it. I've done nothing *but* think about it.'

She folded her hands on the table. 'Maybe it would help to talk it out.'

He met her eyes, frustrated. 'One would think it would be straight-forward—I'm no longer on the case, so attacking my son doesn't help their cause. But even if it had just been Rick Gates acting out as a stupid sixteen-year-old, it's not always that simple. One of my first cases involved a stupid sixteen-year-old who kidnapped the child of his mother's employer. He wanted ransom, but he got flustered when the Feds closed in. He killed the boy in a panic.'

'Oh, Kaj. I'm sorry.'

'So was I. So was everyone involved, but the parents still lost their child. Even if this was only about Rick wanting his brother out of jail, I couldn't predict that he'd stop trying. He's a stupid sixteen-year-old. But the involvement of Sixth Day changes everything. This was a planned, deliberate act. If I get recused, they'll see that their attack got a response. Maybe they'll go after the family of the next prosecutor. Maybe they'll come after Elijah again. I can't predict what they'll do. So, I'll maintain protection and investigation, but for how long? How long do I isolate Elijah? How long before I turn my child into a frightened victim who begins to fear everything? He's smart. He's already thought about what might have happened to him and he didn't sleep all night. He's sleeping now because he feels safe with you here, but he knows the danger could be just outside our door. How long do I leave him in the fear zone?'

Val covered his forearm with her hand, keeping her touch gentle. 'Why not start out with keeping a protection detail for just this week? Keep Burke investigating. Tell Elijah the plan. He is smart, and he's hungry for information. Give him the information and tell him you'll revisit at the end of the week. Seek his input. It will make him feel a little more powerful in a situation where he seems powerless.'

He drew a breath and blew it out, his shoulders slumping. 'That was one of my options, but it kept getting lost in all of the other crap spinning in my mind. It helps to hear it said aloud.' He nodded once, as if to himself. 'And hopefully Burke will come up with some detail that will make my decision at the end of the week easier either way. Thank you, Val.'

She patted his arm, then withdrew her hand, instantly missing his warmth. 'Anytime.'

'I need to go now. My meeting starts soon and I need to put on a tie.'

'For a Skype meeting?'

He smiled. 'Elijah started giving me ties for Christmas and birthdays while Heather was still alive, and he's kept it up. He's filled my closet with them over the years. It's habit now to wear one. My brain isn't ready to go to work unless I'm wearing a tie.' He pushed away from the table, groaning a little as he stretched his back. 'I'm not cut out for all-nighters anymore. My back is killing me.'

She almost offered to massage his back, but . . . no. That was crossing a line if there ever was one. 'You should eat something before your meeting. If you wait until after, you'll spoil your dinner. You run on upstairs and put on your tie. I'll fix you a small snack and bring it up.'

'You don't have to do that, Val.'

'I know, but let me do it anyway.'

'Then thank you again.'

It took her a few seconds before she realized she was staring at his retreating back. And backside. The man's wrinkled khakis hid a very nice ass.

Which I am not going to notice again. Although that might prove difficult. Kaj Cardozo had the kind of body she'd preferred even before . . .

Well, before. Nearly every boyfriend she'd had since she'd started dating again had resembled Kaj in one way or another, but Kaj was the whole package.

No, no, no. This is a job. Elijah's safety was the most important thing. *No perving on the client's dad.* Fussing at herself, she went to the kitchen and made him a plate of veggies and hummus. When she carried it up the stairs, he was coming out of his room, smoothing down a tie covered in bows and arrows.

'You like archery?' she asked, handing him the plate.

'Thank you, and no.' He took the plate, then pointed to his tie with an amused smile. 'It's a "bow tie". Elijah thought it was the funniest thing ever when he was seven.'

Val laughed. 'I like it. Have a good meeting. And remember that Elijah is safe and you don't have to make any new decisions about his care today.'

His smile changed to one of profound gratitude. 'I will.'

He disappeared into his office, leaving Val staring after him, a little shiver racing over her skin. He was a very attractive man, but that smile . . . It did things to her.

And . . . no. Not going there.

Returning to the dining room table, Val refreshed her laptop screen. Antoine had been thorough, as usual. It was going to take her hours to comb through all the information he'd sent.

As she'd told Kaj, much of the Sixth Day information was old and she knew it already, so she'd first focus on the Gates brothers. Corey Gates had seemed sincere in his interview that morning, when he'd agreed that Rick deserved to face consequences for his crime. But she wasn't trusting Elijah's safety to an appearance of sincerity. She'd dig into the Gates brothers' backgrounds to find anything that might tie them to Sixth Day. Because they weren't touching Elijah Cardozo again while she still drew breath.

Mid-City, New Orleans, Louisiana
TUESDAY, OCTOBER 25, 5:45 P.M.

'Oh my God. He's freaking huge!'

At the sound of Elijah's excited exclamation, Kaj looked up from his laptop screen to check the view outside his home office window. A white minivan was parked at the curb, *Marica's Bakery* painted on the door.

A combination of terror, dread, and shame had his shoulders slumping as he stared at the minivan. He'd been so focused on this call with his boss that he hadn't even noticed that someone had knocked on his front door. Or that a vehicle had parked at his curb, fifty feet from his front door—a vehicle nearly identical to the one that had almost spirited his son away. The only difference was the logo painted on the door.

'Cardozo? Cardozo?'

Kaj blinked, his boss's voice cutting through his fear and self-recrimination. He refocused on his screen, where Reuben Hogan's face wore a worried frown. 'Sorry.'

'What happened?' Hogan demanded. 'You look like you've seen a ghost.'

'We have visitors.'

'Go. Check on Elijah.'

Kaj shook his head. 'I can hear him.' The sound of his son's laughter was more of a balm than any of his own self-talk. 'He's with his bodyguard.'

Hogan's brows rose in surprise. 'You hired a bodyguard?'

'I did.'

Hogan's surprise turned into a frown. 'But . . . You're no longer on the case. You no longer have any power over Aaron Gates. Why do you need a bodyguard?'

Kaj shook his head, happy that he'd talked this out with Val. He'd been recused, exactly as he'd expected. 'Because NOPD hasn't picked up Rick Gates yet and we're still not sure who was actually behind the abduction. If it was Sixth Day, I can't afford to assume that they'll immediately back down. And because my son can't sleep and his health is being impacted.' That was the argument that seemed to do it for Hogan, who was now nodding. 'I'll keep the bodyguard for a week and then revisit.'

'I'd likely do the same thing.' Hogan hesitated. 'You do know that your being recused from Aaron Gates's case has nothing to do with my confidence in your ability, right?'

'I know. It's the right thing to do. Every time I think of Aaron Gates, I get so angry.'

'Understandable.'

'I keep thinking that I want to see him punished for putting his hands on my child and then I have to remember that it wasn't Aaron. It was Rick, even though Aaron could have orchestrated it from jail. So as much as I hate losing the opportunity to meet him in court, it's just too personal for me now.'

'Not sure that Aaron is capable of orchestrating anything right now,' Hogan said. 'He's barely coherent. Still detoxing.'

'What about Dewey Talley? Has NOPD found anything on him?'

'Nothing yet, but NOPD says that they have a few leads. They've ramped up the search for Talley and his distribution network. Nobody's quite sure how big it is right now, but it's a top priority. I'll keep you up to speed as much as I can. You're recused, but you have the same right to information as any other victim. If it's any consolation, I'm taking Aaron's case myself.'

Kaj was relieved. 'It is, yes. Thank you.' Hogan wasn't married and didn't have children. The man was married to his job, so there wasn't anyone else in his life who could become a Sixth Day target. 'Should I swap one of your cases?'

He and Hogan had been up to their ears in new cases, as the other prosecutors were occupied with fixing what Hogan called 'a right mess.' They'd recently learned that one of their prosecutors had been guilty of gross impropriety, and all the man's cases were under review.

'Probably,' Hogan said, 'but we can discuss that when you're back in the office. You still have the Doyle/Butler case, after all. Is Miss Butler ready?'

The case against Trevor Doyle for rape was far from a slam dunk, but Bella Butler made a very compelling witness. 'We start voir dire on

Monday. And Miss Butler is about as ready as she's ever going to be.'

'I hate he-said-she-said cases,' Hogan grumbled, 'but I think you've got a good shot at putting him away.'

'I hope so.' Listening to rape victims' stories was always difficult. Bella's had been no different. 'Doyle is slimy.'

'I agree. Go on, now. Spend time with your son. And let me know sooner rather than later if you need to take a more extended leave. If I need to take the Doyle/Butler case, I'll need time to prep with your second chair. Will I see you in the office tomorrow?'

Kaj hadn't thought that his boss would take over the Doyle trial, but it made sense. It would be heavily covered by the media, and his second chair, while an excellent attorney, wasn't accustomed to a trial with this level of exposure. Hogan was a better choice.

Kaj felt better just knowing that was the backup plan. 'I don't think I'll be coming into the office this week, but I'll be available for conference calls if anything comes up.'

'I thought as much. Call if you need me.' Hogan gave him a small salute before ending the call.

Kaj leaned back in his chair, trying to clear his mind. If Hogan was worried that he'd have to bail on the Doyle/Butler case, Bella Butler must be nervous as well.

Kaj picked up the phone and dialed the woman's number.

'This is Miss Butler's office,' a crisp voice informed him.

'I'd like to speak with Miss Butler, please. This is ADA Cardozo.'

After a moment, Bella came on the line, her normally smooth voice thin with anxiety. 'Mr. Cardozo? What's wrong?'

'Nothing with your case,' he assured her. 'We're still starting voir dire on Monday. I wanted to let you know that I'll be there, in case you saw the news about my son and wondered.'

She exhaled shakily. 'I nearly called you, but I figured you'd be out of your mind with worry today and I didn't want to add to it. And every time I rehearsed what I'd say to you, I called myself a selfish bitch.'

'My son is fine and you're certainly not selfish.'

'Thank you. I don't know how I'd focus if something happened to my little girl.'

'I'll focus. Don't worry.' And he would. He might not know how he'd do it now, but by Monday he'd have it figured out. Bella Butler deserved no less. 'You have a good evening.'

'You too, Mr. Cardozo.'

Locking his computer, Kaj left his home office and made his way down the stairs to the living room, where he heard multiple voices. Pasting a bright smile on his face, he stepped off the bottom stair and stopped cold.

Elijah sat on the floor next to a monster dog that looked as if it could swallow him in one huge gulp. Seeing a photo of the dog was one thing, but here? In his living room? 'Holy shit,' he whispered.

Elijah looked up, a grin on his face. 'This is Czar. Isn't he—'

A loud growl cut off whatever Elijah had been about to say. Seconds later the big dog was on its feet—its four huge feet, easily the size of dinner plates.

'Czar, sit.' Val rose from the sofa, touching the dog's head lightly as he obeyed. 'Good boy. Kaj, come and meet Czar. Walk slowly.'

Kaj swallowed hard. 'Uh . . . I don't know about this.'

Elijah's grin faltered. 'He's a nice dog, Dad. Don't be scared.'

Kaj's gaze flicked to the two other people in the room. The women sat on the sofa, holding hands. One was tall like Val, but with long black hair. The other was so small that 'petite' seemed too big a word to describe her. Her hair was braided and pinned to her head just like Val's, but it was bright purple. And she wore a fifties-style dress with an honest-to-God crinoline. Both women appeared to be amused.

'It'll be okay,' the smaller woman said. 'Even I can control him. He's very gentle.'

Val held out her hand to Kaj. 'Come on. It'll be all right.'

Warily, Kaj held his breath and took her hand, earning him a smile as she led him to the hairy beast. He wasn't sure if it was her smile or the fact that Elijah was grinning again that had him relaxing.

She stopped in front of the dog, who hadn't moved a muscle. 'Czar, say hello.'

Immediately the dog's stubby tail began wagging and his tongue came lolling out.

Kaj let out the breath he'd been holding before scratching the dog behind its ears. 'Hi, Czar. You're very large.'

Val chuckled. 'Like I said, nobody bothers me when I'm walking with Czar. These are my friends MaryBeth and Jessica.'

Kaj's lips twitched as he held out a hand to the taller woman. 'Mary Popshins, it's nice to meet you.'

The tall woman laughed as she shook his hand. 'Oh, no. I'm not Mary Popshins. I'm Jessica.' She gestured to the tiny woman. 'This is my wife, MaryBeth. Aka Mary Popshins.'

Kaj blinked at the tiny woman. '*You're* Mary Popshins?'

She stood and, holding out her skirts, properly curtsied. 'I am.' She grinned up at him. 'Don't worry. You're not the first person to make that assumption and won't be the last.'

He was still gaping. 'You play roller derby?'

'She's a jammer,' Jessica said proudly.

'That's the scorer, Dad,' Elijah informed him seriously.

Val winked at Elijah. 'You've been studying.'

Elijah's cheeks pinked up. 'I like to know stuff.'

Val held out her fist for Elijah to bump. 'Me too, kid. Me too.' She pointed to the table. 'I put out some more veggies and hummus, Kaj, in case you're still hungry. Don't eat too much, though. Patty Hebert says dinner's at seven thirty.'

Still half-dazed, Kaj followed the group to the dining room table, where Val had laid out a spread of which Genie would definitely approve. There was also an open box of cupcakes.

'I'm sorry about the cupcakes,' he heard MaryBeth say to Elijah. 'I didn't know about your dietary restrictions.'

Elijah shrugged. 'It's okay.'

'No, it's not,' MaryBeth insisted. 'I make a line of sugar-free cake pops. I'll bring some over.'

Elijah's smile was shy. 'Thank you, ma'am.'

The hairy beast stuck close to Elijah, sitting at his side before curling up on the floor at his feet when Val commanded him to do so.

Kaj had to admit he was impressed. And appreciative, because the pinched look Elijah had worn since the night before had eased. His son seemed more confident already.

He'd have to rethink getting them a dog of their own once Val was gone. He felt an odd pang at the notion of her leaving, because Elijah was laughing at whatever she'd just said, looking happier than he had in a very long time. Possibly even years.

Maybe Val would be willing to visit after all this was over. Elijah would like that.

And you wouldn't hate it, the little voice in his head said slyly.

Stop. Val was a nice woman. Smart and pretty and far kinder than he'd expected. But what he did or didn't hate was immaterial. Val was only here until the danger to Elijah had passed—however long that would take.

'Kaj?' Val murmured.

He startled, surprised to see her sitting beside him when she'd been sitting across the table just a moment before. 'I'm sorry. I must have zoned out.'

Her expression was kind. 'Yeah. You were a million miles away.' She leaned in closer to whisper, 'Have they picked up Rick Gates yet?'

He glanced at Elijah, who was in an animated conversation with MaryBeth about roller derby. MaryBeth was demonstrating how to do a shoulder check, using her much taller wife as her target. 'No,' he murmured. 'Not yet. But I'm off the case.'

Val nodded. 'Maybe they'll turn their attention elsewhere. Until you know for sure, I'll keep Elijah safe and healthy for as long as you need.'

He met her gaze directly. 'I know. Thank you.'

Then all hell broke loose when Czar leapt to his feet and charged the front door, barking loudly enough that Kaj's ears rang from it. 'What's happening?'

Val was already moving to the door, a sleek automatic pistol in her hand. 'Stay back, Elijah. Kaj, call 911.'

7

'WHERE ARE WE going?' Jace asked, keeping his eyes on the road.

'Mid-City,' Corey told him brusquely.

That was Corey's don't-bother-me tone. Jace had learned long ago not to push his brother when he sounded like that, so he didn't ask why they were going to Mid-City. Although he was afraid he might know.

ADA Cardozo lived in Mid-City with his son. The one they'd tried to steal last night.

Were they going to try again? Jace didn't think so. Corey had been furious with them for trying to take the child, so that didn't seem possible.

Jace had been on edge since Corey had tricked him into admitting that Rick had lied about where the order to steal the prosecutor's kid had come from. Corey had been too nice. Too gentle. Too patient. Too lenient, only asking Jace to drive him rather than backhanding him.

Something's wrong. Corey could have driven himself. *No reason to drag me along.*

Something was going to happen, and Jace didn't think he was going to like it when it did. But he stayed quiet because, although he might be stupid, he wasn't a fool.

Jace followed Corey's directions into a nice neighborhood with tree-lined streets and well-kept lawns. People jogged or walked on the sidewalks. A few waved as they drove by.

It was nice. Just like it had been living with Aaron and Dianne before Liam got sick.

'Here,' Corey snapped. 'Stop here.'

Jace obeyed, daring to glance in his brother's direction. 'Why are we here?'

'We're making a delivery.' He shoved a ski mask into Jace's hand, then yanked one over his own head. 'Put this on, since you and Rick are so keen on them. Meet me at the back.'

Bile rose in Jace's throat as he pulled the mask over his head. *Not again. Please.* He met Corey behind the minivan as Corey opened the hatch, revealing a lumpy, rolled-up quilt.

Jace swallowed. Feet stuck out the end of the quilt. Shoeless feet.

He recognized those feet. *Rick.* It was Rick in that rolled-up quilt.

But how? Who put him there? When did they put him there? And why?

'Get it out,' Corey demanded. 'Fireman's carry, just like you did yesterday.'

Jace stood, frozen. 'But—'

Corey shot him an icy glare. 'I said, get it out. Now.'

It. Not him. *It.* Jace shuddered. 'Is he alive?'

Corey gave him a look that chilled him to the bone. 'Get it out of the van now.'

'But—'

Corey grabbed his collar and jerked him so hard that he stumbled.

'You lied to me. Your punishment is to get *it* out of the van and put *it* on the prosecutor's front lawn. Do it now.'

We're turning Rick in? That couldn't be true. Corey wouldn't . . .

But he would. He was.

Tears stung Jace's eyes. 'I c-c-can't.'

'You c-c-can,' Corey mocked. 'And you will unless you want me to leave you here with him. The cops'll be happy to get their hands on you. You can be with Aaron again. In prison.' He unzipped his jacket halfway, showing the gun in his shoulder holster. 'Or I can put a bullet in your head right here and now. Your call.'

Jace stared at the gun, frozen. *Rick said he'd kill us.* Rick had been right.

Corey sneered. 'What? You don't think I'll do it?'

No, Jace knew that he would. He hauled the rolled-up quilt over his shoulder. If he thought about it as a quilt and not as his brother . . . That was the only way he'd be able to do it.

'I'm sorry,' he choked out, hoping Rick could hear him. 'I'm so sorry.'

Please still be alive. Corey couldn't have killed his own brother. *Yeah. He could.*

'Hurry up,' Corey hissed, getting back into the van. 'We don't have all night.'

Jace took a few steps toward Cardozo's front yard but stumbled again. Hefting the quilt higher on his shoulder, he pushed forward. *Just a few more steps.*

And then he heard the barking.

His chin jerked up as he tried to figure out where the dog was. It sounded huge.

The barking grew louder when the front door flew open and a tall blond woman filled the doorway. 'Stop!' she shouted.

'Motherfucker!' Corey yelled from behind him, the van door slamming a second later.

Jace panicked. He lowered the quilt to the grass, trying not to hurt Rick. Then he ran, throwing himself into the van's driver's seat and stepping on the gas as a huge black dog filled his rearview.

Tires squealed as they drove away, turning the corner so hard that Jace was surprised the van stayed upright.

Corey was cackling like this was some kind of game. Jace wanted to yell, wanted to scream. Wanted to hit something. Or somebody. But he'd never raise a hand to Corey. Jace was big, but Corey was bigger. And smarter. And way meaner.

'That dog was a monster,' Corey said, once he'd caught his breath.

Jace didn't laugh. He'd just turned his brother over to the prosecutor to save himself.

I'm the monster.

Mid-City, New Orleans, Louisiana
TUESDAY, OCTOBER 25, 6:15 P.M.

Standing in the Cardozos' doorway, Val stuck two fingers in her mouth and whistled for Czar, who was already halfway down the street.

'What's happening? Where is Czar?' Elijah asked from behind her. Val gently pushed him to the right of her so that he was shielded by the wall.

'He'll come back,' Val said confidently, nevertheless relieved when her dog reappeared at the end of the driveway, his tongue out as he panted hard. 'Czar, come!'

Obediently the dog trotted to her side and she opened the door wider to let him in. 'Down,' she said quietly, and Czar dropped to his belly with a huge doggy sigh. 'Can you get him some water, MaryBeth?'

'Of course,' MaryBeth said.

Jessica was standing behind Elijah, her hands on his shoulders. She'd pulled him farther away from the door.

I'm not the only one who wants to keep him safe. It was a comforting thought.

Kaj, still on the phone with 911, was pale and shaking. But standing protectively in front of his son, his jaw taut. 'Who was it?' he asked Val.

'Two men. Ski masks.' Val closed the door and leaned against it. 'One of them dropped something big on the lawn. Everyone to the back of the house until the cops can check it out. Stay away from the windows.'

'There's windows everywhere, Val,' Elijah said, his voice high and terrified.

Goddammit. The poor kid had been through enough.

'I know. We'll pull the drapes for now, so no one can see in. Sit on the floor with your back to a wall so your head's not near a window.' She exhaled, her adrenaline spiking. 'Find a wall, everyone, and make yourselves comfortable. Elijah, check your blood sugar.'

Kaj guided Elijah to the dining room wall, still talking to the 911 operator as he settled them into a corner. Elijah sat next to him and Kaj put an arm around his son's shoulders.

Val stood in the kitchen, next to the back door but off to the side. Scanning the backyard, she saw nothing amiss, but she didn't trust that the men—whoever they were—wouldn't return. Or that getting them to the back of the house wasn't their intent. Without looking away from the yard, she pulled her phone from her pocket and used voice commands to dial Burke.

'Val. Is everything—'

'Two men were here,' she interrupted. 'Dropped something out front. A rolled-up quilt with a pair of feet sticking out the end. I haven't approached. It's either a body or a trap.'

'Fuck,' Burke hissed. 'I'm on my way.'

'Kaj is on the line with 911. Can you make sure that André knows what happened?'

The NOPD captain was a friend. He'd know what to do.

'Of course. You have everyone safe?'

'Yes. It was a white minivan, like the one from last night. One of the neighbors' security cams may have caught a license plate. Kaj's cameras aren't set for that angle, and I need to fix that. I'd ask around, but I'm not leaving Elijah. Can we add someone to cover the periphery?'

'You bet. I'll do it myself until I can rework schedules.'

'Thanks, Burke. See you soon.' She ended the call and glanced at Kaj across the room. He was calm, which both surprised and impressed her. 'You guys okay over there?'

'Yes,' Kaj said firmly.

'No,' MaryBeth said with a grimace. 'Czar was thirsty. God.'

Which made him a slobbery mess, water dripping from his beard as he tried to sit on MaryBeth's lap.

'Sorry.' Val tossed her a hand towel. 'Elijah, how's your blood sugar?'

Elijah stared at her, his gaze uncomprehending.

'Elijah,' she repeated, but the boy only blinked.

Kaj was checking his own phone. 'It's high,' he said. 'Not dangerous, but high. Give yourself a hit of insulin, Elijah.'

Slowly Elijah complied, then closed his eyes and leaned against his father's shoulder.

'Burke's on his way,' Val said. 'He's going to inform André.'

'Thank you,' Kaj said, still appearing remarkably calm.

But he wasn't calm. Val looked away from the yard long enough to study his face. His eyes were full of fear. He was not okay. She wanted to go to both father and son and comfort them, but that wasn't her job. Her job was guarding Elijah and she'd do that until Burke arrived.

And then she'd make adjustments to Kaj's home security. They were getting more cameras that captured the backyard and a perimeter alarm activated by motion sensors.

And they needed a panic room for Elijah, in case the house was compromised. If she couldn't hide him in a safe house, she needed at least one safe room. She began making a mental list of the ways she'd keep this child safe and immediately felt her stress levels returning to somewhat normal. Lists provided structure, kept her thoughts from racing.

She'd learned this when she'd returned from Iraq, broken and afraid. Therapy had helped her find coping mechanisms. Lists were one of those mechanisms. Buying Czar had been another.

Back in control, she walked to the front windows and peered out. A police car pulled up to the curb, followed by a black SUV. A uniformed cop and a man in a suit got out of the car and André Holmes got out of the SUV.

Thank you, Burke. 'Kaj, André's here. I'll stay with Elijah if you want to talk to him.'

Kaj looked like he'd refuse, his arm tightening around his son. But then he drew a breath and kissed Elijah on the top of his blond head. 'I'll be right outside, okay?'

Elijah nodded numbly. 'Okay.'

Val wanted to touch Kaj's arm, squeeze his shoulder. Something. But she kept her arms at her sides, her gun pointed at the floor. 'He's okay.'

'I know,' Kaj rasped. 'But they came to my *home*. They left a *body* on my front lawn.'

'Or something.' She still thought it could be a booby trap of some kind. 'Don't be too close when they unwrap the quilt, okay?'

'Okay. You'll—' His voice broke and he cleared his throat. 'You'll stay with him?'

She met his gaze squarely. 'Yes. I promise.'

'I did this. I brought this on our heads. On Elijah's head.'

'No, Kaj. You did not. Aaron Gates's people did this.'

His throat worked as he tried to swallow. 'Sixth Day,' he said hoarsely.

'If you have to blame someone, blame them.' She gave in to the urge and clasped his hand, squeezing for a few seconds before releasing him. 'Wait until André gives you the green light before you go outside. I'll be at Elijah's side. I will not leave him.'

Another nod and he went to the front door.

Val joined the others against the wall and sat next to Elijah. 'This sucks,' she said.

Elijah choked on what might have been a laugh. A hysterical laugh, but she'd take it. 'What did they put on the lawn?' he asked, his voice very small.

That pissed her off. How dare they scare Elijah? How dare they make him feel small?

She drew a breath, let it out. 'Dunno exactly.'

'It . . .' Elijah twisted so that he could look up at her. 'It's a body, isn't it?'

'Maybe. We'll have to see.'

'It's a warning,' Elijah said, defeated.

'Let's wait to see what it is before we go all gloom and doom, okay?'

'Okay,' he murmured. 'I wanna go home.'

To New York. Oh, honey. Keeping her weapon firmly gripped in one hand, she draped her free arm over Elijah's shoulders. 'I know. Can't say I blame you.'

He did a little double take. 'You don't?'

'Sweetie, you've just had a super-bad twenty-four hours, and you were missing New York even before that. Of course I can't blame you.'

'Me either,' Jessica said.

'Same,' MaryBeth added. 'You did good, kid. You did what Val said to do and you didn't panic.'

'I should have done something, though,' he said, a little petulantly.

'Like what?' Val demanded. 'I mean, I have a gun and I didn't go running after them.'

'And she's a badass,' Jessica said solemnly.

'I'm more badass,' MaryBeth said, even more solemnly, then stuck her tongue out at Jessica when she made cooing noises, like MaryBeth was an infant. 'You shut up! I am so a badass.'

'Yes, my love,' Jessica said with a sigh. 'You are a total badass, and I quake in fear.'

'That's better,' MaryBeth groused. 'Czar, lick her face. Or shake your wet beard at her.'

'Nooo0!' Jessica laughed. 'Not the wet beard! You are the badassiest of all. I swear!'

Elijah laughed then, a true belly laugh. 'Are they always like this?'

Val smiled at him. 'Silly? Sometimes. I think we all need to get a little silly sometimes.'

Elijah shook his head. 'I'm not silly. Or badass.'

Val tilted up his chin so that she could see his eyes, dark like his father's. 'Elijah. Listen to me. You kept your head last night, you got away, you listened to your aunt, and you pulled Rick Gates's ski mask off his face. That alone was huge. That told us who to look for. You are totally badass.'

He tilted his head, his lips curving. 'I guess I am.'

'Hell yeah,' Jessica said, then *oof*ed when MaryBeth elbowed her. 'I mean, heck yeah. We both said "badass," but I can't say "H-E-double-hockey-sticks"?'

MaryBeth looked stunned and guilty. 'Well, sh—crap. Sorry, kid.'

'It's okay,' Elijah said. 'My aunt cusses all the time, but my dad's not supposed to know. I've learned all the words. I'm just not allowed to say them.'

Val chuckled. 'Good to know. And now that you've admitted your badassitude, we'll work on silliness. Every kid needs some silliness.'

'My friend back in New York was silly sometimes. His whole family was. They had a Tater-Tots fight at dinner one night when I was staying over.'

'You didn't join in?' MaryBeth asked.

'No!' Elijah said, sounding horrified at the notion. 'Which ended up good for me because Jeff had to clean up all the Tater Tots afterward and I didn't have to help.'

Val laughed. 'Smart.'

Jessica nudged him. 'Next time we come we are totally bringing Tater Tots.'

Elijah giggled. 'You are not.'

They continued to talk about food fights, and Val was grateful to her friends for keeping Elijah's mind occupied. A smart boy like him would already be thinking of all the ways this could have ended much worse. Val prepared herself for a restless night. That would be when Elijah would need the most support. This she knew from experience. Nights were the worst.

She was fiercely glad Jess and MaryBeth had brought her dog. Czar would be exactly what Elijah needed.

Mid-City, New Orleans, Louisiana
TUESDAY, OCTOBER 25, 6:35 P.M.

'You okay?' André asked as he and Kaj walked toward the rolled-up quilt.

A pair of feet were visible at one end. *It's a body.* Just as he'd feared.

'No,' Kaj snapped. 'Not in the least.'

André grimaced. 'Sorry. Stupid question. I meant are you all right physically?'

'Yes. We didn't leave the house. Val blocked the front door and sent her hellhound to chase the bastards.'

'Hellhound?'

'Czar. You'll need to see for yourself. The dog defies description. He's enormous.'

André chuckled. 'At least that gave them a little fright.'

'I sure as hell hope so,' Kaj muttered. 'Assholes.' Then something occurred to him. '*Bold* assholes. They just dropped off that bundle like they knew no one would challenge them.'

André slowed to a stop and stared at him. 'Meaning?'

'Meaning it was like they knew there wasn't anyone on guard outside the house. Who knew I'd refused police protection?'

André frowned. 'I don't know, but I'll find out.'

'Thank you,' he said, mollified a little. At least André was taking this seriously. Which Kaj had known he would. André was a good man. A good cop. 'Sorry I snapped.'

'Your son has been threatened and your property breached. I'd be on edge, too.'

'Thanks.' Kaj braced himself. 'Now let's see who they left me.'

A uniformed officer and a detective in a suit stood over the quiltwrapped body.

'I called for an ambulance to take the body away,' the detective said.

Drawing his service weapon, André walked to the rolled-up quilt. 'Thank you, Detective Drysdale. Officer Nolan, can you get a tarp to put under the quilt? I don't want to lose any evidence when you cut him loose.'

Nolan did as asked, then took a knife from his utility belt and began slicing at the quilt.

Remembering Val's warning, Kaj stepped back, and, holding his breath, he watched as the man's body was revealed. He wore nothing but a pair of boxer shorts and began shivering when the quilt was cut away from his torso.

'André,' Kaj said urgently. 'Look. He's alive.'

'The goose bumps?' André asked. 'That's rigor. Dead bodies have goose bumps.'

Kaj shook his head. 'No. He's *shivering*.'

'He is, Captain,' Nolan agreed. 'He's alive.'

'Fuck. You're right. Drysdale, get a thermal blanket.'

The detective went to his vehicle, returning with a thermal blanket as a blue Escalade pulled up behind André's SUV.

Burke got out and jogged over. 'What's going on?'

'He's alive,' André said tersely.

Burke stood next to Kaj, his hand on the gun holstered at his belt. *Protecting me.*

Kaj's concern had been all about Elijah, but Aaron's people probably still believed Kaj held power over Aaron. The press release regarding his recusal hadn't been posted yet.

Eliminating me would not be out of the question. It was unlikely that they'd dropped off an operative in a Trojan quilt who'd fire on them when uncovered, but it never hurt to be careful.

Carefully, Officer Nolan sliced the quilt away from the man's face.

Kaj gasped. 'Holy fuck.'

André took a step forward. 'What the actual hell?'

'That's . . .' Burke trailed off, shaking his head.

'Rick Gates,' Kaj said numbly.

'There's a note, Captain,' Detective Drysdale said.

Squatting, André shone the light from his Maglite on the piece of paper duct-taped to Rick's bare chest. The frown on the captain's face said the note's contents were not good.

'Read it, for fuck's sake,' Kaj demanded. 'Please,' he added.

'"Dear Mr. Cardozo, Rick failed and has been punished accordingly. Set Aaron Gates free or the next body we'll leave you will be that of your son".' André looked up. 'Signed with an S and D entwined.'

'Sixth Day,' Kaj whispered as the detective and the officer dropped to their knees on either side of Rick's still form. 'My God.'

'Elijah is safe,' Burke murmured. 'We're going to keep him that way. Breathe, Kaj.'

Kaj sucked in a breath that burned. *Elijah is safe. Elijah is safe.* Elijah was safe.

But Rick Gates was not. His legs were bound above the ankle and his hands were also bound with duct tape behind his back. Another piece of tape covered his mouth and his eyes were closed.

His chest didn't appear to be moving. Detective Drysdale had pulled on a pair of gloves and was carefully peeling the tape from Rick's mouth. André held out an evidence bag and Drysdale dropped the tape into it, careful to maintain the chain of evidence.

Drysdale hovered his hand over Rick's mouth. 'Five breaths a minute.'

'Pulse is about twenty,' Nolan added.

Kaj was numb as he stared down at the young man lying on his front lawn. This was the boy—no, the *man*, dammit—who'd laid hands on his son. *He tried to take my Elijah.*

'You okay?' Burke asked softly, and it was as if the question unleashed Kaj's emotions. Terror mixed with dread and a raw fury such as he'd never felt before. *He tried to take my son.*

'I'm not going to strangle him with my bare hands,' Kaj said from behind clenched teeth, 'if that's what you're asking.'

'Then you're a better man than I am,' Burke said. 'I don't think I'd be as restrained.'

'I want him to rot in prison. If I strangle him before they can save his life, he won't be able to do that.'

André spread the thermal blanket over Rick's body. 'The paramedics will be here any minute. We'll get him transported and cuff him to his hospital bed. When he comes to—*if* he comes to—he's going to answer a lot of questions.'

Kaj swallowed back the hatred that threatened to choke him. 'I want to be there when you ask those questions.'

André gave him a quick nod. 'Here are the paramedics.'

Hands clenched into fists, Kaj stood next to Burke as the medics checked Rick over and then gave him an injection of Narcan.

'Overdose?' Kaj asked.

André shrugged. 'Likely. If it isn't, the Narcan won't hurt him. If it is, it could save him, but it's a long shot. He seems pretty far gone.'

'His brother Corey did say he'd been using,' Burke said quietly. 'And that he was in with Sixth Day.'

'Officer Nolan, call Corey Gates,' André directed. 'Let him know that we found Rick. Did it work?' he asked the paramedics.

One of them looked up, pulling the stethoscope tips from his ears. 'I think so. His pulse was twenty before. Now it's forty-five. We'll take him in, and hopefully the ER docs can help him.' They moved Rick to a stretcher, then loaded him into the ambulance. 'You coming, Captain?'

'Yeah,' André said, tossing his keys to Drysdale. 'Bring my SUV to the hospital?'

'Sure thing, Captain.' Drysdale turned to Kaj. 'Your son's okay?'

Kaj nodded. 'He's with his bodyguard.'

'Good. I saw the video from last night. Your son is brave, but he shouldn't have to be.' He handed Kaj a business card. 'Please call me if you need anything. I have a daughter. I can't imagine what you're going through right now.'

Kaj took the card, hating that he didn't trust this man, but Sixth Day had known that there were no guards outside his home. Only the NOPD and Burke's group had this information, and he trusted Burke's group. That left the NOPD as the source of the leak. Otherwise, those bastards never would have dared to drive up like they owned the place. 'Thank you,' he forced himself to say, then turned to Burke. 'I need to increase security. Can I add a guard outside?'

'Val already asked and it's already done. You're lookin' at him.'

Smacked by a wave of gratitude, Kaj nodded, hating that his eyes stung. 'Thank you. Val was amazing. And that dog of hers tore after that van like it was a pork chop.'

'Ah, Czar. He's a terrifying teddy bear.' Burke squeezed his shoulder before guiding him up the stairs to the porch, pausing by his front door. 'You may want to consider adding police protection.'

Kaj shook his head. 'I—'

'Hear me out,' Burke interrupted gently. 'Between André and me, we can handpick cops who we trust. At least have them patrol your street. They don't have to come into the house. Sixth Day might be bluffing, but we can't take that chance. Not with Elijah's safety.'

Kaj nodded numbly. 'I know.'

Burke's expression softened with compassion. 'Just think about it. Go on inside. I'm going to do a perimeter check. Meet you inside in a few.'

Burke jogged around to the back of his house and for a moment Kaj could only stand in front of his door, his mind nearly paralyzed with fear for his son. Then he kicked himself into motion, dialing his boss on his cell phone.

'Cardozo? What's happened?'

Kaj told him what had happened, and Hogan cursed. 'I just sent out that press release saying you'd been recused, so it's unlikely that Sixth Day has seen it yet.'

'Or they don't care.'

'Or they don't care,' Hogan allowed. 'Can you leave town for a few days?'

'No. Elijah's doctor wants him close to the hospital in case he has another spike.'

'Spike?'

After being so open with Val and Burke about Elijah's health, Kaj had forgotten that he'd been so closemouthed with everyone else. 'He has type 1 diabetes. The past two days haven't helped. I need to get back inside my house, but I wanted you to know about Rick Gates and the note—especially because you're taking over Aaron's case.'

'You think they might target me.'

'Desperate people do desperate things. They want Aaron freed.'

'Well, that's not gonna happen, but I take your point. I'll have security walk me to my car when I leave the office. Keep me apprised of anything new.'

'I will. Be careful.' Hands trembling, Kaj ended the call. *Elijah is safe. Elijah is safe.* He repeated the words as he pushed through his front door. His son was safe. That was the important thing.

That and finding out every last thing that Rick Gates knew.

Bayou des Allemands, Louisiana
TUESDAY, OCTOBER 25, 8:05 P.M.

'Get out.' Corey shoved Jace onto the dock, sending the boat rocking dangerously. 'You make me sick.'

Jace had cried all the way back to the camp, his posture defeated. Which was exactly what Corey had wanted. He'd break the kid down and build him back to be fucking loyal.

Jace was still sobbing as Corey dragged him to Aaron's quarters. 'You'll stay here until I come get you. You will not leave. You will not speak. Nod if you understand.'

His gaze fixed on his feet, Jace nodded.

'Good.' Corey gripped Jace's T-shirt and yanked him forward, raising his fist. 'And, boy, if you so much as sneeze, you're going to find yourself on Cardozo's lawn next.' Jace cowered. *Good.* The kid ought to be scared out of his damn mind. 'Gimme your shoes.'

Jace blinked up at him, his eyes red and swollen. 'What?'

'Your shoes. Give them to me.' He held out his hand, waiting impatiently. 'Now.'

Jace toed off his sneakers and warily gave them over.

Corey took the shoes and smacked Jace upside the head with one of them. Hard. With a cry of pain Jace clutched his head. 'I bought these shoes, you ungrateful fuck,' Corey snarled. 'I bought your food and clothes and gave you a roof over your head and *this* is how you repay me? By trying to get Aaron back? By *lying* to me? Do not test me, boy. I will destroy you.' He slammed the door behind him, locking the dead bolt from the outside so Jace would stay put.

He'd beat the fear of God into him, if it was the last thing he did. No, not of God. *Of me.*

He walked the hundred feet to his quarters and let himself in, stopping short when he saw Dianne slumped over in his easy chair, a half-empty bottle of vodka on the table beside her. No glass. She'd been drinking straight from the bottle. She was in a drunken stupor once again.

We aren't going to have to keep her sedated. She's doing it to herself. It was hard to watch her slowly killing herself. But drunks were gonna drink. That was the hard truth. After tossing Jace's shoes into his bedroom, he carried her to the bed again.

Leaving the bedroom, he closed the door and leaned against it. He was tired. So damn tired. Watching Dianne grieve was exhausting. He'd had to be strong for her because Aaron hadn't stepped up. Now Aaron never would, not from prison.

Corey would have to tell her that Rick was dead. That was going to rip her apart all over again, especially knowing Rick had gotten involved with a drug gang. But he'd worry about telling her that lie later, once it was safe to take her home. Once the cops were so busy looking at Sixth Day for the abduction attempt and Rick's murder that they'd stopped looking at Corey.

Speaking of . . . He checked his phone, unsurprised to see a missed phone call on his Three Vets phone. This was the number the cops had to contact him in an emergency, and Rick's death would qualify. He tapped the voice mail icon and held the phone to his ear.

'Mr. Gates, this is Officer Nolan with the NOPD. I need to speak with you urgently. Can you please call me back?'

Corey would return the call after he'd taken care of tonight's business. He'd beg pardon for the delay, saying he'd taken a sleeping pill so that he could get some rest. Actually, getting some rest sounded good, but he'd never take a pill. Aaron was the addict. Not me. Never me.

He got to the comm room only to find that Dewey was a bloody mess. The only reason he was still in the chair was because he'd been tied to it. He was missing three fingers from his right hand and two toes from his left foot, and the tic-tac-toe board carved into his chest was sullenly oozing blood. Looked like X's had won.

'Dammit, Bobby. I wanted information. I didn't say you could kill him.'

Holding a scalpel, Bobby grinned a little maniacally. 'I got information. And he's not dead. Not yet.'

Ed looked up from a laptop that Corey hadn't seen before. 'I told him to stop.'

Bobby sneered at him. The two were like children sometimes. 'I got what we needed.'

'He did,' Ed confirmed reluctantly. 'Bobby got all of Dewey's passwords.'

'Including the one to his offshore account,' Bobby said smugly.

'Was his account as big as Aaron's?' Corey asked.

'Not quite as large as Aaron's, but no pittance, either. We've come to the conclusion that the homeless look is just an act. He hid from the cops and caused us to underestimate him all this time.'

'I never thought he was all that stupid,' Corey said, then nodded at Bobby. 'Nice job with the passwords.'

Bobby bowed dramatically. 'Thank you.'

Ed rolled his eyes. 'Don't encourage him. But I do have to admit, he was terrifyingly tenacious. Dewey held out for a long time. Bobby never gave up.'

'How much does he have offshore?'

'Two mil,' Ed said with a grin. 'He had that much, anyway. Now we do. And now we know why Dewey wanted Aaron out of jail so bad.'

Corey pulled out a chair and sat down. 'Tell me.'

'He and Aaron kept a safe,' Ed explained. 'They'd keep putting their profits in it until it was full, then—together—they'd box up the cash and make a run to Miami in Dewey's boat.'

Corey shook his head. 'That boat out there on the dock? They couldn't make it to Panama City in that old jon boat, much less all the way down to Miami.'

Ed turned the laptop around, revealing an honest-to-God yacht. 'This is Dewey's actual boat. He moors it at a marina on Lake Pontchartrain. He's owned it for years—bought it through a shell corporation and used it under the previous Sixth Day leadership. They have a contact in Miami who launders money for a fifteen percent cut. Dewey said it was worth it to avoid scrutiny from the DEA and the FBI. They'd take down boxes of cash, meet up with the guy, hand over the cash, and leave with a deposit into their offshore accounts.'

'Handy,' Corey drawled. 'And here we've been laundering our money through Three Vets, creating all those fake customers and invoices. We could have been doing it the easy way.'

'For real,' Ed grumbled. 'I've been busting my hump keeping our books straight. Anyway, they kept the cash in Aaron's safe.'

Corey shook his head again. 'We checked Aaron's safe. It only had a few grand.'

'Aaron has another safe,' Bobby said, 'right here in the camp.'

'A very fancy safe,' Ed added, 'with a palm scanner for access.'

Bobby waggled his brows. 'Under the floor in Aaron's quarters.'

Then Corey understood. 'Dewey needs Aaron's palm to open it. So how do we get into the safe? Even if we cut Aaron's hand off, those things need live electrical signals from the skin. Don't they?'

'Yes, but Aaron was a lying douchebag.' Ed rolled his eyes. 'Aaron led Dewey to believe that if either of them tried breaking into the safe without both palm prints, it would self-destruct, destroying everything inside. But the safe had an override combination, which only Aaron knew. I've seen the combo in a file on his laptop. I just didn't know what it was for.'

'The safe held a mil in cash,' Bobby said. 'And some more offshore account numbers.'

Corey was floored. 'How many offshore accounts do these guys have?'

'So far,' Ed said, 'I count eight, including the three in the safe. Those were empty. Aaron moved all the money into his own accounts.'

'Which we already took,' Corey said.

Bobby nodded. 'Aaron fucked Dewey over. Stole his share of the profits in the safe and was going to live the high life in the Bahamas with Sandra the Whore, as Dianne calls her.'

'What a dick.' Corey turned his attention to Dewey. 'Did you ask him how he got all that information on Cardozo's kid? Because none of that was online.'

Bobby winced. 'I didn't.'

Corey scowled. 'Dammit, Bobby. I needed to know Dewey's information network. Other than his money, his contacts were the only thing I really wanted from his business.'

'I want that yacht,' Bobby said lightly.

Corey whirled on him, furious. 'Be serious for two seconds, B. I told you I wanted a chance at him and now he's unconscious.'

'Nah,' Bobby said, but he was frowning. 'He's faking it.' He grabbed Dewey's shoulder and shook him. 'Who gave you the intel on Cardozo?'

Dewey didn't say a word.

'Fucking hell,' Corey snapped. 'See if you can wake him up.'

'Can I cut him again?' Bobby asked eagerly, like a giant, deranged puppy.

Corey rolled his eyes. 'Maybe later. Let's wire his balls now. It might be enough to shock him into consciousness.'

'I don't think that's going to work,' Ed cautioned.

But Bobby was grinning again, and Corey watched as Bobby administered shock after shock to Dewey, but the man just lolled to one side, never responding. Not even a moan.

'Bobby,' Corey finally snapped. 'Stop. He really is unconscious.'

'Fucking bastard.' Bobby's initial glee morphed further into rage the longer Dewey didn't respond. It was at times like this that Bobby scared them a little.

'Bobby,' Corey said sharply. 'Dammit. We don't have time for this. You're supposed to be picking up Zach and Allyson at the boat launch to escort them here for our meeting.'

'I'll go with him,' Ed said, 'if you clean up in here. Bobby made a huge mess.'

Corey sighed. 'Fine. Let's get Dewey out to the water. Bring his fingers and toes. We'll dump them in along with him. Then you can get our guests.'

'Can I at least shoot the fucker?' Bobby growled.

Corey rubbed at his temples. 'Yes, Bobby. That you can do.'

8

'THAT WAS SO good,' Elijah said with a happy sigh. 'Thank you, Patty.'

'Yes, Patty,' Kaj added, proud of his son's good manners. 'The shrimp étouffée was delicious. Thank you so very much.' And not only was it delicious, Val's friend Patty Hebert had tailored the recipe to Elijah's dietary requirements. His doctors didn't advise limiting carbs for kids with type 1 diabetes, but Patty had balanced the meal, loading up on the veggies.

'You helped, Elijah,' Patty said. 'You're quite the sous-chef.'

Kaj was beyond grateful to the co-owner of Le Petit Choux, one of New Orleans' best restaurants. She'd distracted Elijah from his anxiety over the intruders better than Kaj ever could have. Czar had also helped mute Elijah's tension, having stuck to the boy like glue.

Kaj, on the other hand, was a mess of roiling fear. He hadn't told Elijah about the newest threat and he didn't intend to. *The next body we'll leave you will be that of your son.* Burke and Val agreed that Elijah was taking the danger seriously enough without needing to be scared further. His son was happy for the moment and he wasn't going to jeopardize that.

Elijah's chest puffed up. 'I want to try it myself next time. I think I can do it.'

'I think you can, too,' Patty agreed, then shifted her attention to the front door, her brows furrowed. 'Val needs to eat. I'd tell her to sit the heck down, but she wouldn't listen to me.'

Val hadn't joined them at the table, instead standing sentry by the front window, not taking her eyes off the street. Burke was on watch in the backyard. Having the two of them keeping such a careful eye was the only reason Kaj had managed to swallow a single bite.

Burke had given Kaj a list of cops that he personally trusted from his days as a detective with the NOPD, and André was working out a protection detail to patrol the neighborhood. The cops hadn't yet been assigned, though, so it was just Burke and Val until they arrived.

'I'll take her a bowl,' he offered, 'if you'll take one to Burke.'

Patty nodded. 'Done.'

Val glanced over his shoulder when he approached, the corners of her mouth turning up when she saw his offering. 'Thank you,' she said. 'Don't stand in front of the window, please. Hurricane glass will stop a hammer or a rock, but not a bullet.'

He moved to her side and leaned against the wall. 'Will you stay here all night?'

'No. I'll need some sleep. Burke and I will spell each other.' She ate a few bites, moaning quietly. Which should not have been as enticing as it was. 'This is so good.'

'It is. Have you seen anything on the street?'

'No. Have you heard anything about Rick Gates?'

'Only that he's been sedated.' Which he'd shared with her shortly before dinner when André had called him with the news. As they'd expected, Rick had OD'd on heroin, but the Narcan the EMTs had administered had counteracted the opioid. Rick had regained consciousness in the ambulance but had begun moaning in pain, so the ER doctors at the hospital had given him Valium, the only painkiller that was both safe and effective so soon after an overdose. 'I hope he wakes up soon.'

'Will they let you observe when they interview him?'

'André said they would.' But Kaj was almost afraid to let himself be anywhere near Rick Gates. *I believe in the law, dammit. In justice.* He was not a vigilante. Still, he wanted to hurt Rick for touching his child. For making Elijah afraid. 'I guess we'll see.'

'It's normal, you know,' she said softly. Her blue eyes were sympathetic, her lips curved in a sad smile.

'What's normal?'

'Fantasizing about punishing Rick.'

He sucked in a breath. 'How did you know?'

'Because I've been there. I fantasized and it scared me, to be honest. It scared me a lot.'

'You wanted to hurt your brother's killer?'

One shoulder lifted in a half shrug. 'Him too.'

Oh. 'You wanted to hurt your stalker.' With whom she'd *had an issue.* Kaj wanted to ask for details, but of course he wouldn't. *Not my business.* But he wanted it to be.

'Yes. I even started planning scenarios. Where I'd take him and who I'd recruit to help me. That's when I moved to New Mexico. I thought if he kept "accidentally" running into me at the market then one day I might snap and follow through on my fantasies. I ended up spilling everything to my brother and he helped me change my name. He even picked New Mexico as my new home. It was a relief, honestly. I moved away and got therapy.'

'Did it help? The therapy?'

'It did.' She returned her gaze to the street. 'You know, Patty told me that you recommended a therapist for her after her uncle was murdered. She said it's helping.'

'I'm glad.' He really was. Patty Hebert and her cousin Gabe had gone through a terrible ordeal last summer as they'd worked with Burke to solve Gabe's father's murder. They were nice people and he wanted them to be okay.

'Well.' She seemed to brace herself. 'You might want to consider that for yourself.'

He blinked. 'Therapy? For me? I was planning to get Elijah a therapist, but I don't need . . .' He trailed off, because he could hear how utterly in denial he sounded.

She gave him a pointed stare, one blond brow lifting. 'Really, Kaj?'

He sighed. 'Even I couldn't pull off that argument. I'll do it. I'll contact a therapist.'

Her smile brightened her face, momentarily stealing his breath. She was a beautiful woman, but when she smiled, she just lit up. 'I'm glad.' She finished the étouffée, then set the bowl aside. 'I wanted to talk with you about two more security features. I'd like to install cameras that face the street and the backyard.'

'Okay. Do it. What's the second thing?'

She hesitated, peeking over her shoulder at the table where Elijah was laughing with MaryBeth. 'Given the continued threat to Elijah, I think he should have a safe room.'

Kaj frowned. 'You mean a panic room?'

'Yes. One of Burke's guys would be able to install one in a day or two. If you're gone and anything happens to me . . .' She shrugged. 'Elijah needs to have a place to hide.'

At first, he couldn't think past something happening to her. But he'd hired her to protect his son and knew she'd be prepared to step between Elijah and a bullet if the need arose, especially after the letter taped to Rick Gates's chest.

God. The thought of Val getting hurt . . . well, it hurt. Like a punch right to his sternum. But she was waiting for an answer, so he forced himself to consider the suggestion. It made sense. 'I'm not against it.

Have you recommended this to your other clients with children?'

'Most of them already had safe rooms. They were either wealthy or celebrities who'd lived with the threat of a kidnapping for years before I was assigned to guard their kids.'

He flinched at the word 'kidnapping'. 'How would it work? Where would you put it?'

'I was thinking the walk-in closet in Elijah's room would be a possibility, but Phin could tell us for sure. He'd beef up the walls, install secure doors, add locks, run a phone line into the room so Elijah could call for help. We'd need to store food and water and even insulin in there, just in case. Phin's very trustworthy. He's Burke's night security and does all the maintenance around the office. He's built safe rooms before. He'll do a good job.'

'Can he come tomorrow?'

'He can. I've already talked to him.'

The next body we'll leave you will be that of your son. 'Tell him to do it.'

She met his gaze, hers calm now, and it made him feel calmer, too. 'I will.'

Their conversation was finished. He should return to the others, allow her to continue her vigil, but he didn't seem to be able to move. Then again, neither did she. He watched, fascinated, as a blush rose to pinken her cheeks. The seconds ticked and he couldn't tear his eyes away.

His mouth dry, he fought for something to say.

She bit at her bottom lip and his skin felt hot. His heart was beating so fast that he felt light-headed. He felt his body leaning forward into her space, and she didn't push him away. Her tongue licked a path across her lip and he wanted to follow it. Wanted to taste her. Wanted to see if her lips were as lush as they appeared.

He wanted to take her hair down and see it spread on his pillow.

And then his phone buzzed in his pocket, breaking the spell. She blinked, her spine going ramrod straight. He thought she shivered and . . .

Shit. He wanted her. The notion hit him like a brick. He'd noticed women since Heather's death, but he hadn't wanted them. *Not like this.* Not like he wanted Val Sorensen.

She made a small noise. 'Are you going to get that?'

Oh. Right. He pulled his phone from his pocket and his body went abruptly cold. 'It's André on FaceTime.' Hands shaking, he managed to hit accept. 'What's happened?'

André's face filled his phone's screen, his expression grim. 'Rick Gates woke up.'

Kaj's pulse went from pounding to stratospheric. 'I'm on my way.'

André held up a hand. 'Wait. When we get him into a formal interrogation room, you can be on the other side of the mirror. I've already asked him a few questions tonight.'

Kaj's temper exploded. 'You promised,' he hissed, cognizant of Elijah in the next room.

'Kaj,' Val murmured. 'Breathe. You know André wouldn't do you wrong.' She laid her hand on his forearm and his rage seemed to crumble into dust.

He felt grounded. And not alone. His throat tightened unexpectedly and he blinked back tears. 'I know,' he murmured back. He angled the phone so Val could see it, too, reducing the volume so that Elijah couldn't hear. 'What did he say, André?'

'He was muttering when he was trying to wake up. Saying "Please, don't. I'm sorry," over and over again.' André exhaled. 'The doctor found evidence that he'd been tortured.'

Kaj's eyes widened. 'What? How? And by whom?'

André grimaced. 'Electrocution to his genitals. The doc found burns on his scrotum.'

'Jesus.' Kaj shuddered, irritated with himself for feeling even a morsel of sympathy for the man who'd touched his Elijah.

'Oh my God,' Val whispered. 'So . . . was he tortured into attempting the abduction?'

André lifted a massive shoulder. 'I don't know and he's not telling. But there was also evidence of other abuse. Old bruises. Healed bone breaks.'

'Did you arrest him?' Kaj asked.

'I did. Mirandized him. He declined an attorney.'

Kaj blinked. 'What?'

'You heard me. He said, "No thank you." Have it on video. I recorded our conversation to submit into evidence, but I can't send it to you.'

'I understand,' Kaj said quietly. He really did. He was recused from the case. Didn't mean he had to like it, though.

'But I can play it for you on my computer while I have you on the phone.'

Kaj perked up. 'Yes, please. Now.'

Val took Kaj's arm. 'Give us a minute, André. There are a lot of people in the next room. We need to go somewhere secure.'

Good thinking. Kaj didn't want Elijah knowing anything about this, either. He allowed Val to lead him into the garage, once she'd explained to Burke what they were doing so he could keep watch on the front of the house. She turned on the light and closed the door behind them, then gently grasped his hand to tilt the phone so that they both could watch. Then her hand dropped to her side and he felt bereft. Alone once again. *Focus, Kaj. Pay attention.*

'Play it, please,' he said, turning up the volume.

'I'd already Mirandized him before this clip starts,' André said, aiming his phone so that his computer screen came into view. Rick Gates lay in a hospital bed, handcuffed to the rail. He appeared to be afraid.

Satisfied rage filled Kaj's chest. *Good. The prick should be afraid.* He was suddenly very glad he wasn't in that hospital room. *I'd have beaten him within an inch of his life.*

And if Rick was tortured into trying to take Elijah? Kaj wasn't able to think that far yet.

'Why did you attempt to abduct Elijah Cardozo?' André asked on the video.

Rick clamped his lips closed and shook his head.

'Were your actions last night directed by your brother Aaron?'

Rick maintained his silence.

'Who was the other man? The driver of the van?' André continued.

More silence.

'Do you know Dewey Talley?'

Rick's breath hitched, and his eyes closed.

'So you do know him. Was Dewey Talley the driver?'

Rick seemed to freeze, then . . . relaxed. Eyes still closed, all of his tension appeared to drain away. 'Yes.'

Yes, Kaj thought triumphantly. They had confirmation.

'What did he hope to gain?' André asked Rick.

No answer.

'Who left you on Cardozo's lawn?'

No answer.

André sighed, his tone softening. 'Who tortured you?'

Rick flinched, a single tear leaking from his closed eyes. Then shook his head mutely.

The video stopped, and André's face reappeared on the screen. 'Other than to decline an attorney, he only said that one word.'

'Do you believe him?' Val asked.

Kaj looked at her sharply. 'You don't?'

She shrugged. 'I don't know. I was asking André.'

'I don't know, either,' André admitted.

'How recent were the burns to his genitals?' Val asked. 'Were they incentive to do the abduction or punishment because he failed?'

'Doctor said they were fresh—more like hours versus a day.' André made an awkward face. 'Plus, no offense, Val, but if he'd had that done to him before, he wouldn't have been able to walk far enough to grab Elijah in the first place.'

Val grimaced. 'Got it. Sorry. Is there anything else you can tell us?'

'Not at the moment. The doctors are keeping him overnight for observation. He'll be transferred to the jail tomorrow. I'll let you know when you can come in.'

'Thanks, André,' Kaj said fervently. 'I appreciate it.'

'It's nothing. Y'all go back on inside the house. I'll call you if I find anything new.'

André ended the call and Val tugged on Kaj's arm. 'Come on. It's chilly out here.'

Kaj chuckled weakly. 'This feels good. You don't know chilly.'

'I lived in Minnesota until I was ten. I know cold. I just don't like cold.' She told Burke they were going back inside and led Kaj back to the dining room, where Elijah was helping MaryBeth and Jessica clean up and Patty was packing up the ingredients she'd brought.

Elijah stopped what he was doing. 'Was that Captain Holmes?'

Lie. Don't tell him anything. But Elijah deserved information. Just not *all* the information. 'Yes, it was Captain Holmes. Rick Gates woke up.' Elijah paled and, once again, Kaj wanted to strangle Rick Gates.

'What did he say?' Elijah asked in the barest of whispers.

'He questioned Rick, but didn't really learn anything.'

Elijah swallowed, his hand moving to pet Czar's enormous head. 'And that Dewey guy? Did they find him?'

Kaj shook his head. 'Not yet. They're still looking.'

'It's going to be okay,' Val said levelly. 'Czar will sleep at your side. I'll be downstairs and Burke is outside on guard duty. You're safe.'

Elijah nodded resolutely. 'I know.'

But his son was still terrified and Kaj blamed himself. *I should have stayed in New York. He'd be safe if we were still in New York.*

Logically, he knew that might not be true. He'd prosecuted all kinds of mob types in New York. Any one of them could have come after his son. But no one had. Not until now.

'Elijah . . .' Kaj trailed off. He didn't know what to say.

'I know, Dad. It's not your fault.' Elijah turned for the kitchen, busying himself with loading the dishwasher.

MaryBeth and Jessica both gave Kaj looks of sympathy. 'He means it,' Jessica murmured. 'He knows this isn't your doing. He's just scared.'

Because Dewey Talley was still out there. Rick Gates had been tortured. What had they planned for Elijah?

Kaj's stomach lurched, bile burning his throat, and he rushed outside, needing the fresh air. He got to the edge of his porch and leaned over, propping his hands on his thighs, trying to breathe. Trying not to throw up. Trying not to cry.

Trying not to get into the car and drive to the hospital to shake the truth out of Rick Gates.

He flinched when a hand settled on his back, working in slow circles. He smelled vanilla. Val.

'You need to come inside, Kaj. It's not safe for you to be out here like this.'

'You should be with Elijah.'

'Burke's got the back. I'm watching the front. Elijah is fine.' The combination of her calm voice and her firm touch helped. He sucked in lungfuls of air and slowly straightened.

'Thank you.'

She smiled at him. 'You're welcome.' She removed her hand and he wanted to beg her to put it back. But they'd nearly crossed the line earlier. He'd nearly kissed her.

He couldn't allow that to happen again. She was here to protect his son.

Soberly, he followed her back inside.

Bayou des Allemands, Louisiana
TUESDAY, OCTOBER 25, 8:45 P.M.

Jace curled up on the bed in Aaron's cabin, numb. His head ached from the crying and the stress. And the chemical smell of Aaron's cabin. But mostly because of what he'd done.

He'd betrayed his own brother.

I'm a coward. I should have stopped it. I should have said no.

But he and Rick had learned a long time ago that they couldn't say no to Corey. At least not without a beating.

Or being shot in the head.

The cops would have Rick by now. That lady who'd run to the door, the one with the dog. She might have been a cop. Jace shuddered at the memory. That dog . . . It had been huge.

What if that dog had attacked Rick? His brother would have been mauled.

If he's still alive.

Jace closed his eyes, his head throbbing and his stomach sick. Why did Aaron's cabin smell so bad? He wasn't sure how long he'd lain there, but the smell was making him sick.

Could he open a window? Corey hadn't told him not to. He'd be madder if Jace puked.

When Jace and Rick had the flu last year, Corey had cursed at them, then left them to take care of themselves. For a whole week. He and Rick had taken turns making microwave chicken soup. But they'd been without Corey's beatings, so it'd been worth having the flu.

Damn. Jace could barely breathe, the smell was so bad. He had to do something.

He inched toward the window and slid it open, pressing his face against the screen to get a breath of fresh air. Gradually the nausea passed, but his head still throbbed. He willed himself not to cry any more. Crying would just make his headache worse.

He'd nearly fallen asleep when the sound of voices jerked him back to awareness.

'Goddamn, this fucker is heavy.'

That was Corey. Cautiously Jace pressed closer to the screen, squinting. What was Corey doing?

The moon was full and shone like a spotlight on the four men leaving Corey's quarters. Ed was there, too, and he and Corey were dragging someone between them. It was a naked man. Bobby followed behind, holding the huge gun he'd worn in his chest holster all day.

Corey, Ed, and Bobby all wore headphones. No, they were the earmuffs they used when they went shooting at the range. Then Jace's gaze zeroed in on the naked man's upper arm.

A dragon tattoo. *Just like mine.* It was Dewey. And he was covered in blood. So much blood. What had they done to him? And why?

They'd stopped at the edge of the water and Bobby was aiming his big gun at Dewey's head.

Jace barely had time to stick his fingers in his ears before the gunshot shattered the air. Open-mouthed, he watched in horror as Dewey's body fell backward into the river. Almost immediately the water began to churn. And turn red. With blood.

The three men took off the earmuffs and Corey's laugh broke the silence. 'Wow. That's got to be a fuckin' record. Never seen the gators come so fast.'

Jace swallowed back the bile that burned his throat. *No. Please, no.*

But it was true. He hadn't imagined it.

Corey, Bobby, and Ed had killed Dewey and fed his body to the gators.

'The cops will be chasing their tails looking for him,' Ed said. 'The mysterious masked driver.'

'Stroke of luck for us that they think Dewey was driving,' Corey agreed. 'I might not slice that tat off Jace's arm for a while, in case we want to blame something else on the old bastard. Jace can be his masked stand-in.'

Jace couldn't breathe. The cops thought Dewey was the driver?

'Not a bad plan,' Ed said. 'Let's get cleaned up and then Bobby and I will pick up our guests. Bobby, you need a shower. You're covered in yuck.'

Bobby only grunted before heading back to Corey's quarters.

Jace quietly lowered the window and sank to the floor. Corey had murdered Dewey.

The cops aren't looking for me.

He crawled to Aaron's bed and climbed into it, curling into the fetal position. His brain was racing. His heart was racing even faster.

Corey had murdered Dewey. Then laughed about it.

Just as he had after they'd dumped Rick onto Cardozo's lawn. Corey had laughed like a crazy man. Maybe Corey *was* a crazy man.

I have to get away. I have to tell someone about Dewey. I have to help Rick.

I have to not be a fucking coward.

He thought about the wallet and keys he'd seen in Dewey's workshop. The keys had to be for Dewey's truck at the boat launch where Corey had left the van when they'd returned from Cardozo's house. *If I can take Dewey's boat . . .*

He heard the roar of a motor and sat up in bed in time to see one of the boats leaving the dock. Ed and Bobby were going to pick someone up. Guests, Ed had called them.

Cops?

No. They'd just murdered Dewey. The last people they'd be bringing would be cops.

I need to get away.

I need shoes.

He climbed out of the bed and dropped to the floor, just in case Corey could see in the window. He crawled to Aaron's closet and slid the door open. *Shoes*. Aaron had a pair of sneakers, so Jace put them on. They pinched, but he wasn't going to complain.

Step one. Got shoes. Step two. Wait until the coast is clear and get Dewey's keys.

Then wait for it to be safe enough to steal Dewey's boat.

He thought of how loud the motor had been when Ed and Bobby had left just now. Corey would hear that and chase him, but Dewey's old jon boat had oars. He could row until he was far enough away to start the motor.

Yeah. That might work.

And if it didn't?

Corey would kill him either way, so he didn't have any other choice. He was going to run. He was going to help Rick.

Bayou des Allemands, Louisiana
TUESDAY, OCTOBER 25, 10:00 P.M.

Corey stood on the dock. Ed and Bobby were approaching with Zach and Allyson, the members of Bella Butler's security force who'd been extorted into aiding them. With Zach and Allyson feeding them Bella's movements, they'd be able to silence her before she ever took the witness stand against Trevor Doyle.

Doyle might have raped the woman. Corey didn't know, nor did he care. Doyle wasn't paying for Corey's approval. He was paying for Corey's expertise.

This was the big time and Corey was ready.

He and Bobby had done a string of small burglaries for more than a year after he'd been discharged from the army, but they'd attracted the attention of NOPD because they hadn't realized that they'd created a noticeable pattern in their thefts. They'd had to stop their operation when Bobby had been told to either resign or be fired and prosecuted.

The failure had chafed both Corey and Bobby—Bobby because he'd lost his job and Corey because he hated to fail. He'd been basically kicked out of the army and his ego had been battered. Nearly getting arrested for theft hadn't helped him at all.

But he'd realized back then that he needed to think bigger and better or he'd be a small-time thief for the rest of his life, just like his father had been—and there was no way Corey would allow that to happen. His father had been a loser who'd spent most of Corey's childhood in a cell in Angola. When he'd finally gotten out, he'd fathered two more children before dying in a puddle of his own blood and piss after losing a bar fight.

Corey had vowed to never be like his father. He'd stumbled a few times after getting out of the army, trying to find his place. He'd tried to get a job but hadn't been qualified for anything that earned a decent wage. Even construction didn't earn him a decent wage. And he didn't want just a decent wage. He wanted more. He deserved more.

He knew how to kill, so that was what he'd decided to do, and now he finally had a profitable business that was only growing stronger.

The idea for their dirty-jobs business had come from one of Aaron's upscale drug customers. Corey had been making a delivery, having driven his construction truck into an exclusive neighborhood. He'd overheard the customer fighting with his wife, who was threatening to expose his drug use in their very ugly custody battle. Corey had casually suggested that the wife could disappear. The customer had said yes and paid him up front in cash, and Corey and Bobby had killed the woman, making it look like an accident.

Ed had joined them shortly thereafter. Corey and Ed had served together in the army, and Corey knew that Ed had bent the rules whenever it had suited him. That had included the diversion of arms and supplies to whoever would pay the most for them. Ed had had quite a little operation going during the years he'd served and had never gotten caught. So Corey had recruited him.

That had been three years ago. Now they were in the big leagues. Doyle was their first celebrity client. He'd been impressed with them because they'd found two people on Bella's security team so vulnerable to extortion.

Discovering vulnerabilities was one of Ed's specialties. Zach's fiancée, a fellow veteran who'd returned from the war with a prosthetic leg and a nasty drug habit, had caused an even nastier accident while driving under the influence. Zach was a paramedic, but claimed he was working security for Bella Butler to pay for his fiancée's state-of-the-art prosthetic leg. In reality, Zach needed the money to continue paying the crash victims for their silence.

He'd folded like a cheap suit the first time they'd threatened to expose the two of them. Unafraid for himself, he couldn't stomach his fiancée serving time for her 'mistake'.

Allyson's sin was actually much worse.

Bella Butler exclusively hired veterans for her security force, so Ed had consulted his network of soldiers still serving about every name on the list. They'd hit the jackpot with Allyson—the rumor mill whispered that she'd slept with an enemy agent while serving in Iraq and that the pillow talk she'd shared with her lover had included the movements of her team. Four American soldiers had been killed in the resulting ambush.

She hadn't been charged by the army, so Corey had had his doubts about the veracity of this information—until he'd confronted Allyson with it. She'd gone so pale that she'd nearly fainted. And then she'd agreed to do whatever he asked if he didn't report her, erasing all doubt.

Corey felt confident that he could control both of them, but that didn't mean he was blindly trusting. And because of that, he'd asked Ed and Bobby to blindfold them.

The boat sped around the bend, the light of the moon revealing Ed, Bobby, and their two blindfolded accomplices.

Ed brought the boat up against the dock, edging past Dewey's old jon boat.

'Welcome,' Corey said jovially, moving out of the way so Bobby could lift their still-blindfolded guests onto the dock.

'I don't feel very welcome,' Allyson said coldly. 'Was blindfolding us necessary?'

Corey ignored her complaint. 'We have a lot to talk about. Bobby and Ed, please escort our guests. We don't want them spraining an ankle, now do we?'

The four followed Corey into the freshly cleaned comm room, where he allowed Zach and Allyson to remove their blindfolds. The two eyed each other warily. Neither had known the other was compromised until they'd met at the boat launch.

He directed them to sit around the table. 'I trust that you'll keep what you hear tonight to yourselves,' Corey said, eyeing each of the two in turn. 'Or your secrets will be found out.'

Both Zach and Allyson tensed, but neither said a word.

Corey smiled. 'Excellent. Let's get started.'

9

JACE DIDN'T WANT to know what Corey was doing with the two blindfolded strangers. It couldn't be anything good. He'd killed Dewey in cold blood, like it was nothing.

And then he'd laughed.

Corey also hadn't blindfolded Jace on the way back from the Cardozos' house. When he and Rick were first brought here, they'd been asleep. Drugged. But this time Corey hadn't tried to hide their location. *Because he doesn't ever plan to let me leave.*

I need to get out of here. But the only door was locked.

The bedroom window was in full view of Corey's quarters, so Jace could be seen if he tried to crawl through it. The living room window faced the back of the property, but it was too small. He'd already tried. He'd need another few inches of space to wiggle out.

He'd searched the other rooms for a way out, but no dice. He had found something in his search, though—a lot of glass bottles that looked like the ones used in *Breaking Bad*. The stovetop was charred black, the countertops bubbled up in places.

Which would explain the smell. Aaron had been making meth here. Jace hadn't wanted to believe it, but it was true. Aaron had not only killed that doctor, but he was a drug dealer, too.

But he couldn't worry about that now. He had to get out of here before Corey shot him in the head and fed him to the gators. *Think, Jace. Think.*

Then he had an idea. If he could pull the window out of the frame, he could get the added space he needed to wiggle through.

Aaron, please have something I can use. On his hands and knees, Jace searched Aaron's bedroom closet, feeling for anything sharp and strong.

Then froze when his fingers touched cool metal. Slowly he pulled the object free and stared. It was an AR-15. And it was loaded.

Corey had taken Jace to the shooting range when he was younger. He still remembered the basics. He didn't want to use a gun, but he would if it meant getting away.

He set the rifle aside, his heart now beating a mile a minute. *Stay calm. Stay focused.* He wasn't going to be able to shoot his way out. Corey, Ed, and Bobby all had guns.

What was this camp, anyway? Was Corey a drug dealer, too? Was Dewey?

Stop. Pay attention. Search for tools.

He touched another metal . . . something. A box. It was a little rusty because it was wet out here in the bayou, but it was just a box, about four inches tall and a foot wide. He lifted the lid and gaped.

Money. Stacks of money. There had to be hundreds—no, thousands—of dollars.

Oh my God. Aaron *was* a drug dealer. *Aaron, why?*

Then he remembered the night he had seen Dianne at her kitchen table, crying about the medical bills. Liam had just been diagnosed and they didn't have good enough insurance to pay for his experimental treatment. Aaron had left his job at the fancy financial firm in New

Orleans to start his own business, but he'd left his good insurance behind, too.

Aaron must have sold drugs to pay for Liam's bills. But that didn't make it right.

Nor would the money help Jace get away. *Focus. You have to get away.*

There was nothing else in the hiding space, so he put the money box and the rifle on the bed, then sat beside them.

He looked up, feeling defeated, then blinked.

Oh. There was a toolbox on the top shelf of the closet. *Okay, then.*

The toolbox had a hammer, a screwdriver, and a chisel that he could use. He'd taken out windows before while helping Corey demo a house they'd been hired to renovate.

It was easier than he thought. He lifted the windows from their tracks and laid them on the floor. Then he took the hammer and pried the metal frame from the window.

It felt like it had taken hours, but it was probably less than thirty minutes before he had a completely open window. *Now, to get out of here.*

He took the rifle, grabbed one of Aaron's dark jackets that he'd seen hanging in the closet, then considered the money box. He'd need some money, but . . . It was drug money.

Don't think about that right now. Just take some.

Hands shaking, he took a stack of twenties bound together with a rubber band and stuffed it into the jacket pocket. Then he squeezed through the window, grimacing when his shoulders still scraped the sides. He dropped quietly to the ground and held his breath, listening.

Nothing but the night.

He crept to Dewey's workshop, exhaling in relief when he saw that Dewey's keys were still on the workbench. Grabbing them, he made his way to the dock, sure that he'd be discovered at any moment.

But he wasn't. *Keep going.* He eased into Dewey's jon boat and untied the rope holding it to the dock. He'd row for a little while—or until he heard Corey coming after him.

Don't think. Just go.

Taking the oars in each hand, he gave a push and . . . he was moving in the direction that he and Corey had come from when they'd returned from Cardozo's house. He wanted to yell with excitement, but he didn't make a sound. He didn't know where exactly he was going, but anywhere was better than here.

Mid-City, New Orleans, Louisiana
TUESDAY, OCTOBER 25, 10:25 P.M.

'Finding anything?' Kaj asked.

Val looked up from her laptop as he put a cup of coffee on the table in front of her. 'Thank you and not yet. I've gone through Aaron's finances and employment history, trying to find out where he connects with Dewey Talley and Sixth Day, since they're so anxious to break Aaron out of jail. If I can find how they know each other, that might give us more details about Dewey's life. Very little is known about him.'

He hesitated. 'Can you take a short break?'

She closed her laptop. 'Of course.'

Kaj took the chair beside her, and dammit, he smelled too good. Like sandalwood and orange. The orange was from the dishwashing detergent he'd used to wash the dinner dishes.

MaryBeth, Jess, and Patty had left shortly after she and Kaj had returned from the garage after talking to André. Val had nearly begged them to stay a little longer, because while she'd taken in stride the information André had shared in the call, she wasn't anywhere ready to deal with Kaj's almost-kiss.

She still hadn't figured out how to think about it. She knew she was flattered. She knew she was interested. Hell, she would have kissed him back without a second thought, even though Elijah and her friends hadn't been even twenty feet away. Luckily André had broken the moment, because she also knew that it wouldn't have been right.

Kaj seemed like the type to want to talk about it, which was why she'd nearly begged her friends to stay. But Patty had to finish out her evening shift at Le Petit Choux, and MaryBeth and Jess always had an early morning at the bakery. So she'd let them go with a shaky wave.

After they'd left, Elijah had gone to bed, Czar at his heels, and Kaj had busied himself with cleaning the kitchen. Burke had called their IT guy, Antoine, to install cameras around the house and pointing at the street. Both Antoine and Burke were monitoring the cameras with their phones, enabling Val to step away from the window for a while. Burke was still outside, watching the perimeter. They were all antsy after Sixth Day's direct letter to Kaj.

Burke paced when he was antsy, so he'd taken first shift outside.

Val had resumed her study of the background information that Antoine had sent her earlier in the day, tuning out the sounds of clanking pots and pans so that she'd been able to hear Elijah's soft breathing through the monitor she'd placed next to her laptop. But the silence between her and Kaj had hung heavy in the air the entire time.

Now it appeared to be time for the talk.

Kaj wrapped his hands around his mug and stared straight ahead. 'I'm sorry,' he murmured. 'I was out of line earlier. I hope I didn't offend you.'

She studied his profile, searching for the right words to say. *Tell the truth.* 'I wasn't offended. I was flattered. And—at that moment— willing. So you didn't do anything wrong.'

'You're kind to say so. But I . . .' He looked at her then, his eyes haunted. 'You never said what happened to you . . . before. With the man who, you know, sought you out.'

Val hated this part. Rehashing past pain. But he didn't seem to be finished, so she said nothing.

'I don't know what you went through,' he continued. 'I don't want to . . . scare you.'

At least she could allay his worry on this. 'You didn't. I'm not afraid of men, Kaj. Not most men, anyway. Big men sometimes trigger bad memories. Like MMA-fighter big. But I've had relationships since then.' Her lips curved. 'Usually with men built like you.'

He exhaled, his relief plain. Then his eyes changed from haunted to interested. 'Yeah?'

'Yeah. But not with men I work for. It's not in Elijah's best interest.'

He nodded once. 'I understand. But after this is all over with and he's safe again?'

'Are you asking me out on a future date, ADA Cardozo?'

He blushed and it was sweet. 'Would you say yes if I did?'

'Yes, I would.'

'Good.' He heaved another sigh of relief. 'I'm so glad that's over with. I'm out of practice. I haven't had a relationship since Heather— my wife. I haven't even been tempted. But you caught my interest the first time I saw you last summer at that party at Gabe Hebert's house. And . . .' He swallowed hard but didn't break his gaze. 'You tempt me.'

Merciful heaven. Her body clenched and Val pressed her palms to her heated cheeks to cool them. 'For someone who claims to be out of practice, I think you're doing just fine.'

He grinned abruptly, making him look carefree. 'Really? Excellent.'

She laughed, her heart suddenly light. 'So we table this—whatever it is—until Elijah is safe and you no longer need me, right?'

He sobered. 'Until Elijah is safe.'

She noticed that he didn't repeat the part about no longer needing her. She liked that.

He pointed to her laptop. 'Show me what you got from Antoine. Now that it's quiet, I think I'll be able to give it my attention.'

She opened the laptop and tilted it so that he could see the screen. 'I told you this afternoon that Aaron used to work at Cunningham and Spector, the same company Van was working for when he died, but then Aaron quit and hung his own financial advising shingle.'

'Right,' he said. 'And?'

'And I've been reviewing the loan and debt statements from his background check. He continued making deposits into his and his wife's joint bank account from his business up until last week. Then all of a sudden, his bank account is cleaned out.'

'Well, he was paying for drugs.'

'True, or at least he was last week when he was high. Did he show signs of repeated drug use?'

'Track marks all over his arms, and the jail infirmary doctor said that the violence of his detox indicates prolonged drug use—both heroin and meth.'

'So he's been using for a while. He was paying for drugs all that time, but suddenly his bank account is empty. Don't people usually do that when they're getting ready to run?'

He nodded. 'That was my conclusion, too. Neither he nor his girlfriend, Sandra Springfield, would talk about their plans, but they're both in detox and not really coherent. So NOPD interviewed Dianne Gates, Aaron's wife, and she said that Aaron and Sandra were planning to go to the Bahamas together. She was quite bitter about that fact, so we might be able to get more out of her if we ask the right questions.'

'Okay, good. Hold that thought. I'm also wondering about his reported income. I inherited Van's house when he died. I'm also the executor of his estate. As such, I had to do his taxes for the year he died. Van was a superstar at Cunningham and Spector, but Aaron, working alone, claimed nearly three times Van's income.'

'You're thinking that Aaron inflated his income.'

'Exactly. Hold that thought, too. Finally, I'm wondering about his relationship with Dewey Talley, a known drug dealer. Did NOPD ask Dianne Gates about him?'

'They did. She said they were friends and that Dewey worked on their cars.'

'They might be friends, but it's more likely that Dewey was Aaron's dealer.'

'Agreed. And?'

'Well, Sixth Day's business was very good before Rico Nova went to prison for killing my brother and before Talley went under. Back then, they focused on lower-socioeconomic areas and students— middle school through university. According to Burke's pal in Narcotics, Talley's rumored to be supplying upper-class clients and society wives. Aaron's clientele from his financial advising business were *also* upper-class clients and society wives.'

Kaj's dark brows lifted. 'You think that Aaron was sending clients Dewey's way?'

'It's possible. It would explain the inflated income numbers. He could have been laundering drug money through his legit business. I think they're in a partnership. It might also explain why Sixth Day is going to such extremes to try to get him back, although that whole angle still doesn't make sense.' She frowned as she organized her thoughts. 'Sixth Day signed that note and they gave up Rick Gates, but Aaron hasn't been charged with drug dealing, just the murder. Yet they've tried, in a very public way, to free him. It's like a neon sign declaring his guilt, even though Aaron had never been tied to Dewey.'

'That's been bothering me, too. Unless they knew that we had the photo of the two of them together. It's incriminating, both because Dewey is a wanted felon and because Sandra hid the images.'

'So it's not out of the question that Dewey and Aaron were working together.'

'Not out of the question at all.'

'Who knew about the photos that you retrieved from Sandra's house?' she asked.

'Me, my boss, my assistant, André, and the NOPD officers and homicide detectives who were searching her house after her arrest.'

She studied him carefully. 'How much are you trusting the NOPD to solve this?'

He sighed. 'André will do his job. He'll go above and beyond. I'm not worried about him. But like I said earlier, I've already made a lot of enemies within the NOPD.'

'And whoever dropped off Rick was bold. That they didn't think you'd have security was one of the first things that occurred to me. Which was why I asked Burke—'

A human whimper came through the monitor, followed by a canine whine.

Kaj jumped to his feet with a gasp. 'Elijah.'

Val pushed past him. 'Me first,' she said over her shoulder. 'Czar isn't barking, so I'm sure he's fine. Let me give you the all-clear.' Of course, he totally disregarded her warning, following her up the stairs.

Gun drawn but at her side, she opened the bedroom door and relaxed. Elijah lay in his bed curled up in a ball. Czar had climbed up beside him, his huge head on Elijah's pillow. Distressed, the dog looked up when Val entered. Elijah was still whimpering in his sleep.

The boy woke with a start, his breath sawing in and out of his lungs. 'What happened?'

'It's fine,' Val said, holstering her weapon before crossing the room to sit on the edge of his mattress. She ran a hand over Elijah's back, then scratched Czar behind his ear. 'You were having a bad dream. Czar was whining. It's what he does when I have a bad dream.'

Disoriented, Elijah nodded. Without his glasses he looked even younger, and her heart hurt. He should never be afraid. But he was. He was also valiantly trying to hold back tears.

She looked over her shoulder to see Kaj hesitating in the doorway. His face was pale and drawn and she wanted to soothe him, too, but Elijah was her priority. 'He's okay, Kaj,' she said softly, then returned her attention to Elijah. 'What did you dream, honey?'

'Them,' he said, his voice trembling. 'Grabbing me. But Rick, not the other guy.'

Val rubbed the boy's back soothingly. 'The man with the tattoo who told you to run.'

'His eyes were sad.' Elijah blinked. 'I saw him. His eyes.'

Val's hand stilled. 'You saw his eyes? In your dream?'

'Well, yeah, but also in real life. Last night. I told the police that I saw them, but I couldn't see what color they were. But I didn't remember how sad he looked.'

Val resumed rubbing his back, unsure if this was a real memory or not. 'Did he say anything? In the dream?'

'He said "I'm sorry." But I don't think he said that in real life.'

'Sometimes your mind tries to re-create or rearrange events to be less painful. It's happened to me, too.'

Elijah frowned. 'Really?'

'Really. Do you think you can go back to sleep?'

'I'll try.' He glanced up at her. 'Will you stay until I do? Dad, too?'

'Of course,' Kaj said, perching on the edge of the bed beside her.

'Of course,' she echoed, tucking the blanket around him, feeling a pang of longing. This was what she'd always wanted. A child to tuck in at night. Which didn't matter. Elijah was not hers. *But I can care for him while I'm here.*

She continued rubbing his back, keeping her touch light. Czar pushed his muzzle into Elijah's neck with a doggy sigh. 'He likes it when I sing to him,' she offered.

Elijah peered up at her owlishly. 'For real?'

'For real. When he was a puppy, it was the only way to keep him from howling at night.'

Elijah considered this. 'You can sing to him. I won't mind.'

Smiling, Val smoothed her hand over his white-blond hair. 'Okay.' She began to sing the old Norwegian lullaby her mother had sung to her and Van. And Val had later sung it to Sylvi, but she wasn't going to think about her sister. It sent her mind into dark places.

Once Elijah started breathing deeply, she quieted her song to a hum, stopping only when he started to snore. Leaning over, she kissed Czar's head. 'You watch over him, okay?'

She rose and turned to Kaj, and her breath stuttered. He was staring at her like she'd hung the moon. Which didn't suck, she had to admit.

She reached out her hand, tugging him to his feet when he took it. Silently they made their way downstairs to the living room, where she crossed her arms over her chest, feeling suddenly vulnerable.

'Heather used to sing to him,' he said, voice unsteady. 'Thank you.'

'He's a sweet little boy. You're very lucky.'

'I know.' He scrubbed his palms over his face. 'What are you going to do now?'

'Check with Burke, then grab a few hours' rest so I can take over duty later. Burke's doing perimeter checks twice an hour and Antoine will be monitoring the cameras while I sleep. Czar is with Elijah, so you don't need to worry.'

He regarded her soberly for a long moment. 'Thank you. I'll sleep with my door open. Yell if you need anything. I'm a pretty light sleeper.'

Bayou des Allemands, Louisiana
TUESDAY, OCTOBER 25, 10:25 P.M.

Corey studied Zach and Allyson. She looked the same as she always did. Tense, but level. Zach was twitching, moving in his chair like he couldn't sit still.

'Ed, can you put the map on-screen?' Corey asked.

Ed did so, then tossed the pointer to Corey. 'All set.'

'Thanks. This is the road from Bella Butler's house. This part here'—he pointed to an area close to Bella's house—'is where we'll strike. Allyson, you've said that she'll be riding in the middle SUV of three. One in front and one in back to guard her. Is that still accurate?'

'Yes,' Allyson said.

'Good. This part of the road has no streetlights. The rest of her security force won't see the threat until it's too late.' He pointed to the exact place they'd scoped out. 'Your job, Allyson, is to get yourself assigned to the first car. Do whatever you have to do to make sure her car slows down as she's passing over this spot. Zach, you're in the last car and you make sure that she can't back up or get away. That's all you have to do. We'll take care of the rest.'

The 'rest' was the planting of the roadside bomb that would take out Bella Butler's SUV.

Allyson remained stone-faced, but Zach swallowed hard. 'What are you going to do?' the medic asked in a voice that trembled.

'Not your business,' Corey said brusquely. 'Your jobs are clear. Allyson makes sure she slows down over that patch of road. You make sure she doesn't back up.'

Zach licked his lips, his skin gone pale. 'You said you were going to hit Bella's car.'

'Yes. That hasn't changed.' Corey tilted his head. 'What has changed, Zach?'

'You're going to kill her,' Zach whispered.

'They were *always* going to kill her, you idiot,' Allyson snapped. 'That's what this has always been about. Haven't you been paying attention? Why else would they want to know her every movement? Why else would they want to know when she's leaving her house for the trial? Good God, man. Are you stupid?'

'No,' Zach snapped back. 'I just thought that it would be a car accident or something. Something she could survive.'

'Well, it's not something she'll survive.' Allyson looked away from him. 'Just do your job, Zach. I don't know what they have on you, but I don't want my secrets exposed.'

Corey leaned into Zach's space. 'What has changed?' he repeated.

Zach swallowed again. 'Bella was going to leave her husband and daughter back at the house for the trial, but she changed her mind. They'll be in the car with her.'

Allyson flinched, but immediately returned to her normal, cold demeanor. 'So?'

Zach jerked his head sideways to stare at her, appalled. 'So? We can't let them hurt that little girl. She's only six.'

Allyson pursed her lips. 'It's either that or a court-martial for me. I'm choosing myself.'

'But—' Tears formed in Zach's eyes. 'She's just a child.'

'Fuck,' Corey muttered, and for a moment Zach brightened as if thinking that having a child die would be enough to stop the operation. Corey motioned to Bobby. 'He's of no use to us anymore.'

Bobby grinned. 'This is my lucky day.' He grabbed Zach by the arm, dragging him out the door. Zach fought but he was only about five-ten, no match for Bobby's six feet, five inches of muscle.

He waited until Bobby and Zach had left before looking at Allyson. Her expression was grim—and unsurprised at the boom of Bobby's overcompensating gun when he shot Zach.

'Well?' Corey asked.

Allyson shrugged like this was no big deal. 'He didn't have the stomach for it.'

Corey was going to say *Good*, but his phone buzzed with a text from Bobby.

Dewey's boat is gone. Did you lock Jace in?

Swallowing back fury and panic, Corey sent a reply. *I did. Did the rope break?*

No. Should I search for the boat?

Yes. Go now. Will check cameras and call you asap.

He noted Bobby's thumbs-up emoji before turning to Allyson. 'We're issuing you a burner for the upcoming job. Keep it with you at all times and watch for further updates. Ed and I will get the burner from the safe in the next room. Get your things together. We're leaving in a few minutes to take you back to your vehicle.'

He followed Ed out of the comm room, locking the door behind them.

'What's wrong?' Ed demanded. 'We still have details to cover and we don't have a safe out here.'

'Dewey's boat's gone.' Using his phone, Corey checked the cameras pointing at the dock, rewinding the surveillance video until he saw movement. 'Fuckin' hell.' There was Jace getting into Dewey's boat. 'The little bastard. We need to find him.'

Ed was also staring at his phone, his mouth set in an angry line. 'How'd he get out?'

'I don't know. Bobby has already started the search. We'll take Allyson back to her car in my boat.'

'Goddammit, Corey. Your brothers aren't worth the trouble they've caused.'

'I agree. I'll check Aaron's quarters. I want to know how Jace got out. You check the camera feeds again once you're back in the comm room to make sure she didn't touch anything she shouldn't. Make sure she sees you do it. I want her sufficiently scared of us.'

'I think you achieved that. She acted all cool when Bobby shot Zach, but she was rattled. I'll meet you at the dock in three minutes.'

'Okay.' Corey made it to Aaron's quarters in less than a minute, struggling with the lock in his haste. He burst into the cabin, grimacing at the lingering odor of Aaron's meth.

Then his heart dropped into his gut.

The window was gone. Jace had ripped it out. *'Motherfucker,'* he hissed.

Rage rushed up in a wave, accompanied by a sense of dread. He stalked to Aaron's bedroom window, and his dread became a living thing. From here, Jace would have had a perfect view of the river's edge—and of them killing Dewey.

I should have thought of that. But he hadn't, so certain that he had Jace cowed. And it was too late now. He needed to find his brother. Yesterday.

At least that solved the problem of what to do with Jace. 'I'm going to find him and I'm going to kill him.' And he'd make it hurt.

Bayou des Allemands, Louisiana
TUESDAY, OCTOBER 25, 11:30 P.M.

Jace looked over his shoulder. No other boats. He couldn't believe he'd gotten away.

Don't count your chickens, he told himself sternly. He wasn't safe yet.

He'd turned on the motor once he'd rowed for five minutes. It was a small motor and he had crossed his fingers that he was far enough away that Corey wouldn't hear it.

Or Bobby or Ed. Or the two people they'd brought in on Bobby's boat.

Who were they and why were they there? Was Corey a drug dealer, too?

He rounded a bend and nearly cried in relief. There was the dock Corey had used when they'd returned from Cardozo's house. Parked on the gravel lot were five vehicles. The minivan Corey had been driving, a Chevy SUV, and Dewey's Dodge truck had been there earlier. The Honda and the Hyundai were new, probably belonging to the two blindfolded strangers.

Carefully, he guided the jon boat to the dock and tied the boat to the piling. Rifle in hand, he scrambled up onto the dock, his heart hammering in his chest. *Almost there.*

He nearly dropped the keys three times trying to unlock the truck but finally succeeded. *Don't celebrate. Don't think. Just go.* He set the rifle on the floorboard at his feet, then cranked the engine to life. Then exhaled. *Almost there.*

He still didn't know where he was going, but he was one step closer to getting away. He'd started to back out of the parking area when the moonlight flashed off Dewey's boat. It was like a neon sign telling Corey where he'd gone.

He jumped from the truck and ran back to the dock, untying the boat and shoving it back into the river. It would float back downstream, toward where Corey's camp was. With any luck, Corey wouldn't think he'd made it this far and would search for him closer to camp.

He ran back to the truck, threw himself behind the wheel, and started to drive. The road was gravel, but it soon dead-ended at a real road. They'd turned left on the way back from Cardozo's, so Jace turned right.

Another road sign, with words he recognized. TO NEW ORLEANS.

That was where Rick was. He'd dropped Rick on Cardozo's lawn like he was trash. *I have to fix this.* He had to get Rick out of Cardozo's hands.

And if you get caught? If someone's found out that you were the driver?

Fear had his chest freezing up. *Breathe. Breathe.*

Jace thought about jail. Then he thought about Corey shooting Dewey in the head and shoving his body into the water for the gators. Then laughing about it.

Even jail would be better than staying with Corey.

And if Rick wasn't at Cardozo's?

I'll find Dianne. She'll help me. Once I sober her up, anyway.

He clutched the steering wheel, forcing himself to breathe. *I got away. I can do this.*

10

'Kaj,' a voice hissed. 'Wake up.'

Kaj swatted at the hand shaking his shoulder.

'Kaj. I said, wake up!'

He opened his eyes, clarity returning in an instant when he saw Val standing over him, a finger against her lips. His heart rate went from zero to racing in a single breath. 'Where's Elijah?'

'In his bed. With Czar. He's fine, but there's someone outside. Come with me.'

Without another question, Kaj followed her into Elijah's room. She knelt by his son's bed and shook him gently. 'Elijah? I need you to wake up.'

Elijah snuggled deeper into the covers. Czar lifted his head and stared up at Val. 'Czar, come,' she said and the dog obediently jumped off the bed and trotted around to sit at her side. 'Elijah. Come on, honey. Wake up.'

'He's a very heavy sleeper.' Kaj scooped his son into his arms. Elijah's head lolled, then settled on his shoulder. *My baby.* 'Where are we going?'

She drew her gun. 'Downstairs, in case we need to leave in a hurry.'

Don't panic. You need to be calm for Elijah. Think. 'We need to call 911.'

'I called André. He's on his way.'

'Good.' Carefully, he carried his son down the stairs and laid him on the sofa. Elijah never even opened his eyes.

Val led Czar to the front door and told him to stay. The dog obeyed, sitting up straight and tall and looking more like a small bear than a dog.

'What happened?' Kaj whispered when Val returned to the sofa.

'I was watching the cameras and saw a truck pass by four times. The driver was circling the block.'

The driver. 'Dewey Talley?'

'Don't know. Burke was asleep on the sofa. I woke him up and he went outside. I went upstairs to guard Elijah.'

Because that was what he'd hired her to do. A sliver of calm worked through him. And then evaporated when a loud noise had him spinning toward the back of the house. It sounded like something— or someone—had been slammed up against the exterior wall.

'Fuck,' Kaj hissed, poised to throw himself over his son. 'What the hell?'

Val was now positioned between the sofa and the front window, standing sentry over Elijah even as she aimed her gun at the back door.

Three brisk knocks broke the silence, followed by the buzzing of her cell phone. Not taking her eyes from the back door, she answered, then listened, then ended the call.

'Burke's going to open the back door, but he wants your permission before he brings our visitor inside.'

Kaj's blood ran cold. 'Visitor?'

'A teenager, says his name is Jace Gates.'

Kaj's mouth fell open in shock. 'Jace Gates? What the hell?'

'Apparently he wants to speak to you.'

'It could be a trap. Distract us, then come at Elijah.'

'It's possible,' she allowed. 'But we're covered. As soon as I woke Burke, we called for reinforcements. One of Burke's guys—Lucien—is only a few blocks away. He should be here any minute. And André's on his way. Antoine is watching the camera feed. We have your house covered. Go and see what the kid wants. I'll stay here with Elijah.'

Kaj knew that she'd keep his son safe. He also knew that he should be terrified. But all he was was furious. He stalked to the back door and threw it open.

Burke stood with a blond man wearing jeans and a jacket. *Teenager, my ass*. The man was at least as tall as Kaj with wide shoulders. His hands were cuffed at his back, but Kaj couldn't see his face because he'd dropped his chin to his chest, his posture one of defeat.

Don't trust him. He's a Gates. They want to hurt Elijah.

But this Gates was controlled, at least for the moment. One of Burke's hands gripped the collar of his jacket. The other held him by the forearm.

'Sorry to wake you,' Burke drawled. 'But you've got company. I frisked him. He's clean. May be better to have a conversation indoors, where the neighbors won't hear.'

Kaj had considered that only a moment before a light flicked on in the next-door neighbor's window. The woman was the worst kind of gossip. He wouldn't put it past her to sell their story to the highest media bidder.

'I don't want him anywhere near Elijah.'

'Agreed. We'll keep him in the kitchen until André gets here.'

Kaj stood back so that the two could enter, then closed the door, both hands balled into fists. He wanted to hit the bastard. He wanted—

God. The kid really was young. In the light of the kitchen, Jace Gates—*if that's who he really is*—had a baby face. A baby face streaked with dirt.

And tears.

'On your knees,' Burke barked, pushing on the boy's shoulders.

The kid's knees buckled like soggy cardboard and he hit the floor so hard that Kaj winced. Hunching over, the kid curled into himself, shaking with silent sobs.

Kaj didn't want to feel sympathy. He knew better.

But he felt some anyway.

Maybe it was knowing that Rick had been tortured. What had been done to Jace?

'Look at me, please,' Kaj said quietly.

It took a moment, but the boy obeyed, sniffling. He had clear blue eyes, not bright sky blue like Val's, but more like a field of cornflowers. Tears tracked through the dirt on his face and he seemed to be valiantly trying to stay in control.

The kid smelled bad. Like sour sweat and chemicals.

No, like cat piss. Kaj had smelled that same odor before—most recently on Aaron Gates. It was meth. But the kid wasn't high. Not at this moment.

'Who are you?' Kaj asked harshly.

'Jace Gates. Sir. I already told him.' He gestured at Burke with a tilt of his head. 'I don't mean you no harm, sir. I'm trying to find my brother.'

This could be a trap. Send Jace in the back while Dewey Talley comes in the front for Elijah. New fear spiked in Kaj's heart and he rounded the counter that separated the kitchen from the dining room to check on his son.

Elijah was, unbelievably, still sleeping. Val was, very believably, still standing guard. She gave him an even nod and he returned to where Jace Gates cowered on his kitchen floor.

A moment later he saw Val back her way to the edge of the counter. She was still close enough to Elijah to protect him, but also close enough to hear what Jace Gates had to say.

She slid her phone onto the counter so that it leaned against a stack of cookbooks, pointing toward the kitchen where Jace knelt. The camera app was open and the red video recording light was on. *Smart thinking*. Kaj checked that Jace was centered in the frame, then gave her a nod before turning his attention back to the crying boy kneeling on his kitchen floor.

'Which brother?' Kaj asked. 'I understand you have three.'

'R-R-Rick,' Jace stuttered. 'Is he alive?'

'He is.'

Jace seemed surprised at this. 'He is? Is he hurt? Did you . . .' He looked up, fear in his eyes, but there was courage, too. 'What did you do to him?'

'Nothing,' Kaj said. 'He was dropped off here earlier tonight and I called the police. They took him to the hospital because he was unconscious.'

Jace pursed his lips. 'Corey,' he muttered, then straightened his shoulders. 'What are you going to do to me?'

Kaj met the kid's terrified eyes. If he was acting, he was damn good. 'Depends. Your brother tried to kidnap my son. He deserves to go to jail. What do you deserve?'

New tears welled in the kid's eyes along with fresh terror. 'I don't know. I just . . . I don't know what to do. I don't want to go to jail, but . . .' He shuddered. 'I deserve that, too. Just please don't hurt my brother. He was wrong, but he was scared. We both were scared.'

The hairs on the back of Kaj's neck stood up straight. *We both were?* Rick certainly had been. He'd had a right to be, based on the burn marks that the ER doctor had found on his genitals. Had Jace also been tortured? And why did Jace believe he deserved jail?

What had been Jace's part in the abduction attempt?

Kaj crouched down so that he and Jace were at eye level. 'Tell me the truth. And start from the beginning. I'll help you if I can.'

'Will I have to go to jail?'

The question sounded so frightened, so vulnerable, that Kaj felt another spear of compassion. 'Depends on what you did. I'll be able to tell you once you come clean.'

'You're young,' Burke said mildly. 'They'll take that into account.' He still stood at the boy's back, and even though his voice had been mild, his expression was fierce. He was prepared to restrain Jace if he made a move. Burke had Jace contained, and Val had Elijah safe.

That was the only thing keeping Kaj from grabbing his son and running for the hills.

Jace swallowed, his Adam's apple bobbing awkwardly. 'My brother Aaron got arrested for killing a doctor. You know that, though, because you're the prosecutor on his case.'

'I was. I was recused yesterday because your other brother tried to kidnap my son. That means I was taken off the case,' he added when Jace looked confused.

Jace winced. 'I'm sorry, sir. Rick wouldn't'a hurt your boy. I swear it.'

Kaj didn't believe that. 'That's a question for the police and the court.'

'Right. Okay. Rick thought that if we had your little boy, you'd give us Aaron.'

'I figured that out myself,' Kaj said dryly.

Jace winced again. 'I'm sorry. You said to start at the beginning.'

'Yes, I did. Please continue.'

'My other brother—Corey—he was really mad at Rick for trying to take your son.'

That was consistent with Corey's words at his press conference yesterday morning.

'Why was Corey mad?' Kaj asked. 'Did he know about it?'

'No, sir. He didn't know nothin' about it. He was mad that Rick tried.'

'All right,' Kaj said calmly, because his gut said the kid knew more than he was saying. There was desperation in his eyes. Plus, he was here. Confessing.

Above them, Burke glanced at his phone, then mouthed, 'Lucien's here.'

That lessened Kaj's tension a fraction more. 'What happened next?'

'Corey took Rick and me to his camp, down the bayou. I'd never been there before. I never even knew it existed. You can only get there by boat. And then he . . .' Jace blinked, sending new tears down his dirty face. 'He hurt Rick. Hurt him bad. He wanted to know who helped Rick plan—y'know. Trying to grab your son.'

'And did Rick tell him?'

'I don't know,' Jace said miserably. 'I heard him scream and scream and I knew they were hurting him.'

Kaj thought about Rick's burns. *Yes, they were.* 'Who was hurting him?'

'Corey and his friend Bobby. And maybe Ed. They work together. They do construction. But . . .' He frowned. 'I think they do more than that. I saw . . .' He rounded his cheeks and blew out a breath, as if bracing himself. 'They killed a man tonight.'

Kaj's brows rose. *Ah.* This was what the kid had been holding back. At least part of it. 'Who did they kill?'

'A mechanic. He worked on Corey's construction equipment.'

'I need a name, Jace.'

'Dewey. Dewey Talley.'

Burke breathed out a curse and Val sucked in an audible breath, the only sound she'd made since coming closer.

'You saw this?' Kaj demanded. 'With your own eyes?'

Jace nodded, his eyes now haunted. Again, if the kid was acting, he was truly good. 'Yessir. They hurt Dewey, too. Then they shot him.' His voice broke. 'In the head. And then they pushed him in the water. Corey *laughed*,' he said, anguished. 'Dewey was nice to me. He didn't treat me bad or call me dumb. He showed me how to work on engines. He said I was good at it. I wanted to go and live with him, but now he's dead.'

Kaj let out a breath, his thoughts churning. The man Jace described did not sound like the drug dealer the cops had been searching for. He certainly didn't sound like the kind of man who'd kidnap a child. But, based on the cops' descriptions, Dewey Talley didn't seem like the kind of man who'd have told Elijah to run, either.

'When did this happen, Jace?' he asked.

Jace frowned. 'Corey took my phone and I ain't got no watch.'

'Make a guess.'

He looked down, his mouth moving as he counted. 'Three hours ago? Maybe four?'

So after Rick had been dropped off with that note taped to his chest. *The next body we'll leave you will be that of your son.* If Dewey had been driving the van tonight, he'd died after writing the note, which meant at least Kaj didn't have to worry that he'd come back for Elijah. Someone else in Sixth Day might, but not Dewey Talley.

However, this Corey character was at least as alarming as Talley. Maybe even more so. 'That had to be terrifying.'

Jace rounded his shoulders, using them to wipe at his face. 'Dewey's dead, Rick's going to jail, Aaron's already in jail, Dianne's always drunk, and I got nobody to help me hide from Corey. I knew he'd kill me next, so I ran.'

'Why did you think you'd be next, Jace?' Kaj asked.

'Because I—' Jace clamped his lips tight, holding his words in.

'Because you what?' Kaj urged, keeping his tone soft and delicate, but his gut was screaming that this was important.

'I wanted to run away,' he finally said. 'Rick and me, we wanted to run away together. From Corey.'

That wasn't what he'd been about to say, Kaj was sure, but he'd go with it. 'Why?'

'Because Corey . . .' Jace looked away. 'He beats us. Especially Rick. It wasn't bad when we lived with Aaron and Dianne. Dianne took care of us. But then Liam got sick and we had to go live with Corey. He was mad about that. He didn't want us. I just did what I was supposed to. Well, mostly. Not school. I'm not good at school. But Rick wouldn't say "Yes, sir." He always argued and Corey would beat him. When Liam died, Corey said it shoulda been Rick who died. He hated us both, but especially Rick. So we tried to get our e . . .' He blew out a frustrated breath. 'Our independence.'

It shoulda been Rick. What a thing to say to anyone. 'Your emancipation?'

'Yes, that. Then Aaron said we could live with him again, but he went to jail and we didn't know what to do. Rick got this idea that if we could get him back, things would be okay.'

If this was true, it explained a lot. It was a harebrained scheme, one a sixteen-year-old like Rick might think up.

'You said that Corey asked Rick, who helped him plan. What did Rick say?'

'Nothing while I was there, but I've been thinkin' on it. Somehow Rick knew where your little boy would be and that the lady with him was too pregnant to fight us.' He looked up, suddenly beseeching. 'She's all right, right? The pregnant lady? I saw her fall.'

Kaj stilled. *I saw her fall.* Genie had fallen backward into the laundromat. She'd been out of view of the cameras recording the attempted abduction. Her fall hadn't been on any of the videos and it hadn't made the news.

Jace had been there.

Kaj kept his voice level. 'Yes, she's all right for now.'

Jace sagged. 'Oh, thank God.'

Kaj leaned in so that he was only inches from Jace's face. 'Jace, were you in the van?'

Jace reared back but went nowhere with Burke behind him. He was visibly trembling, but he lifted his chin. 'Do I get a lawyer? I saw that on TV. I should get a lawyer.'

'Do you need one?' Kaj asked.

Jace's eyes filled with new tears. 'Yes. I didn't mean to do it. I didn't want to do it.'

Kaj let the silence hang for a long moment. 'Do what?'

A sound from behind him caught his attention.

'*Elijah, no*,' Val said.

'I need to see,' Elijah insisted. 'I need to see. Dad, let me see!'

No, Kaj wanted to shout. But Elijah had seen the man. At least he'd seen his eyes. 'Let him come,' he said to Val.

She approached with Elijah, one hand on his shoulder, her gun in the other. 'That's as far as you go, Elijah,' she said, stopping his son ten feet from where Jace was kneeling in the kitchen.

Elijah was still in the dining room, but he had a line of sight to Jace. Kaj wasn't letting Elijah come a step closer.

Neither was Val. She gently pulled Elijah back when he struggled to free himself from her hold. 'No,' she murmured. 'No closer. Try and you're going upstairs. I'm not kidding, Elijah. This is one of those times where you have to do as I say.'

Elijah huffed. 'Fine.'

Jace blanched at the sight of Elijah, then hung his head. 'I'm sorry. I'm so sorry.'

Elijah squinted. 'I can't see him. I don't have my—' He broke off when Val fished his glasses from her pocket and handed them to him. 'Thank you.' Glasses in place, he studied Jace. 'Can you look at me?'

Jace looked up, cringing as if he was expecting a blow.

'Please say "run",' Elijah requested softly.

Jace shuddered out a broken breath. 'Run,' he whispered.

'It's him,' Elijah said. 'The driver. He was the one who told me to run.'

Mid-City, New Orleans, Louisiana
WEDNESDAY, OCTOBER 26, 1:30 A.M.

Val thought she should have been more surprised that Jace Gates had been the driver, but it all made sense. She'd never really believed that Dewey Talley had been the driver.

If Jace was telling the truth, Dewey Talley was dead. Hearing him say so had been a shock. She'd hoped for so long that Talley was dead, but now that he was?

She felt . . . robbed. *I wanted to do it myself.* She certainly didn't want Corey Gates to be the one she thanked. But that was a topic for later. Probably during her next appointment with her therapist. For now, she was here to protect Elijah Cardozo. She brushed some hair off the boy's forehead, more to soothe herself than to soothe Elijah. He leaned back into her anyway.

'You were the driver?' Kaj asked, sounding not very surprised, either. Jace nodded miserably.

'Why?' Elijah said. 'If you didn't want to, then why did you?'

'I didn't know, not until Rick told me to stop the van. I . . .' He dropped his gaze. 'I didn't know what to do and Rick . . . He's my brother. I couldn't leave him there, but I couldn't hurt you, either. Rick wasn't going to hurt you. I swear it. But it was still wrong and I'm sorry. Please.' He was crying again. 'I don't want to go to jail.'

Kaj looked at the boy with uncertainty. Whether it was doubt as to Jace telling the truth or doubt about having him charged, Val wasn't sure. Maybe both. 'There will be consequences, Jace,' he murmured. 'That could mean jail.'

Jace bowed his head. 'I know. Just . . . don't send me back to Corey. Please. I'll go to jail, but please don't send me back to Corey.'

Elijah squatted down, squinting at Jace. He was ten feet away and Val wanted to make it twenty. But Jace seemed docile enough and Burke had him restrained.

'You didn't know what Rick was planning?' Elijah asked. 'Why were you driving him in the first place?'

Jace closed his eyes. 'Rick made up this email and printed it. Said that it was from Corey and that he said we should do what it said. But . . .' He sighed wearily. 'I'm not smart. I can't read. I didn't know why we were there until . . .' He shrugged.

'Until it was too late?' Elijah guessed and Jace nodded. 'Why can't you read? Don't you go to school?'

Jace's cheeks turned a dark, blotchy red under the dirt that streaked his face. Val knew that he was fifteen, but he looked younger in the face. Maybe thirteen. His body, though . . . If the kid wore a mask, he'd pass for an adult with no problem. He was tall and broad, but skinny.

He'll grow. He'll get taller and broader and bigger.

She shoved the thought away. That might have been true, but for now he was a fifteen-year-old kid. A scared kid, unless he was a very good liar.

Jace looked away in shame. 'I went to school, but . . . it didn't take. Dianne homeschooled me for a while and Rick did all my work. When he gave me the paper to read, I just pretended that I knew what it said.'

Elijah turned to Kaj. 'That makes a difference, Dad. It has to.'

Kaj shook his head. 'That's not our call to make, son.'

Elijah's lower lip trembled. 'What'll happen to him?'

'I don't know,' Kaj admitted. 'But I'm proud of your compassion.'

Elijah jutted out his chin, looking very much like Kaj. 'He let me go, Dad. He could have grabbed me, but he let me go. He told me to run.'

Kaj rubbed his forehead. 'This isn't for us to decide. Go on up to bed, Elijah. Take Czar with you. Val? Please take him upstairs.'

'But, Dad!' Elijah looked up at Val imploringly. 'Talk to him!'

Val shook her head. 'I'm just your bodyguard, Elijah. Your dad makes the rules. Come on, honey. Things will be better when you wake up.'

Elijah folded his arms over his chest. 'This isn't fair. He let me go.'

A muscle in Kaj's cheek twitched. 'I said, go to bed. No more arguing.'

Elijah aimed a furious look at his father before—surprisingly calmly—turning on his heel to walk away. But he stopped after two steps and turned back to Jace. 'Thank you,' he said quietly. 'Thank you for letting me go.'

Then he started for the stairs, his anger evident in every step.

Val knew how he felt. She was a little irritated at being dismissed because she didn't want to miss anything, either. And she did have compassion for Jace Gates. But Elijah's safety was her primary concern.

Burke met her gaze over the kitchen counter and lifted his phone. 'Take your phone. Kaj can record on his phone. I'll FaceTime you so that you can listen in from upstairs.'

Val retrieved her phone and stopped the recording. 'Okay.'

Kaj looked contrite. 'I'm sorry. Of course you should know what's going on. But I don't want Elijah to be part of this.'

'He *is* part of this,' Burke countered. 'And if Jace is telling the truth, Elijah might have a valid point.'

Kaj's expression darkened and then he seemed to fold in on himself. 'I don't know what to think.' He looked at Val, beseeching. 'What do you think?'

She considered her answer carefully. 'Elijah knows more than I wish he knew. But yesterday morning, in Burke's office, you allowed him to be a part of the conversation. It seems . . . unfair to dismiss him now.'

'So you think he should be able to listen?'

'Burke frisked Jace. He's not armed. He's cuffed. I'll be at Elijah's side at all times and I am armed.' She crouched, waiting until Jace met her gaze. 'You let him go on Monday night, Jace. That's a stroke in your favor. But make a single move to touch him and I will not hesitate to end you. Got it?'

Jace swallowed hard. 'Yeah. I mean, yes. Yes, ma'am. I never wanted to hurt him. He's a nice boy.'

'He is. And right now, he's the only one on your side, so don't fuck it up.' She straightened and looked at Kaj. 'Ultimately your call.'

Kaj closed his eyes for a long moment. 'Okay. Don't make me regret this, kid.'

'I won't,' Jace said fervently. 'I promise.'

A knock on the front door had them jumping a little. Val checked her phone and saw a text from André. 'Captain Holmes is here,' she said.

'Captain Holmes?' Jace asked, voice quivering. 'Who is that?'

'A cop,' Val said.

Jace curled in on himself. 'He's here to arrest me?'

'Maybe,' Kaj said. 'I don't know. For now, let's take a step back, breathe, and try to make sense of this mess. I still have a number of questions for you.'

'I'll get the door,' Val said. 'Then I'll get Elijah.' She opened the door and let André in.

'I got here as soon as I could,' he said. 'I take it that you've caught your intruder?'

'Oh yeah. They're in the kitchen.' She locked the front door and left André to find his own way to the kitchen while she hurried to Elijah's room. She found him sitting on the bed, his face set in a mutinous frown. 'Hey,' she said.

He glared. 'You let him push you around.'

'Your father? Well, technically he's my boss, so I have to listen to him.' She sat on the edge of his bed, huffing out an *oof* when Czar settled on her lap. 'He's terrified, Elijah. What if Jace was sent by the men who wanted to kidnap you? Your dad wants you safe.'

'He treats me like a little kid.' Elijah folded his arms over his chest.

'I'm only the one who nearly got kidnapped. It's not like I have any say in all this. Which I should!'

'Yeah, well, I happen to agree with you. Which is why, when your dad asked what I thought, I said you should be able to listen.'

His dark eyes widened, made larger by the thick lenses of his glasses. 'You did?'

'I did. Look, I feel sorry for Jace, too, but maybe we're supposed to. This could be a trap. This is the deal. You sit ten feet away and I will stay next to you the whole time. If anything happens, you obey me—to the letter. Got it?'

'Got it. Thanks, Val.'

'Yeah, well. I hope I'm not making a mistake.'

'I knew a kid like Jace, back in New York last year. He was in my class, but he couldn't read. The other kids made fun of him. And his dad hit him, too.'

'What did you do?'

'Told my dad. He helped my friend and his mom get away. They got an apartment of their own and the dad got sent to jail.' He shrugged. 'And I helped him with his reading.'

Her heart melted. 'Did you do his work for him?'

'No! I promise that I didn't. I'd just help him sound out the words once his teacher helped him get tested. He's dyslexic and he gets extra help in school now. Maybe Jace needs extra help.'

She'd thought the same thing when Jace had mentioned his inability to read. She'd had several students with learning disabilities. 'Maybe. But for tonight, none of that matters. Tonight, he's going to be answering questions about a crime he participated in, whether willingly or not. So you listen to me, okay? If I tell you to move, you don't question me. You are my responsibility, not Jace.'

He looked up at her anxiously. 'But who's gonna take care of him? Fifteen isn't that old. He can't have a job. He can't take care of himself. Sending him to jail isn't fair.'

'Maybe, maybe not. We only know what he's told us so far, and that isn't a lot. Let him calm down and get his story straight with Captain Holmes, okay? Then we'll know more.'

Elijah was clearly skeptical. 'Captain Holmes is a good cop, right? I know my dad is nervous about who he can trust in the NOPD.'

That Elijah should know about his father's fear was disheartening. 'I trust André Holmes. He's a good man and a good cop.' She tugged on his hand. 'Let's go downstairs.'

11

VAL AND ELIJAH found Burke, André, Kaj, and Jace sitting at the dining room table. Jace was leaning slightly forward as his hands were still cuffed behind him.

'Thanks, Dad,' Elijah said quietly.

Kaj looked tormented. 'Just stay far away and do whatever Val says.'

Val snapped her fingers. 'Czar, come.' The dog sidled up to Elijah. 'Good boy.'

Jace quailed at the sight of Czar but said nothing.

Val dragged two chairs ten feet from where Jace was seated. Elijah looked disgruntled, but he sat down and began petting Czar's head.

André Holmes turned to Jace. 'I understand you've got a story to tell me.'

Jace dropped his gaze to the table. 'Yessir. But it ain't no story. It's true.'

'Can you look at me, please?' André asked gently, waiting until Jace lifted his eyes. 'Once you escaped the scene of the attempted abduction, where did you go?'

'I called Corey and he told me to meet him at the fried chicken place close to our house. Rick didn't want me calling Corey. Kept telling me not to tell Corey about the email.'

'The one you couldn't read,' André said, and Jace nodded.

'That's when I figured Rick had lied. He made me think Corey had told him to do it. I didn't know what he was going to do until he told me to stop the van and gave me a mask.'

'Why did you put on the mask?' Kaj asked.

'Rick said Corey would be mad if I didn't. I don't make Corey mad. Not on purpose.'

'Why?' André asked.

Jace looked down. 'He hits, sir. And kicks. You can see for yourself.'

André gently lifted the hem of Jace's T-shirt, displaying a large black bruise.

It was a boot print, Val realized. Her heart squeezed painfully. *Aw, honey.*

Elijah made a distressed noise. Val ran a hand over his hair, hoping that he never grew jaded, that he'd always be able to feel compassion like this.

Kaj exhaled. 'Are there more like that one?'

Jace only nodded, his cheeks growing red with shame.

'We'll take photos of your bruises,' André said gently, 'as evidence against Corey.'

'Yessir,' Jace whispered. 'Rick has them, too.'

'I know, son,' André said soberly. 'What happened when you met Corey?'

'He was with his friend Bobby. Corey gave us bottles of water. The next thing I knew, I woke up in Corey's camp in the bayou and it was almost sunup. Rick was still asleep. I guess it hit him harder because he's not as big as me.'

Val frowned. *Bobby.* She'd seen that name in the background check files that Antoine had sent her. She pulled her phone from her pocket and skimmed Antoine's email.

Kaj's brows had lifted. 'Corey drugged you?' he asked.

'Yessir. He hadn't never done that before. I wasn't expecting it.'

'Why would you?' André asked kindly.

Ah. Found it. Three Vets Construction was co-owned by Corey Gates, Ed Bartholomew, and Bobby Landry. There was a lot of information on Bobby in particular.

Val opened a text window to Burke. **Bobby Landry was a cop. He left NOPD under 'mysterious circumstances'.**

I remember him was Burke's reply. *A real psycho. Good job.* Then he slid his phone to André, who looked grim as he read it before passing it to Kaj, who paled but said nothing.

Thank goodness Rick didn't get his hands on Elijah, Val thought. The very idea of the sweet boy in the hands of psychos like Corey and Bobby was too horrible to consider.

'What?' Jace asked, looking at the men around the table. 'What is it?'

'What happened when you woke up?' André asked, ignoring Jace's question.

'Corey wasn't there, but Bobby was. Bobby . . . well, he likes to scare us. He had his gun holstered on his chest. It was a Raging Judge.'

'What's a Raging Judge?' Elijah whispered.

'A frickin' big gun,' Val whispered back. 'Fourteen inches from hilt to barrel.'

Elijah's eyes grew wide. 'Whoa,' he mouthed.

'Bobby called Dewey to come to the camp and fix Aaron's boat,' Jace was saying. 'Dewey asked me to help.'

'Dewey Talley,' André clarified. He pulled out his phone and swiped the screen to what looked like the same photo that Kaj had shown Val that morning. 'Is this him?'

'Yessir. He's . . .' Jace exhaled shakily. 'He *was* the mechanic who took care of Aaron's cars and all of Corey's work trucks and equipment.'

'And he was kind to you,' Kaj said, clearly not believing it.

'Yessir,' Jace said sincerely. 'My brothers . . . They think I'm dumb, and they're right. I can't read. Can barely write my own name. But Dewey taught me about engines. He said I was a natural. That I could come work for him someday.'

Val scowled at that. More likely that Dewey would have had Jace running drugs for him.

'Where is this camp?' André asked. 'And the boat launch?'

'I could show you exactly where on a map. I'm good with maps.'

André looked at Kaj. 'I don't want to uncuff him just yet and I'll need to if he uses the map on my phone. Do you have an old-school paper map?'

'I do.' Kaj retrieved a bound map from a shelf in the living room.

André flipped pages before sliding it over to Jace. 'This is the area.'

Val's burner buzzed with a new text. From Lucien.

What was the make/model/color/year of that truck you saw circling the block?

Dodge/no idea/white and dirty/ten years old? Looked beat-up. Why? Is it back?

Found it parked a block behind Cardozo's. Look what's on the floorboard.

A photo flashed up and Val barely controlled her gasp. It was an AR-15, just visible through the truck's window. *I'll forward to Burke.*

She forwarded Burke the photo. Seconds later, he muttered a curse to himself.

He didn't bring it to Kaj's house, she texted to both Burke and Lucien. *See if he brings it up. But do it soon in case he really is the distraction.*

Agreed, Burke replied. Once again, he passed his phone to André, who scowled. Kaj simply nodded. Hopefully that meant he'd agreed to let André draw the information out of Jace.

She wanted to believe the kid was good. She really did.

Jace looked up from the map. 'I can't point to where it is, but I think I've got it.'

Burke rose and put his finger on the map. 'Right or left of here? Up or down?'

Jace directed him until Burke's finger rested in the correct place. 'That's it.'

'That's deeper in the bayou than my camp,' Burke said. 'But I know the area. If you need a scout, I'll do it.'

'I'm sending someone right now to check it out, but if they can't find it, I'll call you in.' André put his phone away. 'So, Jace. When did Corey arrive at the camp?'

'Around noon. Maybe one? Sun was high in the sky.'

'Was that when he hurt Rick?'

'Yessir. He wanted to know who helped us. He knew I didn't know much. So Corey kept Rick to ask him more questions and sent me back to Dewey's workshop to help with Aaron's boat. But I cut my hand and went to get Corey to stitch it up.'

'Corey's a doctor?' Kaj asked, surprised.

'No. But he worked in a hospital.'

Val glanced over the background check, then texted it to Burke. *As a security guard.*

'He was a security guard in the hospital,' Burke said aloud.

Jace nodded. 'He was, but said he picked up a few things while he worked there. Always laughed when he said it. Bobby, too. I didn't get the joke, but I didn't ask.'

'I'm sorry,' Kaj said. 'I interrupted you. You went to get your cut fixed up?'

Jace looked surprised at the apology. 'Yessir.' He hesitated, then swallowed audibly. 'That's when I heard Rick screaming. Bobby found me and went to get Corey from inside. When Corey came out, I thought he'd hurt me, too, but he didn't. He was really gentle, y'know? But then he tricked me into telling him that Rick had lied.' Jace looked at the table. 'I thought Corey would be mad, but . . . he wasn't. He said he wouldn't punish me, but that I just needed to drive him somewhere.' Jace looked up at Kaj, his eyes shiny with tears. 'To here. He made me put Rick on your lawn, sir. He said if I didn't cooperate, he'd either leave me, too, or he'd shoot me in the head.'

Val's heart hurt for the boy. Elijah looked devastated.

'And then . . .' Jace shuddered. 'That dog chased me and Corey laughed and laughed.'

'Where did you go after you left here?' André asked.

'Back to the camp. He made me wear a blindfold when we were leaving to come here, but he didn't on the way back, and that scared me even more. Like he didn't care if I saw where his camp was. He'd already shown me the gun when he said he'd shoot me . . .' He exhaled wearily. 'I figured he'd beat me, too, but he didn't. He just yelled a lot. And hit me with my shoe.'

'Why?' Kaj asked softly, and Val was glad for his gentle tone. Jace looked ready to break.

'Because I cried. He said I was useless. Then he locked me in Aaron's quarters. It smelled bad and gave me a headache. This was Aaron's jacket.'

'Meth,' Kaj said, and Jace nodded sadly.

'I wasn't gonna tell you because Aaron's got enough trouble, but I figure you'll find it when you go to the camp. I found a lot of glass stuff, like in a chemistry lab. And a lot of money. I took a little when I ran. Just in case. I left it in Dewey's truck. I parked it a block away from here, Mr. Cardozo.'

Dewey's truck, Val thought. *Maybe the rifle belonged to Dewey.*

André nodded slowly and Val thought he'd ask about the rifle then, but he didn't. 'When was Dewey Talley murdered?'

'Not long after we got back. They shot him and pushed him in the water. And laughed.'

'That's when you figured you were next,' Kaj said.

'Yessir. I had to get away. Oh, I forgot. Bobby and Ed left for a while after they . . . well, after Dewey. Then they came back with two people—a man and a woman. I never saw 'em before. They were blindfolded.'

André and Kaj both looked surprised at this. 'Blindfolded?' André asked.

'They kept the blindfolds on while they walked to Corey's quarters. After that, I started looking for tools to take the window out so I could get away. That's when I found the money. And a rifle. I took it in case Corey found me, but I left it in the truck, too. I never fired it. You can check.'

Kaj nodded, looking relieved. *He wants to believe Jace, too.* 'Trust me, we will check. Why did you come here?'

'I was worried about Rick. I shouldn't'a left him here. I was too much of a coward to tell Corey no. I figured I'd hang around, maybe listen if you said anything about where you'd put Rick.' He swallowed. 'I thought he was dead. I needed to know for sure. He's at the hospital?' he asked, looking for reassurance. 'You're sure?'

'I'm sure,' André said. 'I went with him in the ambulance. He'll be okay.'

Jace's shoulders slumped, relief on his face and tears in his eyes. 'Thank you.'

'Didn't you think we'd catch you?' Burke asked.

Jace looked exhausted. 'I thought maybe, but I thought you weren't looking for me.'

André tilted his head. 'Why would you think that, Jace?'

'I heard Corey say that you thought Dewey was the driver because of my tattoo.'

Where had they gotten this information? *Bobby must still have pals on the force.*

Jace flinched when everyone stared at him. 'Didn't you think that? Was I wrong?'

'We did think that Dewey was the driver,' Kaj admitted. 'But you said that my sister had fallen down and that wasn't in any of the videos, so I knew that you were there that night. I figured that you were simply in the van, but then Elijah recognized your eyes.'

The air grew uncomfortably tense. No doubt the three men were thinking the same thing Val was: *Who's the leak in the NOPD?*

Val typed a text to Antoine. *Can you find out why Bobby Landry left NOPD? We have a leak. Someone is feeding info about Cardozo and his son. Maybe to Bobby.*

On it, Antoine replied.

Jace squared his shoulders. 'What's gonna happen to me now?'

Metairie, Louisiana
WEDNESDAY, OCTOBER 26, 2:15 A.M.

'Where the fuck is he?' Corey growled, beyond frustrated.

After Ed and Corey had taken Allyson back to the boat launch and watched her drive away, they'd met up with Bobby, who'd just found Dewey's jon boat floating downstream—no Jace aboard. Dewey's truck was gone, too, and they'd known that Jace had truly escaped.

Ed had gone back to the camp to watch over Dianne, and Corey and Bobby had taken Ed's Chevy SUV to search for the little bastard. They'd driven all over town looking for Dewey's pickup, but Jace wasn't anywhere that they'd checked.

They'd even started to drive by Corey's house, but there were two cruisers parked on the curb and a third in the driveway. The police were still watching his house, with an even greater presence than before. Like they'd learned something new. That wasn't too hard to guess. Jace had run straight to the cops. *Fuck you, Jace.*

They'd abruptly detoured and now sat in the parking lot of a twenty-four-hour grocery store. Bobby was behind the wheel and Corey rode shotgun, each trying to keep it together.

This was very, very bad.

Bobby shoved his fingers through his hair, something he did when he was at his limit. But when he spoke, it wasn't with anger. It was with quiet fear. 'Jace went to the cops.'

Corey's gut twisted and he cursed himself for not killing Jace when they'd returned from Cardozo's. 'Probably. He was really upset about Rick. He figured out he was dead.'

'And Dewey,' Bobby murmured. 'If Jace saw us kill him . . . He loved that old bastard. He was always tagging along after Dewey whenever he came to fix our trucks and stuff.'

'You're right. We have to assume he's told the cops about Rick and Dewey.' Especially with the cruisers in front of his house. No one had tripped the alarm, so they hadn't entered yet, but it was only a matter of time before they got the necessary warrants.

'We should park our vehicles off in the trees behind the boat launch in case the cops do come looking,' Bobby said. 'No need to hand over our wheels if we don't have to.'

'And Zach's car,' Corey reminded him. 'We'll have to dispose of it. But we have to also assume that Jace will tell them about the camp. We need to find a new place.'

Bobby frowned. 'Please don't say we're going to your lake camp. I hate that place.'

Corey's other property wasn't on Lake Cataouatche, but on one of the small tributaries that ran from the lake through the swamp. 'I know it's not a Holiday Inn, but—'

'It's one step up from a tent and pissing in the woods.' Bobby scowled. 'We *are* going there, aren't we? Dammit, Corey.'

'I'll tell Ed to move Dianne and all of our records to the lake camp.

The cops will find Aaron's stuff and accuse us of being in on his business. We need to destroy his and Dewey's buildings. And ours. We have to bring it all down. We have enough explosives.'

Bobby looked pained. 'Even your quarters?'

'Even my quarters. You spilled a lot of Dewey's blood in the comm room.'

'He deserved it.'

Corey pinched the bridge of his nose. Sometimes dealing with Bobby was like dealing with a toddler. 'Any CSI guy worth his salt will find traces of Dewey's blood and maybe blood from the others we've killed there.' They cleaned after each murder, but there would be trace evidence. 'They'd be able to pin a lot of murders on us. Right now, it's just Dewey and Rick, and the cops think both of them are drug dealers, so I don't see them looking all that hard for their killers. If they get blood from all of our other victims, though . . . Well, I'm not going to let that happen. So we take it all down unless you have another plan.'

'No, but . . . dammit. We just got the place the way we wanted it.'

'And when I get my hands on Jace, he'll pay for that, too. The lake camp is livable for now. It's got a generator and running water. We'll grab the satellite dish before we set off the charges. We'll rebuild. You'll like it even better. I promise.'

'Fine. But when you do find that little bastard, I want a piece of him, too.'

'Absolutely.'

Mid-City, New Orleans, Louisiana
WEDNESDAY, OCTOBER 26, 2:45 A.M.

Kaj pressed his elbows into the dining room table and dropped his head into his hands. *What a night. What an awful night.*

Val had moved to sit on his left, Elijah on her other side, Czar at Elijah's feet. André was on Kaj's right, looking grim. Burke was back outside keeping watch and Lucien had taken a still-cuffed Jace into the garage, where they'd remain while Kaj and André decided what to do.

'Kaj, what do you want to do about Jace?' André asked. 'I could take him into custody tonight, but that might be showing our hand to Corey. I've put extra personnel on his house, in case he comes back, but I don't want to scare him underground. I want to find out what that man is up to. The interview he gave is a one-eighty from what Jace described tonight.'

Elijah was watching Kaj warily, and that was a lot of pressure. If Kaj acted callously, what was he teaching his son? But if he'd misread Jace's sincerity and Elijah was hurt as a consequence? He could never live with himself.

'I don't know,' Kaj confessed. 'I want to believe him, but I'm worried that he's here to get under our defenses. And then they'll hurt Elijah.' He turned to Val. 'What do you think?'

'I think he's telling the truth, but I understand your fear. My job is to protect Elijah, not Jace. Let's look at it a different way. If we tell André to take him into custody, we'll be tipping our hand, like André said. But what are the other ramifications? Corey forced Jace to dump Rick on your front lawn. Corey wasn't afraid of security because he likely knew that you'd refused police protection. If André takes Jace into custody, what does that give away?'

'They'll hurt him,' Elijah said spiritedly. 'Whoever blabbed about Dad refusing protection will hurt Jace if André takes him away.'

'André can put Jace in a safe house,' Kaj said. 'My concern is keeping *you* safe.'

'We need to verify Jace's story.' Val squeezed Kaj's arm. 'Because that brings up yet another question. Rick knew exactly where to find you and Genie on Monday night, Elijah. How did Rick know that you'd be at math club?'

'Good question,' André said with approval. 'Elijah, we asked you on Monday night who knew that you'd be there, and you said your math teacher and the other kids in the club. Can you try again to remember if there was anyone else who knew?'

Elijah shrugged. 'Anyone, I guess. Math club is on the schedule on the school's website.'

Val stroked a lock of hair from Elijah's forehead. 'I googled you, Elijah. There's no mention of you in your dad's profile with the DA's office or on the school's website, so neither Dewey nor Rick could have found you or your math club schedule online.'

'I didn't give permission for Elijah's name or photo to be included on any of the school's promotional materials,' Kaj said. 'For exactly that reason. I rarely mention Elijah at work, either. I've never mentioned the math—' He froze as a snippet of conversation flashed in his mind. 'One day Elijah called me. He had a math meet and wanted me to come. I talked to him for a few minutes and noted the date in my calendar. I was in the lobby of the NOPD precinct in the Quarter at the time.'

'So lots of cops could have overheard you,' André said grimly.

Kaj dropped his head back to his hands. *My fault. Dammit.* Then a hand touched his back, gently. Val.

'Not your fault,' she murmured. 'You're a proud father. You should be able to talk about your brilliant son and not worry that there are vipers listening.'

'Dad,' Elijah added. 'Please look at me.'

He did, seeing only concern on Elijah's face. What had he done to deserve this kid? 'Yeah?' he asked, his voice hoarse.

'Val's right. It's not your fault.' He grinned. 'And I am brilliant.'

Eyes burning, Kaj laughed unsteadily. 'You really are. Come here.'

Elijah obeyed and Kaj wrapped him in his arms in a hard hug. 'Brilliant,' he whispered in Elijah's ear. 'And kind. I'm proud of you, son.'

Elijah let himself be held for a few seconds longer before wriggling free. 'This just underscores the reason why you shouldn't let Jace be taken into custody.'

Kaj wiped at his eyes with a sigh. 'Underscores? Really?'

Elijah shrugged. 'I *am* brilliant.'

Val chuckled. 'He's right.' Then she sighed. 'Someone in NOPD is leaking information. Corey knows that Dewey was believed to be the driver on Monday night. Corey knows that you'd refused police protection. Someone told Rick where to find Elijah. Until you know who that someone is, Jace isn't safe in NOPD custody, at least not officially. Once he shows up in the official record, Corey's coming after him. Sorry, André, but that's the way I see it.'

André rubbed a hand over his shaved head. 'Me too, unfortunately. We just need to figure out where to put him.'

Elijah opened his mouth, but Kaj shook his head. 'No. He cannot stay here.'

Elijah scowled. 'It would be the last place that Corey would think to look.'

Kaj opened his mouth, then closed it. His son had a point. 'Dammit.'

'What if,' Val said, 'we hold on to him until André can check out Corey's camp and verify his story? Maybe they'll get lucky and catch Corey and his partners. We'll ask Burke if we can keep Lucien for a little while longer. And we can keep Jace cuffed.'

'Except maybe while he showers.' Elijah made a face. 'He stinks.'

'I'll take his clothes as evidence,' André said. 'Once we know if he's a perpetrator or a victim, we'll know how to better proceed. And I'll need the date and time of that phone call about Elijah's math team. I'll have Nolan or Drysdale go through the camera feeds to ID anyone who was within hearing distance. I want this leak gone.'

'You and me both.' Kaj rubbed his temples. 'I hope I'm not making a big mistake.'

'You aren't, Dad.' Elijah's face was set in a determined look that reminded Kaj so much of Heather. 'You always say that the mark of a man is how he treats other people. That's even true when you're scared, right?'

Kaj sighed. 'I wish I'd brought you up to be a little more self-centered.'

Elijah's lips curved. 'No, you don't. You like me just the way I am.'

'I really do.' Kaj kissed the top of Elijah's head. 'Go on up to bed now. I'll be up in a minute to tuck you in.'

12

'Here.' BURKE HANDED Kaj a cup of coffee he'd poured from a thermos after Kaj stifled a yawn. He'd only slept those few hours before Val had woken him earlier. 'Val makes it strong.'

He and Burke were in an NOPD boat along with André, Officer Nolan and Detective Drysdale, who'd been at his house the night before, a second detective named Clancy, and two police divers. Two other officers had searched the night before but had found nothing.

'Thank you.' Kaj chugged the brew, which was exactly as he liked it. Val had made it for them before they'd left for the bayou—and, hopefully, Corey's camp. So far they hadn't seen anything resembling what Jace had described. 'Do you think Jace was lying?'

Burke surveyed the riverbank. 'Not necessarily. They may not have gone far enough. The bayou can get you turned around, especially when it's dark. My camp is down one of the tributaries. If you don't know where to look, you'll miss it, even in the daytime.'

They rounded a bend and Burke rose from his seat smoothly, not rocking the boat. Kaj seemed to rock it every time he moved. Before coming to New Orleans, the only time he'd been on a boat was the Staten Island Ferry. Not the same thing.

He hadn't complained, though. He was happy that André hadn't fought him coming along as the DA's rep. He was recused from Aaron's case, but this was a new case. The homicide of Dewey Talley.

Not that Kaj would have taken no for an answer even if André had fought him. He needed to see Corey's camp with his own eyes. He wanted Jace to be telling the truth.

'André,' Burke called, getting the cop's attention. 'Just up ahead. There's a dock.'

Using his binoculars, Kaj confirmed what Burke had seen. 'There are no vehicles parked nearby,' Kaj said. 'Jace said there were five there when he ran, including Dewey's truck.'

Two might have belonged to the people Jace had seen arrive blindfolded in Bobby's boat. The other two could have belonged to Corey, Bobby, or Ed. But at the moment, the land behind the dock was bare.

'Bring us closer,' André ordered, and the boat slid up to the dock.

Detectives Clancy and Drysdale hopped out. 'Tire tracks in the grass,' Detective Clancy called down. 'Fresh ones. They head toward the trees.'

Drysdale and Clancy walked toward the woods, skirting the area where the cars would have been to keep from destroying the tire tracks. A few minutes later, they reappeared, joining them in the boat.

'Three vehicles, sir,' Detective Clancy told André. 'A Chevy Suburban, a white minivan, and a Hyundai sedan. None had license plates or VINs.'

'What do you mean, no VINs?' Kaj asked. 'Are they scratched off?'

Detective Drysdale shook his head. 'Gone completely. The VINs have been removed from the dashboards and the labels from the insides of the car doors on all three vehicles. The Hyundai's floorboards were ripped out. That's where the hidden VIN is on that model—

stamped into the chassis. Someone took a blowtorch to the chassis to remove the VIN. We can check the minivan and the Chevy Suburban, but I think we'll find that their VINs are missing, too.'

André frowned. 'Is the minivan the same one that was used on Monday night in the abduction attempt? And last night when Rick Gates was left at ADA Cardozo's house?'

'It's the same make and model,' Detective Clancy said. 'We'll have Forensics check the van. We might get lucky and find fiber evidence that the quilt—or the Gates boy—were there.'

'We know that Jace took Dewey's truck,' Kaj said, 'so that leaves us with one vehicle unaccounted for. That means that someone other than Jace drove away from here last night. It also means that someone— likely Corey—destroyed the three we found. They might have used the fifth vehicle to get away.'

André pointed to Officer Nolan. 'I need you to stay here. Call for a flatbed truck to take the vehicles to Forensics and call for backup to wait with you until they get here. In case Corey and his crew come back.'

With a nod, Nolan jumped onto the dock, and André eased the boat back into the current. 'Let's keep going. Jace said that the camp was downriver from this dock.'

Mid-City, New Orleans, Louisiana
WEDNESDAY, OCTOBER 26, 8:45 A.M.

'Wake up. It's breakfast time and I'm starving.'

Jace blinked, then stared up at the ceiling in a sudden panic. 'Wh—'

Oh. Right. The ceiling belonged to Mr. Cardozo. So did the sofa he was sleeping on. He turned his head to see the man sitting in the chair beside him. Lucien. The two of them had been cuffed together ever since Jace had stepped out of Mr. Cardozo's shower and gotten dressed.

Lucien had been standing in the doorway of the bathroom as he'd showered and changed into the clean clothes that Burke had loaned him. But he hadn't stared or anything. *Just making sure I didn't do anything stupid.*

Which Jace was trying very hard not to do. They hadn't arrested him yet, so that was good. In jail people would watch every little thing that he did. He could deal with no privacy if it meant he didn't have to go to jail. He could deal with being cuffed to Lucien, too. He could deal with anything if it meant he didn't have to go back to Corey.

The man's words registered. *Breakfast.* He was hungry, too. He hadn't eaten in nearly a day. Scrambling to his feet, he followed Lucien to the table.

Val looked up from setting the table. She wore a gun in a holster on her belt, but she was smiling at him. 'Good morning, Jace. I hope you're hungry. Elijah and I made a lot of food.'

The little boy came around the kitchen counter, carrying a platter full of eggs, bacon, sausage, and . . . pancakes. Jace's mouth watered. He hadn't had pancakes in a long time.

'Hi, Jace,' Elijah said cheerfully.

'Good mornin',' Jace blurted out when everyone stopped to look at him and he realized he hadn't replied.

'You can sit here, Jace,' Val said, pointing to the left one of two chairs. 'Lucien, here.'

'I figured that out myself,' Lucien said grumpily. 'Cuffs, after all. I hope you're a leftie, kid, because if you're not, I'm eating first.'

'I am, actually,' Jace said, sitting in the chair indicated.

'Good.' Lucien sat down and immediately began to pile his plate high with food.

Jace was still. He'd wait until everyone had food and then he'd take what was left over.

Val filled a plate and put it in front of him. 'Eat, Jace. I could hear your stomach growling from the sofa.'

He looked up to find her expression kind. 'Thank you, ma'am.'

She patted his shoulder, then sat next to Elijah. 'Blood sugar this morning?'

'Good,' the boy said. 'I can have one of the small pancakes.'

Jace frowned down at his plate. He wanted to ask why a little kid was worried about his blood sugar, but he didn't ask. He glanced at Lucien and saw that the man had nearly cleaned his plate already.

'Eat, Jace,' Val said quietly. 'It's okay.'

Jace obeyed, digging in and barely managing to swallow a moan. *So hungry.* Keeping his eyes on his plate, he ate steadily, listening to the chatter around him.

'Can Czar have a pancake?' Elijah asked.

'No,' Val said. 'Not good for him. You can give him some bacon, but only one small piece. Put it on the palm of your hand and hold your hand flat.'

Elijah's giggle had Jace peeking around Lucien, and he felt his heart skip a beat. The dog was every bit as big as Jace remembered, but he was literally eating out of Elijah's hand.

The dog inhaled the bacon, then stared at Jace like he was considering eating him next.

Jace was too scared to look away. 'Is he dangerous?'

'He'll eat you if you hurt Elijah,' Lucien said.

'I won't,' Jace whispered. 'I promise.'

Val pointed to Jace's plate. 'Eat, Jace. It's not our aim to starve you.'

'Yes, ma'am.' Jace resumed eating, watching the huge dog from the corner of his eye. 'Would he really eat me?'

'If you try to hurt me or Elijah?' Val nodded. 'You betcha.'

Jace swallowed his mouthful of eggs with a loud gulp. 'I wouldn't have anyway.'

Once again, her smile was kind. 'I'm mostly sure I believe you.'

He found himself smiling back, then dropped his gaze back to his food. *Don't talk. You'll say something stupid. They already know you're stupid enough.*

'Can I ask you a few questions?' Val asked casually.

'Yes, ma'am. But can I ask one first? Did that cop from last night find Corey's camp?'

'I don't know. The people he sent during the night couldn't find it, but it was dark. Burke went with them this morning because he knows the bayou.'

'My dad went with them, too,' Elijah added.

'Don't get any ideas because everyone is gone,' Lucien warned. 'I'll take you down just like Burke did.'

'I know,' Jace said quickly. 'I just hope I did the map right.'

If they couldn't find Corey's camp, they'd think he was lying about everything and he'd go to jail. There wouldn't be anything Elijah or Val could say that would stop it from happening.

'Thank you,' Jace whispered. 'For sticking up for me.'

Elijah regarded him with eyes that looked bigger than they really were, because of his glasses. 'You told me to run. You were scared, but you still let me go.'

'I didn't want to hurt you. I swear it. Can I ask one more question? Is my brother out of the hospital?'

Something passed over Val's face. It looked like sadness. 'I'm not sure. He . . . he had some serious injuries.'

Jace fought panic. 'Will he die?'

'No,' Val said, and he relaxed, because he believed her. 'My turn now. Our background check showed that your mother died six years ago, and Aaron and Corey got custody of you and Rick. How did your mother die?'

Elijah looked up from sneaking more bacon to the huge dog. 'My mom died, too. I was five. She had cancer.'

Jace's heart hurt for the little boy. Five was really young to lose a mom. 'She was in a car accident. I was nine. My mom was . . .' He sighed, missing her so much. 'She was really nice. She worked so hard to take care of us, but she was always good and patient, even with me.'

'Was Aaron nice?' Elijah asked. 'He didn't look nice when he was killing the doctor.'

Jace winced. He knew what Elijah meant. 'He was nice back then, but he's been different for a while. I think he started doing drugs after his son Liam got sick.'

'With leukemia,' Elijah said. 'I read about it in the paper.'

Once again, Jace was ashamed. Elijah was a lot younger than him and he read the paper. *Because he's not stupid.* 'Liam died six months ago. He was really sweet,' he added sadly.

Elijah looked sad, too. 'I'm sorry.'

'Thanks.' Jace went back to eating, but everyone was watching him. Slowly he put the fork down. He only had one more bite left, but it felt wrong to eat when they were waiting.

'Keep eating,' Val said. 'We're curious about you, that's all.'

'I reckon y'all have a right to be,' Jace muttered before taking the last bite on his plate.

Val spooned more eggs onto his plate. 'You said last night that school "didn't take" for you but that Dianne homeschooled you. But you went to public school before that.'

'Yes'm. Until my mama died.'

'So until you were nine. Did your teachers talk to you about learning disabilities?'

He glanced up at her, surprised. 'I think so. One said she could help me read, but that was the year Mama died and Aaron took me out of the school. He said the school done fu—um, messed me up, so Dianne would homeschool me. It didn't take, either.'

Why was she asking about this? Was she punishing him for driving the van Monday night? By making him embarrassed about being too dumb to read?

'Well,' she said in a matter-of-fact voice. 'I'm thinking that Dianne wasn't trained to teach kids with learning disabilities, so I'm not surprised that her homeschooling didn't work.'

'I don't understand,' he admitted.

'She's saying that it wasn't your fault,' Elijah said. 'That you're not stupid. Your brain just works differently, so your teachers needed to teach you differently. Val was a teacher.'

'Not a reading teacher,' she said quickly. 'I taught math. Wherever you end up, you can get help with your reading. It's not too late for you to learn to read if you're taught the right way.'

Jace's eyes suddenly burned and he had to bite the inside of his cheek to keep from crying. If he could learn to read . . . *I could have a good life. Get a good job. Not have to live with Corey.* 'You're serious?'

'I am,' she answered. 'You're smart, Jace. Not everyone can work on engines. And not everyone can read a map like you did last night. Or remember their way out of the bayou.'

I did. I read that map. Not like reading a book, but . . . 'You think it's really not too late?'

She smiled at him and it was like . . . sunshine. Warm and bright. 'Not too late at all. Once you're settled, we'll talk. I know some teachers here in New Orleans who can help you.'

Overwhelmed, he turned back to his plate and finished his second helping quickly.

'No more bacon for Czar, Elijah,' Val said, but she sounded like she was laughing.

'He likes bacon,' Elijah said with a grin. 'When does Phin get here?'

She checked her watch. 'Soon. Why don't you clear out your closet so that he can work?'

Elijah looked disgruntled, like he wanted to stay. But he nodded. 'Okay.'

Jace wondered who Phin was, but he didn't ask.

'He's one of us, so don't try anything,' Lucien supplied, but he sounded less angry than before. Maybe he'd just been hungry. 'You're cuffed to me until Burke and André get back.'

'Yessir.'

'Another question,' Val said, checking over her shoulder to make sure that Elijah had gone upstairs. 'Do you think Corey will come after you?'

Jace was glad he'd finished eating, because he wouldn't have wanted any more food after that. 'I think so. He'll want to punish me. If there's anywhere else I can go, I will. I don't want to bring him here. Not again, anyway.'

'Us either. Do you think he'll come after Elijah?'

Jace hesitated. 'I don't know. Before last night, I would have said no because Corey was so mad at us, but Captain Holmes told me about the note Corey had taped to Rick's chest.'

Lucien's eyes widened. 'He told you about it?'

'Um . . . yessir. He asked me about it first—when he was . . .' He dropped his eyes. 'When he was taking photos of my bruises. But I didn't know about no note. I didn't even know that Rick was in the back of the van until we got here. I did know that Aaron was making meth. I told Captain Holmes that I wondered if Corey was a drug dealer, too. So maybe he is. Maybe he meant what he wrote on the note. Maybe he'll try for Elijah again. I just don't know. I'm sorry.'

'It's fine, Jace,' Val assured him. 'You're answering our questions as best you can. Did Corey work with Dewey?'

'I don't know. I don't think so? But . . .' He shrugged. 'I do know that Dewey worked for Corey and them sometimes. He fixed their trucks for their construction business.'

'Didn't you wonder why Captain Holmes had a photo of Dewey on his phone?' she asked gently.

Jace sat back, surprised. 'Not last night, but I guess I do now. Why did he?'

She looked him in the eye. 'Because Dewey Talley is known to the police. He's been selling drugs for a long time, but they haven't been able to find him for the past four years.'

So Dewey had been a drug dealer, too. 'I didn't know nothin' about the drugs. You gotta believe me on that.'

'Would you provide a blood sample?' she asked. 'They'll want to test you, to see if you've been using.'

'They can take blood. I've never used, but I was locked in Aaron's cabin. Will that show up? If I was where he was making meth?'

'No,' she said with a nice smile. 'Are you still hungry?'

He was, but he didn't want to be a pig on top of everything else. 'No, ma'am.'

'Really?'

He didn't think he could lie to her, ever. 'Maybe a little hungry.'

She scraped what was left on the platter onto his plate. 'When did you last eat?'

'Yesterday morning. We had some cereal.'

'Did Corey feed you?' Elijah asked, coming back down the stairs and sitting next to Val. 'When you lived with him, I mean.'

'Most of the time. He'd go away sometimes, on a job, and we'd take care of ourselves. Except a few times lately he forgot to leave food.' That hadn't been fun. 'We had to call Dianne, but she's not the same since Liam died. She drinks a lot. Later, once Captain Holmes finds Corey's camp, I need to call her. If she's sober, she'll be worried about me.'

Val tilted her head. 'Corey does construction jobs out of town?'

'Maybe? But the times he forgot to leave grocery money he must have been doing something else, at least one of the times. Rick and I went to the construction office to see if anyone had left food in the fridge there. All their tools were still there.'

She leaned forward, propping her chin on her hand. 'Do you remember when that was?'

He took another bite, thinking. 'Labor Day weekend and the week after. Why?'

'Corey killed Dewey,' she said. 'He's up to something, don't you think?'

Jace remembered the people who'd arrived in Bobby's boat, all blindfolded. 'Yeah. I think you're right.' And it wasn't good. None of this was good.

Except maybe how nice Val and Elijah had been. That wouldn't last forever, though, so he wasn't planning to get used to it.

Val's phone buzzed and she answered it, but not on speaker. 'Yeah?' Her lips tilted in a smirk. 'I know.' A pause. 'Affirmative to both.' Then her eyes widened. 'What the hell? Are you serious?' She listened a little, then nodded. 'Call me when you know more. Bye.' She ended the call, looking stunned.

'What happened?' Jace asked. 'Is it Corey? Is he coming?'

'I don't know,' she murmured.

'Who was it?' Lucien asked.

'Kaj.'

'Did they find the camp?' Elijah asked.

She grimaced. 'Yes. And no.'

Bayou des Allemands, Louisiana
WEDNESDAY, OCTOBER 26, 8:45 A.M.

Kaj smelled it before he saw it. André had piloted the NOPD boat downriver from where they'd found the vehicles, rounding one bend after another, when the stench of something burning filled his nose. The odor was a mix of the smoky smell of burned wood and the acrid odor of burned plastic. His eyes, intent on watching for Corey's camp, began to water.

A thin plume of smoke rose over the trees, its source visible as they rounded another bend and four piles of rubble and ash came into view. Two large piles, one medium-sized, and one small. There had been four structures here, just as Jace had said, but they were no more.

Kaj blinked, trying to clear his eyes. 'When were they destroyed?'

'We're gonna find out,' André said, frustration evident. 'Fucking hell. What a mess. Jones and Mendez, you guys suit up and start diving. There should be a body down there.'

Whoever had destroyed the structures had left the dock intact, so at least there was that. Burke tied the boat to the dock, and everyone got out except for the divers.

Kaj didn't relish the thought of anyone going into that water with its resident alligators and snakes, but the divers didn't seem too worried. He supposed they had a lot of experience diving in murky, reptile-infested water like this. *Better them than me.*

'It's still hot,' Burke called over from one of the larger piles of debris. 'And I smell the remnants of explosives along with all the other odors. I don't think it's been more than twelve hours since detonation.'

'I agree,' Detective Clancy said. 'That structure over there has a lot of metal pieces sticking up out of the rubble. Looks like engine parts.'

'Dewey's workshop,' Kaj said. 'How long will it take a forensics team to process this?'

'Days,' André said grimly. 'Sons of bitches.'

Kaj stepped aside when the two detectives began taking photos. Lifting his binoculars, he surveyed the riverbanks.

Burke came to stand beside him. 'What are you looking for?'

'Any sign of Corey or his friends, in case this is a trap and they're out there waiting for us.' Kaj wouldn't put it past them, especially as Corey had tortured Rick and murdered Dewey. 'Luring us in and shooting us would be par for the course.'

'Fair point,' Burke murmured.

They were all wearing bulletproof vests, but Kaj was taking no chances.

He froze as an image filled the lenses of his binoculars. 'Shit.'

Burke was instantly turning to search in the same direction. 'What?'

'There's an arm stuck on the roots of that tree at eleven o'clock,' Kaj said. He handed the binoculars to Burke.

'An arm with a tattoo,' Burke added. 'Same as Dewey Talley's.'

Which, they now knew, was the same as Jace's. André had seen it hours earlier, when Jace had given him his clothing for evidence. Jace had admitted that he'd gotten the tattoo because of Dewey, because he'd looked up to the man. Poor Jace. The only person who'd been kind to him was a notorious drug dealer.

'Jace really was telling the truth,' Burke said, lowering the binoculars. 'Poor kid.'

'I was thinking the same thing. At least Val will be able to say she told me so.'

'She will, too. That woman don't take no shit from anybody. Not anymore.'

Kaj opened his mouth to ask what *not anymore* meant, but André was striding up to them. 'What do you see?'

Burke handed him the binoculars and brought him up to speed.

'Fuck,' André muttered. 'I hate it when the bodies are in pieces.' He turned to the divers. 'Start searching over there.' André pointed to the tree. 'Hopefully we'll find more of Dewey than his arm.'

'Glad we brought the big evidence bags,' one of the divers said, and then the two rolled backward into the water.

Kaj checked his phone, surprised to see that he had a signal. 'I'm going to call Val and check on Elijah.' Because he couldn't just stand there doing nothing. He was tired and jittery from nerves and caffeine. He stepped away from Burke and André and dialed Val's number.

'Yeah?' she asked cautiously.

'It's Kaj.'

'I know,' she said dryly.

'Elijah's with you? He's okay?'

'Affirmative to both.'

'We found the camp, but it's gone. Blown up.'

'What the hell? Are you serious?' she asked, sounding stunned.

'Oh yeah. And . . . I think we've found part of Dewey. André's sent divers in.' One of the divers emerged, waving at André. 'I think they found something. I need to go.'

'Call me when you know more. Bye.'

The final word was said with affection and concern, and it warmed him as he walked to the edge of the dock. The diver swam up and deposited a large evidence bag near André's feet.

In it was another arm. Kaj swallowed back bile. Most of one, anyway. The hand was gone. The stump had been gnawed on. *Alligators*. The arm appeared to be male as well, but not the same skin tone as the arm stuck on the tree root. The arm with the tattoo was heavily tanned. The one in the bag was fair-skinned and sticking out of a green sleeve.

'Two victims,' Kaj murmured.

'There's one more pale arm down there,' the diver said.

'Three arms?' André said.

'Well, mostly,' the diver said. 'There isn't much left of the third arm. It's going to take us a while to bring it all up. We'll work for as long as our air lasts.' With that, he disappeared under the water again.

'Shit,' André muttered. 'Two victims. Jace only mentioned one.'

Kaj thought of the three vehicles hidden in the woods. 'Could be one of the people Corey brought out here, blindfolded. One left, taking their vehicle, but one was dead, so Corey had to hide the man's car. Maybe this happened after Jace escaped.' Because he still wanted to believe the boy.

'Probably.' André sighed. 'I was hoping Jace was telling the truth, and so far, everything he's said has been right.'

'And we now know that Corey has access to explosives,' Burke said.

'He was army,' Kaj said. 'He worked munitions. I went through his background when I was investigating Aaron, but I didn't go any deeper than that because at the time there wasn't any indication that Aaron was dealing drugs in addition to using them and even less indication that Corey was involved.'

'I think we can safely assume that Corey is involved,' André said dryly.

'What about Bobby Landry?' Kaj asked. 'He's the ex-cop who's partnered with Corey in their construction business. Did either of you know him?'

'I knew him,' Burke said. 'He had a reputation for being a really cruel bastard. There were rumors that he was told he had to resign the NOPD or else.'

'I knew him, too,' André said, 'and heard those same rumors. He was the definition of a loose cannon and his division was glad to be rid of him. I think everyone was relieved when he went into construction, thinking he was staying out of trouble. Guess that was wishful thinking. I'll check with IA to see what they have on him.'

'Captain Holmes?' Detective Drysdale approached. 'Clancy has something you need to see. I'll stay here with these guys.'

Burke took out his phone and angled it so that Kaj could see but the detective could not. Burke was typing a text to Antoine.

Need a search on Bobby Landry, former NOPD. Find out why he was forced to resign.

Already on it. came Antoine's instant reply. *Val asked me last night.*

'Val's on top of things,' Kaj murmured, feeling a settling in his chest. She was capable and smart. Also very pretty and sweet. He trusted her—with his son's safety and possibly his own heart. That she was interested in him, too, was a relief. He wasn't sure how he'd have handled it if the only woman who'd gotten his attention since Heather hadn't wanted him back.

Burke pocketed his phone and a minute later, André came back, his face angry.

'Cameras,' André hissed. 'Battery-operated, motion-activated cameras. They were moving, watching us. I've seen these before. Most likely a live feed over a cellular network.'

Burke frowned. 'They know we're here.'

'They were afraid that Jace told the police where to find them,' Kaj added. 'If Jace was a target before, he's even more of one now.'

And Jace was with Elijah, putting them both in danger if Corey had tracked Jace to Kaj's house. *Val needs to know. Now.*

Kaj typed out a text. *Corey left cameras at his camp. If he's watching, he knows we're here. He'll know Jace went to the police.*

Shit, she texted back. *We will be on high alert. André's cops finally got here around dawn. They're doing drive-bys around your block. Don't worry. We've got this. Be careful.*

I will. Tell Elijah I love him.

Come back and tell him yourself. A smiley face emoji popped up, softening her tone.

It very nearly made him smile himself.

He put his phone away and met André's even glare. He wasn't going to apologize for keeping his son's bodyguard apprised of danger. 'Did the cameras have audio?'

'I don't know,' André said. 'We disconnected the ones we found, but until I order a sweep, I can't be sure that there aren't others. You got something to say, best type it on that phone and show it to me.'

So Kaj typed: *Put out word that Jace found a cop last night and spilled all. Say it was somewhere other than a police station, so no one will question that they didn't see him. Say he's been taken into protective custody and is in an NOPD safe house. Pretend to let slip which one and have someone you trust be waiting there to arrest whoever shows up. If no one tries to grab him, you can put him in protective custody.*

André read the message and nodded. 'That's a sound plan. I'll make it happen.'

The Quarter, New Orleans, Louisiana
WEDNESDAY, OCTOBER 26, 9:00 A.M.

Noni Feldman smiled pleasantly at passersby as she exited her network's studio, not wanting to attract attention by appearing too anxious. She'd received a text message while she'd been in morning meetings and she needed to call the texter back. The number was a familiar one. It belonged to the anonymous source who'd called her two weeks ago and told her that Corey Gates was up to something.

'Yes?' the woman answered.

'It's Noni. What's going on?'

'I need your help.'

Noni walked around the building, stopping when she was sure she was out of earshot of passersby. 'What is it?'

'I need you to warn Bella Butler that her family's lives are in danger. Someone is planning to ambush her car when she comes into the city. And she's just decided to bring her husband and child with her. If they're in the car, they'll be killed, too.'

Noni slowly released the breath she'd been holding, both at the newest warning and because now she could place the woman's voice. Allyson Meyer was one of Bella Butler's security guards. Noni had met her briefly when she'd interviewed Bella about the trial the month before. Allyson Meyer had also been the one who'd tipped her off about Corey Gates.

That Corey was planning to kill Bella Butler wasn't a major leap.

This was *huge*. It might be the biggest story she'd ever delivered.

'How do you know this?' Noni asked warily. But she didn't doubt Allyson's words. She remembered the posters of Bella Butler hanging in the Three Vets office. It had struck her as odd at the time that Bella was fully clothed in her posters, unlike the nudes that covered the rest of the wall.

'You don't need to know that.'

Yeah, I actually do. 'Do you really think they'll kill them? The whole family?'

A long hesitation. 'They murdered one of us last night.' Allyson's voice trembled, like she was rattled. 'He said no to the job, so they shot him. He was a vet. Paramedic. Dead now. They dumped his body in the bayou. They mean business.'

'Oh my God,' Noni breathed, horrified.

'I just texted you Bella's private number,' Allyson said brusquely. 'Use a burner when you call her. I need to go.'

The call ended abruptly. Noni sighed. Using a burner wasn't an issue. She had one she used for all her sources.

The issue was that Allyson had known something two weeks ago when she'd called the first time about Corey. She'd only looked to warn Bella when her husband and child had become threatened as well. Had Allyson been willing to let Bella die and only now balked at the thought of her child?

How did Allyson know? Had Corey approached her? Threatened her? With what? Energized, she headed back inside the newsroom. She had work to do.

13

'COREY, WAKE UP. Wake up, now!'

Corey swatted at Ed's hand. 'What the fuck? I just went to sleep.' Destroying the old camp had taken nearly all night and he and Bobby had been exhausted.

Exhausted and super pissed off. Corey had sunk three years and a lot of cash into making his camp the way he wanted it. And he'd finally gotten rid of Aaron and Dewey, too. Now everything he'd built was gone.

'The cops found the camp,' Ed hissed. 'They tripped the cameras I had along the boundary.'

Corey sat up, suddenly very awake. *Fucking Jace.* 'Which cops?'

'André Holmes and two detectives. There might be more people there, but I can't see them. You blew up my other cameras,' he added accusingly.

Corey rubbed his palms down his face. Jace had led the cops right to their door, just as he'd feared. *I am so going to kill him.*

'I need coffee.' He got out of the bed and nudged Bobby where he slept in the next cot. 'Get your ass up, B. We got stuff to do.'

'I heard,' Bobby groaned. 'You two are noisier than a herd of goddamn buffalo.'

Corey pulled on pants and dug in his duffel until he found a shirt that didn't smell too bad. 'Where's Dianne?'

'Asleep,' Ed said.

Corey glanced over at him. 'On her own?'

Ed made a so-so gesture with his hand. 'Kind of.'

'We're gonna kill her,' Corey grumbled, 'mixing sleeping pills with her booze.'

'If we do, it's only speeding up what she's doing to herself,' Ed shot back. 'Come on. We need to figure out how bad this is.'

'Oh, I think it's pretty bad,' Corey said mildly even though he felt like a volcano ready to blow. 'Are we "persons of interest" yet?'

'Not that I'm hearing on the police radio. I made breakfast. It's not much. We're going to need to make a run for supplies soon.'

That wasn't as easy as it sounded. This camp was on a tributary off Lake Cataouatche, which connected to Lake Salvador by a narrow strait. Salvador was accessible by road. Cataouatche, only by boat. This area was isolated, with no amenities anywhere close by. Aaron had inherited it from the previous leader of Sixth Day and promptly declared it a dump. Which was fair.

But Corey had traded building Dewey's workshop for this piece of land and he came here alone when he needed quiet time. Unlike Bobby, Corey really liked it here.

He poured himself a cup of coffee and sat in a folding chair at a card table. The chair and table, the cots, one actual bed with a creaky mattress, and a ratty futon were the only pieces of furniture. He thought of his cushy leather sofas in the comm room and once again had to tamp down his rage. *Fucking Jace.* 'If they found the old camp, we have to assume they saw our boat launch. The ground was soft, so there are tire tracks all over the place.'

'André Holmes isn't stupid,' Bobby said, pouring coffee for himself. 'He'll follow the tracks to where we hid our rides.'

Corey shook his head. 'None of those vehicles can be traced to us. We removed the VINs, including the hidden ones. What I meant was that they'll take our vehicles and we'll need to steal another one once we're ready to leave here.'

'We'll get one around Lake Salvador,' Bobby said with a careless shrug. 'Tourists renting those camps leave their cars unlocked. Hell, we could find an occupied camp and take their food. No need to go showin' our faces in a country store.'

'Fine,' Ed snapped. 'But we need to figure out what we're going to do about the Doyle job. If we're tagged as "persons of interest" or plain old suspects—which we will be—we need to either bail on the job or do it fast and run. One or the other.'

Bail? What? Hell no.

'We ain't bailin',' Corey said flatly. This was his business. He'd built it from nothing and, at this point, it was all he had left in the world. He'd been the one to approach Trevor Doyle and he'd also been the one to convince the director that they had a foolproof plan for eliminating Bella Butler before the trial. *I am not walking away.* 'I got too much money sunk into investigating Bella Butler's security team.' Finding Allyson's and Zach's secrets had cost a considerable sum of his own money. 'Her court date is next week. She needs to be shut up before then anyway.'

'And *we* can't move until *she* does,' Bobby added. 'Unless we want to attack her in her safe house, and that's not smart. She's got too much security there. We need to wait until she's on her way into the city before we set the charges and plant the bomb-making supplies in Comic Book Guy's car. By the time the cops trace the online threats to the Discord server and Comic Book Guy, Doyle will have already paid us for a job well done and we'll be long gone.'

'Yeah, I know.' Ed rubbed his temples. 'But this was not supposed to go this way.'

'That's for damn sure,' Corey muttered. 'Bobby, check with your buddy again. Find out when Jace talked to a cop, because he must have led them to the camp. Allyson didn't because she was blindfolded. Nobody else knew where we were. Nobody that's still alive, anyway.'

'Aaron did,' Ed said.

'He wouldn't tell.' Corey was sure about that. 'The cops would have found his lab, his cash, and his stash. He doesn't know we took his money, and he'll be wanting to protect it. Bobby, make the call.'

Corey ate his breakfast while Bobby made his call. When he hung up, he looked satisfied.

'Jace found a beat cop in a convenience store parking lot at four o'clock this morning. Told him everything. Cried like a little baby.'

'I'll make him cry more than that,' Corey said darkly.

Bobby nodded. 'Save some of him for me. My buddy says that he's been taken into protective custody and stashed in a safe house. That information was just released.'

'Where's the safe house?' Corey asked, because he was paying that place a visit.

'My buddy's finding out.' Bobby laid his phone on the table. 'He's going to text me, so you watch for it. I'm going back to bed for a little while.'

Ed turned to Corey as Bobby left the room. 'We need to get to Jace soon. He could jeopardize the Doyle job.'

'He can't do any more damage than he's already done. He's probably told them about Dewey and Rick. We know he told them about the camp, but he doesn't know anything about our other business.'

'Are you sure? None of us thought that Jace was smart enough to get away. We shouldn't underestimate him again. What if he overheard something we said at the office? He was hanging around all the time and Bobby talked about Bella Butler sometimes. You know that Bobby runs his mouth when he's bored.'

Goddammit. That was true.

'I heard that!' Bobby called from the bedroom.

'I don't give a fuck,' Ed called back. 'Go to sleep and let the grown-ups talk.'

'Fuck you!' Bobby yelled angrily.

Corey growled impatiently. 'Shut up, both of you. What could Jace have heard, Ed?'

'I don't know and neither do you. And that's my point. We don't know what he heard, and he isn't under our control any longer. He could be saying anything.'

Corey hated to admit that Ed was right. 'We have Bobby's NOPD friend looking for Jace and we'll take care of him as soon as we can.'

'I still say we should walk away.'

Corey glared at him. He could tell Ed that Trevor Doyle had threatened, in so many words, to kill them if they failed him. But that wasn't going to be a worry because they were *not* going to fail. 'So noted. But we're still not going to.'

'Fine,' Ed grumbled. 'So where are we going once the Doyle job is done? We have enough to retire now, especially since we've taken over Dewey's offshore accounts. We could go to the Bahamas like Aaron was planning to do.'

They had money now, it was true. But it wouldn't last forever, and murder for hire would provide work for years to come. Especially once he'd come through for Trevor Doyle. Everyone would know that someone had intervened to silence Bella Butler, but the cops wouldn't be able to pin anything on Doyle. It was a brilliant plan. *And all mine.*

He'd had nothing when he'd come back from Iraq. He hadn't been able to get a decent job. His ODPMC discharge had seen to that. Damn army shrinks. He hadn't been the only one to rough up the locals. Other soldiers did it all the time. *But they made an example out of me.*

Other Designated Physical and Mental Conditions was a red flag to employers. It wasn't supposed to be, but Corey had been turned away everywhere he'd applied. He'd been forced to get a rent-a-cop job at the ER just to pay his bills. That had been humiliating, but it was made worse by the pittance they called a salary. It hadn't been enough. Not by a long shot.

So he'd made his own way, starting Three Vets and bringing in Bobby and Ed. Now he held the reins. He made the decisions. He made the money. If he kept building his organization, he could branch out. Take on more people. Take on even bigger jobs.

Maybe they had enough to retire. But he didn't want enough. He wanted more than enough. He wasn't walking away now.

'We're not retiring to the Caribbean,' he said. 'Too risky passing back and forth over the border when we have domestic jobs.'

Ed sighed. 'Corey. If NOPD knows about Dewey, they'll be searching for us. For murder. Nobody's gonna want to hire guys who're hiding from the law. We need to run while we still can.'

Ed's words tugged at Corey's gut, but he brushed the uncertainty away, scoffing instead. 'Of course they'll hire us. It's not like they're inviting us to their garden parties now. They meet with us in secret already. It's not like they're expecting choirboys. We kill for money.'

'How are you going to get clients? How will they find you?'

'Same as they do now. We'll either find them, like I did with Doyle, or they'll find us on the dark web or through word of mouth. Why are you arguing with me about this?'

'Because I don't want to go to prison with Aaron,' Ed snapped, then sighed again. 'Will you consider laying low after the Doyle job? It'll be winter soon. We could go to the Bahamas and work on our tans.'

'I'll consider a vacation, but we are not quitting. I'm not, anyway.' He met Ed's gaze and held it, challenging. 'Are you?'

Ed shook his head. 'No. I'm with you.'

Corey clapped him on the shoulder. 'Knew I could count on you.

Wake me when Bobby's buddy finds that safe house. I want Jace gone from the face of the earth.'

Future clients wouldn't care that he was wanted by the cops. They'd only care that he got the job done. But he did need to clean up his own mess if he expected anyone to hire him to clean up their messes.

Jace had to go.

Mid-City, New Orleans, Louisiana
WEDNESDAY, OCTOBER 26, 12:05 P.M.

'Oh my God,' Lucien moaned when the hammering upstairs stopped. He slumped back onto Kaj's living room sofa, where he'd been sitting next to Jace. 'Finally.'

At Kaj's dining room table, trying to focus on the background check of Corey Gates filling her laptop screen, Val heartily agreed. Phin had been doing demo work, preparing Elijah's bedroom closet to become his safe room. Val hadn't anticipated how loud it would be. The fact that she'd had so little sleep was combining with the noise to give her a terrible headache.

'Stop complaining!' Phin yelled from upstairs. 'Unless you get up here and give me another pair of hands, I don't want to hear your whining, Lucien.'

Lucien made a face. 'You can't possibly hear me because you're being so damn loud!'

Beside her, Elijah hummed happily. He was wearing headphones and listening to music as he did his schoolwork.

'Lucien, hush,' Val said with forced patience. 'You're making it worse.'

Lucien turned to her, his lower lip pushed out in a pout. 'But, Moooom. He started it.'

She laughed. 'Shut up.'

Jace lifted the hand that wasn't cuffed. 'I could help. I've been on Corey's demo crew for years. I can do simple things.'

Lucien snorted. 'I don't think so. You're not going up there to see what he's doing.'

Jace lifted his eyebrows. 'He's putting in a safe room. From the sound of it, in the bedroom at the back of the house.'

Lucien glared at Val. 'Did you tell him? We don't know that he's not secretly working with his brother.'

Jace spoke before Val could answer. 'I'm *not* secretly working with my brother. I *hate* my brother,' he added with a venom that he hadn't used before. 'Corey beat the hell out of me. He beat Rick. Not just yesterday, but *all* the *time.*' He glared at Lucien. 'You *saw* my bruises last night. You *know.*' Breathless, he calmed himself. 'I know construction. That guy carried in an exterior door and steel braces for the walls. Nobody uses an exterior door inside unless they're soundproofing or need it to be extra secure. Mr. Cardozo is scared for Elijah and he hired bodyguards, so a safe room makes sense.'

Val's lips curved. 'He's got you there, Lucien.'

Lucien sighed. 'I'm sorry, kid. You're right, I did see the bruises. It can't have been easy for you, living with a guardian who beat you when he should have been taking care of you. But I still can't let you upstairs. Not until André or Burke say it's okay.'

'I understand,' Jace said quietly. 'But I want to pull my weight.'

Elijah had taken off his headphones and was staring at Jace, his expression sad. 'How often did Corey beat you?'

Jace dropped his gaze to his feet, clad only in a pair of Burke's socks. He was wearing a pair of Kaj's sweats, which were only a little too short. His feet, however, were several sizes larger than Kaj's, so Burke had loaned him the pair of socks from his go-bag.

'Every week,' Jace said quietly. 'Some weeks, every day. The only time we felt safe was when he went out of town.'

'When he went on jobs,' Val supplied, and Jace nodded.

'Yes'm.'

Because he'd been kept at home, no one had seen his bruises. No one had intervened.

Until now. Val was going to intervene on this boy's behalf. No matter where Jace ended up, she would be this boy's advocate, because he had no one else.

'Have you remembered any of the other times when Corey went out of town?' she asked, because just knowing that Corey might have done something illegal on Labor Day was pretty much useless. If they had more dates, they might be able to see a pattern.

'No, but I don't keep track of the days. Rick does. Or he did.' He corrected himself with a sigh. 'He was good at school and wanted to go to college. Which won't happen now that he's in jail. Which don't really matter to you, I know that. He did keep track of the dates that Corey was gone, though. He wrote them in the calendar on his phone.'

'Rick does matter,' Val said, because Rick Gates had been an abused kid, too. That didn't make what he'd done to Elijah right in any shape or form, but rehabilitation might be possible. 'Rick can still get an education, even in jail. But we'll figure that out later. For now, do you know why he kept track of the dates that Corey was gone?' Then she remembered what Jace had said the night before. 'Oh, right. He wanted to be emancipated from Corey, so he kept records of when Corey left you two alone with no food?'

'Yes, ma'am.'

'Rick wouldn't talk to André last night,' Val said. 'Except that when André asked if Dewey Talley was the driver on Monday night, Rick said yes.'

Startled, Jace did a double take. 'Why would he— Oh.' He rubbed his free hand over his face. 'To protect me. Rick always protected me. He did my schoolwork and he'd take my beatings, too. Until I got bigger than him. Then I'd take his.'

Lucien looked stunned. 'Kid . . .'

Jace closed his eyes. 'I'm just glad he's alive. Corey kept calling him "it" last night. Kept telling me to put "it" on the lawn. I thought Rick was dead.'

Val tilted her head, studying the teenager. 'Rick was nearly dead when he was dropped off here last night. I wondered why Corey would have chanced turning him over to the cops. I suppose he believed he'd killed him.'

When Jace opened his eyes, they were glassy with tears. 'How could Corey do that? I knew he never wanted us, but . . . Rick's still his brother.'

Val squeezed his hand. 'Rick's still *your* brother, too. And the only word he said last night was intended to keep you protected from the police. He wouldn't talk to André last night, but if he knows that you're safe, maybe he'll be willing to give us more information. It can only help him in his own case.'

Jace rubbed the tears from his eyes, perking up. 'Can I see him? He won't believe you unless he sees me in person.'

'We'll work it out when—' She was interrupted when Czar ran from under the table to the front door, barking his head off. Jace quailed and even Lucien looked surprised.

'What the hell, Val?' Lucien shouted as Val rushed to the front door.

'Incoming,' Phin called as he clomped down the stairs. 'It's Antoine. He's got food.'

A check of the front cameras proved Phin correct. She opened the door wide enough for Antoine—and the three laptop cases hanging from his shoulders—to slide through, then closed the door and took the boxes from his hands. 'What did you bring us?'

Antoine grinned. 'Lunch from Patty at the Choux and dessert from MaryBeth at the bakery. I love your friends, Val.'

She grinned back. 'I love them, too. Thank you for bringing this over.'

He set his laptop cases on the table, winking when Elijah stared in awe. 'Hey, kid. I'm Antoine Holmes. I work on Burke's team.'

Elijah pushed his glasses up on his nose. 'Are you related to André Holmes?'

Antoine's grin flashed brightly against his skin, the color of dark walnut. 'I am André's more handsome and much cooler brother. Just ask Val.'

'Don't pull me into your brother war,' Val stated as she moved her laptop from the table. 'I think you're both equally handsome.' Antoine was, however, the cool one. And, given that the online 'exploring' he did might break a few rules—not that Burke's folks asked, because no one really wanted to know for sure—he was definitely a thorn in André's side.

Antoine gestured to the table. 'Come on, y'all. Let's have lunch. I'm starving.'

Elijah set the table and they all sat to enjoy the food Val's friends had sent.

'Patty says lunch is low carb and she's added the nutritional info so you can calculate your insulin.' Val handed Elijah Patty's note. 'And this note is from MaryBeth. She's sent her sugar-free cake pops. With all the sugar and carb info. Maybe save those for later.'

Elijah's smile was huge. 'I'll write them both thank-you cards.' He leaned around Antoine to see Jace. 'If you want me to write anything for you, I will. Just let me know.'

Jace looked like he couldn't believe what was happening. 'Thank you. I will.'

'I was going to Skype with you, Val,' Antoine said as he filled his plate, 'but then your friends brought the food and I figured I'd just tell you what I found when I saw your pretty face.' He then stuffed his face and chewed, his eyes closing in pleasure.

'Swallow and talk,' Val commanded. 'What did you find out?'

She figured that anything he'd found would be a combination of police chatter and information he'd turned up through hacking into NOPD's files. She wasn't going to start asking too many questions now. She was just grateful for whatever intel he'd gathered.

'First of all, I have an addition to Corey's background check.' Antoine glanced cautiously at Jace. 'Corey's military discharge was ODPMC.'

'I read that,' Val said. 'Other Designated Physical and Mental Conditions. I assumed PTSD.' It was her turn to glance cautiously at Phin, because the man had also come home with severe PTSD. Phin gave her an even stare and a slight nod, so he was okay with the topic.

Antoine didn't miss the exchange and sighed. 'Corey's was different. He nearly killed a local woman, he beat her so bad. It was the final straw.'

'Oh,' Jace breathed, his expression devastated. 'I thought it was only us. Me and Rick.'

'No, kid,' Antoine said soberly. 'Not just you. He's a violent man.'

'And Bobby?' Val asked. 'Is he also known to be violent?'

'He was reported for undue force by several people he arrested. But that's not why he was forced out of the NOPD. At the time he quit, Bobby Landry was being investigated by IA for allegedly breaking and entering houses and stealing valuables. The victims had two things in common. First, they were all wealthy. Second, they'd all been transported to the hospital. Some had died, and the thefts occurred during their funerals. The others had extended hospital stays during which time their loved ones were constantly at their sides.'

'And not at home,' Val finished, her mind racing. 'Which hospital? Please say County General.' Because that was where Corey had worked as a security guard.

Antoine smiled. 'You're very smart. But I already knew that.'

Jace sucked in a breath. 'Corey worked at County when he came home from the army. Are you saying . . .' He slumped in his chair. 'Corey was also stealing from people, wasn't he? That's what he meant when he said he'd picked up a few things while he worked at the hospital.'

'Not too shabby yourself, kid,' Antoine said approvingly. 'It looks like it.' He turned back to Val. 'The thefts went in fits and spurts. They'd stall when the cops were staking out houses of the recently deceased or those in the hospital, trying to catch the thieves. The thefts stopped after Bobby quit the force.'

'Which was only a week before Corey quit the hospital.' Val sat back, thinking about all the pieces and how they might fit together. 'Jace, when did you meet Dewey Talley?'

Jace's brow crunched in thought. 'It was when I was living with Aaron and Dianne. I think Liam had just been diagnosed. It was a bad time. Aaron had started his new company and didn't have good insurance. Liam needed special treatments that his insurance wasn't going to pay for. Dianne cried all the time. Dewey was there for part of that. I remember him hugging Dianne one day when she couldn't stop crying.' He looked at Val helplessly. 'He could be really nice.'

Val briefly squeezed his free hand. 'I'm glad he was kind to you. It doesn't change any of the bad things that he did, but I'm glad he was kind to you. So Dewey and Aaron met right around the time that Aaron needed cash. Because Liam was sick.'

'Which was why Aaron sold drugs,' Jace said heavily. 'Does Corey sell them, too?'

'That's the big question,' Val said, determined to be honest with him. 'Sixth Day was a major player among the drug gangs four years ago. Many of their street dealers got absorbed into other gangs. I don't know how big they are now.'

'NOPD is working on that,' Antoine said. 'The whole Narcotics division is hopping busy, investigating. I'll keep you up to date with what I'm able to glean online.'

Jace drew a sudden breath, like he'd been punched. 'Dianne,' he whispered. 'Did Dianne know about the drugs, too?'

Antoine shrugged. 'The cops are trying to find her,' he said. 'She was supposed to go visit her sister in Houma, but she's not there. She was last seen with Corey, yesterday morning. At the time, NOPD didn't have anything to hold him on, so they had to let him go.'

Jace's eyes grew glassy with tears. 'Dianne wasn't part of this. I can't believe it. I won't.'

Val squeezed his hand again. She wasn't so sure that Dianne wasn't involved, but right now, Jace needed to believe in at least one person in his family. 'Let's wait to see what Captain Holmes finds out.'

He nodded miserably, tightening his grip on her hand. 'If she's with Corey she either knows what he's doing or he took her like he took me.'

Antoine hesitated. 'Would he hurt her?'

Jace shook his head. 'No. He loves her. He loved Liam. Not us. Not me and Rick. But he loves them. He wouldn't hurt her.' But his tone was uncertain.

Val sighed. 'There isn't much we can do from here just yet. Elijah, can you put away the leftovers? Your dad and Burke will be hungry when they come back. Captain Holmes, too, if he's with them.'

'What are you going to do?' Elijah asked, not rebelliously. Just curiously.

'I'm going to keep digging into Corey Gates.' They still needed to find out if Corey was involved with Sixth Day and if that note he'd taped to Rick's chest was a real threat.

The next body we'll leave you will be that of your son.

At this point, they had no choice but to believe that the note was real. Which meant both Corey and Sixth Day posed possible threats to Elijah. And even if Corey didn't pose a continued threat to Elijah, he did to Jace. She'd claimed that keeping Jace safe wasn't her responsibility, but she knew down deep that she couldn't leave him at risk. Her gut was telling her that the times Corey had left town were important to figuring out exactly what the man was up to. She needed to get those dates from Rick. 'Let's finish up. We all have work to do.'

'Not me,' Jace said sadly.

Phin, who'd been silently listening the entire time, patted Jace's shoulder. 'When Burke gives the okay, I could use another pair of hands up there.'

Jace's smile was brighter this time, and Val mouthed 'Thank you' to Phin. She'd known Phin for a few years now but rarely saw him like this, laid-back and talking. At the office, he was usually abrupt and brusque. She knew Lucien and Antoine well, but Phin kept to himself. The man was haunted by memories he never shared, and his PTSD manifested in ways more aggressive than her own. He'd always seemed to have himself on a very short leash. This would be a nice chance to get to know Phin away from the office.

Everyone scattered from the table except for Antoine, who appeared to be setting up shop, arranging his three laptops in a semicircle in front of him. Elijah cleared the table, Lucien and Jace returned to the sofa, and Phin headed back upstairs to work on the safe room.

When it was quiet, Val typed a text to Kaj. *All is well here. But we need to talk to Rick asap. He might have information about Corey but won't talk until he knows Jace is safe. Please advise.*

Bayou des Allemands, Louisiana
WEDNESDAY, OCTOBER 26, 12:30 P.M.

Kaj lifted his hand in a muted wave as the NOPD boat drove away, leaving him and Burke on the dock where they'd found the abandoned vehicles. The vehicles remained parked under the trees, the flatbed truck not yet having arrived to pick them up. Officer Nolan was still here, waiting with his backup in an NOPD cruiser, which sat on the gravel road that led to the launch.

Kaj wiped at the sweat pooling on the back of his neck. He wouldn't admit to anyone that he was glad to have left the crime scene, but hell, he was so glad. The longer they'd stayed, the more body parts the divers had pulled up. Combined with the growing heat of the day and the toxic odors coming off the buildings' rubble, it had become too much.

Burke pulled a bottle of water from the backpack he'd brought with them. 'Drink something,' he said. 'You look a little green.'

'Thanks.' Kaj took the water, draining half the bottle in one gulp. 'I've seen dead bodies, more times than I want to remember.' But it had mostly been in photos. The real thing was much more intense, the evidence of what Burke had called 'gator snacking' undeniable. 'But not like what we just saw. We don't have a lot of gators in New York. Except for the ones living in the sewers,' he added lightly. 'But I'm almost certain that's an urban myth.'

Burke snorted. 'Almost certain?'

Kaj shrugged. 'I'm not going down into the sewers to check it out. At least we got what we came for. André gave us a lot more access than I was expecting, honestly.'

'True enough. We got to view the camp and see remains, and you got to craft his strategy of saying that Jace was in a safe house. I thought he'd send us away as soon as we spied the camp. I actually didn't think he'd let you come at all, so anything we got this morning was bonus.'

Kaj turned toward the trees, squinting for a look at the vehicles that had been hidden there before. He saw a glint of metal that told him they were still there. 'That Hyundai. It makes sense that it belonged to the second body.'

'Yes,' Burke said, waiting for him to go on.

'Corey's got two old friends as his partners in his construction business—Bobby Landry the ex-cop and Ed Bartholomew, who's their accountant.' Kaj paced the length of the dock, trying to organize his thoughts. 'Jace said that Bobby and Ed brought back two people who were wearing blindfolds. Corey didn't trust them if he blindfolded them.'

'With you so far. Especially since they killed one of those people.'

'True.' Kaj grimaced, remembering the destroyed remains. 'Corey made a big show of denying that he'd seen Rick yesterday in that statement to the media. He made an effort to put Sixth Day back in the headlines. I don't know why he'd do that if he's part of Sixth Day, but he is planning something, and I think it's something big. Big enough that he was willing to risk turning Rick over to me. He'd tortured Rick and yet didn't think Rick would tell us. Unless he thought Rick would die from the heroin overdose. We need to find out if Rick shot himself up or if Corey helped him.'

'If he thought Rick had OD'd, he wasn't risking anything.'

'And that's probably the more likely scenario,' Kaj admitted. 'But Rick didn't talk, even when André straight up asked him.'

'Corey has something on Rick.'

'Or someone,' Kaj murmured. 'Corey still had Jace. Rick was too scared to say a word to anyone. Except to say that Dewey was the driver so that we didn't keep looking and find Jace. Whether Corey thought Rick was dead or alive, it doesn't matter. He handed Rick over to divert attention from himself because he's planning something big. The guy who owned that Hyundai is part of it. Dewey must have become a liability after Aaron's arrest, so Corey eliminated him. He couldn't drop Dewey's body off on my lawn because I'd have looked for Dewey's killer.'

'Tossing him to the gators meant we'd keep spinning our wheels searching for a dead man,' Burke said in agreement.

'Why did he need those two people? We need to know what Corey's up to. Corey and Aaron both had cabins here. Aaron *has* to know something. It's time to talk to Aaron again. The last time I had him in an interview room he said nothing, but he was going through detox at the time. It's been over a week and he should be through the worst of it.'

Burke gave him a look full of doubt. 'Your boss won't let you talk to him, will he?'

'No, but Hogan's taken the case and he might let me observe when he interviews Aaron. I'll ask him when that'll be.' Kaj had started to call his boss when his phone buzzed with a text from Val. His heart stuttered in apprehension for a moment until he read the first sentence.

All is well here. But we need to talk to Rick asap. He might have information about Corey but won't talk until he knows Jace is safe. Please advise.

Kaj dialed her number, showing Burke her text as the phone rang.

'Hey.' Her voice was warm and inviting and made him wish he were with her.

'Hi,' he said, feeling his cheeks heat at Burke's lifted brow. 'I'm here with Burke. You're on speaker.'

'Hey, boss. Did you lose my thermos again?'

Burke winced guiltily. 'I left it in the boat. I'll buy you a new one.'

She chuckled. 'You bought that one. I think you've bought my last six. What's up?'

'Is Elijah in hearing distance?' Kaj asked.

'Hold on.' After a pause, she was back, her voice barely a whisper. 'I went to the front door. I can still see him, but he's talking with the others and not listening.'

'What did you mean, Rick has information about Corey?' Burke asked.

'Oh. I don't need to hide that from Elijah. He's heard it already. Jace said that Corey would disappear for days at a time and several of the times he forgot to leave them food. Rick kept a record of all the days he disappeared so that he could use it in his bid for emancipation. Jace said that Corey wasn't doing construction jobs at the time because he didn't take his tools with him. One of these times was the week after Labor Day, but there are others.'

Kaj felt a thrill of excitement. 'That might help us figure out what Corey's up to.'

'But Jace doesn't think Rick will cooperate unless he sees that Jace is okay,' Val said. 'Skype might work, but we'd be sure to get what we need if Rick sees Jace in person. Setting up a meet in the hospital would be ideal, but we don't have much time. Once Rick is released to the jail, our opportunities for getting Jace in undetected go way down. Jace trusts me, so Rick might, too. Is Molly available to guard Elijah for a little while this afternoon, Burke?'

'She is,' Burke answered.

'It won't take long,' Val said. 'We'll get Jace in, talk to Rick, then get out. I'm taking Lucien with me. He'll offer to be Rick's attorney and we'll be his assistants.'

'But Lucien isn't an attorney,' Kaj said, half appalled by the lie and half intrigued.

Burke's lips twitched. 'Yeah, he is. I mean, I'm not against bending the rules for the right cause, but Val's plan is righteous. No law breakage involved.'

Kaj's eyes narrowed. 'Lucien is an attorney? For real?'

Burke lifted three fingers. 'Scout's honor.'

'That part was a lie,' Val said. 'Burke wasn't a Boy Scout. But Lucien *is* an attorney and all his licenses are current. You can check if you don't believe us.'

Kaj winced. 'Sorry. I do believe you. I'm just surprised.'

'Lucien gets that a lot,' Burke said dryly. 'He hated being a lawyer and I don't make him wear a suit and tie.'

'Burke, we need to borrow one of your suits for Jace. Can I ask Molly to go by your place and get one?'

'I think he'd swim in my suit,' Burke said doubtfully. 'He's tall, but too skinny.'

'He can wear one of mine,' Kaj offered. 'Better the pants be a little short on him than way too big. He'd look like he was playing dress-up, and he already looks so young.'

'All right,' Val said. 'I'll make preparations on my end.'

A large engine rumbled the air and a flatbed truck came into view a few seconds later. 'Our ride is here. I'll call you as soon as I can. Be careful, okay?'

'Always,' she said and ended the call.

Kaj glanced at the flatbed. Officer Nolan was directing the driver to the abandoned vehicles, so he and Burke were still beyond their earshot. He didn't distrust Nolan specifically, but he didn't know the other cops and preferred to keep things private until he did. 'I'm going to call André and let him know. If he can let the officer guarding Rick's room know that Lucien is coming with his assistants, it'll ease their way.'

14

STANDING BETWEEN VAL and Lucien, Jace faced the front of the elevator that was taking him to see Rick. He couldn't stop staring at his reflection in the shiny wall. He looked amazing.

He looked like a lawyer who was going to talk to his client, Rick Gates, in the hospital.

Well, like a really young lawyer wearing a light brown wig and a black suit that was a size too small. Val's friend Molly had brought over the wig when she'd taken over guarding Elijah while they were gone. Lucien had helped him into one of Mr. Cardozo's suits—while scaring him with guesses as to how much the suit cost. Jace hoped he didn't mess it up. He hadn't known any kind of clothing could cost so much.

But it was worth it. The wig and suit plus a pair of dark glasses made him look like someone else. Someone smarter. Someone better. Someone trustworthy.

Because he *was* trustworthy. Val and Lucien had uncuffed him. He was free. Not that he'd run, not after they'd trusted him. He stood a little taller, still staring at himself.

'You clean up good, kid,' Lucien said, a grin on his face.

'I do,' Jace said in wonder. Then he shrugged. 'It's like a Halloween costume. I'll never be this.'

Lucien's grin faded. 'This what?'

'This . . . person. I'll never have a suit like this.'

'Well,' Lucien drawled, 'very few people have a suit like that one.' He straightened the lapels of his own dark suit. 'I certainly don't. I bought mine off the rack and it was on sale. Kaj's suits are a step above.'

Jace shook his head. 'I meant, I won't have no cause to wear one, except maybe to go to a funeral. I'll never have a job where I'd wear a suit. I ain't that smart.'

Val nudged him with her elbow. 'You are smart. And if you don't wear a suit to work, that's okay. If you're a mechanic in a garage, that's wonderful. It's a good career, Jace. And nothing to be ashamed of.' She smoothed a hand over her hair. She was wearing a dark wig, too. 'It's almost time. Remember, Lucien is Rick's lawyer and we are his assistants.'

That Lucien actually was a lawyer had blown Jace's mind. Lucien didn't practice anymore and wouldn't say why. 'I know,' Jace said, deepening his voice.

Val smiled at him. 'Just don't say anything until we're in there.' The elevator doors opened. 'This is us.'

Jace nodded once, hard. And said nothing. He wasn't sure he could. His heart was beating so hard that he was a little light-headed as the three of them walked toward Rick's room.

Lucien stopped in front of the cop standing outside Rick's room. Jace didn't react because Val had told him that there would be a cop there.

Jace swallowed hard, scared for his brother. Rick was going to jail. He'd be there with all kinds of criminals who'd . . . He fought off a shudder. He'd seen movies about prison. He knew what to expect.

But hopefully Rick would share info that would help him get a lighter sentence. *That's what today is all about.*

Lucien showed his ID to the cop. 'Hi. I'm Lucien Farrow, Mr. Gates's attorney. These are my assistants. We'd like to speak to Mr. Gates privately.'

The cop studied the ID with a frown, then jerked his head toward the door. 'Yeah, the captain said you were comin'. Go ahead. Get him off easy,' he added sarcastically. 'All he did was try to kidnap a prosecutor's little boy. Fucking lawyers. We lock 'em up, you let 'em out.'

Lucien didn't say another word, just led them into Rick's room. Rick was hidden, a curtain pulled around his bed. The only thing visible was the rolling cart that had a tray of something beige-colored with gravy that had congealed.

Rick didn't eat like I did today. The food had been so good, but the company had made the difference. They treated him so nice. Like he mattered. And Rick wouldn't get that, not for a long time. His heart hurt at the thought.

Lucien closed the door behind them and pulled the curtain, revealing the bed. Rick's face was pale, his eyes closed and his forehead sweaty even though it wasn't hot in the room.

Lucien closed the curtain so that they had privacy. 'Mr. Gates, I'm your attorney.'

'Go away,' Rick muttered. 'I don't want to talk to any lawyers.'

Val squeezed Jace's shoulder. 'Go ahead.'

'Rick?' Jace asked quietly. 'Open your eyes. It's me. Jace.'

Rick's eyes flew open, wide and shocked. He looked like he wanted to shout, but Val put a finger over her lips. 'Keep your voice down, Mr. Gates.'

Still staring at Jace, Rick nodded slowly. 'What the hell?' he whispered. 'What are you doing here? What are you wearing?'

'I'm here to talk to you and this getup is a disguise.' Jace pulled a chair close to the bed and sat down, wrapping his hands around the bed rail. 'We don't have much time, so I have to hurry. Corey made me leave you on Mr. Cardozo's front lawn. Said he'd shoot me in the head if I didn't. I'm sorry. I was afraid, so I did it.'

Rick patted Jace's clenched hand. 'It's okay. Corey told me that he'd make you do it.' He shook his head. 'Why are you here? *How* are you here? Who the hell are they?'

'I got away. I took a boat, then stole Dewey's truck. I went back to Cardozo's to find you, to make sure you were okay, but they caught me.'

Rick flinched. 'Did they hurt you?' His eyes flicked to Val, then to Lucien, before returning to Jace. 'Because of . . . me?' he whispered hesitantly.

Jace understood what Rick was afraid to say. *Because of us. Because of what we did.*

'No. No. They've been nice to me. And they know what I did. They know I was driving that night, but they've still been nice to me. I swear it, Rick. On Mama's grave.'

Rick's lips thinned, but he nodded. 'Okay. Who are these people?'

'Val and Lucien. They work for a private investigator. And they're bodyguards. They're guarding Elijah, the little boy.'

Rick swallowed. 'Is he okay? The little kid?'

'Yeah. And he's nice, too.'

Rick's eyes got glassy with tears. 'I'm going to jail, Jace.'

'I know,' Jace whispered. 'I'm sorry.'

Rick shrugged a shoulder and forced a smile. 'At least I'll get away from Corey.'

Jace clenched the bed rail harder. 'That's part of why I'm here. I've been worried about you, but we also need information. Corey's up to something and it's not good. He's probably been doing it for a while. Remember all those times he disappeared and said he was working?'

Rick's jaw tightened. 'Yeah. I remember. Especially when he forgot to leave us food.'

'You wrote down all the dates on your calendar. If you give us those, we might be able to figure out what Corey's been doing. You might get less time for helping stop Corey.'

'But they're not really lawyers.'

'Lucien is.'

Val leaned close to Rick. 'I'm not going to sugarcoat it, Rick. Only the prosecutors can give you a deal, and it'll be a tough sell, since you tried to abduct Cardozo's son. But if your brother Corey is a bigger fish and you help catch him, it'll be several points in your favor.'

Rick grabbed her arm with the hand that wasn't cuffed to the bed and for a second, Jace was worried. So was Lucien, who started to reach for Rick to pull him off.

Rick dropped Val's arm. 'Sorry. I'm sorry. I just . . . Will you really take care of my brother? Please? I tricked him into coming with me that night. He had nothing to do with it.'

'I know,' Val said. 'I believe what Jace told us. He's already helped us a lot, but you can help more. Your brother Corey is a killer.'

Rick frowned. 'What do you mean? Aaron is the one who killed that doctor.'

Val shook her head. 'Jace saw Corey kill Dewey.'

Rick's face lost all the color it'd had left. 'Corey's going to come after Jace.'

'That's why we need your help,' Val said urgently. 'We need the dates that Corey left you two alone. It'll help us keep Jace safe.'

Jace knew that Val was really trying to keep Elijah safe, but he thought she might want to keep him safe, too. A little, at least. If she did, it was more than he deserved.

Whatever she'd meant, her words had Rick nodding tersely. 'Corey took my phone, but I had it backed up to the cloud. Give me paper and a pen.'

Lucien pulled a notepad and a pen from his pocket and handed it to him.

'I thought that Corey was making drug runs for Aaron and Dewey all the times he was gone,' Rick muttered as he scrawled words on the notepad and gave it to Val.

Jace stared at him. 'You knew Aaron and Dewey were selling drugs? All along?'

'Only for the last year, but I couldn't prove it.' He looked away. 'I was using their shit, stealing from Aaron's stash. I needed a fix Monday night. That's part of why I did what I did.'

Jace's mouth fell open. 'Rick. You said it was so we could live with Aaron again.'

Rick wouldn't meet his eyes. 'That too. I started taking that shit one night after Corey beat me so bad that I could barely stand. I went to Aaron's and I . . . gave in. Once I tried it, I couldn't stop. I had enough for one more hit and I took it in the van when you were driving us to meet Corey. I figured he'd beat me again and I didn't want to be in my head.'

Jace opened his mouth, but no words came out. *How did I not know?*

Val squeezed Jace's shoulder. 'Rick, did you take the heroin last night?' she asked.

'No, ma'am. Bobby shot me up. Told me to say my prayers because I was gonna die.'

'Why didn't you tell me you were using?' Jace whispered, still stuck on that fact.

'I didn't want you to know. You're still a kid.'

'I'm only a year younger than you,' Jace whispered.

Rick swallowed hard. 'I was supposed to take care of you. I fucked it all up. I'm sorry. I'm going to jail and no one will be there to take care of you.'

Jace gripped the bed rail so hard that his knuckles hurt. 'Who's gonna take care of you in jail?' For a moment they stared at each other, both of them miserable. Then Jace turned to look up at Lucien. 'Can you do anything?'

'I'm going to make sure that he gets a fair trial,' Lucien said, and Jace believed him. Jace had wondered on the drive over if Lucien was just pretending, or if he'd really be Rick's lawyer. It looked like it really was the second one, and Jace was nearly dizzy with relief.

'Why?' Rick asked hoarsely. 'Why would you? I did it. I would have taken that kid if his aunt hadn't tased me. I did a horrible thing.'

'I know,' Lucien said. 'You did do a horrible thing. But we like your brother and we know your life hasn't been easy. That doesn't erase what you did, but we might be able to present mitigating circumstances in your defense. You're going to be transferred to the jail soon, and I'll come to visit you there. We'll talk again.'

Rick grabbed at Jace's hand, still clutching the bed rail. 'Come and see me? In jail?'

'Yes. I promise.'

Rick swallowed again. 'Be careful. Don't get hurt.'

Jace wanted to cry. 'I'm doing my best. You too. Stay safe.'

'Rick, I'm leaving you my business card,' Lucien said. 'Call me if anyone tries to interrogate you. Don't say anything to anyone unless I'm with you. Understand?'

Rick nodded. 'Thank you,' he whispered.

Jace didn't want to leave Rick's side, but Val was tugging him, so he let go of the bed rail. 'Soon,' he mouthed before turning for the door.

The three of them were quiet on the ride back down to the parking garage, where Lucien hurried them to Burke's company SUV. They remained silent until the doors were closed and they had left the parking garage.

Val snapped a photo of Rick's log-in information with her phone, texted it to Antoine, then called Burke, putting it on speaker. 'Hey, we're out of the hospital and back in the SUV. Everything went fine. Rick gave us his cloud log-in info and I just texted it to Antoine. He can copy the dates that Corey was gone from Rick's calendar.'

'Excellent. How did Rick seem?'

'Okay,' Val said. 'He's scared, as he should be. Knows what he did was wrong. He did say that he's known for a year that Dewey and Aaron were selling drugs together, so we have confirmation that Aaron is part of Sixth Day and not just a client. Rick also said that Bobby shot him up on purpose.'

Burke sighed. 'At least we have a few more pieces of the puzzle. You okay, Jace?'

Jace exhaled. 'Yes, sir. I just . . . I hated leaving him there.'

'I know,' Burke said gently, 'but Rick did do it. There will be consequences, but we'll do our best to make sure his treatment is fair.'

'Mr. Cardozo won't like that,' Jace said, feeling torn in two. Rick had done something awful. *And he tricked me into helping him.* 'He's mad and he has a right to be. He'll want Rick to have a long sentence. He'll want him to suffer for what he did. But . . . he's my brother.'

Burke sighed. 'I think Mr. Cardozo wants justice done. If the information that your brother gave us proves helpful, then that tilts the scales of justice in your brother's favor.'

Jace closed his eyes because they burned and he didn't want to cry. 'I don't . . . I don't know what that means.'

Mr. Cardozo's voice was a jolt of surprise. He hadn't known that he was with Burke. That he sounded as gentle as Burke was an even bigger shock. 'It means that your brother will almost certainly do time, but his sentence might be reduced since he's cooperating. And it means that we'll try to keep him safe while he serves his time. That's the best that I can do.'

That's more than I have a right to ask for. Tears spilled down his cheeks. 'Thank you.'

'You're welcome,' Mr. Cardozo said gently. 'Val, Burke and I just got dropped off at my car by the flatbed truck driver. We'll meet you back at my house.'

Lake Cataouatche, Louisiana
WEDNESDAY, OCTOBER 26, 3:00 P.M.

Corey had slept for almost five hours, but it hadn't been enough. He still felt thickheaded, and listening to Ed and Bobby bicker was not helping. He needed some quiet to think.

Ed was shaking his head. 'This is *insane*. Why would we go after Jace ourselves if we've been paying off cops for three years? Let one of *them* put a bullet in his head.'

'Because we want to kill him ourselves,' Bobby said, taking a bite of one of the granola bars Ed had brought from the old camp. 'Duh.'

Ed's head fell back and he stared up at the cheap fiberglass-tiled ceiling of the camp's main room. 'Please tell me that you're not going to do this yourself, Corey. It's too dangerous.'

Corey sighed. Ed had a point, but then, so did Bobby. Bobby's buddy on the force had already come through with the location of the safe house where Jace was being kept, and Corey really wanted to be the one to grab his youngest brother. Jace had caused him one helluva lot of trouble. He wanted to see Jace die. 'How many cops do they have guarding him, B?'

'One,' Bobby said. 'Where's the danger in that? It'll be a piece of cake.'

'Famous last words,' Ed muttered. 'Dammit, Corey, what if this safe house is a trap? What if they've got a dozen cops waiting for you? You'll be in jail with Aaron.'

Bobby shrugged. 'We'll shoot 'em up.'

Ed rolled his eyes. 'That's your grand plan?'

Corey's pocket buzzed, distracting him from the arguing. He pulled out his two cell phones—the one he used for Three Vets and the current burner he used for Doyle—and saw that it was an incoming call to his Three Vets number. The caller had tried several times already, he noted with a wince. Actually, he'd missed a dozen calls, all from an unknown number. Not the number that cop—Officer Nolan—had called from last night.

Dammit. He'd meant to call that cop back after last night's meeting, but Jace's disappearance had sent everything to hell. 'Shut up, you two. This might be that cop calling to tell me that Rick is dead. I forgot to call back last night.'

Ed's lips pursed in more disapproval. 'You forgot?'

'I said, shut up,' Corey hissed, then drew a breath and answered. 'Hello?'

'Mr. Gates?'

'This is he.'

'Mr. Gates, this is Dr. Hubble from County General.'

Corey recognized the name from when he'd worked as a security guard at the hospital. Shitty days. 'Yes?'

'I'm calling about your brother Rick. I think someone from the police department also tried to call you.'

Corey injected hope into his voice. 'Have you found him? Is he all right?'

'He will be. I'm calling to let you know that we admitted him last night for a drug overdose. He's still here but will soon be transported to the jail.'

He will be. Corey's blood went cold. 'Wh-what?'

'He overdosed, Mr. Gates, but the paramedics got to him in time. He was given Narcan and was soon breathing normally.'

'Oh my God,' Corey whispered, then his whole body grew hot with rage. He swallowed it back and managed a shuddering 'Thank the good Lord. I'll be in to see him as soon as I can. Thank you.'

'Mr. Gates,' the doctor said. 'Wait. Mr. Gates—'

Corey ended the call and numbly lowered his phone to the table.

'What?' Bobby demanded. 'What is it?'

Corey turned the full force of his anger on Bobby, making the bigger man flinch. 'Rick's alive, you motherfucker.'

Ed gaped. 'What?'

There was a moment of silence that stretched on until Bobby snapped. 'That's impossible. I gave that kid enough heroin to kill four people. If he survived long enough to get to Cardozo's house, then he was doing a shit-ton of H on his own.'

'This is a disaster,' Ed murmured.

'Fucking right it is,' Corey hissed. 'Both of my brothers are out there, telling the cops all kinds of wonderful things.' His anger boiled over. 'Motherfucking hell, Bobby!' he yelled. 'You had one fucking job! To take care of Rick!'

'They're not *my* brothers,' Bobby yelled back, leaping to his feet. 'This is on you, Corey. Not me.'

Corey rose slowly, his pulse pounding in his ears, his fists clenched. Bobby had a few inches and forty pounds on him, but Corey was mad. Bobby's gaze darkened and Corey had shifted his body to throw the first punch when Ed grabbed their shirts and yanked them apart.

'For fuck's sake!' Ed shouted. 'Don't be idiots. Sit down. We have bigger problems.'

Corey lowered to his seat, his gaze on Bobby as he did the same. 'What bigger problems, Ed?' But he really didn't want to know.

Ed turned his own phone around, showing them their own faces. On the NOPD website.

Corey closed his eyes. He'd expected this after Jace went missing, but it was still like a kick to the gut. He'd been so damn careful. *Three years*. They'd been killing for hire for *three fucking years* and in one single week his brothers had destroyed everything.

I should have killed them years ago. He was going to fix that oversight today. At least for Jace. It would take a little longer, but he'd figure out a way to deal with Rick, too.

'We are now "persons of interest",' Ed said quietly. 'Media outlets have picked up the story. We need to be laying low. We may need to bow out of the Doyle job. We definitely shouldn't be taking chances getting Jace.'

Corey clenched his teeth so hard it hurt. 'We will *finish* the Doyle job. We will *not* bow out.' And he was totally killing Jace. It was a necessity now. If for no other reason than his own sanity. He couldn't concentrate with this hatred bubbling through his brain.

Ed huffed impatiently. 'Is Doyle still even on board?'

'As far as I know,' Corey said, reaching for calm. 'He threatened to kill us if we failed, so he hasn't called us off yet.'

'He what?' Ed asked, shocked.

Corey waved a hand absently. 'Posturing. He was angry and desperate.'

'When was the last time you checked for a message from him?' Ed asked.

'Before I went to sleep,' Corey admitted, new dread descending like a thick fog.

Ed grimaced. 'You didn't have a BOLO out on you before you went to sleep. He may have canceled the job once he saw it. Check again. Please.'

Corey pulled his burner from his pocket, dread increasing when he saw the text from Doyle with an attached screenshot. He closed his eyes wearily. *Well, that answers the question of walking away.*

'What does it say?' Ed demanded.

Bobby took the phone from Corey's hand and cursed. 'He says, "If she sings, the NOPD will be the least of your problems."' He hissed out another curse. 'Look at this screenshot of a map he attached. He knows exactly where we are right now.'

He tossed the phone to the table and Ed grabbed it up. 'Fuck.'

'Fuck?' Bobby yelled furiously. 'That's all you have to say for yourself? You said that you scanned Corey's burner for tracking devices!'

'I did!' Ed yelled back.

Bobby leaned across the table. 'Then how does Doyle know where the fuck we are?'

Ed pushed to his feet, leaning toward Bobby, his glare just as vicious. Then he slumped. 'He must have found a way to embed it in one of his messages.'

'So you say,' Bobby grumbled. 'Fucker.'

Ed went still. 'Are you suggesting something, Bobby?'

'Seems like you're pushing us to quit. And then Doyle magically knows where we are.'

'No magic about it,' Ed fumed. 'He's rich. I'm sure he can buy a tech expert, just like he bought our services. And yes, I'm pushing us to quit, because I'm the only one here making any sense!'

'Enough!' Corey roared, slapping both palms on the table. 'I'm fed up with you two fighting. Shut the hell up or get out. We're *not* walking away. We're going to finish the job, then get paid.'

'Corey?' a small voice asked.

Corey spun around to find Dianne leaning against the doorway to the second bedroom, rubbing her hands over her very pale face. He'd all but forgotten about her. 'You're awake.' *Fucking hell.* What had she heard?

'I heard yelling.' She folded her arms over her chest, hunching over. 'Where are we?'

Corey forced himself to smile at her. 'Our campsite, remember? I told you that we were going to get out of the city for a while.'

She shook her head. 'This is a different place.' She frowned. 'At least I think it is. How long did I sleep?'

'A little more than a day,' Ed told her. 'You drank a lot of vodka.'

She looked away, embarrassed. 'I'm sorry. Can I go home now?'

'Not right now,' Corey told her. He got up and took her arm, turning her back into the bedroom. 'We're just finishing up here. Why don't you go back and lie down? I'll bring you some water. That'll help you feel better.'

She rubbed at her head. 'It's so bright in here.'

Corey gently pushed her to the bed. 'That's your hangover talking. Rest. I'll be back.'

'Thank you, Corey.' She pulled a pillow over her eyes with a small moan of pain.

He stood there, watching her as his mind flipped between the two possibilities—drugging her again or killing her. They couldn't take a chance on letting her go home. Not yet.

Not ever.

He closed the door and returned to the table. The three of them sat in silence for a full minute.

'I'll do it,' Ed offered sadly. 'I know you care about her.'

Corey cast him a beleaguered glare. 'So do you.'

Bobby shrugged. 'Ed ain't been in love with her for years, Corey.'

Corey felt like he'd been slapped. 'I . . .' *I can't do it*. He didn't love her. But he did care about her, and she'd been through so much already. He'd been the one to hold her when she cried after Liam's death because Aaron was off fucking Sandra the Whore. Not that Dianne had known that at the time. Which had made it even worse.

Corey had cried with her, missing Liam. Grieving with Dianne. And now . . .

She might not have heard.

He couldn't risk it, though. *What have I done?*

You done fucked up, boy. That's what you've done.

He opened his mouth, but no sounds came out. *I can't do it. God-dammit.*

'I'll just give her extra sleeping pills,' Ed murmured, so softly that Corey barely heard him. 'She'll go to sleep and won't wake up. It won't hurt her. I promise.'

Corey wanted to snarl, because his chest hurt. This was Aaron's and Rick's and Jace's fault. Aaron wasn't supposed to have killed Dr. Singh. Rick wasn't supposed to try kidnapping Cardozo's kid, and Jace wasn't supposed to have been smart enough to get away.

Nothing was going the way it was supposed to.

He exhaled heavily. 'Do it, Ed.'

Ed nodded, his eyes filled with a mix of anguish and anger. He'd been Dianne's friend, too. But Ed always did what needed to be done. 'All right.' He drew a deep breath and let it out. 'What are we going to do about this?' He held up his phone, their faces still staring from his screen.

Corey stood abruptly, his chair clattering to the floor. 'We're going to get Jace. When we get back, we're going to figure out how to get to Rick in lockup. We're going to do what I should have done a long time ago. You got that address for the safe house, Bobby?'

'I sure do.' Bobby patted his pocket, then strapped on his ridiculous gun. 'Let's roll.'

Mid-City, New Orleans, Louisiana
WEDNESDAY, OCTOBER 26, 3:00 P.M.

'Did everything go well?' Molly asked cautiously once Val had kissed the top of Czar's head at the front door and sent him upstairs, where Elijah was taking a nap.

'Yep. I sent the log-in for Rick's cloud account to Antoine. Didn't he tell you?' Val glanced to the dining room table, where Antoine had his three laptops arranged and was typing on two keyboards simultaneously. 'Show-off,' she muttered.

'No, he didn't tell me. I learned a long time ago not to bug him when he's working.' Molly opened the door again when Jace approached with Lucien. 'No excitement?'

'None,' Lucien confirmed. 'Just a dirty look from the cop on duty when I said I was Rick's lawyer, but I'm used to that.'

'Why don't the three of you catch some z's?' Molly suggested. 'Val, go on upstairs. I'll stay on duty until Burke gets back.'

'I will,' Val said, thankful that Phin had taken a break from Elijah's safe room and the house was quiet. 'Or I won't be able to take night duty.'

'I don't think I could sleep if I tried.' Jace tugged on Kaj's tie. 'I just want to get out of this suit before I mess it up.'

'I just want out of the suit,' Lucien said lightly, 'because I hate them.'

Jace stuck out his hands. 'You can cuff me while we go up the stairs.' The teenager shook his head when Lucien looked pained. 'It's okay. I'm grateful I'm not in jail. Mr. Cardozo has been nice, and I don't want to go against him. Cuff me.'

With a sigh, Lucien handcuffed him, then followed him up the stairs.

Molly's brows lifted. 'He's won over Lucien.'

Val snorted. 'The man talks a mean game, but he's a marshmallow.'

'I know. He spends all his extra time at our house, spoiling my sister and Harper.'

'Good. Chelsea and Harper deserve a little spoiling.' Because Molly's niece had survived a living hell, having been molested by her own father.

'So do you,' Molly murmured, because she knew the truth. She was one of the few people who did. Burke knew basic details. Val's parents only knew that she'd had a stalker.

Her brother Van had known the whole truth, too, but he was gone. No one else knew.

Kaj does.

Val blinked, the truth hitting her like a brick. He didn't know everything, but he'd guessed at the basics and he'd cared. Enough to be gentle when telling her that he wanted to see where things would go between them once Elijah was safe again.

'Oh,' Molly said slyly. 'What was that?'

'What?' Val asked, resisting the urge to cover her face.

Molly's eyes sparkled. 'That blush on your face. I was here feeling all sad for you, but you look happy. Almost bashfully so.' She leaned in close. 'Tell me everything.'

Val nudged her away with an embarrassed laugh. 'There's nothing to tell.'

'But there will be.' Molly nodded knowingly. 'I'm sure of it. I saw how he looked at you at the party Gabe threw at the Choux two weeks ago.'

Cousins Gabe and Patty Hebert co-owned the Choux and had closed the restaurant to host Gabe's father's memorial—done in true New Orleans fashion with a zydeco band and dancing. Kaj had been in attendance, but he hadn't been looking at her. Val knew this because she'd been watching him. 'He did not.'

'He did so. I saw him. Even told Gabe. We made a bet on when he'd ask you out.'

Val stared at her. 'When did you pick?'

'Thanksgiving. Gabe said New Year's. Of course, we hadn't predicted that Elijah would be nearly kidnapped, so that threw our timing.'

'Pesky things, attempted kidnappings,' Val muttered.

'You know what I meant. Go and sleep. Maybe you'll be more forthcoming with the juicy details after a nap.'

'Not a chance, because there are no juicy details.'

'Yet,' Molly said archly.

Val allowed herself a small smile. 'Yet.' Then she sobered, remembering why she was there in Kaj's house. Elijah. She was there to keep Elijah safe. 'I'm going to talk to Antoine, then I'll go to sleep.' She turned for the dining room table, but Antoine stayed her with an outstretched hand, palm out.

'Do not bother me,' he said. 'Do not ask me what I know. I've only gotten started.'

Val didn't take offense. When he was relaxed, Antoine was the life of the party. When he was working, he was like a grumpy hermit in a cave. 'Fine. Can I at least know the dates you got from Rick's calendar?'

Antoine made a growling noise but pivoted to his third laptop and typed something. 'I just emailed them to you. Go sleep. Or don't sleep. I don't care. Just don't bother me.'

'Okay, okay. I'm going.' She took a final glance at Molly, who flipped her hand, shooing her up the stairs without a word. 'Fine. I'm going.'

Changing out of her pantsuit and taking off the wig, she stretched her body under the covers of Kaj's guestroom bed. She allowed herself a single moment of wishing she were in his bed instead, but that was all. She closed her eyes, but her brain wouldn't stop racing, so she opened her phone to Antoine's newest email.

And . . . wow. Ten times in the last two years. Ten times Corey had left two teenagers for at least a week at a time—without any food. There were other times he'd left them for days but had at least left a few twenties on the table so that the boys could buy their own food.

Two years ago, Jace had only been thirteen. Rick only fourteen. Fourteen and taking diligent notes to help get himself and Jace out of a horrific situation.

When she'd been fourteen, she and Van had gone to school and played video games afterward. They'd babysat Sylvi when her sitter had to cancel. Their parents had worked a lot, so they hadn't always been physically in their house, but they'd have come home in a heartbeat had one of the kids needed them. They'd *always* fed them. Never beaten them. Her parents had always loved them.

Her heart hurt for Jace, just as it had for every neglected child who'd passed through her classroom. She'd helped as best she could, lining them up with county services so that they didn't go hungry. She still did with the kids who came to her music class at the community center, calling children's services more than once when she'd seen finger-shaped bruises.

Much like the bruises on Jace's skin.

It never got easier to see. It never became possible to unsee.

She wouldn't have it any other way. She never wanted to be numb to a child in need.

Pay attention, Val. She focused on the list of dates but knew that Antoine was better equipped to look for patterns and connections to crimes. At least while her brain was spinning and tired.

She closed that email and opened the one with the background checks on the Gates brothers and their employees. She scrolled past the profiles she'd already studied—Aaron, Corey, Ed the accountant, and Bobby the ex-cop. She'd reread them later.

There was one more profile, the last in Antoine's email. A woman's face stared back at her from the screen. Sandra Springfield had been arrested with Aaron. She was his personal assistant, managing his financial consulting office.

She'd held his coat while he'd beaten Dr. Singh to death. She'd kept photos of Aaron and Dewey on a thumb drive, hidden in her house. She'd known about the drug connection. She'd been high as a kite the day Aaron murdered the doctor.

Val's mind prickled with unease as she studied the photo. Because Sandra Springfield looked familiar. She'd seen her before. But where?

She sat up, concentrating on the photo, zooming in on the woman's face. But no name came rushing into her memory. Just that nagging certainty that she'd seen her before.

She zoomed in on the woman's eyes, her nose, her mouth.

Her hair. A thin line of dark brown ran down the part of her blond hair. *Roots.* Sandra Springfield was actually a brunette.

Val forced herself to walk quietly down the stairs because Elijah was napping. With a frown, Molly looked up from where she sat, nibbling on a cake pop.

'You need to sleep, Val.'

Val nodded, an almost frantic energy propelling her toward the dining room table. 'I know, I know, but I have something.'

Molly jumped to her feet. 'What? What do you have?'

'I don't know.' She stopped in front of Antoine, who deliberately ignored her. 'Antoine.'

'I said don't—'

'Antoine, I'm sorry, this is important,' she persisted, and Antoine looked up, blinking at her.

He leaned back in his chair, giving her his full attention. 'What is it?'

'Sandra Springfield. I know her from somewhere, but I can't remember where. I don't think she was blond when I saw her.' She sat beside him as he brought up both the photo and her profile on one of his laptop screens. 'Can you change her hair to the brown of her roots?'

Molly took a seat on Val's other side, scanning the report on Antoine's screen. 'She grew up in New Orleans. Maybe you went to school with her.'

'I don't think so. Van and I went to a pretty small high school. We knew everyone in our graduating class.'

'And you didn't finish college here,' Molly murmured, 'so it's probably not from there.'

'No.' Val had moved after her first semester at Tulane to get away from her stalker.

Antoine loaded Sandra's photo into his image editing software. He tapped a few buttons and . . . 'Voilà,' he said. 'She's now a brunette. Do you recognize her now?'

Val narrowed her eyes, willing her brain to remember. 'Her hair was shorter then, I think. Level with her jawline.' Antoine made a few changes and the woman now wore a bob cut, just as she remembered. 'Dammit. Why can't I—'

Oh my God. Val's hands flew to cover her mouth to keep in what would have been a shout of disbelief.

I'm remembering wrong. I have to be.

'Val?' Molly asked, her tone still rock steady.

The front door opened and Kaj came into the house, Burke on his heels. Both carried takeout bags from a chicken restaurant nearby.

We forgot to tell them that we have leftovers, she thought. Because it was easier to think about food than the truth that was staring her right in the face.

Kaj locked the door, and then he and Burke both stopped when they saw Val's face.

'What is it?' Kaj demanded. 'Is it Elijah? Where is he? Is he okay?'

'He's fine,' Molly said. 'He's asleep. I checked on him a few minutes ago.'

'Thank God.' Kaj sank into a chair and took one of Val's hands in his. 'Then what's happened? You look like you've seen a ghost.'

'Val recognized the woman who was arrested with Aaron Gates,' Molly explained.

Kaj frowned. 'Sandra Springfield. We know who she is already.'

'No,' Val said numbly. 'That wasn't her name before.' *It can't be true. He wouldn't.*

Of course he wouldn't. She tricked him. The woman *had* to have tricked him.

What if she killed him?

'Before what?' Antoine asked.

'Before she was with Aaron.' Val met Burke's eyes, then settled on Kaj's. 'Her name was Cassie. I only saw her once, but this is her. She was my brother's girlfriend.'

15

KAJ STOPPED HIS Lexus in the driveway. The Kristiansen home was a ranch style, the front yard neatly mowed. 'You're sure you want to do this?' he asked Val softly.

She nodded, a jerky motion. 'I need to know for sure. I need to find out who that woman was to Van.'

He, Burke, Molly, and Antoine had stared at her in stunned silence after her pronouncement at his dining room table. Kaj had been shocked, but his primary concern at that moment had been the stricken look on her face. She'd gone pale and her hands had trembled.

An hour later, she was still pale and her hands still trembled. But she looked determined, just as she had when she'd interrupted their debate of what it could mean for Val's brother to have been dating the woman who was associated with the organization who'd murdered him.

I need to go to my parents' house, she'd said. *There's a photo on their mantel of Van and his girlfriend. I need to know for sure. If he was seeing her, maybe that's why he's dead.*

Burke and Molly had stayed to guard Elijah and watch over Jace, who'd sat quietly on the sofa, his hands cuffed in front of him.

Kaj had volunteered to drive Val to her parents' house. He wanted to know if she'd remembered correctly, but he also wanted to be the one to offer her support, because she clearly needed it. The worried expressions on Burke's and Molly's faces had told him that Val's reaction was not typical. It certainly wasn't what Kaj had observed up until this point. She'd been confident in the face of every challenge, had kept a level head at every threat.

Not so right now.

Kaj cut the engine of his Lexus and turned to study Val's pale face. 'Your parents are going to know that something is wrong.'

She met his eyes, hers tortured. 'I know. I need to pull myself together. My mom's not strong enough to deal with rehashing Van's murder. It nearly killed her four years ago.'

Her hands were clenched in her lap, so tightly that her knuckles were white. Carefully, he reached across the console and pried her hands apart, taking one of them in his. 'What would help?' he asked.

She tightened her grip on his hand. 'This helps.'

'Maybe you should tell me what you remember before we go in there.' She'd refused to say anything more about her brother, regardless of how many questions her coworkers had fired at her. Kaj figured she'd been in shock.

Knowing that your brother was murdered by drug dealers because he'd been trying to keep his younger sister from buying was one thing. Learning that he'd had a relationship with a woman who was a close associate with those drug dealers was something entirely different.

'It was in late November, only a few weeks before he died. Around lunchtime. I was home for Thanksgiving, and I was walking through the Quarter, on my way to see MaryBeth and Jess in the bakery. I remember that I was happy to be home, for the first time in a long time.'

He caressed her hand with his thumb. 'Why?'

She closed her eyes. 'Because Eric Haynes was dead.'

He frowned for a moment, then he understood. 'The man who was stalking you? Who . . . hurt you?'

'Yes. Him. I'd been in the Marines for four years and my family hadn't seen me often then. Only when I had leave. I'd finally come home and not even a year later announced that I was moving again. They tried to change my mind. They tried really, really hard.' She glanced at him. 'I told them that this guy was stalking me. I didn't tell them anything else. My mom's always been a little fragile from a mental health standpoint. I didn't want to cause her to spiral because of what happened to me. So please don't mention it.'

'I won't. I promise.'

'Thank you.' She sighed. 'So . . . I was walking through the Quarter, minding my own business, and came upon a sidewalk café where a couple was going at it, hot and heavy.'

'Your brother and Sandra Springfield.'

'Yes. I was like, "*Van?*" and they jumped apart like they were teenagers caught necking on the front porch. I remember that Van seemed . . . hesitant.'

'Hesitant about what?'

'About introducing me. At least that's how it seemed. So I introduced myself. "I'm Val, Van's twin." She said her name was Cassie. No last name. She seemed amused. Van turned bright red. I asked if she would be joining us for Thanksgiving and Van said no, that she had a family function of her own. She looked disappointed at that and it got awkward. I left, but Van followed me. Told me that he hadn't yet introduced her to the folks, that he wasn't sure how serious it was and didn't want the parental attention. I got that and told him that his secret was safe with me.' She sighed quietly. 'And then he died.'

'Did you ever tell your parents about the woman?'

'I didn't have to. Van ended up bringing her home for dinner about a week before he died. I didn't know that until Mom and I were going through some of Van's things and we found a photo. Mom said, "Oh, Van's girlfriend. She was so nice." But then she started crying and I didn't want to push her.'

Kaj wondered about the circumstances of Ivan Kristiansen's death. That Ivan had followed the youngest Kristiansen sister to where she was buying drugs from dealers who just happened to be connected with his own girlfriend? Seemed way too coincidental.

He wondered if Sylvi Kristiansen had been buying from Sandra. He wondered if Ivan had suspected. He wondered if Sandra had been involved in Ivan's death. But he didn't voice any of those questions. It wasn't the time. Plus, he had no doubt that Val had already thought of all of that.

'So your mother framed the photo and put it on the mantel after only meeting her once?'

'Yes. She was Van's girl and Mom said how happy he looked in the photo. That was how she wanted to remember him. But I never really looked at it. It was hard to look at photos of Van after he was gone. It still is.'

'I get that,' he said softly.

'I know you do. But I don't want to tell my mom that I'm here about the photo.'

'If you're not planning on telling her, what's your excuse for bringing me?'

Val's smile was dry. 'That you're my new . . . friend?'

Kaj lifted a brow. 'Won't she ask questions about what kind of friend?'

'She most definitely will.' Her smile faltered. 'I figured I'd let her wonder.'

'And if she's wondering about me, then she won't notice that you're checking out the photo of your brother.'

'If that's okay with you.'

Kaj brought their joined hands to his lips and kissed her fingers. 'It's fine.'

'Thank you.' She gave his hand a final squeeze before pulling away. 'Let's go. Mom's spotted us.'

'Let me get your door. I like to be polite in front of mothers.' She was wearing a tight smile when he opened her door. If he hadn't gotten to know her over the past few days, he might have believed the smile was real. He hoped it fooled her mother. Gripping her hand, he followed Val into her childhood home, where a tiny blond woman stood just inside the door, waiting.

'Hi, Mom.' Val bent down to kiss her mother's cheek. Val had to be a foot taller than her mother, but the resemblance otherwise was unmistakable.

Her mother kissed both of Val's cheeks. 'We missed you, Ingrid.' Hearing Val called Ingrid was a bit jarring. But it suited her. 'Your father will be so sorry he wasn't here,' she went on. 'He's in a faculty meeting at the university right now.' The older woman aimed a sly look Kaj's way. 'And who is this?'

'Mom, I want to introduce you to my friend. This is Jean-Pierre Cardozo. And this is my mother, Britta Kristiansen.'

Surprised that Val had used his more formal name, Kaj let go of her hand and extended his to her mother. 'But my friends call me Kaj. Spelled K-a-j but pronounced like "pie".' Because if things did go well with Val, he wanted to start as he meant to go on.

Britta took his hand. 'And how else would you pronounce it? It's a good Scandinavian name. Welcome, Kaj.' She hadn't let go of his hand yet. 'Would you like some tea?'

'It's sweet tea,' Val warned, and Kaj laughed.

'I think I'll pass. I'm from New York. I'm still getting used to sweet tea.'

'Understandable,' Britta said and, still holding his hand, she led him to the living room sofa. 'Took me years to get used to it when we moved here from Minnesota. Have a seat, Kaj, dear, and tell me about yourself.'

He sat, but Val remained standing, discreetly wandering over to the mantel. 'Well,' he said, 'I'm from New York, like I said. Born and raised. I moved here about six months ago.'

Britta folded her hands primly in her lap. 'And what do you do?'

'I'm a prosecutor for Orleans Parish.'

'Oh.' Her blue eyes grew round and she pressed her fingertips to her lips. '*Oh my*. You were on the news this week. You and your son. He was nearly abducted, wasn't he?'

Kaj glanced at Val, somehow surprised that her mother would have known who he was. He shouldn't have been, he supposed. Val might have described her mother as fragile, but Kaj wasn't seeing her that way. 'Yes, ma'am, that's correct. My son's name is Elijah.'

She nodded gravely. 'And he's all right?'

'He is.'

'Thank the Lord.' Britta looked over her shoulder. 'Ingrid, stop puttering around and sit with us.' She shook her head. 'That girl has never been able to sit down.' Then she seemed to realize what Val was staring at and her demeanor changed, like a switch had been flipped.

Now Kaj saw what Val had described. Britta's shoulders drooped as her expression fell and Kaj could feel the melancholy roll off her in waves. 'I'm sure Ingrid told you about her brother, Ivan.'

'A little.'

'Bring the picture over here, Ingrid.'

'Yes, ma'am.' Val handed the framed photo to her mother. 'But Kaj doesn't want to hear about Van.'

'Of course he does,' Britta said with a lift of her chin. 'He's a parent. He understands. Don't you, Kaj?'

'Yes, ma'am,' Kaj said gently. The fear that grabbed him whenever he thought about someone hurting Elijah or even Elijah's diabetes hurting him was all-consuming. To have lost a child was something he couldn't begin to fathom. He leaned in to look at the photo—Ivan Kristiansen laughing with a dark-haired woman who was most definitely Sandra Springfield. Kaj had seen pictures of Ivan before, of course. The photo that had once been on his company's website in which he'd appeared sober. Severe, even. The other had been of his body at the scene of his murder in the case files Kaj had read. 'He looks happy in this photo.'

Britta stroked the frame, her smile tender. And fragile. Yes, Kaj now understood exactly what Val had meant. 'He was. This was his girlfriend. Her name is Cassandra, but she goes by either Cassie or Sandra. I think it depends on her mood. And if she's missing my son.'

Kaj had to fight not to show his surprise. 'It sounds like you had a good relationship with her.' He was fishing, but he sensed that there was more here than Val had known.

'Oh, I do. She still visits.'

Val was stunned. Her mouth was open, but no words were coming out. So Kaj rushed in to fill the silence, hoping to keep Britta's focus on himself.

'That's very nice of her. How often do you see her?'

'Oh, every month she comes by with flowers. Just like clockwork.' Britta leaned closer, as if sharing a secret. 'She buys them at my daughter Sylvi's flower shop, God bless her. Sylvi works hard, but she still has a difficult time making ends meet. Cassandra tries to help out however she can. Sylvi always changes the subject whenever I mention Cassandra, but I know she's grateful. She has to be.'

Kaj dared another glance at Val. Her lips were now pursed, her cheeks stained with dark flags of angry red.

Britta must not have seen the news last week, however, because she didn't appear to realize that Cassandra—aka Sandra Springfield— had been arrested on charges of drug possession and conspiracy to commit murder.

'That's good of her,' Kaj said with a smile that he hoped didn't look as forced as it felt.

Val didn't smile. 'How often does Sylvi drop by, Mom?'

Britta turned to her daughter, her irritation as plain as Val's. 'Every week, which is more often than you visit, if you must know.' Kaj winced inwardly as Val winced outwardly. 'Sylvi's changed, Ingrid. She's clean and sober. Has been for four years.'

Val's nod was tight. 'I'm sure she is.'

Translated: *There's no way in hell that she's clean. Not if she's seeing Sandra Springfield.*

Britta closed her eyes and exhaled through her nose, her pose the age-old parental *What am I going to do with you?* 'One of these days you'll wish you'd been kinder, but it will be too late.'

Val's eyes snapped with anger. 'How much money does she ask for, Mom? Whenever she "drops by"?'

Britta's eyes opened, equally angry. 'We will not discuss such a thing in front of company.'

Val looked away. 'I'm sorry, Mom. I worry that she's draining your resources.'

'Your sister doesn't make as much money as you do. She needs help. Which you'd know if you ever gave her the time of day instead of holding on to old hurts.'

It sounded like Val's issue with her sister was bigger than 'old hurts,' but it wasn't Kaj's business, so he remained silent.

Val smiled, but it was totally fake. 'I'd like to see Cassandra again. When does she usually visit?'

'On Saturday mornings, first of every month.' Britta's tone was frigid. 'Come by for coffee. I'd love to see you, and Cassandra would, too.'

Oh wow. There was no doubt in Kaj's mind that the woman had meant the exact opposite of that. 'I will.' Val stood, bending over to kiss her mother's cheek. 'I'll see you soon, Mom. Kaj and I need to go.'

Britta made a frustrated sound. 'But you just got here.'

'We've left Elijah with some friends. Kaj needs to get back to him.'

'Oh. Of course. Please come by and visit again, Kaj. And keep that boy of yours safe.'

'I will,' Kaj said. 'It was lovely to meet you, Mrs. Kristiansen.'

'Britta. You must call me Britta.'

Kaj took her hand, his grip light. 'Britta. Take care.'

She walked them to the door and stood watching while they got into his car. Kaj started the engine, then gave her a little wave. Britta waved back and Kaj pulled out onto the street.

'I'm sorry,' Val murmured. 'That was so rude of me. I shouldn't have argued with her about Sylvi. It made you uncomfortable, and I'm sorry.'

'It's okay.' And it was. He'd known that Val was angry with her sister, but he supposed he hadn't truly understood the depth of it until now. He'd always gotten along incredibly well with his own sister, but if Genie's behavior had led to the death of someone that he loved? He couldn't say how he'd react, so he left the issue alone, focusing instead on the reason for their visit. 'You were right. Your brother was seeing Sandra Springfield at the time of his death.'

'Yes. I took a photo of the picture with my phone. I had no idea that she visited my mother every month. That scares the hell out of me, knowing that the woman who held Aaron Gates's coat while he murdered a man has been so close to my mother. *For years.*' She sighed. 'I suppose I panicked. I couldn't confront her about Sandra, so I punted to what was most familiar.'

Ah. 'It was easier to argue about your sister than to deal with the fact that your mother has been unknowingly welcoming a drug dealer's girlfriend into her home.'

'Pretty much. That it was always on Saturday mornings makes it worse. That's when I teach music at the community center and my dad has a standing golf game. She visited when Mom was alone.'

Kaj hesitated. 'Is it possible that she simply likes your mother?'

She made a sound of disbelief. 'You really think that?'

'I don't know. But maybe we should consider that before we panic.'

'Well, if you're going to be logical,' she grumbled, and he chuckled. 'Yes, it's possible. My mother is very nice to people. Usually only the people who agree with her about Sylvi, but whatever. I personally don't accept that Sandra buys flowers from Sylvi's shop every month out of the goodness of her heart. It's too coincidental. Probably more like she's dropping off drugs to Sylvi every month.'

'You don't believe your sister's gotten clean?'

Val's sigh was weary. 'I want her to be. But of course she'd tell our mother that she was clean.'

'Have you seen her high recently?'

'No, but we don't exactly hang out.' She sighed again. 'I have seen her popping pills as recently as Mom's birthday dinner last month. I asked her if I could help her get into rehab, but she told me to fuck off and mind my own business.'

'Ouch.'

'Yeah. It's . . . not simple. I want to let this anger go, but she's never apologized for getting Van killed. And she keeps asking Mom for money. She and Dad have been trying to save for their retirement. Sylvi asking for their money makes me so mad.' He caught the tremble of her lips from the corner of his eye. 'And I *do* visit my mother. When I'm not on a job, I'm at their house twice a week. I clean and shop for their groceries and fix things that are broken.' She swallowed audibly. 'Dad's your stereotypical absent-minded professor. He forgets to do important things, like paying the electric bill. Mom shuts down when she's overwhelmed, so . . .' She shrugged. 'I quit my job in New Mexico to take care of them after Van died. He'd been handling things. I don't expect my parents to make a big deal about it, but . . .'

'It would be nice if they didn't put your sister on a pedestal,' he finished, reaching over the console for her hand. She slipped hers into his and held on tight.

'Exactly. Thank you, Kaj, for coming with me. If I'd been there alone, I might have yelled at my mother, and I always feel guilty when I do that.'

'What are you going to do next?'

'I don't know. I want to march into the jail and ask Sandra Springfield what the fuck she was doing with my brother. And my mother.' She went still for a beat or two. 'And my sister, too,' she added quietly. 'I'm wondering all kinds of things now.'

'Like?'

'Like, how did Sandra meet Van? How did she meet Aaron? What was her relationship with Dewey Talley? Was she using Van somehow? Did she sell drugs to Sylvi? Sylvi was a troubled kid in high school. Smoked and drank and partied. Nearly didn't graduate because she'd had so many suspensions, but she turned herself around at the end of her senior year. She got into Tulane. Then she got hooked on methamphetamine.'

'To stay awake to study?'

'Yes. After that, everything collapsed.' She slumped in her seat. 'And I feel partly responsible. I was in New Mexico by the time she started college. If I'd been here . . .'

'She may have still bought illegal drugs,' Kaj said. 'You can't play the what-if game. It never works.'

She hesitated, then asked, 'Did you play what-if when your wife got sick?'

His throat tightened. 'All the time. What if I hadn't worked so much? What if I'd taken her to the doctor when she first started feeling tired? It didn't matter. She died all the same.'

Val drew a ragged breath and when he glanced over at her, he saw her wiping her eyes. 'I'll ask Sylvi what was going on with Sandra. And if she's still using, I'll try again to help.'

'I think that's all you can do. You can't force her to quit. She has to want the help. You want me to come with you?'

Her grip on his hand tightened, almost painfully. 'Would you?'

The vulnerability in her voice squeezed his heart. 'Yes. You won't have to be alone.'

She brought his hand to her cheek. 'Thank you, Kaj.'

'You're welcome. I agree, by the way, that Sandra's relationship with your family in general is extremely suspicious. Too many coincidences. Van and Aaron worked for the same firm before Aaron went off to start his own. Sandra was with Van, then with Aaron. Sylvi was there when Van was killed and now Sandra is visiting her every month.'

'You think that Sandra was involved with Van's death?'

'Don't you?'

'Yeah. I do. I thought so as soon as I remembered where I'd seen her. But it's not like I can ask her. She'll lie.'

'No, but I can ask. Or another ADA can, since I'm recused from her and Aaron's cases. She might be willing to talk now that she's been charged with conspiracy to commit murder.'

Val sat up straighter. 'You really think so?'

'We can try. I questioned her right after she was arrested, but she was detoxing.'

'Was that before or after you found the photos of Dewey Talley and Aaron together?'

'Both. She was slightly less confident after but still remained silent on the advice of her attorney. The link to your brother opens things up a bit. I'd like to know more about her before she's questioned again, though. I'm going to do some digging into her background when we get home.'

'Like what? What do you want to know?' Val asked.

'When she met Dewey Talley, for starters. Did she introduce Dewey and Aaron or did they know each other first? How did she meet your brother? Was she connected to Cunningham and Spector, your brother's—and Aaron's—old firm? It wasn't on her employment history, but she could have been a client. Did she meet both of them there? And if not, what is her connection to the two men? How did she go from dating your brother to dating a drug dealer?'

'I could ask Desmond,' she said thoughtfully. 'He's one of Van's old coworkers. They were frat brothers at Tulane and he and I went out a few times when I was home on leave, so I know him well enough. He might not tell me anything, but it wouldn't hurt to ask.'

Kaj frowned, disliking that she'd been out with this Desmond, but he pushed it aside. He was not a jealous teenager. 'No, it wouldn't hurt. Call him when we get back to my house, though. I want to be able to listen in and pay attention, but I can't while I'm watching the road.'

'I don't think I can pay attention right now, either,' she admitted. 'I'm tired.'

'Then sleep. I'll wake you when we get back to my house.'

He thought she'd argue with him, but she remained silent as he approached the entrance to I-10, heading back to Mid-City. When he glanced at her, her eyes were closed and her chest was rising and falling in a steady rhythm. She was already asleep, her face relaxed and serene.

Metairie, Louisiana
WEDNESDAY, OCTOBER 26, 6:16 P.M.

'Well?' Bobby asked, his hands still tight on the steering wheel of the car they'd stolen. They'd disabled the GPS function, so at least NOPD couldn't track them after this latest unmitigated disaster. 'What next?'

Needing a place to decompress, they'd parked behind a boarded-up store after checking to be sure there were no security cameras. Corey was still nervous. *What a fuckup.*

'NOPD was ready for us tonight,' he said.

Bobby huffed. 'Ed was right, as much as I hate to admit it. This was a trap.'

There had been no Jace waiting for them in the small bungalow. Rather, they'd been greeted with shouts of 'Police! Drop your weapons!' Which they hadn't done, of course.

They might have been lured into a trap, but they weren't completely stupid. They'd shot up the house as well as the cops, who'd—unfortunately—been wearing vests. Fortunately, so had Corey and Bobby, because the police had returned fire.

He and Bobby had gotten away before backup could arrive. But it had been too close.

'They know they have a leak,' Corey muttered. 'Better tell your buddy that he might be in danger.'

'Already texted him. He's pissed off.'

Up until tonight, Bobby's friend had been spot-on, although Corey now wondered what else the man had gotten wrong that they'd accepted as truth.

'The cops have Jace stashed somewhere,' Corey said, trying to think past the pounding of his heart. 'They wouldn't have known to use him as bait if they hadn't caught him. So at least your friend got that right.'

'We have to find out what else Jace has told them.'

Corey studied his friend's profile in the semidarkness. '*Did* you mention the Doyle job at the office where Jace or Rick could have overheard you?'

Bobby's angry gaze collided with Corey's. 'No. I did not.'

Corey held up one hand. 'Okay. I just needed to ask. Sorry.'

'What next?' Bobby asked again, his words clipped.

'We still have to find Jace,' Corey said quietly. 'But we might have a hard time getting intel out of NOPD now that they know they have a leak.'

Bobby snorted. 'They've always had leaks. It's like . . . breathing. Give it a day or two. The heat will move on to someone else and my friend will feel fine with talking again. Or we could lean on one of Ed's paid informants. Some of them are placed well enough to overhear helpful things. We have a lot of options.'

'How long you think we should wait before trying again to get Jace?' Because he *would* make the little bastard pay for fucking everything up. *My life was ordered. My business was growing. I had the respect of my clients.* And then Aaron, Rick, and Jace had gone and ruined everything. Aaron was probably going to spend the rest of his life in prison if he didn't get the needle, but Rick would get out someday. And Jace was walking around free.

So Jace would be next. Corey knew he wouldn't get a decent night's sleep until his youngest brother was punished. He'd find a way to deal with Rick, too. *I'm a paid killer, for fuck's sake. I can take out one skinny teenager in lockup.* He'd figure it out.

He had to. How would it look for a professional killer to allow his two brothers to continue breathing after such betrayal? His reputation had already been battered by all this. He would not allow Rick and Jace to ruin his business as well.

Neither of them could continue existing. They simply couldn't.

'At least until we're done with the Doyle job,' Bobby said thoughtfully. 'We get paid, then we can find a place to lay low and hire someone to take Jace out. Not as satisfying, but smarter.' He lifted a brow. 'And don't you dare tell Ed that I said that.'

'I won't. Let's get back to camp. I need to sleep. My brain is too fried to even think about the Doyle job right now. Bella's going to leave her hidey-hole for the city any day now. I need to be alert.'

'Let's steal another car and ditch this one,' Bobby said. 'With our luck, the people who rented it have already reported it missing.'

They were nearly out of the city when Corey's phone buzzed in his pocket. He checked the caller ID and his pulse started to tick up again, because Ed rarely called. He usually texted. 'Yeah?' he answered, putting the phone on speaker. 'What's up?'

'I made some calls to the cops we have on payroll, and one of our guys heard that Rick was visited by a lawyer today.'

Corey rubbed his temples. 'That was inevitable. They had to assign him a public defender.'

'This wasn't a public defender, though,' Ed said. 'Guy's name is Lucien Farrow. Alex Cullen—that's our NOPD informant—remembered his name from somewhere and looked him up. He used to be a prosecutor, but now he's a PI. Works for Burke Broussard.'

Corey frowned. 'Wait. I've heard of Broussard. He was NOPD, too, wasn't he? He's broken some big cases recently.'

Bobby nodded, troubled. 'He was NOPD, yes. Quit because he wouldn't go dirty, or at least that was what the rumor mill said.'

'Why would a PI send a lawyer to talk to Rick?' Corey asked. 'Who's Broussard working for?'

'Oh fuck,' Bobby muttered. He glanced at Corey before returning his gaze to the road. 'You said that there was a woman at Cardozo's house last night.'

Corey nodded. 'Yeah, she had a big dog. Chased us. Why?'

'Oh,' Ed said quietly. 'Cardozo refused police protection, but what if he hired someone private? Broussard does investigations and personal protection.'

'That doesn't make sense,' Corey protested. 'If Cardozo hired Broussard, the last person representing Rick would be one of Broussard's people.'

'Unless they were weaseling information out of him,' Ed said.

Corey closed his eyes. 'Fuck. Find out, Ed. Find out if Cardozo hired Broussard. And find out if any of the guys you've been paying all this time have a contact in the jail. Rick needs to die.'

'Is Jace . . . taken care of?' Ed asked carefully.

'No,' Corey snapped. 'It was a trap. And if you even think the words "I told you so," I'll break your fuckin' nose.'

'Noted,' Ed said. 'Well, what now?'

Corey deliberately misunderstood, because he truly had no idea and that terrified him. 'Now we come back to camp and get some sleep.'

Mid-City, New Orleans, Louisiana
WEDNESDAY, OCTOBER 26, 6:15 P.M.

Kaj brought his car to a stop in his garage, fighting back a sudden wave of fatigue as he lowered the garage door. He hadn't been so tired in a very long time. He rolled his head to one side to study Val, who'd woken about five minutes before, remaining silent as he drove.

She was watching him, her expression as weary as he felt. 'Thank you again,' she said quietly. 'I really appreciate that you came with me.'

The quiet wasn't only in the volume of her voice. It was also in her tone. She was emotionally worn down and Kaj didn't like it. She was strong and confident and made him feel safe, especially with Elijah, but after less than twenty minutes with her mother she was drained and defeated.

He took her hand and squeezed it. 'Are you all right?'

Her smile returning, she squared her shoulders and nodded decisively. It was like watching her don armor. She was the Val he'd known for the past few days, the Val of the past few hours hidden away.

It made him wonder what else she hid. And which Val was the real one.

'Of course,' she said. 'I need to check on Elijah, walk Czar, and then relieve Burke. And you have some company. I saw MaryBeth and Jess's minivan and Patty's VW parked on the curb. I hope that means food.' Getting out of the car as if she hadn't been exhausted a minute before, she waited for him to follow.

Slowly he did, searching for the words that would help her. Because she wasn't all right. Catching her arm before she went into the house, he cradled her jaw in his palm, something inside him settling when she leaned into his touch.

'Tell me the truth,' he said softly. 'Because you're not all right.'

'No,' she whispered. 'My parents are . . . Well, they're not the same people that they were before Van died. Dad used to read three newspapers with his morning coffee. Now he's cut off from the real world, hiding in his history books.'

'Your mother had heard about Elijah.'

'I know. She watches the news and I wish she wouldn't. She becomes upset when she hears about violent crimes and retreats into her own mind, and I don't know what she sees there. If she did see a report on Sandra's arrest, she might have blocked it out.'

'Kind of like they ignore the truth about your sister?'

Her smile was small and sad. 'Kind of like that, yeah.'

Going with his instincts, Kaj tugged her closer, wrapping his arms around her. She laid her head on his shoulder with a shudder and a soft exhale that sounded like relief. He pressed a kiss to her temple. 'I'm so sorry.'

She slid her arms around his waist, under his jacket. He could feel the warmth of her hands on his skin through his shirt and could smell the faint scent of vanilla in her hair. She fit perfectly against him and his body shucked off its exhaustion, his cock perking up with interest.

He hadn't wanted a woman since Heather. He'd nearly forgotten what it felt like to want like this.

It felt really, really good. He brushed his lips over her soft cheek, satisfied when she cuddled closer, nuzzling into his throat and tightening her hold. This felt confident and real. Val was back and he didn't want to let her go.

She pressed a chaste kiss to the exposed skin at his open collar. 'It was easier with you there. I didn't feel so alone.'

He gave his head a shake to clear it, because this was important.

'When this is over, when Elijah's safe, maybe she'd like to meet him? Maybe that would help her connect to the world.'

She pulled back far enough to meet his eyes. The soul-weary, defeated exhaustion had been replaced by interest and heat. 'That's a sweet thought. Now, can we stop talking about my mother?' Then she leaned in to brush a kiss against his lips and his body lit up like fireworks on the Fourth of July.

Groaning, he gripped the back of her neck, greedily taking her mouth. He ran his other hand over her hair, caressing the braid pinned to her head that he wished he could take down. He wanted to feel her hair in his hands, wanted to thrust his fingers through it. Wanted to wrap it around his hands to pull her even closer.

As if reading his mind, her hands slid up his chest and over his shoulders, clasping at the back of his neck. She plastered herself against him, humming into the kiss. She was as tall as he was and it was a different sensation, holding a woman like this. He could feel her from chest to knee and all the places in between.

Her hips pressed hard against his, and she undulated, making him gasp. His hand was on her ass before he knew it. She filled his palm perfectly and he kneaded, wishing they weren't in his garage. Wishing they were in his bed. He pulled back enough to take a single breath, and then he was kissing her again and she was kissing him back. It was hot and wet and everything he'd hoped it would be.

But it wasn't enough, not even close. He needed more. But not now. Not yet.

He ended the kiss before he went too far. She opened her eyes and he nearly gave in to his craving for more of her mouth. More of her. Her lips parted and she was panting, the expression on her face exactly what he needed to see.

Lust and need. She wanted him, too.

He was trembling, his knees close to buckling. From pleasure this time. Not from fear or rage or anguish, like the times before.

With a lovely sigh, she rested her head on his shoulder. 'We probably shouldn't have done that, but I'm not sorry that we did. I needed it. Needed you. Thank you.'

'I might have needed it more. And now that I've really kissed you, I don't want to stop.'

She huffed a chuckle, warm on his skin. 'We might need to, for a little while. Your son is on the other side of that door. And, based on the cars outside, we're far from alone.'

She was right. Her friends had likely made them dinner again. But he wasn't hungry, not for food, anyway. What he wanted was to grab her hand and drag her up the stairs and into his bed, but that wasn't going to happen tonight.

But soon.

'I guess we have to leap into the fray.' Opening the door into the living room, he breathed in something that smelled heavenly before stumbling over Czar. 'Ouch.' The dog ignored him, wagging his stubby tail and staring up at Val adoringly from his position directly in front of the entrance.

Czar was pretty smart.

'Hey there,' Val crooned, kissing the big dog on his head. 'Have you been good?'

'He's been really good,' Elijah said. His son stood up from the sofa and crossed his arms over his chest, his eyes narrowed. 'What's wrong? I heard the garage door. You were in the garage a long time. What happened? Where were you?'

Kaj's cheeks heated and he stumbled over his words. 'We were just . . .'

Val saved him. 'We were talking about my mom and dad. I needed to go and talk to my mother about something and your dad went with me. My mother is . . . well, she's still grieving my brother's death and it's hard for me to watch.'

Burke came around the corner from the kitchen, his brows raised in question. Kaj realized that Val hadn't communicated the results of their trip to Burke yet. Her conversation with her mother really had rattled her, making Kaj doubly glad he'd gone with her.

Kaj gave Burke a nod, then tilted his head toward Val with a resigned expression. Burke's jaw hardened and he nodded back, clearly understanding.

'Oh.' Elijah's brow creased in a frown. 'Is your mother sick?'

'No, honey,' Val assured him. 'Not physically. She's just sad and doesn't know how to live in the world anymore, now that my brother's gone.'

'But she still has you,' Elijah said, and Kaj heard Val's indrawn breath.

Out of the mouths of babes, indeed.

'Yes, she does.' She lifted Elijah's chin with her finger, smiling down at him. 'What's for supper? Did you sous-chef for Patty this time?'

'I did!' Elijah said proudly. 'Patty let Jace do the taste testing. He says that dinner is *really* good. You're staying, too, aren't you, Burke?'

Burke tousled Elijah's hair. 'I would never say no to the Choux's shrimp and grits.' He hesitated, looking down at Elijah. 'Why don't you go help Patty finish dinner, Elijah?'

Elijah's eyes narrowed. 'What happened?' He looked up at Kaj. 'Dad?'

'I don't know,' Kaj said honestly. 'Why don't you help with dinner and let Burke and me talk. If I can tell you, I will.' Elijah opened his mouth and Kaj shook his head sharply. 'There are things you shouldn't know, Elijah. And it's not because you're a kid. It's because I don't want you to have some of the same pictures in your head that I do. Please.'

Elijah's mouth firmed, but he nodded. 'You'll tell me if it involves me?'

'I promise.' *Within reason, of course.*

When Elijah had returned to the kitchen, Burke sighed. 'André called after you'd left for Val's mother's house. I was going to give you the news when you called in after leaving there.'

An unpleasant shiver raced down Kaj's spine. 'What happened?'

'Your trap was sprung. Two men in ski masks attacked the safe house where Jace was supposedly holed up. They shot up the place with AR15s. Injured both cops who were on guard. Camera footage showed two men who fit the physical descriptions of Corey Gates and Bobby Landry.'

Kaj's shoulders sagged. He'd been afraid of this very thing. 'Does Jace know?'

'Not yet. I figured we needed to decide what would happen to him first, because that's going to be the first thing the boy's gonna want to know.'

Kaj mentally stepped back from the memory of Jace pleading with them not to send him back to Corey, focusing on the attack. 'Could Corey and Bobby have been trying to rescue Jace?'

'Unlikely. They breached the door and one of them—probably Corey—opened fire on the bed where the cops had placed a mannequin under the blanket while the other held off the cops with an AR-15. Cops were outgunned. They should have had rifles, but they didn't. The one who'd shot up the bed ripped the blanket off and "swore violently" according to the cops.'

'Oh my God,' Val breathed. 'Okay, so . . . first, will the officers be okay?'

Burke nodded. 'André said that one was treated and released and the other is in a stable condition. They said that the men didn't seem to want to kill them, just hurt them enough that they couldn't fight back.'

'But Corey meant to kill Jace,' Kaj murmured.

'Fucking hell,' Val whispered. 'Poor Jace. I mean, he believed that Corey would have hurt him next, but . . . dammit. We're going to have to tell him.'

Kaj didn't relish that task at all. 'What about the cuffs? Do we take them off?'

Burke shrugged. 'Your house, Kaj. Your call.'

Kaj wanted to tell Burke to take them off. He really did. But . . . 'That kid is terrified of Corey—so terrified that he gave Rick over to me, not knowing what I'd do to him. I know Jace was forced,' he said when Val opened her mouth to protest. 'I *know* that, Val, but that's my point. What if Corey gave him instructions to hurt Elijah if he got into my house? He could still do it because he's scared of his brother. He'll be even more scared when we tell him what happened tonight. I can't risk it. Not yet. The cuffs have to stay on.'

Val slowly nodded. 'I don't like it, but I will respect your decision.' She softened her words with a smile and a brief squeeze of his hand. 'For what it's worth, I think Jace will agree with you. He seems almost comforted by the cuffs. Like if we keep him cuffed, we'll trust him.'

'Which makes me feel even worse about it,' Kaj said with a sigh.

'Will you let him stay here?' Burke asked. 'I think he'd gladly accept the cuffs if you let him stay. I'd take him home with me, but I've been here most of the time.'

'I certainly can't turn him over to NOPD at this point,' Kaj said. 'Not if I want to be able to look at myself in the mirror, anyway. Turning him over to children's services would be just as bad, if not worse. They don't have the security systems in place to keep him safe. They'd have to cooperate with the police and that would put us right back at square one. So . . . yeah. Let's keep him here for at least one more night and then we'll reevaluate. Let's tell him about the attack after dinner, but I'll let him know right away that he can stay another night.'

'Sounds fair,' Val said.

'No, it's not fair,' Kaj said. 'It's not fair to Jace, if he's as completely innocent as we think he is. But it's the best I can offer at the moment.'

'It's better than any of the alternatives,' Val said, her eyes gentle. 'So stop beating yourself up, Kaj. Seriously.' She turned to Burke. 'Has Antoine made any progress with the dates from Rick's calendar?'

'Not yet,' Burke said. 'I called him back to the office for another client's case, but he said he could run the searches on Rick's dates at the same time.'

A clearing of a throat got their attention. Patty stood behind them, smoothing her apron. 'Dinner is ready whenever you are. It's not fancy, but we heard y'all had a trying day, so we decided to pitch in to make it a little better.'

Val gave her friend a hug. 'Thank you. You're the best.'

'And what am I?' MaryBeth yelled from the kitchen. 'Chopped liver?'

'You're all the best,' Val said with a laugh. 'And I'm starving. It's been hours since the last time you fed me. Elijah, give me a hand in setting the table?'

Elijah ran to her side, eager to help, and Kaj saw a future for them—his son and Val, blond heads together, setting the table for a family dinner. His family.

Which was silly. He had no right dreaming of such things after only a few days. But his brain's logic wasn't convincing his heart. He'd have to wait and see.

Elijah eyed Kaj warily as he set out the flatware. 'Was that about me?'

'No,' Kaj said. 'Not directly, anyway. It was about Jace.' Jace already sat at the table, staring down at his cuffed hands in his lap, the picture of resigned dejection. He didn't look up, wouldn't meet Kaj's eyes. 'You'll be staying with us at least one more night, Jace.'

Jace's chin shot up, his eyes wide and so hopeful that Kaj's chest hurt. 'Thank you, Mr. Cardozo,' he said, so very quietly that Kaj barely heard him.

Elijah relaxed, a smile tilting his lips. 'Thanks, Dad. Can you uncuff him? Burke said we couldn't until you said it was okay.'

'Elijah,' Jace said quietly. 'It's fine. I understand why your dad is afraid. As long as I don't have to go back to Corey and he can't find me, I'm okay with the handcuffs.'

Either the boy was sincere, or he was playing them. Kaj still didn't know.

They sat down at the table—Burke handcuffed to Jace so that the boy had a free hand to eat—and dug into the dinner so kindly prepared by Val's friends. Everyone seemed at ease, laughing as MaryBeth animatedly described the time that Val had chased down a purse snatcher in the Quarter, taking him down with a classic roller derby move. Elijah was enthralled and Jace was looking at Val like she was Wonder Woman.

Kaj glanced at Val over Elijah's head, simply enjoying watching her smile. His skin warmed as he remembered that kiss in the garage. He'd forgotten how soft lips could be and how good it felt to be held. To be wanted. It was as if the floodgates had opened, the need he'd shoved down for so many years rushing forth to steal his breath.

He couldn't wait to get her alone so that he could kiss her again.

As if feeling his gaze, she met his eyes. Her cheeks turned the most becoming shade of pink and she quickly looked away, but not before all three of her friends noticed. As did Burke.

All four of them stared at him. He just smiled and dug into his dinner.

16

'I CAN'T BELIEVE YOU had shrimp and grits without me,' Antoine groused from Val's laptop screen. Burke had outside watch duty, so she'd been working at Kaj's dining room table, rereading Sandra Springfield's file when Antoine had surprised her with a Skype call.

Not wanting anyone to hear what Antoine was calling her about, she slipped an earbud into one of her ears and plugged the cord into her laptop. 'We saved you some, you big baby.'

He brightened at that. 'Write my name on it so Phin doesn't eat it tomorrow when he comes to finish the safe room.'

'I already wrote your name on one of the containers. The other is for Phin.'

Antoine narrowed his eyes. 'They'd better both be *huge* containers.'

'Patty took care of you guys. There's plenty. Now what's up?'

Antoine sobered. 'I heard about the safe house attack. Did you tell Jace?'

Val sighed. 'Yeah. After the girls went home.'

Antoine's expression softened with compassion. 'How's he holding up?'

Val looked over to the living room, where Jace sat in an armchair, staring dully at the penguin documentary that Elijah had chosen. He'd tried to react stoically to the news of the attack on his supposed safe house, but Val had seen his flinch and the hurt in his eyes. Kaj had assured him that he was safe with them.

For the time being had hung in the air, unsaid but understood.

Elijah, on the other hand, had been devastated. He'd cried big heaving sobs as he'd patted Jace's hand and said how sorry he was over and over. He'd pleaded with Kaj to let Jace stay until he was safe, finally crying it out. He was now pressed to Kaj's side on the sofa, Kaj's arm around him. She didn't think any of them were truly watching the documentary.

'About how you'd expect,' she said, knowing that they could hear her replies.

'I'm sorry,' Antoine said with a grimace. 'I'm about to add to the good news bonanza.'

'Did you find out what Corey was doing on those dates?'

'Not yet. Burke pulled me onto another case, but I had some searches running in the background. I do this for every protection client—searches for online threats. Chatter.'

Val swallowed hard, new dread clogging her throat. 'What did you find?'

'Well, first, did you know that Kaj is also prosecuting Trevor Doyle? The director accused of raping Bella Butler?'

'Yes, I did know that. It starts next week. Why? What's that got to do with us?'

'There are a number of online communities that have been following this case. Some are pro-Bella. They tend to be out in the open and nonthreatening. The ones of concern are the anti-Bella groups. Some of them just grumble about how a great man can be taken down by a woman's lies and how everything has to be politically correct.'

'I know the type.' She'd been surrounded by them after her assault and had nearly buckled, giving in to the military, who would have preferred to hush her up. It had been Molly Sutton who'd supported her, giving her the courage to move forward, to press formal charges.

She glanced to the living room, seeing that Kaj was watching her. 'Later,' she mouthed.

He nodded and went back to watching the documentary with Elijah, but his posture was far tenser than it had been before.

'You can't speak freely?' Antoine guessed.

'Not right now. I can type out my replies if I need to.' Skype was convenient that way. One could participate in a video call and text within the program at the same time.

'Okay. So. There's another group whose members are a lot more aggressive in their hatred for Bella Butler. This week a few of them noticed Rick Gates's attempted abduction of Elijah.'

Oh no. She thought she knew where this was going. 'And?'

'*And* they understand that Rick did it to get his brother out of jail, *but* these online Bella-haters have run with the idea. They think that Rick had the right goal but a poorly planned execution. They are suggesting kidnapping Cardozo's son to force him off the Doyle case. They've listed his home address online, along with stills of Elijah taken from the videos from Monday night. I don't expect the posts to stay up much longer. The moderators take them down, but the information is out there now. The internet is forever.'

She said nothing, pursing her lips as she held the wave of fear for Elijah at bay. Not wanting Elijah to hear any of this, she texted her reply. ***Don't they know that the DA will just assign someone else to the case?***

Antoine grimaced. 'They posted the name and address of Kaj's second chair, along with the names and addresses of several other ADAs. They're talking about a coordinated strike on several, just to upend the DA's department.'

Val sighed. ***Does Burke know?*** she typed.

'He does,' Antoine assured her, speaking calmly, which helped her calm herself. 'For now, be aware that the threat exists. I told André myself and he's increasing NOPD presence on Kaj's block. He's also got his tech group tracing the identities and locations of the posters, especially the aggressive ones. The posters on the subreddit are going to be the less serious offenders, though. The moderators have been actively purging groups from the platform if they're planning anything illegal. There does appear to be a private server on Discord where they discuss ideas more freely, but you have to be invited to join. I've made a dummy account and I'm trying to get a private invite, but it could take a while to gain the trust of the moderators.'

Are any of the aggressive posters local? she asked, aware that Antoine would have already started checking this.

'So far, most of the ones I've been able to trace are all hundreds of miles from New Orleans. There is one just over the Texas border that I'm keeping an eye on. For now, be aware and vigilant, just as you would be anyway.'

I will. She closed her eyes for a moment, making a mental list so that she could think before typing again. *In the meantime, we need to figure out what Corey's up to. I need to know if that note taped to Rick's chest was a ploy to scare us into chasing after Sixth Day or if Corey actually means Elijah harm. Or both.*

'I'm running searches,' Antoine assured her. 'But if you want something to do while you worry—because you will worry—I'll give you access to the program I'm running to analyze the dates Rick gave you.'

'You know me so well,' she said aloud, keeping her tone wry.

'I do. I'm running the dates through a database of police reports, looking for any criminal activity. I've focused on drug activity because of Sixth Day, but it could be anything. You could start sorting through the results while I work on the other client's case.'

'I'll do that, then,' she said, forcing her words to come out easy and carefree.

'This online chatter could be nothing, but it's better to be forewarned.'

'I know. Thank you, Antoine.' She was about to end the call when an alert popped up on her phone. The perimeter alarm had been bypassed by Burke, meaning he was expecting company and had set the alarm to a text alert instead of a siren loud enough to wake the dead. She toggled quickly to the camera feed around the house.

'Checking the cameras right now,' Antoine said.

'Same,' she told him. 'It's André.'

'Yeah. He said he was coming by to check the NOPD coverage on Kaj's block.'

A text from Burke popped up on Val's phone. *Send Kaj out to the garage. I need to talk to him.*

He doesn't know about the online threat yet. She'd hoped she could break the news to Kaj gently.

Not about that, but I will tell him. André has a package for him.

Val blew out a breath. So much for breaking it to Kaj gently. *Sending him out now.*

Turning to Kaj, she pasted a smile on her face. 'Kaj, can you meet Burke out in the garage?'

Kaj was up in an instant, settling Elijah on the sofa. The little boy had fallen asleep. 'You'll stay with him?'

'Of course,' she assured him. She sat on the arm of the sofa, positioning herself to be able to see both doors. She had the camera feed up on her phone and heard the garage door go up. The garage camera showed Burke and André talking to Kaj.

'What's wrong?' Jace asked quietly.

'Nothing you need to worry about. If you did need to worry, I'd tell you. I promise.'

Jace nodded once. 'I believe you.'

She shot him a quick smile while she switched her earbud to listen to the camera audio. She'd mute it if it was a matter unrelated to the case she was working. Kaj had a lot of ongoing court cases that required confidentiality.

'It's from one of your plaintiffs,' she could hear André say, handing Kaj a flip phone. 'One of my men stopped an SUV that didn't belong in the neighborhood and called me when the man said he was coming to see you. He said that your plaintiff said to tell you "palm tree" and that the number you're to call is saved to the phone's contacts.'

Kaj's face instantly registered understanding as he took the phone. 'Okay. Thank you.'

Then Burke began to speak, telling Kaj what Antoine had just shared with her. As she'd expected, Kaj went pale. He leaned against his car and she wished she'd been the one to tell him. She could be giving him comfort right now.

Kaj nodded numbly, then gave himself a shake. 'You'll keep me updated?'

'Yes,' André vowed. 'But reconsider a safe house. I could keep you safer there.'

'Like you kept Jace's place safe?' Kaj asked bitterly. 'I'm sorry, André. I can't trust that my son would be safe in an NOPD safehouse.'

'We'll involve the Feds,' André said, seeming not to take offense. 'They can hide you.'

'Near a hospital for Elijah?' he asked, frustration on his face. 'Where his doctors can get to him quickly if he needs medical care? If you can do that, I'll consider it.'

André nodded. 'I'll get on it. You have my personal number. Call me if you need me.'

He walked out, and Burke asked Kaj if he was all right.

Kaj just shook his head and held up the plaintiff's phone. 'I need to call this number.'

'Val didn't know about the online threat,' Burke said. 'Not until a few minutes before I texted her. She wanted to tell you herself.'

Kaj nodded. 'Thanks, Burke. You sticking around tonight, too?'

'Absolutely. We'll keep Elijah safe, Kaj.'

He nodded again and brought the garage door down once Burke was back outside. When he came into the living room, his expression was grim.

She stood, crossing the room to him. 'I wasn't keeping this from you.'

'I know.' Anguished, he looked over to Elijah, who still slept. 'I have to take care of a phone call. I'll be up in my office.' He headed up the stairs and, a moment later, his office door closed, leaving her heavy-hearted. She slowly turned to find Jace watching her.

'Did Corey do something new?' he asked.

'No. This is different. Rick apparently gave some other assholes ideas.'

Jace looked away, but not before she saw tears in his eyes. 'I'm so sorry.'

She sat on the arm of his chair, lifting his chin with a finger. 'Stop,' she said when he'd finally met her gaze. 'You didn't mean to do anything wrong. You've done a lot of stuff right. I'm going to get Elijah up to bed, then I'll help you make up the sofa, okay?'

'I can't sleep,' he said miserably. 'Corey tried to kill me. Everyone is after Elijah. Everything is awful.'

She brushed her hand over his hair. 'It seems so. But I've been in that everything-is-awful place quite a few times and . . . it passes. Don't get me wrong—whatever is awful may always be awful. Your brothers have done some awful things. That will never change. But how much it hurts you will lessen over time.'

'Promise?' he whispered brokenly.

'I promise.' With a lot of therapy, of course. She'd make sure he had access to a good counselor when this was over. 'Now, I'm going to put Elijah to bed and then I'm going to get some work done. Why don't you find a movie you've seen before? A really dumb one. That way if your mind wanders and you don't pay attention, it won't matter.'

He wiped at his eyes, looking so much younger than fifteen. 'Did you do that? When everything was awful?'

'I did. *Talladega Nights* is my go-to comfort flick.'

The corners of his mouth twitched up. 'I like that one. Can you help me search for it?'

'I absolutely can. Sit tight.' She crouched next to Elijah, still sleeping on the sofa. 'Elijah? You need to sleep in your bed, baby.'

He didn't move, so she tried a move she'd used on Sylvi when she'd fallen asleep on the sofa, so many years before. Getting Elijah to his feet, she put her arm around his waist. He was probably light enough that she could carry him, but she wasn't going to risk it on the stairs unless he remained dead weight.

'March,' she commanded. 'One, two, one, two.' Elijah staggered forward, awake enough to move his feet, but nothing more. Gradually she got him upstairs, Czar at her heels.

She tucked Elijah in, kissing the top of his head. 'Sleep, honey.'

She was surprised when he grabbed at her sleeve. 'Sing?'

'Of course.' She started the lullaby, keeping it quiet, knowing that Kaj was doing business in his office next door. By the time she'd made it through the first verse, Elijah was asleep again and Czar was snuggled at his side. She kissed Elijah's forehead, then dropped another kiss on Czar's head. 'Keep him safe, big guy.'

Taking the monitor receiver with her, she headed back downstairs, found *Talladega Nights* on one of Kaj's streaming services, and made Jace some popcorn in the microwave.

Finally, she returned to her laptop, finding the link Antoine had sent her. There were lines and lines of entries—police reports for each of the dates that Corey had left his brothers alone with no food.

Sorting through the data would be mindless busywork she could do with half her brain while the other half listened for any new threats.

Mid-City, New Orleans, Louisiana
WEDNESDAY, OCTOBER 26, 9:15 P.M.

Kaj closed his office door behind him, dropping into his chair just in time because his knees were too weak to hold him up. More threats against Elijah.

Because of me. Because of my job. A job Elijah hadn't chosen. Danger his son had not asked for.

He stared at the flip phone in his hand. Another new worry. 'Palm tree' was the code he and Bella had agreed she should use if she ever needed him ASAP, so this was serious.

He blinked hard then shook his head, trying to reset his brain. He needed to think. Unless he recused himself from Bella Butler's case, she was still his responsibility. That she'd used 'palm tree' so close to the start of Doyle's trial could not be anything good.

He found the only number in the contact list and hit send. A moment later she answered.

'ADA Cardozo?'

'Yes, Miss Butler. What's happened?'

She sighed. 'I got a phone call from an anonymous caller today. I recorded it, because I've been recording all my calls since I reported Doyle to the police.'

He'd known she was recording calls. He'd been the one to recommend she do so. Louisiana was a one-party consent state, so she didn't need the other party's permission. 'What did the caller say?'

'That someone was going to kill me on my way to the city from my house. Apparently, the tipping point for the person reporting this was that my husband had decided that he and our daughter needed to be in the city with me. For support.'

For a moment, Kaj's mind raced, unable to come up with a coherent thought. There were too many moving parts in his brain. Finally, he cleared his throat. 'Wow.'

Her laugh held no mirth. 'I know. I just sent a copy of the recording to your burner. The woman who called sounded familiar, but I can't place her voice. It's driving me buggy.'

'Did she say who was targeting you?'

'No. All she would say was that these people are very serious and that they killed one of their would-be operatives who tried to back away when they learned a child would be involved.'

'You believed this anonymous source?'

'I can't afford not to.'

Kaj thought of the threat to Elijah. 'I understand. What are your plans?'

'I tripled my security, leased a helicopter, and found a new hiding place.'

Kaj blinked. 'Excuse me? Did you say "helicopter"?'

'I did, indeed. My head of security has his helicopter pilot's license. We moved to a new location this afternoon and I sent him to your house with the flip phone. He told me that he'd been waylaid by NOPD, but you're calling me, so the phone got to you.'

'Captain Holmes brought it to me.' Kaj puffed out his cheeks, then blew out a breath. 'Will you still be testifying?'

'You bet your sweet ass I will,' she declared, then coughed. 'I mean sweet ass in general, Mr. Cardozo. Not your . . . y'know.'

He laughed, surprising himself. 'I get it. How will you get to the courthouse?'

'In a goddamned armored car. I leased one of those today, too. I'll be accompanied by a virtual platoon of military vets as security. I *will* make that trial and I *will* testify. This is all Doyle's doin'. I know it.'

Kaj thought about the online chatter. 'Maybe not.' He told her what he'd heard.

'I know about that. My security has been watching it for a while. They didn't think it was serious, though. Do you?'

I do now that they've expanded their vitriol to Elijah. 'I don't know, to be honest. But like you said, you can't afford not to.' *And neither can I.*

'Well, unless they have an anti-aircraft missile, we'll be okay.'

'All right, then. What else do you know?'

'Nothing more about the attack. This was enough.'

'Do you know who gave the info about your plans to your would-be attackers?'

'Not yet. The decision for us all to be in that car was made only yesterday. My security head is searching all communications into and out of my old residence and reviewing personnel files. We've put each shift on lockdown as they come in while we search belongings and phones. Anyone who refuses will be handed over to the police as a possible accomplice.'

'So you've told the police?'

'Not yet. I hoped you would. You know who you can trust. In the wrong hands, this information could be lethal to my family.'

'I'll get Captain Holmes involved. He will likely involve the Feds. Witness tampering is a federal offense.'

'I was hoping that the authorities could let the plan to kill us unfold to catch the sons of bitches. Maybe with dummy cars. I don't want anyone to get hurt, but if they don't know that I know, they might get themselves caught.'

'I hope that's exactly what will happen.'

'Thank you. I'm sorry to bother you with this now. I know you've got to be out of your mind with worry over your own son's situation.'

'He's okay and I'm keeping him that way. I've also hired private security. Can you tell me where you are now?'

'I'd prefer not to. Everyone with access to the internet gossip sites knows where I lived. No one knows where I am now except for my security. We didn't even bring the household staff. They're all back at my house, attending to business as usual.'

'Then let's set a time for you to call me every day so I know you're okay. I know you're not going to run, but I worry. Especially until you find the traitor in your household.'

'Is nine a.m. okay?'

'Perfect. An in-person call, please. Texts can be manipulated. And if you're in danger, say "pineapple". Just in case the wrong person heard your security chief tell Captain Holmes "palm tree".'

'Pineapple,' she repeated. 'Thank you again. I'll see you on Monday.'

She ended the call, leaving Kaj sitting in stunned disbelief. He shook himself again, took his personal cell from his pocket, and dialed André.

'Are you in a secure place?' he asked the cop.

'I stopped by my mom's house for some pie. I can go outside. Give me a minute.' A minute later, he spoke again. 'I'm in her garage, sitting in her car with the windows up. Spill.'

Kaj relayed the call with Bella Butler.

'Well,' André said when Kaj had finished. 'I certainly didn't have that on my bingo card. Have you listened to the recorded conversation?'

'Not yet. I figured you'd want to hear it, too.' He hit play and held the flip phone to his cell's speaker.

'*Hello?*' Bella said.

'That's Miss Butler,' Kaj interjected.

Another woman began to speak. '*You don't know me, but I have important information for you. Please don't hang up. It's about your husband and daughter.*'

'*I'm listening.*'

'*Someone is planning to kill you on your way from your home to the city so that you can't testify in the Doyle trial.*'

Kaj knew the voice as well, but he also didn't know from where. Bella had sucked in a startled gasp. '*What? Who are you?*'

'*Someone who doesn't want your family hurt. My source says that*' *you'll have your husband and daughter in the car with you. The people who want to hurt you don't care about your family. They'll kill whoever is in the car with you.'*

Bella shuddered out a horrified breath. *'Who are "they"?'*

'I can't say. My source shared this with me at great peril to themself.'

'How do I know you're telling me the truth? You could be prompting me to take action that would put my family in even more danger.'

The anonymous caller sighed. *'They killed a man—a paramedic— last night who refused to participate in the murder of your child. They dumped him in the bayou. You are in serious danger.'*

Kaj didn't miss André's sudden intake of breath. The cop knew exactly who the caller was talking about.

And then Kaj remembered the unknown pair of arms they'd recovered from the bayou. *Holy fucking shit.* Corey was behind this? This was *Corey's* plan?

'Thank you,' Bella was saying.

'You're welcome. Please be discreet with this information. Don't jeopardize them, please.'

'Why did they contact you?'

'I can't tell you that. Please be safe. Goodbye.'

The call ended and Kaj exhaled slowly. 'Well, hell.'

'Yeah,' André agreed.

'Who owned the Hyundai hidden at the boat launch?' Kaj asked. 'And if you don't know, we can do a search. There can't be too many paramedics who've gone missing in the past twenty-four hours.'

André sighed. 'I already know. I was going to tell you tonight, but then Burke was telling you about the new threat to Elijah and I figured it could wait till morning. His name was Zach Monteith, thirty years old. Army vet, honorable discharge. He left the house yesterday evening, but when he hadn't come home by morning, his fiancée reported him as a missing person. Nobody had followed up, as he'd only been missing for a few hours by that point.'

'Until you pulled up his remains from the bayou,' Kaj finished. 'So that's what Corey Gates is up to. Holy shit.'

'Holy shit, indeed. What are you going to do with this?'

'Send you a copy of the audio file,' Kaj replied, deliberately mis-understanding André's question. The cop wanted to know if he planned to tell Val and Burke. Which he, of course, did plan to do. He'd do *anything* at this point to keep his son safe. 'Miss Butler was hoping you would let the intended crime unfold so that you could catch the perpetrators.'

'I didn't take you for a cowboy, Cardozo. Why are you telling Val and Burke?'

'I'm not a cowboy. But I hired them to investigate this case, to find out who was out to hurt my child. Corey threatened Elijah specifically with that note he taped to Rick's chest. If he plans to kill Bella Butler, too, that's a data point they can use to dig deeper. Corey has threatened my son, André. He has to be stopped and at this point I don't care who does the stopping.'

André was quiet for a long, long moment. Then he sighed again. 'I can't agree with you, Kaj, but I do understand where you're coming from. If it were anyone but Burke Broussard's crew, I'd do what I could to stop you.'

'I'd still do it, André.'

'I know. And I guess we'll have to deal with that later, when we're not in crisis mode.'

'I haven't kept anything from you,' Kaj said, hearing the defiance in his own voice. He didn't care. 'I've told you everything.' Except for the information Rick had shared with Lucien, but that fell under attorney/client privilege and Kaj didn't know the exact dates himself.

It was a fine line, but he'd cross it in a heartbeat to keep Elijah safe.

'I know you have,' André said, sounding exhausted. 'But I'm wondering if Jace has. I'm wondering what he knows about *this* murder scheme.'

Kaj rose, returning Bella's burner phone to his pocket. 'Let's ask him. How quickly can you get here?'

'Let me say bye to my mom. Give me fifteen minutes.'

Mid-City, New Orleans, Louisiana
WEDNESDAY, OCTOBER 26, 10:10 P.M.

Jace watched warily as Mr. Cardozo let Captain Holmes into the house and locked the door behind him. It was only a matter of time before they decided he was too much trouble, even though Elijah's father had promised that Jace could stay with them for one more night.

Two cops had been hurt pretending to protect him. At least they'd be okay. But now Elijah was facing a new threat because of Rick.

I am too much trouble. Jace swallowed hard because both Cardozo and Holmes were giving him an odd look.

'Where's Elijah?' Cardozo asked.

'In bed,' Val told him.

Burke came in from the backyard. 'What's going on?'

'Jace, can you come with me, please?' Holmes asked.

Jace's heart pounded harder. 'Am I going to jail?'

Holmes shook his head. 'Not at the moment.'

'Not tonight,' Cardozo added. He crossed the room, stopping in front of Jace and squeezing his shoulder. 'You're safe here. The only people who know you're here aren't telling anyone your location. I need to share some information with Burke and Val. André's going to take you into the garage for a few minutes, that's all.'

Jace nodded, partially relieved. He still wasn't sure that he'd be staying here, but nobody had lied to him yet. He rose and Holmes escorted him into the garage. The two chairs Lucien had set up the night before—when Mr. Cardozo and Captain Holmes were discussing where Jace would go—were still there, and Jace sank onto one of them. 'Is Rick all right?'

'He is,' Holmes said. 'He's in a protected area of the jail, being guarded. No other prisoners can get to him.'

That should have made Jace feel better, but there was still a feeling of dread that he couldn't shake. 'Did I do something wrong?'

Holmes studied him for a long moment. 'Did you?'

'I don't know anymore. I think I've told you everything.'

Holmes turned one of the chairs around and straddled it. 'Tell me about the two people who visited Corey's camp last night.'

Jace panicked. 'I did already. I told you everything.'

Holmes put a hand on his shoulder. 'Breathe, Jace. I'm not accusing you of lying. I'm asking if there's anything else you remember. You said there was a woman and a man.'

'Yes. That's true.'

'Did you hear them say anything?'

Jace replayed the scene in his mind once again. 'Corey was waiting for them on the dock. He welcomed them to his camp. The woman said that she didn't feel welcome, and was being blindfolded really necessary. Corey didn't yell at her, which surprised me. He'd have beat us good for talking to him like that. He just said that they had a lot to talk about.'

'Did the man say anything?'

'Not that I heard, sir.'

'Do you think you'd remember the woman's voice if you heard it again?'

'Maybe. I'm pretty good at remembering voices. Rick and I would play a game where one of us would play a sound clip from a movie and the other would have to guess the actor and the movie. I won nearly every time.'

Holmes smiled at him. 'That could be a useful skill, Jace. What did they look like?'

'I wasn't really looking at them directly,' he admitted. 'I'd just seen them kill Dewey. It was . . . hard to look.'

'I can understand that. Was Talley the first person you saw killed?'

'In person. I mean, I saw Aaron beat that doctor up, but that was on video.'

'What did you think about that?'

Jace sighed. 'Aaron hated him. Was always talking about how Dr. Singh killed Liam.'

'Did he?'

'He didn't save Liam, but that's not the same as killing him. I tried to tell that to Aaron, but Corey told me to shut up.' He grimaced. 'And then Corey gave me a beating.'

Holmes winced. 'I'm sorry.'

Jace shrugged. 'It's okay. It hurt, but I'm used to it.'

'No one should ever have to get used to that,' Holmes said, his voice a deep rumble. 'I'm sorry no one protected you, Jace.'

Jace wasn't sure what to say to that. 'Thank you?'

Holmes nodded once. 'Do you remember what the man and woman were wearing when they showed up at the camp?'

He thought again. 'The man was wearing dark green. A polo shirt.'

'And the woman?'

'White T-shirt. I couldn't see their pants. They were sitting in the boat and when they started to go to the house I got on the floor because I didn't want Corey to see me watching.'

'Thank you, Jace. That's helpful.'

The door from the house opened and Val's head appeared. 'We're ready for you.'

Jace exhaled. 'That doesn't sound good.'

'You're fine, Jace,' Val said. 'We have a few more questions for you, that's all. Relax.'

He nodded uncertainly and reminded himself once again that she hadn't lied to him—yet. He followed Val into the living room, where Mr. Cardozo and Burke sat on the sofa. Neither looked mad. He sat in one of the chairs and waited, darting glances at the four adults.

Mr. Cardozo leaned forward. 'Did Corey or his friends ever talk about their job?'

'Sometimes,' Jace said. 'Sometimes they took me with them. I can't read, but I'm strong and big enough to do a lot of the demo. Demolition, that is.'

'Have you ever heard of Bella Butler?' Holmes asked.

'I've seen her on TV and a lot of her movies.' She was his favorite actress and she lived in New Orleans.

Holmes bent his mouth, like he was thinking. 'Did you ever hear Corey or his friends talk about Bella Butler?'

'No. Oh, wait.' He stopped himself, remembering. 'They had pictures of her in the construction garage.' He made a face, embarrassed. 'Usually the pictures are of naked ladies. Bobby put up lots of pictures of Bella, though, and she has her clothes on in all of them.'

'When did they put up the pictures?' Val asked. 'Recently? Or were they always there?'

'Recently. Like, maybe a month ago?'

Val smiled at him sweetly, and he let himself breathe. 'Thank you, Jace.'

Holmes cleared his throat. 'Jace is good at remembering voices, Kaj. Maybe let Jace hear a snippet of the recording. I know I've heard her before, too. If he recognizes voices, maybe he can help.'

Cardozo shrugged. 'A line or two won't hurt. Give me a minute.'

He went into the garage and Jace stared at Val, confused. 'What's happening?'

She patted his arm. 'Mr. Cardozo wants you to listen to part of a conversation and tell him if you know who's speaking. We all agree that we've heard the voice before, but we can't remember from where.'

'I can try. I watch a lot of TV and stuff online. Movies, the news, everything.' It was the only way to know what was happening in the world.

Her smile was kind. 'Easier than reading words.'

His face heated, and he looked away. 'Yeah.'

'We'll work on it, Jace. When everything is settled, I'll find some-one to help you.'

He believed her. He needed to believe someone, and he'd do nearly anything to be normal. 'Thank you.'

Cardozo reappeared from the garage, holding his phone. 'All right, Jace. Have a listen and tell me what you think.' He sat on the arm of Jace's chair, holding the phone screen down, but with the speaker pointed at Jace's ear.

'*Thank you.*' That voice he recognized right away. It was Bella Butler.

'*You're welcome.*' A different woman was speaking. He recognized her voice, too, and his heart sped up. He wanted to be useful to Cardozo. Wanted to make it so that the man wouldn't send him to jail. '*Please be discreet with this information. Don't jeopardize them, please.*'

'*Why did they contact you?*' That was Bella again.

'*I can't tell you that,*' the second woman said. '*Please be safe. Goodbye.*'

A few words stuck out. He'd heard them before. He'd heard this woman saying them before. Then it clicked into place in his mind. 'Be safe,' he said. 'It's what Noni Feldman says when she ends the news every night.'

And he *never* missed Noni Feldman. She was almost as pretty as Bella Butler.

Val snapped her fingers. '*That's* who it is. Noni Feldman. She signs off every newscast with "Be safe, New Orleans".'

'I think you're right, Jace.' Cardozo turned to Holmes. 'Does this help you?'

'You bet it does,' Holmes muttered. 'Thank you, Jace. You've been an amazing help.'

Jace couldn't stop his grin. 'That's a relief.' Then he wondered again what was going on. Bella had sounded scared. And why would Noni Feldman ask her not to jeopardize them? Who was 'them'? But he didn't dare ask. It wasn't any of his business. At all.

Cardozo walked Holmes to the door. 'We'll talk soon,' Holmes called before he left.

'He scares me,' Jace admitted as Cardozo was flipping the deadbolt lock.

Val ran her hand over his hair, like she did with Elijah. 'André wouldn't hurt you unless you were threatening someone else, which I don't think you plan to do.'

'No, ma'am.' It felt nice, having his hair stroked. No one had touched him nicely in a very long time. Dianne did, at the beginning, before Liam got sick. His mom had, of course, before she'd died.

He missed his mom. So much.

'You okay?' Val asked, like she really was concerned.

He shrugged one shoulder. 'My mom used to touch my hair like that.'

Val stroked his hair again. 'My mom used to, too.'

'Did she die?'

'No. But my brother did, and she was never quite the same after that. I miss my old mom.' She smiled, but it looked forced. 'Let's get the sofa made up for you. Burke, is Molly coming over soon? I'm about to fall over.'

'In an hour. I'll take care of making up the sofa for Jace and I'll wait until Molly gets here. You get some shut-eye.' Burke pointed to his eyes. 'Bags. You look pretty awful.'

'Gee thanks, boss.' She gave Jace's arm a final pat. 'Try to sleep, hon. I'm going to look in on Elijah, then I'm off to sleep.'

'Good night, Val,' Jace said, and then he turned to Cardozo. Burke was getting the sheets and blankets, so it was just him and Cardozo in the quiet living room. 'Thank you, sir.'

Cardozo gave him a long look, but it wasn't mean. 'For what?'

'For not sending me to jail.'

'I can't promise what will happen when all of this is over,' Cardozo said, and he sounded like he felt bad about it. 'But I'll make sure the DA knows how helpful you've been. That'll go a long way toward leniency. That means they'll go easy on you.' Cardozo started for the stairs, but he stopped and turned. 'Hopefully we'll be able to remove the cuffs real soon.'

That would be very nice.

Burke made up the sofa, then transferred the cuffs on one of Jace's wrists to his own. 'Let's go up so you can brush your teeth and use the head before Molly gets here.'

Burke unlocked the cuff so that Jace could take care of business and wash his hands, recuffing him once they got downstairs. He lay on the sofa, but a worry popped into his head. 'Is anyone watching outside?'

Burke stilled, his voice going cold. 'Why? You plannin' to run?'

'No, sir,' Jace said. 'I ain't got nowhere to go. This is the best I've been treated in a long while, even with the cuffs. I was worried about Elijah. What if someone tries to come in?'

Burke hesitated, then finally said, 'Antoine and Phin installed a perimeter alarm. If anyone comes close without letting us know, the alarm will make a god-awful racket.'

'Good. He's a nice kid. I don't want anyone to hurt him. Especially Corey. He shot up that safe house today. He'd . . . Well, you can't let him get near Elijah.'

'We won't,' Burke promised. 'Sleep now.'

17

KAJ STEPPED OUT of the shower, toweling his wet head. He was exhausted, having been on the go since leaving for the bayou before sunup. Before his shower, he'd called his boss and brought him up to speed with both the newest online threat to Elijah and also the Doyle case and its connection to Corey Gates. Reuben Hogan had expressed worry for Elijah and then complimented him on a job well done. It should have felt good, getting praise from his boss, but all Kaj felt was numb exhaustion.

When Kaj had ended the call, all he'd wanted was to fall into bed, but he'd also desperately needed to get clean. Unfortunately, the shower had woken him up. Or maybe it was what he'd been thinking about in the shower. *Who* he'd been thinking about.

He'd kissed Val. She'd kissed him back.

He wondered what might have happened had they not had a crowd of people waiting in his house. He knew what he'd wanted to happen, what his body had craved.

Her. Val Sorensen. He'd held her in his arms for a few short minutes that hadn't been anywhere close to enough. All he could think about was holding her again. Kissing her again.

And . . . more. He wanted to find out how soft her skin was all over. He wanted to run his hands over her curves. He wanted to bury himself in her body. Wanted to lose himself to heat and need and wild, unbridled desire.

He wanted to hear the sounds she made when she came. She'd throw her head back, her hair spread over his pillow, and she'd be so damn beautiful as she chanted his name as he drove into her over and over and—

He shuddered. *God.* He was hard again, unbelievable since he'd just jerked off in the shower. He pressed a palm to his cock, feeling like he was twenty years old again. It was probably because it had been so long.

He hadn't had sex in . . . *Shit.* It had been six years. The last time had been a year before Heather died, two years into her illness. She'd rallied and they'd been hoping that she'd get better. That they'd have their happily-ever-after.

That wasn't to be. He also knew that Heather wouldn't have wanted him to be alone for so long. *You'd like her, Heather. She's good for Elijah. She's good for me.*

Physically, Val was as different from Heather as day was from night. Heather had been petite with dark brown hair and even darker eyes. Val was as tall as he was and her coloring was Heather's complete opposite.

Inside, though . . . They had a lot in common. Heather had been cheerful and giving. Stoic and strong. She'd loved with her whole heart. He'd thought the time they'd shared would be enough to last him for the rest of his life.

And then he'd seen Val at a party. Fate, in the form of Rick Gates, had given Kaj an unexpected gift—time to get to know her. He'd seen her happy with friends, affectionate with his son, compassionate with

Jace, and almost frighteningly capable when Corey had deposited Rick on his front lawn. He'd also seen her weary and despondent after a visit with her mother and he'd wanted to shake Britta Kristiansen. Couldn't she see what she was doing to her daughter?

No, she can't. Her grief at the loss of her son had blinded her to her treatment of his twin.

He wasn't sure how he'd function if he lost Elijah, but he hoped he'd have the strength to go on for any other children he might have had. He wasn't sure if he should allow himself to judge the Kristiansens or not.

He pulled on pajama pants and a T-shirt, positioning his shoes at the edge of his bed so that he could shove his feet into them if the perimeter alarms went off. Then he opened his door, intending to check on Elijah one last time before he climbed into bed.

And stopped in his tracks.

She was singing again. Val was singing that same lullaby to Elijah, her voice sweet and pure and strong. His shoulders lost some of their tension, a smile stretching his face.

He crossed the hall to Elijah's bedroom door, left ajar. Val was sitting on the edge of his son's bed, the giant dog up on the mattress. She'd showered, too, her long white-blond hair still damp as it streamed down her back. Elijah had one arm around Czar and the other curled up under his cheek and Val was rubbing his back.

It was a very pretty picture. One he wanted so damn badly. He missed having someone at his side, someone to make him feel not so alone.

'Val?' Elijah murmured when she'd finished the lullaby.

'Yes?' Her back was to Kaj, as was Elijah's, so neither knew Kaj stood watching.

'Why didn't you feel safe? You said you didn't always feel safe and Czar helped you with that. Why?'

Kaj stiffened and Val stilled. She threw a glance over her shoulder, her eyes widening a little when she saw Kaj standing there.

'I can go,' he mouthed, but she shook her head before turning back to Elijah.

'I was . . . attacked,' Val said, resuming rubbing Elijah's back. 'Ended up with a broken arm and some bruised ribs. I was well trained in self-defense, but sometimes even someone well trained can be overwhelmed if the attacker is strong enough.'

'He was strong?'

She drew a breath, quietly letting it out. 'Yes. He was.'

'And you had nightmares?'

'Yes. I still do. That's how Czar knew what to do when you had one tonight.'

'I hate them both,' Elijah whispered fiercely. 'Rick and Corey.'

'I know. I thought time would fix my nightmares, but I'm still scared sometimes, especially at night.'

'So you got Czar,' Elijah said, his voice a little muffled because his face was pressed into the dog's fur.

'I did. He was just a puppy when I first got him but he grew fast. I hired a trainer who helped me teach him to protect. And then I finally started sleeping better.'

'Because he was guarding you.'

'That and . . . I felt different. More like my old self.'

'Powerful,' Elijah mumbled.

'You're very smart,' she said with unmistakable affection.

He yawned noisily. 'He makes me feel powerful, too. Do you think my dad will let me have a dog of my own? When you have to leave?'

Kaj's chest constricted and Val's hand briefly stilled on Elijah's back. 'I think you should ask him,' she said. 'Your father loves you and he wants you to feel safe and powerful. And if he's agreeable, I'll help you pick out a dog who'll suit.'

'Will you help me train him?' He yawned again. 'I've been watching videos, but I'm not sure that's enough.' His voice slurred a little. He sounded so much younger like this. Normally Elijah sounded like a mini adult. Kaj missed his little boy sometimes.

'I'd be proud to.' She pressed a kiss to Elijah's blond head. 'Why don't we discuss it tomorrow, when we're both more awake?'

'M'kay. G'night, Val.' He snuggled closer to the dog. 'I'm glad you're here.'

'Me too, honey. Call for me if you need me. Sleep now.'

Kaj backed up so that she could leave Elijah's room. She closed the door behind herself, leaning against it wearily. 'He's okay,' she said. 'He had another nightmare, so I sang to him.'

It sounded like she was apologizing. He stepped closer, cupping her cheek in the palm of his hand. 'I'm glad you did.' His heart did a slow roll when she leaned into his touch, just as she had in the garage earlier. 'I heard the tail end of it. You're good with him. Thank you.'

She smiled self-deprecatingly. 'I'm already way too attached to him.'

Kaj rested his forehead against hers. 'What about his dad?'

'Way too attached to him, too.'

His heart began to pound as he brushed his lips over hers. 'I'm glad. It would have been awful for this to be one-sided on my part.'

'Not one-sided.' She glanced at the stairs. 'But not here. There are people downstairs.'

He grabbed her hand and pulled her into the guest room. He didn't have to pull hard because she was right behind him. Breathless, he closed the door and pushed her up against it and his mouth was on hers before either of them could say another word.

It was instant heat, instant want. Instant need.

Her lips were soft under his and he tried to be gentle, but she wasn't having it. Her arms linked around his neck and she pulled him closer, parting her lips when he traced them with the tip of his tongue. He grabbed a handful of her hair in one hand at the middle of her back and clutched her hip with the other. He was so damn hard that it almost hurt.

Needing friction, he rocked up into her, pressing his cock into her softness. They fit and he couldn't help but fantasize how she'd feel beneath him. She moved fluidly with him, giving him a taste of what it would be like.

Heaven. It would be heaven. He was already so close, even with layers of clothing still separating them.

God. He shuddered, knowing he needed to stop before he embarrassed himself by coming in his pants like a teenager. Breaking the kiss, he trailed his lips along the curve of her jaw, down the length of her throat.

Her quiet moan was his reward. 'Kaj.'

'You feel so good,' he whispered.

'So do you. I want more than I should.'

'Same.' He shifted his hips so that his cock was no longer between her legs and she made a sound of disappointment that made him feel ten feet tall. 'Want you.'

She swallowed and he felt it under his lips. 'Same.' The word was husky and sexy and he had to fight the urge to drag her to the bed. 'But we can't. Maybe we could just . . .' She bit her lip, looking suddenly shy. 'It's been a while since I've just . . .'

Kaj brushed a lock of hair from her face. 'What do you want, Val?' Her cheeks pinked up, and he couldn't stop himself from kissing her again. But he kept it sweet and chaste and very gentle. 'Tell me.'

'Could we just . . . lie down together for a while? Without more?'

'Yeah.' He kissed her mouth again, then ran his lips over the arm that she'd wrapped around his neck. 'We can do that.' He took her by the hand and led her to the bed. Then he climbed in after her and wrapped his arms around her, closing his eyes when she rested her head on his shoulder. 'This is nice.'

'It is.' She'd grown quiet in his arms, but it was a stiff kind of quiet, versus restful. 'I didn't tell Elijah most of it.'

He hesitated, then kissed her hair. 'You don't owe me anything, Val.'

'I know.' She was quiet for several minutes, but he knew she wasn't asleep. He could be patient, though. Finally, she spoke again. 'There were more than one.'

His body went rigid as rage began to build. He had to fight not to tighten his grip, because he might accidentally hurt her. 'Two?'

She shook her head. 'Three. All Marines. All big. They came after me in the dark. I hid, but they found me. I tried to fight, but . . .'

Fucking hell. He didn't know what to say. In his years as a prosecutor, he'd met dozens of victims of sexual assault, and he never knew what to say to make it easier because there was nothing that made it easier. He'd found that firm sympathy usually worked best.

Except this wasn't just any victim. This was the woman he was holding in his arms, and his voice broke when he tried to answer. 'You couldn't.'

She stroked his cheek. Comforting him. 'I'm only telling you because it changed what I can . . . tolerate in bed. I figured we should have this conversation before we went any further.'

Dread was like a lead weight on his chest. 'Did I do someth—'

'No,' she interrupted. 'You were fine. You were a good bit better than fine, actually.'

He couldn't smile. He was too furious for what she'd endured. 'What shouldn't I do?'

'It's mostly my hair. Stay away from my scalp. It was shorter then and it got pulled.'

He felt sick to his stomach. 'I'm sorry. I won't touch it again.'

She reared up, meeting his eyes in the darkness. 'I'm not broken, Kaj. I just need a few modifications. I liked when you grabbed my hair just now. You can even tug on it. Just don't grab close to my scalp. That can trigger a panic attack.'

She was strong, staring him down. He'd be strong for her, too. 'What else?'

'No breath play. Kiss my throat. I like that. But don't put your hands there.'

'Understood.'

'That's pretty much it.' One side of her mouth lifted. 'I like sex, Kaj. I made sure I focused on that when I went to therapy afterward. I wouldn't let those bastards take that away from me. I haven't slept with a lot of men, but when I see one I like, I don't hold back. But I have found that I'm drawn to men who are six-foot-ish, lean muscle, no gym rats.'

He made himself smile. 'Sounds familiar.'

She kissed him lightly. 'I couldn't take my eyes off you, not any of the times I've seen you. I'm glad we're here now. I'm not glad for *why* I'm at your house, but I like you, Kaj Cardozo. I want more of you.'

'I like you, too, Val Sorensen. I couldn't take my eyes off you, either. You're the first woman I've been with in any way since Heather.'

Her brows lifted. 'No pressure.'

'None. Heather would have been angry with me, waiting for all these years. But I wasn't ready. Until I looked up one day and saw you.'

She kissed him again, long and lush and languid, before sliding back down to rest her head on his shoulder. 'I think I can sleep now.'

He tightened his hold. Not enough to hurt her, but enough to satisfy his need to protect her. 'Val?'

'Hmmm?'

'You told me that one of the men was dead. What about the others?'

'They committed suicide, one after a dishonorable discharge and the other after he was released from prison, also with a dishonorable. The Corps tried to convince me to let it go, to let them deliver punishment, but I said no. I pushed back. There was . . . DNA evidence for two of them, but not the third. He was the one who came after me when I got home from Iraq. He blamed me for causing trouble for his two friends.'

Causing trouble. Kaj bit back what he wanted to say because this was not about him. 'So you moved.'

'Yes. I knew he wouldn't go away and I wasn't willing to kill him. So I moved.'

'You said that you didn't tell your folks.' He couldn't imagine how lonely she'd been.

'I told Van, but my parents have never been able to deal with harsh truths. It would have broken them. Telling Van was enough, because then someone in my family knew. He helped me pick Albuquerque for my new home.'

'You must miss him.'

'Every day.' She sighed. 'I'm glad Dewey Talley is dead. But I wish I'd been the one to do it.'

'I understand.'

She curled into him, molding her body along his side. 'I didn't expect that Corey would be planning to kill Bella Butler and her family to silence her testimony. That was . . . whoa.'

'I know. I've had cases intersect in the past, but never like this.'

'It's weird that you had both cases. Is it more than coincidence, do you think?'

'I don't know,' he admitted. 'But my boss and I have been taking on most of the new cases because the rest of the prosecutors are busy sorting through the mess left by the old ADA.'

'I guess his being corrupt means that y'all have to check every case he touched.'

'Exactly. So from that viewpoint, it's not such a big coincidence. At least Corey's desperation to remove the spotlight from himself makes a lot more sense now.'

'Poor Jace,' she murmured. 'He just rolls with it. Like nothing Corey does is a surprise.'

'I know. I hope he's not involved in any of this. I really want him to be innocent.'

'I really believe he is innocent.' She sighed. 'I need to call Van's old friend first thing tomorrow. He had to have known Aaron when he was at the firm. He might know Sandra, too.'

'I can sit with you when you call.' In case she heard things that she didn't want to hear.

She kissed his pec. 'I'd like that. Thank you, Kaj, for listening. And being willing to hold me. That's not always a given thing.'

'It will be with me,' he promised. 'Now sleep. Rest your brain.'

'You won't leave for a while?' she asked, sounding vulnerable.

His heart squeezed. 'Not until you're asleep. Sweet dreams.'

She huffed softly. 'Can't have any nightmares. Your son has claimed my dog. I'll have no one to wake me up.'

'I'll wake you up if you have a bad dream. I'll even lick your face if you want.'

She laughed sleepily. 'Good night, Kaj.'

'Good night.' He held her until her breaths evened out, and then he let himself think about what she'd shared. He had to breathe through the rage once again. Men had put their hands on her. They'd hurt her.

They'd raped her.

They'd made her afraid, yet she'd held them accountable. She'd clawed her way out of her fear, forming her own safe place. Reclaiming her life.

Kaj was so proud of her. He was devastated for her, too. But she'd told him what she needed from him—to not yank her hair at the scalp or put his hands on her throat. Other than that, she wanted to have a normal life.

Hopefully with me, for as long as this lasts. He wanted it to last for a very long time.

There was strength in this woman. Strength he craved as much as he craved her body.

She was fierce. Protective. And yet capable of softness and friendship and joy. And that was the miracle. That after what she'd been through, she could still embrace joy.

He wanted to share her joy.

He wanted to give her a safe place. He wanted to *be* her safe place.

But he wouldn't push. He'd let her make the moves. And he'd be patient, because she was worth it.

Mid-City, New Orleans, Louisiana
THURSDAY, OCTOBER 27, 6:00 A.M.

'Are you hungry, boy?' Val asked Czar as she stepped through Kaj's back door after her run. She'd woken to find herself alone in his guest room bed, but he hadn't been gone long. His pillow had still been warm, which left her feeling warm as well. He'd stayed with her nearly all night. That he'd left before dawn had been wise, even though she would have loved to wake up beside him. If Elijah had woken early, looking for his father, they would have had a lot of awkward explaining to do.

Going to sleep in his arms had been enough. She hadn't slept so well in a very long time.

She could get used to that. Maybe in the future.

For now, she had to feed her very good dog. He'd guarded Elijah all night long. He'd also elicited startled gasps from a few early-rising neighbors during her run. Seeing a Black Russian Terrier in a full run wasn't a usual sight. At least he hadn't been chasing the stunned neighbors. She hoped he'd scared the shit out of Corey Gates.

'I wish you'd bitten Corey,' she muttered as she bent over to fill his food and water bowls.

'I wish he had, too,' Jace said.

Val straightened to find Jace uncuffed and standing a few feet away, next to Molly Sutton. 'Good morning. Did you sleep?'

Jace's smile was wan. 'Not much.'

'Not any,' Molly confirmed. 'We were about to make breakfast when you came in. I told Jace that you sometimes talk to Czar after your run, and we should be very quiet to hear what you had to say.'

Val tried to glare at Molly but laughed instead. 'It's fair. I rarely wish Czar had bitten anyone, though. Usually, I'm just grumbling about the newspaper being all wet or Mr. Boots, the next-door neighbor's cat, because he teases Czar unmercifully. Did you say breakfast?'

Molly chuckled. 'I did. Sit down and we'll make it, then I'm going home to sleep.'

'Coffee first?' Jace asked hopefully.

'Absolutely,' Molly promised.

Val sat down with her laptop, listening to Molly and Jace talking about her horses while they cooked. Jace was telling her that he had always wanted to learn to ride.

Val wanted to promise him that she'd make sure he did, but that wasn't hers to promise. He wasn't her responsibility. Not after all this was over. But maybe the foster system would allow her visitation privileges. She'd make sure it did.

She let their chatter wash over her as she resumed reviewing Antoine's police report data for the dates Corey had left Rick and Jace alone. It had been overwhelming at first sight the night before, but now that she knew Corey was planning to kill Bella Butler and her entire family, she viewed the information through a new lens. Antoine had been focusing on drug deals because of Sixth Day, but Val was thinking murder might be a better direction.

Corey might want to kill Bella because he was a true believer in Trevor Doyle and considered Bella a liar like the online assholes, or he might want to kill her to keep her from testifying. If he hadn't had all those unexplained absences, she'd give more credence to Corey being a true believer in Doyle, but he'd started going AWOL long before Bella had accused the director of rape. It made more sense that Corey wanted to keep her from testifying, and if so, Doyle would be the person who'd benefit the most from Corey's success.

Murder for hire was a sticky crime, especially when it would trigger a witness tampering investigation, but she'd have to come back to that later. For now, she looked for other murders in the police report summary. Antoine had cast a wide net, searching police reports for the entire Southeast.

She worked steadily, mumbling her thanks when a cup of coffee appeared at her elbow. She sipped absently, noting all the murders that had happened on the dates in question. That didn't take as long as she'd expected, because Antoine had built in a search field for the type of crime.

There were still too many to work with, though. She took the first group of murders and began googling the victims. Several random shootings and bar fights, and even more drug-related shootings. She highlighted those. It still could be a Sixth Day turf thing, but the Bella Butler connection made that less likely.

'Oh,' she said aloud, leaning closer to her screen when a particular murder victim caught her interest.

'Oh, what?' Kaj asked, and she startled, her gaze jerking up to meet his. Her cheeks heated, remembering the way he'd kissed her up against the bedroom door. Her thoughts must have been clear on her face, because he winked, making her blush harder.

She pulled her gaze away from his face and studied the rest of him. He looked good this morning, wearing a crisp button-up shirt and a tie with . . . She squinted.

'What are those?' she asked. 'Pigs?'

Kaj smoothed a hand over his tie. 'Hogs. It's a hog-tie.'

Val groaned. 'Oh my God. No punny ties before breakfast. New rule.'

He chuckled, the sound deep and rich. 'So noted.'

'Why are you wearing a tie, Kaj? Are you going somewhere?'

'Nope. But I will have a call with my boss this morning and I always wear a tie when I'm working. Gets my head in the game. What were you doing? I made a lot of noise and you never even noticed I was here.'

'We've been making noise for twenty minutes,' Molly declared. 'She tuned us out, too. Can you take these plates to the table, Jace? Let's eat. I'm starving.'

Val hadn't realized how hungry she was until a plate was placed in front of her. Pancakes, sausage, and scrambled eggs. Biscuits, too. She tried one and couldn't help moaning a little.

'You're getting better at the biscuits, Mol. Is Gabe giving you lessons?'

'He is, and thank you. What are you doing on that laptop?'

'Searching crimes reported for the dates that Corey left Jace and Rick alone over the past two years.'

'Did you find anything?' Kaj asked as he slathered his pancakes with butter. He glanced up the stairs with a guilty look. 'I don't usually eat this way. Elijah can't.'

'I'm going to make him a sausage omelet with lots of vegetables,' Jace told him. 'Molly will cut the veggies, of course. I'm not . . . I won't hold a knife in your house, Mr. Cardozo.'

Kaj smiled at him, a little sadly. 'I appreciate that, Jace. I'm sorry that we even have to be talking about it, but . . .'

'I get it,' Jace blurted out. 'I just don't want you to have any worries about me.'

Kaj squeezed the teenager's shoulder. 'Thank you. I hope this doesn't go on much longer for all our sakes, including yours. You don't deserve this.' He was quiet for a moment and Val thought he might be considering removing the cuffs entirely, but then he turned to her. 'Val? Did you find a connection between the dates and Corey?'

'I may have for one of the dates. It's all I've gotten to so far, but now that I know what I'm looking for, it's going faster. There was a man in Memphis who was found dead in his home. He'd fallen down a flight of stairs and broken his neck. But when I googled him, I found an article saying that after his death, his heirs sold the patent to a new kind of ammunition he'd invented. He'd held off on selling it, turning down millions of dollars. His heirs closed the sale in a matter of days after the will had been read. His girlfriend made a ruckus that he'd been murdered, but the ME found no evidence of foul play and his heirs had rock-solid alibis.'

Kaj's eyes widened. 'You think Corey was paid to kill the man?'

Val glanced at Jace, who'd grown a little pale. 'Sorry, honey. I know this isn't easy to hear, but I think it's a possibility. I'm going to keep looking. I could be wrong.'

Jace shook his head. 'I hope you are wrong, but I think you're probably right.' He frowned for a moment. 'Which day was that?'

'That was this past Labor Day weekend, the time you remembered him being gone.'

Jace's shoulders slumped. 'And you said Memphis?'

Val put her fork down and focused on the teenager. 'What do you remember, Jace?'

'Elvis Presley was from Memphis, right? That's where his house is?'

'It is,' Kaj said. 'What did you see, son?'

'A booklet. A brochure,' he corrected himself. 'One with a lot of writing, but lots of pictures, too. All of Elvis and there was a mansion on the front of it.'

'Graceland,' Val murmured. 'Where did you see this brochure?'

'In Corey's truck. It had fallen under the seat. I was cleaning it for him. That was one of my jobs. When I asked him about it, he grabbed it out of my hand and . . .' Jace absently rubbed his jaw.

'He hit you?' Kaj asked sadly.

'Yessir. Wasn't as hard as sometimes, though. Didn't hurt much. But he was mad that I'd seen it. He crumpled it in his hand and cursed at Bobby under his breath.'

'Do you remember any other brochures, Jace?' Val asked.

'No, ma'am. I'm sorry.'

She smiled at him. 'No, Jace, don't be sorry. You've basically confirmed I'm on the right track. That's huge. I'm going to let Antoine know. He can help me look. Finish your breakfast, okay? Elijah's going to be awake soon and he's going to want that omelet.'

Jace's smile was so sad that it broke her heart. 'I'll try. But . . .' He dropped his gaze to his plate. 'I hate Corey so much. It was bad enough when he was just beatin' on me and Rick. But all of this killing . . . I hate him. Please catch him.'

'We will,' Kaj assured him. 'Don't you worry about that.'

Val quickly cleaned her plate and got back to work. She only had another two hours until she and Kaj would be calling her brother's old friend for information about Sandra. She wanted to identify as many of Corey's victims as possible before then.

Lake Cataouatche, Louisiana
THURSDAY, OCTOBER 27, 7:30 A.M.

'Cardozo has hired Broussard for protection,' Ed confirmed over a breakfast of dry protein bars and truly horrible coffee. 'There seem to be a few main people that are always at his house. Broussard is one of them. The other is this woman, Val Sorensen.' He turned his laptop to show a photo of a woman with white-blond hair and blue eyes that were disturbingly familiar.

'That was the woman who was standing in Cardozo's doorway,' Corey said. 'The one with the giant dog.'

Ed nodded. 'Not surprising. It's not easy to get a list of Broussard's people, but occasionally they're in the news. Sorensen was involved in a double homicide back in August. Two guys came after a woman she was guarding. Sorensen took them both out.'

'She's not to be discounted, then,' Corey muttered. 'I have the feeling I've met her before. Is she from New Orleans?'

'I haven't checked yet, but I will. We need to get the satellite connected to the generator. I'm using my cell as a hot spot internet connection, and the speeds are super slow. It took me over an hour just to get this much information.'

'Bobby and I will install it after he wakes up.' Corey drained his coffee cup with a grimace. 'What did you do with Dianne?'

Ed hesitated. 'She's asleep. On her own.' Then he added quietly, 'I look at her and I see Liam.'

Corey wasn't really surprised. Ed had talked a big talk yesterday about how he'd overdose Dianne on sleeping pills. That he hadn't . . . Well, Corey couldn't blame him too much. 'We have to take care of her. We'll figure something out.'

'Is that coffee?' Dianne asked from behind them. 'And breakfast?'

Both Corey and Ed spun in their seats to stare at her. *Fuck.*

'I needed to use the bathroom,' Dianne said, then gestured at the table. 'I'm really hungry. May I?'

Corey nodded warily. 'Sure. It's just protein bars. They taste like cardboard.'

'I don't care. I could eat actual cardboard, I'm so hungry.' She took one of the bars, but her shoulders slumped. 'I'm going to need a job, now that Aaron's in jail.'

'What do you want to do?' Ed asked, like he was truly interested.

Knowing Ed, he was probably trying to find a scenario in which they didn't have to get rid of Dianne.

She eyed them cautiously. 'I could work for you.'

'At the construction company?' Corey asked. 'Doing what?'

'Receptionist.' She shrugged. 'But if you can't afford to hire me, I understand. I'll find something.' She unwrapped one of the protein bars and shoved the whole thing into her mouth greedily. 'Thank you,' she said around the food when Ed offered her a bottle of water. She drained the water bottle, then unwrapped a second protein bar. 'Um, I could use something stronger than water, if you've got it.'

Without a word, Ed got up and rummaged through the boxes they'd brought from the old camp. He returned with a bottle of cheap whiskey.

Dianne gave it a disgusted look, but she took it, guzzling right from the bottle.

Holy shit. Corey began to wonder if killing her wouldn't be more merciful than letting her kill herself with cheap booze. Her liver had to be suffering.

She wiped her mouth with the back of her hand. 'Where are Rick and Jace?'

'Rick turned himself in,' Corey said. A slight exaggeration, but it wouldn't matter.

Her eyes widened in shock. 'Rick turned himself in? Why? And where is Jace?'

Corey shrugged. 'Rick figured that if he turned himself in, the cops would stop looking for Jace. He did it all on his own. We don't know where Jace is. He ran away.'

She looked distressed. 'But why would the cops be looking for Jace?'

Quickly considering the angles, Corey decided the truth would be okay for this question. 'Jace was driving the van on Monday.'

She shook her head in disbelief. 'Jace is just a big kid. He's not capable of thinking up a crime like that. He'll get chewed up and spat out on the street. I'm sorry. I should have been paying more attention to them. It's . . . the drinking.'

Ed squeezed her hand. 'Don't you think it's time to stop?'

She slumped in the chair. 'I don't know how. Maybe rehab. Except there isn't any money. Aaron spent it all on that bitch Sandra.'

'We can help you figure it out,' Ed said. 'It's going to be okay.'

'But I failed Rick and Jace,' she said sadly. 'We all did.'

Not me. I gave them a place to live and food to eat. Which they were never grateful for.

'We'll find a way to fix it,' Ed said. 'Don't worry.'

But his expression was grim and Corey figured he was thinking about how hard it would be to kill her. Hell, maybe they wouldn't need to. It wasn't like anything she could say to the law would make a difference at this point. His need for an alibi had been decimated when Rick and Jace started talking to the cops.

That he'd killed a drug dealer wouldn't get him that much time, and Jace couldn't tell the cops anything more than that. That he'd tried to kill Rick was really Rick's word against his. And neither of his younger brothers would be alive too much longer. He'd see to it, even if he didn't pull the trigger himself.

But they could not allow Dianne to find out about Bella Butler. If the law even suspected that they'd killed Bella . . . That was a much bigger deal than killing Dewey and trying to kill Rick. Maybe they could just stick to the original plan and keep her drunk until they were ready to head out of New Orleans for their vacation in the Bahamas after they finished the Doyle job.

'I'll try not to worry about anything while I'm here.' She put on her game face. 'So what is there to do while we're waiting for the media ruckus to die down?' She patted her pockets. 'I'm missing my phone.'

'It might have fallen out when we moved you here,' Corey lied again. He'd removed the SIM card from her phone and thrown both into the bayou. 'You can relax outside in the hammock we have around back. Listen to the birds. Or we can do some fishing.'

'I haven't fished in a long time,' she said wistfully. 'I'd like that. I'll fry them up for lunch.'

'That sounds a hell of a lot better than protein bars,' Corey said. 'I'll wake Bobby up and we can get started.'

18

'ARE YOU READY?' Kaj asked, taking Val's hand. They were using his home office to make the call to Van's friend and former coworker at Cunningham and Spector.

'Of course,' she told him, grateful for his presence. 'Van didn't know that Sandra was a dealer. I'm sure of that. But I want to know if Aaron knew Sandra back then. And I *need* to know if Sandra's dealing is recent or if she was doing it while she was with my brother.'

She also wanted an explanation for Sandra's monthly visits to Sylvi's flower shop. Val didn't want Sandra Springfield anywhere near her family, including Sylvi.

'If Sandra did know Aaron when he worked at the firm, find out how they met, if you can,' Kaj said. 'I'd like some background so my boss can plan his interview with Sandra. Find out if she ever had contact with Corey.' Because even though Val thought she'd identified two more of Corey's possible murder victims in addition to the Memphis victim, they still weren't sure if Corey had been part of Aaron and Dewey's drug business as well. 'When we catch him, I want to pin everything on him that we can, and Sandra might have some valuable corroborating information. If she knows anything, she might be willing to talk to get a better plea bargain.'

Sandra had to know about the drug business, especially since she appeared to have been prepared to use Aaron's business relationship with Dewey against one or both men. That she'd kept photos of the two on a hidden thumb drive made those intentions clear.

'Okay. Here goes.' She dialed the central number for Cunningham and Spector and waited for the receptionist to answer. 'Desmond Aurelio, please.'

'Who?' the receptionist asked.

'Desmond Aurelio,' Val said again.

'Oh, he doesn't work here anymore. Have a nice day.'

The woman ended the call, leaving Val blinking. 'That's surprising. He'd been with C&S for years.' She googled him on her phone. 'Oh, he's with a much smaller firm. Only three other financial advisors.' She dialed the number and was put through immediately.

'Aurelio,' the man said, and the sound of his voice made Val's heart hurt. This man had been her brother's best friend since college.

'Des? This is Ingrid Kristiansen.'

'Ingrid!' he exclaimed warmly. 'It's been too long. How are you?'

'I'm good. How about you?'

'Can't complain. Are you in New Orleans?'

'Yes. I've been here since Van died.'

Desmond exhaled. 'We're coming up on the fourth anniversary. I think about him a lot this time of year.'

'Me too. Listen, Des, I was looking at some old photos yesterday and came across one of Van with a woman. I only met her once, but she introduced herself as Cassie.'

He made an annoyed sound. 'I'd hoped not to hear her name again.'

'Why not?'

'I don't like to speak ill of the dead, but I have no idea what Ivan saw in that woman. Well, other than her obvious assets, I suppose. She was incredibly manipulative.'

'Can you tell me how so? The reason I'm asking is that she's been visiting my mother.'

'What?' A chair creaked in the background, like he'd moved suddenly. 'When?'

'Every month since Van died.'

'Oh.' He was quiet for a moment. 'I'd like to be able to say that she probably just cares for your mom, but she was all about herself. Your mother hasn't given her any money, has she?'

'I'm not sure. Did you know that Cassandra was arrested last week?'

'No, I sure didn't.' There was the sound of a clacking keyboard. 'Holy shit, Ingrid. She was arrested with Aaron Gates? I heard about Aaron, but only that he'd murdered the doctor who'd treated his son for cancer. I had no idea that Cassandra was with him again.'

Val shared a startled look with Kaj. 'Again?'

'Oh yeah. The two of them were an item for at least a year before she got with Ivan. That happened to coincide with Aaron losing his job at Cunningham and Spector—and his expense account. If she'd stayed with Aaron then, there would have been no more five-martini lunches.'

She thought back to what she'd read about Aaron Gates. He'd married Dianne nine years ago, which meant . . . 'Aaron was cheating on his wife even then.'

'Oh yeah. Aaron didn't hold much sacred. Maybe his son. He was devastated when Liam got sick. Came and begged for his old job back, but that was never gonna happen.'

'Why not?'

Desmond's hesitation was clear. Then he said, 'Fuck it. I'm going to tell you because Cassandra is preying on your mom. Aaron got caught embezzling. He'd been doing it for quite a while. The partners had to reimburse what he'd stolen from the clients out of their own money. They weren't happy about that, as you can imagine.'

'I suppose not. So how was Cassandra connected to the firm? Did she work there?'

'She was a receptionist for C&S for quite a while, but she worked for a temp agency. Not for the firm directly. She latched on to Aaron pretty damn quick.'

'Did Aaron quit?'

'Yes, or he'd have been turned over to the cops. The partners wanted to keep everything hush-hush to avoid a scandal, but everyone knew. Everyone was . . . well, we were all afraid to tell. The firm threatened to fire and blackball anyone who reported it. Unofficially, of course.'

'Is that why you left?'

'Yeah,' he admitted. 'I couldn't work for them anymore after I found out, but—and I'm not proud of this, Ingrid—I couldn't risk reporting it. My wife was pregnant at the time and I couldn't be blackballed. So I kept my mouth shut.'

'Why are you telling me now, then?' Val asked, suddenly uncomfortable that she hadn't divulged Kaj's presence.

He sighed. 'Because I've been thinking about reporting it for a while. It weighs heavy on my mind every year around this time. Plus, I'm established with a good firm now. It's not as glitzy as C&S, but I work with good people who'd back me up if C&S tried to blackball me now. I guess I'm finally ready to tell. Especially now that Aaron's been arrested for murder. I can't help but think that if I'd said something four years ago, then that doctor might still be alive.'

Val wasn't sure what to say about that. It was a little bit true, but she didn't want to hurt Desmond nor did she want him to hang up on her, so she went on to a point that had struck her as odd. 'Why this time of year? You said Aaron's embezzling weighed heavily on your mind this time of year, but he left C&S in the spring. Not this time of year.'

There was a long pause. 'Ingrid, Ivan was the one who turned Aaron in.'

Val blinked at this. 'What?'

'Yeah. Aaron left without much of a fuss, but when his son got sick, things got bad. He didn't have decent health insurance on his own and he begged the partners to give him another chance so that he could go back on the company's group policy. They wouldn't take him back, of course. They couldn't. Not if they wanted to keep their licenses. It was a clusterfuck all the way around.'

'Did Cassandra leave when Aaron did?'

'No. She and Ivan started seeing each other right after Aaron left, though. She stayed on until Ivan died. Said she couldn't bear to come into the office every day after that, knowing he wasn't there anymore.'

Val's throat constricted, not because of Sandra's sorrow, but for her own. 'I get that. He left me his house, but I lived with my parents for the first six months. I couldn't bear to go in the front door of his place, knowing that he wasn't there. I still haven't sorted some of his things. There are boxes of papers in the attic that I've been putting off. I'm hoping there aren't old parking tickets in them.' She tried to joke, but it came out flat.

'I'm sorry, Ingrid,' he said sadly. 'I should have been there for you. I honestly thought you'd sell the place and go back to . . . where were you back then?'

'New Mexico. I'd planned to do exactly that, but my mom didn't do so well afterward. I stuck around to take care of her and Dad. I'm still here.'

'Still teaching?'

'Yep.' Which was true, just on a volunteer basis at the community center. 'I've moved from math to music.'

'You could always sing like an angel,' Desmond said gruffly.

Kaj smiled at her and Val's cheeks heated. 'Thank you. And thank you for this information. It doesn't really help me know if Cassandra has any ill intentions toward my mother, but I'll know what to watch for. I didn't know until yesterday that she was still visiting. She also visits Sylvi.'

'Your sister? Why?'

'I don't know. She goes to Sylvi's shop and buys flowers, which she brings to my mom. I was wondering . . . Did you ever suspect that Cassandra did drugs?'

Another pause, longer than any of the others. 'Yeah. She did. Coke was her poison, at least back when I knew her. Are you thinking that she and Sylvi are using together? I thought your sister got clean.'

'Sylvi *says* she has,' Val said.

'Ah. I see. Well, I know for a fact that Cassandra snorted coke. I saw her do it.'

Something in his voice sent an unpleasant shiver down Val's spine. A glance at Kaj revealed that he found something troubling as well. 'Did you do it, too?' she asked.

'Once. I didn't like it. And then I had kids and there's no way I'm risking my family. Getting hooked is too easy.'

There was something he wasn't saying. Val's heart began to beat harder. 'Did Van?'

Desmond was quiet for so long that Val didn't think he'd answer at all. Then he sighed. 'Do you really want to dig all this up, Ingrid? It's been a long time. Maybe just let it go.'

Her stomach turned into a lead weight. 'I don't want to dig it up, but I need to know.'

'I know he did coke at parties. I don't know if it was a habit. And during tax season, we were always working long hours. He'd pop a few pills to stay awake. That's all I know.'

Val started to see little black lights dancing in front of her eyes and became aware of Kaj squeezing her hand hard. She'd stopped breathing there for a minute.

'Ingrid?' Desmond asked worriedly. 'Are you all right? I shouldn't have said anything. I'm so sorry.'

'No, no. Y-y-you should have.' She forced the words out. 'I needed to know. About Cassandra. And Van. I won't tell my folks, though. They don't need to know.'

'No, they don't,' Desmond said, his tone soothing. 'I hope Cassandra hasn't dragged Sylvi off the wagon. The last time I saw your sister, she looked really good.'

Val blinked again. 'When did you see her?'

'A few months ago. I'd just finished the 5K charity run that a bunch of businesses in the city sponsor and there she was, coming across the finish line. She looked healthy, Ingrid. I asked her why she was there, and she said that she runs with one of the C&S teams because it was Ivan's firm and it helps her to remember him.'

Val's throat constricted again, this time for her sister. She'd always blamed Sylvi for Van's death, but . . . *dammit.* Sylvi had lost a brother, too. It didn't make what her sister had done okay, but maybe Sylvi was okay. She couldn't run a 5K when she was using, could she?

She cleared her throat. 'What organization was she running for?'

'One of the drug rehab centers, I think. Maybe you should pay her a visit. Ask her about Cassandra's visits.' Desmond was still warm, nonjudgmental. Val felt bad all the same.

What if I was wrong? What if Sylvi really has been clean since Van died?

She swallowed hard. 'I will. Thanks, Des.'

'You're welcome. Hey, I have two kids now. If you want to come over, my wife makes a mean lasagna and you can play with my little monsters.'

'I'd like that, thanks. I'll be in touch.' She ended the call and met Kaj's eyes, stricken.

Kaj was smiling sadly. 'I think you should visit your sister.'

'Yeah,' she said, her voice cracking. 'I think it's past time.'

Kaj kissed her cheek. 'On the positive side, you learned a lot. You did well.'

Val didn't feel like she'd done anything well. 'Van was using, too. Did Sylvi know?'

'You'll have to ask her.'

'I will, but I want to see Cassandra first. I want to know why she visited my mother.'

'I might be able to arrange it. She was detoxing last week and in no shape to talk to anyone, but she should be through it now. She has to agree to see you, though. I can't force her. And you can't ask her about Dewey or Corey, okay? That's off the table for you. Those conversations have to happen with her lawyer present and be conducted by my department.'

'I won't,' she promised. 'I need to know. I need to know about Van.'

Kaj looked pained. 'Why, honey? Why dredge all that up now?'

'Because I put him on this pedestal, and I threw Sylvi away. I need to know what's real. I need to make this right, but I don't know what to be sorry for. Other than harboring anger at Sylvi for all this time.'

'You both lost your brother,' Kaj murmured. 'Maybe focus on building bridges with the sibling you have left.'

'She won't speak to me. I've been awful.'

He pulled her into his lap. 'Stop it. Her addiction led to your twin's death. That's still true. Has she reached out to you?'

'No.'

'Then don't take all the blame. Talk to her, honey.'

'I will. When this is over and I can take some time off. For now, Elijah is my responsibility.'

'And I appreciate that, more than you can ever know. But I think that Burke can take over for a few hours. I . . .' Trailing off, he frowned as though considering his words. 'I'm not a big believer in fate, Val. Things happen randomly in life. People come into your life and sometimes they have to leave. Sometimes they get sick and sometimes they die and it's no one's fault. It's not . . . predestined. But we can make the most of opportunities as they're presented to us. This thing with the Gates brothers—whatever it turns out to be—gave me the gift of more time with you. What if it can give you the gift of a repaired relationship with your sister?'

She stilled, letting his words sink in. He was right. If there was a chance at having a relationship with her surviving sibling, she'd be wrong not to grab onto it with both hands.

'I'll ask Burke if he can take over for a little while this afternoon so that I can see Sandra in jail, then I'll go to Sylvi's flower shop. It doesn't close until seven on Thursday nights.'

And that she knew that fact off the top of her head was telling.

'I can't see Sandra with you since I'm recused from Aaron's case and she's connected to it,' he said. 'I'll have to wait outside. But I can go with you to Sylvi's.'

'I'd appreciate it. I don't think it will be an easy conversation.'

'I know you can do it.' Gripping her chin lightly, he kissed her lips sweetly. It was what she'd needed. 'I'll make some calls and get the visit set up.'

She slid off his lap. 'Molly's got to be tired. I need to get back on duty and let her go home to sleep.' She paused at the door. 'Thank you, Kaj.'

He smiled at her and it filled her chest with warmth. 'You're welcome.'

Mid-City, New Orleans, Louisiana
THURSDAY, OCTOBER 27, 9:45 A.M.

Kaj Skyped his boss as soon as Val left his office. 'Good morning, Reuben.'

'Good morning, J.P.,' Reuben said, and Kaj was caught off guard.

He'd been surrounded by people calling him Kaj for days. It sounded weird to hear 'J.P.'

'What can I do for you?' Reuben asked, a little warily. His wariness was, again, fair. Their conversation last night had been a hodgepodge of Bella Butler, Corey Gates, and the online Bella-haters who'd turned their attention to Elijah.

'I wanted an update. Did you talk to Noni—'

Loud hammering interrupted him and Reuben scowled. 'What the hell, Cardozo?'

Kaj winced at the noise. 'I'm having some work done on my house.'

'I can hear that. Is it prudent to have people in your house right now?'

'I'm having a safe room installed,' Kaj said. 'For Elijah. Give me a second.' He hurried to the door and stuck his head out. 'Hey, Phin? I'm on a call. Can you give me twenty minutes before you start hammering?'

Phin stuck his head out of Elijah's doorway. 'Sure thing. Let me know when I can get going. I'll take a break. I think I hear MaryBeth downstairs. She always brings food.'

'Thank you,' Kaj said, then closed his door and returned to his laptop. 'We'll have quiet for a little while.'

Reuben looked dismayed. 'Dammit, J.P. I wish your son had never been brought into any of this. Has NOPD tracked down any of the online crazies to see if they're still a threat?'

'Not yet,' Kaj said, although Antoine had identified at least one of them, a man living just over the Texas border. Burke had given the man's photo to André, who'd passed it on to all the officers watching his neighborhood. 'But they put my home address online and I'm not taking any chances with Elijah's safety. There's still Corey Gates as well—that note he taped onto Rick's chest. Until I know for sure that Corey's threat against Elijah is an empty one, I'm protecting my son, any way that I can.'

'Unfortunately, all that makes sense. So what were you going to ask me?'

'Have you brought in Noni Feldman, the reporter who warned Bella Butler?'

'NOPD did. Captain Holmes specifically. Feldman would only admit that she'd gotten an anonymous call from her source. She wouldn't tell NOPD who that was.'

'How many people in NOPD know about the threat to Bella Butler?'

'I don't know,' Reuben said grimly. 'It was only Captain Holmes in the interview room with her. Captain Holmes's commander and I were in the observation room. I'm not sure who was in the loop, but Holmes handled everything himself. At any rate, Miss Feldman was allowed to go.'

'Will she have protection?'

'She refused it. Said having cops following her around would "cramp her style".'

'Did she say why this anonymous source chose her?'

'Nope. She was a wall.'

'Does NOPD still have eyes on Trevor Doyle?' They'd put surveillance on the director shortly after the man was released from his arraignment on his own recognizance. Kaj had tried to get him remanded to the jail, but he'd known it wasn't going to happen, even though Doyle was a colossal flight risk. But the surveillance was not constant. There hadn't been enough resources for that.

The bastard had temporarily moved from his lavish home in Hollywood, renting a plantation-style estate outside the city. He would wave to the police sitting outside his front gate, his smile always wide and confident.

'Oh yeah. I bumped it up to twenty-four-seven. But we know he slips past us. We don't see him leave, but we see him return. He does that wave, the cocky bastard.'

'Bella's sure that he's behind the plan to have her killed on her way into the city,' Kaj said, 'and I think she could be right. But finding out that someone wants to silence her made her even more determined to see him convicted, whether he's behind it or not.'

'She's a strong woman.'

Kaj thought of Val, standing up for herself after the military tried to get her to drop her accusations against the men who'd hurt her. 'I gain new respect for these victims every day.'

'As do I,' Reuben said soberly. 'What else can I do for you, J.P.? Are you coming into the office today? You don't need to, but if you decide to, know that the lobby is filled with reporters right now. Word got out about the bodies y'all found in the bayou yesterday morning. I have a press conference scheduled for noon. If you come in, wait until two.'

'Got it. I actually did want to come in today, but it's a more personal issue and I need to ask for a favor. I told you on Tuesday that I'd hired personal security for Elijah.'

'You did. Is that not working out?'

'I'm very happy with his bodyguard.' In more ways than one. 'I hired Burke Broussard.'

Reuben didn't look surprised. 'He's got a good reputation in this town. What does this have to do with me?'

'Well, the security that Burke assigned to Elijah had a personal knowledge of Dewey Talley and his Sixth Day organization.'

Reuben sighed. 'Of course he did.'

'She, sir. Her name is Val Sorensen. Her brother was killed by Sixth Day four years ago. Burke felt she'd be the best choice to protect Elijah because she was familiar with a number of the major players during the Dewey Talley years, because of her brother's murder. She's been exemplary in her role as Elijah's bodyguard.'

Another sigh. 'I sense a huge "but" coming.'

'Yeah, well . . . Miss Sorensen saw a photo of Sandra Springfield.'

'Aaron's girlfriend.'

'Yes. She recognized the woman. Sandra was dating her brother until his death.'

'Sonofabitch, J.P. How many ways does this case interconnect?'

'A lot,' Kaj conceded. 'We also found out yesterday that Sandra has been visiting with Val's mother every month for the past four years. Val is naturally concerned, given the woman's recent arrest. She wants to ask Sandra some questions not related to the Aaron Gates case. She'd like some information about her brother.'

Reuben went quiet. Too quiet. Kaj didn't think that he'd agree, but his boss finally nodded. 'I'll be in the room with her. If Miss Sorensen even starts to stray to the Aaron Gates case, I'll remove her myself.'

Kaj breathed a sigh of relief. 'Thank you, sir.'

'Will you be joining her?'

'I didn't think you'd allow that.'

'I won't. But you can observe. I'll get Springfield set up in an interview room if she's amenable.'

'If she isn't?'

'I'll ask her attorney to explain the value of cooperation. If she'll agree, we'll do this at two p.m. I'm trusting you, J.P. Don't make this a circus.'

'I won't. There have been some lingering issues between Miss Sorensen and her younger sister around the circumstances of their brother's death. Miss Sorensen is hoping to get information from Sandra Springfield that will enable her to heal a family rift.'

Reuben's eyes softened with compassion. 'I've seen a lot of suffering in this job, but regrets for broken relationships left unmended is one of the saddest. Anything else?'

'Did Noni Feldman know that Bella recorded the call?'

'She does now,' Reuben said. 'She was displeased, to say the least. Have you spoken with Miss Butler since she came to your house last night?'

'Yes. She called me this morning, at our agreed-upon time. She's okay.'

'Good. Look, I don't mean to rush you, but I have a meeting in five minutes.'

'That was all I had. I'll see you at two.'

Kaj ended the call and went downstairs, where a group had converged around his dining room table. Elijah was doing schoolwork and Val was at his side on her own laptop. Czar had taken his chosen place at Elijah's feet. Antoine had his three laptops arranged in front of him, and Jace sat with Phin, a blueprint between them. With three of Burke's people at the table, Jace's hands were uncuffed. Kaj wondered when he'd feel safe eliminating the cuffs entirely.

Val patted the chair beside her. 'You want some coffee?'

Kaj sat beside her. 'I sure wouldn't say no.'

'I'll get it for you, Dad.' Elijah bounced into the kitchen, looking happier than he had in a long time.

'Thank you.' Kaj wrapped Elijah in a hug after the coffee mug was on the table. He tickled his ribs, needing to hear him laugh. Elijah giggled before pushing him away.

'No fair,' he protested. 'No tickling.'

'Sorry, not sorry.' Kaj ruffled his hair, then turned to Val. 'Two o'clock,' he murmured. 'You'll get a few minutes with Sandra Springfield.'

She tensed, then nodded resolutely. 'Thank you.'

Jace's eyes widened and both Antoine and Phin immediately shifted their attention to her.

Elijah's gaze darted from Kaj's face to Val's. 'Why are you going to see *her*? She was taking drugs. Maybe selling them, too. Why are you going to see *her*, Val?'

She hesitated, choosing her words. 'Turns out she's an old friend of my brother's.'

Elijah opened his mouth in surprise, then closed it. Kaj could pinpoint the moment that his son figured out the significance of Val's brother being associated with Aaron's girlfriend.

'The one who died,' Elijah murmured. 'He was in the wrong place at the wrong time.'

'Yes. The last time I saw him was on Thanksgiving that year. He was gone by Christmas. I just want to know how he was, those last few weeks of his life. Like, was he happy?'

It was a very sanitized version of the events, and Kaj was grateful that she hadn't told Elijah the entire truth. His son knew far too much about this sordid mess as it was.

Elijah's eyes were wide behind his glasses. 'I hope he was.'

She swallowed hard. 'Me too.'

The Quarter, New Orleans, Louisiana
THURSDAY, OCTOBER 27, 11:15 A.M.

Noni stepped into a private conference room at the station to take the call buzzing on her burner phone. 'Thank you,' she breathed. 'I'm glad you called me back. Are you at work yet?'

'No,' Allyson said. 'I'm getting ready to leave. Why?'

'Because I fucked up. I called Bella Butler, just like you said, but she recorded the call and told the cops.'

'Oh fuck,' Allyson breathed. 'Didn't you tell her not to?'

'No. I just told her to be discreet. I thought she might go to the cops, but I didn't think she'd recorded me. They dragged me downtown early this morning to question me. I didn't give them your name, I swear.'

A beat of silence. 'You know who I am?'

'Yeah. I remembered you from when I interviewed Bella. But I did not tell the police your name. I only called because I didn't want you to be blindsided when you got to work.'

'I was afraid of this,' Allyson said bitterly. 'The head of security sounded off when I talked to him last night. Yesterday and today were supposed to be my days off, but he called everyone in for an emergency meeting this afternoon. Guess I now know why, huh?'

'I'm sorry. I didn't think she'd be able to identify me. I should have altered my voice.'

Allyson huffed angrily. 'Yeah, you really should have.'

'I said I'm sorry.'

'It doesn't matter. Thanks for letting me know. Be careful. If word gets back to . . . well, you know who—'

'Just say his damn name,' Noni interrupted, angry herself now. 'He's not Voldemort. He's Corey Gates and he deserves to be punished.'

Her only answer was dead air, as Allyson had ended the call. Noni wanted to throw her phone at the glass wall of the conference room, but of course she didn't. She composed herself instead. She had to get her makeup on for the news at noon.

She had meetings all afternoon and her final broadcast at six, but after that she'd call Allyson again and make sure she was all right. And then she'd do her job—investigating Corey Gates and exposing him for all the world to see.

19

VAL SAT ON the sofa in Kaj's living room, a notebook in hand. Elijah was curled up in an armchair with his headphones on, watching a video for a science assignment. Czar lay on the floor between Elijah and Jace. Also wearing headphones, Jace was watching a movie on the tablet Molly had loaned him—an older model that had belonged to her niece. The internet was now blocked from the device, but Molly had downloaded a few movies for him. And Antoine had set it up to alert them if Jace tried to send any messages.

Antoine still sat at Kaj's table, his three laptops gathering information on the names Val had identified as potential victims of Corey's criminal organization. She had the feeling that Burke had asked him to work here in case she needed moral support before her meeting with Sandra Springfield. She loved her work family.

Kaj was in his office upstairs, taking advantage of a quiet spell in Phin's construction of the safe room in Elijah's bedroom to make some phone calls. He'd explained that his caseload was heavy and taking this week off was going to put him behind—especially as he anticipated being in court the following week for the trial of Bella Butler's rapist.

Val didn't want to think about that. She'd sat through two trials of her own—and she did think of herself as having been on trial. She'd had to endure the probing questions from the defense attorney and the insinuations that she'd been to blame for what had happened to her.

That even one of the three men had received some prison time had been a shock. She'd known it would be a long shot and she hadn't cared. She'd wanted them to be humiliated and afraid, even if just for the few days of the trial.

She fervently hoped that Bella would get justice. At least Bella got Kaj as a prosecutor. If justice was possible, Kaj would get it for her.

And that was all the mental space she was going to give to the upcoming trial. She had other things to worry about. Like how she'd use the few minutes she was going to get with Sandra Springfield this afternoon.

She'd been staring at her notebook, trying to organize her thoughts, for over an hour. She'd have only ten minutes or so, according to Kaj. She wouldn't have time to think then.

A creak on the stairs had her looking up. Phin waved. 'Coffee break. Want some?'

Maybe caffeine would help her focus. 'That'd be nice. Thank you.'

She expected him to hand her the coffee and go back upstairs, but he surprised her. After giving both her and Antoine a cup, he made himself comfortable on the opposite end of the sofa.

Phin pointed to her notepad. 'What are you doing?'

'Trying to figure out what to ask Sandra Springfield.'

He grimaced. 'Must have been a shock, realizing she'd been with your brother.'

One side of her mouth lifted wryly. 'Understatement.'

Phin hesitated. 'He was your twin.'

She studied him. Phin was never one for gossip or small talk, so he had to be going somewhere with this. 'Yes, he was. It's hard to believe some of the things I've heard about him. I thought I knew him better than anyone else.'

'He was using?' The question was asked gently, but it wasn't really a question. Seemed like Phin had either heard or had figured things out.

Val nodded. 'Seems so. According to his old friend and coworker, anyway.'

'You believe the coworker?'

She shrugged. 'I can't see any reason that he'd lie. I dated him when he and Van were in college. Desmond wouldn't even take free pens from businesses. He was always honest and still seems to be. He left Cunningham and Spector because they covered up Aaron's embezzling. But I don't have a lot of confidence in my ability to read people right now.'

He frowned. 'Stop. You say you thought you knew your brother better than anyone else did. You may have, but he knew you, too. He knew how to hide things from you.'

'Maybe.'

'Definitely,' he said, his voice gone hard.

'Personal experience?'

'Yeah.' He took a big swallow of coffee. 'I'm a twin, too.'

Val stared at him. 'I didn't know that.'

'I don't talk about her. Or any of my family, actually.'

Sadness filled her chest. 'I'm sorry. Were they . . . mean to you?'

He shot her an incredulous look. '*Mean* to me? I'm six-four and two-thirty. It would be damn hard to be *mean* to me.'

But abuse wasn't always delivered with fists. Sometimes it was a parent withdrawing so deeply after the death of a child that they forgot about their surviving children. Sometimes it was a sibling's betrayal.

Except she wasn't sure any longer which sibling had done the betraying. Before yesterday she'd have been a hundred percent sure that it was Sylvi. Now she didn't know, and that bothered her the most.

Because maybe it was me. What if Sylvi hadn't been the reason for Van's death? But even if she had been, Sylvi hadn't meant for it to happen.

Val pushed the uncertainty aside. '*Were* they mean to you?'

'No. They were the best family any guy could ever hope for.'

'Then why don't you talk about them?'

Phin looked into his coffee cup for a long moment before finally meeting her eyes. 'I was the bad twin.'

She frowned, confused. 'The bad twin?'

'My twin sister is a cop up North. Homicide detective. My dad is a cop. Two of my five brothers are cops. One plays the cello with the city's symphony. Two are teachers, and one of them served in the Peace Corps. And my uncle is a priest.'

'And you were a soldier.'

He grimaced. 'Yeah. Still am, sometimes.' He tapped his temple. 'Up here.'

'I know.' She knew he had PTSD. Burke had only shared it so that they knew what to do if Phin had an episode. 'I heard only a little. No one talks about you behind your back.'

'I appreciate that. I told Burke to tell everyone, by the way. He would have "preserved my privacy" otherwise.'

Val thought about her own background. No one at the office knew what she'd been through except for Molly and Burke. 'He's good about preserving privacy.'

'He is.' Phin exhaled. 'I don't know good words to say. But I do know something about keeping secrets from your twin. Don't you blame yourself, Val. If he didn't want you to know he was using, he would have known how best to keep it from you.'

'Did you?' she asked quietly. 'Keep secrets from your twin?'

'Yeah. I came home from Iraq a different person, but not that different. I just wasn't able to hide it as well afterward. Scarlett thought we were the same because we were twins. She thought that we were both good. But I was always angry and I didn't know why. When we were younger, I could stuff it down and pretend like it wasn't there. Once I came back, it was harder to control and I started drinking. I hadn't done that before I served.'

'Did she get angry with you?'

'No. She never did. She should have. My whole family should have. I couldn't take their understanding. My family watched me like I was a wounded dog, ready to bite them.'

'Their concern was a weight around your neck.' She'd felt that. Her family had also known she was different when she'd returned. She'd allowed them to believe that it was the things she'd seen and not that she'd been raped by three big men who'd made her feel powerless. 'I get that. How long since you've seen your family?'

'Five years. I was shot in a bar fight. Scared my family real bad. It was my twin sister that took it the hardest. She tried to get me help and I . . . wasn't ready. So I ran.' He stared into his cup. 'They looked for me. And Scarlett would send photos to my phone. She still does.' He patted his shirt pocket. 'I keep the same number even if I never use it. Just for her photos. She has a daughter now and I've never seen her in person.'

'Why not?'

'When you saw your brother with the woman, with Sandra Springfield, how did he act?'

'Shocked. And . . . shy. At least I thought so. Now, knowing what I know, I think he didn't want me to know about her. He didn't look me in the eye the entire week I was home.'

'You were a reminder of what he should have been.'

She thought about that. Van had helped her choose Albuquerque when she'd wanted to leave town. She'd been thinking Charleston so that she could still see her parents occasionally, but Van had insisted she move far away. Was he using back then? Was that why he'd wanted her out of his life? Because she was a reminder of what he should have been?

Maybe. But she wasn't going to get answers from Van, so she focused on Phin. 'Is that why you haven't seen your family? They remind you of who you think you should have been?'

He smirked. 'I see what you did there. Who I *think* I should have been.' Then he sobered. 'It's real, Val. I hated myself for so long for so many things. I kept thinking I'd go home when I'd figured everything out. Now I've been gone so long . . .'

'You think they've forgotten about you? That they don't love you anymore?'

'No. But I think their lives are settled and they don't need me fucking it up for them.' He met her eyes and his were haunted. 'They found me a few years ago. In Miami.'

'Where you lived before New Orleans. Is that why you left?'

'Yeah. I was walking to my apartment and I saw Scar outside. She was with her fiancé and his brother. I . . . hid. It was an awful neighborhood. I was ashamed that they knew I lived there. That I lived like that. I thought they'd go back to Ohio and give up on me.' He shook his head. 'The next day I figured it was safe enough to go back to my place. Her fiancé's brother was waiting outside my door. Told me that Scar was desperate to find me. That he'd seen me hiding.'

'Was he a cop, too?'

'No. He's some investigative reporter or something. Damn good eyes. I thought he'd pull Scarlett out of a dark corner and say "Aha!" But he only patted my shoulder. Told me that I should come home, but that I had to be ready. Not perfect, just ready. He said he'd keep my location quiet. And then he gave me his card. Said I should call him if it got bad. That he was a recovering addict and he understood not feeling worthy.'

'He sounds kind. You ever contact him again?'

He nodded. 'I call him a few times a year. Get updates on my niece.

Our niece, I guess. Look, all I really meant to tell you is that being a twin doesn't mean you're mind-melding. If you didn't know what was happening with him, it's because he hid it from you. And if you're anything like my sister, you're feeling guilty about not being "there for him" or some such shit. Don't. He made decisions all on his own. He knew you'd be there for him. He *knew* that, Val. So don't feel guilty, because you're in no way responsible for his actions.'

She hadn't known how much she needed to hear that from someone who hadn't kissed her. Kaj had told her the same thing, but he might have been a little biased.

'Thank you,' she whispered. 'But I might be the bad twin. My younger sister was there when my brother was murdered. I was so sure she was totally responsible because he was only in a drug dealer's den to stop her from using, but now . . .'

'You're not so sure?'

'I'm not sure about anything anymore. Except that I was wrong. About Van and about Sylvi. Even if Van was there that night to keep her from buying, she still wasn't responsible for his murder.' She looked away. 'I've been so bitter toward her all this time and I was wrong.'

'I can understand that. Both this epiphany and your anger toward her. If someone killed my sister or even did something that caused her death, I'd never forgive them.' He pointed to the notepad. 'So, what do you really want to know from Sandra Springfield?'

'If Van was there to buy or if he was there to keep Sylvi from buying. Not sure I want the answer, but I need it.' She glanced at Jace and Elijah again, satisfied that they were still focused on their videos. 'Not sure if you heard, but Sandra's been visiting my sister and my mother with regularity.'

Phin nodded. 'Burke told me. Sounds like you want the truth about the night your brother died and the truth about why she's kept contact with your family. It might be innocent, but based on everything else? I'd sure want to know.'

Val realized that those were really the only two things she needed to know. She wrote the questions down, then paused, pen still on the paper. 'I didn't lie to Elijah. I do want to know if Van was happy. He looked embarrassed the day I saw him and Sandra together in the Quarter, but he must have figured things out. He introduced her to the family after Thanksgiving that year.' *But not to me.*

'But not to you?' Phin said with a sad smile.

'No, not me. Maybe because I'd already met her, but . . . that hurt. Not gonna lie.'

'I'd rather have a root canal without novocaine than spend five minutes having my twin sister look like she was disappointed in me.'

Her shoulders sagged. 'I wasn't the same when I got back from Iraq and I didn't spend much time with my family, either. Even before I went to New Mexico, I kept to myself.'

'You're wondering if he thought you'd closed the door between you, so he didn't come to you for help with his drug problem?'

That was exactly it. 'Bingo.'

'Still not your fault. Everyone's life is like a spinning top. We just have to keep our own top spinning. It's not fair to expect someone else to give us a spin or to be expected to do the same. Occasionally, yes. But not all the time. Did your brother know why you were distant?'

'Yes. He was the only one I told.'

'There you go. He knew you trusted him. He knew he could trust you. If he didn't, it was his choice.'

That was true. Completely true. That Van hadn't come to her . . . *Not my fault.*

She smiled at him, feeling a sliver of peace. 'Thank you, Phin. You helped.'

He shifted where he sat, uncomfortable with her praise. 'What's your plan today?'

'To see Sandra at the jail, then see my sister at her flower shop.'

'You'll be careful?'

'Always. I should be getting ready to go. Burke will be here any minute to take over guard duty. How long before the safe room is done?'

'If Kaj's okay with me working into the evening, I can have it sanded and painted by eight o'clock tonight. Then the paint just has to dry. I'll be back in the morning to show them how everything works. Elijah will be safe in there.'

'Thank you, Phin. It means a lot to Kaj. And to me.'

'Elijah's a nice kid. Would be hard not to get attached.'

'Guilty as charged. Thanks again. Has anyone else ever heard you talk this much?'

He laughed. 'No. And I don't plan to make it a habit.'

She hesitated. 'Do you think you'll go home? Ever?'

'Yeah. I'm thinking about going after the holidays. And I haven't told anyone else that.'

'Should I nag you about it?'

He looked grateful, she thought. 'Yes. Thank you.'

She couldn't bring Van back, but maybe she could repair her relationship with Sylvi. And if she could help Phin reunite with his family?

That would be icing on the cake.

Lake Cataouatche, Louisiana
THURSDAY, OCTOBER 27, 12:45 P.M.

'Fuck,' Bobby whispered as he stared at his phone. '*That bitch.*'

Corey turned from the table to the ratty futon where Bobby sat. His friend's whispered curse was more alarming than a shouted one. 'What?' Corey demanded.

Bobby looked up, his expression one of shock. And fury. 'She sold us out.'

Corey's blood ran cold. 'Explain.' Surging to his feet, he checked the window for Dianne. She was sitting on the riverbank with Ed, so Corey turned back to Bobby. 'What's happened?'

'Noni Feldman met with the cops this morning because she placed an anonymous call to Bella Butler yesterday, warning her that someone was going to kill her along with her husband and child to keep her from testifying.'

He stared at Bobby. '*What?*'

Bobby nodded grimly. 'When Bella didn't believe her, Feldman told her that a paramedic was shot and killed when he wouldn't go along with the plan.'

Corey couldn't move. Couldn't think. This was a disaster. 'Allyson.'

'Yep,' Bobby said, his jaw taut.

Corey rose, his legs shaky as he paced the small room. 'How do you know this?'

'My source inside NOPD just texted me. Said they interviewed Feldman this morning, but he couldn't get away to buy a new burner phone until now. He destroyed his last one.'

'Doyle's going to kill us.'

'Not if he can't find us,' Bobby said. 'We need to go. Run. Find somewhere to hide.'

'*No.* We're *not* going to run like scared children. We are going to *finish* this damn job. We're going to *get* our money and we're going to do it in spite of everything.'

'Corey, no. We *can't.*'

Corey stopped in his tracks, pointing his finger at Bobby. 'Yes, we *can*. Yes, we *will.*'

'It's not just that Bella knows. She's moved to a new location and the cops don't even know where she is. There is no more job.'

Corey's mind was racing, trying to sift through the shit and find the action steps that would enable them to finish this damn job. 'Does Doyle know about this?'

'No, I don't think so. The cops aren't saying anything. My guess is they're hoping we go through with it. It's a trap now.'

Corey continued pacing. 'If Doyle doesn't know, we're still good.'

'No, Corey, we are *not* still good. If the cops know, they'll be watching Doyle like a hawk now. He won't be able to do anything, including paying us.'

'He has resources. He'll find a way. And the same logic still applies. No witness, no trial. They can't connect him to us or vice versa. So we continue as planned. We kill her and frame Comic Book Guy and his online friends.'

Bobby huffed, exasperated. 'Didn't you hear me say that Bella has gone into hiding?'

Corey glared at him. 'Then we find her. We have three and a half days until the trial starts.' A thought occurred to him. 'Longer if we can delay the start.'

Bobby's frown deepened. 'And exactly how do you plan to do that?'

'By taking out the prosecutor,' Corey said.

'There's a second chair,' Bobby said.

Corey shrugged. 'We'll take them both out. You already got all that information on the second chair just in case. We'll post some more anti-Cardozo shit on the online boards and let the basement dwellers make a plan. Ed can nudge the conversation in the right direction again so they're still the suspects when the dust clears. With both Cardozo and his second out of the way, they'll have to assign a new prosecutor and that will take a little time. All we need to do is delay. And find that bitch Bella.' Another thought occurred. His brain was finally kicking back into gear, his shock wearing off. 'I bet Cardozo knows where she is. She's his star witness. I bet *he's* hiding her.'

'Then we'd better not kill him,' Bobby said sarcastically.

Corey gave him a sour look. 'Smartass. But you're right. We need to get one of Ed's guys to watch Cardozo's house. I want to know when Cardozo leaves and where he goes.'

'He's got police protection now. On the block, anyway. Happened right after you dropped Rick on his lawn. Not in his house, just around the block, patrolling his neighborhood.'

'According to your mysterious buddy?'

'Yep.'

'Fuck.' Corey scowled. 'Guess I should have expected that.'

'Yep,' Bobby drawled, his tone laced with something that Corey did not like.

Corey turned on him with his coldest look. 'What crawled up your ass?'

'I'm frustrated. All *three* of your brothers have sabotaged our plans without even knowing it. They couldn't have fucked us over better if they'd tried.'

'I know. But we can't change that part. We move forward and for that we need Cardozo's movements. We'll grab him and ask our questions. If he knows where Bella's hiding, he will tell us with the proper incentive.'

'His life or his kid's,' Bobby said.

Corey smiled. 'Exactly.'

'What about Allyson? She might know Bella's new location.'

'Depends on when she last worked. Ed's been tracking her car ever since we tagged her as a possible way into Bella's inner circle.' Corey opened the door to the outside. 'Ed? Can you come in, please?'

Ed immediately joined them in the cabin. 'What do you need?'

'Allyson blabbed,' Bobby said baldly. 'She told Noni Feldman to warn Bella Butler. Now Bella's gone under and we don't know where she's hiding.'

Ed paled. 'Fuck.'

'Don't say we need to cut and run,' Corey cautioned. 'I swear to God I will fuck you up if you do.'

Ed drew a breath. 'Okay, but know that I'm thinking it. What do you propose we do?'

'We're going to make either Cardozo or Allyson tell us where Bella is,' Corey said firmly. 'First, I need you to track Allyson's car. Has she been anywhere other than Bella's home in the past day?'

Ed sat at the table and opened the laptop. 'Checking now. This'll go a lot faster now that the satellite is up.' He clicked some keys and tensely waited for his screen to fill. 'Allyson's car is sitting in front of her house right now. It's been there since Tuesday night, probably when she returned from the old camp.'

Corey felt the spear of disappointment. 'She hasn't been to where Bella's hiding, then. She hasn't even been to work since we saw her.'

'She told us that she had the next two days off when we were taking her back to her car,' Ed reminded them. 'She wasn't supposed to report back until tomorrow.'

'So she probably doesn't know,' Bobby muttered. 'Dammit. Cardozo it is, then.'

'We need someone in the pack of cops that's watching his neighborhood,' Corey said. 'Ed, your cop friend who ID'd the lawyer—what's his name? The cop, not the lawyer.'

'The cop that I've been *paying* for *information* is Alex Cullen.'

'Whatever. Get him within sight of Cardozo's house, however he needs to do it. I want to know when the man leaves, where he goes, and who he's with.'

'Where are you going?' Ed asked when Corey started filling his backpack with guns and ammunition.

'For supplies. And Allyson. Even if she doesn't know anything, we need to take her out. Nobody betrays us and lives.' It was not only a matter of principle, it was also a matter of survival. Word spread among people looking to have dirty jobs done. If an operator appeared weak, he wouldn't get the plum assignments that brought in the big bucks.

Corey's brothers had already weakened him enough. Allyson wasn't going to make it worse. He would survive this and he'd be even stronger.

When he'd finished packing his guns and ammo, he met Ed's

worried gaze. 'While we're gone, I need you to take care of Dianne. Put something in her drink. I want her comatose until we're ready to move on. We'll drop her somewhere that she can be found when we leave town, but I don't want her overhearing anything in the meantime. Especially if we end up bringing home guests.'

'Will do.' Ed opened one of the boxes he'd brought from the old camp and pulled out a small medicine bottle. 'I'll add a few of these to the whiskey she's been sipping all day. She'll fall asleep and won't be a problem.'

'Don't kill her,' Corey instructed. 'Just knock her out.'

'I got it, Corey. Now go. Bring us back some decent coffee, okay? And some beignets. I'm gonna miss beignets when we leave town.'

So will I. Because of his fucking asshole brothers, they were going to have to leave the city and set up somewhere else. He'd lived in New Orleans all his life, except for the years he'd spent in the military. He didn't know how to live anywhere else.

But he was going to have to learn.

20

K AJ PRESSED HIS palm to Val's back as he herded them through the throng of reporters waiting outside the jail. Reuben had warned him that there would be a lot of media outside after his press conference, but dammit, this was a bigger crowd than Kaj had been expecting.

'Are you going to see Rick Gates?' one shouted.

'What will you say to Rick Gates?' another shouted.

'Who's the lady?' someone else yelled.

Kaj said nothing and neither did Val. She allowed him to guide her, but she stood straight and tall, one hand resting on the gun in its holster at her hip.

Ever the bodyguard.

Kaj shuddered out a breath once they were in the lobby. 'I don't normally get so rattled.'

'It's personal,' she murmured. 'For both of us.' She gave up her firearm to security, saying no more until they reached the observation room, where Reuben held out his hand.

'Miss Sorensen. I'm Reuben Hogan.'

She shook his hand. 'Thank you for allowing me to do this. I know you're busy.'

'J.P. speaks highly of you.'

She faltered a little at Reuben's use of 'J.P.,' then nodded. 'The same of you.'

'Sandra's on her way,' Reuben said. 'She's still a little shaky from the detox, but her attorney says that she's willing to talk to you. We'll see what happens.'

Val just waited, her body stiff. Her tension grew with every second that passed.

Finally, a woman was led into the interview room, accompanied by a police officer and a man in a suit. 'That's her court-appointed attorney,' Kaj said. 'Jay McLeod from the public defender's office. He's sharp.'

'So noted,' she murmured. 'I don't think he'll have an issue with what I need to ask.'

'I'll be in there with you,' Reuben said, not unkindly. 'If you stray toward any unapproved areas—like Aaron Gates or any of the Gates brothers—I'll have to escort you out. It's time. Follow me.'

She did, the fisting of her hands at her sides the only indication of her stress. Otherwise, she appeared calm.

Kaj studied Sandra through the glass. Her skin was sallow and she had dark circles under her eyes. Her hair was clean but unbrushed. Detox had not been kind.

Val sat in the chair opposite Sandra, Reuben standing behind her. 'Thank you for agreeing to see me.'

'Don't feel too special, honey,' Sandra said with an edge to her tone. 'I'm only doing this because the DA told me that I might be able to help with "another matter" and that my cooperation would be noted. I'm bored enough to see what—' But then her gaze fell on Val's face and she gasped, staring. 'Who are you?'

'Ingrid Kristiansen.'

Sandra sagged back in her chair, her sallow skin growing pale. 'Kr-Kristiansen?'

'Yes. Ivan was my brother.'

'Oh my God,' Sandra whispered. 'You have his eyes.'

'I didn't remember you, to be honest. Not until I saw your photo after your arrest. Then I did remember that day we met, there in the Quarter.'

'It was Thanksgiving week,' Sandra whispered. 'I remember now.'

'I didn't get to talk with my brother that whole week. He was so busy. And then . . .'

'He died,' Sandra said quietly, but flatly.

'He died,' Val repeated. 'I have questions. See, I've blamed my younger sister for Van's death, all this time. I've thought for so long that Sylvi had gone to buy drugs that day and that Van was stabbed when he tried to stop her. But I now understand that Van was also using. I was hoping you could tell me why he was there at the Sixth Day café that day. If he was buying for himself or trying to stop Sylvi from buying.'

Sandra leveled a sharp stare across the table. 'You shouldn't ask questions that you don't want to know the answers to.'

Val's shoulders slumped. 'He was there to buy, then.'

'Not exactly.' Sandra leaned over to whisper in her attorney's ear.

The attorney's brows shot up in surprise. 'I don't know. We can ask Mr. Hogan.'

Reuben took the seat next to Val. 'Ask me what?'

'Miss Springfield has information about a murder. She's wondering what it's worth.'

'It depends,' Reuben said. 'Let's hear it and we can decide.'

Sandra and her attorney shared another look, and then he nodded. 'Go ahead.'

Sandra turned to Val. 'Be sure. Once I tell you this, you won't be able to unhear it.'

Val visibly braced herself, but Kaj could see her hands trembling. 'I'm sure.'

'Sylvi wasn't there to buy. She'd followed Ivan, trying to keep *him* from buying. She didn't know who he really was.'

Val swallowed audibly. 'Who he really was? What does that mean? Who was he?'

'Ivan ran Sixth Day. He was at the café because the business was his.'

Holy shit. Kaj hadn't expected that at all.

Val stared in shock, and Kaj wanted to hold her. He wanted to drag her out, take her away to where she wouldn't have to hear these things.

'*What?*' Val whispered, her voice breaking. 'He was *what?*'

Sandra's smile was grim. 'The big kahuna. Ivan didn't make the drugs, but he directed those who did. He decided which dealers got which routes, how much they got to sell, and what they'd charge. And he took a generous cut.'

Val's mouth opened. 'I . . . I don't understand. This can't be right. You're lying.'

'I'm not. He had a lot of very influential customers. Movers and shakers. Society wives. And, of course, all the normal junkies that Sixth Day had sold to before he took over, but he made his real money off the rich bastards. He was a classy source. An acceptable source.'

'Why should I believe you?'

Sandra shrugged. 'You asked. I'm just giving you an honest answer.' She looked at Reuben. 'The names of the movers and shakers is a separate deal.'

'Why?' Val demanded. 'Why would Van sell drugs? This is insane.'

'Why does anyone do it? Money. He'd had to pay his firm back for some . . . irregularities. He needed the cash.'

Val continued to stare, her expression tortured. 'Irregularities?'

'He embezzled a shit ton of money from Cunningham and Spector.'

'No. That was Aaron.'

'Well, him too. But Aaron got caught. So did Ivan, but he brought in a *lot* more money than Aaron. The firm didn't want to lose him and Ivan knew it. So Ivan made a deal. The firm fired Aaron and paid his debts and let everyone think that Ivan was the whistleblower, which was kind of true. An internal auditor found Ivan's thefts and the firm confronted him. That's when Ivan gave Aaron up, to help save himself. The firm agreed that they could lose Aaron, but wanted to keep Ivan. So Ivan kept his job and looked like a hero to his coworkers but paid his own debts. He was broke after that. He was about to lose his house.'

The house that Val now lived in. Kaj sighed. *Oh honey.*

'So Van just . . . started selling drugs?'

'He'd been using before. Coke and H. Some meth during the busy season, but mostly at parties during the rest of the year. He made a deal with Dewey Talley. Dewey had been his dealer. Ivan would sell to his rich friends and clients and he and Talley would split the profits. Ivan was good at business and grew Sixth Day's. He and Talley became full partners.'

Val's hand shook as it lifted to cover her mouth.

That explained a lot, Kaj thought. Aaron wouldn't have had access to the rich clients after leaving the firm, so he couldn't have developed that part of the business. He'd inherited Ivan's clientele.

Sandra sighed. 'I'm sorry, but it's the truth. You can ask Talley, if you can find him.'

'He's dead,' her attorney said.

Sandra's eyes widened, shocked. 'How? When?'

'His body was found Wednesday morning,' her attorney told her.

'Holy shit,' Sandra murmured, then shrugged. 'Well, the asshole lived a lot longer than I thought he would.'

Val was visibly trembling, her voice thin. 'If Van was the boss, who was Rico Nova?'

'One of his managers. Rico owned the café on paper. He was really one of Ivan's front men.'

'All right.' Val lifted her chin. 'You said you had information about a murder. I assume you meant Van's murder. Why did Rico Nova kill Van?'

'He didn't.' Sandra pressed her lips together, then whispered in her attorney's ear once more.

'Oh,' the attorney said. 'I don't think Mr. Hogan will allow that.'

'It's not like it's connected to Dr. Singh,' Sandra argued.

Val gasped again, this one small. Like it was her final breath. '*Aaron* killed Van?'

Sandra just stared at her.

'But why?' Val demanded brokenly.

Sandra looked up at Reuben. 'Your call. I can tell her or not. No skin off my nose either way. But I want it on the record that I've been a virtual ray of cooperative sunshine. I want credit for this, and I want it to reduce my sentence.'

Reuben took out his phone and started to record, giving the date, time, and participants. 'Please proceed, Miss Springfield. I'll consider incorporating whatever you share today into a plea deal, but I'm not promising anything until I hear what you have to say.'

'Tell them,' her attorney urged. 'It can't hurt.'

Sandra's expression grew hard as she returned her focus to Val. 'Remember, Ingrid, you asked for this. Aaron had lost his job at the firm because he'd been caught embezzling. He started his own firm, but he was struggling. I left him because . . .' She lifted a shoulder. 'I was accustomed to a certain lifestyle and he could no longer provide it. Then his son got sick.'

'Liam,' Val whispered.

'Yes. Aaron was desperate because Liam was going to need expensive treatment that his insurance wasn't going to cover, so he went back to the firm to beg for his old job.'

Kaj held his breath, waiting. All of this was consistent with what Van's old friend had shared that morning.

'But the partners said no,' Sandra went on. 'One of them said that they'd all had to give up their bonuses that year to replace the money he'd taken. Like I said, Aaron was desperate. He told them that Ivan had been stealing, too. And the partners said they already knew. One of them told Aaron that Ivan had paid back everything he'd taken from his own pocket. Aaron hadn't been given that option and demanded to know why. They told him that Ivan brought in more money. Aaron told me that he'd been ready to get down on his knees and beg. He offered to be an assistant, to take a pay cut. Anything to get back onto the firm's payroll and insurance policy. He asked them to bring Ivan in to vouch for him, that he'd do a good job. And that's when one of the partners—one of the five-martini-lunchers who was always a little drunk in the afternoons—laughed and asked Aaron who he thought had turned him in. That's when Aaron realized that Ivan had thrown him under the bus.'

She paused, then sighed sadly. 'You gotta realize—I loved Ivan like I never loved anyone else. Aaron was a pale replacement. Ivan and I were going to get married, and he was going to quit the drug business. He kept saying so, anyway, but I doubted it. He was making way too much money, plus he was back in the black at the firm. Earning again even after repaying what he'd stolen. Most of Aaron's clients at C&S had gone to Ivan and were doing better. Ivan was simply better with money. Aaron was good, but Ivan was something special.'

'Just tell me what happened that day,' Val said from behind clenched teeth.

'Fine. Aaron followed Ivan to the café in Freret. Aaron didn't know about the drug business. He thought he was going to an actual café to confront Ivan. Aaron was furious because—in his mind—Ivan had caused him to lose everything, and now his son was dying. He was desperate. He burst into the café and confronted Ivan. I was there. So was Dewey Talley. And Rico Nova. Rico was next in line for the throne, after Dewey. And I didn't know it at the time, but Sylvi was at the window and saw the whole thing go down. Aaron screamed at Ivan, that he'd betrayed him. That he was killing his son. Ivan kind of shrugged. Then . . . Aaron pulled a knife from his pocket and he stabbed Ivan.' She swallowed hard. 'Gutted him.'

She stopped for a moment and studied Val, something like pity flickering in her eyes. But the pity disappeared and Sandra's eyes went back to being cold. 'I tried to help Ivan, but he was already dead. I screamed for Dewey to help me, but Dewey said that Ivan deserved it. And . . . when the shock passed, I had to agree. That was a really shitty thing for Ivan to have done. Dewey was impressed with Aaron and figured that Aaron would know all of Ivan's rich clients. That their drug business could go on. So Dewey offered Aaron a partnership and Aaron said yes, partly because he wanted the money and partly because he wanted what had been Ivan's. Which included me, I think, but I was okay with that once I'd found out what Ivan had done. There was, of course, the issue of Ivan's body. So Rico Nova dragged him out while Aaron got in the shower and washed off Ivan's blood.' She paused again. 'I saw Sylvi running away. Dewey didn't see her and . . . well, she was Ivan's sister. I liked her. I didn't want her to die, too. But I also didn't want her to tell.'

'You convinced her not to,' Val said, her tone numb.

'Yeah. I told her that if she told, the same thing would happen to her—and her parents. Dewey wasn't a kind man. Except for one person, I can't think of anyone he was nice to.'

'Aaron?' Reuben asked.

'Well, yeah. Dewey was nice enough to Aaron, but they were equals. Business partners. I'm talking about Jace. Dewey was always so nice to Jace. Kid can't read or write. Not sure what's wrong with him, but he's not the brightest bulb in the chandelier.'

Not true, Kaj thought defensively. Jace was smart. He now saw what Val had seen right away—an abused kid who just needed some kindness.

'I thought I'd convinced Sylvi not to tell, but Rico's trial was coming up and Sylvi was going to tell anyway. That wasn't the only time, either. Her conscience gnaws on her from time to time and she feels this need to tell the truth.' Sandra gave Val a look of contempt. 'Mostly because of you. You didn't make any secret of how you felt about her after Ivan died. But if she told, Dewey and Aaron would kill your whole family and . . . I grew to like them.'

Val was dangerously pale. 'You visit my mother. You take her flowers.'

'Yep. I stop by Sylvi's first. Just a little reminder that she should stay quiet. Then I spend an hour or two with your mother. She's lonely, you know.'

Val flinched. 'She thinks you really like her.'

'I really do. She's a nice lady, nicer than my own mother. And she makes amazing cinnamon buns.'

Val clenched her jaw. 'And your visits are in no way a threat?'

'Well, more like another reminder to Sylvi of what she has to lose. But I'm not getting out of here for a while, so I won't be able to continue my Saturday morning coffee klatch with Mrs. K.'

Val was trembling now, her whole body shaking. 'What about Rico Nova? Why did he admit to killing Van?'

'Because he's got a family, too,' Sandra said with no shame at all. 'Dewey threatened to kill all five of Rico's kids. So Rico said he did it. I imagine with Dewey being dead, you'll be hearing from Rico's attorney real soon, Mr. Hogan.'

'How can I know any of this is true?' Val asked, sounding so damn lost.

Sandra smiled cuttingly. 'Ask your sister what she saw.' She looked at her attorney. 'I'd like to speak with you privately and then return to my cell. And Mr. Hogan? I've got a lot more information. This is only the tip of the iceberg, so I'm hoping you'll help me drastically shorten my stay with the state of Louisiana.'

'We'll see,' Reuben said brusquely, then helped Val to her feet. Even from the observation room, Kaj could see that his boss's touch was gentle. Bracing himself, Kaj went to the door into the hall and waited for Reuben to exit with Val.

She stumbled into Kaj's arms, and her body began to shake with silent sobs. She'd held herself together magnificently and he was proud of her, but his heart was breaking with hers.

Reuben turned off the volume of the interview room speakers to give Sandra and her attorney privacy. 'The room next door is empty. I don't think Miss Sorensen would appreciate it if Sandra heard her cry.'

'Thank you, Reuben,' Kaj said, his own voice rough.

'You're welcome, J.P. Take good care of her.'

Kaj hesitated, then blurted out, 'Kaj. Spelled K-a-j but pronounced like "pie." That's what my friends call me.'

Reuben smiled, but it was somber. 'You're welcome, Kaj.'

Kaj helped Val into the empty room, closed the door, then collapsed into one of the chairs, pulling her into his lap as she cried. He didn't whisper platitudes. Didn't tell her it would be all right. He just stroked her hair and let her grieve.

Finally, the storm subsided and she took little shuddering breaths. 'I'm sorry.'

'For what?'

'Messing up your expensive suit.'

'You're more important than any suit.' He pulled a pack of tissues from his pocket. He'd figured she'd be needing them at some point but had thought it would be after seeing her sister. 'What do you need from me?'

'This. Just this.' She wiped her eyes with the tissue, then blew her nose. 'I hate to cry. It's weak.'

'It is not weak. Val, you're one of the strongest people I know.'

'I sometimes cry when I'm angry. I hate it.'

'Well, stop. You have a right to be angry. I'm angry for you.'

'I'm angry *at* me. And at Van and Sandra and Aaron *fucking* Gates.' Her voice broke. 'He killed my brother, Kaj. And he got to walk free for four years. And now that he's finally in jail, it's not because he killed Van. When he gets life in prison, it won't be for Van.' Another sob shook her. 'And I can't even say that Van deserves justice. Not if any of this is true.'

'I know.' He stroked the back of her neck, keeping his touch light. 'Why are you angry with yourself, Val?'

She stilled in his arms. 'Because I tossed my sister aside like she was nothing.'

'You were misled. You can make it right.'

She nodded, then winced. 'My head hurts.'

'I brought water and Advil. It's in my car. I thought you might need it.'

'Thank you.'

He kissed her forehead. 'You're welcome. You still want to see Sylvi today? Or save it for tomorrow? This has been a lot for one day.'

'Today. I need to make this right *today*.'

'Okay. I've got her shop's address programmed into my phone. Even with traffic, we can be there in less than an hour.'

'I must look awful. Those reporters are going to get pictures of me looking like this.'

'I've got a hoodie in my office. Some dark glasses, too. Sometimes I like to sneak in and out, so I keep an incognito costume on hand.'

She huffed a pained laugh. 'You bad boy, you. We should go.'

He put his arm around her waist. 'If you change your mind, you just have to say so.'

She shook her head slowly. 'It has to be today.'

Kenner, Louisiana
THURSDAY, OCTOBER 27, 3:45 P.M.

Val stared at the flower shop. It was in a small stand-alone building nestled between a house that served as an accountant's office and a diner that served only breakfast and lunch, so it was closed already. A tire shop sat on the other side of the diner, anchoring the row of businesses.

Val had driven by Sylvi's flower shop several times over the past four years. She'd even parked once. But she'd never been inside.

Kaj hadn't said a word. He'd held her hand while her mind churned and her heart ached.

Sylvi had been going to tell, Sandra had said. *Mostly because of you. You didn't make any secret of how you felt about her.*

'What if she throws me out?' Val murmured into the silence.

'What if she doesn't?' Kaj said gently.

'I don't believe what Sandra said,' Val stated. 'She's got to be lying.'

'Okay.'

He was studying her, his dark eyes so damn kind that hers burned. *No more crying.* Her aching head couldn't take any more. 'Van was ruthless in business and everything else. I knew that. He would do almost anything to win. But he wouldn't steal. He wouldn't sell drugs.'

The hand that held hers squeezed lightly. 'Sandra told quite a story,' he murmured.

'I don't want to believe any of it.'

He squeezed her hand again but said nothing.

'How could I not have seen this?' she asked, hearing her own desperation. 'How could I have missed that my brother had . . . gone so wrong?'

'You wouldn't be the first—if it's true. Talk to your sister. Ask her. You might not feel better, but at least you'll know.'

He was right and she was stalling. 'Give me a minute.'

'As long as you need.'

Hands shaking, Val called Desmond's new firm and, fearing what she'd hear, didn't put it on speaker, pressing the phone to her ear instead. She didn't want to get Desmond into any trouble or put Kaj in an awkward situation. 'Desmond Aurelio, please,' she said when the receptionist answered, then held her breath as the seconds ticked by.

'Aurelio,' Desmond said. 'How can I help you?'

'Des, it's Ingrid again.'

'Hi,' he said cautiously. 'What's up?'

'I, um, I went to see Sandra Springfield. At the jail. She told me some things.'

'Oh.' The tone of his voice spoke volumes.

Val's heart hurt. But she needed to know. 'You said that Van did drugs at parties with Cassandra. She pressured him to do it, right?'

Desmond sighed. 'Ingrid.'

'Des, *please.*'

He blew out a breath. 'Other way around. Ivan got her to start using. He was . . . persuasive.' He hesitated. 'What else did she tell you?'

Val shuddered, her eyes filling with new tears. *Dammit.* 'Did Van embezzle, too?'

'Fucking hell,' Desmond muttered.

His response was as good as an actual confirmation.

'It's true?' she asked hoarsely. She could feel Kaj watching her, his gaze a sad caress.

'From what I heard, yes,' Desmond admitted. 'The official word was that he'd turned Aaron in, but watercooler gossip said he'd been caught, too. I also heard that he paid it all back, but it had to have been quite a lot. The partners didn't want him to just pay back what he'd stolen. They charged him fines and penalties. Nearly doubled the amount he had to repay. Again, all this was rumor. I have no idea how he would have even gotten his hands on that kind of money.'

I do, Val thought. *Now I do.* 'Did you ask him?'

A long pause. 'No. I didn't want to get involved in whatever he was doing. That's when I left C&S. I'm sorry.'

Goddammit. So Desmond had believed the rumors. 'No. You had a family. I get it. I really do.'

'Oh, Ingrid. I'm so sorry. I didn't want you to know about any of this.'

'Did you notice . . .' She let the words trail off, unsure of what she wanted to ask. 'Was Ivan . . . nice?'

'Nice?' Desmond echoed. He sounded cautious again. 'What do you mean?'

'Would he have . . . hurt someone if it helped him?'

'I think I need to go.'

'Wait,' Val snapped. 'I'm serious, Desmond. You knew him better than I did. You *knew* him. *Tell me.*'

'Okay,' Desmond said, defeated. 'But I don't know why you're dredging all this up now. It's not healthy.'

'Please,' she whispered, staring at Sylvi's store window. It was filled with flower arrangements, mockingly cheerful. 'Please.'

'Fine. Ivan was ruthless. People called him Ivan the Terrible, but he'd just laugh. He'd sell trash stocks and make them sound like gold. When the client lost their money, he'd shrug. Making a profit for the firm, and then for himself, was all that mattered. It affected our friendship.'

'It did?'

'It did. We were friends in college, but there were times that I didn't . . . that I wasn't comfortable with him. He'd walk over people to get ahead. Once he manipulated a study partner into doing the bulk of work on a project, then claimed she'd slacked off when the woman wouldn't go out with him. The prof believed Ivan had done all the work, and the other student got a failing grade. No one wanted to be on Ivan's bad side, but we were friends, so I was loyal. For a while, anyway. I'd already started pulling back, but by the time he started using drugs, I was done. I didn't make a big deal of it. Just said no when he'd invite me out. He gradually got the message. The thing with Aaron was the final straw for me, though. I never would have told you any of this if you hadn't pushed. You practically worshipped him. I didn't want to hurt you. But . . . he wasn't the man you thought he was.'

Wasn't the man you thought he was. Such simple words. Yet they held the weight of a thousand unsaid things. 'I need to go. Thank you for your honesty.'

'Are you all right?' Desmond asked worriedly.

No. Not at all. Not even a little bit. 'I will be.'

He sighed. 'Since Sandra's let the cat out of the bag, I'll file a statement with the police, telling them what I heard while I was employed at C&S. I imagine someone in law enforcement heard what she told you. There'll be an investigation. This is my chance to clear my conscience. So . . . thank you for that.'

'You're welcome,' Val whispered. 'Be well, Des.' She ended the call and reached for the car door, checking their surroundings out of habit. With internet crazies trash-talking Kaj, she needed to be alert, despite her personal turmoil. The parking lot was about half-full of cars, a semitruck taking up the other half as it unloaded tires to the tire shop two doors down, effectively blocking the parking lot's entrances. It was as safe as they were likely to get. 'Let's go.'

Kaj didn't ask her what Desmond had said. He didn't ask if she was certain. He simply met her at the front of the car and kissed her softly. 'You can do this.'

She wasn't sure about that, but she forced her feet to move to the front door of her sister's shop. 'She owns this place now,' she murmured. 'She bought it from the previous owner when they retired. I should have been proud of her for this.'

Kaj squeezed her shoulder. 'You still can be. But not from out here.'

21

VAL OPENED THE door to Sylvi's shop, hearing a beep as she was hit with the fragrance of hundreds of flowers. She inhaled and stepped inside, Kaj behind her.

Sylvi came in from a back room, her arms laden with long-stemmed roses. 'Can I h—'

For a long moment they stared at each other. Sylvi was small like their mother, but she had their father's coloring—hair the color of a deer's hide, all the browns and golds combined.

'Hi,' Val managed to choke out. 'If this is a bad time, I can come back.'

'No, no.' Sylvi laid the roses on the counter. 'What can I do for you, Ingrid?'

'I'm . . . I don't know where to start.'

Sylvi's smile was sad. 'Let's talk in the back.'

'Thank you. This is Kaj. My . . . boyfriend?'

Kaj placed his hand on Val's back. 'Kaj Cardozo. It's nice to meet you, Sylvi.'

'Likewise. Mama said you two stopped by yesterday. Give me a sec.'

Flipping the sign to CLOSED, she led them to a room dominated by a worktable and shelves filled with vases. She opened three folding chairs. 'Please, sit.' She folded her hands in her lap. 'What brings you by?'

'I'm sorry,' Val blurted. 'I'm so sorry.'

Sylvi's brow wrinkled in confusion. 'What?'

Val drew a ragged breath. 'I visited Cassandra Springfield at the jail.'

Horror froze Sylvi's features. 'What did she tell you?'

'The truth?' Val shrugged. 'I don't know. But I never asked you what happened. I am now. Will you tell me? Please?'

Sylvi shook her head. 'I can't.'

'Yes, you can,' Val said gently. 'Everyone who was in the room that day is either dead or in jail. Aaron Gates and Sandra are in jail. Dewey Talley is dead. You're safe now. And if you're not safe, I can make sure that you are.'

'And Mom and Dad?'

'I'll keep them safe, too,' Val promised. 'Tell me. Please.'

Sylvi covered her face with her hands as a sob broke free. 'Aaron Gates. He killed him. Killed Van.'

Val slid from the chair to kneel in front of her sister, gently pulling her hands free and holding them in hers. 'I should have done better by you. I should have listened. If you'll let me, I want to listen now.'

'You won't believe me.'

'I think I will.'

Sylvi looked up, uncertain. 'Why would Sandra have talked to you?'

'She's looking to plea-bargain. I know that she visited you once a month. I know that she visited Mom, too.'

'She saved me. Kind of.' Sylvi exhaled. 'She could have let those men kill me, but she didn't.'

Instead, Sandra had kept Sylvi too afraid to talk, all these years. Val waited silently, giving Sylvi's hands an encouraging squeeze.

'Van was using,' Sylvi said.

'I know. Now. I didn't know then.'

Sylvi's eyes widened, then narrowed with a flicker of anger. 'So you believed *Sandra?*'

'Only because Desmond corroborated what she said. He said that Sandra and Van did coke at parties.'

'Coke and heroin. And meth,' Sylvi murmured. 'He'd pop pills when he got busy. That's where I got my first hit.'

Val flinched. 'Van gave you drugs?'

'No. I stole them from him. I was so tired, and I needed to study for an exam. I knew it was risky, but I was desperate.' Her gaze searched Val's. 'And then I was hooked.'

'You knew all this time that Van was using. Why didn't you say something?'

'Who would have believed me? I was the fuckup kid in high school. You were a Marine and then a teacher like Dad, and Van was successful at work, and I was . . . just me. I got in trouble and got suspended all the time and . . .' She sighed. 'I cleaned up my act because I wanted college to be different. *I* wanted to be different. I wanted to be like you and Van. I wanted to get straight As, but I couldn't hack the workload. That's not an excuse for using, but that's where my head was then.'

'Did Van know you were using?'

'Yes. He cut me off, but I'd steal money from him. He was always using, but he managed it somehow. He'd use and become Superman. I'd use and become a junkie mess.'

'You got clean.'

'I did. I didn't want to be the fuckup Kristiansen any longer, so I got some help. Went to the campus clinic and they found me an outpatient program. I got clean. Van kept using. He was a charming junkie,' she said with a sad bend of her lips. 'Life of the party.'

'He was hyper the last time I saw him,' Val said. 'That Thanksgiving. I thought he was just busy or embarrassed that I'd seen him with Cassandra, but now I'm realizing he was high.'

'He was high all week. He said he'd stop after Christmas. He didn't live that long.'

'How did you end up at Sixth Day's café that night?'

'I'd been sitting outside his house, practicing my "it's time to get clean" spiel. He got in his car, so I followed him. I recognized the place when we stopped. I'd bought there before. It looked like a normal café, but the back room had all the goodies. I saw him go in and knew why he was there. I figured that would be where I'd start—that he was so far gone that he'd risk his reputation by being seen in a place like that. That maybe he'd even get arrested. I had my speech all planned, but he didn't come out. So, I peeked in the window.'

Val braced herself. 'What did you see?'

'Van was fighting with Aaron Gates.'

'How did you know his name?' Kaj asked softly.

Sylvi startled, as if she'd forgotten he was there. 'I didn't then. Sandra told me later. But that day he was so angry with Van. Yelling that Van "threw him under the bus," and that his son would die because of Van. He pulled out a knife and . . . stabbed him.' Sylvi swallowed. 'I didn't know what to do. There was blood everywhere.'

'I'm sorry,' Val whispered.

'Me too. I was so fixated on Van and Aaron Gates that I didn't see the other people in the room right away. But then I did, and I just froze. Cassandra was there. I stood at that window, staring at her. She was trying to save Van, but . . . he was already gone.' Her lips trembled. 'Cassandra looked up and saw me. So I ran. I didn't try to save him. I'm sorry.'

Val couldn't hold back tears. 'There wasn't anything you could have done. When did Cassandra find you?'

'Later that night. She knew where I lived. She'd given me a ride home from Ivan's house—now your house—a few times when I went to have dinner with them, and she told me that she wanted to be a sister to me. I guess I was lonely. You were different when you came back from Iraq. Colder. Not yourself anymore. And then you left for New Mexico. So when Cassandra offered to be my sister, I said yes.'

It was as if Val could see her life from thirty thousand feet. She'd been so scared of the man who'd raped her that she'd run and changed her name, her life, her everything. Leaving her sister behind, confused and hurt. She opened her mouth, but no words came out.

Sylvi frowned. 'Are you all right?'

Warm arms wrapped around her as Kaj helped her back into the folding chair.

'I was having some personal problems,' Val confessed. 'I shouldn't have shut you out.'

'I thought that it was me,' Sylvi said, her pain clear.

'*No*. It had nothing to do with you. It was something that happened over there.'

'Mom said that a man was stalking you.'

'Yeah. It was . . .' She exhaled, debating what to say. *The truth. Just say the truth*. Because keeping it hidden hadn't helped any of them. 'I was assaulted over there. One of the guys walked on the charges, and he came after me when we were both home.'

Sylvi's eyes widened. 'Oh my God. Ingrid.'

Val waved a hand. 'It's done. I got therapy. Mom and Dad don't know the full story, and I'm only telling you because I don't want you to think that it was your fault in any way. I've hurt you enough.'

Sylvi's expression softened. 'Maybe we hurt each other. Like that one time you offered to get me into rehab, and I snapped your head off. I wasn't using that day, just so you know. My doctor gave me meds for anxiety. They're non-habit-forming so they're okay for addicts like me. I was freaking out all the time back then.' She hesitated. 'Especially when I had to see you. You were so angry and—'

'I'm—' Val started but Sylvi stilled her with a raised hand.

'I was going to say that based on what you knew, you had a right to be. I wanted to tell you the truth.'

'But Sandra convinced you not to.'

'She said the man who killed Ivan would hurt Mom and Dad, and I couldn't let that happen. Rico Nova was there that day, but he didn't do it. Sandra told me that Rico was taking the fall and not to say a word. I've felt guilty for so long. I let him go to prison.' She looked at Kaj. 'Is there a law about that? Saying I should have told? If I have to face some charges, I will. I deserve that much.'

'We can figure it out,' Kaj said kindly. 'But I don't think you'll face any charges. You might think that Sandra saved you, but she was really threatening your life. Now, you said that Aaron and Ivan were there. Dewey and Sandra. Rico Nova. Anyone else?'

'There was one other man. I'd never seen him before. I think he came with Aaron.'

Val stilled. Beside her, Kaj drew a long, slow breath before speaking. 'Can you describe him?' he asked.

'Tall, big like Aaron. Bald head. Both Aaron and this man looked like they were about Van's age.'

Val pulled up a photo of Corey Gates on her phone. 'Him?'

Sylvi flinched. 'Yes. That's him. Is he in jail, too?'

'Not yet,' Val said grimly. 'But he will be.' She brushed aside thoughts of Corey and Aaron Gates and focused on her sister. 'Kaj, can you give us a minute?'

'I'll wait in the front.' He left them alone, closing the door quietly behind him.

'Can we fix this? Us?' Val held her breath, waiting. And hoping.

Sylvi's smaller hand covered hers. 'I thought that's what we were doing.'

Val really looked at her sister. She was clear-eyed and healthy. 'I'm glad you're clean. I'm sorry I wasn't around when you needed me. And even if Van had gone to that café to keep you from buying that night, it shouldn't have mattered. Can you forgive me?'

'I think I did a long time ago. A part of me always understood why you were so angry with me. Van was your twin. You two were so solid. That was a relationship I couldn't compete with, no matter how hard I tried.'

Not so solid. Otherwise, Val might have guessed at the secrets Van had kept. 'Maybe we can be solid together.'

'I'd like that.'

Val wrapped her arms around her sister and held on. Sylvi held on right back. 'You could have died that night, too,' Val whispered.

'There were times I wished I had.'

'*No.* Don't say that.'

'Van went there that night because I'd taken his stash and thrown it out.'

'No, he didn't. Van had secrets neither of us knew about. He wasn't just using. He was selling. He was there that night because he was part of the business.' She held back that Van was the boss. That was a bombshell for another day. If ever. 'No more blame. For either of us.'

'No more blame,' Sylvi agreed. 'What happens now?'

'We catch up on our lives. I want to meet your friends and I want you to meet mine.'

Sylvi's grin was sly. 'Like Kaj?'

Val blushed. 'Yeah. He's got a kid. Who I need to be getting back to. Elijah Cardozo was nearly abducted a few days ago. Kaj hired me to be his bodyguard.'

Sylvi's eyes widened. '*That's* what you do now?'

'Yeah. It's why I'm gone so much. I . . . appreciate you spending time with Mom.'

Sylvi's smile faltered. 'It's not easy. She's so different. I don't know that she'll survive knowing the truth about Van.'

'She'll survive knowing he was using, but we can't tell her about the selling.' And if it became public knowledge, she prayed her mother would block it out like she'd done with Sandra's arrest. Val drew Sylvi close for one more hug. 'Thank you. For forgiving me.'

'Thank you for coming. I know it wasn't easy.'

'I couldn't let another day pass.'

The two walked to the front in a comfortable harmony, Val smiling at Kaj when she saw him sniffing one of the roses that Sylvi had laid on the counter. Sylvi took it from his hand, stripped off the thorns, and handed it to him.

'In case you want to give it to a girl,' she said slyly.

Kaj smiled. 'Thank you. Please visit us. My son will want to meet Ingrid's sister.'

'Soon,' Sylvi promised. 'Y'all go on now. I'll text you when I'm free.'

'You have my number?' Val asked as she and Kaj opened the front door.

'I've always had your number,' Sylvi said and waved goodbye.

Out on the sidewalk, Val drew a deep breath. 'That was easier than I expected.' *Easier than I had a right to expect.*

Kaj took her face in his hands and kissed her. 'I'm proud of you. First with Sandra, then with Sylvi. You've had a busy day.'

She smiled at him. 'At least we know how Aaron and Dewey met. And that Corey was aware of Aaron's drug business from the beginning.'

'We'll need to meet with the others and share what we've learned.'

'Right away.' She glanced over when a gray sedan pulled into the lot, but instead of parking, it continued driving. Slowly. *Too slowly, with an open driver-side window* was all she had time to register before she saw the barrel of a gun pointing straight at them.

The car stopped twenty feet away but directly in front of them, giving the shooter a straight line of fire.

They had no cover. No trees. Not even a potted plant. The parking lot had cleared while they'd been inside and only Kaj's car remained, but it was too far away to hide behind. The alleys between Sylvi's shop and the two businesses on either side of her were too far away to crawl to.

So she shoved Kaj to the sidewalk, pulling her own gun from its holster as she covered his body with hers.

'Val, what the—'

He was interrupted by a single gunshot that shattered the air around them—and Sylvi's display window behind them as well.

Val blocked out the scream from inside the shop and focused on the sedan. It stopped, a man with a ski mask emerging from the passenger side, a rifle positioned at his shoulder.

Val aimed at the man's chest and pulled the trigger, knowing that she had to hit him first. Her Glock was no match for his rifle and if the man got a second shot, Kaj would be hurt.

The man reared back with a roar of pain, but he didn't go down.

Too late she saw his body armor. She fired again but she missed the shooter. *Dammit.*

'When I say go, you crawl to your car,' she hissed to Kaj, cursing the fact that she'd left them so vulnerable to attack. His car was only ten feet behind them, but it might as well have been ten miles. 'I'll cover you.'

'Not without—'

The man repositioned his rifle and Val fired again and again. The man staggered back, but the driver took over, aiming his handgun her way. Still lying on the sidewalk covering Kaj, Val fired, getting off one more shot before a large body landed on her back, forcing the breath from her lungs.

Trapped. I'm trapped. Size and weight were that of a man. A big man.

No. No, no, no. Battling against panic, she started to fight, but the masked rifleman let out a barrage of shots. The body above her jerked with each shot, moaning in pain.

'It's me,' the man above her breathed. 'Phin. Don't fight me.'

Phin. Oh my God. He'd been hit. He lay motionless atop her now and she fought off a different panic. *Please, don't be dead.*

Val pushed Phin's arm out of the way and unloaded her magazine into the sedan. Doors, windows, the driver and the passenger—anything she could hit, until she heard the clicking of an empty chamber.

There was silence then, broken only by her own unsteady breaths and the labored ones of Kaj beneath her. Was Phin still breathing? *Goddammit.*

The sedan's driver-side door opened, one foot landing on the asphalt of the parking lot. The passenger crept around the side of the car, rifle still at the ready.

Fuck. This was it. She'd failed Kaj. She'd failed Phin.

And then the loud wail of a police siren broke the silence. The cops were close.

The driver and his passenger hesitated for a moment, then cursed and got back into their car. A second later, the sedan was gone in a squeal of tires.

Val shuddered out a breath and eased out from in between Kaj and Phin before gently rolling Phin to his back. Kaj lay on the sidewalk, staring up at the sky.

'Kaj?' She cupped his face. 'Kaj?'

'I'm okay. The wind's knocked out of me. What the fuck just happened?'

'They tried to kill you.' Val pivoted to Phin, noting with relief that his body armor was level IV. The ceramic inserts had probably saved his life. He was breathing but not moving. 'Phin's down.'

'I'm not dead,' Phin muttered, sitting up with a groan.

Val let out a squeak of surprise. 'Fucking hell, Phin. You scared me to death.'

'Pot . . . meet kettle,' Phin wheezed.

Kaj barked out a laugh, then groaned. 'I think I have bruised ribs. You weigh a ton, Phin.' He sat up, wincing. 'Where are you hit?'

'Not hit. Body armor.' He exhaled a shuddering breath. 'But damn, it hurts.'

Sylvi. Val shot to her feet and pushed through the shop's door just as a police cruiser screeched to a halt in front of them. 'Are you all right?' she asked her sister.

Sylvi popped up from behind the counter, face pale, her cell phone in her hand. 'I called 911. What happened?'

'That's a damn good question. Oh shit.' Two uniformed officers had their guns drawn on Kaj and Phin. She pulled out her phone, unlocked it, and handed it to her sister. 'Find Burke Broussard in my contacts list. Ask him to get here ASAP and to contact Captain Holmes.'

'Broussard and Holmes,' Sylvi repeated. 'Got it. I'm glad you're all right. I just got you back.'

Val managed a smile. 'Me too, kid. Me too.'

Kenner, Louisiana
THURSDAY, OCTOBER 27, 4:50 P.M.

Yanking at the steering wheel, Corey pulled the car behind a convenience store, fury and pain burning him from the inside out. 'Fuck.'

The bitch had hit him, and the bullet was still lodged in his forearm. His arm was on fucking fire.

'Let me see,' Bobby said. He'd been hit as well—twice—but those bullets had struck his vest. He had some bruised ribs, but he'd be okay. He grabbed a T-shirt from his duffel and wrapped it around Corey's arm. 'The bleeding has slowed, but we need to get this bullet out. And soon. Too bad we killed Zach. He could have fixed you up, being a paramedic and all.'

Corey's laugh held a hysterical edge. 'Fucking hell, Bobby. Shut up.'

Bobby grinned. 'Couldn't resist. What now?'

'I need to get this bullet out.'

Bobby scrunched up his face, in deep thought. 'Is it Wednesday?'

Corey blinked at him. 'Thursday. What the hell, B?'

'Thursday is way better than Wednesday for where we need to go. Okay, let's switch places. I'll drive. You'll wreck us and then our day would start to suck.'

'*Start* to—' Corey huffed a laugh when Bobby winked at him. 'You're an idiot.'

'And for a second you weren't thinking about your arm. Come on. Switch.'

They switched places and Corey leaned back to rest. His arm was bleeding again, so he grabbed a handful of napkins from the glove compartment and pressed them to the wound, applying pressure with his good hand.

I am going to kill that woman.

They'd followed Cardozo and the woman from the jail and had been ready to make their move an hour ago when they'd first arrived at the flower shop, but a damn semitruck had blocked their shots. By the time they'd moved for a better angle, the two had disappeared into the shop. He'd been so sure that they'd had it covered when Cardozo and the woman had reappeared.

They'd planned to kill the woman and take Cardozo alive. But the woman had not been as distracted as she'd first appeared to be. Corey might have admired her reflexes if he didn't want to strangle her with his bare hands.

Bobby gingerly positioned himself behind the wheel, his ribs clearly sore. But he was in better shape, so it was better that he drove.

Then a lucid thought broke through Corey's fog of pain. 'We need to steal another car. The cops will be watching for this one.'

'Already on it,' Bobby promised. 'I know where we can pick one up, and the owner won't even know it's gone until Saturday. It's not far from here. We'll keep to the back roads.'

Corey really didn't have a choice. 'We lost our chance to grab Cardozo and get him to tell us where Bella is. He'll be guarded even more heavily from now on.'

'I know,' Bobby said grimly. 'And we're not in very good shape to launch another attack. You won't have full use of your hand for at least a few weeks. Maybe longer.'

'Don't need my left hand to shoot,' Corey muttered. 'I want that blond bitch in my sights. She'll be the first one I take down.'

'You got that right.' Bobby navigated the back roads, turning again and again, until Corey had lost track of their path.

'Who was the big guy there at the end?'

'I don't know,' Bobby said. 'We're going to find out, because he's on my list as well. I'm betting he works for Broussard. Another of his bodyguards.'

'Makes sense. Where are we going?'

'Old girlfriend's house. She's a flight attendant. She has the TransPacific route that leaves on Thursday and returns on Saturday.'

'How long ago were you together?' Corey asked.

'We broke up a month before I left the force.'

'Four years ago? Are you crazy? She's probably changed routes.'

Bobby flashed another lazy grin. 'Of course I'm crazy. You've always known that. We're not together anymore, but I still drop by every few weeks. She's not shy about texting me for a booty call when she's in the mood. When she's on duty, she leaves her car in her garage and takes an Uber to the airport. I know where she keeps the extra key to her house and the keys to her car. Don't worry. I have this.'

'I have nothing *but* worry. Cardozo was our best option to find Bella Butler and he's slipped through our fingers.' Along with any plans Corey had made for his future.

He *had* to finish this job. He *had* to find Bella. And then he'd do what it took to force her to recant. She would not win this war. She would not make him fail.

'We're here.' Bobby pulled into the driveway of a small house on a quiet street, leaving the motor running. 'I'll be just a minute. Keep your head down.'

Corey slumped down so that his head wasn't visible, the movement making his arm throb. The image of strangling the blond bitch with his bare hands filled his mind.

'Goddamn woman.' He wasn't going to simply kill her. He'd make her pay for what she'd done. She would suffer. He'd see to it.

But he didn't have to take care of Val Sorensen now. He could kill her when his hand healed. All he needed to do was find Bella Butler.

Corey lifted his head when a garage door rumbled and rose. Inside was a black Volvo.

Perfect. Nobody would be looking for them in a Volvo.

Bobby slid into the driver's seat beside him and shook a medicine bottle. 'I raided her medicine cabinet. Found some oxy so you can knock yourself out. Take one.'

'I will, once we have Bella.'

Bobby sighed wearily. 'Fine.'

Corey glared at him. 'What does that mean?'

'It means that we're all banged up. We're going to need to over-power Allyson to bring her in if we expect to keep any of the respect we've built. And we still need to get Cardozo—or someone—to tell us where to find Bella.'

'Fine,' Corey grunted. 'So let's go.'

'Not yet. We're going to get that bullet out first.'

Corey cringed. '*You're* going to do it?'

'Well, it's not like we can walk into a hospital, can we?' Bobby pulled into the garage, parking their stolen car next to the Volvo, which had darkly tinted windows.

Even better.

Bobby lowered the garage door. 'Come on. I already set out the things we'll need. Luckily Paulina's a prepper. She's got a storage room full of food and medical supplies.'

Corey followed him into what was a tidy little house. The kitchen table was covered in bandages and other first-aid equipment. Uneasily, he sat down. 'You ever done this before?'

'Nope. But I've seen a lot of old movies and I know what to do.'

Corey pushed to his feet. 'No.'

Bobby laughed. 'Sit down. I've done this before. One of my old buddies on the force shot himself in the leg when he was fooling around with his gun, trying to look macho. He didn't want his old lady to know, so I took care of it.'

Corey slowly sat back down. 'He thought he could hide a gunshot wound from his wife? How'd that work out for him?'

Bobby snorted as he quickly arranged the supplies in a way that actually did give Corey a little confidence. 'About like you'd expect. I never said he was one of my smarter buddies. Ended up sleeping on the couch for a month. Take one of those pills, Corey.' He glanced up, now totally sober. 'I'm serious. One won't kill you. It won't even impair you that much. It'll take the edge off what's gonna be a shit ton of pain.'

Corey scowled at the little bottle of pills. 'I do not want to become Aaron.'

Bobby's smile was uncharacteristically gentle. 'I won't let that happen.' He took a bottle of water from the pile of supplies and handed it to Corey. 'Take one.'

Corey complied, shuddering as it went down. 'My dad was a drunk. A stupid drunk. My brother is a stupid addict. I will kill you if I get addicted to this shit.'

'You won't,' Bobby said. 'Lay your arm flat on the table and bite down on this.' He handed his leather belt over the table. 'Like in the movies.'

Corey grimaced. 'I'm not putting your disgusting belt in my mouth.'

'God, you're a baby. I cleaned it with alcohol. Just do it.'

Corey did, looking away when Bobby began probing his wound with a scalpel. Nausea rolled through his stomach and he clenched his jaw harder. *Not gonna throw up, not gonna throw up.* He chanted the words in his head until he heard the slight *ping* of metal as it hit a stoneware bowl.

'It's out,' Bobby said unnecessarily. 'You can spit the belt out if you want. That was the worst of it.'

'You're not a bad medic,' Corey admitted reluctantly.

'Aw, shucks,' Bobby deadpanned. 'You're embarrassing me.'

Corey chanced a look at what Bobby was doing. 'What's that?'

Bobby held up a small tube of what looked like ointment. 'Liquid stitches. It'll close up the wound and you'll be back to your old charming self.'

Corey laughed, but it came out as a moan. 'Fuck off.'

Bobby applied the liquid and bandaged him up. 'All done. Sit there while I gather all the bloody bandages. We'll take them with us and burn them later. I'm also going to raid her pantry. I'm starving.'

'See if she has decent coffee for Ed while you're at it,' Corey called, then dropped his chin to his chest. His arm hurt, his head hurt, and he was so fucking pissed off that he didn't know what to do.

Yes, you do. You take out your anger on Allyson and then you go after Cardozo again. Then you find Bella, kill her, and get paid.

'Sure,' he muttered. 'Easy as pie.'

A few minutes later Bobby returned with a few bags of groceries. 'You okay?'

'Sure,' Corey drawled. 'I'm just peachy.'

'Good to hear,' Bobby said cheerfully. 'Let's haul ass to Allyson's house. I'm looking to punish a bitch.'

'Sounds like exactly what I need.' Corey stood, gritting his teeth when the world tilted. He breathed deeply until it passed. 'I want to get my hands on the bitch who shot me, too.'

Corey followed Bobby to the garage, sliding into the passenger seat of the Volvo, then frowning when Bobby started the engine. The *quiet* engine. 'Is this a *hybrid*?'

Bobby laughed. 'God, the look on your face. Yes, it is, but it's got the best acceleration of all the hybrids. I helped her pick it out.'

'Then why didn't you make her get a car with something bigger than a golf cart engine?'

'Because she cares about the environment. Look at it this way—we can sneak up on people with a quiet car.'

Corey grunted. 'Nobody was gonna be looking for us in a Volvo. Nobody's really gonna be looking for us in a *hybrid* Volvo. I just hope we don't have to get away fast.'

Bobby only sighed as he put Allyson's home address into his phone's map app. 'You're always such a ray of sunshine, Corey. Don't ever change.'

Mid-City, New Orleans, Louisiana
THURSDAY, OCTOBER 27, 6:55 P.M.

'You okay, Dad?' Elijah murmured from where he sat on the arm of Kaj's chair.

They'd finally made it back to his house in one piece—him, Val, Sylvi, and Phin. Burke had one of his part-time people in Sylvi's shop, putting plywood over the shattered window. The cops had given Val a hard time about firing her weapon until André had arrived. They'd confiscated her gun, but they'd all been cleared to leave.

André was still at the crime scene but had promised to let them know if they found any evidence identifying the shooters. As if they needed evidence. It had been Corey and Bobby, Kaj had no doubt.

Now that his adrenaline was crashing, his mind was playing what might have been.

'I'm okay. It's just . . .'

'Sinking in?' Elijah asked. That his son understood was unacceptable. *They tried to take my son and then tried to shoot me?* He hoped he'd be there when the bastards were caught. He had some pent-up anger to release.

He wrapped an arm around Elijah, exhaling quietly when his son rested his head on Kaj's shoulder. 'Yes. It's sinking in.'

Sitting on the floor with her back to Kaj's legs, Val sighed. 'All I wanted to do was visit my sister.' She threw a harried smile at Sylvi, who returned it.

'Thank you for inviting me to your home, Kaj,' Sylvi said. 'I live over the shop and wouldn't have slept a wink tonight.'

'You're welcome for as long as you need to stay,' Kaj said sincerely. If there was one good thing to come of this day, it was Val's reunion with her sister.

Burke returned from the kitchen, a bag of ice in each hand. He wrapped the bags in towels and carefully laid them on Phin's back. Phin was sprawled facedown on the sofa, his back bruised but not bloody. None of the bullets had pierced his military-grade body armor, thank God. The armor was designed to withstand high-velocity rifle fire, which was the only reason Phin was alive right now.

When they'd asked why he'd been there, he'd said that Val was distracted and that had worried him, especially with the online threats. He'd followed them from the jail and had been waiting in the narrow alley next to the flower shop, planning to follow them back once they were done talking with Sylvi.

Wearing the armor had been a last-minute decision, he'd told André, looking embarrassed. Helped him reduce his anxiety and stave off a panic attack.

Kaj was waiting for a quiet moment to express his gratitude. Phin didn't strike him as the kind of man who'd want to be the center of attention as Kaj thanked him. Besides, the man was looking pretty miserable at the moment.

Phin hissed at the ice but settled quickly with only a slight grumble. 'Thanks.'

'You're welcome.' Burke looked over his shoulder to the table where Antoine sat with his three laptops, Jace at his side. 'You tap into the security cameras around Sylvi's shop yet?'

'Yep,' Antoine said. 'Nice shooting, Val. I think you hit the driver in the arm.'

Antoine was right. Val had done some fine shooting, considering one of the gunmen had been using a semiautomatic rifle.

'Wish I'd hit him in the head,' Val muttered. 'There didn't appear to be any blood at the scene, but André said they're looking for the gray sedan. He might have bled on the upholstery.'

The gunmen would probably ditch the stolen car and steal something else.

'Can I?' Jace asked, tugging at Antoine's laptop. 'I want to see.'

Kaj had agreed to release Jace from his cuffs while both Burke and at least one other of his people were in the house. Jace had been grateful, but not insistent. Nevertheless, Kaj had gathered all the kitchen knives and any sharp implements Jace could use as a weapon. He still wasn't sure that he trusted the young man, but he really wanted to.

'That's Bobby,' Jace said, pointing at the screen. 'The guy with the rifle. He moves like Bobby and has the same shoulders.'

'And the driver?' Val asked.

'It's not Ed,' Jace said. 'Ed's a smaller guy. He's built more like my brother Rick. So that leaves Corey behind the wheel. Why would they try to kill you, Mr. Cardozo?'

And wasn't that the one-hundred-thousand-dollar question? 'At this point, I'm betting it has to do with Bella Butler. Captain Holmes insisted that they kept the knowledge of Bella's recorded phone call to a minimum, but we know there's a leak somewhere in the department.'

Val shrugged. 'Noni Feldman also knows about the call, since she placed it. Maybe she told the wrong person.'

Val was right. As much as the Feldman woman wanted to protect her source, she might have inadvertently disclosed the truth. 'We should talk to Miss Feldman,' Kaj said. 'Just to make sure. But there's also a chance that, even though André was careful about who knew about his interview with Noni this morning, the NOPD leak found out and told Corey and Bobby. Also, André never said if he found out who was standing close to me when I took that call about Elijah's math meet. We need to ask him about it. We need to find the leak.'

'That might have gotten bumped down the list,' Burke said. 'A lot has happened since we first talked about it in the wee hours of Wednesday morning.'

'Antoine?' Kaj looked to the dining room table, meeting Antoine's eyes. Antoine gave him a wordless nod without him having to actually ask Antoine to hack into the surveillance cameras in the lobby of the NOPD's headquarters. 'Next question. How did Corey and Bobby know we were going to the flower shop? I'm assuming they followed us from the jail.'

'Probably,' Val said quietly. 'We were at the jail for forty minutes, tops. If they were informed as soon as we arrived, it's possible that they could have arrived in time to follow us.'

'No, they couldn't,' Jace said, then bit his lip when all eyes turned to him. 'Sorry. I'll be quiet.'

'No, Jace. Don't be quiet.' Val went to sit at the table. 'Why couldn't they?'

'Because I think they came from the bayou. Can you rewind the video, Antoine?'

Antoine did as he was told until Jace said, 'Stop. There. When the driver puts his foot on the asphalt, his boot's covered in mud. It could be old mud, but I don't think so because it ain't dry. If it was dry, it would have started to crack and slough off. If he was on the water, it would have taken him more than forty minutes to get to the jail, even if they were told as soon as you got there.'

Everyone was silent, then Burke clapped. 'Very good, Jace. You've got a good eye.'

Jace blushed. 'It's nothin'. I just . . . notice stuff, that's all.'

Val squeezed his hand. 'It's not nothing. It's a good thing, Jace. I'm proud of you.'

Jace frowned. 'But what does it mean?'

Val blew out a breath. 'I think it means they were already headed into the city before we got to the jail. Someone told them where we were and they went to the jail, waited, then followed us from there. That person either worked at the jail or followed us there from this house. Is it possible that someone is watching us?'

'André stepped up police presence on the street,' Kaj said. André had insisted on more coverage after the newest online threats came out that—thankfully—they'd managed to keep from Elijah. 'They've been stopping anyone who doesn't live on the street.'

'And nobody suspicious has approached the house,' Antoine stated. 'I've set up cameras on the street to check traffic flow, and I haven't noticed anyone hanging around. They're far enough away that we don't see them, but close enough for them to know when you leave.'

'I'll talk to André again,' Burke promised. 'But what about Noni Feldman? We need to find out what she knows. I'll go talk to her. She might be more willing to talk with me than she was with the cops this morning.'

'Yes,' Val agreed. 'We do need to find out what she knows. But Burke, maybe you should stay here with Kaj and Elijah. Miss Feldman may be more comfortable talking to me. You can be a bit . . . much. You know . . . big.'

Burke scowled. 'I'm a pussycat.'

Jace opened his mouth, then snapped it shut, but his expression was clear. He was still a little afraid of Burke.

Burke sighed. 'Fine. I'll keep watch here. But you can't go alone, Val.'

'I know,' Val said. 'That's why I texted Molly fifteen minutes ago and asked her to swing by and pick me up. She'll be here any minute.'

Kaj gave Elijah another squeeze before shoving himself out of the chair. Damn, his ribs hurt. Phin really did weigh a ton. But he was more than grateful the big man had followed them. Val might not be alive if he hadn't. *Or me.*

'You'll wear a vest?' Kaj asked her.

'Absolutely.'

He pulled her into the kitchen, away from prying eyes. 'Be careful. Promise me.'

'I promise. I don't want to leave you and Elijah right now, but this could keep you safe.'

He carefully threaded his fingers through her hair. She'd let it down after the attack and now wore it loose around her shoulders. He made sure he didn't grab anywhere near her scalp, keeping his touch gentle. 'I want you safe, too,' he whispered. 'You're important.'

She tugged him close, kissing him the way he'd hoped she would. It was warm and comforting, which was exactly what he'd needed.

She ended the kiss on a quiet sigh. 'Stay inside. Don't go anywhere.'

He let her go. 'I won't. You'll be with Molly, so I know you'll be in good hands, but just . . . We don't know that they were shooting just at me. If they took you out, I'd be . . .'

Lost.

'I'll be careful. I promise. I'll be back soon.' She kissed him lightly. 'I promise.'

'Val,' Burke called. 'Molly just pulled into the driveway. Get a move on.'

'On my way,' she called back.

Kaj watched her go, trying not to let his worry show. He shouldn't have bothered. Elijah was at his side in seconds.

'She'll be okay, Dad. She's a Marine and carries a gun. And she's a roller derby queen.'

Kaj kissed the top of his son's head. 'She's a lot more than that.'

22

COREY SURVEYED ALLYSON Meyer's neighborhood as they approached her town house. The oxy he'd taken had finally kicked in. While his arm still hurt, it was nowhere near what it had been.

Bobby slowed as they drove through the parking lot in front of Allyson's town house. All the lights were on. 'Looks like she's home, but I don't see her car. I thought Ed said her car hadn't moved.'

'That was hours ago. Let me call him.' Corey dialed Ed. 'Where's Allyson's car?'

'Same place,' Ed said. 'It hasn't moved since yesterday at noon, like I told you.'

'It's not here,' Bobby said. 'She drives a Honda Civic, right?'

'Right,' Ed said. 'No other cars are registered in her name. Her car has to be there. I'm sending you a link to the tracking screen.'

Corey clicked on it when it arrived in his inbox. 'Ed, we're standing right next to the dot and there is no Honda Civic to be seen.'

'Fuck,' Ed muttered. 'Check the car adjacent to her space.'

'On it,' Bobby called. He was crouching next to the car that was where the app said Allyson's should be. After a minute, he rose, a tracker in his palm. 'Ed, she found the tracker you put on and put it on this other car.'

'So we've lost her,' Corey said flatly. 'Track her credit cards, Ed.'

'Doing that now.' Keys clacked on his keyboard, followed by Ed's sigh. 'She hasn't used them. She's either on the run or she went to work as scheduled, just in another car. If the second is true, she knows Bella's new location. Either way, she won't be easy to catch.'

Bobby was staring up at Allyson's town house window. 'Unless we can draw her back.' He pointed to the window where the silhouette of a woman quickly passed by. 'Someone's in there.'

'And I know who.' Corey pointed to the Audi he'd seen only a few days before parked in front of his own house, then again in front of the Three Vets office. 'Noni Feldman.'

Bobby's lips curved. 'Let's take her instead. She'll make great bait.'

'She might even know where Bella is,' Corey said.

Bobby's grin grew. 'I bet I could make her tell me.' He drew his gun and aimed it toward the ground. It wasn't the Raging Judge he'd been wearing in a chest holster. This was a sleek Glock with a suppressor. The Judge was Bobby's fun gun. The Glock was all business.

'Ed,' Corey said, 'do what you can to find Allyson. We'll keep you updated.' He slid his phone into his pocket. 'Noni wanted to talk to us on Tuesday. Let's give her an interview.'

Gentilly, New Orleans, Louisiana
THURSDAY, OCTOBER 27, 7:15 P.M.

Noni sat on the edge of Allyson's bed, staring into the empty closet. The woman was gone. Her car was gone, as were her clothes, and there were no suitcases anywhere. She'd left a key under the doormat, though, and a note to her landlord saying she'd had a family emergency and wasn't coming back.

Noni hoped that Allyson had left of her own volition. When Noni's calls had gone unanswered, she'd pictured Allyson lying dead somewhere, a victim of Corey Gates.

Noni had risen to leave when she heard the tinkle of broken glass. *A window. Someone's breaking in.* She ran to the bedroom window that looked out to the backyard in time to see a familiar bald head seconds before it was covered by a ski mask.

Corey Gates.

Corey Gates is here. For Allyson. But he wouldn't find Allyson. *He'll find me.*

Fear gripped her gut and, for a second, she froze in indecision. *Move, dammit. Do something.* She found her cell phone in her pocket and called 911.

Nothing. With growing horror she saw that she had no cell phone signal.

Cell phone jammer.

No one knew she was here. No one would look for her.

She was on her own.

Hide.

She ran for the bathroom but stopped to strip off her coat and stuff it under Allyson's bed. Her newsroom ID was in the pocket. If someone came looking, they'd know she'd been taken.

Then she crept into the bathroom and climbed into the tub, pulling the shower curtain closed. Heart pounding, she plastered herself against the tile wall, wishing she had a gun.

For what seemed like forever, she stood there, holding her breath. Listening for footsteps. None came. She quietly exhaled. They were gone. They hadn't found—

The shower curtain was yanked aside, revealing an enormous man. Holding a gun. With a silencer.

She sucked in a breath to scream, but he leaned forward and slapped a piece of duct tape over her mouth. Yanking her out of the tub, he twisted her arms behind her back, making her cry out. Before she could blink, he'd taped her wrists together and pulled her flush to his body.

'Found you,' he whispered in a singsong voice, then laughed.

Her fight instinct finally engaged and she kicked at him, but he just laughed again and taped her ankles. *I'm going to die. He's going to kill me.*

Gentilly, New Orleans, Louisiana
THURSDAY, OCTOBER 27, 8:15 P.M.

Val tugged at the itchy Kevlar she wore under her sweater as Molly entered Allyson Meyer's neighborhood. 'We're nearly there, Kaj,' she said into her phone, hoping this house would be more fruitful than the last.

Noni Feldman hadn't been home when they'd knocked—or she hadn't answered—but Kaj had called as they were headed back to his house, telling them that he'd just talked to Bella Butler. She'd informed him that two of her security guards hadn't shown up for an emergency meeting that afternoon—Zach Monteith and Allyson Meyer.

Her head of security had tried calling their cell phones multiple times but had received no answer. Visits to their respective homes had also yielded no answer. But one of Zach's neighbors had informed him that the police had been by their house earlier in the day. It had taken Bella several hours to find out that Zach was the dead paramedic that Noni had mentioned in her anonymous call, his body found in the bayou.

Val and Molly had immediately detoured for Allyson Meyer's address.

Kaj had been understandably irked that Bella hadn't called him right away when they'd realized the two hadn't shown up. But she'd wanted to be sure before she accused them.

'I called André to tell him,' Kaj said, 'but got his voice mail. I left him a message to call me back urgently. If you get there and anything is off, back away and call 911.'

'We will, don't worry,' Val assured him. Of course, his definition of 'off' and hers were likely very different. But she'd have Molly at her side.

Alone, Val knew she was strong and extremely good at her job. Partnered with Molly Sutton, they were a formidable force.

'Did Bella have any idea of why Zach would be working with Corey?' Molly asked Kaj.

'Only that he needed money for a state-of-the-art prosthesis for his fiancée, but she pays her staff very well. She paid Zach even more because he brought medic skills to the team. Antoine is trying to get into his financials. Bella still wasn't sure if Allyson was involved. She said the woman seems impenetrable.'

'Everyone has vulnerabilities,' Val murmured. 'Secrets, even.'

Molly cast her a sympathetic glance. Val had shared her conversations with Sandra Springfield and Sylvi. Molly had baggage of her own, so she'd understood.

'True,' Kaj said. 'It's not clear if Zach was being paid by Corey or extorted. Noni Feldman did tell Bella that he'd been killed because he refused to participate, so he could have been forced.'

'Let's hope that Allyson just has a bad cold and that a NyQuil stupor is to blame for her being AWOL from work,' Molly said briskly. 'But we're prepared for whatever happens, Kaj. Don't worry. I have Val's back.'

'Don't hang up,' Kaj said. 'Burke is here and we want to listen. Just in case we need to call 911 for you.'

'Will do.' Val slipped her phone into her pocket, and together she and Molly approached Allyson's front door. Val knocked and they listened. No answer and no sounds came from inside.

'She ain't here.'

They turned together to the adjacent town house. A boy around thirteen years old leaned against his doorframe trying to look bored, but he was studying them with obvious interest.

Val smiled at him. 'We're friends of hers and she didn't show up for movie night tonight. We got worried. Do you know where she went?'

He straightened a little, his chest puffing out with importance. 'Hospital, I think.'

'Why do you think that?' Val asked.

'She got carried out by some guy. Like she was sick or something.'

Cold dread raced down Val's spine, but she feigned simple alarm. 'Oh my. We were worried about that. When was it?'

He consulted his phone. 'Forty minutes ago exactly.'

'Exactly?' Molly asked. 'How do you remember exactly?'

'Because I was talking to my mom—she's at work and was checking on me—and the phone just cut out. I was coming outside to get a better signal and that's when I saw them. One was carrying her out to a black car, all wrapped up in a blanket, and the other got into another car.' He shrugged. 'They drove away.'

'Did you happen to see what the guys looked like?' Val asked.

The boy frowned. 'Did I do wrong? Should I have stopped them?'

'You didn't do anything wrong,' Val assured him. 'We're just . . . you know, overly protective of her. If they took her to the hospital, they're probably friends of ours, too. We need to ask them where they took her. We're her friends. Girls worry.'

'Yeah, I know. My mom worries *all the time*,' he added with an eye roll.

'Did you see what they looked like?' Val asked again.

'No, ma'am. They were wearing baseball caps. And it was dark. I'm sorry.'

'Don't be,' Val said. 'We'll make sure we tell her that you were a help when we catch up to her.'

'Do you happen to have a key to her place?' Molly asked.

'Nah. I don't even know her name. She keeps to herself. My mom doesn't like her. Says she's a snob. But I think she's nice. She feeds the stray cats.'

Val smiled at him again. 'Thank you. We're going to check around the back. She sometimes leaves it open for us. See you later!'

She and Molly stepped down the stairs and began walking quickly down to the end of the row of town homes.

'Corey,' Molly muttered.

'And Bobby, it sounds like. He's big enough to carry a woman like that.'

Molly slanted her a look of concern as they started up the narrow alley behind the row of town homes. 'You okay with this?'

Val knew Molly was referring to the fact that men Bobby's size often triggered her fear. 'I'm fine.' She really was. 'I'm far more worried about Allyson Meyer.'

They opened the gate into Allyson's back courtyard and immediately saw that a window had been broken and the door was ajar. They shared a quick look before pulling on gloves and drawing their weapons. Val pulled her phone from her pocket.

'Call 911,' she whispered to Kaj. 'Already done,' he replied. 'Be careful.'

He didn't urge her not to go in, which was a surprise. She wouldn't have listened, so maybe he knew her well enough already not to bother trying.

Molly pointed to herself, then down. *She'll go low, I'll go high.*

They crept into the house and found all the interior doors open, but no one was there. They cleared each room, then went on to the next, then climbed the stairs. Again, they found the doors open. There was a spare room with a monitor, but no computer.

They finally got to the primary bedroom. They'd seen nothing out of place anywhere.

'You think they drugged her?' Val murmured.

'Don't know. It's possible. Allyson was army. She knew how to defend herself, but there's no sign of a struggle. I'd have thought that if she was able, she'd have fought. Closet's empty.'

'So are the drawers,' Val said, checking the dresser. 'Allyson was planning to leave. But the kid next door didn't say anything about the guys carrying suitcases. Just a woman.'

Molly nodded. 'I was thinking the same thing. I'll check the bathroom.'

Val looked over the rest of the bedroom, immediately noticing that the bedspread was rumpled in only one small area. It was the only thing out of place in the entire house. 'Someone sat on the bed. Everything here is perfectly placed and Allyson was army. I think she would have smoothed it over. At least I would have.'

'I agree,' Molly said, coming out of the bathroom. 'I couldn't have walked away from a rumpled bedspread, either. There are dirty shoe prints in the tub. Someone was wearing heels. She must have been hiding.'

'There's nothing else here.' Val had started for the door when a flash of color caught her eye. 'Hold on.' She crouched down to check it out. 'It's a coat, all balled up.'

'That's different. Hurry. We need to be out of here before the cops get here, which will be any minute.'

'Will do. I don't want André to have to rescue me twice in one night.' Val winced when her back protested her position, but the pain was worth it. 'There's an ID badge on the carpet. It fell out of the pocket.' Reaching her phone under the bed, she snapped a photo of the badge, then showed it to Molly, zooming in on the image. 'Oh my God. This is why Noni didn't answer when we knocked on her door.'

Molly blew out a breath. 'She was here. What do you want to bet that Allyson was already gone and Noni came to check up on her source?'

'Yeah. Let's go.'

They hurried down the stairs and out the back door, jogging down to the end of the row as the police pulled up in front of Allyson's house.

Molly pointed to the direction from which they'd come. 'We asked our boss to call you. We came to check on Allyson Meyer because she didn't show up to work today. Signs of forced entry at the back.'

The cop stared at them. 'And you are?'

Molly smiled at him sweetly. 'Private investigators. We work for Burke Broussard.'

The cop just nodded. 'Please wait on the sidewalk. I'll have someone take your statement.' He narrowed his eyes. 'Did you go inside?'

'Only to see if anyone needed help,' Molly said. 'When we saw that no one was home, we left immediately.'

Kind of true. It seemed good enough for the cop. 'All right. Please wait.'

Val quickly sent the photos she'd taken to Burke and put the phone to her ear to hear him swearing. 'They got Noni Feldman?' he exclaimed.

'Fuck,' Kaj swore softly.

'I know,' Val said grimly. 'Molly saw shoeprints in the tub, like she'd hidden there. It looks like Noni shoved her coat under the bed before hiding in the tub. The kid next door said that his cell phone stopped working right before he saw two men carrying her out. He thought he was looking at Allyson. They'd wrapped her up in a blanket.'

'Cell phone jammers,' Burke said, annoyed. 'If Noni called for help, she wouldn't have been able to get through.'

'All of your theories make sense,' Kaj said. 'But everything just got worse. If Corey and Bobby were there, it means they know that Bella knows about their plans.'

'Which reinforces an NOPD leak,' Burke finished. 'André is going to be very unhappy, because this also means that someone he trusts is dirty.'

'You should put your phone back in your pocket now,' Molly said, tilting her head toward the cruisers starting to arrive. A sedan pulled up behind the cruisers, and two detectives got out.

'Stay tuned,' Val said to Kaj and Burke before sliding her phone into her pocket. 'I recognize the one with silver in his hair,' she murmured to Molly. 'He was at Kaj's the night Rick was dropped off on the lawn. Name's Drysdale. One of André's team. I didn't talk to him, but he gave Kaj his card and told him to call if he had any problems.'

Drysdale was not smiling as he approached with the other detective. 'Ladies,' he said with an undeniable air of superiority. Val wanted to bristle but kept her cool.

Once again, Molly smiled sweetly. It was a deceptive expression that often fooled overly confident people into dropping their guard. 'Detectives.'

The other detective stepped forward. 'I'm Detective Clancy and this is my partner, Detective Drysdale. Your boss called this in?'

'He did,' Val confirmed.

'And you entered the home?' Drysdale asked, his jaw clenched.

'Only to render first aid if needed,' Molly said. 'None was needed, so we left.'

Val had always been impressed with how Molly could lie and tell the truth at the same time. It was truly a gift.

Val pointed to the town house next to Allyson's. 'The boy who lives there saw a woman being carried out. You might wish to speak to him.'

Detective Clancy nodded his thanks, leaving them with Drysdale, whose expression grew even more sour. 'You shouldn't have gone in the house. What if the intruders were still there?'

Molly's mouth tightened almost imperceptibly at the corners. 'We would have been fine. We're trained for situations exactly like that.'

He was quiet for a long moment. 'You seem like nice women. Will you accept some advice?'

Val was curious as to what he'd say, so she nodded. 'Sure.'

'Stay away from this investigation. Find a safe job and leave the PI-ing to the rest of Broussard's men. This is too dangerous for you.'

Molly blinked. 'Excuse me?'

Val swallowed a sigh. It wasn't the first time she'd faced a patronizing attitude from a man. It wouldn't be the last.

Molly met the man's gaze head-on. 'We're Marines. We'll be fine.'

Well, Molly still considered herself one. Val had shucked off the mantle when she'd realized that her military career had been over the moment she'd pushed to press charges against the men who'd raped her.

Still, Val nodded. 'Like Molly said, we'll be fine. But thank you for your concern.'

'Suit yourself.' Drysdale started to turn away, then pivoted back to stare into Val's eyes in a very aggressive way. 'But if three big guys come at you, are you gonna faint?'

Val froze, unsure if he'd meant what she thought he had. *'Excuse me, Detective?'*

She glanced at Molly, who wore a similar expression of shock.

His lifted a brow. 'Just a question.'

'Who the hell are you to ask me something like that?' she demanded.

'I'm a father. I'd tell my daughter to be careful around strange men who mean her harm. I'd also tell her not to put herself in harm's way. Again.'

Val's mouth fell open. *Again?* Like it was her fault the first time? *What the fuck?* In her mind she snarled the words, but her mouth wasn't cooperating.

Swallowing hard, Val straightened to her full height, making the detective look up. It was a small thing and perhaps petty, but it felt good. 'With all due respect, Detective, fuck you.'

'I'm really trying to help you,' Drysdale said quietly. 'I'm sorry if the truth hurts.'

'We'll be going now,' Molly said brusquely, finally regaining her power of speech. 'Call us if you need help with your case, Detective. But we charge for investigative services. A lot. Consider this a freebie for the NOPD out of the goodness of our hearts.'

Molly turned on her heel and all but marched to her car, but Val stood there a moment more, staring at the detective, who continued to stare back at her.

'How did you know about that?' she asked.

He shrugged. 'You killed a couple of men last summer when you were on the job. You walked away because it was self-defense. It was the first time you popped up on our radar, Miss Sorensen, so we did a background check. All kinds of things came up, including the fact that you've been involved in other homicides while working for Broussard. Interestingly, your military . . . *history* did not come up. Not under your current name, anyway.'

Val felt her eye twitch and she forcibly calmed it. 'I see. And if I were to do a background check on you, Detective, what would I find?'

His expression grew dark. 'I was *trying* to *help* you,' he said in a soft snarl.

She smiled coldly. 'Well, you know what they say. You can't help someone who doesn't want to be helped. Have a good evening.'

She kept her steps slow as she ambled to Molly's car and got in, closing the door carefully. 'Drive,' she said from behind clenched teeth.

Molly pulled away from the crime scene. 'Take your phone out of your pocket. We need Burke in on this.'

Val obeyed, on autopilot now. Her hands were shaking as she connected her phone to Molly's stereo. 'Did you hear that?' she asked, grateful that her voice didn't break.

'I did,' Burke said, his fury fully evident. 'What the actual fuck?'

'Are you all right?' Kaj asked, his fury mixed with concern.

'I'm sorry, Val,' Burke said. 'I should have asked that.'

'I'm okay. Not happy that NOPD knows my personal history, but it is what it is now. I mean, we run background checks as a matter of course. I suppose I get why someone might have been concerned when I killed people, but I still hate knowing my private life is no longer private.'

'Just come home,' Kaj said. 'We can figure out what, if anything, you want to do about him.'

For a few minutes, it was silent in the car, Molly driving and Val nursing her wounds. Val didn't end the call because she found that the connection with Kaj comforted her in a way she hadn't expected, even if neither of them said anything at all.

'He seemed like he really wanted to be helpful, as ugly as he was about it,' she finally said.

'Or,' Molly countered, 'he was trying to make us angry about NOPD doing background checks on us so that we'd stop thinking about the fact that Noni Feldman was just kidnapped by Corey and Bobby.'

'Or that,' Burke said wryly. 'Thank you, Molly.'

Val didn't speak again until Molly had pulled into Kaj's driveway and Kaj rushed outside to open her car door. 'Come on,' he urged. 'You're home now. Are you coming in, Molly?'

'Not now. I may come over later to spell Burke, but tonight was Gabe's night off, so I have a delicious dinner waiting at home.' She squeezed Val's arm. 'Don't give that bastard Drysdale another thought. He was trying to distract us.'

Kaj pulled Val out of the passenger seat and into his arms. 'She's right. Don't give him another thought. Just come into the house and let me take care of you.'

Mid-City, New Orleans, Louisiana
THURSDAY, OCTOBER 27, 9:30 P.M.

Kaj pulled her into him as he walked them up the front porch steps, where Burke stood waiting, his weapon drawn. 'What are you *thinking*, Kaj?' he hissed. 'Are you *insane*? You were just shot at a few hours ago!'

Kaj faltered. He hadn't been thinking. She'd needed him and he'd just reacted. 'I'm sorry,' he said to Burke. 'It won't happen again.'

'It better not.' Burke paused at the door, his expression softening to concern when he saw Val's face. 'Come in, all of you. It's time to stop working.'

'I'm okay,' she assured him as she walked through the door. 'Just pissed off.'

Kaj wasn't so sure. She said she was pissed off, but he had the feeling that the detective's words had cut far deeper than she was willing to admit. Bringing up her assault had undoubtedly brought up a host of bad memories. Kaj hated to think of the images that had to be running through her mind right now.

'Hey.' Val's tone was casual as she entered the living room, upbeat even. 'What'd I miss? Where's Elijah?'

'He went to bed,' Sylvi said. 'Took your dog up with him. He helped me make dinner for everyone while you were gone—well, Elijah did, not the dog. Leftovers are in the fridge. Elijah said to tell you that I'd "fed and watered" both him and Czar.'

'Thank you, Sylvi,' Val told her with a smile that Kaj recognized as forced.

Sylvi must have seen the same thing, because she glanced at Kaj, concerned.

Phin still lay facedown with ice packs on his back. 'We're fine. You okay?'

Val nodded. 'Just really tired all of a sudden.'

'It's been a crazy day,' Jace murmured from a sleeping bag on the floor. He was sitting cross-legged, the tablet Molly had loaned him on his lap. He was cuffed, but only one arm. The other cuff was attached to the bookcase, which weighed a ton, so it wasn't going anywhere.

Kaj had tried to take the cuff off because they'd decided that he didn't need to be restrained when Burke's people were in the room, but Jace had shaken his head. He'd said he'd prefer to stay cuffed if it meant keeping out of jail, and that he didn't want to have to worry that he'd be sent away, cutting Kaj's heart to the quick. How could such a sweet kid have come from that toxic environment?

Jace was currently studying Val with a critical eye. 'You look different, Val,' he said quietly. 'Are you really okay?'

She smiled at the young man but, again, it was forced. 'Like you said, crazy day,' she deflected. Jace was clearly unhappy with the lack of answer, but Val changed the subject before he could say anything more. 'Antoine? Anything new?'

Antoine glanced up from his laptops with a distracted frown. 'I've matched a few more of the dates that Corey wasn't in town to victims who either died in what appeared to be an accident or who disappeared and were never seen again. So far, there are six murders for hire and two arsons. You were absolutely right, Val. He's been doing this for at least three years. I still don't know how he's attracting his business, whether he's actively recruiting or clients come to him through word of mouth or some method of dark web advertising. But I'll figure it out.'

'Murders for hire?' Jace asked, his voice small. 'And arson?'

Antoine turned to Jace. 'None of it's on you, kid. You helped us figure it out. This information will help the cops charge him with more crimes.'

'Which means he'll never get out of jail to hurt you again,' Burke added.

Jace nodded sadly. 'Or hurt anyone else.'

They were quiet for several heartbeats, Jace's melancholy affecting them all.

Then Antoine pointed at one of his laptops. 'I've also been viewing the footage from the shooting this afternoon at Sylvi's shop. From the angle of Sylvi's outdoor camera, it wasn't clear where the gunmen were aiming, but one of the businesses across the street has a wider view. I don't think they were aiming at you, Kaj. I think they were aiming at Val.'

Val didn't look surprised by this, and Kaj wasn't, either. Not really.

'And you didn't think to mention this?' Burke snapped, perturbed.

'Because I just found it,' Antoine snapped back.

'I thought that might be the case,' Kaj said, trying to soothe the tension. The stress was starting to wear on them all. 'Taking me out doesn't make sense. But Corey obviously knows that Bella called Noni. He accurately assumed his mole was Allyson Meyer. Maybe he thinks I know where Bella is hiding, and he was going to force me to tell him.'

'But you don't know where she is,' Jace said, worry bunching his brow.

'He doesn't know that,' Kaj told Jace. 'For the record, I do not know where she is.' He shot a quick glance up the stairs. 'But if he thinks that I do, Elijah could become a target again.'

'We've got him covered,' Burke said confidently.

'Right,' Val echoed. 'We do.'

But the confidence was gone from her tone.

Val made a show of yawning. 'I'm plumb tuckered. Sylvi, I think you should take the guest room. I can sleep in Kaj's exercise room. It's close to Elijah's room and there's space for me to bunk on the floor.'

A flurry of comments met this declaration, mostly from Phin, who lumbered to his feet to offer Val the sofa, and from Sylvi, who was refusing to take Val's bed.

Kaj held up his hand. 'Sylvi, take the guest room. Val, take my room. Phin, you can take the sofa. I'll sleep in my recliner. I've done it before. Jace, I've got a blow-up mattress you can use so that you aren't on the hard floor.'

'I've slept in a lot worse places, Mr. Cardozo.'

Another slice to Kaj's heart. 'Well, you won't have to here. Burke?'

'I'm on watch,' Burke drawled. 'Don't you worry 'bout me.'

'I'm going home soon,' Antoine said. 'So don't worry about me, either.'

'Burke, I'll be down to relieve you in a few hours,' Val said as she went for the stairs. 'See you later.'

'She's not okay, is she?' Sylvi asked once Val had left the room.

'She will be,' Kaj promised. 'Guest room is last one on the left.'

'Thank you,' Sylvi said. 'For everything. You'll take care of her?'

'I will,' he promised. He turned to Burke when Sylvi went upstairs. 'I'm going to get some work done in my office upstairs. If you don't see me for a while, that's where I am.'

That was a fib. He didn't intend to even try to work. He intended to hold Val until she went to sleep. He might even sleep with her for a few hours.

Burke gave him a knowing look. 'Tell Val that I'm calling Molly to relieve me later. Mol got to sleep today, so she'll be fresh. Val can sit tonight out.'

'Thanks, Burke.' Taking his leave, Kaj started up the stairs but stopped halfway. Sylvi was standing outside Elijah's door, her hand over her mouth. Kaj hurried the rest of the way, understanding her reaction once he reached the landing.

Val was in Elijah's room, quietly singing to him as she sat on the edge of his bed, rubbing his son's back. Elijah was curled up with Czar, mostly asleep. He was murmuring something to Val that Kaj couldn't hear, but whatever it was, it made Val look sad. Kaj wanted to rush in and make it all better, but he held himself back. Not yet. Not in front of others. He'd wait until Val was alone and offer her whatever support she needed.

And if she didn't want him to touch her after being reminded of her past trauma, he'd keep his distance. *Whatever she needs.*

Sniffling quietly, Sylvi turned for the guest room. Kaj followed, stopping in her doorway. 'You okay, Sylvi?'

She smiled wistfully and it was then that Kaj saw the family resemblance. She and Val had the same smile. 'Ingrid used to sing me to sleep like that. She's ten years older than I am, but she never ignored me. She taught me to do all the fun things, like riding a bike and spitting really far. And how to swear in Norwegian, of course.'

'Of course.' Kaj's lips twitched up. 'The important things.'

Behind him, he heard footsteps and then his bedroom door opened and closed. Val was in his room now. He'd give her a few minutes to herself before he'd ask to join her.

'Exactly,' Sylvi said. 'Mom and Dad both worked long hours back then to make ends meet, but Ingrid was always there. She got me up in the morning and made my breakfast. She put me to bed and read me stories. She sang to me and taught me to play the piano, even though I'll never be as good as she is. She let me tag along with her and Van. She was always there,' she repeated. 'Until she wasn't.'

'She joined the Marines.'

'Yes, but that's not when things broke down. I was only eight when she joined up, but she would write me letters and emails and tell me funny stories. I was so excited when she came home on leave. When she came home for good, I was beside myself. But she wasn't the same. At the time, I thought it was me, but now I guess I know. It was the assault.'

Kaj swallowed. 'Yeah.'

'You know the details?'

'Some. But it's not my story to tell.'

'I understand. Back when she went to New Mexico, when all we knew was that she had a stalker, Mom and Dad would sigh and say, "That's just Ingrid, being dramatic again."'

Kaj pushed back the surge of anger at the elder Kristiansens. Val hadn't been being dramatic. She'd been raped. But she hadn't told them that, so they couldn't have known. Anger morphed to sadness for all of them. This family had stopped communicating long before Ivan was killed.

Sylvi was watching him. 'Of course, even if it had been just a stalker, Ingrid was entitled to react exactly how she did. Mom and Dad loved us. They did. They do. But they've always been more sympathetic and patient with people who aren't their children.'

That surprised Kaj. 'I thought your mother was very sympathetic to you.'

Sylvi's smile was wry. 'She'd make you think so. Reality is a different thing. Mom doesn't let me forget how Van died. Ever.'

'It must have been hard to keep that secret for so long.'

Sylvi's eyes grew pained. 'You have no idea. At least Ingrid knows now. Go take care of her. She looked like she'd had another shock. Let her know that I'm here if she needs me.'

'I will.' Pulling her door closed, he went to check on Elijah. His son was sleeping deeply, Czar cozied up next to him. Between Val and Czar, his son felt safe.

We're going to have to get a dog of our own when Val leaves. Because even if he and Val continued whatever it was that they'd started once this was all over, she wouldn't move in. She wouldn't be a constant presence in their home like she'd been for the past few days. And Czar would go home with her.

Kaj hated the very thought of it.

He leaned over Elijah, pressing a gentle kiss to his son's bright white-blond head before giving Czar a stroke down his back. 'Thanks, big guy.'

Czar let out a doggy sigh, lowering his head to Elijah's pillow.

23

'SHE LOOKS SKINNIER on TV,' Bobby grumbled as he carried Noni Feldman from the boat to the camp. 'I thought the camera added ten pounds. Hers must be hiding fifty.'

'Fuck off,' Noni snapped, then whimpered when Bobby punched her in the kidney.

'You'd be wise not to provoke us,' Corey said. She'd been like this since they'd pulled her from the Volvo's trunk—refusing to answer questions and cursing them at every opportunity.

Breaking Noni Feldman's spirit was going to be a real treat.

A shadow passed in front of the window. Ed had waited up.

'Bobby, dump her in the room we're using,' Corey told him. 'We'll let her stew while we take care of business.'

'But I want her,' Bobby whined.

'Bobby,' Corey warned.

Bobby huffed. 'You never let me have any fun.'

Ed took a step toward them when they entered, then stopped. 'Is that . . . Noni Feldman? What the hell are you doing with her?'

'She was in Allyson's house.' Corey dropped into one of the folding chairs at the small table. His arm was killing him. 'Allyson will come to us if we have Noni. She had a key to Allyson's house, so they're either friends or related. Maybe even lovers. Do we have any ice?'

'No,' Ed said. 'This is insane. Everyone will be looking for Noni Feldman. What were you thinking?'

'That we can't let Allyson's betrayal go unpunished,' Corey snapped. 'And that she might know where Bella's hiding. So what if anyone knows she's gone? They can't track her here. I got rid of her car and her phone. Goddammit, Ed. If we don't have any ice, do we have any Advil?' He wasn't going to take any more of the opioid that Bobby had stolen from his old girlfriend, but his arm *hurt*.

He was never going to become an addict like Aaron. Aaron was weak and now everything he'd built was destroyed. Corey was better than that. He'd figure this out without any drugs.

Ed produced a bottle of Advil, his gaze falling on Corey's bandaged arm. 'What happened to you?'

Bobby returned, joining Corey at the table. 'First things first,' Corey said. 'Where's Dianne?'

Ed took the other chair. 'Asleep in the bedroom where she's been all this time. I put a few of the pills in her whiskey bottle. She drank it all. She'll be out for hours, at least. So what happened tonight? I've been on pins and needles, waiting for word from you two. All you told me was that Allyson found the tracker, moved it to another car, and hit the road, and that you were going to check out her roommate.'

Corey downed the Advil with some water. 'We missed Cardozo. His bodyguard got off a lucky shot. Got me in the arm.'

'Fuck.'

Bobby rubbed his face. 'Succinct and accurate. Have you been able to track Allyson's credit cards?'

'Nope. She hasn't used them. I've been checking traffic cams around New Orleans, trying to figure out which direction she went, but so far, no dice. If she ditched her Honda Civic and is driving something else, I might never find her. If she's got her phone on her, she's turned it off. How do you plan to let her know you've got Noni so that you can draw her back here?'

Corey and Bobby looked at each other, and then they both shrugged. 'We hadn't thought that far out,' Bobby admitted. 'Maybe when Noni doesn't show up for work tomorrow, the media will announce that she's gone missing.'

Ed opened his mouth, then closed it, along with his eyes. 'This is insane. We need to leave, Corey. We need to destroy our laptops, pack up our shit, and leave Louisiana.'

'Fuck that!' Corey roared, tired and in pain. 'I am not quitting now. If I do, I'll have nothing. And that is not okay.'

He didn't miss the glance Ed and Bobby shared.

Bobby put out his hands like a traffic cop. 'Settle down, everyone. I'm going to be the voice of reason, bizarre as that might sound. Corey, breathe. Ed, we want Allyson because letting her go unpunished will kill what's left of our reputation. Future clients would see us not killing her as weakness, just like not killing Rick and Jace is weakness.'

'We won't *have* any future clients,' Ed bit out. 'We are wanted men. If we're caught, we are headed for prison. I don't intend to spend the rest of my life behind bars.'

Corey narrowed his eyes. 'Are you quitting?'

'Maybe.' Ed narrowed his eyes as well. 'Are you going to kill me, too?'

'Guys, guys,' Bobby said, shaking his head. 'Everyone, stand down. Corey, you're hurt and irritable. Take another oxy. I mean it,' he snapped when Corey started to say no. 'Ed, stick with us until we finish this job, then we can talk again. I don't see this as doomsday as you do. It won't be easy, but we can have jobs after this mess. And the way that we dig ourselves out will let our clients know that we aren't quitters. That's important.'

Corey nodded, struggling to find his calm. Struggling not to panic at the thought of Ed leaving them. He depended on the man. A lot. Maybe too much. Which pissed him off, too.

'Discussion of our future clients can wait for a few days, like Bobby said. Our priority is finding Bella Butler because if we fail Doyle, he will retaliate. I know you are afraid you'll be looking over your shoulder for the cops, but Doyle could be an even bigger threat, because he has money to hire someone to take us out.'

Ed rolled his eyes. 'He's not going to take us out. He's posturing.'

Corey fought the urge to smack him. 'Possibly, but do you want to take the chance? We don't want on his bad side. He could retaliate in other ways. He knows our résumé.' They'd had to give Doyle examples of their past work to prove their competency. 'He could turn us in for a helluva lot of killin'.'

'Not without exposing himself,' Ed said, then sighed. 'Unless he does it anonymously. Fuck. Okay, so we don't want on his bad side.'

Corey nodded, relieved that Ed was finally agreeing with him. 'Now, Noni says she doesn't know where Bella is, but Bobby hasn't had a chance to work his magic yet.'

Ed sighed. 'And if Noni truly doesn't know?'

'We go back for Cardozo,' Corey said. His stomach churned, but he attributed that to the pain and the Advil. Not to the fact that they'd failed today. They'd get the ADA, one way or another. 'He's the prosecutor on the case. He's got to know. And if he doesn't, he can get Bella to tell him where she is.'

'How did Cardozo get away tonight?' Ed asked.

Bobby's grin faded. 'His bodyguard—y'know, the blonde.'

'Val Sorensen,' Ed supplied.

'Yeah,' Bobby grumbled. 'Her. She threw herself over him and my first shot went through a flower shop window instead.'

Ed frowned. 'Cardozo went to a flower shop? Now, with all this going on? Why?'

Once again, Corey and Bobby looked at each other. 'I don't know,' Corey said slowly. 'But we should find out.'

Ed looked like he was losing his patience. 'I'll do it. So, let's back up to the beginning when you two left here. You'd docked the boat and were headed into the city when Alex Cullen—my guy inside NOPD—called to say that he'd followed Cardozo to the jail. I assume you caught up with Cardozo as he was leaving the jail.'

'We did,' Bobby confirmed. 'We followed him and the blonde to the flower shop and they were in there for a good half hour. We tried to get him on his way in, but a truck was blocking the way and we didn't have a clean shot. Once they came out, he and the blonde stopped to talk. Looks like he's sweet on her. But then she noticed us driving past. She shoved him down and hit the deck. Started shooting back at us.'

'And hit Corey,' Ed said.

'And Bobby,' Corey added. 'Hit him in the chest. His vest caught the bullets. Bobby was opening fire with the rifle when this big guy came around the corner of the shop and threw himself on both of them.'

'Had to have been another of Broussard's guys,' Bobby said with a sneer. 'He must have been wearing some level IV armor because it took three rounds from my AR-15.'

Ed rubbed his temples. 'Did you need me to dig out the bullet?'

Corey shook his head. 'Bobby did it. We need to figure out the best way to get our hands on Cardozo.'

'Or his kid,' Bobby said.

'Or his kid,' Corey agreed. 'Grabbing his kid would be a better way to get Cardozo to talk anyway. Rick had that part right, at least, which really hurts to say out loud.'

Ed sighed. 'I'll see what I can find out. The message boards have been actively discussing using the boy against Cardozo to stop Doyle's trial, so at least we'll have someone to blame if we have to go that route. My hope is that Noni Feldman knows something, and we can leave Cardozo and his kid alone.'

'Your mouth, God's ears,' Corey agreed. 'But if we have to grab him, where is the best place to do it? We *must* find Bella and make sure she can't testify. I'm not accepting a failure on this job.'

'No failure,' Ed said wearily. 'I get it, Corey. But your time is running out. The trial starts Monday and tomorrow is Friday already. Now that Cardozo's been shot at, he'll be sticking close to home.'

Bobby rubbed his bruised chest absently. 'We'll have to hit his house.'

'He's got security,' Ed warned. 'Broussard's people are hanging out there. My NOPD source added himself to the rotation around Cardozo's neighborhood. Nobody questioned him because the brass had upped their numbers. The guys on legit duty figured he was supposed to be there, so they gave him all kinds of information. The cops who'd been there since Wednesday morning said that Broussard ups the staff at Cardozo's house during the night. Lots of people are going in and out during the day, but their coverage is lighter.'

'Who comes in and out?' Corey asked. 'I'd have thought they'd be locked down tight.'

'Some ladies that work in a bakery,' Ed said. 'Marica's.'

'They have good stuff,' Bobby said, then frowned when both Ed and Corey stared at him. 'They do. Best in the Quarter. Run by a couple of girls. Great cupcakes.'

'Like real cupcakes?' Ed asked. 'Or is this code for breasts?'

Bobby snorted. 'Nah. They're lesbians.'

Corey rolled his eyes. 'Focus, B. If they're in and out all the time, we can use that to our advantage. I'll give it some thought. Who else?'

'Burke Broussard,' Ed said, counting on his fingers. 'Antoine Holmes, his IT guy.'

'Related to André?' Corey asked.

'Younger brother,' Ed answered. 'A medium-sized blonde—Molly Sutton. She seems to be on duty when the others take breaks or go somewhere. I'm guessing the big guy you shot at earlier would be in and out. Then there's the tall blonde, Val Sorensen.'

Corey nodded. 'Who visited the jail with Cardozo today before going to the flower shop. She could be a target, too. They were looking really cozy outside the shop.'

'But I think she'd been crying,' Bobby said thoughtfully. 'Her eyes were puffy and red. They were in the shop for a while, so it was personal. Unfortunately, whatever happened didn't impact her reflexes.'

'So,' Ed said, 'if we can't get to Cardozo, we'll grab her and use her as leverage to make Cardozo tell us where Bella is. I think taking his kid would get him to cooperate faster, though.'

Corey pushed himself to his feet. 'We'll work through the details after we sleep. Bobby, you got those pain pills? I need to sleep, but my arm is killing me.'

Bobby handed him the bottle. 'What about Feldman?'

'Let's chat with her now. If she continues to be difficult, we'll go at her in the morning. Let her spend tonight worrying about what we're going to do to her. She ain't going anywhere.'

Mid-City, New Orleans, Louisiana
THURSDAY, OCTOBER 27, 10:00 P.M.

Kaj left Elijah's room and knocked on his own bedroom door. 'Val? Can I come in?'

'Yes, of course,' came the muffled reply.

Kaj slipped into his room and closed the door. She sat on the side of his bed, staring at the far wall, looking lost.

'It shouldn't matter anymore,' she said. 'I shouldn't care what

Drysdale said. I shouldn't care that NOPD did a background check on me and knows my whole life story. *It shouldn't matter.'*

'But it does matter,' Kaj said quietly, sitting next to her on the bed. He took her hand. 'It was a terrible time in your life. It changed you. How could it not matter?'

'I went through therapy. I'm not supposed to feel like this.'

'First of all, therapy isn't a cure. We both know that.'

'Yeah,' she said grudgingly. 'That's true. Is there a "second of all"?'

'I would never start with "first of all" if I didn't have a "second of all".' He kissed her cheek. 'Second of all, you feel what you feel. Which—if you don't mind my asking—is what?'

She sighed. 'Conflicted. I'm furious that Drysdale knows—that any of the NOPD know—but I think he meant well. He was warning me off this case. Like a dad would.'

'Does it matter how he meant it?'

'I think so. Because now I'm wondering if he's right.' She met his eyes, hers troubled. 'What if three big guys come at me when I'm guarding Elijah? What if I freeze?'

Kaj had to take a breath, because her question hit him hard. If she froze when she was guarding Elijah, what might happen to his son?

And then he realized he might have read her reaction all wrong. 'I thought you were upset because he reminded you of what happened.' As soon as the words left his mouth, he wanted to take them back. 'But I suppose you don't forget, do you?'

'No. It's always there, hovering in the background. Sometimes I'll see a big man and I . . . y'know. I remember. But years of therapy taught me coping mechanisms. I took self-defense lessons and, while I'm not a multiple black belt like Molly, I can hold my own. I even deliberately sparred with big guys.'

That made him frown, just thinking of her putting herself in that position. 'Why?'

'I was afraid and didn't want to be. I figured practice with body types that triggered me would help me to develop muscle memory, so that if someday I was in that position again, I'd react as trained. The one time I couldn't control my fear was when I was asleep.'

'So you got Czar.'

'Exactly. And I dated men who weren't taller than me because I didn't want to push the boundaries of my control with romantic relationships.' She dropped her gaze to her hands. 'When I was intimate with someone, I wanted to be in the moment, not always on guard.'

He didn't want to picture her being intimate with anyone else but shoved the irritation away. *This is not about me.* 'That makes sense.'

'I was never drawn to the linebacker types like Burke, so avoiding them afterward wasn't a conscious choice. Intimacy was hard for a long while, I'll admit, but I had a nice boyfriend back then. He helped me through it. We didn't work out, but I'm grateful for his patience.'

'I'm grateful to him, too,' he said, and it was no lie. The man had helped her find her balance after the assault. But insecurity tugged at him. 'Why didn't it work out with him?'

He wouldn't want to make the same mistake.

She met his eyes with a directness that had him focusing all his attention on her reply. 'He was a fixer. We were good together as long as I was broken, but when I'd found my feet, he grew frustrated. I wasn't willing for him to keep fixing me, so we parted ways. It wasn't an easy decision. I loved him. Part of me always will, but he wasn't good for me long term and I wasn't what he wanted.'

Point made. 'You're not broken.'

She nodded once, watching him warily.

He cupped her face in his palm, caressing her cheek as he chose his words. 'I won't try to fix you. But you will tell me if I do something you don't want?'

She nodded again, clearly relieved. 'I will. Just be patient.'

'I will.' It came out sounding like a vow.

'I believe you. There's kindness in you, Kaj. Tenderness. I trust you. I did the first time I saw you. So, to go back to your original question, no, I'm not hyperventilating about my assault.' She sighed. 'However, my career confidence is a little shaken.'

Which was probably Drysdale's intent. He'd wanted all of Burke's people so furious over this breach of Val's privacy that they'd stop butting into the investigation.

'Have three big guys come at you before?' he asked.

She nodded. 'Remember the case I told Elijah about? When the CEO's teenage daughter slipped out to meet her boyfriend?'

'Her boyfriend had been hired by kidnappers to lure her out,' Kaj recalled. 'You saved her, but the kidnappers killed the boyfriend to snip off loose ends.'

'Yes. The kidnappers were all big. I shot two of them in the leg, disabling them, but I had to grapple with the third because he'd grabbed the girl. She got away and ran back into the house. Grabbed her little brother and took him to the panic room, just like we'd practiced. The third guy was very unhappy with me.'

Kaj's gut tightened. 'Did he hurt you?'

'Knocked my head into the driveway, but nothing else. I kneed him in the nuts and he let me go. The two I'd shot dragged him to their van. The boyfriend was trying to get to the van, too, but one of them fatally shot him as they drove away. He could ID them, I guess.'

'How did you catch them?'

'The cops were already on their way. I'd called them as soon as I realized the daughter was gone. I'd shot out the van's windows and tires, so the vehicle was easy to spot.'

'And you didn't freeze or freak out.'

'It was close, but I held it together until I was off duty and alone in my room.'

He hated to think of what she'd gone through, all alone. But she didn't want pity and he wasn't her fixer. He'd remember that, no matter how difficult it was. 'Any other times you were faced with big men and you came close to freezing?'

'No.'

He wrapped his arm around her. 'Then why are you worrying about it now?'

'I'm not sure. Maybe because I'm already attached to Elijah. Or maybe because Drysdale's the first person to have confronted me with it.'

'In the guise of meaning well,' he said coldly. 'It was a dirty shot, intended to distract you. Maybe even hurt you.'

One corner of her mouth lifted. 'Gonna beat him up for me?'

He rested his forehead on hers. 'Not today. I make no promises if he does it again.'

'You're not worried that I'll freeze up?'

He considered, then decided to be honest. 'If you're not worried, then I'm not. If you are, then your mind is compromised, and we should reevaluate our business arrangement.'

Her shoulders sagged. 'Maybe I'm *not* the best bodyguard right now.'

'Good thing you have the night off, then,' he said lightly. 'Burke's already called Molly to take the night shift. You had a rough day.'

'Burke is a good boss, but I think he believed I was stronger than I am, giving me this case. I really thought I could handle it.'

Kaj kissed her firmly. 'Stop. When he gave you this job, he believed Dewey Talley and his drug organization were behind the abduction attempt. He had no idea that you'd learn about all the shit your brother did, and neither did you. So stop it.'

She sighed softly. 'You're right.'

He kissed her again, more gently. 'Say that again? I didn't hear you the first time.'

She snorted inelegantly. 'You're right, okay?'

He grinned at her. 'Just making sure we have open lines of communication.'

She leaned her head against his shoulder. 'Thank you. You seem to know exactly what to say to me to make everything better.'

He hugged her close, his heart happier now. 'You ready to go to sleep now?'

'Will you stay with me? At least until I go to sleep?'

'Yes. I'll stay for as long as you want me.'

'I might want you for a while.' Her tone was light, but her eyes were serious.

He'd want Val Sorensen for a very long while. *Starting* now. He shifted when his pants suddenly became too tight. 'Then that's how long I'll stay.'

'Thank you.' She brushed a chaste kiss over his mouth. 'Let me take a quick shower and change.'

She took her things into the bathroom and he tried not to think of her naked in his shower when the water came on. Because nothing was going to happen until she decided the time was right.

Which isn't likely to be tonight.

Needing a distraction, he sniffed himself and shuddered. He needed a shower as well. Badly. And he needed to change the bedding. He normally did the wash on Monday, but this week hadn't been normal in any way. He busied himself with changing the sheets. For Val.

He paused, the stack of fresh bedding in his arms. He was going to have a woman in his bed for the first time in five long years. He'd held Val the night before, but that was in the guest room. It wasn't his bed.

Tonight, he'd see her on his sheets and he'd commit the sight to memory.

He'd just finished putting on new sheets when she emerged from the bathroom in a cloud of vanilla-scented steam. She wore a thin cotton tank top that hugged her breasts and a pair of sleep shorts that showed off her long, long legs.

'Um . . .' Kaj swallowed hard and reflexively pulled a pillow over his crotch to hide his erection. 'Pick a side. I don't care which one. Your choice.' He was going to hold her tonight. That was all.

'Thank you.' She pulled back the sheets and got into bed while he watched each movement greedily. 'Kaj?' she asked when he continued to stare.

Shit. He ripped his gaze away. He wasn't going to make her uncomfortable. If that meant taking care of things in the shower, that was what he'd do.

'Sorry. I'm . . .' He exhaled. 'You're very beautiful.'

She smiled, and it was somehow both shy and sultry. 'Thank you. Are you getting in?'

'No. Not yet.' He pointed to the bathroom with the hand that wasn't still holding the pillow. 'Have to . . . shower. Yes. That.'

She smirked. 'Are you planning to shower with the pillow?'

His face flamed. 'No.' He handed it to her and her gaze dropped to his pants, lingering for a long moment. Then she met his eyes. No longer afraid or devastated, they were warm with arousal. She wanted him, too. Maybe not tonight, but soon.

'Hurry, Kaj.'

He obeyed, taking the fastest shower ever. And he did not take care of things. He wanted her to know what she did to him. When he returned to the bed, she was curled up on her side. He climbed in and wrapped her in his arms, spooning her.

She hummed, content. 'Good night, Kaj.'

He kissed her shoulder. 'Good night, Val. Sleep now. I've got you.'

Lake Cataouatche, Louisiana
THURSDAY, OCTOBER 27, 10:15 P.M.

Noni bit back a groan as she tried to find a less painful position on the floor of the dark room. Her hands and feet were still bound with tape and she thought she might have a broken rib. They had not been gentle, throwing her on the floor when they'd arrived here. Wherever 'here' was. Somewhere on the bayou. Like that helped at all.

They'd taken the tape off her mouth, and while that had stung like a bitch, she could breathe better. Although that also meant that they didn't mind if she screamed. They'd shown her their faces, too, and called each other by name. They didn't care that she could ID them.

Don't think about that.

Corey and Bobby had already tried to get her to tell them where Allyson was, once they'd driven out of Allyson's neighborhood. Luckily for Allyson, Noni had no clue where she'd gone.

Which is unlucky for me. Because they'd kill her. She had no doubts about that.

The door to the small room opened and the two men entered. The first kick stole her breath. The second made her moan, even though she tried to hold it back.

'Where is she?' Corey demanded.

Noni said nothing.

'You'll tell us,' Corey said. 'You'll scream and you'll beg us to kill you. But we won't. Not until you tell us where we can find Allyson.'

'I. Don't. Know,' Noni repeated.

'She's gonna be stubborn,' Corey said.

'More fun for me,' Bobby said, sounding gleeful.

Corey got in her face. 'Where is Bella Butler?'

'I don't know. I only had a phone number.'

'Where did you get the phone number?' Corey demanded.

From Allyson, where do you think, you idiot. 'From the newsroom manager,' she lied. 'We interviewed her last month.'

'She's lying,' Bobby said coldly. 'She knows where Bella is.'

'We'll be back,' Corey promised. 'And you will tell us.'

Noni shuddered. No one knew she was gone. No one would be looking for her.

Still, she prayed to whoever might be listening. *Help me. Please.*

Mid-City, New Orleans, Louisiana
FRIDAY, OCTOBER 28, 5:15 A.M.

Normally it was soft, clean cotton that Val felt beneath her cheek as she woke. This morning was a million times better because beneath her cheek was soft, warm skin. She'd fallen asleep with Kaj spooned against her back, but she must have rolled over in the night, because she was now using his chest as a pillow. One thing hadn't changed, though— his arms were still wrapped tightly around her.

When she'd first started therapy after her assault, she'd worried that she'd never wake this way again. But she had. Not with many men, but she'd had a few boyfriends over the years. This felt different.

This felt special.

She nuzzled her cheek into the hair on his chest. It was fine and soft and he smelled so good. Woodsy and clean. His chest expanded with a deep breath and she knew he was awake.

She propped herself on her elbow and smiled down at him. He smiled back, all sleep-mussed, his usually tidy hair tousled. He looked ten years younger like this, and she realized she was seeing a relaxed Kaj for the first time. Before, he'd been either working or worrying about Elijah.

Or me. That he'd worried about her last night was sweet. It would continue to be sweet as long as he kept his promise not to try to fix her. She wasn't perfect, but she was not broken.

Holding her gaze, he lazily stroked her hair. 'You're a morning person, too?' he murmured gruffly.

'I am. Czar and I are usually out for our morning run by now.'

'I'm usually working out in my exercise room. Elijah will sleep for another hour, at least.'

She dragged her fingertips through his chest hair. 'I could let you get up and work out.'

One side of his mouth lifted. 'You could, but I think I'm already up.'

She grinned, sweeping her hand down his chest and under the waistband of his sleep pants to find him very *up* indeed. He was erect and hard and hot. She wrapped her fingers around him and gave him a gentle stroke, making him groan quietly.

'Is this okay?' she whispered.

He leaned his head back into the pillow, arching his throat. 'Yes. Please. Feels so good. Forgot how much.'

'How long has it been, Kaj?'

'Six years.'

He'd been with no one since even before his Heather had died. The knowledge made her sad. He must have been so lonely. So heartbroken.

But right now, he was looking at her with heat. Longing. And lust.

He's not broken anymore, either.

She leaned in to kiss him, stroking his cock more firmly now. 'What do you want?'

He shuddered, thrusting into her grip. 'This, if it's all you want.'

She kissed him harder. 'What do you want, Kaj?'

Stilling, he panted out a few breaths. 'I want to be inside you.' His voice was a low growl. 'I want to feel you come around me. I want to see you come apart for me.'

It was her turn to shudder. 'Good answer.' She released him and slid from the bed. 'Give me a second.' Digging through her overnight bag, she found a condom in one of the zippered pockets. She didn't use them often, but she was never unprepared. She straddled his hips, aware that he'd been watching her every move. She wriggled against him, shivering at the feel of him right where she wanted him. Or almost where she wanted him.

'You're wearing too many clothes,' she told him.

His gaze raked her up and down, lingering on her breasts. 'So are you.'

'Then do something about it.'

Without warning he lunged up, gripped the hem of her T-shirt, and tugged it off, tossing it to the floor. She barely had a moment to process before he took her nipple into his mouth and sucked. Hard.

Just as she liked it. She pressed her hand to her mouth to stifle a cry of pleasure. He pulled away, glancing up at her, gauging her reaction for a split second, before turning to her other breast. His hand covered the breast he'd already suckled, lightly pinching the nipple he'd made hard and tight. He wasn't rough, but he wasn't gentle, either.

Just right. Just right. It was a chant in her mind. Everything felt just right. *Perfect.*

And then she was tumbling to her back and he was between her legs. His mouth was at her neck, kissing his way to her shoulder as his hand swept down her side, over her thigh, tugging her leg until she bent her knee. He repeated the action on the other side until she was cradling his hips.

'You've got the most gorgeous legs,' he muttered. 'Go on for miles.'

She couldn't respond. She was breathing hard and . . . feeling. It was so good. *Just right.*

When she thought she'd caught her breath, he was gone, up on his knees. Staring down at her, his lips wet.

'Yes?' he asked, his voice a harsh rasp. 'I need to hear you say it.'

She swallowed. 'Yes.'

'Lift,' he commanded, and he pulled her shorts off and tossed them on top of her T-shirt. 'Oh.' But he didn't voice the word. It sat on his lips as he looked his fill.

She should have felt self-conscious, but she didn't. She felt worshipped.

And then she felt impatient. She tugged on his sleep pants. 'I want to see you, too.'

He got out of the bed and switched on the lamp on the nightstand, sending low light over the bed. 'Is the light okay?'

'Yes.' It was perfect. Not because she needed assurance that he wasn't a monster from her nightmares, although she had wanted that in the past with the men she'd slept with. Now, she wanted the light because he was beautiful and because she wanted to remember every moment of their first time.

He was strong, his pecs defined. Not bulging. No six-pack. Just long, lean muscle.

He dropped the sleep pants and . . . *Oh dear Lord*. The man was perfect. Long legs.

Long cock. He was going to feel so good.

She held out her hand and he took it, returning to kneel between her legs. He pointed at the condom she'd tossed on the nightstand. 'Put it on me.'

Hands trembling, she rolled the condom over him, then waited to see what he'd do next.

He simply looked at her for the longest moment, a smile curving his lips. 'You look good in my bed, Ingrid.'

'I feel good in your bed, Kaj Jean-Pierre. I'd feel better if you'd hurry it up.'

He chuckled. 'So bossy.' But he lowered himself, bracing his weight on his forearms so that he could kiss her.

He was a very good kisser. He owned her mouth, making her want so much more. He slanted his head, kissing her one way then another. He nipped her lip, then licked the sting away.

She lifted her hips, writhing impatiently. 'Kaj.'

'Taking my time,' he murmured between slow kisses. 'Don't rush me. This is important. *You* are important.'

She understood then, stilling, letting herself savor each kiss, each stroke of his tongue. This was more than sex. The way he kissed her . . . It was almost sacred.

And then he was kissing his way down her chest, sliding down her body. When his tongue finally found her clit, she was wet and trembling. '*Kaj.*'

'Ummm' was his only reply, and the vibrations against her sensitive flesh nearly made her come. He was very good at this, too.

'Kaj,' she whispered. 'If you want to feel me come all around you, you need to hurry.'

He looked up with a lazy grin, then kissed his way back up her body, finally—*finally*—sliding inside her as he claimed her mouth once again. He was every bit as big as he'd looked and she locked her heels around his ass, holding him tight as he began to move.

Her moan was muffled against his lips that tasted . . . *Like me*.

It was erotic as hell and sent her hips into overdrive, meeting each of his thrusts. Like before, he wasn't rough, but he wasn't gentle. He was perfect, and her body began to tighten, her skin to tingle. She felt . . . electric.

She'd missed this.

She wasn't sure she'd ever truly had this.

She never wanted to lose this.

And then, without slowing his rhythm, he reached between them and pressed his thumb against her clit, and she gripped his hair, pressing her lips to his to muffle her crying out his name as she flew apart.

She'd closed her eyes but forced them open. She wanted to see him. He was staring down at her, hungry and passionate and on the brink. She tightened around him and he gasped.

Then, his eyes still wide open, the muscles in his arms quivering, he came on a quiet groan. Panting, he rolled them to their sides and rested his head on the pillow. His eyes slid closed and he wore a smug, satisfied smile.

They lay like that as the seconds became minutes. Val brushed his hair from his forehead and trailed her fingertips over his stubbled cheek.

'We have to do that again,' he murmured.

She laughed softly. 'We really do.'

'I didn't hurt you, did I?'

'No. It was perfect. You were perfect. Exactly what I needed. And wanted.'

He couldn't hide his relief. 'Good. Don't move.' He pulled out of her and disappeared into the bathroom to deal with the condom.

Val didn't move. She wasn't sure that she could. She wasn't tired, but her body was deliciously worn out.

Kaj climbed back into bed and drew her close. 'Thank you,' he whispered. 'I knew I was lonely before, but I don't think I knew exactly how lonely I was.' He kissed her forehead. 'Can we just stay here all day?'

She smiled. 'Nope. But we can stay a little longer. Go back to sleep.'

'Don't wanna. Don't want to miss a minute.'

She kissed him, sweetly touched. 'We'll have lots of minutes, Kaj. You can sleep through a few of them.'

'Uh-uh,' he insisted. A minute later, he was snoring softly.

In a few more minutes, she'd get up and start her day. Be Elijah's bodyguard once again.

But for a few more minutes, she'd be Kaj's lover. She figured they'd both earned a few minutes of peace.

24

Pinning her braid to her head, Val tiptoed out of Kaj's bathroom so that she didn't wake him. He needed the rest.

'Hey,' he said sleepily. He sat up in the bed. 'You're dressed. Where are you going?'

'Going to check on Elijah and walk Czar. You can sleep more.'

'No. I have work to catch up on.' He rolled out of bed, stretching with a groan. But he was smiling at her, and she couldn't help but smile back. 'You look remarkably awake.'

'And I feel amazingly good.' She walked into his arms, snuggling into the warmth of his body. 'I feel like me again. Thank you, Kaj.'

He kissed the side of her throat. 'I would be happy to make you feel like yourself anytime you wish.'

She grinned. 'I'm going to take you up on that. Get dressed. I'll see you downstairs.'

Closing the door behind her, she peeked in on Elijah. He was still asleep, his arm around Czar. Last night when she'd checked in on him, he'd asked her to help him choose a new dog once it was time for her to go. She'd agreed, although the thought of leaving Elijah and his father had left her a little sad.

Part of that had been the crisis of confidence she'd gone through the night before. She'd attribute it to being exhausted, both physically and emotionally. *I feel so much better now.*

She clucked her tongue. 'Come on, boy,' she whispered. 'Time to go out.' Czar slid off the other side of Elijah's bed, so careful not to disturb him. 'Such a good boy.'

She crept down the stairs, Czar at her heels, then came to an abrupt stop in the living room. MaryBeth sat at the dining room table with Molly, Phin, Antoine, and Jace, who, Val was pleased to see, was uncuffed.

Once this was over, she was making sure this kid had the best home ever. *Maybe even with me.* The idea stunned her momentarily, but the more she thought about it, the more she liked it. *I could be certified as a foster care provider.* Later, she'd google how that worked in Louisiana. But not until after breakfast.

Because everyone had coffee and one of Marica's breakfast sandwiches.

'Are you in charge of feeding us now?' Val asked MaryBeth with a smile.

MaryBeth waved her over. 'I can't stay long, but I know you guys have a lot going on and I didn't want Elijah to miss any meals.'

Val winced. 'I didn't do a very good job of feeding him yesterday, did I?'

Molly frowned. 'It's fine, Val. We fed him exactly on time and his blood sugar was in control. We're here to help. You don't have to carry this alone. Stop feeling guilty for things that aren't your fault.'

'Wow,' MaryBeth said to Molly with exaggerated awe. 'You do know her, don't you?'

Molly arched her brows. 'She's not very hard to figure out.'

'She's right here,' Val said, unoffended. 'I need to walk Czar and then I'll eat.'

Molly rose, Czar's leash in her hand. 'I'm doing it this morning. You stay in here. No getting shot at on my watch.'

And, of course, Molly was right. Val patted Czar's back. 'Go on, boy. Go to Molly.'

Czar padded obediently to Molly, allowing her to clip the leash to his collar. 'We need to find a way to get him some real exercise today.'

Phin took a swig of coffee and pushed away from the table, wincing a little as he stretched, but he looked loads better than he had the night before. 'There's a treadmill upstairs. Can dogs use those?'

'Czar can, but he doesn't like it,' Val said. 'Where are you going?'

'With Molly,' Phin said. 'Nobody goes out alone. Burke's new rule.'

Val took a seat at the table next to Antoine. 'I thought you were going home to sleep.'

Antoine looked like he hadn't slept a wink. 'I am. Soon.'

'He worked all night,' Jace said quietly.

Antoine glared. 'Tattletale.'

Val gave Jace a sympathetic look. 'He says the same thing to us when we try to take care of him. Don't take it personally. Right, Antoine?'

Antoine sighed. 'Right. Sorry, kid. I'm . . . frustrated. I need more coffee.'

'I'll get you a refill,' Val said. 'I got some sleep, so I'm good.' She refilled his mug, then poured herself a cup, then gasped in delight. 'MaryBeth!' On the counter were a dozen cake pops, decorated like pumpkins, vampires, witches, and ghosts. 'Did you make these?'

'I did,' she said cheerfully. 'Halloween's on Monday, so we've made a lot of these. They're sugar-free and low-carb but tasty, so you can all have some. I made him pumpkin cookies that you can freeze for later, too. They'll thaw well.'

'I forgot all about Halloween. Poor Elijah. If this continues into next week, he'll miss his school party.'

'I took care of that,' MaryBeth said. 'I called the team.'

Val blinked. 'The team?'

'Drink some coffee, girl. You need to jump-start your brain. The QuarterMasters.'

'Your roller derby team,' Jace added helpfully.

Val's cheeks heated. 'Don't you tell anyone that I forgot about them.'

'I won't,' MaryBeth promised. 'This time. Anyway, we're going to have a Halloween party when it's safe for Elijah to leave the house. I told all the girls with kids not to pack the costumes away. If we're still here next week, we're going to do a trick-or-treat at the arena with nonfood prizes for kids who have food allergies and sugar issues.'

Val's eyes stung. 'You're the best.'

MaryBeth did a little wiggle. 'I am. You can come, too, Jace. You're a little old for trick-or-treat, but I'll fix you up with a lot of candy.'

Jace's eyes widened. 'Really?'

'Really. You're a nice kid. We like you.' She rose when Molly and Phin returned from walking the dog. 'Can someone walk me to my car? I have to get back. Jessica has our part-timer working with her this morning, but we're slammed with people buying treats for all the Halloween parties happening this weekend.'

'I'll walk you,' Phin said, waiting by the door.

Val gave MaryBeth a crushing hug. 'Thank you. You really are the best.'

MaryBeth hugged her back. 'You look good this morning. I'm glad you got some rest.' She pulled away and grinned wickedly. 'Call me. I want details.'

Val's face heated. 'I take it back. You're not the best. You're mean and hateful.'

MaryBeth curtsied low. 'You love me.'

'I do. Be careful.' She returned to her seat and leaned over to look at the closest of Antoine's three laptop screens. He didn't even react, and that was unusual. He normally would have angled the screen so that no one could see what he was doing. 'Is there any news on Noni Feldman?'

Antoine shook his head, the movement slow and . . . numb. 'No. Not yet.'

Val frowned. 'What's wrong, Antoine? You're scaring me.'

Antoine looked at her, his eyes bleary and full of worry. 'Remember the video we wanted to look at? The one where Kaj was in the lobby of NOPD talking to Elijah and mentioned the math meet?'

Val nodded. 'André was going to get one of his people to review it, to ID whoever's leaking information. Did you find it?'

'No. It's gone.'

Val's frown deepened. 'What do you mean, it's gone?'

'It's gone,' he repeated. 'There's ten minutes missing from the video stored on the NOPD server. It starts out fine, even shows Kaj coming through the lobby doors, then it disappears. Ten minutes later it restarts.'

'Someone erased it,' Val murmured. 'Did you tell André?'

'I've tried. Left him a bunch of messages, but he hasn't called me back.' Antoine looked ill. 'He always calls me back.'

'Maybe he's gotten a lead on Noni's whereabouts,' Val said, but she was worried, too.

'Maybe. I hope so. I'm getting ready to call Farrah.' André's fiancée was a favorite among Burke's group. 'She usually wakes up about now to go to work. André's usually been up for an hour by now. He goes running every morning.'

'He's got a lot on his plate. This isn't his only case.'

Antoine forced a smile. 'I know.'

Val didn't know what else to say, so she finished her breakfast and listened as Molly drew Jace into a conversation about her garden. Jace was wistful, saying that his mother had grown her own vegetables and he missed helping her.

The boy needed a garden. *I could make that happen for him.*

Foster parent certification. Val pulled out her phone to google it but paused when Kaj came down the stairs.

He pulled up a chair and sat down. 'What's wrong with Antoine?' he murmured.

'André's not answering his calls or texts,' Val murmured back. 'He might be working or asleep, but Antoine is worried.'

'I'll make some calls,' Kaj said. 'His boss might be able to tell us where he is.' He found André's boss's contact info and was about to dial when Antoine's phone began to buzz.

Antoine snapped it up. 'Farrah? Is he home?' His eyes filled with fear. *'When?'*

No, no, no. Val could feel Antoine's anguish. *Not André.*

'Where did they take him?' Antoine demanded. 'Okay. Hold on. I'm coming. Do Mom and Dad know? And DeShaun?' After listening for another minute, he ended the call. 'She found him outside their house, in the backyard. He's been stabbed, at least twice. Once in the gut. He's still alive, but it's not good. I need to get to the hospital.'

Molly and Val looked at each other, trying to figure the best way to support Antoine while maintaining security for Kaj and Elijah.

'You should drive him, Molly,' Val said.

'I can drive myself,' Antoine insisted.

'Uh, no,' Molly said firmly. 'Nobody goes out alone. Plus, you haven't slept and you've had a terrible shock. Phin and Val can stay, and I'll come back as soon as you're settled.'

Val hugged Antoine hard. 'You'd do the same if it were one of us. You know this.'

Antoine nodded, his shoulders shaking. 'I can't lose him.'

Val took Antoine's face in her hands. 'You won't. You go and be there for Farrah. I'll call Burke and we'll hold down the fort until backup gets here. We love you. Now go.' She led him to the door,

Molly right behind her. 'Be careful,' she told Molly and hugged her, too.

She watched them leave, then turned to Phin, Jace, and Kaj. 'How's that panic room coming, Phin?'

'I never got to finish painting, but it's done except for that.'

'Why don't you show Kaj how it works? Y'know, just in case.' Because they were very low on staff and the timing felt very suspicious. 'I'll stay down here and call Burke.'

'Cuff me,' Jace said, holding out his hands. 'I'll be down here with only one of you. Burke's rule.'

'No,' Kaj said with a tense smile. 'You're good. No more cuffs.'

Jace stared at Val as Kaj followed Phin upstairs. 'I'm good?'

Val squeezed his hand. 'You're very good, Jace. Don't forget that.' She dialed Burke and he picked up on the first ring.

'Yeah?' Burke barked by way of greeting.

'We need you here. André's been stabbed and Molly's taken Antoine to the hospital. It's just me and Phin.'

'Shit. Prognosis?'

'I don't know, but this feels connected. Can you send someone over? Is Lucien back in town?' Lucien had been assigned to emergency protection duty for another client.

'Not yet,' Burke said grimly. 'I expect him back later this morning. I'm on my way.'

She ended the call and smiled weakly when Czar put his head in her lap, sensing her worry. 'Good boy.'

'What's happening, Val?' Jace asked quietly. 'Who hurt Captain Holmes?'

'I don't know, but I'm sure NOPD will find out. It'll be okay, Jace.'

But she wasn't sure who she was trying to convince—Jace or herself.

Lake Cataouatche, Louisiana
FRIDAY, OCTOBER 28, 6:45 A.M.

'Corey, please,' Ed murmured raggedly. 'She doesn't know anything. Make Bobby stop. He's going to kill her.'

Standing in the doorway, Corey surveyed the bloody woman on the floor impassively. Noni Feldman had continued insisting that she didn't know where either Allyson or Bella were. And Bobby had really tried to break her.

In the end, he'd broken her physically, but they still had no information.

Ed looked like he'd be sick and, as much as Corey despised the woman for her aggressive reporting, even he found himself disturbed.

'Bobby,' Corey said sharply. 'Stop. She's unconscious.'

Bobby looked up, an unholy light in his eyes. 'So?'

'*So*,' Corey said, wondering how far Bobby might have taken it if he hadn't stepped in. 'If she's dead, she's no good at luring Allyson to us.'

Bobby scowled. 'Fuck. I never get to have any fun.'

Corey thought his friend had had way too much fun. Like, Bobby-needed-therapy amount of fun. 'Go shower, Bobby. You look like an extra from a horror movie.'

Corey followed Bobby out, pulling the door closed behind him. Bobby went off to the tiny shower and Corey sat at the small table. He'd slept like shit, his arm throbbing all night long.

'Ed, can you make some coffee?' he said wearily. 'We brought some back with us last night. I need to think.'

Ed sat down as the coffee dripped. 'What are we going to do?'

'Find Bella. That's the first priority.'

Ed sighed quietly. 'That's what I thought you'd say. I think it's a very bad idea, but I'll help you finish this job since it's so important to you. But after this, I'm not sure. I'm worried about you, Corey. You're going to have to learn when to walk away or the law's going to catch you. Or kill you. And anyone standing next to you. Which might be me.'

Corey ground his teeth, torn between relief that Ed was going to help him and irritation at the man's condescending worry. 'I'm fine,' he bit out. 'Tell me how we can get Cardozo so I can get to Bella. After that, you're free to walk away.'

'I don't want to walk away,' Ed insisted. 'I just . . . You're . . .' He shook his head. 'Look, I owe you a lot. You gave me a job when I got out, and I've had fun. I admire what you've built in the last three years. What we've built. I've admired that you've never given up, in spite of the odds. Until now. I'm worried you're about to throw it all away.'

'But you're no quitter, either,' Corey said, meeting Ed's gaze, challenging him. 'Are you? Because if you are, I'm not letting you take any of Aaron's money with you.' All of which was still in their joint offshore account. 'Look, I owe you a lot,' he said, deliberately parroting Ed's words. 'You've organized us and made this job easier and safer. I need you to finish this one final job. Then you can go your own way with your share of the money, and we'll replace you. Eventually.'

Ed's shoulders sagged. 'I don't want to go, Corey.'

'Then don't. Instead, help me finish this job so that Trevor Doyle doesn't send his triggermen after us.'

Ed blew out a breath. 'Will you promise to go on a nice long break after this is done? We'll find a house in the Caribbean and drink cocktails on the beach.' He leaned across the table, his expression imploring. 'You've been pushing yourself hard ever since Liam died. You can't see it, but I do. You're grieving, just like Dianne. She crawls into the bottle. You crawl into your job. Your determination is becoming an obsession. Not a lot different from Aaron's drug addiction,' he added gently. 'You deserve a break. You *need* a break. We all do.'

The words hit Corey hard. He hadn't had a break since . . . well, ever. He looked down at himself, realizing he'd pressed the heel of his hand to his chest. Because it hurt. Losing Liam had hurt. Grief hurt.

And for the first time he didn't hate Aaron as much for killing that doctor. He still hated him, just not as much. Because grief sucked.

He released a shaking breath. 'I promise. I will go with you guys to the Bahamas or wherever and I will take a break. But, Ed, I *need* to finish this job. Will you help me?'

Ed studied him for a long moment before nodding. 'I will.' He opened his laptop. 'So, I've been thinking about Cardozo. Alex, my guy in the NOPD, may not have all the answers that Bobby's buddy has, but he's still surveilling Cardozo's house. He's taken up residence in one of the neighbors' homes. He's watching through the front window and will use the neighbor's car if he needs to leave. The NOPD patrolling Cardozo's neighborhood aren't stopping cars registered to the residents.'

'What did your guy do with the neighbor?'

Ed shrugged again. 'I didn't ask. I don't want to know. Anyway, he says that the guys on patrol told him yesterday that bakery van— Marica's—shows up at Cardozo's place at least once a day. It parks in the driveway, right up close to the house.'

'So if we had the van, we could get close.'

'Yes, but the house is locked down. We'd have to get them to let us in or draw them out.'

'You're thinking that we use the baker.'

Ed turned his screen to a photo of two smiling women. One was tall and fierce-looking. The other was small and wore a fifties-style dress. 'The tall one is Jessica. The little one is her wife, MaryBeth.'

'I say we use the little one. The big one looks hard to control.'

'Agreed. The little one arrived at Cardozo's house at five thirty this morning and left a little while ago. She arrived with a few bags with the bakery logo and left empty-handed.'

'So we hijack the van with the little one in it, take it to Cardozo's, make her get out with some bags of food, and when they open the door, we rush in?'

'Cameras on the perimeter,' Ed said. 'They'll see you coming.' He poured two cups of coffee.

Corey gulped it down, the burn taking his mind off his throbbing arm. Fucking blond bitch. He'd make sure she'd paid for shooting him before he left town. 'How about this? We hijack the van, drive it to Cardozo's, force the little one out with bags of food and when she's a foot away from the front door, we shoot her. Not dead. We want them to open the door to save her. And when they do that, we shoot our way inside.'

'That could work,' Ed said with a nod. 'We won't have much time. They're sure to have the house alarmed. We'll have a minute, tops, before the alarms go off. Probably less time than that. We'll have to get in, get out.'

'I'll get Cardozo. You get the kid. Cardozo will be a lot more cooperative about telling us where Bella is if we have his kid. Bobby can take care of the bodyguards.'

'I want the blonde,' Bobby said, drying his hair with a towel as he came in from the bathroom. 'She and I need to have a chat.' He pointed to his chest, where a black bruise had spread over his pecs. 'Look what the bitch did.'

Corey pointed to his arm. 'I get dibs.'

Bobby dropped into a chair. 'That's fair. So Cardozo, his kid, and the woman are our targets, in order of importance?'

Corey nodded. 'Sounds like a plan. Ed, can you ask your cop friend Alex to be ready to assist?'

'What are you going to want him to do?'

'Be prepared to shoot anyone who isn't Cardozo, the kid, or the blonde.'

Ed considered it. 'He can probably do that, as long as it can't be traced to him. He likes his job on the force and wants to keep it.

We don't pay him enough for him to risk his job.'

'At least ask him. I feel better knowing we have coverage. How do we know where the baker's van is?'

'I guess we wait outside the bakery,' Ed said.

'We?' Bobby asked.

'We,' Corey said. 'We'll all go. We need all hands on deck for this one. Feldman's not going anywhere. I hope she's still breathing when we get back. You gotta learn control, B.'

Bobby shrugged unapologetically. 'I didn't kill her, okay?'

Corey sighed. 'Whatever. What about Dianne? We need to make sure she doesn't wake up while we're gone.'

'I gave her some more booze and sleeping pills before you all started on the reporter,' Ed said. 'She'll sleep until late afternoon, at least. What are we going to do with Cardozo after he tells us where Bella is?' Ed asked.

At least that was an easy answer. 'We kill him and frame the online assholes, just like we'll do with Bella.'

'And his kid?' Ed pressed.

'We use the kid and the woman to get Cardozo to talk,' Corey said. 'Then we'll dispose of them. Cardozo gets a bullet, quick and easy. I get the woman, because she's going to feel some pain for shooting me before I kill her. We'll give the kid some of Dianne's pills. He'll just go to sleep and not wake up.'

Ed nodded grimly. 'Okay.'

'I get a crack at the blonde, too,' Bobby said. 'No fair keeping her all for yourself.'

'Fine,' Corey huffed. 'What about the cops watching his neighborhood? If they search the van and find us, it's game over.'

Bobby grinned. 'Let me take care of that.'

Corey finished his coffee and pushed to his feet. 'Then let's do this.'

Mid-City, New Orleans, Louisiana
FRIDAY, OCTOBER 28, 7:00 A.M.

Kaj hadn't wanted to think about the panic room in his son's closet. He had thought about it, of course. Phin's constant hammering had made it impossible to forget.

But he hadn't *wanted* to think about it. Hadn't wanted to think about the fear Elijah was feeling all the time, even if he hid it well.

Because of me. Because I'm a prosecutor.

He and Phin had been quiet, hoping not to disturb Elijah's sleep, but they needn't have bothered. Elijah was sitting on his bed, dressed and tying his shoes.

He looked up with a tired smile that made him look far, far older than ten, and Kaj's throat constricted. *Dammit.*

'Morning, Dad.'

Kaj had to clear his throat. 'Good morning. How are you?'

Elijah slid his glasses on. 'Fine. Sugar's normal.'

Which Kaj knew, of course. The data from Elijah's blood sugar monitor fed to Kaj's phone and alerted him whenever the numbers were trending up or down. That his phone wasn't constantly dinging was a miracle. 'I'm glad. Phin's going to show us the safe room.'

Elijah glanced at his closet, his expression going neutral.

Guilt grabbed at Kaj's gut and twisted. Elijah felt the same way about the safe room.

It had seemed like a good idea three days ago. It still seemed like a prudent precaution. But not one that should have been required.

'Can I look at it later, Phin?' Elijah asked quietly.

Phin's expression was not neutral, and the difference was striking. Gone was the stoic, I'm-an-island mask. Warm compassion had taken its place. 'Maybe after breakfast? MaryBeth brought breakfast and some special cake pops for you. Y'know, for Halloween.'

Elijah perked up at that. 'Cool. I didn't think I'd get any Halloween this year.'

Another stab to Kaj's heart. 'I'm sorry, Elijah.'

'It's fine, Dad. I can't trick-or-treat because of the candy anyway. But dressing up would have been fun.'

'There's a costume party at your school on Monday,' Kaj said, remembering with dismay.

'Dad, it's fine. I'm not really sad or anything.' He smiled then, looking young again. 'But don't tell MaryBeth that. If she feels sorry for me, I'll get more cake pops.'

Kaj chuckled as Elijah headed out of his room. 'Your secret's safe with me.'

Phin mimed zipping his lips.

Elijah stopped in his doorway, suddenly serious again. 'Thank you, Phin. I know you did a lot of extra work to get this done so fast. I appreciate it and I'll be back up soon.'

'Whenever you're ready,' Phin said.

Elijah gave them a little wave, then bounded down the stairs, calling for Czar.

'It's not your fault,' Phin said quietly.

Kaj's gaze jerked to meet Phin's, surprised that the man had read his mind. 'What?'

The big man shrugged. 'My dad's a cop. Up in Ohio.'

'Okay,' Kaj said slowly.

'My mom was a teacher. When I was a kid, I always thought my dad was the stronger one, you know? Because Mom isn't big and tough.' He opened the closet door, exposing the safe room door within. 'We had a storm cellar, of course. It was Ohio. Tornadoes.'

Kaj followed him to the closet, wondering where this story was going. But Phin seldom spoke, and when he did, his friends listened. So Kaj would listen, too.

'My friends went to their basements and hung out until the tornado warnings were over. But we had a special room in our basement. It had reinforced concrete walls and a steel door. And it was big enough for all of us—and that's saying something. I'm one of seven kids.'

'Wow.'

Phin's mouth quirked up. 'You have no idea. My poor mother. But anyway, she decorated our storm room. It had a phone and snacks. Pillows and blankets and flashlights. A radio. She even pasted glow-in-the-dark stars on the ceiling in case the flashlight batteries ran out. Whenever the tornado sirens would blow, we'd all rush down to the storm room and Mom made it like a party. We were never scared. We'd sing and play cards.'

'Your mom sounds nice.'

'She is. But I'm sure you're wondering why I'm telling you this.'

'A little.'

'One night she woke us all up. Had to have been two in the morning. Told us that there was a storm coming and we had to get down to the storm room. I remember asking her why there wasn't a siren. She said she'd heard the warning on the radio while she was waiting for Dad to come home because he was working that night. So we all tromped down to the storm room and she locked the door from the inside. I'd never seen her lock it before.'

Kaj thought he knew where Phin was going now. 'How old were you?'

'About Elijah's age. I almost asked Mom why she'd locked the door, but then I realized that I was the only one who'd noticed. She just shook her head at me.'

'Asking you not to say anything.'

'Exactly. She started passing out snacks and we stayed there for hours. Looking back, I can see that she was terrified. But then I thought she was worried about the storm. I wasn't scared. I'd asked my dad all kinds of questions about the storm room's structure and I knew that even if the house fell down on our heads, we'd be safe. I'm not sure how much time passed, but it was just getting light outside when we finally came out. The phone had rung in the storm room and Mom started crying when she answered it. It was Dad and he was outside the storm room door. Mom unlocked it and we all went upstairs. It was a Saturday morning, so we didn't have school. She made us waffles that morning and it was like any other day.'

'Except?'

'Except there was no storm. Never had been. I heard my parents talking later that day because I was eavesdropping. I needed to know what had happened. I'll never forget it. Mom was sobbing and Dad was crying, too. I'd never seen my father cry. Never. It was unsettling.'

'I guess so. I take it that someone had tried to attack your home?'

'Yes. And Dad was blaming himself. He'd called my mother the night before to tell her to get us to the storm room. Some guy had a grudge against my father and had threatened us. He broke into our house but thought we'd run away. He didn't know about our storm room. Eventually, cops confronted him a few miles away and it lasted for hours. Dad told Mom that the only thing keeping him sane was knowing we were in the storm room.'

'Had he built it to be a storm room or a safe room?'

'I don't know. All I know is that I'm glad we had it. Dad told Mom that the man was armed with enough ammunition to have killed us all ten times over.'

Kaj shuddered. 'Jesus.'

'Yeah. But then Dad said he was going to quit the force. That him being a cop wasn't as important as the safety of his family, and my mom let him have it. She told him that she'd taken care of us, and didn't he trust her, and had he married a helpless woman?'

Kaj found himself chuckling. 'Questions a man answers only one way.'

'Exactly. Dad said of *course* he trusted her and of *course* she wasn't helpless. She told him that he was a good cop and she wouldn't let him quit. That situations like this one were like plane crashes. Planes fly safely every day, but we only hear about the crashes. Cops do their jobs every day, but it's only once in a blue moon when their work threatens their family. We'd had our blue moon and survived. So he should shut up about quitting and feeling guilty.'

'Did he?'

Phin shrugged. 'He shut up about quitting. I don't think he ever got over it, though. I'd catch him looking at us with this haunted expression. Which is how you were looking at Elijah.'

'Did your dad quit?'

'No. He kept on being a cop and helped a lot of people. My sister and a few of my brothers followed in his footsteps, and now they're helping a lot of people. You do good work, Kaj. Burke respects you and that tells me everything I need to know. It's your call whether you continue being a prosecutor, but you have friends in this town. Friends who aren't helpless.'

Kaj let Phin's words sink in. He'd have to process them later. 'Did you hate the storm room after that?'

'I looked at it differently, for sure. But I'd look to Mom whenever we had to shelter. I knew that if she locked the door, I needed to be afraid. She'd always meet my eyes when she pulled the door closed, like she knew I was watching her. She only locked it that one time.'

Kaj drew a breath. 'Show me the safe room?'

Phin opened the closet door, revealing a rack full of clothes. 'His closet's a lot smaller now, but it seemed like most of his clothes were in his dresser drawers anyway. I hung some of them up here. If he needs to go into the room, he can spread them out before he closes the door. It won't hide the door forever, but it might buy time for help to come. One of the secrets of having a panic room is that no one knows it's there.'

He opened the exterior-style door that led into the safe room and followed Kaj inside. The space was unbearably tight with the two of them, but it would be fine for Elijah.

A small fridge was nestled under a shelf stacked with blankets and pillows. And snacks. And a phone and a radio. Even a plastic urine bottle for if he was trapped for a long time, God forbid. There were books and a deck of cards and a Lego model airplane set. And the ceiling was covered with glow-in-the-dark stars.

It was both Phin's childhood storm room and a hideaway with Elijah's favorite things.

'There's a router in here, so he can get Wi-Fi and communicate with you,' Phin said. 'Insulin's in the fridge. I called your sister yesterday to ask about it, since you weren't here. She told me where in your kitchen to find it and how much he'd need for a day. Just in case. She also had me give her the ex-date so that she could text you when you need to replace it. There's juice in the fridge, too, in case he has a sugar low.'

Kaj exhaled. 'He'll want to spend time in here even if there's no threat.'

'I kind of hoped so,' Phin said quietly. 'He's only ten. I didn't want him to be afraid of this room. I hope he never needs it because of a threat and sees it like his personal space.'

A wave of emotion crashed over Kaj and he had to close his eyes because they were stinging. 'Thank you,' he whispered. 'This is more than I expected.'

'You're welcome. Let me show you how the lock works, in case you need to come in here with him.'

Phin demonstrated and Kaj was amazed at how much he'd been able to accomplish in a short time. Phin immediately unlocked the door and stepped out, exhaling on a shudder, vibrating with anxiety.

'Are you okay?'

'Not a fan of small spaces,' Phin explained. 'I'm going to get a cake pop now. You should, too, before they're all gone.'

Recognizing the deflection, Kaj followed him into the hallway and stalled him with a brief touch to the big man's arm. 'Thank you, Phin. For the safe room and for being there for us yesterday. I didn't realize you were one of Burke's bodyguards.'

Phin's shrug was almost bashful. 'I'm not. I'm night security and the handyman. Val's the bodyguard, but she was off her game, worrying about talking to Sandra Springfield. There was enough online chatter about taking you out to delay Doyle's trial that I figured you might be a target. On a normal day, she's the perfect bodyguard, but yesterday wasn't normal. I didn't want either of you hurt because she was distracted.'

'Well, thank you.'

Phin's cheeks flushed. 'You're welcome. I need to go.'

'That was nice,' Sylvi said from behind him. She closed the guest room door and stepped into the hall. 'Phin seems like a good guy.'

'I think he is.' Kaj gestured to the stairs. 'Breakfast awaits. Coffee, too.'

Sylvi let out a little moan. 'Coffee. Thank you. I'll have some, then I'm heading over to the shop. I've got cleanup to do.'

'Make sure one of Burke's people walks you to your car.' Kaj started down the stairs with her. He could use another cup of coffee before starting his work for the day. But the buzzing of his cell phone stopped him. It was his boss.

'Cardozo,' Kaj said, stepping into his office.

'Kaj.' Reuben's voice was tired. 'You're okay?'

'Yes. A little bruised, but okay. Turns out Val and Phin are heavier than I expected. And if you tell anyone I said that about Val, I'll call you a liar.'

Reuben's chuckle was weary. 'So noted. I have news.'

'About André Holmes? Do you know what happened to him?'

'He was stabbed twice in the backyard of his home and his fiancée found him bleeding and unconscious. He's in surgery now. That's all I know.'

Relief mixed with fear. André was still alive, but surgery couldn't be good. 'That's more than we knew before. Antoine went to the hospital, but we hadn't heard anything yet.'

'NOPD's all over André's house and yard, processing the scene. I haven't received any updates yet.' Reuben hesitated. 'That wasn't my news. Since I've taken on Aaron Gates's case, I've been visiting him every day. Up until this morning, he was still in the infirmary. He no longer is, so I had a conversation with him. He's through detox and was more coherent than any of the other times I'd seen him. I told him that you were recused because of what Rick did. I told him what Corey did to Rick and how he tried to kill Jace. He was surprisingly angry. Especially that Corey had tortured Rick.'

'At least he has some humanity,' Kaj muttered.

'Not much,' Reuben said. 'But he does seem to care about the two younger brothers. He was furious that Rick's in jail and very worried about Jace. But the big deal coming out of our chat is that he's ready to talk about Corey. He wants to talk to you.'

Kaj blinked. 'Me? Why? I'm recused.'

'I told him that. He's insisting it be you. Look, Kaj, I need some answers. I want to know where Corey is, because the NOPD is no closer to finding him than they were four days ago. We've got eyes in the air, but if Corey and his men are under tree cover, we won't see them.'

'You want me to talk to Aaron?'

'If you would.'

Kaj considered it. Molly and Antoine were with André in the hospital. Lucien was out of town. 'I need to wait until Burke gets here. Security is scant at the moment.'

'Hurry, Kaj. We need Aaron to tell us what he knows.'

'I will. Listen, did André ever ID who overheard me talking about Elijah's math meet at NOPD headquarters?'

'Not that he told me. Why?'

'It appears that the portion of surveillance video that we were looking for has been erased.'

'*What?*'

'Yeah,' Kaj said grimly. 'We have to find out who's leaking information.'

'You're right, of course. I'll see what I can find about the video.'

'Thank you, Reuben. I'll call you when I'm on my way to the jail.'

Mid-City, New Orleans, Louisiana
FRIDAY, OCTOBER 28, 8:30 A.M.

'I don't like it,' Val said for the tenth time. That Aaron had asked to see Kaj after André was stabbed and Noni Feldman was abducted felt very wrong.

'Neither do I,' Kaj said, also for the tenth time. He put his arm around her, drawing her close on the sofa. 'But I need to go. If he tells us where to find Corey, we can bring Noni home.'

Jace was watching a movie with earbuds, and Phin was showing Elijah the safe room, but Val lowered her voice just in case either boy could hear her. 'If she's still alive.'

Kicked back in Kaj's recliner, Burke folded his hands over his stomach. 'NOPD doesn't have any leads as to who took her or where they took her.'

'You know who took her,' Val said, frustrated. 'Corey Gates and Bobby Landry.'

Despite his relaxed position, Burke's eyes were shadowed with worry. Antoine and Molly were sitting with Farrah in the hospital because André was still in surgery. Burke had been friends with the Holmes brothers for years and he was taking this hard.

'Yes,' Burke said, 'but there's no proof. They left nothing in Allyson's house for the CSU team to find. Corey and Bobby have been smart. Bobby survived in the Narcotics division for years. He knows what not to do so that he doesn't get caught. Right now, Aaron is our best bet for information. If he wants to talk to Kaj, we need to listen.'

Val exhaled. 'I know. I know you're right, but it feels . . . wrong.' So wrong. Her skin felt too tight and every nerve was screaming 'danger'.

'If it's any consolation,' Burke said, 'it feels wrong to me, too. But we don't have a choice.'

'That's not a consolation,' Val muttered.

Kaj kissed her temple. 'What are you worried about? That I'm going to be hurt when I leave or that Elijah will be in danger when I leave?'

'Both.' But she reined in her emotions. It was time for logic. 'Who's going with you? Lucien's still a few hours out and I'm not leaving Elijah. Burke, can you go?'

Kaj glanced up the stairs. 'What about Phin? You and Burke can stay with Elijah.'

Burke and Val shared a long look. 'He was good yesterday, Burke,' Val said quietly. 'He saved our lives. My Kevlar wouldn't have withstood rounds from an AR-15. He was calm and collected. He didn't lose it. Even when the cops came with all the sirens and questions.'

Kaj looked confused. 'What am I missing?'

Burke sighed softly. 'Phin's . . . complicated. His PTSD sometimes requires him to break away if he gets too anxious.'

'I saw a little of that,' Kaj murmured. 'He fought off a panic attack when he was showing me the interior lock in the panic room.'

Val stared at Kaj and Burke's eyes widened. 'He went inside?' Burke asked, stunned.

'Yeah,' Kaj answered cautiously. 'He had to. He built it.'

'But for the most part, the door was open when he was building it,' Burke said. 'He doesn't do small spaces.'

'That's what he said. But he seemed okay while we were in the room together. When the door opened, he kind of shuddered. He seemed in control, though.'

'That's really good to know,' Burke said sincerely.

'Can he legally carry a gun?' Kaj asked.

Burke nodded. 'He has a concealed carry permit, but he doesn't carry often. He's a good shot, though. Sniper good. We can ask him. If he says no, we'll respect that.'

'If who says no?' Elijah asked, skipping down the stairs, Czar at his heels. 'Dad, did you see the room? It's like a little library. And there's a Lego airplane kit! So cool.'

Kaj smiled. 'I saw. Phin made it perfect for you. Did you thank him?'

'He did,' Phin said. 'I'm happy he likes it.'

Elijah's eyes abruptly focused in on where Kaj's arm lay on Val's shoulders and a little smile curved his lips. 'I knew it,' he stage-whispered to Czar.

Kaj huffed a laugh. 'Come on, kiddo. You have schoolwork to do.'

'I did it all already. For the whole week and part of next week, too.'

'Good job,' Kaj praised. 'Let's go upstairs and call Aunt Genie. I bet she's bored silly, having to stay in bed.'

Elijah's eyes narrowed. 'What's going on?'

'Your father wants you out of the room so that Burke and I can talk to Phin,' Val said.

'Why didn't you just say so?' Elijah demanded. He waved at Jace, who took out his earbuds. 'Come on. You can meet my aunt on Skype. You'll like her.'

Jace looked at Kaj, uncertainty all over his face. 'Mr. Cardozo?'

'It's fine, Jace,' Kaj said kindly. 'Come with us.'

'All right.' Jace picked up the handcuffs from the table, but Kaj shook his head.

'No need. Leave those there.'

Jace slowly put the cuffs on the table. There was such hope in his eyes that Val's breath hitched in her chest.

'Yes, sir.' Jace gathered his things and followed them up the stairs to Elijah's room.

'Tell your aunt I said hi,' Val called, then patted the sofa. 'Have a seat, Phin.'

Phin approached warily. 'Why?'

'Kaj needs to visit the jail today,' Burke said. 'He wants you to go with him.'

'As his bodyguard,' Val added.

Phin blinked. 'Me?'

'If you're not ready, no one will blame you,' Burke assured him. 'But you kept your shit together yesterday. Kaj feels comfortable with you.'

Phin sat so quietly he might as well have been stone. Just when Val was sure he wouldn't answer at all, he nodded. 'I can do it. I want to do it.'

Burke smiled. 'Good enough.'

Val studied Phin. He looked . . . determined. And satisfied. 'Have you wanted to do more than night security and handyman work all this time, Phin?'

'Yes,' he admitted. 'I wanted to work with you, not for you. But I wasn't ready before.'

'What changed?' she asked. 'I'm not judging. I'm just curious.'

'Therapy,' he said gruffly. 'Burke found me someone. It helped.'

'Okay, then.' She squeezed Phin's arm. 'Take care of Kaj. He's . . . important.'

'You know I will.'

'Wear your vest,' Burke said. 'Kaj, too. Hopefully this will be a short trip to the jail, but we need to be prepared.'

'Of course,' Phin said, all business. 'I think we should hide the fact that he's leaving the house. We know someone's been watching the place and reporting back to Corey.'

The cops patrolling the neighborhood hadn't been able to find who was watching them and neither had Burke. All the cars on the street belonged to neighborhood residents. No vehicles had anyone lurking inside.

'I asked André to start a door-to-door search,' Burke said. 'André said he would, but then . . .' He trailed off, angry and sad.

Because their friend had been stabbed and the NOPD still had no leads.

'I'll bring the company Escalade into Kaj's garage,' Phin said.

The SUV was fitted with bullet-resistant glass and reinforced side panels. That Phin planned to use it for Kaj made her feel a bit better.

'Kaj can lie down in the back under a blanket,' Phin went on. 'Will he fight me on that?'

'No,' Burke said. 'He's not a stupid man. And he likes being alive.'

A cold shiver ran down Val's spine. *This feels wrong.* But this was the situation and she'd deal. 'What about next week? Kaj's got the Doyle trial on Monday. Bella Butler will be back to take the stand. He'll need security. Who'll go with him?'

'We'll provide someone,' Burke promised. 'For now, let's get through this meeting with Aaron Gates.'

'Okay.' But Val needed a word with Kaj before he left. 'I'm going upstairs for a few.'

'Tell Elijah's aunt we said hi,' Burke said slyly, and Phin smirked.

Val snorted. 'Shut up.'

She found Elijah in his safe room with the door open. He'd called his aunt on his tablet, which he was sweeping around so that Genie could see it, too. Jace sat on the side of Elijah's bed, looking uncertain as he petted Czar, who lay at his side. Czar was enjoying the attention.

Kaj stood off to one side watching Elijah, a smile playing on his lips. Val slid her arm around his waist.

'Phin's in,' she murmured.

Kaj nodded, unsurprised. 'Figured he would be. We'll be fine. Don't worry.'

Val nodded, faking confidence. She tugged Kaj into the hall. 'Be careful. Please.'

He cupped her face in his hands and pulled her in for a sweet kiss. 'I will. But this might be the break that we've been waiting for.'

Val rested her forehead against his. 'I don't trust Aaron.'

'I don't, either. But we can't keep living like this. I want Elijah to be able to go back to school and not be afraid. I want Jace to have a good life, too.' He kissed her again, longer and lustier this time. 'Now let me go.'

'Mr. Cardozo?' Jace stood in Elijah's doorway, still looking uncertain. 'While you're at the jail, do you think you'll have time to check on Rick?'

'They may not let me see him since I'm recused from his case. I'm only seeing Aaron because he insisted on it. But I'll try. Do you have a message?'

'Just for him to stay safe.'

'If I can, I will. If I can't, I'll ask my boss to check on him, to make sure he's okay.'

Tears shimmered in Jace's eyes. 'Thank you, sir.'

25

'REUBEN.' KAJ NODDED to his boss, who waited outside an interview room at the jail. 'This is Phin Bishop. Phin, this is Reuben Hogan.'

Reuben inclined his head. 'Are you one of Broussard's people?'

'I am. Where do you want me to wait?'

'In the hallway is fine,' Reuben said. 'Aaron's public defender is with him. We've also got two officers in there.' He thumbed over his shoulder, pointing to the interview room door. 'He won't try anything. New info before you go in there—Ballistics matched the bullets from the rifle used on you last night to those found at the fake safe house that supposedly held Jace.'

'No surprise,' Kaj said grimly. 'Let's see what Aaron has to say.'

Aaron Gates sat at the table, his hands and feet shackled. The chain connecting the shackles was secured to a steel ring in the floor. Considering the brute strength he'd used when he'd killed the pediatric oncologist who'd treated his son, Kaj was grateful for the precaution.

Of course, Aaron had been fueled by meth that day.

Today he appeared exhausted and gaunt, his skin stretched tight over his cheekbones. But his eyes were sharp as they studied Kaj.

Kaj could see some resemblance between Aaron and Jace. Their eyes were the same blue, but Aaron's were calculating and cold. Jace's were either frightened or grateful for the smallest consideration.

How a sweet kid like Jace could have come from the Gates family was a mystery.

Kaj didn't speak, patiently waiting. Aaron had asked to speak to him. He'd let the man make the first overture.

After a silent minute, Aaron spoke. 'Mr. Cardozo.'

'Mr. Gates.'

Reuben stood along the back wall. The two officers stood at the ready on either side of Aaron's place at the table. The public defender sat quietly next to them, watching.

'Have you seen my two younger brothers?' Aaron asked.

'Jace, yes. Rick, momentarily.'

'You put Rick in jail,' Aaron accused.

'Rick committed a crime,' Kaj said mildly. 'And he was delivered to my front lawn, unconscious and rolled up in an old quilt. He was almost dead from a heroin overdose.'

Aaron's eyes narrowed. 'Who left him on your lawn?'

'Jace, because Corey forced him to do it.'

Aaron leaned back in his chair, trying for nonchalant. 'You've spoken to Jace?'

'I have. He's a nice kid.'

Aaron's cold eyes softened the slightest bit. 'I didn't want him involved in any of this.'

'He's being cared for. He's okay. Confused and scared, but okay.' Kaj hesitated, then shrugged. 'He's got a good eye for detail. He remembers things. He's really very smart.'

Aaron scowled. 'No, he's really not. He can't read or write.'

'He's probably dyslexic.'

Aaron blinked. 'What?'

That made Kaj angry. 'You're a well-educated man, Mr. Gates. How could you not know?'

'I . . .' Aaron exhaled. 'I wasn't paying attention. My own son was dying.'

And before that? Kaj wanted to demand, because Jace had been Aaron's responsibility for more than two years before little Liam had become ill. But he calmed himself. 'I'm sorry for that. I'm a father, too. I can't imagine how terrified you must have been.'

Aaron looked down. 'Every damn day.'

Kaj didn't trust this man, but he could believe that he'd loved his son. 'Jace said that he asked Dewey Talley to be his guardian after your arrest.'

Aaron's gaze shot up, filled with rage. His fists clenched on the table. '*No.*' Then he frowned, appearing confused. 'But he can't now, can he? Mr. Hogan says he's dead.'

'I saw Dewey's remains,' Kaj confirmed. 'His body was . . . not intact.'

Aaron grimaced. 'Gators?'

Kaj nodded. 'Yeah. Not pretty.'

'No, it's not,' he said. 'Corey killed him?'

'That's what I'm told.'

Aaron's eyes narrowed. 'By whom?'

'By Jace. He witnessed it.'

Aaron flinched. 'Where?'

'Corey was holding them at your camp. Well, your former camp. Corey blew it up.'

Aaron sucked in a startled breath. 'He did *what*? What an asshole.'

'He's hunkered down somewhere else now. Do you know where he might be?'

'He really blew it all up?'

'There appeared to have been four buildings impacted. Nothing was left.'

Aaron swallowed hard, then shook his head. 'He blew up his own quarters, too.' He glared over Kaj's shoulder at Reuben. 'I got a few things to share, Mr. Hogan. I want them recorded so that a judge will take them into consideration when I'm sentenced.'

Aaron seemed to assume he'd be found guilty. That would make things easier. It was always harder when they were in denial.

'This session is being recorded,' Reuben said. 'I already told you that.'

'Hold on,' the defense attorney said, speaking for the first time. 'Aaron, I recommend you share nothing.'

'I'm interested only in Corey,' Kaj said. 'I won't be pressuring Mr. Gates to admit anything about himself.'

The attorney considered. 'I still recommend you share nothing.'

Aaron turned his glare on his lawyer. 'I want my brother to pay. I'm not admitting to any of my own shit. I'm not that stupid. But I have information on Corey, and I'll share it for the sheer pleasure of seeing him taken down a peg or two. If you can shave a few years off my sentence, then that's a bonus. I'll save disclosures about the stuff I did—along with the names of the city's fancy people who're doing worse than I ever did—to help myself. Are we clear?'

The man shrugged. 'Suit yourself.'

'What do you know about Corey?' Kaj asked, steering the conversation back on track.

'What do you want to know?' Aaron asked, abruptly cagey.

Kaj wanted to roll his eyes. Guys like Aaron couldn't help themselves. Everything was a transaction. So Kaj pulled out the big guns. 'Corey tried to kill Jace.'

Aaron went still. 'When?'

'After Jace escaped the camp. He'd seen Dewey murdered and knew that Corey had hurt Rick. Jace figured he'd be next, so he got away and found help. Law enforcement suspected they had a leak, so they planted a false story that Jace was being held in a safe house. That night, two masked men whose body types matched Corey and his business partner Bobby entered the safe house and sprayed the place with gunfire, injuring the two officers who were waiting for them. Jace remained unhurt because he wasn't there, but that told law enforcement that Jace wasn't safe from his brother.'

Aaron's expression grew murderous, and Kaj saw the man who'd beaten another man to death with his bare hands. 'Can you prove this?'

Kaj lifted one shoulder. 'Bullets in the safe house matched the bullets found at a crime scene last night where Corey shot at me.'

'Well, the thing about Corey is that he thinks he's smarter than everyone else. He's been operating a murder-for-hire racket out of his quarters that he blew up. I wasn't involved,' Aaron stated. 'Corey thinks he's so clever that nobody knew he was doing it. But I knew. I'm not sure exactly what kind of shit he was doing, but I know he's killed one or two people at least. Robbed a few others. He does the dirty work for rich folks who don't want to soil their own hands. He runs the show, but his friend Bobby works with him. Bobby's an ex-cop who still has a lot of friends in the NOPD.'

Kaj listened, not letting on that they'd already figured all that out. 'I thought Corey and Bobby ran a construction company.'

Aaron rolled his eyes. 'It's a front.'

'Corey's not at his camp any longer. Where would he go?'

'You'll make sure you catch him?' Aaron asked. 'And that Rick and Jace will be safe?'

'I will,' Kaj promised. 'Rick will have to do some time, but we can make sure he's in a safe place. And we will take care of Jace.'

'Okay then. Corey's got another camp. Not in his name.'

Kaj's pulse began to pick up speed. 'Where?'

'On the bayou. Close to Lake Cataouatche.'

'You'll have to be a little more specific, Mr. Gates. The area around Cataouatche has been searched.'

'It's a little tributary. Hard to find without a guide. I could find it for you.'

Kaj blew out an impatient breath. 'Do you want Corey arrested or not? If you do, tell me what you know. Because you know we're not taking you with us as a guide.'

Aaron grinned. 'It was worth a try. The property belonged to an old friend. Ivan Kristiansen. He left it to me.'

Kaj couldn't control his shock. His mouth dropped open and he snapped it shut.

Aaron's eyes narrowed. 'You know him?'

'He came up in a conversation with Sandra Springfield,' Kaj said.

Color flooded Aaron's face, a vein abruptly throbbing in his temple. 'She talked to you?' He lunged at Kaj, but one of the officers shoved him back down. 'You're lying.'

'We're done,' the defense attorney said. 'Please leave. I need to talk with my client.'

Kaj stood and took a step back, keeping Aaron in his sight. He didn't breathe again until he was in the hallway with the interview room door closed behind them.

Phin immediately straightened. 'Are you all right?'

Reuben was frowning at him. 'Does Miss Sorensen know about this property? It was her brother's, after all.'

Kaj looked at Phin first. 'I'm okay. Just surprised. Aaron kind of lost it there at the end. Reuben, I'm sure she doesn't know. She would have volunteered the location if she'd known. I need to get home.' They needed to search for that property. 'You'll personally check on Rick?'

'I said I would.' Because Reuben had said no outright when Kaj had asked to visit. 'We'll see you on Monday?'

For the trial of Bella Butler's rapist. 'Absolutely.'

Kaj said nothing more until he'd reached their vehicle, Burke's highly secure Escalade. 'I'll sit up front on the way back. It doesn't matter if they see me coming back in, does it?'

'Maybe, but I don't want them seeing you, period. Duck your head down when we get close.' Phin opened the front passenger door for Kaj, then opened the hatch to retrieve his gun from a safe bolted to the floor at the rear of the SUV.

'Where to?' Phin asked when he was behind the wheel.

'My house. But first I need to call Burke.' Kaj dialed Burke's number and the man picked up immediately. 'Aaron said that Corey has another property on a tributary off Lake Cataouatche. Says it was owned by Ivan Kristiansen.'

Burke gasped. 'You're fucking kidding me.'

'Nope. Aaron smirked and said that Ivan "left it to him".'

'I'm starting a property search as we speak. You're coming home?'

'We're in the car now. See you soon.' Kaj ended the call. Phin was staring at him, the vehicle still in park.

'Ivan Kristiansen? That's Val's brother? How did he leave property to Aaron Gates?'

Kaj sighed. 'How much do you know about Val's brother?'

'Not much. I know he was killed trying to keep Sylvi from buying drugs or something like that, but that he was also using. I know that Val and Sylvi have made up. Something else is going on, but I didn't ask questions. Val looked . . . fragile last night.'

'She was.' Until they were in bed together. Then she'd transformed back into the strong woman he was quickly falling for. 'Val's brother and Aaron worked together in a financial firm for a few years. Ivan was also the leader of Sixth Day before Aaron took over.'

Phin's eyes widened. 'Holy shit. *That's* what she found out yesterday?'

'Yes. She was devastated, as you can imagine. She also found out that Ivan wasn't killed because he was in the wrong place, wrong time.'

'He was there because he was selling the drugs, not just using them.'

'Yes, but he died because he did a shitty thing to Aaron Gates and Aaron killed him.'

'Poor Val. That woman—Sandra—she told her all of this?'

'Yes. Sylvi verified it. She saw her brother murdered.'

'My God. All this dredged up those memories for Sylvi, too. No wonder she cried herself to sleep last night.'

Kaj lifted a brow. 'How do you know that?'

'I couldn't sleep. I was doing rounds and checking on Elijah. I heard her. I figured she was upset because her store got shot up.' He started the engine. 'Any other bombshells?'

'Only that one.'

'Then I'll get us back to your place.'

The Quarter, New Orleans, Louisiana
FRIDAY, OCTOBER 28, 10:00 A.M.

'Finally,' Bobby grumbled as the tiny woman emerged from the bakery into the alley behind it, her arms laden with bags bearing the bakery's logo as she got behind the wheel of her minivan. She appeared to be going on a delivery run, which was perfect for their needs. Bobby fixed duct tape to his jeans to restrain her. 'She took forever.'

'She took twenty minutes,' Ed corrected. 'Which is not forever, unless you're a toddler.'

'Enough,' Corey snapped, and they quieted. 'We need to be focused. Everyone ready?'

They'd taken two boats out of the bayou, leaving one at a boat launch on Lake Salvador, and then the three of them had taken the remaining boat to a second launch closer to the city, where they'd stolen a car. Having an escape route from two different boat launches seemed prudent, given that they'd almost certainly be running from the police once they'd finished their task.

They parked their stolen car across the narrow alley, forcing the bakery van to come to a stop.

'Go, Bobby,' Corey said, his gun drawn. Just in case.

Ed was behind the wheel of their stolen car. He'd follow until they were a block from Cardozo's house. Then he'd park the car and join them in the bakery van. If things went south, he was to grab the Cardozo kid and haul ass to the car. Corey and Bobby would meet him at the first boat launch if they could. If not, Ed was to take the first boat and head to camp. Corey and Bobby would find a way to get to the second boat and meet him.

Bobby had forced his way into the bakery van's passenger seat before the woman had time to become impatient. Corey followed a few moments behind, pushing his way into the van's back seat. Hands clenched on the steering wheel, the baker glared over her shoulder at him.

'You,' she hissed.

Bobby sat in the front passenger seat, his Glock shoved into the woman's side. He held up a small pistol. 'Little tiger was armed. Luckily mine is bigger.'

'Let's go, lady,' Corey ordered.

Her lips trembled, then firmed. 'No.'

'Fine. We'll do this without you.' Corey leveled his gun at her head. 'One more chance.'

She lifted her chin. 'I won't help you hurt them.'

'Then you'll die.'

She swallowed hard. 'Then I die.'

'Well, fuck, Corey. I like her.' Bobby was grinning. 'I'll tie her up and shove her into the footwell. She's so tiny, she'll fit. Cover me.' He grabbed her by the collar, covered her mouth with one of his big hands, then dragged her across the console.

Corey looked behind them. No one was in the alley, but one of the store owners would eventually come out of their store and wonder what the fuss was. 'Hurry.'

Bobby yelped. 'She bit me!' He slapped one of the lengths of tape over her mouth, but the woman transformed into a wildcat, her elbows jabbing Bobby hard enough to make him snarl. 'Fucking hell. That hurts.' He backhanded her, stunning her into immobility for long enough to restrain her hands. Her feet were next, and then he shoved her into the footwell.

Leaving her on the passenger side, he marched around to slide behind the wheel. He yelped again when he could barely move, yanking at the seat release. The seat slid back, and Bobby exhaled.

'That was harder than it needed to be.' He put the van in gear and gave the finger to Ed, who was laughing his ass off.

'Let's go, Bobby,' Corey urged. 'We've been sitting here too long.'

Ed moved the stolen car and Bobby eased the van into traffic. Hopefully they were all tourists and wouldn't realize that the men in the bakery van were wanted by the NOPD.

Traffic moved quickly once they got out of the Quarter and headed for Mid-City, where Cardozo lived. Finally, Bobby pulled over while Ed parked the car a block away from NOPD's checkpoint.

Ed hopped in and gave Corey a nod. 'Do we free the woman before we send her toward the house or shoot her and let them find her?'

'We free her feet,' Corey answered, 'but not her hands or mouth, or she'll scream and warn them. Remember the plan. Bobby, you take care of the bodyguards. According to Ed's friend, there are two—Broussard and Sorensen. Kill Broussard. Grab the blonde. I'm after Cardozo. Ed, you grab the kid. And whoever encounters that monster dog first, shoot it.'

'Dammit,' Bobby whined. 'I don't want to shoot a dog.'

'You'll do it,' Corey snapped. 'Now focus. We have one shot at this. Just one.'

He held his breath when they approached the police who'd been watching Cardozo's neighborhood, but the man simply waved them through. Didn't even look into the window.

'How did you do that?' Corey demanded.

Bobby smirked at him in the rearview mirror. 'My buddy's got juice.'

'When this is over, you have to tell me who he is.'

Bobby shrugged. 'When this is over, I don't plan to let him live long enough to introduce you two. We're here.' He backed the van into Cardozo's driveway, then leaned forward to yank the baker onto the seat. He slit the tape binding her feet, then shoved her hard so that she stumbled out of the van and a few steps up the walkway. She started to turn to run the other way and Bobby fired a single shot to her leg. With the silencer, all they heard was a pop.

Down she went.

Showtime.

Mid-City, New Orleans, Louisiana
FRIDAY, OCTOBER 28, 10:25 A.M.

Val stared across the dining room table at Burke. 'Corey's second camp belonged to Van?'

'That's what Aaron told Kaj.'

'But Van never told me about any property he owned in the bayou.'

'Van didn't tell you a lot of things, Val,' Burke said gently.

'True.' She sighed wearily. 'My brother was a total stranger.'

Jace fidgeted. 'I don't know where it is. I didn't know that Corey had the first camp.'

'Oh, honey.' Val squeezed his arm. 'Nobody's expecting you to know.'

Jace dropped his gaze to the table. 'I want to be useful. To earn my keep.'

'Jace.' She waited until he was looking at her. 'No one expects you to earn your keep.'

His brows crunched. 'Mr. Cardozo said I didn't have to be cuffed anymore. Why?'

She smiled at him. 'I think he wanted to ditch the cuffs a few days ago, but he had to think about Elijah. So he waited until he was sure. I guess he's sure now. Don't worry, honey.'

'But . . .' Jace shook his head. 'Never mind. You have to look for Corey.'

'Tell me,' Val insisted gently.

'Just . . . where will I go when this is over? What's going to happen to me?'

Val needed to reassure this boy without promising too much. But she wanted to promise him everything. She settled for honesty. 'I don't know exactly. But we will make sure you're okay, wherever you go.'

Czar began to growl a second before both Burke's and Val's phones buzzed—the perimeter alarm had been triggered.

'Someone's here,' Burke said.

Val stood, drawing her gun from its holster as Burke checked the camera feeds on his phone. Then he smiled and she relaxed.

'It's MaryBeth,' he said. 'I think she's brought us an early lunch.'

'She's spoiling us,' Val said, holstering her gun as she walked to the front door.

'She should ask us to walk her inside,' Burke grumbled, still watching the camera feed.

Val started to unlock the front door. 'I'll do it.'

'No, wait. She's coming now and—*Oh shit*.' Czar's low growl filled the air as Burke's chair hit the floor. 'MaryBeth's hurt. She just collapsed out front. I'll go to her.'

This is it. This was what had been nagging at her all day. 'Wait. I'll get Elijah to the safe room.'

Burke paused, his hand on the door as Val ran to Elijah, yanking his headphones off and dragging him to his feet.

She pulled Elijah to the stairs and gave him a little shove. 'Elijah, safe room. *Now*.'

His face going sheet-white, Elijah ran.

'Czar, protect,' she told the dog, and Czar chased the boy up the stairs. 'You go, too, Jace. Upstairs to the safe room. *Now*.'

Jace glanced at Burke before taking the stairs two at a time.

Burke was on the phone, dialing 911, calling for help, asking them to alert the cops André had assigned to neighborhood security. Hands steady, Val checked the camera feeds. MaryBeth was on the ground, her blood pooling on the front walk.

There was no one else in view.

'This is a trap, Burke,' Val murmured.

'I know, but MaryBeth could die. I'll carry her into the house. You keep Elijah and Jace safe. Close the door as soon as I'm through it. Watch the camera and let me in when I'm close.'

Burke opened the door, started through, then dropped like a rock. *What the fuck?*

'Burke!' Val shouted. She shoved on the door to close it, but Burke was in the way.

He was too heavy. He was dead weight.

Panic clawed up her throat. *No, no, no. Not dead.* Her brain was shouting at her to close the door at the same time it was pleading with her to help Burke. To drag him inside.

Elijah and Jace. She threw her whole body into the door, but it flew back when it was shoved open from the other side. She was forced into the coat closet door, the impact leaving her dizzy, but not so much that she couldn't see the man coming toward her.

He wore a ski mask and body armor. *Lean, about five-ten, one-eighty. You can take him.* Aiming, she emptied her magazine into his face and head. He staggered, then fell on top of her.

She shoved him off, jumped to her feet, flicked the magazine release with one hand, and dug into her pocket for a spare magazine. Shoving it into place, she racked her pistol and leapt for the front door, only to have it fly open again. The door smacked her in the face and she took a clumsy step back, blinking away the pain and focusing on the two men who were forcing their way inside.

Two very big men. They were . . . big.

Her mind started to shut down, but she fought it. *Details.* Both wore ski masks, but she had no doubt who they were. One was six-three. *Corey.* The other had to be six-five. *Bobby.*

She was still blinking, her mind still struggling to catch up, when the men stopped cold, staring at the dead man at her feet—probably Ed Bartholomew. *One down. Two to go.*

She'd lifted her gun when Corey snarled, 'Fucking hell. Drag her to the van. Hurry.' Then he charged toward the stairs.

Toward Elijah. Toward Jace.

No. She started after him, but Bobby crowded her into a corner.

No. Not now. You will not lose it now.

From upstairs she heard Czar barking and Corey yelling. 'Where the fuck is he?'

Then Jace was screaming. 'Get away!'

God no. He was supposed to be in the safe room.

She heard vicious barking. *Czar, rip Corey apart.*

Then . . . a single gunshot.

Her chest froze up. *Elijah. Jace. Czar.*

Bobby reached to grab her by the throat and her muscle memory finally kicked in. She dropped into a crouch, surprising him, then sprang up, twisting to throw her shoulder into his chest.

Classic roller derby shoulder block.

Stunned, he staggered back a step. Then fell on his ass.

He'd tripped over the dead man.

Val fired at Bobby as she vaulted over him, but he caught her ankle and yanked her down, making her shot go wide. She kicked and fired again, but that shot missed him, too.

Bobby pointed his gun at her face. 'Drop the gun. Now.'

'Motherfucker! Where is he?' Corey's distant shout of rage startled Bobby for a split second.

Corey was still up there. With Elijah and Jace.

Val kicked free of Bobby's grip and sprang to her feet. She shot at his arm and this time he dropped the gun on a roar of pain.

Gotcha. She'd steadied her hand for the next shot, but another shot was fired. Upstairs.

26

J ACE'S HEART WAS going to explode out of his chest as he chased
Elijah up the stairs. 'Hurry, Elijah. Hurry!'

White-faced with terror, Elijah stumbled into his room and toward
his closet.

Jace pushed past him, opening the safe room door. 'Get in. Now.'

Elijah grabbed Jace's hand. 'You, too. Val said! You and Czar.'

But Jace had let Rick down, and he was not letting Corey put his
hands on Elijah Cardozo. He thought fast and realized Elijah's hands
were empty. 'Where's your phone?'

Elijah blinked at him. 'I don't know. Downstairs.'

'I'll get it. You need it to check your sugar.'

Elijah yanked on his shirt. 'No.'

'I'll be right back,' Jace promised. 'Close the door and lock it. Don't
open it until I say "Midway."' It was the code word Elijah had set with
his father before they'd called his aunt.

'Then you take Czar,' Elijah insisted. 'Please, Jace.'

They didn't have time to argue. Jace grabbed Czar's collar, not relaxing until he heard the lock engage in the safe room. 'Stay,' he commanded, hoping the dog obeyed, then pulled the clothes across the closet pole, hiding the door. He first closed the closet door, then the bedroom door, trapping Czar inside, then ran for the stairs just as Val yelled, 'Burke!'

Jace froze. Gunfire. One, two, three . . . He lost count, the bullets came so fast.

He's here. Corey was here.

Move, you idiot. Move. Do something. But Jace's feet wouldn't move.

He felt like a bug trapped in a spider's web. Paralyzed.

And then he heard it. Corey's voice. 'Fucking hell. Drag her to the van. Hurry.'

Val. Jace looked around frantically. Need a weapon. He ran into Mr. Cardozo's room, hoping to find something to save Val. To save Elijah.

But footsteps thundered up the stairs and the door to Elijah's room was thrown open. 'Where the fuck is he?' Corey screamed.

Elijah. Corey had come for Elijah.

Czar was growling and snarling. Corey would kill the dog. And then he'd get to Elijah.

He's safe. Locked in the safe room.

But Corey would find a way. Corey always got what he wanted. His brother could blow things up. He'd blown up his own camp. He could blow open the safe room.

Elijah would be killed.

'No,' Jace whispered, then grabbed the lamp from Mr. Cardozo's nightstand and ran for Elijah's room. Corey was aiming his gun at Czar. Jace didn't stop to think.

'Get away!' Jace shouted as he swung the lamp, but Corey had seen movement in Elijah's dresser mirror and ducked at the last minute.

Corey screamed when Czar sank his teeth into his arm—there was already a bandage there. From where Val had shot him. Jace felt satisfaction deep down. *You go, Val.*

Corey aimed his gun at Czar again, but Jace threw himself against his brother as he pulled the trigger and the shot hit the ceiling, showering them with plaster. Czar let Corey's arm go, but stood over him, growling, teeth bared. Jace yanked Corey from the room and slammed the door, once again closing Czar in Elijah's room.

For a moment Corey stared at Jace, his mouth open. Then color flooded his face. 'You sonofabitch,' Corey hissed. 'You've been here all this time? Where's the kid?'

'Not here,' Jace lied. He backed toward the stairs. *Get him away from Elijah.*

'Motherfucker! Where is he?' Corey's nostrils flared, his eyes blazing and his lips curving coldly like they did before he'd beat them. But this time Corey aimed his gun at Jace's chest and pulled the trigger again.

Pain instantly burned from the inside out and Jace fell backward.

Mid-City, New Orleans, Louisiana
FRIDAY, OCTOBER 28, 10:32 A.M.

Val stared in horror as Jace tumbled down the stairs, landing at her feet. A crimson stain was spreading across his T-shirt. No.

Bobby rolled to his feet, holding his arm, gaping at Jace. 'He was *here?*'

Corey came down the stairs, his face a mask of pure fury and a gun in his hand. 'They've been hiding him the whole time.' He kicked Jace in the side.

'*No.*' Val swung her gun to point at Corey, dropping to her knees when Bobby's fist connected with her head. The pain was excruciating, and she had to blink to see.

Her vision blurry, she shot at Corey's leg. But it didn't stop him. *Missed. Dammit.*

The barrel of a gun was shoved against her skull. 'Drop it,' Bobby repeated.

'Fuck off,' she slurred, and fired one more time before Corey raised his hand and brought the butt of his gun down on her head. She crumpled, landing on Jace, who moaned pitifully.

'Sorry, Val,' he whispered. 'Tried to stop him.'

'Take her,' Corey snapped.

'Where is Cardozo?' Bobby demanded. 'Where's the kid?'

'Not here. Take her and go. The cops will be here any minute.'

'What do we do with him?' Bobby asked, pointing to Jace.

'Leave him. I don't care anymore. If he lives, he can tell Cardozo that I've taken his woman.'

Val gasped when Bobby grabbed her collar, yanking her off Jace. She fought, but her head was spinning and she couldn't see. Blood, she realized. Her head was bleeding from where Corey had hit her with the butt of his gun. She tried to wipe the blood from her eyes, but Bobby grabbed her hands, taping them behind her with duct tape. She kicked, but he rolled on her legs and secured her ankles. Another piece of tape was slapped across her mouth.

She bucked, but Corey hit her in the head again and nausea rushed over her in a wave.

'Take her guns and toss her phone,' Corey said. '*Hurry*. The cops have to be coming.'

'It'll be fine,' Bobby said, removing Val's backup gun from her ankle holster before hoisting her over his shoulder, jarring her joints. But she couldn't move. Couldn't fight.

Bobby took a giant step and Val wiped her eyes against Bobby's back. Her cry of horror was muffled by the tape. He had walked over

Burke, who lay on the front porch, not moving.

MaryBeth lay beside him, blood smeared on the front walk. It looked like she'd dragged herself from where she'd fallen. Burke's gun was next to her hand.

That's why Bobby and Corey took longer to enter the house, Val realized dimly. MaryBeth had tried to hold them off. Tears fell as grief and love mixed, making it hard to breathe. MaryBeth was her oldest friend. Together since high school. That she'd sacrifice herself was who MaryBeth was. *Don't you die, dammit.*

Val cried out again when she was tossed into the back of MaryBeth's van, another punch hitting her head.

'That was for Ed, you fucking bitch,' Corey snarled. Then the two climbed into the front seats and the van was moving.

'She'll pay for killing Ed, too,' Bobby said viciously. 'Dammit.'

'We'll think about Ed when we're out of here. We have to get away. The cops are going to be here any minute.'

'My buddy's gonna slow the cops down,' Bobby said confidently. 'Don't worry.'

'Who's your buddy that he has *that much* juice?' Corey demanded. 'Don't tell me it's a secret. If he's got that much power, I need to know.'

'Name's Drysdale,' Bobby said smugly. 'He's one of André Holmes's detectives.'

'Huh,' Corey grunted. 'Gotta say I'm impressed.'

Drysdale? *But André trusts him.* Val thought of André getting stabbed right outside his own home. He would only have let someone he trusted that close.

'What about Ed's guy?' Corey asked from the driver's seat. 'The cop? Alex Cullen.'

'I'm sure Alex is gone already,' Bobby said as they turned a corner.

'He didn't tell us that Cardozo and the kid had left the house,' Corey fumed.

'I know, but his shot that took Broussard down was sheer perfection.'

'It was,' Corey agreed begrudgingly. 'But he's still on my shit list. How's your arm?'

'Shot. It was a through and through, but it needs stitches.'

Corey laughed, the sound more than a little hysterical. 'Too bad you killed Zach. He could have fixed you right up.'

'You're an asshole.'

'Yeah, well, the dog got me. I went looking in the kid's room and the dog attacked. Bit my sore arm, the fucker.'

'Did you shoot it?'

'Tried to, but my shot went wide when that little prick brother of mine attacked me.'

Czar's okay. Thank God.

'I didn't see that comin',' Bobby admitted.

'Me either,' Corey said, his anger clear. 'I hope Jace chokes on his own blood.'

He might, Val thought dully, thinking of the bright crimson staining the boy's shirt. But Corey hadn't found Elijah and Kaj was safe.

'Since we don't have Cardozo,' Corey said, 'we need to get in touch with him to deliver our demands. We should have dumped the contacts from the blonde's phone to get his number. Can Drysdale get the number for us?'

'I'll ask him when we're safely away from here.'

The van came to a stop and Val was grabbed again and frisked. They dumped her in the trunk of a car, her body shoved into a fetal position. The trunk slammed down and it was dark.

Val fought to push back the fear. *Stay alert. Be ready. Fight back.*

Mid-City, New Orleans, Louisiana
FRIDAY, OCTOBER 28, 10:40 A.M.

Kaj stared at the blood sugar monitor app on his phone, dread like icy fingers down his spine. 'Oh no.'

'What?' Phin asked.

'Elijah's blood sugar is dropping. Fast. His levels get fed to my phone.' He dialed his son, but the phone just rang, then went to voice mail. 'Something's wrong.'

'Duck your head down,' Phin said. 'We're approaching your neighborhood.'

But Kaj's phone rang and he immediately answered without glancing at the caller ID. 'Elijah? Why's your sugar dropping? Take some of that glucose gel.' It was fast-acting and would bring his sugar back up.

'Kaj, it's Antoine.' And he sounded frantic. 'Where are you?'

'With Phin, on our way back from seeing Aaron at the jail. Antoine, what's wrong?'

Phin glanced down to meet Kaj's eyes. 'Speaker, please.'

Kaj did so. 'You're on speaker. How's André?'

'In recovery. But, Kaj, you need to get home right away. Elijah's there alone.'

Kaj couldn't breathe. Elijah's blood sugar was continuing to drop. *'What?'*

'Intruders,' Antoine said. 'My phone alerted when the perimeter was breached. It was MaryBeth's van, but . . .' His voice hitched. 'She was hijacked. Shot in front of your house. Burke was shot on your porch when he went out to help her.'

But what about Elijah? *Elijah, be okay. Please be okay.*

'MaryBeth was bait,' Phin said tightly.

'Yeah,' Antoine choked out. 'Burke's hurt. Real bad. Cops are just arriving, but they should have been there already. Kaj, they carried Val out.'

'Who did?' Kaj demanded, fighting back the panic that closed his throat. 'The cops?'

'No, the men who broke in. They wore ski masks. Three went in. Two came out carrying Val.'

Terror froze him. *They took Val. Val is gone.* 'Elijah?'

'They didn't bring him out. Jace either. They're still inside.'

The safe room, Kaj thought, his mind in a tailspin. *Please be all right.*

'Had to be Corey, Bobby, and Ed.' Phin was grim.

'Tell the cops that the shot that hit Burke wasn't from any of the three guys, either. It had to have come from the house directly across the street from Kaj's, probably a long-range rifle. The men in the van couldn't have gotten the right angle. Tell them that the rifle was suppressed. There's no gunshot on the camera audio.'

'Got it.' Phin accelerated. 'Stay on the line, Antoine. Keep watching the cameras. Can you track Val's phone?'

'Cops are there now,' Antoine said. 'EMTs too. I called 911 as soon as I saw MaryBeth and Burke go down. Val's phone is in the house.'

Phin pulled into his driveway and Kaj was out before the vehicle had come to a stop.

'Kaj!' Phin yelled. 'Wait!'

But Kaj couldn't wait. Phone clutched in his hand, he ran to his house, shoving at the uniformed officer who tried to block his path.

'Get out of my way,' Kaj shouted. 'Now.'

A familiar face approached. 'ADA Cardozo,' Detective Drysdale said gravely. 'We need you to wait outside.'

'No!' Kaj shoved the detective hard, twisting out of his grip. 'My son is in there.'

'No, he's not,' Drysdale said. 'We swept the house. Your son's not in there.'

'Did you check his bedroom?'

'There's an out-of-control dog in there. We opened the door enough to see that there was no one else in the room.'

'Fuck that,' Kaj growled. He shoved through the first responders, stumbling to a stop when he saw EMTs working on both Burke and MaryBeth. 'Oh my God,' he whispered.

One of the EMTs working on Burke looked up. 'Are you Kaj?'

Kaj could only nod.

'He wants to talk to you,' the EMT said. 'Make it fast. We need to load him up.'

Kaj dropped to one knee beside Burke's stretcher. 'I'm here, Burke.'

'Val,' he whispered. 'Took her.'

'I know. Antoine told me. We'll find her. Where are Elijah and Jace?'

'Safe room,' Burke said. 'Told them to go. I'm sorry.'

'Sorry, sir. We gotta go.' The EMTs wheeled the stretcher into the ambulance and Kaj turned to the next EMT team, who were putting an IV in MaryBeth's arm.

'She's unconscious,' one of the EMTs said. 'She's lost a lot of blood. Do you know who her emergency contact is?' he called over his shoulder as they wheeled her to a second ambulance.

'Her wife. Jessica. They run a bakery. Marica's in the Quarter.'

'I know the place,' one of the uniforms said. 'We'll send someone to the bakery to inform her wife and take her to the hospital. But ADA Cardozo, please step aside. We have to preserve the crime scene.'

Kaj wheeled on the man, letting his fury free. 'My *son* is in there. Stay the fuck out of my way.' He barreled up the front steps and into his house, staying clear of the pools of blood.

So much blood.

There was more blood inside the house. A man in black lay in front of the coat closet, a ski mask over his head. But the ski mask was dark with blood.

And then . . . 'Oh my God. Jace.' A third set of EMTs crouched by the young man, transferring him to a stretcher. His T-shirt was solid red. Jace reached a bloody hand to Kaj.

Kaj grasped it. 'Jace.'

'Sir. They took Val. Corey and Bobby. They came.'

'I know.' He managed to keep his voice level even though a sob was rising in his throat. 'What happened, Jace?'

'Elijah. He's in the safe room. I pushed him in. Made him lock the door.'

Relief had Kaj's knees buckling. 'Corey didn't find him.'

'Corey was so mad.' Jace groaned, his grip on Kaj's hand tightening. 'I . . . got him out of Elijah's room. Tried to stop him from hurting Val.'

'Did Corey shoot you?'

'Yeah. Hurt Val. Please, sir. Get her back.'

'I will. Molly and Antoine are at the hospital already. I'll make sure one of them meets you in the ER. You won't be alone, son.'

'I'm sorry, Mr. Cardozo. I'm so sorry. I tried.'

Kaj pushed the boy's hair off his face. 'Don't say that. You were brave, Jace. Thank you. I'll come and see you as soon as I can.'

'Find Val.'

'I will,' he promised, then stepped back when the EMT pointed to the door.

'We need to go. Do you know his next of kin or guardian?' the EMT asked. 'He says he's only fifteen.'

'Me,' Kaj said. 'I'm his guardian.' He'd make it true somehow. 'The brother with legal guardianship was the one who did this to him, so use my name for now.'

'The hospital will have to call children's services,' the EMT said, 'since he's a minor. But we'll note what you said in the report.'

Jaw tight, Kaj wiped his bloody hand on his pants as he took the stairs two at a time. An officer stood outside Elijah's bedroom door, blocking Kaj's entry.

'Sorry, sir. There's a violent dog in there.'

'I'll take care of the dog. He knows me and is protecting my son. Please move.'

'I can't, sir. I'm under orders not to let anyone inside until we've dealt with the dog.'

'He's my girlfriend's dog. *Move.*' Kaj shoved him to the side and opened the door enough to slide through. Czar stood in front of Elijah's closet door, snarling. Closing the door behind his back, Kaj swallowed hard. 'Czar. Settle down.' He held out his hand, hoping the dog would recognize his scent.

He wasn't sure if the animal was mentally present. He was snarling and pacing in front of the door like a caged lion. 'Czar, easy.'

For a tense moment, Kaj stared the dog down. Then Czar lunged, but instead of a bite, Kaj felt a cold nose nuzzling into his hand as Czar whined pitifully.

Kaj exhaled, his heart pounding. 'I know, boy,' he murmured. He petted Czar's head, then stepped around him to open the closet door. The clothes were spread out over the safe room door, obscuring it. Jace had to have done that, too.

Jace should have been in the safe room with Elijah. *Why did you do it, Jace?*

But he knew the answer. Jace was trying to earn safety. A home. Love.

Tears burned Kaj's eyes. 'Elijah?' he called hoarsely. He pushed the clothes aside, exposing the door to the safe room. 'Elijah, baby? It's Dad. Please open the door.'

Czar shuffled into the closet and leaned against Kaj's legs.

'Elijah?' Fear began to tighten around his heart again. 'Come on out, son.' And then Kaj remembered the code word they agreed to only hours before. 'Midway, Elijah. *Midway.*'

Relief swamped him when he heard Elijah disengaging the lock. The door opened and his son flew into his arms. 'Dad,' Elijah sobbed.

Kaj dropped to his knees, wrapping Elijah in his arms. 'Oh God, you're okay.'

'Jace. He wouldn't come in with me.'

'I know, I just saw him. He's on his way to the hospital.'

Elijah pulled back, his mouth open, his breaths coming too fast as he hiccupped between sobs. His skin was clammy, his face pale. 'Corey hurt him?'

Dammit. Of course Elijah hadn't known. 'Yes, but the hospital will fix him up.'

'Where's Val?' Kaj went still and then Elijah did also. 'Dad? Is she . . . here?'

Kaj knew what his son was asking. *Is she alive?* They were the words Elijah had used as a little boy when they'd been sitting at Heather's deathbed, wondering if his mother was still breathing. That Elijah used those same words now nearly broke Kaj's heart into two.

'Val was taken.' Elijah's body shuddered and his sobs grew more intense as he cried, 'No, no, no.' Kaj held his son tighter, the same words throbbing in his own mind. *No, no, no.* 'We're going to bring her back.'

I'm going to bring her home.

But where do I start?

With Corey. Corey had taken Val, just like he'd taken Noni Feldman. Corey was still trying to get his hands on Bella. He'd taken Noni either to force her to tell him her source—a traitor in Corey's organization—or in the hopes that Noni knew where Bella was.

That was why Corey had tried to get to Kaj yesterday. Corey thought that Kaj knew where Bella was hiding. He'd come here today looking for Kaj. Looking for Elijah.

Corey had planned to trade Elijah for Bella's location. Just like Rick had planned to trade Elijah for Aaron's freedom. But Corey hadn't been able to find him, so he'd taken Val. Because they'd seen him with Val yesterday in front of Sylvi's shop. They knew that Val was important to Kaj.

So damn important.

Aaron had been certain that Corey would go to the camp near Lake

Cataouatche. *All I need to do is find that camp.* He'd have Antoine start searching the property records, but Kaj would also ask Val's family. Ivan might have left a record. Or a deed. *Something.*

Kaj backed out of the safe room and closed the closet door. He tilted Elijah's chin up so that their gazes met. 'Did you give yourself insulin?'

Elijah nodded, his eyelids fluttering shut.

'How much?' Kaj demanded, but Elijah didn't answer. *Oh no.* He was passing out.

Kaj checked the app that received the data from Elijah's glucose monitor. It had dropped even lower. Hands shaking, he found a tube of the glucose gel he'd always carried in his pocket since the last time Elijah had become hypoglycemic and squeezed it onto his son's tongue.

'Swallow it, baby,' he urged, stroking Elijah's throat until he swallowed. Then he scooped Elijah into his arms and ran out of the room, Czar on his heels.

'What the hell?' the officer standing guard asked. 'Where was the kid?'

Kaj didn't answer. He ran outside, meeting Phin on the front lawn and ignoring the startled cries from the cops at the sight of Elijah. 'Get me to the hospital. Please.'

Phin opened the back driver-side door so that Kaj could lay Elijah on the seat, then opened the hatch for Czar to jump into. Kaj sat in the back with Elijah. 'Hurry. Please.'

27

'STOP STARING AT me like that, Dad,' Elijah said wearily. 'You're stressing me out more.'

Kaj dropped into the chair next to Elijah's bed in the ER bay. His mind was racing and his heart was still pounding. Burke was in surgery, as were Jace and MaryBeth.

And Val was still gone.

Dr. Ross, Elijah's pediatric endocrinologist, parted the curtain surrounding them. 'Elijah's right. You gave him glucose and got him here quickly. He's going to be fine.'

Elijah had unintentionally taken too much insulin while waiting in the safe room. When he'd woken up in the SUV, he'd told Kaj that he'd figured his sugar was rising because of the stress, as it had done the previous times that week, but he hadn't had his phone to test his levels. So he'd guessed and, in his fear, had guessed wrong.

'That's not what has him so upset,' Elijah confided. 'Not the only thing, anyway.'

Dr. Ross nodded. 'I heard about what happened. If you need to step away and do . . . whatever, please know that we'll be taking good care of Elijah.'

'I can leave soon, though,' Elijah said. 'Right?'

'Depends on your definition of "soon",' the doctor countered. 'If you remain stable, you can leave sometime this evening. Okay?'

Elijah sighed. 'Okay.' He waited until the doctor had left the cubicle. 'Dad, you have to find Val. I don't need you right now. She does.'

'I'm waiting on a few phone calls,' he said instead, which was true. The one he was most anxious about was from Corey, who still hadn't called with his demands. 'Molly said she'd call when she found someone to stay with you, so that I can search for Val.' As Burke's second, Molly was coordinating security for both Elijah and him.

'Is Molly still with Antoine?'

'No, she went to get Sylvi.' He brushed the hair off Elijah's forehead, which was thankfully no longer clammy and cold. 'When they get here, I'll need to step away.' Because Val's sister was bringing the boxes of Ivan's papers that Val had stored in her attic.

That was where they'd start looking for the property that Aaron had been talking about.

'Hello?' The curtain parted, and Molly stuck her head in. 'How are you doing, kiddo?'

'Better than Dad is,' Elijah said. 'Do you have news?'

'Not yet. Everyone's still in surgery except for André. He should be waking up in recovery soon.'

Elijah nodded. 'Jace tried to save me. Again.'

Molly's expression became so sad that Kaj's eyes burned. 'I know, honey. And we'll make sure he gets the very best care. I promise.' She turned to Kaj. 'A moment?'

Kaj rose and kissed Elijah's forehead. 'I'll be just outside the curtain.'

Elijah grabbed Kaj's shirt with the hand that wasn't hooked up to an IV. 'Dad. Find Val. *Please.*'

His throat thick, Kaj just nodded and kissed Elijah's forehead again. 'Love you.'

'Love you, too. Now go.' He looked over at Molly. 'Tell him that I will be fine here.'

'Of course you will,' Molly said firmly. 'Lucien is back in town. He and my sister are on their way in to stay with you.'

Elijah's relief showed. His son had been talking a brave game but clearly hadn't relished being alone, and he already knew Lucien. 'Thanks.'

'You're welcome.' Molly waved, then tugged Kaj out of the cubicle.

Kaj found Phin waiting outside the curtain. Molly pulled it shut behind them, shielding Elijah from their conversation. 'I can't think,' Kaj admitted.

'Yes, you can,' Molly said in a no-nonsense tone. 'At least enough to go through the papers that Sylvi brought. Phin's going to sit with Elijah until Lucien and Chelsea get here. Now, let's go. The staff said we could use a family waiting room.'

Smiling wryly, Phin held up a deck of cards. 'Got these in the gift shop. Kid'll probably kick my ass, but it'll keep his mind off you. Go. I've got this.'

'Thank you,' Kaj said, gratitude washing over him.

He followed Molly to a small room with a lumpy sofa and a few hard plastic chairs. Sylvi stood against one wall, trembling, two boxes at her feet.

'How's Elijah doing?' Sylvi's voice broke, her eyes red and puffy.

Kaj cleared his throat. He would not cry. If he did, he might not stop. 'Much better. Thanks for bringing these. We're hoping that there's something in Van's records that will help direct us to the property.'

'Aaron really said that my brother owned the land?' Sylvi pressed. 'Why would Aaron help us? He killed my brother.'

Kaj had sent Molly to Sylvi's shop to tell her that Val had been taken. Sylvi had been in shock but had rallied quickly. The younger woman was as strong as her sister.

Molly had a key to Val's house, and the two of them had retrieved the boxes of papers.

'He did,' Kaj confirmed. 'Aaron's angry that Corey tried to kill Jace and Rick. Whether he was telling the truth remains to be seen.'

'Let's find out.' Molly handed them sterile gloves. 'Put these on.'

'Shouldn't we give these papers to the police?' Sylvi asked.

'Technically, we are handing them over to law enforcement,' Molly said. 'Kaj's the ADA.' She moved one of the boxes close to the sofa. 'Kaj?'

He blinked, realizing he'd zoned out, worrying about Val. 'Sorry.' Kaj pulled on the gloves and took the other box. 'My mind is racing.'

Molly shot him a look of sympathy. 'I get that. Rein it in. Get to work.'

Her tone was exactly the shove that Kaj needed. He pulled out a stack of papers. 'These are financial records,' he said after a few minutes. 'Ivan seems to have had a few aliases.'

Sylvi took a tablet from her purse. 'Tell me what they are. I'll take notes.'

The list of aliases was ten long by the time Kaj had made it through the first stack. 'These names are listed as owners of bank accounts. I wonder if the accounts are still active.'

'Does that matter?' Sylvi asked. 'I don't want his drug money. Neither will Ingrid.'

'If these are still active, they could be autopaying things like property taxes or insurance,' Kaj explained. 'I need a laptop.'

Molly dialed her cell phone. 'Antoine, we need one of your laptops.' She listened, then told Antoine where they were. Two minutes later, Antoine joined them, his three laptop bags hanging from his body.

'You rang?' he asked, his eyes haggard and worry-worn.

'Have a seat,' Kaj said. 'We need you and your machines to do internet searches.'

Antoine opened his laptops, typed in the passwords, then gave one to Molly and another to Kaj. He glanced at Sylvi. 'I have my own Wi-Fi. I'll send you the password so you can use your tablet. What are we searching?'

'Property records,' Kaj said. 'The property that Aaron thinks Corey's using as a hideout is west of Lake Cataouatche, which is in St. Charles Parish. Look up their property records website and start searching on the Ivan aliases we've found so far.'

'Makes sense,' Antoine said. 'Let's do this. What's the first name?'

Sylvi grimaced. 'John Smith.'

Kaj typed it in the search page. 'Less than ten results.' He plugged the addresses into Google Maps. 'None of them in the bayou. Next name?'

Thirty minutes later, they'd found no properties in the bayou or elsewhere under any of Ivan's names, and Kaj's anxiety was ramping up.

'Back to the box,' Molly said and pulled out another stack of papers. A folder of photographs spilled onto the floor, and Sylvi knelt to pick them up.

'Oh my God,' she whispered, horrified. 'What is this?'

Kaj knelt beside her and his stomach rolled. 'Fucking hell.'

Lake Cataouatche, Louisiana
FRIDAY, OCTOBER 28, 12:45 P.M.

Noni didn't want to open her eyes. Everything hurt. Hell, maybe she was dead. She heard music. Yes, there was music. Familiar music. *Humming, maybe. Yes. Quiet humming.*

I know this song. 'Tears in Heaven.' So sad.

Maybe I am dead, she thought and hummed along until even that started to hurt.

'Are you awake?' a voice whispered. 'Honey, you need to wake up. We need to get out of here.'

'Sing,' Noni managed. She didn't want the voice to talk. Just hum.

Something pressed against her lips, making her whimper.

'Take a drink. Just a sip. It's water. Only water.'

The voice was a woman. Not a man. Not the one who'd hurt her.

'Come on, honey. Open your mouth. Just a little bit.'

Noni tried and a little water filled her mouth.

'That's good,' the woman said soothingly. 'Now swallow.'

Noni swallowed. The water felt good. 'Than—' The word wouldn't come. *Thank you*, she thought and hoped the woman would understand.

A hand stroked her hair. 'You're welcome, sweetie.'

Noni struggled to open her eyes but could not.

'It's okay,' the woman whispered. 'Don't open your eyes. There's nothin' to see here.' The woman's breath hitched. 'I think we're gonna die here.'

'Who . . .' Noni tried.

'My name is Dianne and I'm stuck here, too. I'm so sorry,' she said mournfully. 'I couldn't make them stop. I was in the other room. I could hear them, but . . . I couldn't do anything. I was too scared. I'm so sorry.'

'S'ri,' Noni whispered. It was all right. There wasn't anything Dianne could have done.

Dianne. Aaron Gates's wife was named Dianne. *Same woman?*

Noni's thoughts began to clear. *'Tears in Heaven.'* It was about a child's death. Dianne's son had died.

Dianne Gates is here. What is she doing here? 'Why y—?'

'Why am I here?' Dianne guessed. Her hand stroked Noni's hair, and Noni thought it might be the only place on her body that didn't hurt. 'I'm not completely certain. The last thing I really remember is Corey doing that interview in front of his house. You were there. Next thing I knew I was in a little house on the bayou. Someone left me some vodka and . . . well, I drank it. Next thing I knew, I was here. I heard Corey and Ed talking—yesterday, I think. I think they were talking about killing me to keep me quiet, but Ed had said that when he sees me, he sees Liam.' Dianne shuddered out a heartbreaking sigh. 'Join the club. When I close my eyes, my baby is all I see. Most days I wish I could die, too.'

'Ssssry,' Noni tried. *Sorry.*

'Thank you,' Dianne said sadly. 'But I guess I don't really want to die because Ed gave me a bottle of doctored booze last night and I only pretended to drink it. So . . . I was awake and heard them this morning. Doing that to you. My God. Bobby's an animal. I never knew.'

So tired. Don't wanna think. Don't wanna remember.

'I want to get you out of here,' Dianne went on. 'But I can't carry you and I'd be afraid to drag you, even if I had anywhere to drag you to. They took both of the boats.'

She resumed humming that sad, sad song and Noni let her thoughts drift away.

Lake Salvador, Louisiana
FRIDAY, OCTOBER 28, 1:45 P.M.

Corey brought the boat to a floating stop next to the second boat they'd left behind as an emergency getaway. It was supposed to have been for Ed, in case they got separated.

They had gotten separated, but permanently. Corey's throat closed up, partly in grief and partly in panic. Ed was a critical part of their operation and now he was gone.

The blonde would pay for that, too. But he couldn't let himself think about Ed yet. He needed to secure their hostage. *Later.* He'd worry about Ed later.

'You take it back to the camp,' Corey told Bobby. 'I'll stay in this one.'

Bobby eyed the tarp-covered figure in the boat's belly. 'I can take this one.'

Corey didn't trust Bobby to be alone with their prisoner. They needed the blonde as leverage against Cardozo first. 'That's all right. I've got her. I'll meet you back at camp.'

Bobby frowned like a spoiled child deprived of a toy. 'You never let me have fun.'

The truth was that Bobby's fun was getting out of hand. He'd gotten way too excited with Noni Feldman that morning. They'd be lucky if the woman was still alive when they returned.

'I have to have something of value to trade to Cardozo.' Because Cardozo wouldn't want to comply. He wouldn't want to give up Bella Butler, but in the end, he would. 'Besides, I get dibs. We've been over this. If I let you go first, you won't leave any of her for me.'

'You'll have plenty left over of her,' Bobby said, almost whining.

'Like you left plenty of Noni Feldman this morning?' Corey demanded.

Bobby's jaw hardened. 'I didn't kill her.'

Only because Corey had made him stop. 'We need Feldman to draw Allyson.'

'Can I have Allyson?'

'Yes. You can have her all to yourself.'

'And this one?' Bobby asked, nudging the Sorensen woman. 'Can I have her after you're done with her?'

'Yes,' Corey snapped, exasperated. 'But not until we have Bella *in our hands*. Do you understand?'

'Yeah, yeah,' Bobby grumbled. 'I understand.'

I swear, the man is like an insane toddler. 'Good. Take that boat back to the camp. I'll meet you there.'

Bobby began to move from one boat to the other but stopped,

holding his phone, which was buzzing with an incoming call. 'It's my buddy.'

Bobby's buddy, who was one of André Holmes's trusted men. Always master of the understatement, was Bobby.

'Answer it. Put it on speaker.'

'You gotta be quiet,' Bobby said. 'You're not supposed to know who he is.'

Corey mimed zipping his lips and Bobby accepted the call. 'What's up?' Bobby asked.

'I did what you said to do,' Drysdale said, and he sounded afraid. 'Send me my money.'

Corey frowned at Bobby. 'What money?' he mouthed.

Bobby waved as if it were no consequence. 'You'll get it when this job is done. I haven't gotten my share yet, so I can't pay you. We discussed this.'

'I have to get out of town. Out of the country. I've waited too long as it is.'

'Look, I didn't tell you to gut Holmes. You did that on your own.'

'Because he knows. He called me last night, said I had to meet him this morning at work, early. I knew something was up because he sounded too casual. Everyone knows he runs at the same time every morning, so I went to his house early and waited for him to come out. He saw me and we fought. He told me that he knew it was me, that he saw me near Cardozo on video.'

'What video?' Corey mouthed.

'What video?' Bobby asked.

'It was work I was doing for Talley. He wanted to know Cardozo's weak spot, which is his kid. But Talley couldn't find anything on the kid, so he asked me to investigate.'

'You were on Dewey's payroll, too?' Bobby asked, surprised.

'How do you think Talley stayed hidden all this time?' Drysdale demanded.

'Huh. So what's this about a video?' Bobby asked, serious now.

'I was standing in the lobby of NOPD in the Quarter and heard Cardozo take a call from his kid. The kid had come from a math competition and Cardozo was excited for him. I looked up math competitions for all the schools and figured out which one Cardozo's kid attends. It's some small private school, which is why the boy was so hard to find. I told Talley and he was going to grab the kid on Monday night.'

'But Rick did it instead,' Bobby said slowly.

'I don't know why the Gates kid did it. But Cardozo figured that was how his son's schedule was found out—from that overheard conversation. Holmes asked me to view the tapes, to figure it out. I scrubbed that part of the tape.'

'But Holmes found it,' Bobby said.

'Yeah. There was another server—a backup—that I didn't know about. Holmes found the video and confronted me.'

'Why didn't you just kill him?' Bobby asked.

'I tried. I didn't want to fire my gun. We were outside his house and his fiancée would have heard a shot, so I stabbed him. I really thought I *had* killed him, but the bastard didn't die.' Drysdale's voice ratcheted louder and higher as he spoke. 'His fiancée found him and now he's out of surgery and waking up. I waited as long as I could. I helped you today. I made sure no one checked who was driving the bakery van *and* I redirected the cops to give you time to get away from Cardozo's house, but I need to get out of here. *Now.*'

'Ask him where Cardozo is,' Corey mouthed.

'Okay. I'll get you the money. I promise. As soon as I get to where I'm going, I'll put it in your bank account. But I need a little more info. Where is Cardozo now?'

'In the hospital with his kid. We didn't know it, but his kid was in a safe room inside the house. The kid's here now, along with Broussard and all of the others.'

What? The kid was there all along? Fucking Cardozo. Building a fucking safe room. *Fucking dog keeping me out of the room.*

'With Broussard?' Bobby clarified. 'He's alive?'

'Yes.'

'Well, fuck. I thought we'd killed him. What about the bakery girl? And Corey's asshole little brother?'

'They're all still alive.'

'Damn,' Bobby muttered. 'Did you know Jace was there?'

'Hell no! I would've told you. When will I get my money?'

'Tell him to follow Cardozo,' Corey mouthed. 'We're going to call Cardozo in a minute.' To demand he tell them where Bella Butler was hiding.

'I need you to do one more thing while I'm getting your money together,' Bobby said. 'I'm about to call Cardozo and give him our terms of release for the blonde. I want you to keep tabs on him.'

'No. I told you, Holmes is in recovery. When he wakes up, he's going to tell who stabbed him. I do not want to be around when that happens.' The man drew a breath. 'I have more information that you'll want, but I want my money.'

'What is it?' Bobby asked. 'Tell me and I'll tell you what it's worth.'

'This is worth a lot. You can use it to make Cardozo do whatever you want.'

Bobby snarled. 'Tell me.'

'Sorensen got raped by three guys when she was in the Marines. Other Marines. Big guys. She hid at first, but they found her. One of them taunted her, "Come out, come out, wherever you are." It was in the trial transcripts. If you tell Cardozo that you'll do the same to her, he'll fold in a heartbeat.'

'How do you know this?' Bobby asked suspiciously.

'I have access to Holmes's email and files. He had background checks run on the Sorensen woman last summer when she killed two intruders while on a job for Broussard. That's also how I knew

Cardozo's personal cell phone number, which I also gave you like you asked. So give me my money.'

Bobby's brows lifted as he shared a greedy glance with Corey. 'You have Holmes's passwords? I want them.'

'I'll give them to you when I get my money.'

'If you want your money, you will keep tabs on Cardozo,' Bobby said coldly.

'Landry, I did what you asked,' Drysdale whined.

'And you'll continue to do so,' Bobby said angrily. 'We want to know what Cardozo's doing. Knowing him, he'll give us a fake address for Bella and arrange for a bunch of snipers to be waiting for us. You get close to him and find out what he's up to.'

'I'm not going back into the hospital. There's cops crawling all over the place right now. I couldn't get close to him if I tried.'

'You will do as I say,' Bobby snarled, then gentled his voice. 'Look, I know you're doing this for your kid. But if you want little Laurel to keep breathing, you'll do what I say. Otherwise, we'll do to her what those Marines did to Sorensen. What *we're* going to do to Sorensen. Depends on you.'

Drysdale gasped. 'You're a bastard.'

'I really am.' Bobby ended the call and grinned, his humor restored. 'I figured threatening his kid's virtue or her life would have equal results. He'll make sure Cardozo isn't pulling a fast one on us.'

'Why exactly *is* Drysdale doing this? What's going on with his kid?' Corey hoped she didn't have cancer. That would hit too close to home.

'He needs the money. His kid's at some fancy college up north that costs like seventy, eighty grand a year.'

'A *year*?' Corey asked, appalled. 'You're shitting me.'

'Nope. I didn't know he was working for Dewey, but his daughter's a senior now, so he would have needed the money right around the time that Dewey went under after Ivan kicked it. You gonna call Cardozo now? I want to listen.'

'Let's call him right now.'

'Are you going to use the info Drysdale just gave us? About the Marines?'

'Not yet. I'll use it to prod him along if he drags his feet.' Corey frowned. 'Ed never mentioned that the woman had a military record.'

It made him wonder if there was anything else that Ed had missed, but he'd never know.

Goddammit. Panic started to rise at the thought of replacing Ed, but he pushed it away. *Focus. Now. You'll figure Ed's replacement out. You always do.*

Mid-City, New Orleans, Louisiana
FRIDAY, OCTOBER 28, 2:00 P.M.

Kaj stared at the photos that had come from Ivan's box. Three bodies. All men. Two were hanging from nooses. The third had a bullet through his head.

'The folder has Ingrid's name on it,' Sylvi said. 'What is this?'

Kaj had a terrible feeling that he knew exactly what this was. Each photo had a name printed on it. The victim who'd been shot in the head was Eric Haynes, and Kaj knew that name.

This was one of the men who'd assaulted Val. The one who'd stalked her when she'd come home. He could only assume that the other two were also her rapists. Val had told her brother about her assault, and Ivan had 'taken care' of things.

He let out a breath, aware of the others staring at him. 'It's not my story to tell.'

Sylvi shook her head. 'But—' Kaj could see the moment that she understood. She covered her mouth with her hand. 'Oh.'

He slid the photos back into the folder and set it aside. 'She didn't know that Van did this,' he murmured.

Molly grabbed the folder, scanning each photo, her face growing more and more upset with each one. 'Of course she didn't know,' she snapped. 'Goddammit.' She closed her eyes for a moment and when she looked up again, she was back in control. 'She told her brother?'

Kaj was startled until he remembered that Molly was one of the only other people who Val had told. *And then she trusted me with this, too.*

'Yes, but no one else in her family.' He glanced at Sylvi. 'She didn't want to worry your parents.'

'Oh, Ingrid,' Sylvi said sadly.

Antoine shoved the photos into his computer bag. 'I don't want to know, and Val doesn't need to know. Agreed?' He stared at each of them until they nodded. 'Fine. What's next?'

'We keep looking for a deed to the bayou property,' Kaj said grimly. He took the rest of the papers from his box and set them on the floor. 'Oh.'

At the bottom of the box were two thumb drives.

From one of his bags, Antoine pulled a fourth computer, a no-frills model.

'Four laptops, Antoine?' Molly asked. 'Really?'

'This is my junk machine,' he explained. 'It's not hooked up to the net and can't be hacked.' He plugged in the first thumb drive and scanned the list of files. 'All spreadsheets.' He clicked on each one and shook his head. 'Lots of information about his cash flow along with account numbers, but that isn't what we're looking for right now.' He tried the second, a smile spreading across his face.

Kaj felt hope for the first time since he'd discovered Val had been taken. 'What?'

Antoine grinned. 'A list of his shell corporations. I'm betting that his properties weren't bought under the aliases, although we could have connected them had we continued to dig. The aliases we searched for are all "officers" in said corporations.' He recited the names of four of the corporations and they each looked one up in the St. Charles Parish property records.

The first ten corporations owned no property in the bayou. All owned homes in the New Orleans suburbs. 'I wonder if he was making or dealing his drugs out of these places,' Kaj said.

'Yes to at least one,' Sylvi said. She turned her tablet so that they could see the pin on the map. 'This address is the café where Van was killed.'

'Got it,' Molly crowed. 'A parcel west of Lake Cataouatche.'

Kaj nearly doubled over in relief. 'We found it.'

But the relief was gone seconds later when his phone rang. 'It says "Private number",' he said, regarding his phone like a snake ready to strike.

'Put it on speaker,' Molly said.

Kaj activated his phone's recorder, then put it on speaker. 'Cardozo.'

'We have her.'

Kaj's blood ran cold as he recognized Corey Gates's voice. 'Where?' he asked, abject terror threatening to steal his breath. He knew he sounded scared, because he was scared. Even though they might know where Corey was hiding, it didn't mean they'd get to Val in time.

'Someplace you can't find,' Corey said. 'I want Bella Butler.'

It was as Kaj had suspected. 'I don't know where she is. She didn't tell me.'

'Then you'd best find out,' he said. 'You have two hours until I call you again and at that time, you'll give me Bella's coordinates. If you don't, we'll start in on your girlfriend. It's real simple, Cardozo. Give us Bella or you'll get your woman back in pieces.'

Kaj froze as panic spread through him from the inside out.

Molly mouthed, 'Stall him.'

Kaj's breath stuttered. 'I . . . can't. I only communicate with Miss

Butler once a day. She contacts me to tell me that she's okay. I don't know where she is.'

'You've got your little team of super friends,' Corey said mockingly. 'Have that computer nerd brother of André Holmes trace her calls.'

'He'll need more time.'

'He's supposed to be a genius. Make him work. Two hours or your bodyguard will die.'

'Wait,' Kaj said urgently. 'I want proof of life. I want to talk to her.'

'Sorry. She's asleep right now.'

Kaj swallowed audibly. 'Asleep or unconscious?'

'Dunno and don't care. You have one hour and fifty-eight minutes. And I'd advise you tell your computer guy not to bother wasting his time trying to track this call. He won't find me. Use your time to find Bella.'

Lake Cataouatche, Louisiana
FRIDAY, OCTOBER 28, 2:35 P.M.

Noni was fading in and out. Everything still hurt, but she wasn't alone. Dianne still sat with her on the floor, stroking her hair. And singing.

Dianne's humming abruptly stilled, as did the hand stroking Noni's hair.

What? Noni wanted to ask but couldn't call up the breath to force the word out.

'Boats,' Dianne said, her dread a palpable thing. 'Two of them. They're coming back. I have to get back to my room. Pretend you're unconscious. They'll leave you alone if they think you're passed out.' She scrambled to her feet and Noni heard the closing of the door as Dianne ran back to wherever she'd been kept.

Noni wouldn't have to pretend to be unconscious. She was so tired and there was peace in the darkness. *Just let go.*

But Noni kept breathing. Her heart kept beating, even as she willed it to stop. *Please don't hurt me anymore.*

'Put her in with Feldman,' a man said. Corey.

'C'mon, Corey,' another man whined, and Noni's beating heart stuttered. *Bobby.* The one who'd . . . 'Just let me play a little. You'll still be able to trade her. I won't leave any marks.'

'No,' Corey barked. 'Put her in with Feldman.'

They were coming closer.

Put who in the bedroom? Trade her? To whom? For what?

Footsteps pounded across the floor before there was a thud. Like they'd dropped something. *Or someone.*

'Leave her,' Corey ordered. 'And check Dianne.'

Bobby's footsteps pounded again, coming close to Noni's head, but he didn't kick. Instead, his footsteps faded and there was quiet for a while. Until Bobby came back.

'Dianne's still passed out,' Bobby reported. 'Is Feldman still breathing?'

Corey came closer, knees popping as he crouched beside Noni. She tried to flinch away when he pressed fingers to her throat, but . . .

So tired.

'She alive?' Bobby asked.

'Barely,' Corey said, then straightened. 'Let's clean up. I need to stitch up your arm and clean out mine where that fucking dog bit me. All I need now is an infection.'

The door slammed closed and Noni wondered who they'd dropped beside her. She wondered if the woman would ever be able to tell her her name.

I'm sorry, whoever you are.

They'd be dying here together.

28

K AJ STARED AT his phone, shaken from Corey's call and fighting the need to throw up. 'Is that true, Antoine? That you can't track his phone?'

Antoine's expression was grim. 'It's a burner. Makes it . . . difficult.'

Kaj's heart sank. If Antoine said it was difficult, that meant close to impossible. 'We need to get there fast.'

'This property can't be accessed by road,' Molly said steadily, studying a map on her laptop screen, and once again, her no-nonsense tone helped Kaj get ahold of himself. 'Antoine, Farrah's still here with André, right? We need her boat. Her folks have a camp on Lake Salvador,' Molly explained to Kaj as Antoine called Farrah. 'It can be accessed by road. From there we'll take their boat to Lake Cataouatche. Farrah's family allows André and Antoine to use the boat anytime, but we need to make sure it's in working order.'

Antoine ended his call, then slid two keys from his key ring. 'These go to the lake house and the boat. Farrah says the boat is tuned up and gassed up. Who's going?'

'Phin and me.' Molly glanced at the incoming text on her phone. 'Lucien's with Elijah, so Phin's going to meet me at Burke's SUV. Antoine, you stay here. Keep us updated.'

Sylvi stood uncertainly. 'What about me? Should I go?'

'Stay here with Kaj,' Molly said kindly. 'We'll contact you as soon as we know something. And do not mention this to anyone. No cops, nobody.'

'I'm not staying behind,' Kaj said, gearing up for a fight. Elijah was being guarded by Lucien. But Val was still gone.

Molly sighed. 'It was worth a try. I've got an extra gun in the SUV. Can you use it?'

Kaj nodded, surprised that she'd agreed so quickly. 'Not as well as you, but yes.'

'You wearing Kevlar?' she asked.

'Yeah. Under my shirt.' Burke had insisted he wear it that morning.

'Good. Although it won't stop a high-powered rifle bullet. That's what got Burke. He was wearing a vest and now he's having a bullet removed from his thoracic cavity.'

'It'll have to do,' Kaj said, trying not to think of Burke on that stretcher, struggling to breathe. 'Unless Phin's got extra of the militarygrade armor.'

'He doesn't. Antoine, can you keep Ivan's papers safe?'

'Of course. And I'll sit with Jace when he comes out of surgery. Farrah and half of the NOPD are in with André, Jessica's here for MaryBeth, and Joy's here for Burke. I don't want Jace to wake up alone.'

Molly nodded once. 'Then let's go.'

Sylvi followed them out, her eyes shadowed with fear. 'Please bring her home.'

'We will.' Kaj squeezed her arm. 'Go to the surgical waiting room. Burke's office manager Joy is there. You can sit with her until we get back.'

Antoine walked Sylvi to the waiting room, and Kaj and Molly hurried to the parking lot. 'We're going to be cutting it close,' Molly said. 'There's no fast way to get there.'

'Get where?'

Kaj and Molly spun around. Detective Drysdale was giving them a suspicious look.

Kaj faked a polite smile when he really wanted to hit the man for making Val second-guess herself last night. 'We're going out for some food.'

Drysdale's smile seemed forced. 'Then you won't mind if I tag along.'

Molly shook her head. 'After what you said to Val last night, you have some nerve, Detective. We can't stop you from following us, I suppose, but you're not riding with us.'

She and Kaj got into Burke's SUV just as Phin slid into the back seat.

'I don't like him,' Kaj said tightly.

'I don't, either.' Molly started the vehicle. 'We're going to lose him.' She left the lot, checking her rearview mirror. 'He's in pursuit.'

'Too bad I dropped Czar off at your sister's place, Molly,' Phin said. 'I'd like to let him deal with that asshole cop.'

Kaj sent a text to Elijah. *Had to leave for a bit. Be back as soon as I can. Love you.*

Love you too. Elijah's reply came with an attached photo of him in his hospital bed with Lucien and Molly's sister, Chelsea, standing by his side. Kaj had only met the woman a few times, but she was nearly as fierce as Molly.

'Elijah's fine,' Kaj said aloud. 'Who's guarding the others, Molly?'

'I called in some of the guys Burke uses on a part-time basis,' she said. 'Burke, Jace, and MaryBeth are covered, just in case Corey or Bobby are closer than we think and go after them. It's not likely, but we'll err on the side of caution. André's family is with him. His dad's a retired cop and called in some of his buddies to stand watch. Everyone is fine.'

'Good.' He was sliding his phone into his pocket when it buzzed with an incoming call from a number he didn't recognize. His heart started pounding again. 'Yes?' he answered, praying that Val was all right.

'ADA Cardozo, this is Drysdale. Tell Miss Sutton to slow down. She's driving erratically at a high rate of speed. If I didn't know better, I'd think you were trying to lose me.'

'I'll tell her.' Ending the call, he gave in to his urge to snarl. 'Drysdale says to . . .'

'Tell me what?' Molly asked.

But Kaj was staring at the phone in his hand. His *personal* phone.

'Kaj?' Molly pressed. 'What did Drysdale say to you?'

Both Drysdale and Corey had called him on his *personal* phone. Kaj only gave his number to those he allowed to call him Kaj, as a general rule. And Elijah, of course.

Val had it, as did the rest of Burke's group. Genie and her husband, René, had it.

He hadn't even given it to Reuben yet.

His breath hitched. 'André,' he murmured. André had had it, too. And that was all.

'Is André all right?' Molly scowled at her rearview. Drysdale must have still been behind them.

Drysdale. Kaj had thought that the man was a misogynist after he'd thrown Val's assault in her face, but now it was clear. 'Drysdale is André's leak.'

'Say more,' Molly said calmly before taking an abrupt turn onto a side road. Horns behind them blared. 'Because he's still behind us.'

'I have two phones. You all have my personal number, but not many people do. I gave it to André. Drysdale just called me on my personal cell.'

'You think André gave it to Drysdale?' Phin asked.

Kaj shook his head. 'André wouldn't share my personal information, but Drysdale might have found it in André's phone after he stabbed him, because Corey called me on my personal cell, too.'

Molly sucked in a breath. 'Sonofabitch.'

'And André had asked him to check the surveillance video to figure out who'd overheard me talking about Elijah's math meet,' Kaj added. 'Now that portion of the video's gone.'

'What do we do about him?' Phin asked coldly.

Kaj clenched his jaw. 'I want to kill him, but we can use him to redirect Corey. I need Corey away from Val or at least to distract his attention from her.' Because if Drysdale knew a piece of information, odds were good that Corey and Bobby would, too.

'What do you want to do?' Molly asked.

'We tell him that we're following a lead to find a missing witness,' Kaj decided. 'If he's working with Corey, he'll know that means Bella Butler.'

Molly nodded. 'We'll give him a fake address. He'll tell Corey, who'll go after Bella.'

'If we're lucky,' Phin said, 'Corey might take Bobby with him, but that's less likely. If I were Corey, I'd want my leverage guarded while I checked out the tip. If that's true, we've at least split the two up and only have to deal with one of them when we extract Val.'

'How do we feed information to Drysdale without him becoming suspicious?' Kaj asked.

'You'll tell him that you need to go back to the hospital,' Molly said, 'because Elijah needs you. I'll say, "I need to get to a witness ASAP to protect her, but now I have no ride." I'll go with Drysdale, directing him to the fake address, and have him park a block away. I'll get out to do recon and that'll give him a chance to call Corey.'

'Doesn't Bella have a lot of security?' Phin asked. 'I heard Antoine saying that that was the reason the online haters hadn't stormed her house yet.'

'Good point,' Molly conceded. 'I'll tell Drysdale that it's urgent because her security didn't show up today and she's worried about being alone. Corey will know that Allyson and the paramedic were involved in Corey's plot, so he might assume they're the ones who didn't show.'

Phin nodded his approval. 'Corey won't be able to resist that.'

'Exactly,' Molly said. 'Kaj, you'll tell your boss what's happening, and he'll get André's boss on board. He'll know the cops we can trust. They'll arrest Drysdale for stabbing André and all the other things he's done and then they'll wait for Corey to arrive. Ask André's boss to also bring a few of the cops to meet me. You two get to Farrah's boat and I'll bring the cops and meet you there. That will give us backup at Corey's camp, and we can get Val—and Bobby if he's there—while the cops get Corey when he comes to the fake safe house looking for Bella.'

Kaj shook his head. 'There are so many things wrong with this plan, Molly. You can't go alone with Drysdale.'

'I can if he doesn't suspect. Trust me, Kaj. Unless you have a better plan.'

He didn't. 'How will Phin and I find Corey's camp? How will we operate a boat?'

'I know how to operate a boat,' Phin said, 'but I don't know the bayou that well.'

Molly used her hands-free to dial on her cell phone. 'Farrah, it's Molly. Can your father guide Kaj and Phin through the bayou?' She listened, then thanked Farrah before ending the call. 'She's texting you the address, Kaj. Her father will meet you. He knows the bayou, maybe even better than Burke does. Are we all in agreement? Because we're wasting time.'

'Yes,' Phin said.

Kaj forced himself to breathe. 'Yes.'

'Then let's make this count, guys.' Molly put on her blinker and pulled her car to the side of the road. Drysdale stopped behind them. 'Showtime.'

Lake Cataouatche, Louisiana
FRIDAY, OCTOBER 28, 3:35 P.M.

'That stings,' Bobby whined, taking another swig of whatever rotgut was in the bottle he'd claimed from Ed's stash.

'I swear to God, you are such a baby,' Corey muttered as he cleaned out the gunshot wound in Bobby's arm. *We should have taken his exgirlfriend's first-aid kit.* Those liquid stitches he'd used on Corey had done the job. 'Hold still and stop the drinking. You're a crazy bastard when you're sober. I don't like you much when you're plastered.'

Bobby guzzled some more before setting the bottle aside. 'My arm hurts.'

'So does mine, and you don't see me whining all over the place. Now hold still.' He bandaged Bobby up, then leaned back in his chair to take a deep breath. 'Ed's dead.'

Bobby just looked at him. 'Yeah,' he said in a *duh* voice. 'Are we going to replace him?'

Bobby didn't sound too torn up about Ed's murder, but neither was Corey. Not yet, anyway. They were still running on adrenaline. Or adrenaline and booze, in Bobby's case. The loss would hit them soon enough. Remembering how devastated he'd been at Liam's death, Corey wasn't in a hurry to go through that again.

So he simply nodded. 'We'll need to find another tech guy. But let's get the Doyle job finished first.'

'We are going to lay low for a while after that, though, right?' Bobby looked uncharacteristically worried. 'We're beat up and hurt, and I need some downtime before we do this again.'

'We'll lay low.' He'd promised Ed that he would, and now the guy was dead. Keeping his promise seemed like the least that he could do.

'Good. I'm going to take a nap. I slept like shit last night and today has sucked balls. Wake me up if Drysdale calls.' He tossed his phone to the table and ambled toward the other bedroom.

'No,' Corey said sharply. 'You're not going in that room with Feldman and the blonde. I don't trust you. Sleep on the floor next to Dianne.'

Bobby gave him an icy glare. 'Fuck off, Corey. I'm not sleeping on the goddamn floor. My arm hurts.'

This was why Corey hated it when Bobby drank. He rose and grabbed Bobby's good arm, directing him to the outer door. 'Then snooze in the hammock.'

'Right,' Bobby drawled. 'Fine. I'll sleep outside. But call me if anything happens.'

'I will.' Corey watched Bobby make his way around to the back of the house where the hammock was strung between two trees. Then he closed the door, wishing he could rest, too. But he needed to stay awake until he'd dealt with Bella Butler.

After that, I'll find a beach and I'll sleep for a week.

It had been about an hour since he'd given Cardozo his deadline. Maybe it was time to up the ante a bit. Taking his phone, he went into the bedroom where they'd put Feldman and the blonde. He crouched beside the reporter and pressed two fingers to her throat.

Her pulse was even slower now. She didn't have long. *Dammit.* He was going to have to hunt for Allyson without having Feldman as bait, and he didn't have Ed to help him search.

He turned to the blonde. She kept her eyes closed, but her body was tight, like she was coiled and ready to spring. Corey wasn't too worried since she was restrained, but he wasn't taking any unnecessary risks.

'I know you're awake. Best open your eyes and say cheese.' Her eyes remained closed. 'Fine. Suit yourself.' He dialed the number Bobby had gotten from Drysdale—Cardozo's personal cell. Putting it on speaker, he waited for the man to pick up.

'Cardozo,' the prosecutor bit out.

Corey smiled when the blonde twitched. 'You find Bella? You've only got an hour left.'

'Not yet,' Cardozo said, his tone clipped. Anxious. Terrified. 'I have a lead, but I need more time.'

Corey's smile broadened at the man's fear. 'I'm sending you a photo. She's alive but refuses to open her eyes.' He snapped a photo of Val and texted it. 'She is unhurt.'

Cardozo made a noise like a strangled puppy. 'Her face is covered in blood.'

'Head wounds,' Corey said. 'Bleed like a bitch. Whatcha gonna do?'

'Let me talk to her.'

'She's gagged. She's not going to be doing any talking. What she will be doing is reliving past traumas if you don't hand over Bella Butler.'

Cardozo was silent for a long moment. 'What does that mean?' he asked quietly.

'It means that we know what happened to your girl over there. In the sandbox. Three big guys, taking turns with her. We only have two big guys left thanks to your bitch, but Bobby and I'll make her wish that those other guys had killed her when they had the chance. Do you understand?'

'You sonofabitch.'

'Do you understand?'

'Let me talk to her,' Cardozo snarled.

'Ball's in your court, Cardozo. Give me Bella, you get your woman back. One hour.' He ended the call and gave the blonde a swift kick in the hip. To her credit, she didn't move. She didn't even flinch. Had it not been for that tiny twitch when she had heard Cardozo's voice, he might have believed she was unconscious. She was good. Very good.

I'm better. 'Sit tight. I'll be back in an hour.'

Then, if Cardozo hadn't coughed up Bella's location, he'd start the hard stuff. He'd let Bobby have five minutes with her while he sent Cardozo the live video. But he didn't think he'd have to. Just the threat of it would be enough to get Cardozo to break.

He went back out to the common room and lowered himself into a chair, suddenly exhausted. He had an hour. He could close his eyes for that long.

He laid his head on the table and was almost asleep when Bobby's phone began to ring. Instantly alert, Corey grabbed it. Phone in hand, he ran to the hammock and poked Bobby in his good arm. 'Wake up. Your phone's ringing. It's Drysdale.'

Bobby lay sprawled, snoring loud enough to wake the dead, but unfortunately not loudly enough to wake himself. The bottle of whiskey was mostly gone.

Bobby was passed out drunk.

Corey wanted to kill him, especially when the phone stopped ringing. He grabbed the collar of Bobby's shirt with his good hand and shook, but Bobby didn't wake up. The fucking little baby. He couldn't take a little pain.

I'll show him a little pain.

But then the phone began to ring again and Corey answered it. 'Yeah?'

'Oh, I have the wrong—'

'No, you don't,' Corey interrupted. 'You're Bobby's friend, right? He's not here right now. Did you have a message for him?'

After a moment's hesitation Drysdale spoke again. 'Tell him that I know where his special lady is.'

Corey wanted to yell in triumph. 'Where?' he asked, pretending that he didn't know exactly who he was talking to. 'This is his friend, Corey. I work with him.'

'Tell him he needs to pay me first.'

Drysdale wanted money, but Bobby's threats against his daughter had gotten more traction. 'Look, I know he owes you money and he will pay you. But if he doesn't finish this job, there won't be any money. And I'll be pissed. I understand your daughter Laurel is in college up north. I'll kill her and send you the video so that you can watch it over and over.'

'No,' Drysdale gasped.

'Give me the address for our special lady.'

'Okay, but don't hurt Laurel.' And he spilled out the address.

Bella was in Metairie, not too far from Corey's house. And Drysdale said that she had no security because two of her security personnel hadn't shown up for work—Allyson being in the wind and Zach being dead. *Excellent*.

'That wasn't so hard, was it?' Corey asked Drysdale. 'Don't worry. You'll get paid. But if our special lady isn't at this address? Laurel's dead. So don't be wrong.'

Ending the call, he gave Bobby another shake. The asshole was in no shape to fetch Bella. But leaving Bobby alone with the three women? That was a stupid idea.

Except that Bobby would be sleeping like the dead for hours with all the booze he'd consumed. Especially on an empty stomach. They hadn't eaten since before they'd grabbed the little baker.

Corey pocketed Bobby's phone in case Drysdale called again, reloaded his Glock and his rifle, loaded up his pockets with full magazines, then grabbed a handful of Ed's protein bars.

He'd get real food after he got Bella.

He loaded the weapons and ammunition into his boat. He'd be back with Bella before Bobby woke up. But Bobby wouldn't be getting the blond bodyguard. He hadn't earned her, and Corey wasn't giving her back to Cardozo.

She'll be my reward.

Lake Cataouatche, Louisiana
FRIDAY, OCTOBER 28, 3:45 P.M.

Val stared up at the ceiling, struggling to stay calm. She couldn't cry anymore, not with the duct tape covering her mouth. She'd nearly suffocated in the damn trunk of that car, unable to breathe through her mouth when the tears had caused her nose to become stuffed up.

Corey had her. The man who'd watched while Aaron Gates gutted her brother had her. The man who'd tried to kill sweet Jace had her. The man who now knew exactly how to make her suffer by 'reliving her past traumas' had her. Hearing Corey threaten Kaj with her rape had nearly had her crying out in terror, but she'd managed to hold it in. Had managed to maintain her facade of calm.

She wanted to kill Corey Gates, but she wasn't sure she'd survive to do it.

The NOPD hadn't found Corey's hideout in days of looking. Kaj had less than an hour. He'd sounded so scared just now. Scared and angry.

Me too. Because, barring a miracle, she was on her own. *Do not panic. Think.*

She pulled her body into a sitting position, the movement sending pain burning from her ribs to her hip to her back. Corey and Bobby had kicked her hard, but she didn't think anything was broken.

Not like Noni Feldman. Val gazed sadly at the woman, who lay unmoving. Corey had said she was barely alive. Bobby had broken her and didn't seem to have a shred of empathy.

I have to get us free. And she didn't have much time left.

Okay, okay. What do I have? Not her gun. They'd taken her primary and backup weapons before they'd left Kaj's house, and then Corey had patted her down before moving her from the trunk to the boat, taking both her boots and the knife she kept in one of them. He'd searched her in a clinical way, refusing to let Bobby do it. Because Bobby was apparently insane.

Can I have her after you're done with her? he'd asked Corey in the boat.

Me, Val had thought. *He's talking about me.*

Val shuddered, panic like a vise around her throat. *I have to get out of here.* She glanced at Noni's motionless figure once again. *That could be me.*

No, because you're going to fight. You're going to get loose and you're going to fight.

But how?

She looked around the room. There were two cots with simple metal frames. If she could find a nick in the metal, she might be able to saw the tape off.

Grimacing, she spun around so that her back was to the bed and began using her feet to propel herself backward.

Careful. Don't touch Noni. She didn't want to make things worse for the poor woman.

She finally made it to the bed, half expecting Corey to come in again, but he didn't. She paused at a loud noise in the next room, holding her breath to listen.

It sounded like a door slamming.

A minute later a motor revved. A minute after that, the motor's noise had quieted and she sat in silence once again.

Get moving. You're running out of time.

Awkwardly, she began feeling for a sharp place on the metal bed frame. It was too damn smooth. This wasn't going to work. She let go of the frame, letting her shoulders slump.

Then jumped when the door to her room quietly opened. Val didn't move. The steps behind her didn't sound like they belonged to Corey or Bobby.

She barely swallowed a gasp when cool fingers touched her hand.

'Shh,' a woman whispered. 'I'll try to help you, but they can't know I'm awake. Turn your face toward me.'

Val obeyed. It was Dianne Gates. That was why the NOPD hadn't been able to find Dianne. As Jace had feared, Corey had had her all this time.

Why is she here? Was Dianne a prisoner or a participant? Was this a trap?

Guess I'll soon find out.

Carefully, Dianne peeled the duct tape from Val's upper lip. It was enough for Val to suck in a breath.

'Thank you,' Val whispered. The tape was still stuck to her lower lip and right cheek.

'Keep it on your face, just in case they come back. I'll have to run back to my room. They can't know I helped you.'

Val nodded. 'Got it. Can you loosen my hands?'

'I'll try.'

It seemed to take forever, but it must have been only a few minutes before Dianne found the end of the tape binding Val's hands and began to work the edge loose.

'Are they both gone?' Val finally whispered.

'I think so. Last time they took both boats. This time it was only one, but no one was in the main room when I came through.' Dianne renewed her efforts and finally Val could move her hands.

Wincing, she slowly brought her hands from her back to rest on her outstretched legs. Her fingers were numb. She shook her hands to restore circulation.

'I'm Val Sorensen,' Val said quietly, leaning forward to start picking at the tape binding her ankles. 'Why did they bring you here?'

'I think that they think that I know too much, but I don't know anything. And you?'

'I'm leverage. Corey thinks my boyfriend knows where Bella Butler is hiding. Corey aims to kill her to keep her from testifying against the man who raped her.'

'What?' Dianne breathed, looking shocked. 'Why?'

'He was hired by the man who Bella accused of raping her. Noni found out about Corey's plan and warned Bella.'

Dianne looked sadly at Noni's still form. 'I couldn't help her.'

Val caught the edge of the tape on her ankles and pulled until her feet were finally free. She ripped the tape off her face, then crept toward Noni to check her pulse. Still alive, but—as Corey had said—barely.

'She likes when you stroke her hair,' Dianne whispered.

Val did so, using one finger to brush hair off Noni's forehead. Her red hair was matted with blood and her face was so bruised that she was unrecognizable. The woman's eyelids fluttered, but she didn't open her eyes.

'We're going to get help,' Val promised, then inched her way to the door and listened. 'I don't hear anything.'

Dianne's mouth firmed with determination. 'We have to run while we can. There's still one boat out there.'

'Let me check for weapons. We'll be safer if we can defend ourselves.' Val slipped from the room to find an enormous gun on the table, and Val remembered Jace telling them that Bobby liked to scare people with his Raging Judge. *That's gotta be it.* She picked it up with both hands because it was fucking heavy.

She checked the cylinder. Six shots and fully loaded. Yes.

A backpack sat on the floor and Val grabbed it. It held duct tape and one empty magazine. She put the huge gun in the backpack and shrugged into it. She needed her arms free to get Noni outside.

Tiptoeing back to the other bedroom, she found Dianne wrapping Noni in a sheet.

Oh no. 'Is she dead?'

'No, but she has open wounds. I don't want her to get help only to die later of infection.'

Val figured that Noni's wounds were already infected, but she simply nodded. 'Let's get Noni to the boat.'

Dianne pointed to Val's feet. 'You don't have shoes.'

'Don't worry. I'll be okay. Help me with Noni.' Crouching, she slid her arms beneath the woman's back and carefully lifted her. 'Get her feet. Hurry.'

Dianne did, but she was petite and struggled with Noni's weight. But they made steady progress, Val walking backward and Dianne shuffling forward, Noni between them.

Out of the bedroom.

Through the small common room that doubled as a kitchen.

And out the door to the outside. *Almost there.*

'Just a little more,' she whispered to Dianne, who was stumbling now. Val looked over her shoulder to check the path to the dock. There weren't any obstacles she might trip over.

'Can you operate a boat?' Val asked. She could, because Burke had loaned her his boat all of the times she'd searched the bayou for Dewey Talley after Van's death.

'Yeah,' Dianne panted. 'I can.'

'You'll need to drive. I've got Bobby's gun and I'll be watching for Corey.'

And then they were on the dock. 'Let her go,' Val instructed, and Dianne lowered Noni's feet to the dock. 'Good. Now get in and I'll hand her to you.'

Dianne got into the boat, but it rocked dangerously. She turned and held out her arms, like Val was going to toss Noni to her like a ball.

'Crouch down,' Val said. 'Be steady. She's heavier than you.' She dragged Noni closer to the edge of the dock. 'Can you grab her feet?'

Dianne did and Val inched closer to the edge of the dock, sliding Noni into the boat as Dianne guided her.

And then they were done. Noni lay in the bottom of the boat, still motionless.

Val hoped they hadn't killed her by moving her, but if they'd left her behind Bobby would have finished the job. Val was about to step into the boat when a roar broke the silence.

It sounded like a bear. *A bear would be better.*

Because it was Bobby and he was running, a pistol gripped in his hand.

'Shit,' Dianne hissed. 'Hurry, Val. Now.' She yanked the pull cord and the motor coughed, then started. 'Get in!'

Val was trying, but the boat was rocking and she kept trying to time her leap. She'd set one foot in the boat when Bobby fired. The bullet caught her arm.

A graze. Only a graze, but it was enough to send her sideways. The boat rocked and she . . . tumbled.

Her head hit the dock and she slid into the water. But the water smacked her back to alertness and she kicked her way to the surface. Bobby was nearly on the dock now. There was no time to climb into the boat.

'Go,' Val commanded. 'Get help.'

'He'll kill you,' Dianne screamed, her face sheet-white.

Val shoved at the boat ineffectually. 'Just go!'

Bobby let out another roar, firing again and again. Val heard a shrill scream as Dianne threw the throttle forward. Dianne had been hit and there was no way for Val to know how bad it was.

Be safe, she wished. Wishing was all she could do for them at this point. She'd gotten them safely away. Now she needed to think about saving herself.

The boat took off downriver, its wake swamping Val. She swam beneath the dock and slogged her way to the bank, wedging herself between the shore and the wood above her.

Bobby fired several more times before abruptly ceasing.

The boat was gone. They'd gotten away.

But I'm still here. And Bobby still had at least four bullets left in his magazine.

'I know you're there,' Bobby said. 'Come out, come out, wherever you are,' he added in a mocking singsong.

Val shuddered and fought a wave of nausea. She'd heard Drysdale tell Corey and Bobby about her ordeal, about what the men had said to her, how they'd taunted her. She'd expected Corey and Bobby to use it against her, had tried to prepare herself for the words, but for a moment she was back in Iraq and she was young and she was scared and she was escaping into her mind. They couldn't hurt her when she was in her mind.

Stop. You're not that Ingrid. You're Val. You're strong. You're Kaj's. And you have Bobby's big-ass gun.

Hands trembling, she shrugged out of the backpack and unzipped it. The backpack was designed to be waterproof, but the gun was still a little damp. Luckily, guns could fire when wet. Holding the gun gave her an infusion of courage. *You can do this.*

The splash made her jump and all of a sudden he was there, in front of her, bent over so that his head didn't hit the dock above them.

Her courage wavered. He was big.

So big. Big hands.

Which reached for her.

She scrabbled away but was stopped by the piling at her back. Her hands were under the water. The gun was submerged. But she could hear her Marine trainer's voice in her ear. *Modern guns can be submerged for weeks and still fire.*

Bobby grinned and it was a terrifying sight. 'Nowhere to hide,' he crooned.

But Val wasn't going to hide. She was going to fight.

'Nothing to say?' he mocked. 'Well, you will. You'll say "stop" and "please" and "don't." You'll beg. Oh, I'm going to enjoy you.'

She didn't say a word. She didn't need to. She simply lifted the big gun out of the water, pointed it at his chest.

And fired.

She wouldn't forget the expression of shock on his face for as long as she lived. The bullet struck his chest and he fell backward into the water, but she could still see him. The water was shallow and Bobby was big.

The gun's kick hadn't been as bad as she'd expected. She was still standing, unlike Bobby. Still, she wasn't giving him a chance to rise out of the water. He'd never put his hands on anyone, ever again.

She fired again. And again. And again. And again.

And watched as the water turned red with his blood.

Blood. In the water. Get out. Get out.

Because things lived in the water that would be drawn by his blood.

Her ears ringing painfully from the noise of the gunshots, Val dragged herself out of the water and onto the shore, just as two alligators approached, gliding under the dock.

Fitting. *Bon appétit, guys.*

She was exhausted, but she was too close to the water's edge. Too close to those gators.

Fucking hell. Fighting nausea, she clawed her way up the riverbank to the grass, where she dry-heaved.

And then collapsed. Bobby was dead.

But I'm alone. No one knows where I am.

Except Corey. And Dianne.

She hoped Dianne found help before Corey came back. If he was anywhere close by, he'd have heard the gunshots. Her ears would be ringing for some time.

Bobby's Raging Judge had a six-bullet capacity. She'd used five. That left just one for Corey.

I better make it count.

29

FARRAH ROMERO'S FATHER slowed the boat and turned to Kaj and Phin. 'We're close to the bayou that connects Salvador to Cataouatche. You've got two choices. I can open the throttle completely and cross Cataouatche at full speed, or we can keep to the shoreline. It'll be slower that way, but you'll have stealth. Which should I do?'

Oscar Romero had been waiting at his Lake Salvador camp as promised and had them on their way within minutes of Kaj and Phin's arrival. André's no-nonsense future father-in-law knew how to drive a boat, and Kaj didn't have words to express his gratitude.

The NOPD would be arriving soon as well. When Kaj had called Antoine about Molly's plan, he'd learned that André had woken up and told them that Drysdale had been the one to stab him. André's commander had been there for both André's revelation and Kaj's call and had sent out a team to aid Molly with Drysdale's capture. Another team had been dispatched to the coordinates of Corey's property on the water, but Kaj and Phin had had a head start.

I should have told NOPD as soon as we discovered the location of the

Lake Cataouatche property in Ivan's records. But he hadn't known who to trust. Not with Val's life.

He'd be facing a reprimand, for sure. But if they got there in time, it would be worth any price he had to pay. Especially since Drysdale had been the first cop he'd seen after discovering Val's whereabouts. If he'd told Drysdale that they knew where Val was, Corey would have been told. And Val would have been dead. Or moved to where they couldn't find her in time.

Please, let us be in time. Please.

'I think we cross the lake fast,' Kaj said, 'then slow when we get to the tributary that leads to Corey's property. Our time's running out. We need to get there before Corey . . .'

He couldn't finish the thought, but he didn't need to. Phin and Oscar had heard his most recent conversation with Corey Gates. If Corey hadn't taken the bait of the fake address for Bella, then their time had already run out.

Phin nodded. 'I agree. When we get close, I'll take the wheel and, Oscar, you get down.'

'That's the plan,' Oscar said grimly. He wasn't a cop, but he knew how to fire a rifle and had brought his own along, just in case. Opening the throttle, he guided them down the waterway connecting the two lakes.

Kaj's phone buzzed in his pocket, and he was relieved to see Molly's name on the caller ID. Pressing his phone to one ear, he plugged his other ear with his finger to block the noise of the motor. 'Are you okay?'

'Yeah. Drysdale's in custody and Burke's out of surgery. They say it looks good.'

'And MaryBeth and Jace?'

'MaryBeth's still in. Her surgeon told Jessica that it was taking longer than they expected, but that she shouldn't despair.'

Kaj's heart skipped a terrified beat when she stopped talking. 'And Jace?'

Molly hesitated. 'He's alive. Antoine said that the surgeon told him it was touch and go. They lost him once on the table but were able to bring him back. The surgeon said that Jace is young, so they're hopeful. Where are you?'

They'd passed through the bayou between the two lakes and Mr. Romero opened the throttle full-out, the boat taking off like a small rocket. 'Just got to Lake Cataouatche. Where are you?' Kaj shouted over the roar.

'Des Allemands. Burke keeps a boat docked here. It's how he gets to his camp. I studied the maps. I can get there from Burke's place, so I'll come from the opposite direction.'

'Be careful,' Kaj ordered.

'I'll be fine. My sister says that Elijah is fine, by the way. The doctor will let him go home in a few hours.'

'He texted me, but thanks.' Elijah had been sending an *I'm okay* text every thirty minutes because he didn't want Kaj to worry. *What a great kid.*

'Gotta go. If you can, wait for me. But if it comes to waiting or saving Val, save her, okay? Let Phin go first. He's still a soldier. He's got this.'

'I will.' Kaj ended the call and relayed their friends' status to Phin.

'They'll be fine,' Phin said stubbornly. 'They have to be.'

Because they were Phin's family. The man had been increasingly twitchy for the past hour and Kaj was worried he was going to have an episode. But so far, so good.

'Where is the tributary we're looking for?' Kaj asked Oscar.

'At eleven o'clock. I'll start slowing down in a minute or two.'

'When we turn away from the lake, we want you to get down,' Phin said.

Farrah's father was wearing tactical gear, including a helmet, but they weren't taking chances with his life.

Oscar nodded. 'My wife already told me that I better not be a dead hero.'

Shielding his eyes, Kaj checked out the shoreline around the point where they'd be heading into the bayou. It was quiet. No activity—

'Fucking hell,' Kaj snarled. 'Look.' He pointed at eleven o'clock. A smaller boat was emerging from the tributary, heading into the lake.

'Corey,' Phin hissed.

'Should I slow down?' Oscar shouted over the motor. 'Head for shore to hide?'

Kaj nearly said yes. But Corey had already seen them. *Fuck*.

Corey steered the smaller boat in a circle, heading back the way he'd come.

Heading back to Val.

No fucking way.

'Follow him!' Kaj shouted.

Lake Cataouatche, Louisiana
FRIDAY, OCTOBER 28, 4:50 P.M.

'Fuck,' Corey snarled. Drysdale had lied. This was a trap.

The boat racing toward him held Cardozo, the bodyguard who'd protected him at the flower shop, and a third man whom Corey had never seen before.

They'd known where he was. Cardozo had already been on his way when Corey had called him an hour ago. The lying bastard.

Corey turned his boat in a tight circle and headed back. He still had the advantage.

He had Val Sorensen and Noni Feldman as leverage.

He also had Bobby to cover him while they loaded their leverage into the boats. Because there were other ways out of the bayou. Other ways he could escape. Tributaries where they wouldn't be looking for him.

He was driving too fast. He was going to hit a sandbar and rip the bottom out of his boat. But the clock was ticking.

I'm running out of time.

He wouldn't get to Bella Butler, not anytime soon. He wouldn't finish this job. He wouldn't get paid or make that name for himself. Doyle would smear his reputation. He might even hire killers to end Corey and Bobby.

I'll have to start all over. At least he had the money. He and Bobby would split everything that would have been Ed's. Everything they'd stolen from Aaron and Dewey. He'd live on it until he could resurface with a new name. A new reputation. He'd be okay. Not today, but soon. He'd be okay.

But today he *could* kill Cardozo, and he would. The man had ruined him.

He skipped across the water, narrowly missing submerged roots. But Cardozo was gaining. Corey could see the man's face, grim and angry.

A bullet whizzed past Corey's ear.

Fuck. Too close. Another glance over his shoulder revealed the big bodyguard from the flower shop, pointing a rifle right at him.

Corey made it across a shallow spot, then drew an easier breath when the bigger boat behind him had to slow to go around or risk grounding itself. He'd just bought himself a minute, but no more. He sped up, slowing only when he saw his dock.

With no boats tied to the piling. *Where the fuck is Bobby's boat?*

Adrenaline spooled into fury. *If Bobby's left, I will murder his fucking ass.*

Corey brought his boat to a stop, jumped out to tie it, then ran down the dock, drawing his weapon. 'Bobby!' he screamed. 'Bob—'

His feet stopped moving.

Val Sorensen sat on the grass, a look of exhausted determination on her face. And Bobby's Raging Judge in her hand.

They were at a standoff, it seemed. He aimed at her head, she aimed at his.

But then Sorensen stood and the gun in her hands shook. She was tired. She had to hurt. Her strength was ebbing fast. She wouldn't be able to hold that gun for long. She might not even be able to fire it.

'Where's Bobby?' he demanded. 'Bobby!' he yelled.

Sorensen didn't blink. 'He's under you,' she said, her voice like gravel.

Corey stared at her. 'Under me? What the hell?'

Her expression remained stony, her eyes cold. 'Put your gun down. You're done.'

He laughed. 'You won't shoot me.'

'I wouldn't bet on that. I shot Bobby. Now he's dead.' She smiled and the sight sent a shiver down his spine.

Corey nearly looked down, but that was what she wanted him to do. All it would take would be a momentary lapse of attention and she'd shoot him dead. 'You're lying.'

She shrugged. 'Fine. I'm lying. Drop the gun, Corey.'

He took a few steps forward. Sorensen didn't move. She didn't shoot him. He didn't think she would. 'How 'bout you drop yours?'

'You won't shoot me,' she said. 'Cardozo won't trade anything for me if I'm dead.'

She was right about that. But she wasn't simply leverage anymore. With Cardozo on his tail, she was his ticket to freedom. He started walking again, making it to the end of the dock. She hadn't shot him yet.

She wasn't going to.

He made it to the edge of the grass. She hadn't moved. The gun was shaking a little more now. He was almost close enough to grab it.

'Stop,' a male voice said at the same time that the barrel of a gun shoved up against the back of his head.

'Cardozo,' Corey snarled.

'Drop your gun, Corey,' Cardozo demanded.

'Okay, okay,' Corey snapped. *Like hell I will.* He twisted out of the way, still aiming at the blonde as he pulled the trigger.

Lake Cataouatche, Louisiana
FRIDAY, OCTOBER 28, 5:02 P.M.

Don't look for Val. Don't look. Kaj leapt from the boat as soon as Oscar touched the dock, running to stop Corey. *Stay focused on Corey.* Because Corey was pointing a gun at Val.

She's all right. She was standing with a massive revolver in her hands.

I'm not too late.

Holding his breath, he crept up to Corey and shoved his pistol against Corey's head. '*Stop,*' Kaj ordered, almost hoping Corey would fight back.

Just try me, motherfucker. I want to shoot you. But he also wanted Corey Gates to stand trial for his crimes. Kaj believed in the justice system. However, he also believed in not giving a bad guy the chance to kill you.

'Cardozo,' Corey snarled.

Kaj's stomach churned and his mind raced because while he'd never actually shot a live person before, he'd do it. For Val. 'Drop your gun, Corey.'

'Okay, okay,' Corey snapped, but he twisted his body to duck away from Kaj's weapon.

Kaj had fully expected Corey to lie just before making his move.

Adjusting his aim to where Corey's temple now was, Kaj pulled the trigger.

But instead of a normal gunshot, a ground-shaking boom filled the air.

Corey flew backward, landing on his back in the grass.

As did Val, except she quickly sat up, the gun still aimed in Corey's direction, her face expressionless. Like she was no longer there.

Phin rushed up from behind, Oscar's rifle in his hand. 'What the hell?' he shouted, but Kaj barely heard, his ears ringing from the blasts.

Kaj spared a look for Corey. He had a neat hole in his temple.

He also had a giant hole in his chest.

Both Kaj and Phin stared at Val. She lowered the huge gun to her lap and closed her eyes.

Kaj approached on trembling legs. 'Val? Honey?' He dropped to his knees beside her, barely conscious of Phin scooping up the huge gun.

Kaj put his arms around her, but she didn't move. Didn't react. Not for long, long seconds that felt like years.

Finally, she shuddered. 'Kaj.' He couldn't hear her, but he saw his name on her lips.

Relieved, Kaj sat beside her, pulling her to his lap. 'Can you check the house?' Kaj shouted to Phin.

'Will do. You should get out of the open area,' Phin shouted back. 'Bobby might still be around somewhere.'

Val shook her head. 'Under the dock,' she said dully.

Kaj and Phin shared a look. Phin walked midway up the dock, then knelt so he could look over the edge. A minute later, Phin was sitting on the dock, his eyes closed. His body rocking slightly, he was mouthing, 'No, no, no,' and his face had become as expressionless as Val's.

Whatever Phin had seen had pushed him into a PTSD episode. Kaj had known he'd been twitchy. He'd hoped Phin could hold it together, but it appeared that the man had had enough.

'Where's Bobby?' Kaj asked Val softly, letting her see his mouth.

She pointed at the dock again. 'Under. I killed him.' She drew a breath and let it out. 'Alligators.'

Kaj swallowed back bile, remembering the scene at Corey's old camp. That had been one of the more gruesome things he'd ever seen. But it was also a fitting end for Bobby Landry.

Now that Kaj was looking, he could see that the water around the dock was tinged red. Bobby had bled a lot.

He gently touched a bloody patch on her shirtsleeve before cupping her cheek. 'Did Corey hurt you? Did he shoot you?'

'No. Bobby grazed my arm. Corey's shot went wide.' She touched her fingertips to her side. 'I have a few bruised ribs maybe. From their boots.' She looked up suddenly, fear in her eyes. 'Dianne and Noni. Did you find them?'

Kaj shook his head, confused. 'Dianne? Aaron's wife?'

'She was here. Noni too.' Tears filled her eyes, devastation mixing with the fear. 'They hurt her, Kaj. Noni. She was almost dead. I got them out. They took the other boat. You didn't find them?'

'No, baby. But we'll search. I promise.' The NOPD had to be close by now.

Oscar leapt nimbly to the dock and came close enough that they could see his mouth. 'She's okay?' he shouted.

Kaj didn't think Val was okay. At all. 'Physically, yeah. Did you see another boat? With two women in it?'

Oscar shook his head. 'I'll get on my radio and put the word out.'

'Please do.' Kaj held Val closer, rocking her gently. 'I've got you.'

She shook her head. 'Noni. I need to find her.'

Kaj's phone began to buzz in his pocket. He nearly ignored it but yanked it from his pocket at the last minute and was glad he had, because it was Molly.

He didn't answer, texting instead. *Where are you? Can't hear you. Ears ringing. Gunshots.*

You okay?

Yes. Corey's dead. Bobby's dead. Val's here w me. Don't think she's hurt. She says 2 women escaped by boat. Dianne Gates and Noni Feldman.

I've got them. They went the wrong way. We're headed to Des Allemands. Medevac on its way for Noni. Sent NOPD to help you.

It was several seconds before Molly's next text came through. *It's not good. Tell Val we'll get Noni to a hospital ASAP.*

I'll tell her. Hold on. He tipped up Val's chin so that he could see her eyes. 'Molly has Noni. She's getting her to a hospital.'

Val closed her eyes and nodded once.

Thx. How is Phin? Molly texted.

Kaj looked at Phin, still sitting on the dock. Still saying, 'No, no, no.' Oscar had knelt beside him and was saying something that Kaj couldn't hear.

Not okay, he texted back.

Fuck. I knew it was too soon.

Kaj didn't know what to say to that. *Any more ppl we need to worry about?*

No. All dead/arrested. U can breathe now. Gotta go. Medevac here.

He dropped the phone and pulled Val closer. 'All the bad guys are dead. You took care of them, baby. You can let go now.'

Val nodded once, then turned her face into his neck and began to quietly cry.

Her tears broke Kaj's heart. He hoped they were cathartic tears. Tears of relief. He hoped she'd be okay once she'd cried them all out. And if not, he'd stay with her until she was.

He stroked her hair and for some reason that made her cry harder. So he rocked her where they sat until her sobs quieted to hiccups.

She stiffened in his arms. 'Drysdale's the mole.'

'We know. He's in custody. NOPD handled it.'

She frowned. 'You trust them?'

'André's friends rallied around him. They're on their way, in fact.'

'Okay.' She was silent another moment, then stiffened again. 'Elijah.'

'He was in the safe room. He's good. His sugar dropped and I took him to the ER, but he's fine. He told me I had to find you.'

'And Jace?'

'He's . . . hanging on.'

'I need to get to him.'

'We will. Let's wait for André's people to get here. We should still get back before Jace wakes up.'

She hesitated. 'Burke?'

'In recovery. MaryBeth was still in surgery, but she should be out by now.'

'Czar?'

'He's perfect. He kept Corey out of Elijah's room. Corey never even had a chance to figure out there was a safe room.'

'Good. How did you find me?'

Kaj paused for a moment. 'This property belonged to your brother. Aaron took it after your brother died. Corey trying to kill Rick and Jace made him angry, so Aaron told us where to look for Corey.'

She blew out a breath. 'Van hurt a lot of people. He sold drugs to children. He wasn't the man I thought he was. He didn't deserve to die, but he didn't deserve to be free, either.'

He kissed her temple. 'I'm sorry, baby.'

Her smile was small and sad. 'I know.'

Kaj looked at Corey's dead body. 'Why didn't you shoot Corey when he was on the dock?'

'Only had one bullet. Needed to make sure I hit him.' She lifted her hands, still trembling. 'Was afraid I'd miss.' She blew out another breath and he could see her tension easing degree by degree. 'You came. I knew you would.'

'Of course I did. Now rest. Everything is going to be okay.'

Kaj thought of Jace and hoped he hadn't lied.

Kaj held her on the riverbank in the waning sunshine while Phin and Oscar Romero sat on the dock. Finally, three NOPD boats arrived with officers, divers, and a CSU team.

One of the officers approached. It was Nolan, who'd been there the night that Rick had been dumped on his lawn and who'd accompanied them into the bayou the morning they'd found the remains of Corey's camp. And the remains of Dewey Talley and Zach Monteith. Kaj relaxed, confident he was one of André's good guys.

'Are you all right?' Nolan asked. 'Do you need medical attention?'

'We're okay,' Kaj said, able to hear a bit better now. He glanced at the dock and saw that Farrah's father was standing over Phin protectively. 'No immediate medical attention needed.'

Nolan looked sympathetic. 'We have a few questions and then we'll get you back to the city.'

Val lifted her head from Kaj's shoulder. 'Make it fast, please. I have a child to see.'

Jace or Elijah? Kaj wondered, then knew. Jace and Elijah.

When Jace recovered, Kaj was making sure that kid had everything he needed. Starting with a family who loved him.

Once Nolan had asked his questions, Val stood up and extended her hand. Kaj took it and together they went to where Phin still sat, silent and haunted.

'You ready to head home?' Val asked Phin. When he didn't answer, she knelt beside him and cupped his face in her hands. 'You did so well, Phin. You saved Elijah. You saved Kaj. And you saved me. Thank you.'

Phin looked up. 'You had to kill him.'

'Bobby? Yeah.'

'Don't you *dare* feel guilty,' he said fiercely.

'I won't,' she assured him, and Kaj wondered if she knew something about Phin's past that he did not. 'Burke and the others are waiting for us. Let's go home.'

Phin nodded once and followed them into the boat, steadfastly looking away from whatever was left of Bobby Landry under the dock.

Val, on the other hand, didn't take her eyes off the sight until they'd rounded a bend. She looked grimly . . . proud. But not okay.

None of them were okay.

But they would be.

30

V AL SHIFTED UNCOMFORTABLY in the chair in Jace's ICU room, but she wasn't going to leave. She'd promised Jace that she'd stay. She wasn't sure if he could hear her, but it didn't matter. He would not be alone when he woke up.

His surgeon was hopeful, so Val would be hopeful, too.

Burke was expected to make a full recovery. He'd had a room full of people when she'd stopped by to see him. They still hadn't found his shooter, but the NOPD was searching.

CSU had determined that Burke had been shot from the house across the street. NOPD had searched the home, finding the owner tied up and blindfolded in an upstairs closet. The woman couldn't tell them who her captor had been, but she wasn't permanently injured.

Val, however, had remembered Corey and Bobby talking about Burke's shooter when she'd been tied up in the back of MaryBeth's van. They'd said 'Ed's guy' was a cop named Alex. After hearing that name, many of the cops who'd been patrolling Kaj's neighborhood remembered seeing Officer Alex Cullen asking questions. Because he'd been a fellow cop, none of them had thought twice about it—until one of them realized that he'd never been listed on the protection detail. There were BOLOs out for Alex Cullen, but so far, he was still missing.

MaryBeth was also awake, but the doctors had told Jessica that she'd need more surgery and physical therapy because the bullet had shredded one of the muscles in her thigh. She might never skate with the QuarterMasters again. But she was alive, having ripped her crinoline skirt to use as a tourniquet for her leg.

Val was intensely grateful. And proud. Her friend was badass.

Val had seen Elijah when she'd first arrived at the hospital. He'd broken down in sobs when she'd hugged him. So she'd held him, rocking him, singing to him until he shuddered in her arms. But he was alive. Physically whole.

Val would be grateful to Phin for the safe room for the rest of her life.

She rested her forehead on Jace's bed rail as she lightly held his hand.

'I'm so mad at you, Jace. You should have hidden with Elijah. You're not allowed to risk yourself. You don't need to earn your place. You don't need to carry your weight. You don't need to be useful. You just need to be with us. With me.'

A knock on the doorframe of Jace's room had Val turning to look. She'd been hoping it was Kaj, but he was probably still at his sister's. Elijah would stay with Genie and her husband tonight, but Kaj had promised he'd be back as soon as Elijah was asleep.

Val's eyes widened. 'Dianne.' The woman had sustained a minor gunshot wound to her arm while fleeing Bobby. She'd been treated and released, but she looked very pale. And shaky. Almost like she needed a fix, and Val remembered Jace saying how Dianne was always drunk. She wasn't drunk right now.

Dianne Gates stared at Jace's still form. 'Can I come in?'

'Of course.' She gestured at the other chair. 'Please.'

Dianne was Jace's remaining legal guardian, since Aaron was in jail and Corey was dead.

Because I killed him. And I'd do it again.

But Dianne's presence had Val's hackles rising. She hadn't realized how much she'd built up the dream of fostering Jace until it had been ripped away. She could only hope that Dianne would continue to let them be a part of his life.

Dianne stared at Jace for a long time before she spoke. 'I failed them. I knew that Corey disciplined them, but I didn't know how bad it was. I didn't let myself know. I was taking care of Liam, but that doesn't make it right. I shouldn't have left Rick and Jace with Corey for so long.'

Val couldn't disagree with that, but she wasn't going to say that out loud. This woman had lost her son. And she'd shown compassion to Noni Feldman.

Dianne sighed. 'Jace has always been so big, so self-sufficient. I sometimes forget how young he is.'

Val wouldn't forgive her. She couldn't. But this wasn't hers to forgive. It was Jace's and Rick's. They'd been neglected, pushed aside, beaten, and tormented.

Dianne drew a breath and let it out. 'Corey was angry when I told him that the boys wanted Aaron back so that they didn't have to live with him, but I never thought he could be so cruel. Not until he let Bobby hurt Noni Feldman.'

Val swallowed hard. 'I haven't checked on her in a while. Not since I got here.' The woman had been in surgery at the time. Her source, Allyson Meyer, was still missing.

'She . . .' Dianne choked on a small sob. 'Noni died.'

'Oh.' Val felt like she'd been punched. 'Oh no.'

Dianne wiped at her tears with her hands. 'You tried. You tried so hard. Thank you for that. You could have left her there. You and I would have gotten away.'

Val shook her head. 'I couldn't have left her there.'

'I figured as much.' She was quiet a little longer before sighing again. 'I'm a drunk.'

Val met her eyes. 'I know. Jace told me.' *And the system's going to let you have him back. That's not right.*

'I started drinking six months before Liam died. Just at night after he went to sleep. After he died, I started drinking all day long. If I hadn't been a drunk, I might have been able to help Rick and Jace and none of this would have happened.'

Val couldn't disagree with that, either. So she said nothing.

Dianne closed her eyes. 'I'm going into rehab. And then I'm going to fix my life. I have to figure out how to support myself because Aaron's never getting out. But I don't know what to do about Jace. He deserves a lot better than me.'

Yes, he does. He deserves a family who loves him. 'Would you sign custody over to someone else?' Val asked, refusing to hope. Not yet.

Startled, Dianne's eyes flew open. 'That would depend on who it was. I don't want him to go into the system, but a good foster family would be better than what I can give him now.'

Hope unfurled. 'Sign custody over to me.'

Dianne stared at her. 'You? But you've only known him for a week.'

'I've grown attached. Plus, I can help him get the reading help he needs. He's most likely got some form of dyslexia. He's smart, Dianne. He deserves a chance to learn and to grow in a safe place.'

Dianne closed her eyes again, tears escaping to roll down her cheeks. 'Do you mean it?'

'Yes. I was going to apply to be a foster parent so that I could take him, but if you sign over custody, we can do this quickly—as long as Jace agrees, of course. It'll be up to him. But if he does agree to live with me, I'll take care of him. I promise.'

'I believe you. You took care of me and Noni when you didn't have to. And you made me leave you so that we could get away.' She wiped her face again, murmuring thanks when Val handed her the box of tissues next to Jace's bed. 'He has dyslexia?'

'I think so. I'll get him an official diagnosis.'

Dianne nodded. 'Thank you. I . . .' She exhaled. 'Just thank you. If Jace is okay with it, I'll get the papers drawn up. Can . . . Can I still see him sometimes?'

'Of course. We'll work it out.'

'Thank you.' Dianne stood, kissed Jace on the forehead, then left the room.

Leaving Val with a full heart. She took Jace's hand in hers. 'I'll take care of you,' she said quietly. 'I promise.'

Then she sang the same lullaby she'd sung to Elijah, hoping Jace could hear her. Hoping that he understood that he mattered to someone now.

The scent of flowers hit Val's nose after the third verse, a slim arm sliding around her shoulders. 'Hey, Ingrid.'

Val smiled. 'Hey, Sylvi.'

'You look awful,' Sylvi said honestly. 'But I'm so glad to see you.'

'Me too.' Val laid her head on her sister's shoulder. 'I heard what you did, how you helped Kaj and the others find me. Thank you.'

'I'm glad it worked.' Sylvi let her go, then sat in the chair Dianne had vacated. 'I saw Dianne in the elevator. She told me that she's giving you custody.'

Val's lips curved. 'I know. I can't believe it.'

'You'll be a good mom to him. You were a good mom to me.'

Val's throat closed. 'Don't make me cry.'

Sylvi chuckled. 'Fine, fine. I'll save the mushy stuff for another day. I do remember you singing me to sleep with that song, though. It's nice to hear you sing again.'

Val held out her free hand and Sylvi took it, squeezing hard. 'You smell like flowers.'

'I went to the shop,' Sylvi said, 'and made arrangements for all of your friends, for when they're out of ICU. I left one in my car for Kaj to take to his sister since she's on bed rest.'

'That was nice of you.'

'I needed to work off some energy. Stress plus idle hands isn't a good combination for recovering addicts.' Val hadn't even considered that. Her expression must have given her concern away because Sylvi's smile was wry. 'I know my limits and my triggers, Ingrid. I'm okay.'

'I'm so glad,' Val said fervently.

Sylvi squeezed her hand again. 'You know about Noni Feldman?'

Val sighed. 'Dianne told me.'

Sylvi looked away. 'I'm not going to be charged for staying silent when Rico Nova confessed to Van's murder, according to Kaj's boss, Mr. Hogan.'

'That's good. Right?'

'Of course. I just feel like I should do something. Make amends.'

Val smiled at her. 'Then we'll find something and do it together. There are so many ways we can help.'

Sylvi leaned into her. 'I'm so glad I have you back.'

'Me too. How are Mom and Dad?'

Sylvi shook her head. 'They know you're okay. They send their love. I don't think they have a full appreciation of what nearly happened today. I don't think they can, y'know?'

'I know,' Val said sadly. 'I guess we keep taking care of them. There are some consequences we can't fix.'

'Mom wants to visit Cassandra in jail, so she's admitting that she got arrested.'

'Baby steps. I'm not sure how we keep Van's connection from them, though.'

'I don't think they'll believe it. They could read it in a thousand newspapers and not believe it. But we may just have to accept that. Oh, and they weren't giving me money. Mom told me that she'd let you believe that. They loaned me money to buy the shop and I've been paying them back. I nearly have their loan paid off.'

'Thank you for telling me. And I'm sorry I thought the worst.'

'Mom helped with that. Now I'm going home. I'm going to have a hot bath, eat a pint of ice cream, and sleep for a week.' She kissed Val's cheek. 'Call me. Love you.'

Val's eyes filled. 'Love you, too.'

'Sing to Jace some more. He'll hear you.'

Mid-City, New Orleans, Louisiana
FRIDAY, OCTOBER 28, 11:30 P.M.

'Kaj!'

Kaj stopped in the ICU waiting room, having nearly missed seeing Molly and Joy, who were drinking coffee at one of the tables. 'I'm sorry. I'm on autopilot right now, I think.'

'Want some coffee?' Molly asked.

'Say no,' Joy stage-whispered. 'It's awful.'

Molly grimaced. 'It really is, but it's caffeine.'

'I'm overcaffeinated, but thank you.' Kaj sat next to Joy's wheelchair. 'Any news?'

'MaryBeth's awake,' Molly said. 'She's trying to get Jessica to go home and sleep, but that's not happening.'

Kaj breathed a sigh of relief. 'Mary Popshins is gonna be okay?'

Molly waggled her hand. 'She'll be out of work for a while. Jess is going to need help at the bakery.'

'Luckily one of my kids has baking experience,' Joy said, 'and needs a job, so we should have them covered, at least in the short term.'

'I love how you guys rally around each other,' Kaj said with a wistful smile. 'I don't know what I would have done without you this week.'

'We're not going anywhere,' Molly informed him. 'You're one of us now. You can't get rid of us.'

That turned his smile from wistful to happy. 'Thank you.'

'Elijah get to sleep okay?' Joy asked him.

'Yes, especially after Molly brought Czar to my sister's house. When I left, the two of them were cuddled together in Genie's spare room. Thank you, Molly. How's Burke?'

'Cranky,' Molly said with pure relief. 'They'll move him to a regular room tomorrow.'

Kaj hesitated. 'Jace?'

Molly shook her head. 'Still hasn't woken up, but the nurse says his vitals are strong. But the good news is that Dianne Gates is signing over custody to Val.'

Kaj's heart squeezed happily in his chest. 'Val texted me. I'd been worried about what would happen to him. Is she still here?'

Joy rolled her eyes. 'We can't pry her from Jace's bedside long enough to eat. That's why we're here. We brought her food. Have you eaten?'

'Yes, ma'am. My sister's husband fed us. I'll sit with Jace so Val can eat.' He buzzed the nurse at the ICU desk, who let him through. 'I'm here to see Jace Gates.'

'Your girlfriend has a lovely voice,' the nurse said.

Kaj smiled at the nurse. 'She's been singing to Jace?'

'For the past hour. She only stopped ten minutes ago.' The nurse peered into Jace's room. 'Because she sang herself to sleep.'

'Ah. Thank you.' Kaj slipped into Jace's room, closing the door softly. Sure enough, Val had propped her elbow on the edge of Jace's bed, her cheek resting on her clenched fist. But she was wobbling.

Kaj started to reach for her, then stopped short. Jace was awake, staring at Val with something like awe.

Jace noticed him and whispered, 'Is Elijah all right?'

'He's fine. I'm going to tell a nurse that you're awake.' Gently he shook Val's shoulder and she sat up straight with a gasp.

She calmed quickly, though, her smile breaking wide when she saw Jace. 'Hey, kid.'

'You're okay,' Jace whispered, his voice dry and rough. 'You stayed.'

'I am okay. And I will always stay.'

Kaj moved to the door and signaled for a nurse, who hurried over. Val stood on shaky legs, backing away to give the nurse room. Wrapping his arms around her from behind, Kaj urged her to lean against him. 'He's okay, Val.'

'I know. I know.'

Fortunately, everyone would eventually be okay.

Except for Noni Feldman. Kaj hadn't had a moment to grieve for her. She should have been more forthright with them, telling them what she knew. She might be alive right now.

But Val was alive and he was so thankful. He tightened his hold until she sucked in a sharp breath and he remembered her sore ribs. 'I'm sorry.'

She kissed him. 'Don't be. You feel good. You make me know I'm okay.'

They waited while the doctor and nurse did all their checks and left the room, promising they'd be back later.

'Are you going to tell him about Dianne?' Kaj whispered in Val's ear.

'I think so. Hopefully she won't change her mind, but it will ease his, so yeah.' Hand in hand, they sat in the chairs next to Jace's bed.

'You sang to me,' Jace said sleepily. 'Was like . . . far away. Followed the sound.' He drew a shallow breath. 'What's going to happen to me?'

'Do you mean your injuries?' Val asked carefully.

'That too. I'll be good again?'

She nodded. 'You will. And I'll take care of you until you're back to normal.'

'So will Elijah and I,' Kaj said. 'You won't be alone, Jace.'

He closed his eyes. 'And after? When I'm all better?'

Val reached for Jace's hand. 'Dianne said she'd sign custody over to me, if that's okay. She's going to get some help with her alcohol issues.'

Jace's eyes flew open, and they were filled with hope. 'You're not lying to me.'

'Nope,' Val said. 'You're stuck with me and Czar. And Kaj and Elijah, too.'

Tears filled Jace's eyes. 'I can live with you?'

'Yes,' Val said. 'I have to figure out where I'm living, though. I can't live in my brother's house anymore. Not knowing how he paid for it. You can help me look for a place, so get better fast.'

Jace's mouth curved up and he looked so young and eager it made Kaj's heart hurt.

'Jace,' he said, closing his hand over Val's where it gripped Jace's. 'Thank you for protecting Elijah. I will be forever grateful. But you didn't have to do that. We still would have wanted you.'

Jace made a contented sound. 'I know there's still problems, like, Aaron and Rick are still going to jail, but . . . this feels like one of those movies where everyone is happy.' He abruptly frowned. 'Did you catch Corey and Bobby?'

Kaj and Val shared a glance. 'Jace,' she said gently. 'They're gone. They're dead.'

Jace's expression hardened. 'Is it wrong that I'm glad?'

'No,' Kaj assured him. 'You have every right to feel that way. Now, it's late. You need to rest and so does Val. It was a busy day. She needs to have a meal and go to sleep. We will be back first thing in the morning. Don't worry.' He wrote his cell phone number on the notepad next to Jace's bed. 'This is my personal number. You need me, you call.'

'Okay, Mr. Cardozo.'

'Kaj. Call me Kaj. Elijah and I will see you tomorrow.'

'Promise?'

'I promise.' Kaj brushed the hair from Jace's forehead. 'Get some rest.'

Jace swallowed. 'Thank you.'

Kaj tugged Val to her feet, but she turned to kiss Jace's forehead. 'You and I are going to be family, you understand? And that'll include Burke and Antoine and Phin and Molly and Kaj and Elijah and everyone else.'

Jace's smile was bright. 'I understand. Go to sleep, Val.'

With a final caress to his cheek, she let Kaj lead her from the room. 'I'm tired.'

'So am I. You want to stay with me tonight at Genie's? Czar is already there. Molly brought him by for Elijah.'

She smiled up at him. 'I'd like that.'

EPILOGUE

WIPING HIS DAMP palms on his jeans, Jace took a seat in the visitation room of the jail.

'Breathe, Jace,' Val said from beside him.

He appreciated that she didn't tell him it would be okay, because it wouldn't. Not for Rick.

Jace's breath caught in his throat when the door opened and Rick shuffled in. His legs were shackled, but he wasn't handcuffed, so at least there was that. He didn't look hurt, either.

Jace had been afraid that Rick would be beaten in jail. Or worse.

He rose as Rick approached the table, not sure what to do with his hands. 'Rick.'

Rick smiled tiredly. 'Hey, kid.' His glance flicked to Val and his eyes widened. 'You visited me in the hospital. Your hair was brown then. Val, right? I mean Miss Sorensen.'

'I was wearing a wig that day,' Val said. 'Please, sit down. Jace won't until you do and he's still not at a hundred percent.'

Rick slid onto a chair and folded his hands on the table, his gaze searching Jace up and down. 'You were shot. I saw it on the news.'

Jace sat because Val was right. It still hurt to stand. 'I'm better. But that's why I haven't visited until now.'

'I knew you were hurt. Lucien said that you nearly died.' Because Lucien had taken Rick on as a client and Jace hadn't been able to say thank you enough times.

Jace winced. 'Yeah. Corey shot me. Here.' He pointed to his chest, where he'd likely have a scar.

Rick's mouth thinned. 'I heard. I also heard that Corey's dead.'

'Val and Kaj did it,' Jace said, and if he sounded proud, he wasn't going to apologize. 'Both of them shot him.'

Rick looked at Val, his expression sober. 'Thank you. Thank you for taking care of Jace and thank you for . . .' He sighed. 'For taking care of Corey.'

Jace saw her flinch, even if no one else did. She still had nightmares about that night. He'd heard her mumbling 'No, no, no,' in her sleep, followed by Czar's little whine as he woke her—usually because Jace wasn't asleep, either. He hadn't slept well, unable to get Corey's rabid fury out of his mind. But he would, eventually. His new therapist had said so.

He and Elijah went to the same therapist and once they'd gone together. A joint session. That had been hard. Knowing that his family had caused Elijah so much harm . . . Jace hated it.

It was like Jace had a younger brother now. But he still missed Rick. A lot.

'You're welcome,' Val said. 'I came with Jace because he's underage. I don't want you to think I'm spying.'

'No, it's okay,' Rick said quickly. 'Like I said, I'm grateful you're looking out for him. I've been worried. What will happen to him? Will he have to go into the system? I asked Lucien, but he said it wasn't his to say.'

I'm right here, Jace wanted to say, but he didn't. Rick had always taken care of him. It wasn't going to be easy for him to stop just because he was in jail.

'Dianne signed custody of me over to Val. She's my guardian now.'

Rick's eyes popped wide. 'Really?' His gaze shot to Val. 'You did that for him?'

Val smiled at Jace. 'We've grown to love him. He'll be well taken care of, I promise.'

Slumping in his chair, Rick closed his eyes and Jace was stunned to see tears on Rick's face. Jace's eyes burned and he had to suck in a deep breath to keep from crying, too. 'Rick?'

'I'm fine. It's . . . I didn't want you to go into the system. Dianne really signed papers?'

'She did. She's in rehab now. Her sister helped her get into a good place.'

Rick nodded once. 'Good.'

'And you, Rick?' Val asked. 'How are you doing? Going off heroin cold turkey couldn't have been fun.'

Rick shuddered. 'It wasn't. But I guess I have time to kick the habit while I'm here.'

'How long?' Jace asked, even though Kaj had been keeping him updated. Rick had accepted a deal, pleading guilty to attempted kidnapping and possession of a firearm.

Rick squared his shoulders. 'Five years, but I'll be eligible for parole in two with good behavior. Lucien says I probably would have gotten less if I hadn't had the gun. I'll serve it in juvie, not with the adults.' Jace must have shown how upset he felt about Rick spending even two years in juvie because Rick's hand shot out and gripped his arm. 'It's okay. I did it. And now that I'm sober? I don't know what I was thinking. Mama would be so mad at me.'

Jace swallowed hard, trying not to cry. 'I'll come see you.'

Rick smiled. 'Yeah?'

'I'll try to come every week, but I need someone to bring me since I'm not eighteen.'

And neither was Rick. Kaj said the judge had taken that into account—Rick's age and that he'd been abused by Corey.

Jace was still amazed that Kaj could look at him, knowing that Rick had tried to kidnap Elijah. But Kaj had a good heart. As did Val and Burke and all of them.

My new family.

He did cry then, because Rick was going to be in jail while he was free and living with good people.

'Don't,' Rick pleaded. 'Please. I can't handle it.'

Jace tried to get hold of himself. And then he felt Val's fingers in his hair, soothing him. For another minute he cried even harder, but then sucked in a breath and wiped his eyes. Val's hand rested on the back of his neck and he took strength from that. 'Val says you can keep up with school.'

Rick nodded. 'I know. I'm working on that.'

Jace sat a little straighter. 'I'm going to learn to read.'

Rick's eyes widened once again. 'Yeah?'

'Yeah. I'm dyslexic. The letters . . .' He waved his hand. 'They move around. But Kaj and Val found me a teacher and she's going to tutor me.'

Rick exhaled, his eyes once again filling with tears. 'I'm glad. Really glad.'

Jace pointed a finger at him. 'Do not cry or I'll start again.'

Rick's laugh was watery. 'Deal.' He sobered. 'Have you seen Aaron?'

Jace shook his head. 'I don't know if I can.'

'I know.' Rick shook his head. 'I might change my name once I get out.'

'Me too.' Val had, after all. Not for the same reasons, but she'd already told him that she'd help him do it if he really wanted to. 'Hey, I got a job.'

Rick blinked. 'Yeah?'

'Yeah. One of our friends got hurt when Corey . . . Well, she got hurt and they need help in her bakery. I'm going to do deliveries on a bicycle and keep their delivery van tuned up.'

'When the doctor clears you,' Val said with raised eyebrows.

'Soon,' Jace said, and Val just shook her head. They'd been having discussions about him pulling his weight. 'At least when I'm sixteen. Maybe. But I do have a dog now. Val's dog, Czar. I'd show you a picture, but I couldn't bring my phone.'

Val pulled a stack of photos from her pocket. 'I printed these out for you.'

Jace grinned his thanks and started taking Rick through each one. 'This is Elijah. Well, I guess you know about him.' He quickly moved to the next photo. 'This is Czar.'

Rick's mouth fell open. 'Holy shit.'

'He bit Corey.'

Rick grinned. 'Fuckin' A.'

'Right? And this is Kaj. And Burke. And Molly. And Phin. He builds things. Says I can help him soon. And this is Val at the track.' She'd taken him and Elijah to a QuarterMasters game and they'd had an amazing time. 'This is Patty. She's a chef. And MaryBeth and her wife, Jessica. They own the bakery where I'm going to work. And another of Czar.'

It'll be okay, Jace thought as he talked about his new friends. Maybe, in time, Rick could get to know them, too. Except Kaj and Elijah. He wasn't sure their hearts were that big. Although maybe if Rick proved himself . . .

Maybe.

The Quarter, New Orleans, Louisiana
MONDAY, NOVEMBER 14, 4:30 P.M.

Kaj waited in the doorway of Burke's big old house in the Quarter, watching Val and Jace sitting in her car at the curb. He'd been worried the whole time they'd been gone. They were safe now, he knew that, but it was hard to shake the feeling that danger still lurked.

Detective Drysdale was in jail, having taken a plea bargain. He'd still serve life in prison, but they'd house him in a prison out of state so that he wouldn't be in the same population as the criminals he'd put away. Kaj wished they'd left the man local and wasn't sorry for it.

Sandra Springfield had bargained her way down from conspiracy to commit murder to accessory after the fact. That, along with the drug possession charge, had earned her ten years in prison. She might be out in as little as five, but they'd worry about that in five years. The names of the city's wealthy buyers of Aaron's drugs that she'd provided had gone a long way toward reducing her sentence and would keep Kaj and the rest of the DA's office busy for a long, long time.

Once Noni Feldman's death had been announced on the news, the city had mourned her. As had Allyson Meyer, who'd been found dead in the tub of a cheap hotel room, having eaten her own gun. She'd left a letter detailing what had happened and why. Corey had found out about the affair she'd had with a foreign agent in Iraq that had resulted in the deaths of American soldiers. She'd likely be posthumously courtmartialed.

Her confession didn't matter so much from a legal standpoint because all of the players were dead, but it did help answer a lot of questions.

NOPD had finally located the dirty cop, Alex Cullen, who'd been feeding Ed Bartholomew information. Cullen had been slinking into a bus station in a tiny town in Arkansas when a sharp-eyed ticket seller had called the local police. He'd also taken a plea bargain and would serve at least twenty years. Good riddance to bad rubbish.

Everyone who'd wanted to hurt his little family was either dead or in prison, but Kaj still worried about the psychological effects of the aftermath on all of them. At the moment, his concern was focused on the woman and teenager in the car at Burke's curb.

'I told you they'd be fine,' Elijah said as he leaned against him, Czar at his side.

Kaj ruffled his son's hair. 'You did and you were right.'

They'd been staying at Burke's house while their house was being fixed. There were bullet holes in all the walls and blood had soaked into the hardwood floors. Kaj wasn't sure if he'd be able to live there once the repairs were done, but he'd try. At least Elijah didn't carry the memory of their friends bleeding—and of Ed Bartholomew's body.

Elijah had been passed out by then and hadn't seen anything outside his bedroom.

Small mercies.

Val had been staying in the room across from Kaj's, but usually only half the night. He'd hear her nightmares and would spend the rest of the night holding her. Czar would hop off her bed and climb into Elijah's, comforting his son when he inevitably woke as well. From there, he'd move on to Jace. Kaj wasn't sure what they'd do without the monster dog with the sweet heart.

Somehow, they managed to get through the days on little sleep. It was getting better, though. So was Burke, thank goodness. MaryBeth was still on crutches, but Burke had installed a ramp for Joy's motorized wheelchair years before, so the house was accessible.

Kaj didn't know what Val would do about housing. She wouldn't go back to her brother's house, knowing how he'd paid for it. She was looking for a place to rent—a place that allowed behemoth dogs, of course. She and Jace would stay with Burke while she sorted things out.

'What's wrong with them?' Elijah asked, concerned.

Val had leaned across the console of her car, her arm around Jace. 'Maybe visiting Rick was harder on Jace than he expected.'

'And he expected it would be really hard,' Elijah said sadly. 'I'm not sure if I'll ever like Rick, Dad.'

'I know what you mean. But we can love Jace, right?'

'Duh.'

Kaj leaned down to kiss Elijah's head. 'I love you, y'big doofus.'

Elijah smiled up at him, eyes big behind his glasses. 'Same. Oh, they're coming. We should wait inside. Jace won't want us to see that he was crying.'

My sweet boy. Kaj let himself be led back inside, where a party was going on. Burke's people were there, and Gabe and Patty were cooking for them. They were eating well tonight.

Burke sat in his recliner, hands folded over his belly, his lips curved in an indulgent smile as he watched his houseguests laughing. Lucien and Molly's sister, Chelsea, were dancing while MaryBeth and Jessica sang—badly—to the song on the stereo. Joy sat next to Molly's niece, Harper, and they were deep in conversation about Joy's experiences as a cop, because Harper had apparently added police officer to her very long list of things she wanted to be.

Sylvi was fiddling with a flower arrangement on the table. Beside her, Molly placed bowls filled with the food Gabe and Patty had prepared. Farrah was setting the table and André was arguing with Antoine about how many points the Saints would win by on Sunday. André was mostly healed, but his eyes held a haunted sadness from the betrayal of one of his own men. He'd be all right, though. And he was already rebuilding his team.

Kaj now knew many more NOPD officers that he could trust if he ever needed guarding again. Which would not be happening. He hoped. He'd thought a lot about what Phin had shared that day he'd shown him Elijah's safe room, how his mother had told his father that having one bad guy come after them was the one plane crash among thousands of safe flights.

That had kept him going for the past few weeks. *Only safe flights from here on out.*

Phin had run. After they'd returned from Lake Cataouatche, Phin had simply disappeared. He periodically texted Burke to say he was okay, which might be physically true. But psychologically, the man was scarred and there didn't seem to be much they could do for him other than be there when he came home. But everyone still worried about him.

Finally, Val and Jace came through the door. Both had red eyes, but they were smiling. Val came straight to Kaj, wrapping her arms around him and holding on.

'Hey,' she whispered.

'Hey, yourself. You okay?'

'Yes. And no. He cried all the way back.'

'I'm sorry.' And he was. He was also conflicted because as much as he cared for Jace, he did not want Rick to walk. The kid had tried to kidnap Elijah and if he'd succeeded . . .

Kaj still shuddered at the thought. At least Rick had agreed to a deal and it wasn't too lenient. It gave him two years behind bars at a minimum and the chance to complete his education. As candidates for rehabilitation went, Rick was a good one. So they'd wait and see.

For now, he'd enjoy having Val in his arms. He glanced to where Elijah and Jace sat together on Burke's sofa. They were an unlikely pair, but Elijah had taken Jace under his wing.

'What's he doing?' Kaj wondered when Elijah put an Amazon box on Jace's lap.

Val turned to see, a smile lighting up her eyes. 'A present. He used your credit card.'

'What is it?'

'Colored overlays for books. It helps dyslexic readers focus on a line at a time.' She chuckled. 'And the first *Captain Underpants* book.'

Jace studied the gifts with wonder, then gave Elijah a hard hug and a big smile.

'Elijah talked to Jace's tutor and she recommended them. He's an amazing little boy, Kaj. Your wife would be so proud of how you're raising him.'

Kaj's heart stuttered and his eyes burned. 'Thank you.' Val wouldn't try to make them forget about Heather. She mentioned her often, always with fondness.

She also sang Elijah to sleep every night and was teaching Jace to play the piano on Burke's old upright. Thankfully Heather's piano hadn't been damaged in the shootout, so they could use that when the house was habitable. Again, small mercies.

I have many small mercies. So much to be thankful for.

He nuzzled Val's neck, letting vanilla tease his senses. 'I visited the animal shelter on my way home from work today,' he whispered so that Elijah wouldn't hear.

Val's gaze was knowing. 'Where's the dog?'

He chuckled. 'Still at the pound, but they're holding him. I thought you and I and Elijah and Jace might see him tomorrow.' Because eventually Val and Jace would find a home and Czar would stay with Val. 'A boy needs a dog.'

Val kissed his cheek. 'You're the sweetest man. Of course we'll go. I can't wait.'

'Yo! Lover boy and girl.' Patty held a frying pan and a spoon, banging them together to get their attention. 'Soup's on. Plus lots of other stuff.'

'We've been summoned,' Kaj said. 'Let's eat.'

They converged on Burke's table and Kaj sat there for a moment, letting it soak in. Genie would be joining them the next time they all gathered. She'd had her baby the week before but was cautious about bringing his new niece around so many people so soon.

Sylvi was laughing with Val about something. One of the good things to come from their week of horror was that Sylvi and Val had been spending a lot of time catching up.

'Those flowers are beautiful, Sylvi,' Kaj said. 'Thank you for bringing them.'

'Thank you, kind sir, but they're not from me and they're not for you. I did the arrangement, though.'

Kaj frowned. 'Who are they from and who are they for?'

'I had a visitor to my shop today,' Sylvi said with a grin. 'One Bella Butler. She said she wanted to send you flowers, but I didn't think you'd be allowed to accept them, so she sent them to Val.'

'Loophole,' Kaj said. 'I like it.'

Sylvi's smile softened. 'She says she's doing well and wanted to thank you again.'

The trial had commenced and, as expected, Trevor Doyle's attorney had tried to shame Bella on the stand, but Bella had stood firm. After two days of deliberations, Bella had heard the judge read the jury's guilty verdict.

The FBI, with a little anonymous help from Antoine, had located and arrested the ringleaders of the online Bella-haters who'd tried to instigate violence against the DA's office. Once the leaders had been arrested, the rest of the chatter seemed to fizzle away. Kaj was still afraid for Elijah and might always be, but the threat was being monitored and had dissipated for now.

Justice won sometimes. Another silver lining. It had come at a very high price, though. So many hurt. A few people gone forever. But everyone in his circle had made it through.

Large mercies.

'She wants to do something for the women in the city who've been assaulted,' Sylvi said. 'I told her that I knew some people who'd like to help.'

Val gave Sylvi a hug. 'I told you that we'd find some way to help.'

Molly tapped a spoon to her cup. It was plastic and didn't carry the sound as well as glass, but everyone laughed. 'We made it through,' she said, echoing Kaj's thoughts.

Everyone's thoughts, probably. It was hard not to think about how lucky they'd been.

'And now,' Molly continued, 'we've made our family a little bigger. So here's to Kaj, Elijah, Jace, and Sylvi. Welcome.'

'Welcome,' was the resounding reply.

Kaj couldn't speak. His throat was too tight.

'He says thank you,' Elijah said cheekily, making everyone laugh.

But Jace was staring at everyone with wonder and Kaj had to agree.

He'd lived in another city his entire life, but at this moment, he'd never felt so much at home.

ACKNOWLEDGMENTS

The Starfish—Christine, Cheryl, Sheila, Brian, Kathy, and Susan—for all the plotting.

Marc Conterato, for all things medical. And for so much more. Thank you.

Andrew Grey, for word counting with me every day.

Sarah Hafer, for all the editing.

Robin, Jen, Liz, and Claire, for all your support as I wrote this book. Thank you.

As always, all mistakes are my own.

Karen Rose's New Orleans series
continues in . . .

BURIED
TOO DEEP

Coming Summer 2024.

Available to order now

HEADLINE

A gripping new series from Karen Rose begins with . . .

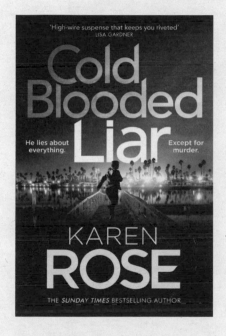

Available to order now

HEADLINE